The Bitter Smell of Almonds

THE BITTER SMELL OF ALMONDS

Selected Fiction

ARNOŠT LUSTIG

NORTHWESTERN UNIVERSITY PRESS

Evanston, Illinois

Northwestern University Press
Evanston, Illinois 60208-4210

Printed in the United States of America

10 9 8 7 6 5 4 3 2 1

ISBN 0-8101-1902-1

Library of Congress Cataloging-in-Publication Data

Lustig, Arnost.
    [Selections. English. 2001]
    The bitter smell of almonds : selected fiction / Arnost Lustig.
        p. cm. — (Jewish lives)
    Translated from the Czech.
    Originally published by Northwestern University Press as 3 separate works: Street of lost brothers (1990), Indecent dreams (1998) and Dita Saxova (1993).
    ISBN 0-8101-1902-1 (pbk.)
    1. Lustig, Arnošt—Translations into English. I. Title. II. Series.

PG5038.L85 A2 2001
891.8'6354—dc21

2001034534

The paper used in this publication meets the minimum requirements of
the American National Standard for Information Sciences—Permanence of Paper
for Printed Library Materials, ANSI Z39.48-1984.

Contents

STREET OF LOST BROTHERS

Stories

Four things disquiet man: war, misery, pain, and death.

Morning till Evening

I'm back," he said.

"Yes," said the woman.

Emanuel Mautner, taking off his coat, whistled the melody of a song from the Italian front. He stood there, thin, with soft black hair. His narrow, nut-brown face camouflaged the fatigue of nighttime.

"How about something to eat?"

"Were you there?"

Emanuel Mautner dropped his eyes. Her glance—as at night with the unfathomable sound of broken branches and the leafless stumps of wood— filled the echo of what she would only suggest. He was glad there was plenty of light coming through both windows of the kitchen.

"Did you look everywhere? All the time you were at the railway station?"

"Now Emily," he tried once more.

He looked at the table, the blue tablecloth, which he had bought before the war, marked with imprints of plates and glasses. The stove was cold. The dishes from yesterday were in the sink.

"Did you talk to anyone?"

The skin on Emanuel Mautner's cheeks furrowed up to his eyes. He held out his coat for her. (When he was leaving that morning, at nine, she had promised to sew on the torn coat tag. The velvet collar was ripped.) She sent him to the railway station and the other places where efforts were being made to locate missing persons.

It occurred to him that they could move from here, from this apartment, this house, this street. Maybe he should prepare Emily for the thought of a retirement home somewhere far away. For a moment he pictured the company they would keep: old women with dyed hair or wigs, wearing heavy make-up like they do in the theater or in the circus.

"Button up, mamitschko," he said.

Emily stood there in her robe, a washable fabric, with nothing under it. She looked at him remotely. He smiled at her. She had blue eyes, tired from the previous night's sleep. Her complexion was smooth and pallid.

"You know what you are."

Emanuel Mautner looked at the floor and slipped into the corner of the kitchen by the window. His cheeks twitched; then the corners of his mouth lifted. He felt an old pang. She had hinted at his origin, as though echoing what had been said daily since the war and Miroslav left.

"You ought to button up," he repeated.

"What happened when you spoke to the building supervisor?"

"They will repair the elevator."

"I can imagine what you told her. What would you be talking about if you couldn't bring me into it?"

He felt a desire to caress her, but he reprimanded himself. For thirteen years he hadn't touched her. When her headaches started, he convinced himself that things were better this way. He smiled a little bit again. The bright daylight whitened him now.

Emily looked at the torn coat tag and then at Emanuel. In his eyes she noticed a moment of retreat. He looked like a bird whose vision has lost the trees or the sky above and the earth and rivers below. She waited to see what he would say. Maybe he would talk about Italy, which he knew during World War I at the river Piave, or about applesauce and coffee, whose prices had soared again because of the frosts in Colombia.

Maybe he would invite her to the Zoological Garden, to watch endangered species like condors, Mongolian horses, or Chinese bears.

He wouldn't let her see the mailman for the same reason he'd given up one newspaper and his subscription to *The Jewish Gazette*. He also terminated his membership in the stamp collectors' society. He even made several trips to a secondhand bookstore to sell their books dealing with the war and, later, Miroslav's book about the famed Lafayette Escadrille, the American volunteer who joined the French Army as a pilot before America entered World War I in 1917.

"Come on, mamitschko," he said, "let me button your robe."

She tore herself away. He wanted to hold her so she wouldn't fall, but her back hit the edge of the stove. Emily pursed her lips slightly. In her mind there circled a planet whose axis revolved without her instructions. It made her pretty and at the same time diminished her beauty.

The sleeping pills had dropped from her pocket. He bent over and picked them up.

He had just gone to the corner drugstore. He continued to buy sleeping pills, not only for the holidays and the end of the year. (Sometimes he played cards for small sums no one would worry about, and this helped him to forget during the hours spent awake.)

"I don't believe a word you say," she told him.

She flushed out a moth that flew up and then perched, its transparent wings fanning on the shade of the kitchen lamp. Emanuel straightened himself. He tried to guess whether she had found out what he and the superintendent had been talking about.

"I'd give anything, darling, to know he's still alive," he whispered, but to be sure, inaudibly, "even if I were never to see him again." In his mind he saw a picture that he'd never confided to his wife.

2

There was a highway leading from the downtown of Landsberg to an adjoining town, Kaufering, known during World War II for its eleven prison camps, some large, others pocket-sized. It was a cold winter day in 1945;

there was snow on the ground. The heavy white flakes glistened at night. They covered the mud, the swamps, the rocks and fields. Miroslav walked with the last row of prisoners. By morning he couldn't continue, and in stopping he moved from the path into a ditch. The column moved on. Some had fallen in the snow before him.

Miroslav knew the order of the two gunmen who walked at the rear. He saw the two escort men at a distance of twenty steps, then heard the bang of their pistols, dry, as though they were firecrackers.

An alder tree grew from the ditch Miroslav sat in. In the dark, his hands could feel the hard bark of its trunk. The tree creaked about close to him. He was glad it wasn't a man. But when he attempted to lean his back against the tree to rest his head, the trunk seemed to move away.

Miroslav knew he was going to freeze. He knew that before freezing one has a sense of warmth, as children do when falling asleep. The breath of the snowstorm began to brush against him. The snow seemed soft.

Suddenly the windy night turned quiet. Before the gunmen could see him, he grew torpid. That was the last he was aware of, no longer conscious of the men who stood over him, neither when they were approaching, nor when they stopped.

First they tried to summon a response by kicking him.

"My nose is frozen," said the first one.

"This will take care of itself before you can blink an eye," the other said.

They tried to awaken him once again. There was no response. They heard only the cracking of bones.

"As they say within the city limits of Landsberg," said the first, "it isn't enought to aim. You must hit. Not all who snore are asleep."

"There are fewer of them," said the second one. "But it seems there are more all the time."

They didn't hear what echoed in Miroslav—Emily's embrace, a mother carrying her frozen son in her blue eyes. Nor could they see the movement of Miroslav's lips, a kiss intended for his father.

Miroslav didn't hear when the first gunmen instructed, "Don't shoot. Save two rounds. He is frozen already."

"We won't lose this war because of one bullet," the second gunmen said. He needed to restore circulation to his fingers before the shot. He took off his gloves.

"As the saying goes in Kaufering: When the apple's ready, it will drop," said the first soldier.

The blast of two gunshots, fired in succession, split the air. The boy's body twitched as though someone were trying to wake him, but no one did. The column moved on. The smell of gunpowder dissolved in the freezing air. The stars didn't move.

3

"Why are you looking at me like that?" Emily asked. "What happened?"

"Nothing," Emanuel Mautner said. "I'll have to be going again."

"You haven't had breakfast."

"I'm not hungry. I'll eat when I return."

"I know you weren't there." A little while later she added: "So many smart people have left. It could have been different."

"You shouldn't blame yourself, mamitschko."

"Don't call me mamitschko. Swear that you were there."

He raised his hand. His fingers were steady.

"Put that hand down for God's sake!"

He avoided her glance. He heard the alder groves falling in his mind—sparks heard in the crisp, biting air of the Polish wasteland. He was looking at Emily, at her head and hair, at her throat and flat breasts. She stood with her shoulders stooped, head almost on her chest because of her dropped chin. In a split second, he recalled the story of how his son had spent his first night with a woman, just before he was to leave Theresienstadt in the fall of 1944 for the East. From there they went into Germany. Some said that Miroslav hadn't been shot, but had his frozen legs amputated.

"You've always been able to rely on me."

"You should be going to work."

"I will shortly."

"Come back as soon as you can."

"It's a nice day," he said.

"Don't leave me alone."

"I like this kind of light, don't you?"

4

An hour and a half later, Emanuel Mautner found himself on Ridders Street watching a grocer arrange a crate of Meissen apples according to size. The apples were bright red and round with well-defined stems and smelled of fruitful lands.

For a moment he imagined that he was strong and careless like people who don't need to worry. Light makes them stronger and, maybe, weaker at the same time. He thought of Emily.

The biggest apples were on the bottom, the smaller in the middle, and the smallest on top, forming a pyramid.

"Would you like to buy some?" the grocer asked. He had his crates stacked so they looked like stockades. "This fruit is all from the same tree."

"No, thank you. Maybe on my way back," Emanuel Mautner told him. The apples reminded him of Miroslav's red cheeks.

The grocer was removing the apples that were damaged or beginning to rot and discarding them into a little bin under the counter. "You should buy while there are still some left," he muttered casually. "Those who wait too long miss the boat."

Emanuel Mautner slowed his pace and looked into the shops and into the apartment windows with curtains. At an inn by the roadside, daily patrons were drinking lemonade, beer, and coffee at their tables.

In a conspiratorial tone he said, "Of course, mamitschko, I know and you know, too." And then he added, "I don't have time to criticize anyone." He smiled. "Joy and sorrow are sisters." Earlier in his life he would measure each year from spring to spring. Each day by every night. He liked the daylight as much as the darkness. As a traveling salesman for the umbrella company on Carpenter Street, he took his vacation with his family in August. Three people: blond and blue-eyed Emily, fair-haired and blue-eyed Miroslav, and himself. Every year they talked about going skiing, but were content with Miroslav's ice skating and sledding in the winter at home.

"*Dis si pasce di sper anza, muore di lame.* He who lives on hope dies fasting," he said again, somewhat loudly. "It's hard to get money out of an empty pocket." The streetcars, numbers 10, 15, and 23, rang their bells, sounding at once into the streets, and screeching their brakes.

When Miroslav was a child, they had met a man on this same street who talked to himself in the way Emanuel found himself doing now. The man would tell stories about himself until he either laughed or cried. Emanuel had explained to Miroslav that some people went crazy from being alone and advised him to stay out of the man's way.

"I'm here with you, mamitschko," he said now.

No one paid any attention. He delivered the last parcel at the corner of Peters Street and Peters Square. He ran errands for the workshop electricians. He could come and go; it was understood he was to make deliveries on the neighboring blocks Goldsmith, Carpenter, and Spinner Streets.

Across from the workshop, before the war, two brothers had owned the umbrella factory he had traveled for. He no longer knew where they were or where they emigrated to. He didn't know that the brothers had left during the last possible days in 1939, just before the fifteenth of March. On the sixteenth, when the Germans had already invaded the country, Emanuel went to work and the clerk told him the two brothers were out. At first he thought that the clerk meant on an errand; maybe they had stopped for some cappuccino in the Arco Café, or at the Café Roxy on the first floor at Long Street.

"Where do people vanish to all of a sudden?" he asked aloud.

Many people had left. Those who remained were the shreds of families without fathers or mothers, parents without children, or brothers without sisters.

He thought how "hope" was an old word whose meaning was taught to him by the Italians. He imagined the word as an old woman who knows about fate. Or the soldiers in Italy who compared luck and hope to an aging whore.

After the war, Emily had gone to a palmist. For two crowns the Gypsy told her that Leo would unite with Virgo and that the number forty would be important. There would be a train for Emily, the palmist read, but she must not entrust her passage to any engineer who had derailed once before—even if that were his first and only mistake.

Miroslav left in 1942 for Theresienstadt; they expected him to return in 1945. He left Theresienstadt in September of 1944 with a transport headed for the East. The number forty was on all of his documents.

The Gypsy also told them that the Revolutionary National Council of the Second District in Prague had found Emily a job as a cashier in the box office of the Anchor movie house.

Emanuel Mautner passed the Anchor movie house at the beginning of the Avenue of the Revolution. It was a year since he and Emily had gone to see a movie. The last one was called *Steam Over the Pot.* The newsreel showed an Italian Saint Bernard receiving a medal for faithfulness from the War Ministry; for twelve years after the war, the dog went to the bus station and waited for his master. He was a rust-colored salivating dog with weeping eyes.

Maybe he'd made a mistake with Emily by not meeting with those who had a similar fate. Why does everybody think his fate will be exceptional?

Emanuel crossed the square looking in both directions so he wouldn't get hit.

"I can't do it, mamitschko," he said as loudly as he could. "There is no sense in doing it. Let's start again, mamitschko. Come on. You understand why I'm not doing it anymore, don't you?"

In the main hall of the central station, Emanuel Mautner inhaled the sweet clouds of smoke. He followed the yellow signs with black letters—schedules of stations and trains, timetables of departures and arrivals. On the other side of the hall, two strong women were washing the stone floor. Although it was the middle of the day, the hall was illuminated with big yellow lamps hanging from the ceiling. Emanuel stood in the way of a railway employee who was riding on an electric cart.

"What train are you looking for?" the employee asked. "An express?"

Since Emanuel didn't answer, the man in the uniform volunteered some information. "There are several changes. Summertime and wintertime. Some trains have been added."

"I'm not sure it's an express," Emanuel said.

"The locals usually go through Main Station and a few of them go to Prague-Center."

Emanuel thought that the blue eyes of the employee in the spotted uniform saw him as a lost man—as a scarecrow with his wrinkled yellow tie and torn black umbrella under his arm.

"A train from Germany," Emanuel Mautner told the man. "Kaufering II—does that mean anything to you?"

"Kaufering II. Sure it means something to me," the man answered. "Like Buchenwald or Dachau or Landsberg, right? Did you say 'Kaufering II'? I drove freight cars to Theresienstadt in 1943. The Little Fortress and the Big Fortress. Then I went there in May of '45 when the typhoid epidemic broke out. I drove Czech and Russian doctors there. And three German ones."

The railway employee noticed the dark circles under the small man's eyes. He thought how people like this lived during the night, like some insects so preoccupied with sustenance that they don't notice their wrinkled condition. The daylight doesn't make them well. Then he noticed the throbbing veins in Emanuel's temples and forehead.

The railway employee spoke again. "The interstate and express trains have been arriving at the Main Station—which used to be the Wilson Station—for the last nine months."

The employee looked one last time at the slight man with the umbrella. Emanuel was dressed in a pinstriped woolen suit, as though it were not the end of summer. At the same time, the railway employee thought that this man's thin, straight Jewish nose, greasy skin, stooped shoulders, and diffident eyes reminded him of a moth or a mayfly that lives for two days as if born by mistake.

The railway employee saw that the little man was blinking as though he had cinders in his eyes.

"Haven't we seen each other before?"

Emanuel Mautner shrugged his shoulders. He headed for the door to the main hallway. Behind him he heard the departing electric cart, loaded with baggage and mailbags.

At the corner of Goldsmith Street—next to the Imperial Hotel, which housed the Union's Recreational Center—a girl to whom Emanuel used to deliver parcels bathed in the sunshine. She called to him from the first floor window, reminding him to listen to the radio in the evening. "A lovely day, isn't it, Mr. Mautner?"

Again he passed the house of the lost brothers. His memories were an invisible tissue made of multicolored silk, Indian bamboo, and local imitations of rain and dreams.

The two brothers—what did they look like? He tried to remember their voices or the sound inside their voices when business was good. He had begun selling for them in small towns, moving up to more important positions, until he became sales representative for Prague.

He looked at the wooden umbrella on the facade of the house in Carpenter Street facing Peters Square. It was displayed on the wall between the first and third floors. There was nothing next to it. The children of future parents would wonder about the origin of the wooden umbrella on the building. It had been raining the day the two brothers left the country.

Maybe they were living somewhere far away in an unknown place and would never come back. People who emigrated to who knows where. Maybe they were selling umbrellas somewhere in New Zealand. Or they joined one of the armies that helped defeat Nazi Germany. He imagined men who defended the lives they were in charge of, armies that didn't fail, officers who died rather than jeopardize the lives of their troops.

He passed through the street with another look at the wooden umbrella. He wondered what time it was.

5

"Why aren't you eating?" Emily asked.

"Look. I brought some money."

"Did you have a lot to do?"

"Only some envelopes to deliver and one box and a roll of copper wire."

"Would you like more soup?"

"This is really good soup, mamitschko. Did you water the plants?"

"Why aren't you eating?"

"I have a little heartburn. It looks like we're going to have a long warm spell. We still have time. They are predicting snow for the winter. The snow is good, really, because there isn't enough water."

"How do you know?"

"It was on the radio. They know all about the Ice Age and about the next five winters."

Emanuel Mautner wiped his lips. He wanted to clear the table, but he felt Emily's glance and then something frightened her, as she abruptly swept the bills from his pay envelope off the table with her hand. The bills fell to the floor.

"What are you doing, mamitschko?" When she looked at him he added, "Don't worry, nothing's happened. I'll pick them up myself."

Emanuel bent down to pick up the bills. He put them back into the pay envelope. "Everything's OK, mamitschko. That young bookkeeper in the shop gave me some ten-heller red stamps with a picture of Albert Einstein when he taught in Prague."

"What do you need stamps for? What will the people say?"

"She had some extras."

When he'd collected the bills, she said, "What's new?"

"In the shop? Nothing. It's better when there's no news." He smiled. "They explained that England exported her criminals to Australia. Now the new generations have to pay for the sins of their fathers."

He was squatting on the floor. Emily watched her husband as though he were part of a night's dream. But her dreams weren't just summer storms with their thunder; the lightning was like a fiery serpent penetrating the streams of falling waters.

"Button your dress, mamitschko."

Did she know the contents of the telegram from the postwar Center for Repatriation in Vienna? Emanuel Mautner thought he had hidden it from her. *Castelles Strasse 57 Stop*, the telegram read. *They are supposed to be missing.*

Emily was not far from the night when she dreamt they arrived in Kaufering II in the dark while the disinfection carriage waited for them. In the canteen near the former Frauenbunkers, people ordered beer and sandwiches. The nearby stand sold souvenirs, bookmarks, and postcards. Where the camp had been before, the ground was blackened. The man who sold flowers kept lying to them or changing the conditions of the sale. The only hotel to sleep in was in Landsberg or Kaufering I, where warehouses and apartment buildings were built on mass graves. Emanuel Mautner tried to entertain her all the way, as though they were going to a variety show. The gravedigger was in a hurry, even though they had paid him for a full day's work. He was trying to convince the mother of another son that the crust of civilization is thin. The gravedigger folded Miroslav's body as though it were frozen or as though it had no legs. He did it as if stacking wooden logs.

The gravedigger in her dream covered the pit with the broken earth that had given him so much trouble. With soft earth, he could work faster. Sometimes he came upon huge holes in the ground that were capable of hiding a battleship. But could he be sure that under all that dirt, all the way down, Miroslav really lay there?

"No one reproached you for being out so long?" she said.

Emanuel Mautner placed the envelope on the table. "I don't take it that way, mamitschko. Fortunately, no one checks my time."

She thought about the part of Emanuel Mautner that was guilty as well as the part that was innocent. Was it because of his dark hair, the curve of his nose, or the olive tone of his skin that he looked like the

Spanish grandee to whose ancestors he was related? Or was it that sign of his race or purity performed on a Jewish man once in his life, the rite she didn't allow Miroslav to have? Why then wasn't she able to save Miroslav by herself, with his bright blue eyes, straight nose, and fair hair?

She looked through the kitchen windows into the bright sunny light and at the reflections of light on the windows across from them.

"Did they give you a raise on their own?"

"I didn't ask for one. It sure made me happy."

"Sometimes I think they'll let you go."

"You're too trusting."

"They need people everywhere these days."

He handed her the envelope with his pay. "Will you take care of it?"

The corners of his mouth moved up. It was only half a smile. *Tempi passati.* He knew she would be afraid to kill a fly. They were both swallowed up by the bright sun; the kitchen was full of light.

6

Dusk poured in—an end to a day. The kitchen windows faced the courtyard. Across the street, from the entrance of the inn to the garrison in number 23, a man's voice was shouting to the woman in a window.

The water in the kettle was boiling; Emanuel Mautner made tea. He threw a vial of sleeping pills into Emily's cup. He poured water into the cups, making sure not to confuse the two. He looked at Emily's light hair, her blue eyes. Afraid that she could read his thoughts, he blushed, grateful for the dusk.

"I'm afraid I'm going to have dreams again," Emily said.

He held the gas valve of the stove between his thumb and forefinger and lowered the heat by turning the knob until the flame quieted. Whenever he turned the valve, the same thought came to him: how lovely she once was, not so long ago. Only thirteen years. He was still holding the gas valve on the range between his fingers. Then the flame died down.

Her silence sounded like the flight of a bird whose wings are tired but still has a long way to fall before shattering on the ground. It embraced her silence, her voice, thousands of silences and voices he'd never heard. His fingers let go of the gas valve.

"We've grown old together."

"I don't want you to look at me like that," Emily said.

That sound was flowing through her voice again, just as in the mornings, the burning remains of smoldering wood—her unfathomable voice of trees and broken twigs, a dry crack that cut the wind and frost that carried the sounds afar.

He imagined birds perched in big cages and how he used to sell Latin American umbrellas with handles that resembled lion's claws or cock's heads.

He brought the cup with the dissolved sleeping pills. "Drink it while it's hot."

"I can't drink it so hot. I'll burn my tongue." Then she added, "I don't feel anything." It seemed to her that the tea had the taste of soft clay. She inhaled a couple of times to get rid of the taste.

Emanuel Mautner took a sip of his tea, then waited until the first signs of fatigue formed in her eyes. Sleepiness fell silently on the apple shade of Emily's cheek, and on the dark, almost transparent semicircles of muscatel spots under her moist eyes. All of a sudden, her eyes seemed small. He wondered where her eyes disappeared to during sleep. He was thinking about the idea he dreamt about so often, how good it would be if they would die, to have it all over with. Unconsciously, he didn't want to make it gas, and he was afraid to die first, also. He felt dead tired and deeply ashamed.

He started coughing. He was not at all sure he hadn't mixed up the cups. Both contained sleeping pills, but there were more in hers.

Someone across the street lit a candle in a window. It looked like a slender sun praying in the windowsill; the rosy clouds drifted from east to west until the sky grew dark. Then the candle went out.

He watched Emily falling asleep. Later, when he himself was half-asleep, it seemed to him that she sat up next to him on the bed.

"Go and open the door," she said.

Emanuel Mautner rose and walked through the hall. He passed the wardrobe and the coatrack by the door. There was the chest they'd bought during the war—for storage and to have their traveling things ready all the time. Next to it, there were suitcases stacked in the hall. He unlocked the security lock, loosened the chain, and opened the door.

Outside stood a young man who had visited them right after the end of the war, on the morning of Tuesday, May 19, 1945. The slanting scars across his forehead made it look as though his skull were separating under the skin. He wore honey-colored corduroy pants, a dark blue flannel jacket, and a red kerchief around his neck. He asked, had Miroslav also returned home? This "also" confused Emanuel Mautner. Might they have parted somewhere on the corner, by the garrison or just across the street from the Ideal Hotel? Emanuel Mautner's heart stood still. Could it mean that Miroslav was only delayed somewhere?

"No," Emanuel Mautner answered; he couldn't breathe. "Miroslav hasn't come yet. When was the last time you saw my son?"

"In Theresienstadt, in 1944," the young man answered. "We were sent East on different transports."

"Of course." Emanuel Mautner understood at once, though not understanding anything.

The boy then began a story about a girl with whom he and Miroslav had spent their last night in Theresienstadt in September 1944. Emanuel Mautner remained silent then, not wanting to spoil the young man's homecoming.

"It's been a long while," Emanuel Mautner said now.

"I hope you have forgiven me for confusing you then."

"You look well."

"How are you?"

"What do you do?"

"It's not bad. I'm an aeronautical engineer. I wanted to be a pilot, just like your son, but that didn't work out. They told me I don't have the best vision. Unless I would be satisfied being a navigator. How are you doing, Mr. Mautner?"

"How do you manage to make it so well?" Emanuel Mautner countered with a smile. "Do you have an apartment of your own? If you hadn't been in a hurry then you could have had the bedroom of a German untersharführer who occupied a Jewish apartment, number sixteen next door."

Emanuel Mautner led the young man into the hallway. "My wife is home. Be careful. *Di salto in salto.* She draws rather rash conclusions from everything."

Emily was stretched out on the bed. She rubbed her eyes.

"Was that you ringing just now?" Emily turned to the young man. "We always ring three times."

"You haven't changed, Mrs. Mautner," the young man said.

"None of us is getting any younger," Emanuel Mautner added. "So we live in our memories of a better past." And before Emily could say anything, "We must have sent him a hundred and fifty parcels during the war. Isn't it so? We still have some postal receipts."

"They must be somewhere—I haven't thrown out a thing," Emily said.

"Don't even ask how much it cost," Emanuel said. "All of Emily's dowry, her jewelry and our savings. It was fortunate that I could work; they raised my commission before Miroslav left. We were lucky to send one parcel a month, including things bought on the black market." And again, before Emily could add anything, "Tell Emily about where you and Miroslav spent the last night before leaving Theresienstadt with a transport to the East."

"In good company," answered the young man. "She was a half-German Jewess. Twenty-two. Pretty, strong. Her name was Inge. She had pink cheeks, dark eyes, and black hair. She looked healthy. Someone told us that she had TB. We all ended up falling in love with her, although some of us only after we looked back on it. She loved your son the most, I would say."

The young man didn't say that Miroslav received few of the parcels they sent him and always shared the ones that did come. And that this half-German and half-Jewish girl Inge, the last name unknown or forgotten, was sent to Theresienstadt directly from the streets, with a police note in her papers, being *vollblütdirne aus Café Ammarkt,* a full-blooded prostitute from a notorious café.

When she heard about it for the first time it was obvious that it pleased Emily, just as it pleased Emanuel Mautner, but now, like her husband then, she felt embarrassed.

"I hope the girl survived," she said.

"No one's heard of her," the young man answered. "The only thing of hers that survived was her parting gift to us." He smiled.

"We're never too old to learn," Emanuel Mautner said. *"Non si e mal vecchio per imparare."* He was thinking: is it true that a liar should have a good memory?

"Stop by again," Emanuel told him. "Let us know beforehand so we'll be home."

8

Emanuel Mautner tossed about in bed. His throat and forehead were wet. So were his groin and armpits.

He imagined the room with the dozen boys, all the same age as Miroslav, and how the girl was able to make each one feel as if he were the only one. Inge. He heard the echo of a sound as though someone were ringing a bell. He always disconnected the bell from seven in the evening until eight in the morning.

He thought again about his son's first moments with a mature woman. He tried to breathe softly in order not to wake Emily. He dried himself with the blanket. He was thankful for the girl. He tried to imagine her face and her hair and whether she was allowed to use lipstick in the camp. What did she look like?

"What's the matter?" Emily asked, half-asleep. She still held the cup in her hand.

"Didn't you hear the bell, mamitschko?"

"Can't you be at peace with yourself, at least at night?"

"I thought I heard the bell."

"I sleep as though I'm on water. I would know if it rang. Wipe your nose."

The cup from Emily's hand fell to the floor, breaking into pieces, the sound of shattering china.

"It's still night, mamitschko."

"I have to sleep," Emily repeated.

He watched her fall asleep again. He felt her dying soul. He wished to breathe life into her. He felt that with her soul his soul would die, too. The freshness of youth dissolved from Emily's face. The wind outside howled, sounding like the branches from trees, and whispers between boys and girls, men and women; or like the peeling paint of distant pictures—signs that one no longer understands; like ashes crumbled by frost, or reeds in Polish or German swamps; or faraway lakes filled with human bodies that disappeared from foreign maps. Only an echo contained the color of ladies' umbrellas and gentlemen's canes with ornamental mother-of-pearl or silver handles.

The night was flowing through the darkness. Everything Emanuel Mautner saw before him looked like hot rain, smothering chips of alder wood—layers that flowed downstream, ashes thrown from trucks into rivers during the war before they were lost in the oceans. He thought about the strange tides between people, like an ocean of fish that struggle to eat one another, only to be caught by fishermen and gulped down; there were acquaintances with strangers, the dead, the living, the real, the imagined, and those in the past with those yet to be born. He felt a force that passed him in the night with a motion that went from nowhere to nowhere, beyond man's control, that you could touch only the way the stars touch each other. He remembered days when Emily was beautiful, when she became his wife, before he could compare her with the unknown girl in Theresienstadt.

The fool who mumbled to himself when Miroslav was still a child flashed into his mind. He asked himself whether the man only wanted to be happy. A thin bald man in greasy shirt and shorts, unkempt and unshaven, with sparse rotting teeth. Sometimes he ran around Goldsmith, Carpenter, and Peters Streets singing an aria from *Aida*. Where are all those people who have disappeared from Germany, like Inge and the fool from their street?

The image of the girl Miroslav slept with remained with him. The wind from the street sounded like cobwebs, like broken gossamer nets, a lullaby, frozen snowflakes.

Someone was returning from the night shift out on Carpenter Street. Emanuel heard the downstairs entrance gate slam and then the door of the inn. In front of the Ideal Hotel, a brief strain of a woman's laughter broke out, followed by a man's voice saying how difficult it was to bring up daughters. Is it right that the eldest daughter receives money and the youngest beauty? Is it true that when a woman behaves well, she will have a baby boy? Then everything was quiet.

Emanuel Mautner kept returning to the girl, to Miroslav, to the fool in the street, who had to rely on his own world because the surrounding planet of men had failed him and he had failed it, and to how Emily, tired from sleep extracted from sleeping pills, could remain so beautiful, at least in the dark. He thought how those who were together remained alone. Again he wished to live longer than Emily, even if by one day or a few hours, so that he would be able to bury her with his own hands. He felt the throbbing of his veins in his temples. Then he saw an image of the Landsberg camp and contours that he had been trying to avoid the entire time, which, against his will, completed what he'd seen so many times in the same way.

9

Slowly he began caressing Emily. He stroked her forehead with his palm. He touched the edge of her hair, which was done in a tight twist. It wasn't the first time she had fallen asleep without undressing. The murmur of her double sleep, which he had provided for her, swept past his greasy forehead.

"I didn't wash or undress yesterday either, mamitschko." He knew that she had drunk all of the sleeping pills.

"I will carry you over, mamitschko," he whispered. "It's not comfortable. Come on. I'll unbutton it for you."

He was relieved when he felt movement in her. "It's a shame we haven't gone out together in such a long time."

Emily blinked and ran her hand across her forehead. "Why do you keep waking me?" she asked. Then she added, "No one has ever confirmed it for us." She was dreaming about ships suddenly taken by a storm and never heard of again. But the wives and mothers of the sailors, nevertheless, believed their husbands and sons lived somewhere, forgotten and safe.

Emanuel Mautner carried Emily in his arms. She was easy to carry, almost like a child. Only he knew. In the darkness her skin looked like weathered wood, exposed through the years to heat, to frost-beating sun and prolonged rain. He remembered again how young and fresh she used to be and how her parents wanted only the best for her. It seemed to him that her heart beat like that of a caged bird, trembling with fear even in sleep. He held her with one arm under her knees and the other around her neck, but even so, her legs and head felt limp.

"I have to change your clothes, mamitschko."

"I wouldn't leave anyone behind."

He put her down carefully. He folded her underwear, her dress, and her robe on the armchair next to the bed. He dressed her in a white batiste nightgown that covered her up to her neck. Then, he lay next to her. He first put his cheek to her shoulder, then to her breast. It seemed to him that her small, almost unwomanly breast smelled of geraniums. He felt her dry coarse skin. He stroked her with his palm and pressed his lips to her chest.

"Where are they?" she asked. "Where are they all?"

"Sleep, mamitschko."

"I don't understand you. What do you want to do with your own hands?"

He turned on the radio, which looked like a big white seashell. He remembered the girl on Goldsmith Street who had reminded him to listen tonight. While the lamps of the radio warmed up, he thought of Miroslav. Emily opened her pale blue eyes and looked at him. The wind streamed in through the window and the starlight skimmed over her blanket, passing over her face and disappearing into the hall. It was the light of dead and living stars. Both of them heard the words of the song on the radio:

> *While the red orchids bloom*
> *Our flower will bloom for everyone . . .*

"I have to sleep," Emily said.

"Sure, mamitschko."

The nightly news came on the radio for a minute. The newscaster was talking about an eruption of a Pacific Ocean volcano next to some faraway Australian island. He reported that silent volcanoes thousands of miles apart talked to each other.

"Let it play if you want," Emily said.

"Remind me in the morning of what I wanted to tell you. We'll go out somewhere."

He put his cheek on the pillow next to Emily. Through the window, the winds, flowing from the Ideal Hotel to the inn at the garrison, from the Avenue of the Revolution to Peters Square, carrying the song and words, seemed like a funnel through which everything flowed into him. He held Emily around the shoulders, as though they weren't lying down but standing and about to go out, with their arms around each other the way they used to hold each other. Then he waited for her to fall asleep. He huddled up beside his wife as though he were lying and walking and guarding, killing his and her loneliness at the same time. He lowered the arm that held her around the shoulders. He felt her heartbeat, her rattling breath. He felt the layer of freckled skin. For a moment he felt removed from everything, like a distant star in a nightless sky.

"I'm not dreaming of anything," Emanuel Mautner whispered when he was sure Emily was asleep. He thought about the soul of words never uttered and the soul of unchallenged memories—and about the things one never knows. Did he want to know now? What good would it do Emily to know?

She didn't answer. Her palm was touching his hand. The music on the radio was already wordless.

"After all, no twig is only green," he said in Italian. He felt younger.

Emanuel Mautner felt like a ship that had sailed through the fog in waters full of unexploded and forgotten mines, past rocks and whirlpools. He felt like a volcano of the sea, which erupts each night to spit out an island touching the surface, penetrating it. He closed his eyes. They walked through a garden where men were firm, where mothers and fathers were not afraid of daylight or volcanoes or the voices of silence; where all the flowers, trees, and grass looked different from those they had known before. Their long undeclared war had ended; daily strength had been taken, and in its place, this nocturnal truce had formed. The sun rose and set, and the winds and rain came and went again. The shadows were soft and indicated only by beginnings and endings. Time was no longer their master, and night and day filled its waiting.

"Mamitschko," Emanuel Mautner said softly, so as not to wake her.

In silence, the sound of pistol shots faded like dry firecrackers.

He kept repeating to Emily that it was all right, that everything was good because no one could live with joy alone, and they didn't have to die for suffering either. The wind's melody carried the voices of Miroslav and of the German-Jewish girl who was his son's friend on the last night before he was shipped East. It separated smell and strength, kisses and tears, as well as anguish and doubt, the life that was, the life that continues, and the life that would like to be.

Emanuel Mautner held Emily in his embrace without waking her. He wished her a dreamless night. He felt like a twig grafted onto a dying branch. He wanted to penetrate Emily so that neither of them would feel like a fallow field or a dead tree. It was the strength born of weakness, like the flight of birds.

And then, very much later, when the white shell of the radio receiver, with its strange names of cities and countries, had turned silent but the station panel continued to send its green lights into the depths of the bedroom, he turned to her once more and said, "Good night, my love."

INFINITY

During the night I dreamed that I was an SS officer and was in charge of the gas chamber selection. In the dream, the lager commandant asked me how I was doing. I answered that I felt as if every day I trampled underfoot thousands—tens of thousands—of ants on the flat stone, but it didn't seem to lead anywhere. I cannot destroy the breed of ants. The ants will go on living even when I trample a hundred times more under my feet. Then the commandant changed into a voice. It could speak, and listen, and it was omnipresent. I have had similar dreams in the camps many times already. Once I dreamed an octopus was reaching for me and every tentacled arm pulled me toward its mouth and I tried to resist. But it had the ability to speak and announced to me that the average life span in Auschwitz-Birkenau is fifteen minutes. During the course of the day I forget the dreams, but as I prepare for each night of sleep I fear what I will dream of.

We got the upper bunk for the three of us: Harry Cohen, Ervin Portman, and myself. We did not have blankets. They were taken to the laundry in the Delousing Station because they were so full of lice and infested with typhus bacteria. We pressed against each other to make the most of our bodies' warmth. Portman was quietly repeating the number tattooed on his forearm, as he usually did before going to sleep, so that he would remember it if someone woke him up in the middle of the night. He preferred to lie on his left side so that he could see the number, in case Rottenführer Schiese-Dietz came to make his night selection.

Before sounding the taps, Rottenführer Schiese-Dietz had made the rounds with his whip. It had a long handle like the whips used by coachmen driving teams of horses. The whip itself, twice the length of the handle, was braided leather made from human skin, fastened at the end with a double golden ring (cast from gold teeth) into which a Jewish jeweler in the camp workshop had engraved his initial. You could never be sure when Rottenführer Schiese-Dietz would get the idea to come to the barracks. He'd learned to crack the whip like a lion tamer. It sounded like gunfire. If the tip of the whip happened to touch someone it would slice the skin. A little while ago, satisfied that the barracks were quiet and that he'd seen nothing unusual anywhere, he had returned to the SS quarters and played the piano. He could play Bach, Schumann, or Mozart from memory, proud that he remembered so well everything he had learned. He had a different whip before, from somewhere in Saudi Arabia or from some German enterprise exporting whips to the near Orient, to make camels go faster. He was told that a camel never forgets a blow, even a baby camel, and that they sometimes run away in the middle of the desert. This couldn't happen here. People never escaped. There was nowhere to go. He had worn out his camel switch by using it too often and too hard, to beat out of people their habit of asking futile questions about boredom, or why they were living or why they were born or, most often, why their lives were so miserable. It was up to his whip to show them why they were still alive, and what had to be accomplished and why they were dissatisfied with their lives.

Somewhere in the night, a German voice called out: "*Laufschritt! Laufschritt!*" On the double! On the double! And again silence spread over the camp. Everywhere was mud. It was good at least to be under a roof.

A half hour later, Portman asked me, "Why aren't you asleep?"

"I'm cold," I said.

"Quit lying. What are you waiting for?" asked Portman.

"They'll begin soon," I blurted out.

"Get some sense into your head," Portman reprimanded me.

He must have known what I was waiting for, and he was right. I was waiting. I knew that he must have been waiting too, if he was not asleep. Maybe he waited for the same reasons I did and maybe at the same time it was because he wanted to refute what I wanted to verify for myself once it began. I felt a secret shame and didn't know exactly why. It encompassed many other shames, and all were present in one question: how and why were we born as we were born? And probably Harry Cohen was also waiting, although he said, "You shouldn't wait for it. It gets on your nerves. It isn't half as encouraging as it would seem."

"You'd better sleep," said Portman. "Be glad that we can sleep and they're not driving us to do some loading or unloading. In the mud it's obnoxious. It goes right through my rags." He trembled. "You keep wiggling. Who can put up with that?"

I did not answer. I did not want to be talking to Portman when they began. There were the usual noises in the bunks. Someone was quietly praying and somebody else told him to shut up and leave him alone and let him sleep in peace. And close to them, someone had a dispute with his Creator. The Creator didn't answer but the man had madness in his voice.

The wrangle finally stopped. Harry Cohen got a bit of gossip from his neighbor: that morning, the grüppenführer in the office of the Gestapo had been found dead, shot by his own hand.

Harry Cohen put his arm under his head. "That Chinaman who once said that the more a man knows, the luckier he is, was wrong," he whispered. "It's just the opposite. The more you know, the more your world is filled with misfortune. Shit. I think I'm already dead. Don't let me oversleep. Do you know how long it's been since I've had a dream?"

"It's better to wait for the swallow to come back in the spring than to wait for *them*," said Portman.

He stretched out his arms. He had long arms. He believed that was a sign of luck, and that, when necessary, he could reach farther and easier than Harry Cohen or I. His ears stuck out and he was convinced that this was a sign of someone who was satisfied with his lot; he was always sleepy and tired, but at the same time he had great willpower, although not the best talent for choosing friends. He did not have much patience. It was good that Harry Cohen did. In his former existence, Harry Cohen had had a lot of good luck, both in cards and in love, and was very successful in business undertakings. Portman considered my kind of patience morbid. He could not understand how I could go on waiting.

But Portman still wasn't asleep. Maybe he could still hear the rotten-führer cracking his whip. Maybe he could imagine that golden ring, cast from teeth that were knocked out of corpses and sometimes, just for the gold, out of the living. Most of the gold went into sealed railroad cars to the underground safes of the Berlin State Bank, but quite a bit of it slipped through the fingers of the SS men. Sometimes he dreamed about his little sister, up the chimney four months ago already. Her skin was very fair, with a touch of pink or peach; she was so white he could still see in his mind the blue veins beneath her skin. Her soft skin smelled like spices, maybe like flowers. Her fingers—not rough or damaged by manual labor—were long for a child of eight, and she also had long, dainty feet. Perhaps Portman envied the dead just as you would envy the living. Yesterday he had mumbled something in his sleep about Samson, and no one wanted to remind him of it. On Monday he dreamed that he had gotten typhus, on Tuesday that he had diarrhea and couldn't stop it, and Wednesday morning he realized that it had been both a dream and a reality. It wasn't hard to figure out what brought Samson's name to his lips. Samson was definitely the last resort.

"The rabbis know what they're talking about when they say that Noah was wrong to send out a pair of doves to bring the news that the flood had subsided. Maybe it drove him mad," Harry Cohen said. "To go mad—that's not the worst there is. The worst is when you know it. This afternoon when we were coming back from the soccer field, they were picking out women who had no shoes and those who were sick. The deaf and dumb are gone already and so is that shipment of war invalids from Vienna."

"Did you think they would be feeding them white bread and milk here?" asked Portman.

"Half of the people that they added to make up the count for the transport were healthy and strong—something was going on," added

Harry Cohen. "They're in a hurry now. But why do they want to get rid of the women first?"

"The Nazis don't like women," said Portman. "They're dead set in their beliefs that women are the source of all evil, just as we are. I heard Rottenführer shouting at the women in the laundry that they like to screw, especially when they were menstruating, so that they could infect everyone with syphilis and other infectious diseases. He yelled at them that here they would lose all their bad blood. He told them that he knew a woman could not wash laundry properly when she had her period and then he threatened to send them all to the bath and burn them with their dirty rags. And then he said point blank that he would shoot down any woman who got closer than three steps to him or dared to touch him."

"There are places where the men believe that if you glance at a menstruating woman your bones will go soft and you'll lose the ability to have children," said Harry Cohen.

"I hope it happens fast," I added. "At least without having to stand in the snow and mud." I liked Harry for never complaining about anything. Whenever they beat him he never moaned a minute after. Maybe he believed human dignity lies in never speaking of pain, especially afterward. In Prague he left an Aryan girl, Maruschka. Sometimes at night, when he was looking at the stars, his big lips would have a tender smile like the Mona Lisa's. Once the rottenführer caught him with that tender smile and beat him to chase it away. Cohen opened his mouth, but didn't complain.

"Why don't you both go to sleep?" Portman said.

I couldn't sleep. I waited for them to begin. Maybe they wouldn't.

When the killing came so close that he couldn't pretend not to see it, Portman would always get nervous. The blood would rise to his brain, and he would take it out on me. I could imagine that he was putting the blame on both the living and the dead, on people who had already gone through it, as well as those who were still waiting. I did not confide in him that for the last few nights I had been seized by a vision of crashing stars that in a fraction of a second would crush the whole camp and the planet on which the Germans had built this camp with our hands. It was a strange wish and it actually had something to do with Samson—only it was not just a matter of a few columns holding up the roof of an ancient palace. My vision encompassed the destruction of everything and everybody: the crushing of the earth, down to the very last pebble. It embraced the transformation of the planet into stardust—together with all and with everything, down to the last crow and the last ant. It was a very disturbing yet comforting obsession, and I knew it would depart with the first sleep or when the women from the adjoining camp would begin. It was safe as long as the Germans only killed new transports and picked out the sick and those people who were guilty of being old, of having gray hair or wearing glasses. The old-timers still held on to some hope or illusion, which turned into a new truth when the Germans started killing even the healthiest and strongest, those who could still work for them.

I did not want to miss it when the women from the adjoining camp began. It was always the beginning of something else as well. The beginning and the continuation of something that had no end even when it was over.

There were two women's camps. One was for Jewish women from Hungary and Slovakia and the other was for both Jewish and non-Jewish women from other occupied countries. They worked in the hospital ward, in the showers where water actually flowed from the sprinklers, and in the delousing station where they exterminated lice and insects with Cyclon B. The latter came from the same cans as those which were used in the underground showers next to the disrobing stations and the crematoria from number one to number five, and was used in fourteen-hour cycles, necessary for the proper extermination of vermin. The women also worked in cleaning stations, laundries and kitchens, and in the warehouses where shoes, gems, underwear, hair, orthopedic devices, and costume jewelry were stored. These women also had opportunities to work through all seasons as performers in the whorehouse or in the concert hall. Polish and Ukrainian henchmen and guards and German criminals wearing purple triangles took their opportunities in the brothel, although they had to pay two Reichmarks from their wages or other remuneration for the services. One mark was for the whore, and the other went into a special account which the commander of Auschwitz I, II, and III had been ordered from above to keep aside.

In the family camp B2b, which was burnt to ashes during the night of March eighth, there were kindergartens and nursery schools, and their teachers, before being killed, had rehearsed theatrical productions and gymnastic performances which the SS would come to watch.

Would they begin? They really ought to begin. If they were planning to, they should begin now.

As far as Portman was concerned, I had not been behaving like a normal person for the last few days. It was not the first time he had caught me waiting for them to begin. He knew why I had stared at the wooden ceiling with my eyes open, why I stared at the open, glassless window under the roof where I could see the stars or the moon or snow or smoke, waiting all the time. Sometimes my teeth would chatter with the cold and Portman would hear it and it would upset him because we lay so close to get heat from each other. He would blame me for not sleeping because I waited for the women to begin. He was mad at the women for what the camp had done to them instead of being mad at the camp. He thought that the women were crazy. Their faces had become coarse and some had hair growing on their cheeks, which made them look old.

Sometimes Portman would get furious, though at the same time he was afraid to vent his fury. That made him stutter, although maybe it was because he could not speak out loud. Yesterday, for some unknown reason, he had broken a tooth and thought he would die of it. Harry Cohen mentioned that people who had such widely spaced teeth as Portman did would always have to look for their good fortune far away from home. Well, as long as he was here, he was far enough from home, but what good fortune could he have when his teeth were crumbling, even though they had not sent him to the showers yet? Sometimes he became speechless when I waited for the women, but not now. He also feared he had tuberculosis. He believed that he would pull through if

he could make it through the next month, unless Rottenführer Schiese-
Dietz would spoil everything with his next selection, needing one more
for the showers. It was already the twenty-seventh of October. He told
himself that October was not a good month for those who have TB,
and he fixed his mind on November. Portman sometimes blamed it all
on his mother, whom he had never known because she left when Portman
was born. Sometimes the thought came to him that it would be rather
ironic if his mother had not been Jewish. He also believed that he could
get rid of his suspicion of tuberculosis if he could take one gulp of milk.

It was strange that the image of women was associated in my mind
with the image of milk, but I preferred not to mention this to Portman.
My back drew the heat from Portman's belly and I pressed my stomach
and chest against Harry Cohen's back. That afternoon I had given
Portman a piece of my bread and blood sausage because I knew what
he was afraid of. He gulped it down at once. Now he had the hiccups.

Everything was permeated by the smoke that rose toward the sky
during the day and during the night, smoke from the dead who would
not have a grave. I remembered what Rabbi Gans once told us in the
Vinohrady synagogue: that when they were in the Sinai desert, Moses
had ordered his successor, Joshua, to bury him in the ground so that
no one would find his grave. The Germans were now doing it on a
grand scale.

Portman hiccupped again. "I washed my rags in the latrine and the
rottenführer came there and whipped me out of the hole. He yelled at
me in his Bavarian German: 'Höre doch auf, Mensch!' He told me to
stop it or he'd take the handle of his whip and press me out through
the hole in the planks to see if I could swim."

"They should have started," I said.

Portman yawned. "It's better if they stay quiet. It won't help the
dead. And the living should stick with common sense. You don't want
them to run into bayonets, do you?" Then he added, "It brings them
bad luck, just like the night air. Don't they know that? It's making their
brains soft. Or they've gone crazy already. They sound like men. I don't

miss it. And most of them don't have periods anymore even if they're sixteen."

Harry Cohen was feeling his chest, his body, the last thing that he owned. He was at rock bottom. He had used up his last bit of willpower and self-control to pretend otherwise. He did not say that here in Auschwitz-Birkenau everything, even breathing the wind, a draft, or still air, brought people bad luck. The good luck of one always meant the bad luck of another. Everyone who lived, lived at the expense of someone who lived no more. It was not his fault. It was the Germans' organized way of killing. There were batches that were sent up the chimney for punishment, and the rest were picked to feed the crematoria according to numbers. And so there would be no cheating, these numbers were tattooed on each person's forearm. People could live in the camp only until it was their turn to go to the showers or into the furnaces and crematoria, because even the best German engineers could not figure out how to burn them all at once. The Germans loved order and kept better discipline than the Frenchmen, Englishmen, Italians, Czechs, Belgians, and other nationalities which the Germans deported to this camp for liquidation. Even those Germans who had no more than a seventh-grade education, like Rottenführer Schiese-Dietz, managed to command order, even when the situations got very confusing.

Harry Cohen lay with his mouth shut not only to avoid wasting energy talking, but in order to breathe through his nose so as not to inhale the germs of typhus and tuberculosis. Neither his former nor his future elegance were of any use to him here. Every memory of the past that could be uplifting was at the same time depressing. Everything that could heal could also wound. Once in Theresienstadt, Faiga Tannenbaum-Novakova ruminated about the omnipotence of the devil. The devil now seemed like an amateur compared to what the German Nazis had dreamt up in Auschwitz-Birkenau and its subsidiaries. Harry Cohen felt the skin in the middle of his chest with the balls of his fingers, trying to ascertain how much there was; it was thinner than wrapping paper, and he wondered how long it could last. He was probably thinking of all those things the tired, frightened minds were thinking, all those who hadn't yet managed to fall asleep.

"They're burning the old Hungarian women who came Monday," said Portman. "The Polish and Romanian railway engineers who brought them were completely drunk because the women stank so much. Somebody said he'd never seen women so full of lice. When the old women stripped at last, because they did not understand what they were supposed to do—since most of them did not understand a word of German, just like the Italians or Frenchmen—the barbers asked for double disinfection before they started cutting their hair."

His words became lost in the thick air of the barracks. Words were the first thing to become silent and lose their meaning. There were no innocent or inexperienced people among us. We had all been there too long, even a single day or a single night. None of the people believed any longer that they were going to take a bath, even if they actually went to baths to be deloused and disinfected before the journey. Nor did they believe that the Germans would send them to work in one of their dominions because they were experienced tailors, goldsmiths, blacksmiths, or automobile mechanics—or that they could find work in the German armaments industry. Everyone knew where he was going if the order was to take the road to the left or turn on the road to the right. The road to the right led out of the camp, into a room which had doors without door handles, and they knew that no one who entered the room came out alive. No one was fooled by the notices about cleanliness and health, by the cursing and light banter of the Nazis.

"The dental technicians had a hell of a job prying the gold teeth out of those old women," Portman added. "As usual, they searched everywhere, up and down, back and front, to see if they didn't have some hidden gold, bank notes, or diamonds. Most of them had used them already at home. A couple of them were beaten just because nothing could be found on them in any of the places that women tend to hide things."

The words faded again. They were lost in the rotation of the earth— which did not fall between the two crashing stars as I had wished—and in the thickness and smell of emaciated bodies, covered with sweat, but at the same time getting numb, because it was already the end of October and it was cold, made more so by the wind. Most of the men were quiet. This silence sounded like the dried-up language of the dumb, like the very last silence of the earth as it will one day be heard by the last human generation, even without Auschwitz-Birkenau, when the sun will approach with its enormous ball of fire, and all that is human will turn into fire, ashes and ice, before the planet earth turns into an infinite night, like this night, but much more desolate, much more silent, and much more cold. In my imagination it came sooner.

For the third time Portman said, "I'll bet anything, including your bread and blood sausage, that they will beat it out of them five minutes after they've begun."

Harry Cohen did not say anything. He was, as always in the rare moments of quiet, concerned with the number of possibilities every situation seemed to offer, while really offering only one. It encompassed all possible endings.

"It's not worth it," Portman repeated. "They should be glad that they had time to undress. They wouldn't even have to bother dressing again."

Women over forty, just like girls under fifteen, usually went into the furnace right away, directly from the ramp, or by the first or second selection. They had to wait only if the dressing rooms and the crematoria did not have time to process them all. Although it was cold now—not like during the summer heat—the Germans were afraid that the corpses might decompose and epidemics would start, and so the old women had waited since Monday afternoon. Their lice-infested underwear, clothes, and shoes were burned. And so they had to wait naked, some for hours, some for days and nights, in the wind, rain, and snow, and no one bothered to give them water or anything to eat. About two hundred thousand Hungarian Jewish women had come here since the summer. It was said that in Hungary there remained, until the beginning of 1944, about eight hundred thousand Jewish men, women, and children, and the Germans had now decided to liquidate them quickly, just in case Hungary changed sides in the war.

In a few hours the Hungarian women stopped asking what happened to their husbands, their children, and their families. They wanted to go into the showers and get it over with. When the women were undressed and their belongings taken away, they had no poison they could take, nor knives with which to slit their wrists.

"What's today? It must be Friday. Right, it's Friday," said Portman.

"Or maybe it's already Saturday," said Harry Cohen. "And it will begin all over again. But actually, why should it?"

No one had a watch. A watch was the first thing the Germans stole from you in Auschwitz-Birkenau. The first day here, Harry Cohen made up his mind that he should lie and tell them that he was a trained watchmaker in order to get a cushy job, but fortunately he did not do it.

"You were probably born like a rabbit, with open eyes," Portman grumbled in my direction. "Or do you sleep with your eyes open?"

I didn't say anything. I was waiting for the women to begin. Portman probably debated with himself whether he should continue his talk about food. He knew as well as anyone that talking about food made one hungry. Someone would tell him to shut up. Once, when Portman served as Rottenführer Schiese-Dietz's orderly, he got outside the camp and carried back an image of deep and silent woods that only here and there were fenced with barbed wire. These were endless woods, pines, firs, and sometimes deciduous trees, full of game and silence. The SS men went out to hunt, but they did not shoot deer, does, and hares—they shot people.

Outside, the flames cut through the night and the snow. The sparks flew out of the darkness. The wind howled. Now and then you could hear the crows across the evening sky. They were evil omens. They were flying to the left. That, according to Portman, was the worst. If they flew to the right, that meant he should be cautious. And he could make a wish, as when you see a falling star. All sorts of superstitions came back, and many of them resembled crows. Crows were always an omen of death, of the worst there is. In the night I could imagine the curved flight path of the crows. Portman believed that they talked to each other. But according to him, they talked only because some farmer and some village children had slit open their tongues. The crows held court and they sentenced individuals from their ranks; and a male and a female carried out the sentence together, pecking the culprit to death either in flight or on the ground. But Portman would reverse this sometimes and insist that crows are capable of helping the weakest ones in the flock, the young ones and the weary. A squadron of crows will send out a patrol from its midst to save the weak, the falling or ailing ones. And they know how to warn others of danger.

Already on Monday, before it got dark, Portman, Harry Cohen, and I saw the old Jewish women who spoke Hungarian or Yiddish. We knew what awaited them. We hoped it would be quick. But our wishes did not matter. I also wished that the crows would fly somewhere else with their cawing and hoped they would fly in a straight line without detours. Their sounds reminded me of the worst things: of humiliation, hunger, cold, of illness, weakness, and helplessness. I envied them— their life, their flight, their freedom. I couldn't understand how they could live a hundred and fifty years. But it occurred to me that they could collect endless secrets in that time. I thought of all that they had lived through and wondered where they could take it in their flight.

Portman talked only about the living. He pretended that he had never seen the dead in the camp, as if there weren't any dead here, not to mention the dying. He did not see them. He did not look. Or maybe he looked elsewhere. He forced his hungry red eyes not to see, his brain not to comprehend, as if he had heard about the dead only secondhand.

I wasn't even thinking about the selection that Rottenführer Schiese-Dietz had come to perform. He made the prisoners walk over the long stable-chimney that ran horizontally about knee-high all the way through the barracks ever since the days of the Austro-Hungarian empire when the cavalry was garrisoned here. The prisoners had to walk over the chimney bricks naked, so that the overseers could quickly discern their healthy or sickly condition. Men whose penises had turned black, who were skin and bone, or those with exalted feverish eyes went at a trot down the whole length of the chimney; and only the healthy ones, when the thumbs-up sign was given, could jump off and go back to their bunks. The others who did not get the thumbs-up were selected to continue to the end of the chimney and then through the back entrance down a plank to be loaded onto a truck that took them to the showers. If someone's penis got hard as he was running down the square chimney, either from excitement, from fear or cold, or from some nervous disorder, he had to run to the end of the chimney down the plank, into a car, and into the disrobing rooms, where Germans would make short shrift of his Jewish lust as well as of him, in the surest possible way.

In the women's barracks there had been today—like every day including Saturday and Sunday—two, three, perhaps even five routine selections. For the Germans, it was both a necessity and a pastime. Naked women, in the presence of two or three well-built and elegant SS men, would run or walk along the chimney as if on a stage, waiting for the sign of the thumb. Women with sagging or dried-up breasts, the skinniest ones who had turned old overnight or all of a sudden, women weakened by menopause and with fear of illness or nervousness in their eyes, women without husbands and children, swollen or again thinner than dying mares, women with male traits and beards which they had no time to pluck out, women who were bleeding in the groin but could not clean themselves up, or just women who were splattered with mud and dust—they all waited for the sign of the thumb. Up, horizontally, down. Down and horizontally. The SS would take turns. They had enough women so that among the three hundred and thirty-three, each one could choose his own figures. Each time it was ten or twenty women who got the sign to walk or run to the back entrance at the back of the truck.

"Now," said Harry Cohen all of a sudden, just one second before I wanted to come out with it.

"I know," I said. "I can hear them."

"They're like swans," said Portman. "Women are always faithful beyond the grave to someone, just like swans. Or maybe like geese. But they're wrong if they think they're laying golden eggs in the darkness. How will this help them? I bet they haven't eaten. Are you telling me that you both knew they'd begin, as if nothing had broken them?" Sometimes, after the selection, the women would sing. They would wait for darkness to cover the camp, when everything except the fires had died down. No one could guess how long it would go on. Sometimes the guards sicced dogs on them, and sometimes the guards would fire a few volleys from a machine gun from the door to silence them. Sometimes a few shots were enough, sometimes a few magazines. It was always only a question of time. But before that there was the question whether they would begin, or whether they would give up even this, the very last thing they had. And now they began. It evoked a horror that most people could no longer sense. It gave a new birth to something that had perished long ago. They filled the void that spreads from space, like waves over a calm surface rippled by a wind out of nowhere. It was like a stone that had been given a voice.

"The heat from the chimneys gets on some people's brains," said Portman. "They must all be mad, or they wouldn't be asking for it. Do they want to drive everybody crazy?"

I could not yet identify the words of the melody, but I felt how they filled the space of the camp and of the whole night, the space of the world and beyond, extending into infinity, the incomprehensible void, which they filled with their voices, with their melody that was only beginning to take shape. I imagined a labyrinth, bodies, voices, wooden bunks in the dark, a maze from which the women tried to find a way out—like all the blind, deaf and dumb, drugged or poisoned, tottering from blows to the head, driven nearly out of their minds.

"All the rats have left the women's barracks," said Portman.

The women sang for all those who had lost someone, someone selected at daylight to be sent up the chimney and now no longer among the living; they sang to distract the bereaved from thoughts of the fires and of those who were alive only a few hours ago. The women who sang belonged to the Cleaning Outfit, which scrubbed even the trucks, scrubbing them clean of the dirt left behind by the condemned ones.

The singing filled the night with double voices. Double darkness. Double eyes. Double blood. Double snow, and far above the snow clouds, in a double star-filled sky. Double memory. Double hope and illusion. It filled it with all the things that man possesses only once in his life and loses.

"They make me nervous as a cat," said Portman.

You could not see the flames, you could only hear them. The women who had lost someone already—yesterday, the day before, last week or last month—sang for the mothers who had lost a daughter, for the daughters who had lost a mother, for the sisters without sisters, and for friends without friends and acquaintances who had lost someone they knew. At first the singing was low, then louder, and finally quite loud. They would sing for a short time and sometimes longer, although never too long, and their singing was joined by those who were afraid at first. Finally they were joined by those that were stricken, until in the end, everybody was singing.

"If you sing at night or in bed, that's bound to bring you bad luck," Portman said again. "If you sing at night, you'll be crying before dawn. If you're singing because you don't have a reason for doing it, someone will give you hell for it."

The whole month Portman had argued that even here there were good days and bad days. And that only children and old people could not survive their uselessness.

I waited, as did all the men in the camps, for the first tune—just as you wait for the first evening star, making believe that it has some special significance for you. I tried to imagine the faces or figures of the women from Norway, Belgium, and Holland, the women and girls from Rome, Warsaw, or Sofia, women and girls from Berlin, Paris, or the island of Corfu who had come here by boat and then by train, half dead with thirst. That which they were singing was, at least for the moment, beyond the reach of the hierarchy of the ruling and the humiliated, those who condemned them while they still had the chance to do the condemning. It reminded one of a fortress crumbling invisibly, even though its ramparts were strong and remained tall and unassailable.

The singing came from the darkness distorted, as if from a great distance. I felt something that no one could understand. It contained everything that I had ever waited for, everything I was afraid of and which filled me with mystery and fear, as well as with the wonder of life, because death had become simple, comprehensible, and ordinary. This is the world in which the killers were born together with us, but by killing would live without us; this was the world in which each one of us was the last in the world, before he disappeared and left behind a sliver of ash in the museum of an extinct race, remembered as someone who happened to appear for a couple of thousand years on the surface of this earth. It filled me with something resembling chloroform, which knocks you out like a fragment of a dream.

I waited to hear it interrupted by the rattle of the train on the ramp or a volley from a machine gun or a revolver. At the same time I hoped it would not stop. I wished that the women would sing, just as I wished to see the only thing that would make up for the destruction of justice: my image of two stars flying toward each other before they crash and crush the world that had culminated in this camp and in the killing of innocence in the name of an idea. It embraced something that I never could explain and which I probably would never be able to explain. Everything that man is and is not.

In those women's voices I heard all that is insignificant as well as all that is great, that which is pitiful and full of a silent glory, that which is comprehensible and incomprehensible, like every man and everything he has gone through and still must go through in the future. I understood that man in his smallness and misery is part of something greater, something that has had and will have many names, something that is unfathomable and great like the sea and the earth, the clouds and trillions of stars or galaxies, and at the same time lost like a grain of sand in the desert, or a fish or drop of water or salt in the ocean; that for which man wants to live, even in a place like this, permeated with death and killing, just as the sky is permeated with stars or a snowy night with snowflakes. I understood why man has the strength to die when it is his turn, so that someone else will not have to die in his place; and what he will share, when he has nothing left but his body heat and a spoon carved from an alder branch so that he can eat his soup and not lap it up like some dog, wolf, or rat.

I expected to hear the barking of dogs from the darkness of the night. I felt a different kind of fear and anxiety, different from what I experienced in the afternoon while I looked at the barbed wire, at the German uniforms, at the whip with the golden ring in the hand of the Rottenführer Schiese-Dietz. When I closed my eyes, I had the feeling that I was witnessing the birth of a new planet which was yet to be peopled, a feeling of going way back into time, into the very oldest times when the cooled-off planet earth had just become inhabited. I felt a new infinity, that infinity upon which man trespasses now and again with every breath, word, act or even the blinking of an eye. Something closer than closeness and more distant than distance, something so loud that it deafened me, and something so soft that it was like an incomprehensible whisper.

"Who cares about this," Portman growled. "I'd give them a better idea."

It probably seemed to him that he was watching how they would beat or shoot his mother, if he had ever known her. I don't know. Harry Cohen, too, let Portman's words float by as if Portman had not said anything the whole evening. This bothered Portman. It was a funeral rite, the singing that was born here and was not performed elsewhere, nor would be in the future. It probably both comforted and disturbed him that there would never be witnesses anywhere to this funereal singing that sounded like a martial song and like a suicide challenge, the invisible gauntlet thrown into the face of the enemy, because those who sang were in mortal danger. I don't know, I really don't know. For me it was something that I had lacked so I could perceive my life as less incomplete, and it was something that I do not understand to this day, somewhat like perceiving an echo that exists only in the memory, or a shadow that fell long ago, or a cry that memory has blurred.

"I don't want to hear them sing so I won't have to hear them cry," Portman added.

The women's voices were still mixing with the snowflakes, with the fire and the darkness. The singing came out of the wild night into which the women had brought it to subdue this night when people were being killed, like every night, every day, Friday, Saturday, and Sunday, on high holidays and on every working day, before the stars came out and when they were already fading in the sky. It came out of the night where words meant less than wind, snow, slivers or clumps of ash before they disintegrate, out of the night where innocent people were being killed in one part of the world, while in another part makeshift barracks were being slapped together for more and more prisoners, until all of Europe was German.

Not very far from us was a whorehouse to which prominent Jewish prisoners, henchmen and informers, and Jewish collaborators were occasionally admitted. We hated and despised them and at the same time feared them almost more than we feared the Germans. A little farther away there was another brothel for the soldiers, and yet a few steps further, mothers and wives of the soldiers and clerks of the Totenkopf SS garrison (entrusted by the Nazis with the cars of the prisons and prison camps) were reading fairy tales to their children about Hansel and Gretel and about the brave Siegfried. In one block, German doctors cut pieces of skin from healthy prisoners for grafting on frostbitten German soldiers from the Eastern front, or frozen airmen fished out of the English Channel. In another block two Jewish women pianists played a concert of Beethoven sonatas before being sent up the chimney. The prisoners and the jailers slept under the same stars.

The voices of the women came from the openness and closeness of the night, flowing together like a refuge created from nothing, like a shelter where you can hide for a moment without fleeing, where you can rest and gather strength or save the remainder of your strength. Their voices became a battleground upon which danger, for a few seconds, did not seem so dangerous. For just a moment, pain changed to painlessness and indifference to solidarity.

Over Auschwitz-Birkenau, below the low-lying snow clouds, in the thick smoke of the chimneys of the five crematoria, the singing of unknown women continued. Their singing came from the darkness, for a few seconds, almost a minute, two minutes or three, from the ever renewing sea of life and death, from the darkness and out of the wind, from the lips of women and from the depth or shallowness of the universe.

I was afraid that the women would stop. Then everything would be quiet. And then the only sound in the night would be that of ashes, snow, and wind.

"They're probably feeding the dogs in the kennels now," Portman mused.

Harry Cohen plucked hair from his nostrils and his ears, so that he would look all right in the morning lineup.

The singing of the women sounded like a river overflowing its banks. It colored the night the way the flames colored it or the red morning sky for those who are still alive to see it and for those who can only imagine it before they perish. It marked the night with a forgotten strength, forgotten tenderness, forgotten defiance, and forgotten understanding.

"How can anyone in Germany today think that a thousand years or ten thousand years from now this will be forgotten?" Harry Cohen asked.

"I can't stand the realization that all that remains of them is song and ashes," Portman said. He did not say that he divided people into those who'd already gone through it and those who were still waiting. He divided women into those whose families had perished long ago and those who had lost them to the trucks only this afternoon or at dusk.

"It's like catching sparrows in a cage," Portman added. "Everyone knows what to expect for that." His voice was full of anger and death. "I wish they'd shove it," he added.

Harry Cohen held a piece of bread and a bloody pork sausage under his ragged jacket. Was he about to eat it? He had to be hungry. But he did not eat. Was he waiting for the women to stop, just as I was, in the same way as before, when we waited for them to begin?

"They've lost their minds," Portman said. "They're more stubborn than I thought. They're more persistent than salt."

I could imagine the way the women looked. Some were swollen from hunger and irregularity, while others for the same reasons lost weight. Some sold themselves for a piece of bread, while others sold a piece of bread for a bowl of water so that they could wash. Sometimes I saw them humiliated because they had to strip naked before the SS soldiers or the Ukranian guards, or doubly humiliated because their heads had been shaved, destroying their femininity. They had already lost their capacity for bearing children. But now they were singing.

"What's the good of it?" Portman asked. "Why don't the smarter ones make them shut up?"

"With what? With ashes?" Harry Cohen asked.

"It makes my teeth hurt," Portman said. He was afraid that he would get another toothache and that without his teeth he would never be the same.

Did he huddle up so that he would not hear them? Did he pretend that the song no longer interested him? Was he interested only in his own breath? I no longer understood Portman and probably neither did Harry Cohen. The more we exposed our lives, the less we understood each other.

The women sang lullabies that they had brought from their homes, songs about love and joy, about the freshness of children. Their voices brought back a world which no longer existed.

"Yesterday Schiese-Dietz picked out the redheads," said Portman. "He probably knew why."

Portman feared who the rottenführer would pick out in the morning. Sometimes he picked out people who had prominent chins, or those who had small receding chins—sometimes people with white teeth and sometimes just the opposite. He'd picked out people with small heads and small brains, or with big heads in which he expected big brains even though the selected one would stare at him with the eyes of an idiot. Portman did not know when Schiese-Dietz would start selecting people with big ears or untrimmed fingernails, with thin or flat lips, with thick or sparse eyebrows, cross-eyed ones and people with long fingers.

But Portman sometimes dreamed about being selected for the Canada commando special unit, who cleared the arriving transports and had lots of food and drink, at least for a day, for themselves and their friends—bacon and bread and strawberry or plum jam, and thermoses with coffee, cocoa or hot tea, and vodka or schnapps or French cognac. He dreamed about this in spite of the fact that it also meant clearing the ramp and the railroad cars of dead infants and small choked children, carrying a bunch of them at once like bananas or shot hares or killed or choked hens. Portman dreamed around the clock of a full belly, but there was no chance of his making it into the Canada commando.

"It's my father's birthday today and the anniversary of his death," Harry Cohen said. "I'm as old today as he was when he died. He died in his bed. He was reading a book, closed his eyes and whispered that the end had come."

"Congratulations," replied Portman. "Do you think this has some special meaning here? That it's perhaps some kind of prophecy and you have a right not to let me sleep?"

Suddenly I realized that I was holding on to Harry Cohen's elbows and wrists and that Portman was pressed between us. Our lice crawled from one collar to another. I took their warmth and they took mine.

The unknown women had sparked an image of what could be because it had been once before. From time to time, the wailing wind interrupted the singing. Then the voices became clearer again, although the wailing wind did not die down. They floated through the network of electrified barbed wire, somewhere into infinity. I no longer waited for what Portman would say to mask his envy of the living and the dead. He was sometimes afraid of the dark so he had to talk to hide his even greater fear of the Germans. The singing roused something in him that he thought was dead. It was somewhere on the limits, the nakedness of everything that was still living. It was the heart of his existence, on the thin border of his moral and physical strengths, like the moments of selection, dependent upon decisions made by someone else, but also upon his own decision on how to accept it. Only he and his consciousness, no traitor to himself.

"I'll give them another minute," said Portman. Suddenly it sounded as if he did not have enough air in his lungs. Maybe he had tuberculosis already. "Count to sixty."

The women were singing a popular German song: *"In den Sternen steht es alles geschrieben, du sollst küssen, du sollst lieben..."* Probably those who went into the chimney were German or Austrian Jewish women. It was an old coffeehouse hit, but in this moment it carried some immediate, close, pure and direct sincerity and courage, some surprising truth about who is who, no matter where or when. There was in that song now everything that was still unselfish or honorable, even when it was weak and abased.

"Well, really, who cares? When it takes so long it's no good," Portman added. He was being sarcastic about the thought that someone here was singing about kissing and passion or the desire from which children are born.

I held on to my wish that the women would not stop. Did Portman want them to stop because he feared for them? Besides the fact that in the end he turned his anger upon himself?

"Do you want to cry for them?" Portman asked. "This is idiotic solidarity and does no one any good. It just makes the Germans madder. The women have paid for it a couple of times already, as far as I know. Wouldn't it be better to let the Germans sleep at night at least? Do they want to test whether it's true that the devil never sleeps at night? Do they think they're in America—where they can sing whenever and whatever they please?"

Portman turned his face to the planks of the bunk. "They'll knock their teeth out if not worse. I've seen a lot of toothless ones here. And then later I didn't see them anymore, precisely because they had lost their teeth."

I held on to the last bits of the melody, which was already becoming blurred against the night. My brain, along with hunger and the smell of human bodies in the barracks, was floating off into the numb wakefulness that precedes sleep. I suddenly realized that I needed to have Ervin Portman beside me, even with his anger and superstitions and fear, and I needed Harry Cohen, just as they both needed me. Even when the people—both the living and the dead—get on each other's nerves because they have nothing to offer each other and just vegetate, even on the way to the showers. What makes a man forgive others is not born of weakness or of strength, but from the fact that human life is irreplaceable and that nothing else matters.

Portman was bothered by my lice and by Harry Cohen's fleas. Portman picked them out from the ends of his short hair before it would be cut again for blankets and army coats. He pinched them with his nails and threw them down from the bunk in a curve resembling the flight of crows. When someone below grumbled, as though he'd swallowed them, Portman stopped. I felt Portman's hot breath, just as Harry Cohen felt mine.

"When I was a kid, my mother used to believe that if two people started singing the same song it brought them luck," Harry Cohen said.

"I never sing or whistle when I play cards," Portman said. "That's sure to make you lose. I don't rush headlong into hell if I can remain at least a little while at hell's entrance. I prefer to look at smoke instead of looking straight into the fire. That's one thing they've taught me: that it's better to have your hand in the water than to have it in the fire."

"Hell isn't down below, in the center of the earth, in the crevices of mountains, rocks, and passes. It's up above, on the surface of the earth, like scales on the body of a fish. It's in every man, under the stars, under the snow, under the enormous firmament," Harry Cohen said. "It's in every uniform, in every whip, bullet, or dog that is set against people. I think that hell exists fivefold—in each of the five crematoria. Or in the eight-meter pits where they burn people when it's not snowing or raining."

"They're still singing. They're more persistent than salt," I said. "They're braver than geese or wild swans. I wish I had their marrow in my bones."

"A lot of good it would do you. You'd really end up in a fine mess then," Portman said. "Don't count on me."

The uniqueness and worthlessness of human life—like two sisters—floated through the night, over the camp and over all of the camps of Germany and the occupied territories. This is what in five, six years the German war had done. This is what made one doubt man and his existence, victory and defeat, good and evil. What caused the first to be last and the last to be first. The wind distorted the singing of the women. It drove the snow against the wall of the barracks and filled its enormous arms with ashes which it carried away farther or closer, spreading them on all sides—ashes that will remain on the face of the planet like a birthmark, even if every last Jewish man, Jewish woman, or Jewish child should perish.

The ashes silenced the echo of the first shot. It lasted only a few seconds. Definitely less than half a minute. The singing mixed with the shooting, then there was only shooting and its echo. It definitely was nothing unexpected; Portman was right about that. It sounded like the rottenführer's switch for camels. Last time, Harry Cohen remembered that a camel will never forget if somebody wrongs it. But, Harry Cohen added, they never forget the good that someone does for them, either. I was sure that he was now in his mind with that Aryan girl in Prague, Maruschka. Maybe she could read his mind, but she could never know what he knew.

In the air, among the snowflakes, a kind of echo remained from the shooting of the machine gun. It was all ordinary, just like the snowflakes. Like the smoke from the chimneys. Like mud.

"They could have figured it out," Portman said. "Unless they've become blind, like moles in the winter."

"Maybe they did figure it out," Harry Cohen replied. "But I don't believe it, just as I don't believe that moles go blind in the winter."

"I'll go to sing with them, once they get the idea of throwing rocks at the rottenführer and at the scharführer at the same time," Portman said. And then he added, "No one will give a damn."

Someone went to the bucket. Nothing had changed in the least in the daily routine of the barracks. From the sounds of the steps and movements you could tell who had diarrhea, who had dysentery or even typhus, who had tuberculosis, pneumonia, or only asthma—who would not make it till morning or midnight and who would manage to infect his bedfellows before he died.

I bid farewell to the singing of the women and looked forward to tomorrow's, just as I had looked forward to my grandmother's bedtime fairy tales. Where does a man find strength when all that he has is weakness?

"Schiese-Dietz believes that Jewish children are born hairy, like animals," Portman said. "He also selects the hairy girls first, even before those who are skin and bones."

I knew that I would be able to hear the women singing again, and yet it occurred to me that they would be singing when I wouldn't be there—nor Portman, nor Harry Cohen. I thought about life and death in Auschwitz-Birkenau. What is the purpose of human existence? Why is man plagued by feelings of futility and worthlessness? How do you find out how to do the right thing when it comes to it? It was again a moment of unanswerable questions. But there was some change in the air, even if there were no answers. How many people had they shot? What would the women appeal to tomorrow with their singing? I was lost in the echo of their chorus. I felt the snow, the ashes, and the silence around me. I felt the urge to go outside, for which the guard would immediately shoot me before I got to the barbed wire. I wanted to touch with my lips a sliver of ash or snowflake. I listened. There was no sound. The women had sung themselves to sleep. Others cried themselves to sleep. And still others had been shot into an eternal sleep.

"At last," said Portman.

It did not sound like relief or satisfaction, though sometimes Portman thought that women had nine lives, like cats. Perhaps he hoped that it was true. Everything that had to do with cats Portman believed to be ill-fated, an echo or foreboding of misfortune, even when it was born only in his head.

"Couldn't they have gone to sleep long ago?" Portman asked. "Tomorrow they'll be dropping like flies, even those who were not hit." And then he continued, "There's no sense in wasting your time or your strength. It's a waste of every drop of blood when you spill it on your own and for nothing."

I tried to call back the echo of the women's voices, the image of birth, of something that for me was always connected with women, something which I knew little about and probably never understood. I felt the familiar shame, but for the first time, maybe knowing why.

"Do you have the shakes or what?" Portman addressed me. And finally, "They'll drive me nuts with their singing."

Portman curled up to sleep. I wished the remaining women would fall asleep and not be cold. Harry Cohen began to chew his bread and blood sausage. He was, maybe, concerned with the number of possibilities everything and everybody had, has, or should have, or doesn't have at all. He wished to be somewhere else, someone else, where people do not live a miserable life, where they don't have to ask every other second why they were born, about things for which there were no solutions.

Portman's fleas and lice were feasting on me. The smoke rose slowly toward the sky. Black snow was falling. I have never forgotten the black snow with ashes in Auschwitz-Birkenau, which that night I saw for the first time in my life before I fell asleep.

"Good night," Portman said in a conciliatory tone. He repeated to himself the tattooed number on his right forearm. He probably no longer envied the dead.

"Good night," Harry Cohen said. It was one of the possibilities.

"Good night," I managed sleepily.

We were swallowed by the silence into which Samson once disappeared and in which every night and every man seems to be the last. Infinity engulfed us.

A Man the Size of a Postage Stamp

❖

Don't react to a mad man if you don't want to be like him.

Answer a mad man's madness so he doesn't think how wise he is.
——Jewish Proverb

Nobody knows anything. Nobody is going to know anything.
Not even we know anything.
——Heinrich Himmler

The dead can't carry the dead.
——German Proverb

1

H ey, still the hair and whiskers?" said Feldwebel Karl Oberg, a leader of the garrison band.

He was as surprised as he had been on Thursday that nothing showed on the teacher's face. "What do you think is so smart about not shaving or cutting your hair? You still believe that he who lives to see next spring will survive for one whole year?"

Karl Oberg's coat had been tailor-made for him when he had been the military bandleader in the Warsaw garrison. Polish nobility patronized the same tailor. Feldwebel Oberg said he didn't expect the teacher to reply. He hadn't answered last Thursday, either. The teacher hadn't said a word the whole day there and back. The commandant had ordered him to bring the old man again. The feldwebel wondered what the commandant could want from the teacher.

They were halfway there. Alongside the old teacher, Feldwebel Oberg felt like a strong young sapling in springtime next to an old tree. Thinking about an old tree, he could imagine the labyrinth of roots, a hiding place for poisonous snakes. The old man's back was bent. His eyes were dim. The bandleader's eyes were blue. He was slender and well built, and there wasn't a speck of soot on his well-shaven face. His black shoes were well shined. He was careful to keep his shoes clean.

They passed the bakery and the storehouse and the office of the accountant and the camp's army-supply depot. After that, the two were joined by the bandleader's German shepherd.

"Come here, Suicide," said the feldwebel. "What are you doing loose here? Isn't it dangerous to run free? There must be a bitch around somewhere."

It was cold. The wind was still. The coldness lay across the land like silence. It patched the marshes together.

"Still got all that hair and all those whiskers," said Feldwebel Oberg. "Yet we can't import seaweed, mattress stuffing, or sponges from all over the world anymore like we used to."

He exhaled and his breath came out like white steam. "Doesn't all this ever remind you of the sea? Or perhaps a rock at the bottom of the sea? Hey, wake up, Whiskers! We still got a few minutes to go."

Feldwebel Oberg had gone to the trouble of arranging one of the Jewish melodies in the morning. He put its funeral-like rhythm into a march. He would introduce it next Thursday evening at the casino.

You could hear trains coming and leaving on the ramps.

"Some people keep silent to make themselves feel bigger," the Feldwebel said. "We're almost there, Whiskers."

Karl Oberg began to whistle "The Entry of the Gladiators." Something occurred to him.

"You not only have all your hair and whiskers like you did last week," he said, "I understand you've still got your name, huh Whiskers? But you've got a number too, and a tattoo on your left forearm, isn't it so? Still got everything, hair and whiskers, the name, even your civilian clothes. You ought to be more grateful."

He kept on whistling. He glanced briefly at the teacher's face.

They were almost there, and Henryk Bley tried to straighten up so he could keep pace with Feldwebel Oberg. Walking warmed him up a little, but it exhausted him as well. The dog kept circling and jumping, sniffing and snarling. Not even the rapid pace was enough to keep the teacher warm. He had once told the children in the camp orphanage to stand in clusters and hug each other to keep warm.

The German shepherd stopped in front of the commandant's house.

"Take it easy, Suicide." The feldwebel addressed the dog. "Don't you like *Menschentieren*?"

The German shepherd eyed Karl Oberg from the doorway. His nostrils quivered in anticipation.

"Faster, Whiskers. Try to catch Herr Commandant, if we haven't missed him already like last Thursday."

Karl Oberg let the teacher pass through the gates between the sentries and then followed him. The guard told the feldwebel that his escort should stay in the waiting room.

2

Herr Commandant Oscar Adler-Bienenstock was with his son at the park. He didn't have a wife, only a twelve-year-old son who had come here afterward. Herr Commandant had been wounded at the Eastern front. They both liked engines and music, which, as Schopenhauer said, mimics the world, the mystery of life, the great nothingness; the melody to which the world's text is set. But that was all they had in common.

Herr Commandant had taught his son reading and writing, physics and arithmetic. He taught him the mysteries of birds and animals, the importance of discipline, and the secrets of engines. In winter the marshes froze, and in the springtime they melted. It was hell for engines. But worst of all was keeping the machines going and repairing the engine's disorders.

People began to whisper that Herr Commandant's little son, a blue-eyed, fair-haired little angel who did not look like Herr Commandant but probably resembled his mother, wasn't quite right in the head. He had big bloodshot eyes that were wet and glassy, a skull that narrowed in the back, a high forehead, and big ears. Only his complexion was lovely, just like his shiny hair, like a girl's. His bottom lip was large and wet from the way he kept running his tongue over it; even if he wasn't eating or drinking he found something for his tongue to do.

The boy listened to his father's explanations. Had the father forgotten the time? It seemed that the boy liked to look at things backward. Trains coming and going—and vice versa. Sometimes the boy seemed scared and other times indifferent and still, or aggressive before submerging into his indifference again.

Islands of leafless forests stretched above them and into the countryside. The sound of engines carried far into the marshes.

Herr Commandant ordered the forests cut. He had the timber hauled off for the Reich. That way, not even the maimed forest could give shelter to the fugitives. Only miles from here there were forests untouched, silent and deep; in their midst, wrapped like a gossamer in needle leaves, was T.II., the brother camp.

"What happens to animals when they're with people?" asked the boy.

"Why?"

"Because of these children here."

"Oh, I see," Herr Commandant said.

But he wasn't sure. Was it that the boy saw the children in the camp, as he did the rest of the prisoners, as animals? Hopefully, the boy didn't know any more about the people they put behind the wires.

But the boy saw them, every day. He would grow with it as German children were growing among farms and gardens or factories and schools. They were coming and never leaving, but their numbers didn't increase.

Sometimes the boy thought it was strange. Were they entering some underground river, disappearing into an invisible sea?

Herr Commandant grabbed his shoulders and called him a man; but the boy didn't like his embrace. For a second, he looked through his father as though he were a stranger.

"Which side of the fence was my mother on?" the boy asked.

"Your mother?"

When it was too cold to watch the band practice outdoors, or to watch and listen to the engines, the child's attention was captured by the waves of greasy smoke that rolled in on the wind from the marshes or over the forests from the camps at T.II., and the dumping station. The boy watched as the wind pulled the smoke across the sky and created letters, numbers, or signs. Sometimes the clouds were thick, and black ash fell from them like rain. And sometimes the clouds resembled engines and trucks. The pond was half frozen.

"You're going to like the military maps," Herr Commandant said.

"Why?" asked the boy.

Military maps weren't what the boy liked. He was fond of new army trucks with red crosses painted on them. Three weeks ago he had seen soldiers taking out stiff human bodies. At first, Herr Commandant forbade the boy to watch, but it became routine, everpresent.

The pond resembled a sunset in the midst of the day, reflecting dry clouds split from a dark ocean. The boy looked up at the smoke writing its incomprehensible messages in the sky.

There was no river in the town or at the camp at the side of the marshes, so there were no bridges. Only once had the boy asked for the bridges he remembered from Germany. All that was left of the church was the bell tower. German pilots had aimed at it when the town was still Polish. After that, the young German cannoneers used it as a training target. A small handful of military families comprised the German garrison. It was the army that created the atmosphere in the town, even though it was represented by few people—the way a country was represented by a ship, a flag, or a reputation. The boy didn't like other German boys, and vice versa.

"In a map you can taste the time, like you can tell the taste from the smell of an apple," said the father. "There are many things you can taste and feel—time, tradition, courage. Maybe later, a woman like your mother."

Was it too complicated for the boy?

The boy seemed not to listen. There was an inscription on the garage that fascinated the boy: "We Germans came into the world in order to die." It reminded him of the truck with red crosses on its sides and on its roof. The ambulances had no windows, like birds without wings or heads. Something was missing, or rather, had been added—a sheet metal neck that led into the strong, eight-cylinder motor. And instead of legs, it had two big exhaust pipes, like the wings of a bird in flight, curving like fins; but why did they have no windows? The boy wondered. Why did the exhaust pipes curve inward instead of out? What happened to people from the moment they stepped into the ambulance until the cab was empty again? Man never asks, the father had said. The boy's thick, fair hair was combed back, like a mane, and his blue eyes shone.

It struck Herr Commandant that his son looked like an angel. Only angels do not know and ask why. There is no why for people in command. Why did this happen to me? That brought to mind some lines from Nietzsche about the dead god who had killed the conscience— who said that beauty is watching someone you have helped to create (in this case his boy) glide across the pond's level, performing the backstroke. It was necessary to scorn death, maybe to love death. The killing and the possibility of being killed. To understand life and death as one. How to teach that to his son? How to introduce him to the great killing, teach him to despise and defy life?

One's name—being a father—being a son means very little in the light of some things, Herr Commandant thought. The new kind of love is tough, not fragile like Christian love—or, forgive me, that of the Jewish swine who ended up on a Roman cross and good riddance to him—I've got a feeble-minded son—thanks to whom?—I must love him in a tough way, like a master without weakness. But the commandant was thinking about the Reich's laws and institutions like Brandenburg, Hartheim, or Eglfing-Haar hospitals or a mental hospital in Kaufbeuren, and what was called "the merciful act."

When he took the boy out of school to look after his education himself, his son confused the points of a compass, north, east, south, and west. He could never remember the four elements, fire, water, earth, and air. There was some fifth element between his temples. He had trouble with everything that included four, the ideal number of Pythagoras. He only comprehended the number three of Aristotle. He didn't know that swamps can belong to both elements, water and earth. He would concentrate on light, or on sounds, and always on voices. But he could never get them all together.

It seemed as if the boy's interest could not be aroused by talking about animals and what happens to animals in the company of people. Only about engines. Then he started to make wet circles with his small, full, red tongue.

"Why don't you listen when I speak to you?"

"I'm looking," the boy said.

"At what?"

"At the ambulances. They look like birds. Like fish. Like swans."

"They're good cars."

"They don't have windows."

"They're disinfection trucks," the father told him. "Yesterday, three of them broke down. They've got new engines already, or I hope so. I will show you four new ones."

"They've got exhaust pipes like elephant trunks," said the boy.

Maybe he should have been born a girl, Herr Commandant thought. What am I going to do with him? And through the father's mind flashed the thought how the boy would be better off.

The boy looked up at the sky, at the picture the smoke was drawing in the still air and at the rolls of huge, black, sooty, vaporlike balloons. The blue sky was endless.

"There will be a concert this evening," Herr Commandant said. "'The Entry of the Gladiators.' That's a nice march. *Einzug der Gladia-toren.* Will we go listen in the casino?"

The father looked on as the son played ducks and drakes with flat pebbles. He always took three stones at once. Then the boy threw the stones into the water and watched the circles. They never touched the icy margin.

"Why don't you say something?" asked the father.

The boy remembered the morning he visited his mother in her bedroom in Berlin. It was a clear day, and his mother had said that she would have nothing more to do with his father. His father hit her in the face with his fist. Her back and head struck the wall of the bedroom. She bled from her nose. His father became furious at the sight of her blood and he hit the boy's mother again and threw her onto the bed, tearing her dress and her underwear from her. "I can't stand you," said the mother. "Go away. You're disgusting." The boy was hidden in the wardrobe with his mother's dresses and shoes and flacons of perfume. Nobody knew the boy saw. His father didn't know he was there. The boy could only guess what it meant, why the mother refused to share the bed with the father, why the father had gotten so mad. He left her lying in her blood, her face toward the ceiling.

Sometimes the water brought it all back to him. Or the smoke. And sometimes the trucks. But near his father he always remembered it. When he was four or five years old, his father broke into a fit of anger at having an imbecile for a son and beat him with his fists about his head and face and nose and eyes, and that happened often. Only later, after his mother left, did he stop beating him.

"To understand animals is to understand people; and to understand people is to understand war," said Herr Commandant.

"Why do animals fight?" asked the boy.

"From an instinct for survival," answered Herr Commandant. "To live."

"Look there," said the boy.

"Where?" asked the father.

He looked up at the sky where the smoke was thinning out and into a stream from the castle at T.II. Puffs of it floated in the sky like a map that Herr Commandant could follow—the same way sailors at sea can read the stars, or the way a blind man can move with confidence along a familiar path. The smaller dots were towns and villages, and the tiniest circles were camps.

"Let's go, I have a meeting at the Commandatur and Führesheim. You wish to go with me?" He touched the boy's shoulder.

His eyes flickered with a distaste he couldn't put into words. He thought about fathers and children. Four elements. He looked back from the ambulances, away from his son and the inscription over the garage door and back to the sky.

3

Henryk Bley waited, as Feldwebel Karl Oberg told him to, in the commandant's waiting room. Ever since last Thursday, the teacher had racked his brain about why Herr Commandant summoned him, then sent him away without bothering to see him. He ruled out the possibility that the commandant had wanted to ask him to teach or advise him on his son. But he hadn't ruled out the possibility that he might be interested in knowing his views on his son. The teacher had years of experience in that field. Last week, Feldwebel Oberg had mentioned that at the castle at T.II.—they weren't just exterminating bedbugs and lice and rats with Cyclon B.

There was a loose-leaf calendar on the right side of the door leading into Herr Commandant's office. Easter Monday was printed in red. The teacher could hear Feldwebel Karl Oberg talking with an orderly at the other end of the hall. They both laughed. The noises of trains on the ramps were coming and fading again.

The orderly, Sturmman Fritzinger, on the way to the ambulances, had a good story for the bandleader in his native German about what the last Gypsy king had said: "Big in his own eyes, small in the eyes of others."

The office of Herr Commandant was in the left wing of a stone building whose windows overlooked a garden with huge poplar trees. From the corridor and the waiting room you could see the frozen trees wrapped in ice which melted at midday and froze again in the afternoon, forming droplets of ice like pearls. Stubby icicles hung from the drain-spouts, reflecting the feeble afternoon sun. The corridor was decorated with framed portraits of German military leaders, right up to the most recent one, who had brought the Reich together. Some of the portraits had mourning bands across the right hand corner.

The teacher heard footsteps in the hall. Herr Commandant had lost one leg below the knee fighting on the Eastern front in Suwalki, Lithuania. That place was marked on his map in red.

Henryk Bley stared at the toes of his shoes. He tried to concentrate on Easter Monday, or on a distant picture of the city of Susa, in Persia, where he'd been once. The muddle of the village came closer and then faded away—fragments of an image. There was also a man in a regal robe, embroidered with pearls, gold, and rubies, who'd wanted to exterminate them some hundred and fifty generations ago but had decided not to at the urging of the queen, one of his wives—maybe a little whore in the king's harem—but certainly someone clever, brave, and most probaby just.

The teacher tried to imagine the woman who had kept the king from killing them. He was brought closer by comparing her to the eldest girl in his orphanage here, Noemi Astach.

But thinking about the black, deep, sad eyes of Noemi Astach reminded him again of Herr Commandant's boy. The teacher's stomach rumbled. At one time that would have embarrassed him. He paid no heed. It gave him a slight pain. What was worse? Hot or cold? Hunger or fear? The silence from behind the woods? Fear now or fear five minutes later? Which fear is the worst of all man's fears? Which fear takes away from him and which fear gives him strength? How long had he been here already?

The waiting room was clean and warm. The pellets of ice in the old man's beard were melting. Some of the drops looked like wet salt. Why doesn't man have the quality of salt? The teacher licked the drops from his lips. His stomach growled again. He dared to raise his eyes to read the sign again and glance at the calendar marked for Easter Monday; the teacher's eyes were hazy—like the haze when evening falls; or in the morning before it lifts. He didn't want to think of being hungry, of fear, of Easter Monday, or of the deep, black, sad eyes of Noemi Astach.

He remembered the breakfasts and the suppers in the orphanage before the war and the way the children were taught. How the cook explained to them how she couldn't hear when they all talked at once.

It was when they only spoke one at a time that their words, wishes, and explanations were understandable and could be listened to—sometimes even when they just whispered. The teacher thought about the fibers that bind the past with what no longer exists.

The rumble of his stomach echoed into his thoughts of how they had arranged the tables and chairs, deciding where each should sit, where he should keep his clothes hanger, bath and hand towels, or from which plate he would eat. He recalled how the children came into the dining room in groups: first, second, third. Or which children had to nap after lunch and which ones preferred to play.

The commandant's waiting room reminded him of the house from which he had just come—the way the day reminds of the night, the dryness of the damp, or the way being hungry reminds of being fed, and thirst conjures up an image of a glass of water.

The door of the commandant's office remained closed. After thirty minutes, Feldwebel Oberg reappeared in the waiting room. He had a dog at his heel and was holding its collar.

"Come on, Whiskers," said bandleader Karl Oberg. "Pull yourself together. It's too late for our turn. Maybe next time . . . "

4

Outside, Karl Oberg mounted a horse and reined it next to the wall on the sidewalk beside the teacher. The feldwebel felt good in cold weather.

"Well, Whiskers, we're back where we started."

They continued side by side, the feldwebel on horseback and the teacher on the ground. They took up the sidewalk. There was nobody around. They went by the warehouse. The feldwebel patted the horse's neck with his pigskin glove. The dog, trotting alongside, barked.

The horse turned his long magnificent neck here and there.

"After the Germans, nobody will return anywhere, not to Poland, not to Germany, Whiskers. And if, thousands of years from now, someone asks, 'What's the difference?' the answer will be 'Yes, this is the difference.' The moment of no return, Whiskers. No exceptions."

The hooves of the horse rumbled on the stones. One, two, three, four. One, two, three, four.

"You're already alive for a few extra Thursdays beyond average, Whiskers," said the feldwebel, from the loftiness of his horse. "Here we are, it's the middle of the week, and it's as though nothing has happened. Just when the band boys are at their best. And I've had to leave them when they're all warmed up."

Sometimes the horse nudged his nose against the teacher, pushing him closer to the walls of the buildings they passed.

Feldwebel Oberg pulled the reins, eased them out. The horse snorted. The dog bared its teeth at the marshes; maybe it sensed what a person or a horse couldn't. Or just a bitch; dogs can smell a bitch for miles.

"Hair and whiskers," mused Feldwebel Oberg. "As if you didn't know, Whiskers, that what's appropriate today can be a drawback tomorrow. You've outlived your old woman, your family—many families. You enjoy surprises you can't take credit for, don't you, Whiskers? Who knows what will happen by the time next Thursday rolls around? Come on, faster. You've got legs like a ballerina. And you don't say a word, Whiskers, as if you were trying to tell me something. By now you ought to have some idea of how far it goes, your being an exception. In winter, everybody's got thin skin. Yours must be like paper."

The horse stumbled because the feldwebel had pulled on the reins. Then he recovered and resumed his pace. Stones stuck out of the pavement.

Feldwebel Oberg patted the animal. His ruddy face looked sunburned. The feldwebel's black calfskin riding boots pressed against the horse's flanks. He eased up on the bit. "Whoaa . . ."

The teacher also stopped, without the feldwebel even telling him to.

They were in the middle of the camp in front of the home for Abandoned Children, Street and block Ch. 13. Farther from here was the canteen, blockführer house, and the hauptwache next to the casino.

Henryk Bley said nothing. He waited for the bandleader to dismiss him.

"Your hair and whiskers are like rocks at the bottom of the sea," Karl Oberg chuckled. "By the way, Whiskers, wouldn't you like to know what happened at T.II. with the lady of your heart? Children were with her. Does that make sense to you, Whiskers? You certainly know what I mean, Whiskers. And even when you shave and get your hair cut, it will still be like a stone at the bottom of the sea. So, go, go, go, Whiskers—*dalli, dalli, dalli* . . . "

5

"I'm here," said Henryk Bley when the door closed behind him. He listened to the echo of his words. He wanted to assure himself that he was speaking, breathing, still living. Was he?

Inside the house he could feel the moldiness, the smell of cold, stagnant air. The teacher waited. Where are the rest?

Man is a stranger in the world, but there are some places where he's more a stranger than others. And places that are good, at least a little better than others. That brought his thoughts to the postage stamps. He remembered his collection, which the Germans had taken as they'd taken everything. One of them had a silhouette of Flavius Josephus, the Jewish military leader and historian from the years 37 to 100 in the common era. During the Jewish war against the Romans, the largest war ever fought against Rome, Flavius led and gave up a rebellion in Galilee. He commanded the fortress of Jotapata and handed it over to the Romans. He claimed that in surrendering he had at least saved the lives of some of his people, even though he'd taken the honor and dignity of those who'd already fallen and of those who survived. The teacher sighed. He prepared himself for the first thing he'd say. It's a miracle we're all still alive, he thought. The teacher had only a few teeth left. Almost every day he was beaten. Only the first beating is memorable.

The cold came in through the windows the children had plugged with paper and rags. It's a good thing there's no wind, he thought. An icicle hung from the waterspout. He knew the children were in bed already, pressed close together to keep warm. This was something he didn't have to teach them to do. He thought about the silence that swallows up all voices together.

"I'm back," the teacher said.

He continued on his way toward the stairs that rose from the long corridor on the ground floor. The stairs led up to the attic. He had his bunk next to the hallway where fifteen-year-old Noemi Astach, the eldest girl in the house, slept. The rest of the children slept downstairs. As the teacher went upstairs, the treads and planks creaked, as did the wormy boards. He told them to stay in bed as long as possible, the longer the better, to beat the hunger and the cold.

The teacher stepped on the third stair and its squeak sounded as it had since last Thursday, echoes of two hundred children whose faces, voices, and names he couldn't remember. He was afraid these faces would get lost, because later, from afar, a person is not much more than a face, and when all that is left is a memory, the face is the first to get lost. Then one forgets the name and, finally, the memory of the memory.

In his mind's eye he could see the window the sun came through, against which the wind blew. He thought about what the children learned: German, English, Spanish, Hebrew, French. Syllables, substantive nouns, adjectives. Subtraction, addition. Division. The mysteries of Ludolf's number. Numbers and principles of Pythagoras or Archimedes. The beauty of Baruch Spinoza. He could hear the song all the way in his office when the windows were open in the spring, summer or fall. He recalled the lines he'd written for the children to read. Isn't it terribly cold here? Not as bad as outside, at least.

What did he really want them to know? What's good and bad? Right and wrong? Just and unjust? Why man lies, steals, and kills? Why he doesn't lie, steal, and kill? Why man is born? Why he dies? It seemed so simple. He wanted to make them forget today and yesterday and to look for tomorrow. But that was a lie. He thought of how he'd called them into his office for their medical examination. He breathed in the cold, musty air.

"I am here," he repeated.

6

Noemi Astach came in before he could draw the blanket in front of his bunk like a curtain.

"They took away a third child while you were gone," she said. "Natasha, Diana, and Aneta are gone."

"Aneta." The teacher's voice sagged.

"They said she needed medical treatment. And that you knew about it. They loaded Aneta into an ambulance."

"Without a window? When?"

"An hour after the feldwebel took you away."

"Who?"

"The driver and his helper. Herr Commandant's son was with them. He was sitting in the front cab."

"I don't know anything," Henryk Bley replied. It was as if with each word he were wiping away each thought, vision, and echo he'd brought here to his nook. The girl looked at him before lowering her eyes.

"Last Thursday when you left the ambulance came, too."

Noemi Astach wore a kerchief on her head like an old woman. Her reddish hair was closely shaved.

"It's cold in here," the teacher said.

"Where were you?"

"At Herr Commandant's headquarters."

"What did they want you for?"

Three girls gone, why? Noemi Astach was eight years old the day her parents had been stoned to death in their country town and people sent her to him. Now she had a piece of burlap wound around her neck, the same piece she wrapped her feet in during the night. It was an old coat sleeve and she wore an even older coat. Henryk Bley knew that she had nothing on underneath. She'd given her clothes and underwear to the younger children. She'd given her sweater to Aneta, the girl they'd taken away during the time he'd been gone. Before that, she gave her socks to Diana and traded her shoes for Natasha's.

He glanced at the walls. Flies, lice, and bedbugs were frozen against the stone. Some had been killed with pins. That morning the children had found a rat frozen in the cellar. The teacher took the blanket left hanging in front of his bunk and wrapped it around her shoulders.

"I don't want to think only about what they're doing," he said.

Patches of mold grew on the walls. They'd scraped them off the evening before, but they were there again in the morning. Blotches of dampness appeared, encircling the mold. The roof leaked only when the ice on it melted at high noon, not during the evening or at night.

"I knew they were going to take someone away when you weren't here," Noemi Astach said.

She looked at him. It was a double anger against herself, the teacher, and the rest. She had brown eyes.

His lips quivered, purplish with the cold and moist from the melting ice. Was he still preparing himself for what he was going to tell the children about Easter Monday? He looked at the moon. Framed inside the icy hole in the roof, its craters were visible. The teacher recalled in a half voice the names of the seas and mountains and valleys of the moon. It was all very distant. The icy tart that was the moon looked remote and thinking about it brought to his mind the image of Herr Commandant's boy—his blue eyes, the strange way his small but long tongue kept rolling around inside of his mouth like a windmill, and that curious, amazed, inexplicable expression of his. And it brought home the resemblance of Noemi Astach with her sad eyes to the German child. He knew his first impression was not mistaken when he had gone away and then come back. Easter Monday, he thought to himself. And again he was overcome by the premonition he'd feared. The moon sailed through the clouds. It looked like a round jellyfish in an icy sea. It was only after a while that he realized that Noemi Astach had left.

7

Henryk Bley was awakened by the cold. How long had he slept? He looked up through the hole in the roof. A few minutes? Or seconds?

It was a long time since he had had dreams at night. As unbelievable as they seemed to him, they frightened him before he could forget. In his first dream, there had been the blind girl and deaf boy he taught walking along the sunny beach—both of them healthy, healed of their muteness and blindness, but twenty years older, bathed in sunbeams and reflections of the blue water of the Mediterranean. Things had shifted into the future. The image even had fragrances—of cypress and warm, dry air, white, wet sand, and salt water. The once-blind girl had met her sister as if she hadn't stayed behind at T.II., and they walked together, side by side, along a sandy path, and their shadows were cast on yellow and white rocks. Along the bottom of the rocks a moss grew. But high on top, the rocks were bare and smooth. Beyond the rocks lay Haifa, the port, and the hills of Carmel. The highway next to the path curved toward the new town of Tel Aviv. Both young women were pushing baby carriages. The path and highway were bordered by magnolias and oleander bushes. Far ahead, the oranges in bright green trees stirred in the wind, and so did the lemon trees, half of whose fruit was still green, half just beginning to turn yellow. On the left the water was heaving, tireless, a sea with its white and silver waves and foam. Glistening fish leaped above the surface and then plunged back again in a game that's lasted unchanged, and will last until the sun goes out. The young women passed a garden restaurant where music was playing. The restaurant took up a long stretch of beach where palms grew.

In his second dream, Henryk Bley was chatting with Herr Commandant Oscar Adler-Bienenstock about his son, as if the Commandant had requested his advice. From his papers, Herr Commandant knew that Henryk Bley was a teacher and a physician, an educator and writer, or rather, he had been all that before he came here. In his papers were hints that the inclinations of the teacher weren't completely comparable to others, but at the same time there were enough records of dates with women to whom the teacher had been close in his years. Herr Commandant asked the teacher to sit down. Henryk Bley sat on the edge of his chair. It occurred to him that he'd leave later, and when he returned to his children, the house would be empty. Herr Commandant was staring at the globe. Germany was right there in its place, close as a hand in a glove.

"We're turning the world back to the way it used to be and forward to where it should be," Herr Commandant said.

On the small Polish mahogany table—the kind a little lamp or vase of flowers belongs on—there was an empty white bird cage. A full bookcase was against the wall.

The teacher noticed that there was no clock in the room.

"*A bove majore discit aratrore miror*—the bull learns to plow from the ox. *Absent naeres non erit*—the absent one will not inherit," said Herr Commandant.

He stretched as if he wanted to get up, but it was only the upper part of his body that moved. His crippled leg with the prosthesis and his other leg with the amputated toes remained immobile.

"In the breast of many a father, a mother's heart beats," said Herr Commandant.

Outside, the orderly Fritzinger opened the door of the stove and threw in a shovelful of coal. The wall shook and the door of the desk opened. The inside of the door was inlaid with bits of colored wood.

"Even if you wanted to shave and have a haircut, I'm afraid you're going to have to wait until Monday. Isn't it Easter Monday?"

His face grew sober. The door creaked. Herr Commandant's son came in.

"Three," he said.

"Four," Herr Commandant smiled. Then he said, "We can't move ahead by always looking back." Then he went on, "I'm sorry, old friend, but I'm the Commandant here; I'm not the Commandant there." He said no more.

Suddenly Henryk Bley didn't know whether he heard his own voice or Herr Commandant's. Everything, even the castle at T.II., was transformed into a small railroad station with a garden and a field and a forest at the end of the meadow. This was his third dream. The guards

opened the doors of the freight cars—forty men and twelve horses—
and ordered the children to get out. The children looked around, dazzled
by the sun.

"Yes, Herr Hauptman," the stationmaster said.

"Of course, Herr Kriminalrat."

"Where is orderly Fritzinger?"

An auxiliary engine pushed the rest of the train toward the gateway.
The air was clear. Everything was still. The blue sky was the color of
the sea, and flowers were blooming in the meadow. They went across
a long path in the grass and as far as the woods, but not quite to the
trees where the meadow turned into a plain. All went in silence as if
in the night. The blue sky was still full of sun. The children began to
sing. It was the song Henryk Bley had composed with them before they
went.

> *When you go into the unknown, far away,*
> *Take just the flag and hope*
> *So board, my little ones, the longest train . . .*

He could still hear the children's voices and see the meadow, the
forest just ahead, and the sunshine; where the forest began and ended.
The children kept going and singing. Suddenly the pine trees turned
into German soldiers, spread out on chairs, their legs apart, with machine
guns in their hands. The machine guns were aimed at the children, but
the soldiers didn't shoot. The children kept on opening their mouths,
but their singing couldn't be heard anymore. All became mute. You
couldn't even hear the machine guns. Led by him and Noemi Astach,
the children melted into the stillness of the forest at the edge of the
abyss; no matter where they turned, each of the trees became a German
soldier.

The teacher forgot all three dreams at once. He saw the chunks of
ice on the roof again. The moon was full. Stars glittered in the sky.

8

"On Monday we're going to move," the teacher said.

"It's Sunday already. Where to?" asked Noemi Astach.

"We don't need to worry about packing," he added. "That's good."

You could hear the whistles of two trains as they passed each other at the ramps. One was just arriving and the other was just leaving.

"Did you find out any details about my 'brother from the band-leader?" asked Noemi Astach.

"No. He talked about Leona."

"Are they going to kill us today?"

Noemi Astach's dark eyes deepened, like a well in which the first and last thing drowning was fear.

Henryk Bley knew who the girl reminded him of, although it wasn't just a likeness. He remembered his friend before she'd boarded the train to T.II. She was tall, firm-breasted, and narrow-shouldered, and her hair was black as coal and smelled of cinnamon when she washed it. She still had long hair when she got out of the freight car. He remembered her hands.

"Don't be afraid, and don't let the others fear," he said to Noemi Astach.

"It's easy to say."

The teacher was preparing for what he was going to tell the children—that they should look upward and not slouch when they walked or rode away, as if they were about to spot Allied planes in the sky, coming to punish Germany. He thought about both things at once, about how many times the Germans had postponed what should have and what was supposed to have happened in Warsaw or in T.II. The teacher was listening to the trains. By morning one was gone, the other already empty.

When they were downstairs, he looked at the children. "I want to tell you about Susa in ancient Persia. I was there once when I was still a young man."

The teacher saw relief in Noemi Astach's eyes and questions in the eyes of the other children, except the blind girl and the deaf boy. He glanced around the floor for a trace of the rat that had lost its life here—a bit of hide maybe, but he found nothing. The teacher thought about what the blind girl wouldn't see and the deaf boy wouldn't hear. "About good things," he added.

Through the tear in the window's paper cover, the clouds could be seen floating slowly. The first light of dawn was pushing back the night. The walls had long since begun to sag and the teacher wondered whether the house might not collapse. It had been a short night.

Smoke and the stench of fire came from the marshes beyond the town. The earth breathed with the approaching spring, with the smell of winter, of mold, darkness, and ice that was turning into slush. It mingled with the smell of mold on the rotting walls.

"There are some things that are good for us," he said.

The morning star was still visible like the evening star had been the night before. It was before five. The teacher caressed several of the children. Their skin was rough, dirty, and chapped. He tried to cling to the image of the rocks by the Dead Sea and Easter Monday in Susa. He heard a motor. He knew he had just a moment left before the ambulance with its red cross stopped in front of the house at Ch. 13.

The teacher calculated how much time he had before bandleader Karl Oberg would bang at the door or somebody else would come to tell them where they were going to be moved. He thought that he would tell the children of his pleasure at how quickly they'd awakened and gotten ready.

He talked fast about the bloodshed which had once been prevented against their people in Susa and how many fathers had stood before their children like he was standing with them now. Those fathers had probably thought at that moment about what they'd done right, what they refused to do differently, and about the mothers who had given them life and what it all meant. About how a brave woman was found (a distant cousin of one of them, or all of them), one of the wives of the Persian king at the time. He'd always envisioned her as slender, pale from fear or from the chill that ran along her spine. She couldn't help being afraid of what was coming, of what was so close already, of what she alone could handle—or couldn't. She'd heard the stories that were later confirmed to her by her uncle, a dignitary in the king's court, when they ate at the table with the king.

Henryk Bley spoke more quickly; he heard the noise of the ambulance and then the brakes, and the door opening and then banging shut again.

He tried to breathe life into his words with the image of the king's table in far-off Persia, spread with a white damask cloth, the crystal vases filled with flowers, and bowls the servants carried to the tables. Henryk Bley described the wine goblets on the royal table, the water, and the platters of the finest food. He realized that he was describing acorns, which the children had gathered last fall, and bran, which neither belonged nor would have appeared on any royal table. He described the glow of candles in hammered silver candlesticks that stood on the tables, and the light of more candles in golden chandeliers that hung from the stucco ceiling, thinking about the wax that must have dripped on the table when they burned low before their lights went out. And then he talked about the king's throne and cushions.

In the meantime, he couldn't help hearing what the children were hearing, the omnipresent footsteps of the feldwebel and of two other pairs of feet in high jackboots, the kind people wore in this part of the country during the winter and early spring. He heard a dog bark. The children turned their heads and looked at him, but he kept talking as though he couldn't hear what everybody else had.

He spoke of the king's wives—who sat on the king's left at the table and who resembled his friend, Leona—and their mothers, and Noemi Astach, looking the way the children remembered her from before.

Henryk Bley heard the bandleader's first thump on the door. Without talking about it, he went on imagining the desire and gentleness the woman beside him had aroused in the king long ago, and the events that set one against the other because somewhere someone took the first step that made the other steps inevitable and prepared the way for the massacre of everyone who'd been born of the same mothers as the queen.

Before he'd become the director of the orphanage in Warsaw, Henryk Bley had had a stone paperweight that had been found at the bottom of the Dead Sea. The sea was shallow. It had just as much strength as the thousands of years that crush stones. He could see the stones, softened as a sponge.

"We'll all stick together," the teacher said now. "This will be good." And as he nodded to Noemi Astach to go and open the door, bandleader Karl Oberg kicked it open with his polished boot.

"Good, good," the feldwebel said in German. "Of course. *Sehr gut.*"

The feldwebel grinned at the teacher. "Still all that hair and whiskers, Whiskers, as if nothing had ever happened?"

His face was ruddy from the cold. "The mud stinks here, Whiskers," said Feldwebel Oberg.

Beside the ambulance stood the driver and the commandant's son.

"Are you ready?" asked Karl Oberg. "You'll get warmed up in a little while."

There was a quickness in Oberg's voice, a kind of exuberance and a reconciliation with fate, either with what he was missing or because he had again to abandon his military music-makers. "Hair and whiskers—still like the rocks at the bottom of the sea. You won't listen to reason, old man." He turned to the commandant's son. "Have you ever heard of a *seeschwein*—a sea pig?" His eye was caught by the teacher's tuxedo trousers with the satin ribbon down the sides. "How many are you, Whiskers?" the feldwebel demanded.

"Where are we going?" asked Henryk Bley.

"Far and near, Whiskers. Don't worry about that. Just resettling. A little to the East as always."

The feldwebel knew that the teacher and the Commandant's son were hanging on to his every statement. "I don't want to overload the ambulance."

"Ten," said Henryk Bley. "Eleven with me."

"That's all right," said Feldwebel Oberg.

"Where are you taking us?" asked Henryk Bley.

For a fraction of a second, the teacher thought of those who were no longer living. At the moment he needed to concentrate on those who were.

9

The ambulance stood twenty paces from the entrance of a half-ruined house called the Institute for Abandoned Jewish Children, at the edge of the camp. The vehicle was angular, like German ambulances, manufactured during the Second World War by BMW and by Mercedes-Benz.

"Come on, get going, Suicide," the feldwebel said to the dog at his feet. With its tail between its legs, the dog growled and ran over to the ambulance. It sniffed as though it were on the scent of something that would lead him home. It didn't dare to jump inside.

The ambulance stood with its back to the house, facing the little garrison town which, in honor of the forty-second birthday of Herr Commandant Oscar Adler-Bienenstock, had been given a new name on the maps of Germany—Festung Adler-Bienenstock. Marshes stretched out on every side, under maimed trees of what had been forests. The driver watched what the bandleader was doing, always as if for the first time. The commandant's son stood beside the ambulance, his mouth wide open.

"Everybody is to get in and sit down as soon as I say so, Whiskers," started Feldwebel Oberg. "But only one at a time. You'll have two minutes from the time I give the word. Everything's got to click. But first, I've got to have your signature on this paper, stating that you're moving and leaving the house in order."

The feldwebel drew a folded piece of paper from his sleeve and spread it out in front of the teacher.

The driver opened the rear door of the ambulance.

"If you don't want to sign, I'll have to leave you here and the children will go ahead," the feldwebel continued. "Since your bed is made, you must lie in it."

Even before he caught Noemi Astach's eye, the teacher signed his name.

"Well, now we're quits, Whiskers. I can see you don't want to stay by yourself if there's a chance to go somewhere together," said the feldwebel.

The driver closed the door. The commandant's son had noticed there was no handle on the side of the door. Then he noticed there were scarred and scratched wooden benches on both sides of the van, a little window behind the driver's seat with bars on it, and a curtain of steel chain which could be opened and closed but only from the driver's side. The ambulance had no other windows. The floor, sides, and roof of the vehicle were steel plated like a police van. That was why it went so slowly and made such a lot of noise, like a troop transport. It showed signs of wear, as though it had gone several times around the world.

It looks a bit like an iceman's van, the boy thought to himself, or like one of those trucks that transports gold and money to banks. Like a watertight steel safe-deposit vault.

He was disappointed the children hadn't sung the song he'd expected. Even though, there'd been a gleam in his eyes since he was witnessing something so strange as the trip they were taking—going from somewhere to nowhere.

The bandleader's words echoed in his head. The commandant's son had finally understood what it meant to move from somewhere into nowhere, the trip whose destination was the swamps. Was that what his father meant when he said the worst is the best and the best is the worst, making sense of things that hadn't made sense before?

"All right, Sturmman Max Hans," Feldwebel Oberg said, sitting up in front as the commandant's son, the sturmman, and the dog got in the cab of the ambulance. "Let's go."

The driver switched on the starter and the vehicle moved off. The feldwebel looked content. He'd already rehearsed the afternoon concert for Herr Commandant. It would start off with "The Entry of the Gladiators." Then "Alte Kameraden," "Vöglein Singen," and "Bummelpetrus."

"Some people don't ever shape up," the feldwebel said at length. "How many times have I told that old man to shave and get himself a haircut?"

He turned to the commandant's son, who was sitting to his left. "By the time you're a few years older, you won't have to wait to know how things are. I can see you're not as scared this time."

The commandant's son was thinking about the words "disinfection" and "resettling" and about lice. About the posters in the garrison and in the camp: One louse means your death. *Eine Laus dein Tod*. What was it his father, Herr Commandant, had said? *Jedem das Seine*. To each his own. He thought about the animals in the jungle, where the elephants go to die, and about what he felt but had never understood.

Dim geographical zones—the whole world at once—floated through the boy's head the way nightfall swallows the last sources of light, changing sunset into darkness. He thought about what he'd overheard. Then he thought about the scorpions that hid in the sewer pipes, in the shower faucets, in garages, and in clothing when it wasn't changed often enough.

The boy thought about fleas. He always seemed to arrive at fleas even when he started with elephants. Then he thought about bees, which carry poison along with their sting. Then snakes, fish, and birds. Finally about lions, tigers, and crocodiles, which knew how to kill men. These thoughts also made him think of rats.

The commandant's son was thinking about the rats that seemed to spread faster than people. As his father had said, the spreading was dangerous because it robbed people of food. He thought about the fearlessness of his father. And finally, the strength of engines.

"What are you thinking about?" asked Feldwebel Oberg. "About the sweet land of forgetfulness?" Maybe they should at least castrate these people, like so many others, he thought to himself.

"What happens to animals when they're with people?" the boy asked.

"What do you think?" replied the feldwebel.

The boy didn't answer yet; he was thinking about what was going to happen before they reached the marshes. For a moment, he had the feeling that as they approached the marshes they were melting into them, as if the marshes could think, and as if, at that moment, he could guess what it was the marshes thought about at times like this. Bubbles rose to the surface from the dead bottom of the swamp, like swollen stars that burst in silence down below. There were three bubbles. Again three.

His eyes caught fire as if he had chills and fever at the same time. The next time his father started telling him about how and where the elephants die in secret places in the jungle and how Indian tigers get a taste for human flesh and blood, he would say, "No, it's the marshes. It's the engines. The trucks. Ambulances without windows. Exhaust pipes like elephant trunks. Like birds without wings. Or like fish with wings and birds with fins."

All of a sudden from somewhere, his father's eyes looked at him.

"Is it true that they call them in Polish *duschegubky*—soul-eaters?" the boy asked suddenly.

"Are you telling us or asking us?" the feldwebel wanted to know.

Where could the boy have known it from? One of the young German inventors, SS-Untersturmführer Becker, invented these ambulances, and came here to test them. They forced carbon monoxide into the van instead of outside. The head of SS-Einsatzgruppen, Otto Ohlendorf, had objected to the unloading because it was not a stimulating view for German soldiers to look at the *menschentiere* in their own blood and saliva and excrement. The SS-Untersturmführer rode around to the single units of the SS-Einsatzgruppen to teach the drivers how to handle his invention correctly: not pushing the accelerator to the floor right away, but gradually and patiently at the very beginning; putting the prisoners to sleep and then choking them, not the other way around. That will get rid—he claimed to the soldiers of the SS-Einsatzgruppen—of the view of distorted faces, of the people who had expelled what they were not able to digest when they were unloaded.

When the boy didn't answer, the feldwebel went on. "Are you coming to the concert? How about you, Max Hans?"

The feldwebel decided that there must be strange ideas getting themselves entangled at the moment inside the head of the commandant's slow-witted son. Should he test him on the four cardinal points of the compass and the elements?

"How much farther are we going to go?" the commandant's son asked. His glittering eyes were like marshes at sunset.

"It'll take twenty to twenty-five minutes before we get there," replied the feldwebel.

"Where?" the commandant's son wanted to know.

"There," answered Feldwebel Oberg.

"There—nowhere," the commandant's son echoed.

It was as though understanding had suddenly come to him from afar—of everything it meant and encompassed—and now was carrying him on implacably toward the same goal the children inside the ambulance already sensed.

The mystery of the marshes, he thought to himself. The mystery of the engines. The secret of animals who were killed because they were animals. He turned to the little barred window. It was more transparent than the points of the compass and the elements—water, air, earth, and fire—which canceled themselves out in his head. One, two, three, and one is four. He toyed with his tongue. It was better than trying to make a difference between the north and water.

They drove past the stables, warehouse, the dog kennels. They passed the command headquarters casino and turned off toward the marshes where the camp began. The vehicle left hardly any exhaust fumes behind.

"They haven't emerged from paradise yet," the feldwebel said to the driver, who didn't answer. "Sometimes it feels like an eternity from Thursday to Monday. Or sometimes the opposite, from Monday to Thursday." He chuckled. "Are you giving it the gas, Max Hans?"

"Full gas ahead," replied the driver, who was wearing an SS-Einsatzgruppen uniform and had a gas mask at his feet.

"Step on it, Max Hans," said the feldwebel after a while.

"It won't go any faster," replied the driver. "The gas pedal's right to the floor."

Karl Oberg grinned. The commandant's son looked at him. There was an innocent understanding between the two of them that excluded the Commandant Adler-Bienenstock. Everything was going the way it was supposed to.

"Good, no?" asked the feldwebel. "The world's a fine place. As long as you know how to get by. *Jedem das Seine. Eine Laus dein Tod.* We Germans were born to die." He calculated how far it was to the marshes. "Do you feel like a regular fellow?" asked the feldwebel. "I think so."

"You're a regular fellow," echoed the commandant's son, as if he'd just discovered what it meant to be mature, to be grown up, to be a *man*, and he gazed at the bandleader with his watery blue eyes. His eyes were like bluish stars, like an angel's bells. His mouth, in which his tongue revolved, was rosy.

The SS driver kept his eyes on the road and the vehicle he was driving. "Forty kilometers an hour here is probably like driving ninety on an empty autobahn," he declared.

"Can you give us a little heat, too?" asked the feldwebel.

"Why not?" the driver replied.

The lights in the ambulance and in the cab were watertight. After about ten minutes, Karl Oberg switched them on, turned around, and looked inside. A second later he switched them off.

"They seem to be coughing," remarked the commandant's son.

"They are coughing. It's cold," the feldwebel confirmed.

"Yeah," the driver declared.

"It'll soon be spring," said Karl Oberg.

"Yeah," agreed the driver.

"It's about time," admitted the feldwebel.

"It's dull here in the springtime," the driver said.

"That's the truth. Not much grows here. Too many wars have passed this way," the feldwebel said.

They listened for a while to the sound of the motor. Then the bandleader asked the boy if he liked the springtime.

"I wish I were with them now," said the boy.

"Where?"

"There," replied the commandant's son.

The boy began to sweat. Tears started rolling down his face, which was twisted as if he were laughing. But he wasn't. He was thinking about the sheet metal neck on the ambulance. About the strength of the engine. Although he didn't dare to turn around and look into the back of the van like Karl Oberg had done, he had it before his feverish blue eyes. There was the closeness in the eyes of Oscar Adler-Bienenstock's son and a distance, too—an emptiness. His ears were singing with the song he'd heard once about distances, strange flights, about souls that flutter in the wind like flags. About trains going somewhere.

The glassy light on the roof inside the ambulance gleamed in the dark like an icy full moon. Like a fish eye, like an empty eye socket. They were already in the marshes and the vehicle lurched along. Karl Oberg rapped his knuckles against the glass of the cab to the rhythm of "The Entry of the Gladiators."

10

The driver shifted the lever, changing the course of the engine's exhaust. When he did that, Henryk Bley's words and thoughts were snapped off as if a fragile thread had been torn. The children and the teacher pressed rags instead of handkerchiefs against their noses and mouths.

That was when the commandant's son heard the first noises in the back of the van. It was as if sacks of potatoes were falling on the floor, or as if those sacks had ripped open and the potatoes had rolled out, or as if the teacher and children inside were fighting. That was when it occurred to him that the exhaust pipes looked like the trunks of old, sick, dying elephants in some unknown jungle. Drops of sweat stood out on his childish, almost girlish forehead. His tongue remained quite still inside his mouth.

That was when the children and the teacher began to choke. The teacher already forgot his vision of the black-haired queen; there were no palms in the corner of the banquet hall anymore where the king and queen were dining, nor was the sky above the couch in the royal chambers, nor were the amorous murmurs of the king interrupted by the pleadings of his wife who, more than saving her own life, wanted to prevent mass murder. The queen's adversary, the minister, was not there either. He was drawing lots to find out what would be the best date for the massacre and he'd hit on the spring festival. Susa, which had been a populous city at that time in Persia, had become just a heap of mud and greasy stone in Henryk Bley's day. But then it was a place of gilded silks and brocade draperies with heavy fringe in the shape of pine cones or bells or flowers, a city of carpets woven with blue and crimson horses and dogs' heads and bodies of bronze leaves with veins like a candelabra. And the statues of men like Hercules, capable of strangling a lion with their hands. That was all gone. Henryk Bley, sensing all the emptiness and terror and relief that surrounded him, felt the weariness that stars must feel when they're dying. The sun had gone out. The volcanoes grew silent. He heard his coughs and the coughs of the others who were choking to death with him. He heard cries, including the cry of the deaf boy and the cry of the blind girl, all of which were lost in the turmoil of everybody else's screams. But it was only for a fraction of a second. He could feel Noemi Astach lurching against him, her head bumping his forehead as if she'd had some kind of seizure. He could feel her finger digging into him on one side and the blind girl clawing him on the other. But he couldn't speak anymore.

Like the rest of them, he began to cough and scream although he had told them not to scream, not to let themselves be broken at the last minute, gasping, choking, on their way to distant places far away. Finally he began to cough up blood and foam from his mouth and nose, like a person drowning. This was the end. He didn't want to think about himself. But now he did. It was the last moment of his consciousness. He felt how alone they were, how alone he was. Just one of many. It was only for a fragment of a thought, maybe just an echo of a thought he'd fortified himself with while waiting for this moment. His mouth closed when he bit one of the fingers on his left hand. Then his face became distorted. There was only darkness, which veiled and swallowed everything up.

The ambulance pulled up to the swamp. There, above the gateway, was the inscription made of pine branches and brushwood: "Next Year in Jerusalem."

11

The commandant's son listened for sounds from the back of the van. He couldn't hear anything. His tongue rotated like a windmill inside his mouth and he kept repeating to himself north, south, east, west, wagging around his saliva like a paintbrush. He felt something he couldn't understand.

"They're done for," said Feldwebel Karl Oberg. "*Vollgefressen*. Fully eaten up."

"I've got to dump them," the driver said.

"Don't lose too much time," the feldwebel said.

"Hope not."

"I don't want to hang around here too long," repeated the feldwebel.

"It might take five minutes. I've got to do it by myself," the driver said.

"Five minutes is all right."

"We don't waste time."

"I've got a concert this evening."

While the driver unloaded the bodies, the boy and Karl Oberg left the van and walked over to the deepest point in the swamp. They didn't speak. The sky was high. Already the moon was visible. There was silence all around. No wind. It was far from the barracks to the lager commandant bureau, his adjunct's office, telephone central and block-führer's house, far from the lager post office.

Finally, the bodies and heads disappeared like dead hens in the swamps. The driver splashed the blood and excrement from the bodies in the truck with a few pails of water.

"Ready, finished," the driver called.

"Yeah, one moment," the feldwebel called back.

The bandleader Oberg threw a stone into the water. As soon as it sank, circles appeared. The boy's eyes were foggy.

"Are you looking?" asked the feldwebel.

"At what?"

"At the circles."

"Yeah."

"Still?"

"Yes. Those are the largest."

"All the time?"

"Yes."

"Do you still see them?"

"Weakly."

"And now?"

"A little."

"Still?"

"No."

"So you see."

"I don't see anything."

"That's it."

"What?"

"Nothing."

"Nothing?" asked the boy.

"That's just what happened."

"What?"

"Nothing."

"How come?"

"That's the difference between right and wrong," the feldwebel said. "There's no difference in them when you don't see what you don't want to see. You see? It is just like when you throw a stone into the water. It doesn't stay. You throw a stone, it whirls up the circles on the surface, and then they spread out and disappear. And now imagine it's foggy.

Nebel. Do you know what *vernebling* is? Fog. Night. Like brother and sister."

"No," the boy replied.

"You'll see in a moment," the feldwebel promised.

But from the boy's expression it was obvious he knew what to expect.

"What is it now?" he asked.

The feldwebel still didn't explain the main thing to the boy, just as his father hadn't explained it to him before and wouldn't explain it later.

Feldwebel Oberg turned to the commandant's son. "Well, you've seen it. They're just *Menschentiere,* as your father rightly said. Nothing more than *Menschentiere. Schweinehunde.* Sow hounds. When you're studying the elements, don't forget about fire, water, earth, and air. The fifth element is us." He grinned. *Das Tausendjährige Reich.* The thousand year Reich. *Blut und Boden.* Blood and soul. The Nuremberg law for protection of German honor and blood. He pulled on his yellowish pigskin gloves, as if he didn't want to touch anything anymore. Sometimes ashes fell into the marshes. That made them look like pools of black water lillies.

"It's good, isn't it?" he asked.

The driver circled the van. Then he entered the cab and started the engine. The smoke coming from the exhaust pipe seemed to poison the air around them. The dog was trembling, looking at all three of them, and then at the commandant's son.

There was a light in the boy's eyes that almost set his forehead aglow. It was like the sun, like springtime and fire. Or just water? The marshes seemed brighter and even the little islands of ash, several layers of it, were flooded with daylight at the meridian. He was dripping with sweat, as if he were in a steam bath. The sound of the motor reminded him of the song he'd heard once and never afterward, and he had the feeling he could hear it now, even though he couldn't make out the words. He was happy to listen to the strong engine. They went back to the van.

"Would you like to ride in the rear?" asked the feldwebel before they boarded for their return trip.

"Yes," answered the boy.

"Go ahead. Get in."

"Thanks, *danke*," said the boy.

"*Arbeit macht frei,* and here is the number *drei*," said Karl Oberg as he smiled.

The commandant's son had the feeling he was looking at his father's face, eyes, words. Three, not four. Number *drei*. He looked in the ambulance and out, where there was a dumping station in the swamp. The dog jumped into the cabin.

"Everything for a good German family," said the feldwebel.

He closed the door of the van. Karl Oberg coughed. Then he turned to the driver.

"I've got a new march based on a Jewish funeral tune, like the idea I got last Thursday to turn a Gypsy wedding melody into a funeral march. It makes sense when you turn it all upside down. Don't you want to come to the casino and listen?"

"If I've finished my work at the garage," replied the driver. "Too much overtime work. Then I have to go to the dentist at his apartment. I think his phone extension is 34."

"Yeah, you're right. It is 34. Did you get a new motor?"

"Yes, but I doubt it's a brand-new one. It's probably been over-hauled," the driver answered.

The driver thought to himself that it wasn't nice to confuse the feebleminded boy with talk about the elements, since even the birds in the trees talked about how he couldn't keep the points of the compass straight in his head.

But the boy wasn't thinking about elements now. He was still thinking about how the exhaust pipes looked like elephant trunks. How strong, beautiful, and powerful the engines were. He thought that knowing why elephants wander off and why tigers hunt people instead of people hunting them was more important than knowing the points of the compass

The three of them—two in front and one inside—drove back faster than they'd come. The truck felt lighter as it bounced and jiggled along the road to the marshes like a young horse. The red cross, painted three times in brilliant military colors, looked guileless, as though it were offering something. The motor rumbled, and black, sooty vapors sputtered out of the exhaust pipes that looked like a swan's neck or fish fins. They left thick, oily fumes behind, and because there was no wind, it took a while before they dissipated in the fresh air. But soon the smoke from the ambulance disappeared altogether and left the air behind it clean. The dog was quietly grooming itself.

They were on a huge plain in the middle of a spreading wasteland between the Baltic and Azov and Black Seas, reaching out in all directions like a frozen spiderweb, an occupied country, like an island to which no ships come sailing, lost in the leafless forests and lost in the world. Far away but still visible by eye, as a tiny line on the horizon, were green forests growing from time immemorial, so deep and high and thick that everything disappeared in silence, as though every living thing would stop.

It was a cold, still day at the end of winter and the beginning of spring. Easter Monday. The ash settled in between the empty husks of grain and snow which, at noontime, had turned to slush. Crows flew, cawing high above the untilled fields. They were huge birds, darkening the sun.

For the fourth day and fourth night, rolls of black smoke floated across the sky. There was still no wind.

NIGHT

❖

1

The moon swung low and was swallowed by the river. A trail of sedge and gray ashes from the ghetto was washed ashore.

"Enough," rang out a strict voice.

A small crowd of men came to a standstill.

"Get on," the voice continued. "Anyone opening his mouth . . ."

On the white road made gray by the night, a truck waited. Four benches placed close together were in the back, under the canvas. The men climbed in. The policemen who had come with them stepped back into the darkness. The young SS officer who had taken them over looked from one to another with half-closed eyes.

"Let's go," he said in the direction of the driver. The engine turned over.

"Where are we going?" asked a voice, quiet and tired, like an old man's.

"Shut up!" bellowed the young SS officer.

Suddenly the truck left the road. It went around something like a fortress or a plowed field, and the sharp whine of the brakes cut into the night. The man with the tired, old-sounding voice was big and strong and

belonged to a commando of carpenters and diggers. The child beside him
was his son.

"Out!" bellowed the young SS officer.

From somewhere nearby came the acrid smell of burnt ground. The
night was dark and no one could see anything. They walked, holding each
other by the hand.

"Hold on to me, boy," said the tired, old-sounding voice.

2

The SS officer said, "Stop." He wore a green field uniform. Apart from
the burnt ground, the spring night was full of the smell of rye fields and
young meadows, and from the distance the wind brought the smell of
potato fields in June, of flowers, and a certain chill. The young SS officer
went ahead to report to his superiors.

They had been picked out of bed earlier, but none of the policemen
told them what was going on, where they were going, or why—except that
they had to be male. Then the young SS officer and a German driver took
them over. They had already taken away one unit the day before, and
nobody knew where they had gone or where they were now, because they
had not yet returned. That unit had contained thirty-six men, and today's
unit comprised another thirty-six.

"Sixteen and twenty men, Herr Brigadenführer."

"Good."

"What are your orders, Herr Brigadenführer?"

"Send them here."

"Yes, Herr Brigadenführer."

The young SS officer returned to the group from the ghetto. The acrid
smell of burnt ground still lingered, along with the ugly taste of timber
doused with petrol, and paraffin set on fire, and the taste of charred
thatched roofs and walls which the wind kept carrying away and returning.

When he brought them, he reported: "Unit is ready, Herr Brigadenführer. Attention! Sixteen and twenty men, Herr Brigadenführer."

"Take a deep breath," said the general.

Then he waited and said, "There was a village here. Now it's gone. You're going to work. A bullet for the first one who opens his mouth."

A silence spread again over the hilly countryside. In the darkness the trees were invisible. The more distant hills and the remnants of the village were also invisible. Later, birds flew across the sky.

Their gaze penetrated the darkness a short distance ahead of them. There was a village here, but now it is gone. From somewhere close by, the cry of a crow rang out. From nearby came the bleating of goats.

"Show me that wall," said the general.

"Here, Herr Brigadenführer. A hundred and seventy-three men. At dawn we identified them with the help of the village records. Immediately afterward . . . "

"Enough, thank you," said the general.

"The wall, Herr Brigadenführer."

"Carry on," said the general. *"Weitermachen."*

3

"There are goats here," said the tired, old-sounding voice. He leaned toward the boy and supported himself on the boy's shoulder.

"I saw sheep, geese, and ducks," the boy added.

"Don't cough," the tired, old-sounding voice added. "Don't draw atten- tion to yourself."

The boy was irritated by the smell of the burnt earth. Smoke from the other end of the village, from where the fire was no longer visible, still penetrated everything.

"Quiet!" somebody in the general's entourage shouted toward them.

"These are Jews from the Terezin ghetto," a different voice said to the brigadenführer.

"Who ordered this?" asked the general.

"You, Herr Brigadenführer."

"Oh," said the general. "All right. Let's move."

"Yes, Herr Brigadenführer"

A tractor rattled somewhere nearby, rolled over a hillock, and disappeared into the darkness. The voices of the men from the general's entourage,
who were no longer visible, could be heard again. Suddenly the wind
brought the smell of quicklime.

When the general's entourage reappeared, the general said in the direction of the young SS officer who guarded them, "Let them know."

"Men," said the young SS officer. "You must dig a mass grave. You're
going to bury the dead. A hundred and seventy-three bodies."

The general added, "By morning this will be flat earth."

Before the young SS officer took them to the marked pits, they heard
somebody in the general's entourage say, "Pioneers will be deployed here,
Herr Standartenführer—one commissioned officer, one noncommissioned
officer, and thirty-five men. This squad won't be able to manage it, Herr
Standartenführer. It's necessary to deploy two strong squads, equipped with
the best implements, for a fortnight."

"Nonsense," said the general.

Where the pits were to be dug, the smell of freshly turned earth was
added to that of the burnt ground.

"Get on with it," sounded from the group of men in leather coats.

"Get on with it," shouted the general in the direction of the young SS
officer.

"Get on with it," shouted the young SS officer, as the pistol in his hand
gleamed darkly.

"What are they going to do to us?" the boy whispered.

"Don't be afraid," the tired, old-sounding voice whispered back. "We
are here together. All together."

"Here," said the young SS officer. "Get working."

Then they heard, "We have deployed three squads of Reichsarbeitdienst,
which will also be used as a clean-up unit in order to secure further
valuables—such as farming machines and metals suitable for scrap—Herr
Standartenführer."

The first man lifted his pick. Its head flashed through the darkness.
They started to dig and toss out earth. They could only think that they
were digging, throwing out, and treading on the remnants of a village that

had lost its living souls during the night—a village which had succumbed to fire and was now to lose its dead. They heard fragments of what the unit officers reported to the general. They could not connect the work they were doing with the idea of the village.

Because of the darkness, it was impossible to guess how big the village had been. Only shadows and darkness covered the plain and the hillock, the remnants of the houses, as if it were a derelict fortress.

They could hear the sound of the picks, the birds of the night, the soft blades cutting softly into the spring soil, which was ready for summer. They could hear the gentle clink of spades striking against flint, a buried horseshoe, or a discarded cooking pot. They could smell the scent of the earth piling up beside the pits, hear the touch of metal on soil, the breath of the men digging, and the sounds of the night.

"Three meters deep," said the young SS officer.

"That'll be enough," said the general. And to somebody in the crowd of men in leather coats, "Let them be useful again for a while."

Somebody laughed.

4

The men who were digging were almost up to their shoulders in the ground. They kept throwing out earth as birds flew overhead, along with insects, in a gentle spring breeze. With the advancing night, the wind brought a chill that was made greater by the fresh earth. They dug and cast out earth for those who had still been alive the day before, for those who had owned houses and the land on which the houses had stood. They listened to the wind, the birds, the trees, the horses, the goats and the sheep, and now and again to a cockerel whose call failed to separate night from day.

They were forbidden to speak, even though the young SS officer had disappeared into the darkness. Soon they were in the ground, the earth looming over their heads. Sometimes, a star would appear among the spring clouds, disappearing when the clouds thickened again. At one moment in the middle of the night, a falling star came tumbling down and the sky resembled a pit being dug out of the earth. The men were no longer visible; only the mounds of earth which they threw out were. From time to time, the general of the security police, or the men in the leather coats, or the young SS officer would appear near the hole in the ground.

"Don't cry, son," whispered the tired, old-sounding voice. "Don't look there."

"Quiet," said the general.

"Quiet, men, or else ... " said the young SS officer.

"Ten blows with a stick for interrupting work," said the general.

"I could think of a stricter punishment," said the standartenführer.

"Yes, Herr Standartenführer," said the young SS officer.

"Put it away," said the general, looking at the mound of bodies.

The general and the men in leather coats were leaving.

"It's my son, sir," said the tired, old-sounding voice.

"Who asked you?" said the young SS officer.

"He has never seen a dead man," said the tired, old-sounding voice.

The smoke crept into their noses and throats. Every now and then the wind would spin around in circles. The clouds dropped. It looked as though it was going to start raining.

The men at the top began handing down the first bodies, where they were lined up along the charred wall like logs, to the men at the bottom of the pit. Some of the bodies were half-dressed, others only barefoot, others in their underwear.

"Perhaps some of them are still alive," whispered the boy.

"No," said the tired, old-sounding voice.

"More earth, faster," said the young SS officer.

"Come on," the tired old voice prompted the boy.

The boy looked toward the charred wall that the village men had been facing, hands up, before they were shot. He continued throwing earth onto the corpses while looking at his spade, the earth, the wall that the dead had been touching with their hands before they fell. The wall had been blackened by flames. The first signs of morning appeared in the distance, but it was not morning yet—just a brilliant ribbon, the first touches of light, the final touches of darkness. The eyes of the boy, accustomed to the darkness, started to distinguish the ground plan of the village, which until that moment had been one with everything else. He did not want to look at the dead. He did not want to look at the earth that was falling on the fingers, noses, and eyes of the dead. Here stood a house, here a shed, here a barn. This is where a fence stood, a lane ran by, here the tractor had driven through earlier. This could have been the school, this the savings bank. Before them, behind them, beside them, under them, above them was a village that no longer existed. He threw the earth very quickly, in order to see the first bodies covered and from then on to see only the earth. The echo of the young SS officer's words that they should throw more earth, faster, faster, reverberated in his ears. The handle of his spade was warm from his hands, moist with his sweat. The dirt rained down. The dead had no shoes. They were burying them barefoot. He kept looking at their feet. Sometimes a shower of dirt threw up an arm, moved a finger, a head. Their feet were already covered.

"Enough," said the young SS officer. "You've five minutes for a meal. You can go eat."

5

The young SS officer took them to a tarpaulin on which stood bottles of water, bread, and a round of cheese.

"Eat up, Jew-boys. There's a feast for you," he added. Then he went to one side and squatted down near a mound of earth.

"Son," said the tired, old-sounding voice. "Stay close beside me."

"Ten blows with a stick," whispered the boy.

Here they were, those thirty-six people who had left the day before and had not yet returned, the village which was and is no more, the smoke that rose to the sky all through the night and which was carried away and brought back again by the wind—those one hundred and seventy-three men shot and dead, another life, strange or familiar, distant, which had come and gone.

They could see one another as much as they had been able to before they had been moved onto the truck the previous night—before they had been brought here.

The echo of words, fragments of reports that they overheard. Forty eiderdowns, seventy-four cushions, three baby carriages. Eighteen radio sets. Ninety-six pairs of men's shoes, eighty-three pairs of women's shoes. The food they were now eating. Grain, oats.

There were stars in the sky, clouds.

"You don't need to," said the man with the tired, old voice to the boy.

"Nobody?" asked the boy.

"People will pray for them later, perhaps, somewhere abroad where there aren't any Germans," said the tired, old-sounding voice. "And perhaps even somebody, somewhere in Germany."

"Nonsense," said the younger of two brothers nearby. "They wouldn't have given us anything to eat."

"I can't," said the boy.

"Where are we?" hissed the elder of the two brothers. "Does anybody know anything?"

"It's a mining area," said the younger brother.

"Do you have to talk?" asked a man with glasses. "Isn't it enough just to look?"

"And for you?"

"I hope you don't feel like the Maccabees," said the man with glasses, swallowing a piece of bread and cheese. "Perhaps for that matter we have only our bodies and muscles." And then he asked, "You're not going to eat?"

"It's burnt out as though they had the plague," said the elder of the two brothers. "This was not the act of pioneers. I'm sure you know who I have in mind, though."

"Did they drive us for an hour, or was it two?" somebody asked. "I've lost all sense of time. I only know that it was night and now it is morning."

Steps, noise, snatches of voices could be heard. The answers were contained in the questions. After they had eaten and finished the work, will they also . . . ? The young SS officer returned. They fell silent.

"Finished?" he asked, looking at the tarpaulin. Most of them had not even touched the round of cheese or the water or the bread.

"You can take it with you," the young SS officer said. "Put a little life into it. Get a move on. The unit before you wasn't even given a scrap. The general wasn't here. You're lucky. You've escaped the stick. You've done a good job." And then he quietly added: "If any of you find anything—a ring, money, or something like that—hand it in." He started whistling "Heimat deine Sterne." He rubbed his hands as if they were frozen.

"Into pairs," he ordered them in the end, until they were all paired off again, a digger and a man with a shovel.

6

"Faster," bellowed the general.

He stared at his watch. The sky was still dark, but only above them and further toward the west. In the east, day was already breaking. He tried to guess how long it would be before it was actually daybreak. The young SS officer swallowed dryly. It was chilly. Dew glistened in the grass.

"A littler more dirt here, where I'm pointing. Cover it up properly."

It seemed to him that the man with the tired, old-sounding voice embraced the last dead body on the pretext of moving a stone. Could he be putting it under his head? Why did he throw so little dirt on him? What did he see in the dead man? Was he perhaps the mayor? A priest? An assassin?

"*Scheisse*," said the young SS officer. "Have you lost your head? Do you want ten blows with a stick? A bullet? What are you doing with him? Cover him up. This minute. Make him eat dirt."

The glow of daybreak swept over the pale face of the dead man, who could not have been much more than sixteen, eighteen at most.

The man with the tired, old-sounding voice did as he was told by the young SS officer, but he looked away from the boy, who tossed dirt down to him from above, farther to the west, where it was still night, as if he could not hear or see and could not perceive things through the reflection of the night.

"Cover him up properly," repeated the young SS officer. "I won't tell you twice. Throw a few shovelfuls on top of him." He started toying with the leather tongue of his gun holster.

"Throw all the quicklime in there, nothing left over," he added. "Do you hear me?"

The man with the tired, old-sounding voice watched his son pour out a sack of quicklime, then stepped back and climbed up. They all emptied sacks of quicklime.

"That's it," said the tired old voice.

The young SS officer spat. Then he went to report to the commander of the security police, who stood erect, as though he were also making a report as well as listening to one. By the light that was now spreading over the land, the commander could see that the earth and lime had filled the pit, the communal grave, up to the brim. A tear in the clouds spilled light softly onto the scarred earth. Beyond the tear, day had arrived. Once more, they could imagine that this had been a village. They could imagine the days, the months, the centuries through which it had flourished. The place where the church had stood. The path that had been trodden by foundrymen, miners, their wives, mothers, sisters, children. The fields plowed by the men now in the pit, their necks, heads, and chests pierced by gunshot wounds. The women who had been taken away the day before and who had given bread and milk to the children they would see no more. Their relatives and friends who would learn about this from the next announcements following the news from the German Supreme Command.

The general looked around the plain, the mound; his eyes returned to the remains of the village.

"Excellently done, gentlemen, I think," he said and put his hands into the pockets of his overcoat.

He looked around over his shoulder, toward the men in leather coats. These men had nothing to do here now. Their cars drove up at 4:30. They got in.

The general stayed behind. He cast an eye over the village ground plan once more, noting what no longer existed. The clouds drew apart and the moon sailed out once again. The general watched the wisps of smoke, which no longer had the strength to float high but were torn by the wind and kept near the ground in curls, as though the burnt earth and the freshly-dug pit was a body of water.

But there was no longer anything here, apart from the wisps of smoke that merged with the morning mist. The bleating of the sheep and goats could be heard again, like the cry of the departing night, of the arriving day.

"Back to the truck," ordered the young SS officer.

Beside their truck and behind the mound, which up until this time had been invisible, there was now another truck, the two like brother and sister. On the other side, the general's black limousine waited. The right mudguard sported a flag of the commander of the SS security police.

The man with the tired, old-sounding voice now looked like an old man who had aged overnight, in a morning, in a single journey. He motioned for the boy to climb up.

"Get down," said the young SS officer. "I haven't given the order to line up yet."

The white bodies of the goats and the white wool of the sheep emerged from the misty morning.

"Load them on," said the young SS officer. "Half of them onto each truck. Sixteen men and sixteen sheep. The goats that won't fit onto the vehicles will be taken away by a different unit. Make space for the animals. I don't want them to suffocate."

"No," the general interrupted him. "Take the animals separately."

"It's a hundred and forty-four goats, Herr Standartenführer," said the SS officer.

"OK, put the goats onto one truck and the unit and the sheep and a few goats, perhaps, onto your truck," added the general.

The SS officer did as the general ordered and signed a piece of paper, which he handed over to one of the military policemen.

"Let's go," said the general.

"Let's go," said the standartenführer.

"As you command, Herr Standartenführer," said the young SS officer. And to the men he said: "To your places. Quick. Faster."

7

They rode along with the animals, through the misty morning in which the stars no longer shone. For half an hour nobody spoke, even though the young SS officer sat in front, in the driver's cabin. Nobody drew the canvas aside, not even a crack, so they could see which way they were going. There was the chemical reek of blast furnaces, the breath of the coal shafts and of the plain, swept by a raw wind, a wind carrying the odor of the brown-coal surface mines and even still the smell of burnt ground—then the noises of towns, small or perhaps large, of crossroads, of railway crossing barriers and of the road, cut in half by the railway line. They traveled a road that followed the railway line and ran through a mountainous region, and perhaps through a pass, before reaching the lowlands again. The man with the tired old voice was silent, as they all were, not knowing at that moment, as they did before and later, whether they would reach their destination. The truck was loud with the clipped bleating of the sheep, the braying of the goats. The sheeps' eyes were dull, without interest or fear. The space was made warmer by the breath of the animals. They pressed themselves into the front half of the vehicle. Even in the twilight, under the canvas, the animals, thick with wool, gleamed white. Now and then, light could be seen as it bore down on the canvas from above, before the invisible sky became once more overcast with clouds.

The landscape through which they passed was silent. The truck drove through the sound of its own engine. It was still early morning.

They could only surmise which way they were going from the maps they held in their memories.

"It's behind us," said the tired old voice to the boy.

"Right," said the boy.

"Perhaps. Let's hope so," said the elder of the two brothers.

It was first and foremost the village that was no longer, the people who were and now are dead. The village that had disappeared from the face of the earth, as a river running dry, a fire dying out, a breath merging with mist. The men, shoes removed, shot, some of them undressed, trousers gone, left in their underwear, without papers, faces to the wall—nameless, jobless, futureless. The village that had disappeared like a mountain swept away by an earthquake, as night fades into morning, day into evening. An extinct volcano, a burnt-out star, a village. A village become a mass grave, filled with earth, night, day, quicklime. A pit that will become overgrown with grass, trees, and weeds.

When the canvas loosened from the long journey and the bottom straps were fluttering in the air, the men saw a river. The driver followed a road nearby. An early morning moon, as white as quicklime and blood red, floated on the water. The water was turgid—banks of mud and occasional stones.

The man with the tired, old-sounding voice put his arm around the boy's shoulder. He could feel how cold the boy was. He was cold, too. It was a chilly morning.

After an hour, the truck stopped.

"Get out," said the SS officer on the embankment.

The young SS officer looked back, probably waiting for the other truck, which they had lost on the road.

The men got out. The tired, old-sounding voice suddenly said, "I want to stay with my son."

"Why?" asked the young SS officer. "Do you want ten blows with a stick?"

"I want to stay with him no matter what happens," the man repeated.

"Help the animals, carefully. Unload them," said the SS officer.

"What is going to happen now?" the man asked the young SS officer. And to the boy he said, "Stay with me."

The man with the tired, old-sounding voice looked at the river and held the boy. He looked at the river, but his gaze was turned inward. He saw a village, one hundred and seventy-three men shot dead, one hundred and ninety-eight women imprisoned, ninety-eight children abducted, a pit filled with earth and quicklime. At the same time, he saw the river, himself, and the remaining men. Those other thirty-six who had left the day before and had not returned. The men by the wall before they had been shot, with the priest, who like the rest no longer had shoes on. Who was he, the man who had been forced to remove even his underwear? The houses doused with petrol and paraffin and set alight—the first house at seven in the morning, so that by ten o'clock all would be on fire. A blaze, kindled according to the instructions of the German military police officer, so that there would be no need for firemen to control it.

The man with the tired, old-sounding voice breathed in mist with the wind, which his son also inhaled, and watched the river flow, the moon recede.

"Take the animals down," said the SS officer. "Carefully. Whoever harms those goats and sheeps . . ."

Just like his father with the tired, old-sounding voice and the others, the boy did not mutter a word.

"Keep your traps shut back there," said the SS officer, describing an arc with his right arm in the direction of the river. "Otherwise . . ." And he drew two tightly closed fingers across his throat.

8

The banked walls of the military town were illuminated by the late spring morning. There were no longer any soldiers in the fortress, only fortifications and ditches, in the south, in the north, the west, and the east. The fortress now served as a town donated by the Führer to the Jews, and as a warehouse and off-loading point. The moon hung over the town, blood red with circles of dirty gray around the sharply defined crescent. Everywhere, above and below, clung mists.

They passed a Jewish guard beyond the no-man's-land, surrounded by old battlements and new police boxes.

"*Heil*," the young SS officer hoarsely greeted a senior constable. To the men, he said, "Take the animals to the gardening area. You will make a sheep pen." To the police, he said, "These men can sleep all day."

"Yes, sir," answered the senior constable, nodding to a policeman on the other side of the fence and to the Jewish guardsman, who had a wooden truncheon and a cap bearing a yellow ribbon.

The animals trickled through the gate, their hooves gently clattering on the stone pavement.

"Son," said the tired, old-sounding voice. "Give me your hand. We are back safe and sound. We are alive."

The man with the glasses said, "I don't feel like pretending we were the Maccabees. They've the right to say that the first bird to stick his head up will be shot."

"It's just as well that it was at night—you couldn't see anything," said the tired, old-sounding voice.

"Right," replied the boy.

"Back there," said the tired, old-sounding voice. "Everything there, what happened there. Poor people."

"I didn't see anything. I didn't look," said the boy.

"Good," said the tired, old-sounding voice.

"Nothing, nothing, nothing," said the boy.

The man with the tired, old-sounding voice looked at the entrance to the barracks, from which they had been picked up at the beginning of the night before, at the paraffin lamp with its painted blue shade which allowed its light to fall only close by, in line with the blackout regulations. Suddenly he remembered the smell. He sniffed around several times and felt that the barracks didn't smell as it used to. His nose was full of burnt ground.

The boy remembered the emphasis which his father placed on his last word.

"Good," the boy repeated. Then he leaned against a ram, and with his palm, covered in calluses—some of which had broken and were marked with loose skin and blood—he grasped the coarse curls of wool on the animal's back and on its neck, touching the leather collar at the animal's throat. The ram looked at him with dim dull eyes.

The elder from the barracks, together with the elders from their ward, came out to meet them.

"At last," said the elder from the barracks. "Are you all back?" At the same moment he recognized on the man and the boy the smell of burnt earth. It was the kind of smell that couldn't be washed or scratched off, as if it were a tattoo.

"All of us," answered the tired, old-sounding voice.

"Sheep?" asked the elder from the barracks.

"Sheep, goats. Perhaps even horses, cows, and pigs," answered the tired, old-sounding voice.

"They demolished houses and undressed and removed the shoes from the dead. They pulled their socks off."

"Yes," said the tired, old-sounding voice, stroking the boy's head as though he wanted to cover his ears.

"Did they beat you?"

"No."

"Have you eaten?"

"What's he got there?" asked the man with the tired, old-sounding voice. "What are you holding on to?"

"Nothing. A collar," answered the boy.

In fact, it was nothing more than a leather strap from which someone had torn off the bell.

They looked for an owner's name, but didn't find anything, even later when they inspected the leather by the light of day, except the name of the blacksmith who had been and was no more, or the name of the harnessmaker who was no more. There was indifference in the dull eyes of the animals.

"You can go and get some sleep," said the tired, old-sounding voice to the boy.

It seemed to the boy that daybreak would not come for a long time. The moon turned the color of the sheep's hair and blood and eyes, and of the dirt of something that was impossible to name. The moon drifted above the river again. Slowly, the sun began to shine.

FIRST BEFORE THE GATES

❖

1

I t was rumored that Captain Johann Wolfram von und zu Wulkow, with his silvery hair and polite, reserved manner, was a German count who spoke fluent French, English, and Latin, and wore a magnificent uniform. His signature glittered on the public notices glued to the passages in the houses and the walls. During the last week of April, he built his headquarters on the highest hill in the center of Prague, near the monastery and the steel lookout-tower above the Moldau River, overlooking the city from all sides of the Compass Rose. Nobody had seen him in the streets, down in the quarter. It was said that he was ready to leave the city as a warrior, without looking back. Though he never made speeches like his predecessor, he was said to speak to the people in his mind, never for more than a minute. And it was rumored that the Captain had a teenaged illegitimate son somewhere in Germany. But everybody knew that Captain Wulkow's new military camp lay by the cemetery wall. At the thought of the cemetery, the old woman, Maria Kubarska, about whom the story later came out, said at the end of the night to herself, "It won't be long and I'll by lying there, too, like so many others. In a few days I'll be seventy-two. I've lived long enough." She had other thoughts, too. There was a feeling

in her that the boy didn't understand her, that he didn't understand himself
and what was going on.

"Child," she whispered, "you are like a sieve and your head like a
leaking pot."

The words "rite of passage" passed over her lips, followed by the word
"Nazis." Small things of great significance and great things disappearing
into nowhere. She often repeated words from an old prayer book that she
found in a trash can where Emanuel Bloch was deported to the East,
together with his mother. It was said that the old woman was ninety-eight
years old and was not permitted to sit in the streetcar but had to stand
on the platform of the second car, the place for dogs and freight.

Each time the night streetcar, number seven or twelve, drove through
Carmelite Street past the Church of the Triumphant Virgin Mary, where
Maria Kubarska prayed on Sundays, the glass-paned door of the house
rattled. She thought about why, at the end of the six-year-old war, the life
of one person was so valueless, as if nobody cared whether you lived or
died. And why so many people were going about their business as usual
in spite of the fact that day after day so many people were being killed in
camps, on the gallows, and in places of execution.

"Why aren't you asleep?" asked the boy drowsily. "Why don't you
pray during the day? If I don't get enough sleep, I'll feel like a fly by
morning."

"There's a new big shot among the Nazis here, Johann Wolfram von
und zu Wulkow, a count."

"I saw people tearing down all the posters with his German name,"
said the boy.

She felt contempt in his voice and it came, first, because she kept him
up at night, and second, because he didn't see the sense in something she'd
picked up from a trash can almost three years ago, and kept like a treasure.
He didn't like it when she repeated the Jewish prayers like an echo of an
echo, from far beyond. The old woman returned to the rumors she heard
on the block about Captain Wulkow from the fresh military unit which
had pitched his tent only a couple of streets west of their house on the top
of the hill. What kind of man was he? A notorious killer who had come

directly from Russia or Poland, where survivors still told tales about him? Or from France or Italy, where they had already chased away unwelcome Germans? The grocer insisted that he was a German of noble origin who talked without shouting, read poetry, and listened to music, and seemed not unaware or unconcerned about the end of the war, which was quickly approaching, but wanted it his way. Somebody heard that he was stationed in Paris during the summer of 1943.

The darkness of the new moon had deprived Maria Kubarska of sleep for six years, just as on this night. She had gotten used to her insomnia. She didn't need so much sleep now. She couldn't blame it on the boy, whose bright red hair shone in the dark, nor could she blame it on Germany, old age, or even the grocery store owner's noisy rooster. (It had finally been slaughtered and eaten for Easter, so the old woman couldn't hear it crowing.) She didn't even blame her insomnia on the grocer's five years of cooperation with the Germans. Only sometimes did she fear nightmares in which death was a woman in black rags, resembling her, coming to the foot of the bed to announce that it was time to stop lounging and to come.

"Why are my nights so heavy—my thoughts an endless maze?" she wondered.

"It's night still. Sleep," said the boy.

"I can't," she said. "I wish. You should sleep. Sleep, please."

Was it the dead who talked to her—her husband and her daughter and Mr. Emanuel Bloch and his mother? Deprived of sleep, she thought about her man, who had been executed on June 23, 1942, not far from here on the shooting range of Kobylisy, near the water tower and the old Jewish cemetery. She kept quiet. She thought about the reasons the boy would wet the bed, often three times in one week. The feeble person is of no use to anyone. Children need protection. Did he have bad dreams? Was he sick? I have to be strong, she thought.

Maria Kubarska thought about Mr. Emanuel Bloch and his ninety-eight-year-old mother. They were part of her thoughts when she was scrubbing the floor, the restrooms, and the cloakrooms at the railroad station, and when sweeping the hall around the bumpers of the railroad cars—triple blocks of cement ending in a dull pyramid which stopped the

train. In her mind she saw Mr. Emanuel Bloch drink water from the faucet
in the hall or go to the common restroom with his hands folded as in
prayer. Was it true that Mr. Emanuel Bloch and his mother prayed facing
east? Was he dead like his mother, like her husband and her daughter?
Who ate at his table now? Who sat in his chair, slept in his bed?

Sometimes it occurred to her that she linked the living and the dead
through the language of Mr. Emanuel Bloch's prayer book. *Who is he who
possesses wisdom? It is he who learns from every man, it's said. From all
who can teach me I learn. Who is he who possesses strength? It's he who
overcomes his own desire, as it is said.*

"God," said the boy in a half-whisper. "You must be crazy from all
that. Are you trying to be Jewish or what?"

"Don't blaspheme. Did you forget to buy bread? I can go to the monks
for sheep's milk before daybreak . . . Here, take a bite, suck my blood," added
the old woman. "Today we have to go to the doctor. I've got a summons
to show up with you—a subpoena." She prayed from the book of an old,
and by now, dead Jewish man to prove to herself that the Nazis couldn't
destroy her mind—but maybe the body. *It is said, sometimes a man goes
to his mate, and sometimes his consort comes to him. A man is easily
appeased, but not a woman.*

2

Otto Kubarsky, Maria Kubarska's grandson, waited only two minutes
to make sure the old woman was asleep. At every night's end she was
exhausted from waiting for something to happen, so at dawn she closed
her eyes as if dead and slept. Should he burn the book or throw it away—
back into the trash can where she'd found it? For a split second he thought
about how she became silly, while blaming it on him. Did she really believe
that the prayers of a dead man could save her life? He had to forget about
the old woman and her accusations that, in his mind, changed into the
fear of weakness.

He thought about bats—how they're equipped to fly on a starless night and avoid invisible cobwebs; and about chipmunks, small as distant stars, leaping from tree to tree somewhere in Bolivia; and about butterflies so weak the wind can carry them off, yet able to fly over an ocean. Sometimes he wanted to be one of the birds he'd read about, to fly thousands of miles alone, to fly across the world twice, from north to south and from south to north, only to return next season right to his nest, to the same tree or roof or cliff he'd started from.

He thought about Nazi tanks, like the Königstiger, King Tiger, the Panther—the best tank of the war, or the Hummel, Bumblebee. He also thought about soldiers, the *Panzergrenediers,* always part of the Nazi army in Prague, essence of the Blitzkrieg, which had now lasted for six years.

In two or three minutes he faced the hill with the stairs to the cable cars and the steep slope close to the Hunger Wall on the way to the Premonstrate's monastery. There was no moon and the skies were black and starless. He trembled with cold, fighting the moist wind and fear as well as the muddy path, coming closer to the monastery's rear wall with its narrow wooden door.

From his place now he saw the tents of the military camp; the guard didn't see him and the dogs couldn't smell him. In the distance near the cemetery was the tent, a flag with a swastika flapping in the wind. Otto Kubarsky, too, had heard the commander was a count, von und zu Wulkow, and that he had a whole cable car to himself going up and down the hill, always alone except for his adjutants. He recognized the big guns, looking from the top of the hill down on the city in all directions. For another split second, he imagined the old woman could see him. Her Jewish prayers would come in handy. He stood and watched how they unloaded artillery and ammunition from cable cars.

Five minutes later, carrying a pot of milk, he passed the long shadow of the big tank guns. He went back the same way, his feet wet and trembling from the cold, looking forward to being in his bed again.

3

"Oh my God, boy, you'll be my death," the woman whispered.

She stroked the boy with her hand. Her palm was hard like a scrubbing brush, soaked so many times in hot or icy water and full of oil, dirt, and grease. So now he's become a thief as well? What next? *To whom does God give wisdom? To one who is modest? To the brave and honest who don't steal and lie? A woman prefers a poor young man to a wealthy old man.*

"It's cloudy," she said without looking outside. His shoes next to the bed were wet and covered with mud and grass. "Where have you been? You must be sick in your head. Isn't there a German military camp out there?"

Outside, the loudspeaker announced five A.M.; then came the military march. The old woman lifted her arm and her head. The headquarters of the high command announced that tank traps, which forced some troops into a tactical retreat, and then to reassemble as in the Ardennes, had caused temporary difficulties. Beethoven's march was played. There was static and squealing in the loudspeaker.

"Are you working today?" the boy asked.

"You talked about bleeding in your sleep. A doctor ought to look at you. Ready?" said the old woman. "Let's go."

She had a harsh voice. Maybe it was the way his eyes were spaced that made him seem so far away. They were set wide apart, close to the sides of his face, so that the pupils always seemed to be unfocused, as though the world could run together. His eyebrows too were set high above his eyes, making the skin beneath lengthen and cast shadows at the corners. They were like the eyes of her daughter, Marta, with their hooded faraway look. But they were also selfish eyes, though she couldn't say in what way, except that he proved a thief, stealing at night, and he didn't see the danger of the German camp. And to steal so close to a cemetery—wasn't that blasphemy? Life is a sorrow, yes. Were his the eyes of a child and a man at the same time? He was small for his years and had thin shoulders, long tapered fingers, and a narrow face that gave him a girlish look. He was one of the smallest boys in his class.

"Put on a sweater or you'll catch cold," the old woman added. "This is the birth of Jack Frost. It's blowing in from everywhere. It came early this year." Then she said, "I won't let them kill you as they killed your Grandpa, or Mr. Bloch and his mother. What did you dream? Tell me."

The boy didn't answer. It was better thinking about birds and butterflies that could overcome great distances in spite of their weak wings, or about the chipmunks of Bolivia.

She almost threw the coat over his head. It had been her daughter's and she had altered it for the boy. She watched as he fastened the buttons with his fingers. Then the old woman started drinking the rest of the milk.

The dark May daybreak lingered above the courtyard. She could see from her bed the contour of the garage with its caved-in roof, the ash cans, and rotten wooden cages left by the former landlord, who had raised budgies and finches. Sometimes on sleepless nights she imagined the grocer being forced to exchange his apartment with them as a punishment. Many people became rich during the war, but the poor became poorer.

Her bones creaked. Her coat had wide lapels and sewn-on rabbit skin. "Comb your hair. Your head looks like a rooster tail. And tie your shoelaces."

4

The German doctor was tall and bony, with black hair plaited into braids pasted close to her head. She had the cheeselike complexion of a person who hasn't slept. Her lips were close, thin, and mannish. Her white coat was buttoned under her arm. Maria Kubarska had never seen such a coat. Inside the office was a couch covered with white, waxed linen and a table full of papers. The doctor stood at the desk with her legs apart.

"Am I supposed to examine you," the doctor asked the old woman, "or the boy?"

"Him," the old woman answered.

"Such a handsome young man," the doctor said. "What's wrong with you?"

"He wet himself twice during the night," said the old woman.

"Nothing so bad," the doctor said slowly. "I've seen such cases. The mother smothers the boy and won't let him be a man. What kind of proceedings are you in, criminal or civil?"

"We're not in any proceedings," the old woman said.

"Many people are sick today," said the doctor, who looked at Otto Kubarsky and then asked, "What do you dream about?"

The old woman's face reddened. So did the boy's, which the doctor noticed without moving her lips. The old woman looked at the doctor's nostrils. Could the doctor incriminate them merely for his dreams? The doctor looked the same way the secret police officer with the hunter's hat and the driver who showed them the way to the door had.

"I dream about fire," the boy said, trying to relieve the old woman. "One time a viaduct was burning, a transport was moving on it, they called for help. I had a fire engine and hurried to put it out."

"What else?" the doctor wanted to know. She had been interested in aberrations of behavior, in the structure of certain chambers of the brain, its parts, its composition; she'd been promised the brains of criminals, including German deserters, from the Gestapo office. They were giving them away after execution. The expression on the doctor's face was suddenly animated. Interest grew in her eyes.

"It's always some fire," added the boy.

The old woman grabbed the boy by his hand.

"It was only a dream, doctor. It has nothing to do with politics. We're alone. All our people are dead," Maria Kubarska said.

"Of natural causes?" the doctor wanted to know. "Give him less to drink in the evening. I don't know if I can place him in the German institution, especially now. There are no more free places in Castle Hartheim. Maybe next time."

The old woman's brow was wet with perspiration. Her chin shook, chilled by the cold. Her thin wrinkled skin was covered with little black hairs.

Once they'd left the doctor's office, she said, "They're making a fool of you."

"I won't drink," said the boy. "That's all. Why did you drag me here?"

He thought of the birds, flying over thousands of miles. The old woman's feet hurt and the veins in her leg were swollen. The speaker in front of their home on Carmelite Street was noisy. *Das Obercommando der Wehrmacht gibt bekannt.* Behind the hillside the glossy material of the tents reflected in the sun.

"Johann Wolfram von und zu Wulkow," Maria Kubarska said in the midst of the announcement. "Yes, no more than Chanan, John, or Ivan. The lamentations of Jeremiah . . . She will never see you. Only how she stared at you. You're not an animal, I will cure you. Just wait and see." And she quoted the papers from the trash can of the old man, *man is paired with the woman he deserves.* And, *a man should not think evil thoughts in the day as they might lead him to uncleanliness by night,* and then, *for a man whose wife dies in his lifetime, the world is deepened.* But how is it vice versa?

"What did you say?" she asked.

"Nothing," the boy answered.

The boy thought again about birds and butterflies and about boys who poured sugar, if they had it, into the gasoline tanks of German automobiles and sand and dust into the oil cylinders of wheels on the railroad freight wagons where the old woman worked. He knew the old woman would start her prayers again.

5

In the evening, Captain of the Wehrmacht Johann Wolfram von und zu Wulkow noticed a boy in a black flannel coat standing by the fire.

He put away his personal field mirror, saying to himself, "*Avoir des Cheveux d'argent.*" Silver hair. "*Silberne Hare.*"

The captain went to inspect the condition of the troops and to decide whether the fire was breaking safety regulations. He liked the new moon and the dark sky; the stars, hidden by clouds, seldom shone. The wind wafted through the city like a vanishing song. It was Rainer Maria Rilke's city, the place he described as a "miserable town of suborned existences." "*Reiten, reiten, reiten, durch den Tag, durch der Nacht, durch den Tag. Reiten, reiten, reiten. Und der Mut ist so müde geworden und die Sehnsucht so gross* . . . (Riding, riding, riding, through the day, through the night, through the day. Riding, riding, riding. And courage has grown so weary, and longing so great.)"

The captain smiled to himself. He held the monocle to his eye. In the distance there was the sound of a streetcar clanging, the roar of a military motorcycle, and the whistling of a long freight train. He was surprised that he remembered a railroad station, the faces of people who had been sitting in a compartment of a train when he'd gotten on, how much the ticket cost, and how the telegraph poles flashed by.

He watched the slender body of the boy. He thought about what the military camp of the victors meant to a child of a close enemy tribe. Captain Wulkow thought then of history, of what makes it greater than man.

To sit in an open city like Prague wasn't the worst of fates, he thought as he watched the boy by the fire. It was almost time for taps. The soldiers had returned from the local beer halls, "Under the Lookout Tower" and "At the Local Gimlet." You can't change human nature. He saw his soldiers as men of force, as the oldest, most ancient yet contemporary men, prepared at any second of the day or night. But the war was going to be over soon, and he was going to leave and not turn his head back, maybe never.

In the glare of the fire, Captain Wulkow noticed three wrinkles on the top of the boy's forehead. From the nearby monastery, the chapel bell sounded for late evening services, and from the other side of the hill the bells from the Church of the Triumphant Virgin Mary called back. The men gathered around the corporals, who were roasting a ram on a spit. The meat was partly a gift and partly booty from the Premonstrate's sheep fold. Only the strongest and most ruthless will survive this time, this place, this world, the captain thought, not the most civilized. The monks thought it was good to buy the favor of the soldiers with a flank of mutton. The walls under the observatory in the middle of the gardens, a broken plow forgotten since last fall, and the tall and bushy pear trees—all reminded Captain von und zu Wulkow that the ram from the monastery's flock was something slavishly pagan. On the inside he smiled again.

In German nothing sounded as it did in the Slavic language. He could take the words "rock," "rifle," "fire," and each was always just what it said. He tried it in French, Latin, and English. Tell me what language you speak and I'll tell you who you are, the captain thought, and he resolved to enter this observation in his diary. It was a long war, a lost war. Most probably it was not his last. It was not over yet, of course, but it would be. No turning back. There was something very old in his mind; he couldn't say exactly what, but it was older than the first water, heavier than the stars and the air, and more unattainable than the darkness.

The captain watched the fire, the roasting ram, the soldiers half German, half French, both corporals and the boy. It reminded him of a woman he had been in love with in Germany as a cadet in a military school. She was the wife of the commanding officer, professor of strategy and tactic, a leading expert of the army. The commander was proud to have a son with features resembling his lovely wife. The captain sighed. The boy reminded him of that German-French woman. It was the past, a bridge where a man shouldn't turn his head backward. But he did, in secret, for himself.

He stayed in the shadows where he knew they wouldn't see him until he chose to make his presence known.

Earlier the captain had read through the evening military mail and the posted orders. Then, before sunset, he looked at the city camp and studied its architecture with the aid of a map. He was fascinated by the gardens. This city, he knew, had been built by the German architects Parler, Brokoff, and Braun. The beautiful churches linked the inhabitants to Germany, whereas the neighboring Poles—while they still had a country—turned to Rome. The presence of the churches brought peace to the captain's soul, a hazy idea of Slavic tribes, even though during his entire stay at Prague he had never crossed their threshold. His mind was full of foreign landscapes, strange faces, and distant languages.

Captain Johann Wolfram von und zu Wulkow felt the invisible solidarity and the intangible presence of thousands—hundreds of thousands—and millions of German men in arms: flyers in the air, men in submarines in the dark waters deep under the sea wherever they were, from Gibraltar to the Caribbean Sea and from the Atlantic to the Pacific Ocean. He felt their spiritual, almost physical, presence here in Prague at the top of the highest hill, under the low-lying wet heaven, in the only world where there was never enough space and air for all, for the victims and the defeated.

The boy stood by the fire. The sentry had brought him there when he muttered that he had gone to the cow shed at the monastery for a pot of milk. They had scared him by saying that traitors would be hanged on one of the pear trees that grew in the park or on the hillside leading up to the camp. The boy was impressed and scared at the same time. He barely succeeded in hiding his nervousness in the presence of the soldiers. The black and blue mark beneath his left eye had been put there by the sentry's rifle butt as he urged him toward the camp at a faster pace.

Corporal Rudolf Kalkman said to the boy, "Everything that lives must die, but there are two catches: not everything that dies will be born again, whether an animal, man or flower; and each person makes that decision at different times."

The second corporal agreed. His name was Maurach, and he felt right at home in the Eastern European regions. He collected articles about the lives of Aryan Slavs fit for Germanization—he noted their conditions, signs, and inclinations. It's unbelievable how much depends on ears, noses, and chins, on the color of eyes and hair, and on the mouth. What was the curse of the weak who made brothers of his servants? There were only too many exceptions.

The corporal showed the boy a bayonet covered with blood. (The boy had offered earlier to bring an animal from the monastery, which he did.) Corporal Kalkman smiled, grinning in his coal black eyes.

"Good evening," Captain von und zu Wulkow greeted. "Is the animal perfect? You can tell the men to stand at ease, Corporal."

The second corporal, Maurach, began to play the harmonica, *Heimat deine Sterne*. The fire roared as the ram roasted, crackling as it came apart at the joints. The captain, his eye behind his monocle, peered into the fire. He watched the movement of the animal's skin touched with gold. Corporal Kalkman had been a butcher in civilian life. Now he refreshed his skills; he hadn't forgotten anything. In a stable, goats protect horses from diseases and bring luck and money to the farmer. A goat's horn under the pillow cures insomnia. But sheepskin also has its mysteries in daylight, and in moonlight, and in different seasons.

There was hesitation in the flames, and in connection with the sheep it created strange music in the captain's ears.

"The meat is superb, Captain," Corporal Kalkman answered. "It was a black sheep. That doesn't mean calamity when you cut its throat fast, Herr Captain."

His eyes were bloodshot. He'd been standing very close to the fire and hadn't slept for several days before the camp had moved to the hillside. He watched the drops of fat running down the skin of the animal and into the fire. Tufts of black hair protruded from the corporal's nostrils. He was careful never to show weakness to anyone. He kept away from Hungarian and Romanian soldiers in order to avoid any suggestion that he looked Jewish, or, as he once said, Mediterranean. He didn't like Italian, Romanian, or Hungarian soldiers. He envied Corporal Maurach's blond hair and light brows as well as his thin beard, light as straw, and his blue eyes. He was glad Captain Wulkow was not blond and blue-eyed. Captain Wulkow was a silvery brunette, with green-gray, almost colorless eyes.

"Come with me to my tent, I'll see that you're well treated," the captain told the boy.

The captain thought about how his mother believed that seeing a sheep at night meant a storm or a death, and that only a ram drives away the evil spirits of man.

They walked next to each other in the soft grass under the dark pear trees. The first star appeared on the north side. Captain von und zu Wulkow felt a tension in the boy he thought he could explain.

In the tent he had the boy pronounce certain Czech words. He enjoyed the musical quality of the language. As soon as the German and Atlantic armies jointly defeated the Russians, the language of the Czech tribe would die out as would the language of the Jews—like the mysterious language of the Aztecs or of the lost continent of Atlantis which had died thousands of years ago.

So weit die braune Heide geht . . . The captain opened the portable record player he took along with him wherever their expedition went— from Moscow to Kiev, from Kiev to Paris, from Paris to Warsaw, from Warsaw to Prague. He wound the spring. The melody was Beethoven's Sonata in G major, opus 30. A bat passed through the air behind the tent; then an owl hooted. The captain smiled. By taking only one step backward, he felt as though he flowed back to the times of the twelve Teutonic tribes. The tent and the large travel trunk were covered with small carpets of Turkish and Persian design.

What was it? What was the boy awakening in him? He thought of his secret, half French-half German woman and the son of the commanding officer and teacher of strategy and tactics in the military school thirteen years ago. The captain looked in his field mirror. He thought about the boy's frailty and the slash marks on his face. He thought about the many German boys who had fallen, and about secrets of fathers and sons, unknown fathers and secret sons.

He picked up the telephone. It would be necessary to announce that today, May 4, 1945, at 8:16 P.M. winter time, the criminal elements in town abused a German soldier. Punishment must be handed out.

Captain Wulkow took the boy by the shoulders and led him back to the fire. The fire swished and crackled. With the back of his hand he touched the frail, white face, the chin and the nape of the slender neck. He urged the boy to walk faster and slapped him a few times on the shoulders with his gloved hand.

6

At that moment, the German doctor wrote an inquiry to the Gestapo's Prague office, asking them to provide her with more brains of local criminals. It was similar to a request she'd made yesterday when the skirmishes and attacks against German soldiers began on the streets. The Gestapo advised her also to ask the commanders of local units. Only a few German university laboratories were busy with similar research. She hypothesized that there were connections between head trauma in childhood and aggressive attitudes toward German occupation and forces in general—particularly with aberrations in behavior.

Comparing the addresses of the two Kubarskis, she wrote a second letter to Count von und zu Wulkow. She took pains to explain her purpose and the future importance of her brain research. It would be ideal to be able to conduct the experiments on some people before and after execution. She had already studied the brains of ten hanged criminals and of twelve others shot or frozen in the laboratories of a certain castle. She had no doubt that her research could contribute to science and the scientific prestige of the Third Reich. There was no better place than Prague, the center of Europe.

She thought about the front line, about where Schörner's army, with one million fresh German men, was now and what obstacle presented itself to this city, its inhabitants, their future being closed in by the American army. She thought of the pride of this city, of how some of the people demonstrated pure madness. Did they think they could defeat Germany? No one should underestimate German capacity and resolve or Nazi ability to act with ruthlessness. Nobody is permitted to touch Germany. It was a pleasure to know that her commander had a fun-

damentally different approach than the mad dogs in Prague expected.
She sent her letter by her personal messenger under her seal to the
quarters of the Count von und zu Wulkow.

7

The wind brought the fragrance of the blue and white lilacs and the
pear trees to the fire, which mixed with the night and the scent of the
roasted animal. Below, the town seemed submerged in darkness. Planes
occasionally hummed overhead. Down on the street, a streetcar or
motorcycle droned in the dark.

"Are you cold?" the captain asked the boy. "Get closer to the fire."

Corporal Kalkman gave the order to stand at attention and then at
ease. He handed the captain a metal plate with a helping of meat. He
knew the captain would refuse it, but would let the boy be served.

The captain thought about the boy, about what he would do with
him. The town below reminded him of a sacrificial ground that German
knights in armor once rode to with clanging weapons and spirited horses.
It was Friday, the fourth of May, a new moon. The moon seemed to
be hidden behind a dark curtain through which it would break, a tiny
crescent, perhaps tonight or tomorrow morning. The captain thought
about their Teutonic past. That age didn't seem so far off. Nor did it
seem difficult for him to look forward a thousand years. At one time,
the Teutonic tribes ruled Europe with an iron hand. They were strong
and healthy. Had they let themselves become dominated by the Greeks
and the Romans or by the dubious wisdom of the Jews? On the hillsides
overlooking the city, he felt close to all of that. He absorbed it with
every breath, with every step he took in the grass under the cool spring
sky. In the dark, he had the taste of something that even the German
language had no words for. He thought about how the dead and the
living penetrated from the depths of the past to the present, to this
place, to the fire under the sprawling pear tree, into the wood and the
aroma of the roast. Here they were, his Teutonic ancestors: lethal as
wolves, keen as hawks, proud as eagles. He breathed deeply in and out.

Again, in his thoughts he was with the wife of the commanding officer in the military school.

The captain turned away from the fire and looked out into the darkness over the city where black towers jabbed the sky. Smiling slightly, he thought about how all that was German flowed up at this moment, and he felt how one thing was connected to another. History didn't just follow. It is the result of individuality and resolve and conduct in unstable times. History made Captain Wulkow tell the soldiers to bring a small barrel of rum for those who were not on duty.

The captain stood next to the boy and looked into the fire. The boy's eyes also belonged to the fire, as though the fire itself was in them. But on his back he felt the wind shiver with hunger. The wind rustled in the treetops. The grass flattened, then stood again. The captain was observing how the boy caught the warmth of the flames with his forehead and chest and the palms of his hands. Does he think about me, wondered the captain? Does he think about light, sound, and voices? About childhood associations, in reverse, about the visions of his unknown future? Someone handed him a small slice of military bread. He ate slowly. The bread tasted like the pressed and baked sawdust bakers mixed with flour. From the other side of the fire, Corporal Maurach threw him a linen towel so he could wipe his hands and mouth.

It occurred to the captain that there was no other army in the world as companionable as the German army, descendants of the Teutons, knights of the Middle Ages, the Crusaders: born of song, blood, and the land, of honor, light, and voices, as hard as tungsten steel, lithe as a leaping panther, mighty as an ocean. That was the army keeping Europe *maustod,* dead as a mouse. The army which made the enemy *mundtod,* deadly silent.

In the evening, the town reminded the captain of a poem written by invisible hands, one that has lost its meaning. He left for his tent.

"We will put out the fire, you can pee with us into the flames," said Corporal Kalkman, and he smiled.

When he was leaving for his tent, the voices of the corporals and the soldiers merged in the captain's ears with the humming wind in the pear trees. He didn't turn.

8

"You're not going there anymore," said Maria Kubarska. "Only over my dead body. I won't let them shoot you like a dog."

"Living like dogs is OK?"

"Don't you understand?" she asked. "It's just not worth the risk." The old woman fell silent again.

The new moon edged toward its end. The dark blue curtain of the sky, purple and velvet on opposite ends, sailed through the clouds above the courtyard. Maria Kubarska lay next to the boy and wondered: What will happen? Am I prepared for it? The spring always asks how the winter was, or the past six winters.

"They'll kill you as they did your grandfather. They'd love to kill everyone." And then she said, "I wish you were my bird again."

The house and the courtyard were dark and quiet. Friday was falling into the past and soon Saturday would arrive.

She lay on the bed and looked across the room at the geranium. She had placed a geranium in the window that faced the courtyard. She wondered if it would start raining.

She thought of all those who'd been killed because they'd listened to Radio London or Radio Moscow, about all the maimed who'd gone to Gemany and worked in the Ruhr, Essen, or Westfall and were forbidden to talk to the German population, just allowed to work for them. They'd never returned, like Mr. Emanuel Bloch and his mother. They were condemned to *Todschweigen.* Killed into silence, as the Germans said.

"What are you doing?" the old woman asked. "Have you lost your tongue?"

"I'm asleep," the boy lied. "What did Grandpa actually do to them?"

"He didn't dispatch the trains at the freight station," Maria Kubarska answered. "Because of him something was delayed. And then the SS Gauleiter Reinhard Heydrich, general of the German secret police and the first deputy of Hitler, his darling, was assassinated in May 1942 like a stray dog. They killed him and Mr. Emanuel Bloch and his mother.

They dispatched three Jewish transports, thousands of people on each, and destroyed one entire mining village. Now we're going to pay for it. I can feel it in my veins. In these bad veins of mine, and in my chest. No, you're not going anywhere. There are others here. Grownups. They've waited for six years."

"There's too much on your mind," the boy answered.

"It's quiet; I don't hear any shooting anywhere."

"If it starts raining, I'll go right away," the boy said. "I'll be back in the morning. Where's my coat?"

"I sewed it and reinforced it with my own hands. It would break my heart if something were to happen to you. My veins would open, even where old wounds have healed. My breath is loud, just like Marta's. Turn toward the wall. You're the last of the Kubarskys. Marta wanted it that way, for your name to be Otto just like your grandpa and your father. Look out. I smell the stench of trash cans all the way here. I don't want to live here anymore, not even one more day. In the morning we'll go out together."

"Do your veins hurt?"

"They're open," the old woman nodded.

The night became darker. "Everything will be different," she whispered. "When it's possible to defeat Adolf Hitler, any vision—no matter how distant—is close enough. You have to be reasonable, my little boy. They're worse than you imagine."

She waited for the dawn when the birds would come—the sparrows and the swallows, in great crowds on their paths between the land and the skies—hunting and nesting, flying day after day, year after year. She envied the birds. She didn't know exactly why. Maybe it was their freedom, or maybe it was something more—and at the same time less.

The night seemed to her the darkest in six years. The Germans were here, astute and strong, though in other ways already weak. From one side the Russians were coming; on the other side the Americans were waiting for their prey. What would they be like? Maybe it was the last night of the war. She thought of everything that made the nights heavy and dark, as if they had no end. As if someone had killed all the roosters that separated daytime from evening and night from morning.

9

On Saturday, the fifth of May, when the field artillery pieces on the Petrin hillside and around the lookout tower were no longer covered with waterproof linen caps, a small, boyish figure brought two sheep from the Premonstrate's fold, tied to a rope. No one on the hillside suspected him. The monk who saw him didn't say a word about the boy taking the sheep. The sheep bleated and the boy pulled the animals behind him and wiped the sweat off his forehead.

On each side, three men in raincoats stood by each of the guns, prepared to shoot. The safety catches on their personal weapons were uncocked. Johann Wolfram von und zu Wulkow's unit was prepared. It was cold.

"Stop. Where are you going? Not a single step forward or you'll be full of lead," the voice of Corporal Kalkman cried out from behind the boy.

"I'm bringing you some sheep. You said you'd get hungry and you wanted another roast. I couldn't come during the day, there was shooting. I had to wait."

"Move on or you're going to trip over your own carcass," the corporal mumbled.

Corporal Kalkman passed him and looked into his face, at his darkly circled eyes. The corporal pressed the point of the bayonet into the back of the black flannel coat that had once belonged to the boy's mother. The boy felt the sharpness of the point, and the corporal guessed by the slight degree of resistance that he'd touched the boy's back near the heart. The shadows were pitch black. Once in a while the wind blew the remaining drops of afternoon rain off the leaves and branches of the nearby pear trees.

He ordered the boy to wait by Captain Wulkow's tent. With his heels and toes together, slightly bent forward, he announced to the captain that the boy was here again and that he'd dragged in two sheep. They were on their way to the field kitchen near the supply wagon.

The captain sat looking over a map near an oil lamp. He was in uniform with high riding boots, and across his arms lay a coat with silver epaulets. He was uneasy about the large number of streets and connecting roads by which the rebels could attack or—after the attack— retreat. There was the winding Swedish Street; and to the north, Belcredi Avenue as well as a clump of streets around the Institute for the Blind; and from the east, Italian Street. This led to the market and to Carthusian Streets, a channel of roads with many windows and doors. He'd come to an agreement with the High Command of General Reitman's staff that he would assume alert status. But someone had cut the telephone wires and disconnected the electricity five minutes before. And now Corporal Kalkman had interrupted him.

Captain Wulkow's silvery hair flashed in the darkness. "Did you frisk him to see if he had any weapons?"

The captain put on his coat and buttoned it up. He heard the bleating animals and it occurred to him that someone could zero in on a unit by following their noises. He didn't say a word. He saw the boy under one of the pear trees. Voices were coming from the direction of the guns. From the monastery, the evening bells rang.

"Once, Corporal, you told the men that your father wanted to beat you over the head with a chair. A man like you only attains age in life, nothing else. You remind me of a lumberjack who cuts down a tree for his friends to make a casket for him. You're still only a butcher, Kalkman. Destroy the animals on the double."

"I'll destroy them on the double, sir."

The captain thought: To obey is as beautiful as to give orders, but on a lower mental plane. For people like Kalkman, only one rule applies: to bend and be bent. Man is his muscle and not his sorrow; life is an orgy, not higher principles. Only the present time—no eternity. Simple matters, no concern for the cosmic; no harmony, only chaos. Light, sound, and voices, but what kind? From where?

Corporal Kalkman killed each sheep with a single blow. He rammed the bayonet through their hearts. They gave a single bleat, then fell, washed by blood in their white wool.

"You don't understand a thing," Captain von und zu Wulkow said, and in his mind added, *avoir des mains de boucher. Hände wie ein Fleischer.* He saw the corporal's hands covered with blood. Captain Wulkow departed from the corporal and went uphill along the line of pear trees to his staff, hidden in the dark. He took no notice of the boy.

In three circles, sentries made their way noiselessly around the camp. They stepped quietly in the grass between trees, as if they were separating from their shadows and merging with them again. The rain began, small cold drops.

On the other bank of the Moldau River, a fire not even the rain could dampen was burning. Several German squadrons were flying east to west.

The lights of the flames didn't disappear until they were high in the sky.

They boy looked at the holster of Kalkman's pistol, put aside just like the coat on the open bed of the Mercedes truck. Only for a moment did he place his hand on the pistol. At that instant, he felt Captain Johann Wolfram von und zu Wulkow's gloved hand. The other hand that gripped him belonged to Corporal Kalkman.

"You know just a few types of meat, Corporal," the captain said. He let go of the boy's arm. The boy's shoulder shivered for a moment. To the captain, the boy's bones seemed frail under the thin flannel woman's coat. He remembered how once, right before the war, he'd run over a fawn during manuevers in the forest in Berlin. How strangely everything changes. Light, sounds, the mood. He coughed. Then he said: "Tie him to the cannon barrel of your tank, Corporal."

"*Zum Befehl*, Herr Captain," said the corporal.

"The most dangerous animal is a wounded one, Corporal. The worst war is a lost war."

"*Zum Befehl*, Herr Captain."

"Fire three rounds, Corporal."

"*Zum Befehl*, Herr Captain. Tie him to the tank barrel and fire three rounds."

The bell had stopped tolling. An old woman was coming from the bottom of the ruined walls, passing the cemetery wall. She crossed the peak of the hill. The guard's searchlight shone its bright light directly upon her. She reminded the captain of an owl and the corporal of a bat. She reminded the boy of an old bird who had wings but couldn't take off, a creature who could only move about with difficulty. She was seventy-two years old, to the day and the hour. In the searchlight, her wrinkled face flashed, her eyes squinted. Her mouth was open. Her lips were chapped. For another second, veins showed in her face and on her temples.

"In the morning, at ten, you'll be driving through the city streets in the center of the Wenceslaw Square, so shoot sharp," said Count von und zu Wulkow.

Maria Kubarska was coming in the black dress she had worn to her husband's funeral on June 12, 1942, with her head tied in a scarf and her hands clenched in fists, with the dark brown spots on her neck and aching feet. The old woman was fading in the night, tripping, as low branches hit her in the face, hands, and chest. She kept moving in order not to lose a second. Flashes of light blinded her, but she pressed on, determined not to lose a single step. Her arms were glued to her body; she didn't even use her right hand to protect her from the branches.

In the next flash of light the captain could see why. She carried the black prayer book tightly under her arm, protecting herself only with her left hand. The branches snapped against her wrinkled body.

A split vision of a man and his ancient fate many years ago passed through her mind. She walked slowly and with difficulty, as if her head weighed as much as the earth, the stars, and the universe. Her shoes were flat and worn. Her ankles, wrapped in muslin rags, were round and swollen over the tops of her shoes. She walked with slow determination, aiming directly, making way. So broadly do men carry their will against time and mountains.

The old woman moved her lips; she squinted her eyes and fought on, as if she wouldn't let herself be stopped by the night, the dark wild bushes, or the blinding light.

Everyone has his fool, and I have two at once, the captain thought again. *Wie Man sich bettet, so liegt Man.* As you make your bed, so shall you lie in it. The boy moved, as if he wanted to run and meet the old woman, but the corporal held him.

The woman caught sight of the three shapes near the pear tree, and she headed straight toward them. She felt her feet getting heavier all the time, but she went on over the wet, seaweedlike grass toward the pear trees.

The captain thought for an instant how bountiful their fruit must be. What year did the trees produce sweet and rich pears, full of succulent juices? What years not? Why can nature be virile at one time and barren the next? He imagined blossoms falling during the heat of summer; and then the fall reckoning what only the virgin knows. He thought how similar nature is to human beings, yet how people cannot narrow the border.

The old woman tripped in ditches and over hillocks, overturning pieces of turf and rocks. She was humming through bitten lips. *Let me not fall into the hands of man.* She whispered to herself and then almost aloud.

She thought about Emanuel Bloch, who liked to refer to some of his ancestors, most of them murdered. *Any man, alive or dead, will never be born again; some people are only born to do one good thing during their life—and maybe only to act out a notion.* She marched slowly and persistently forward, step after step, far up the hills, her eyes as dark and cold and hard as ice.

The old woman finally saw a man in a corporal's uniform gripping the boy's shoulder. When she came closer, she heard the crowing of a rooster cut into the night along with the breath of the boy and the voice of a man in a captain's coat, who said, "Do you have enough rope, Corporal? The old woman as well."

Clock Like a Windmill

❖

*The town hall burned first in a fire started by the French in 1689 and again
in the ghetto conflagration of 1754. The two clocks were repaired in 1855.
The one in the tower has Arabic numerals; the second, in the gable under
the tower in the northern side facing the Altneuschul—the Old-New
Synagogue—across the narrow street, has Hebrew letters. The hands of the
Hebrew clock turn backward like leaves in a Hebrew book. According to
the Jewish calendar, it is 5,705 years since the creation of the world.*

veryone in the cellar was captivated by the woman sitting on the
chopping block beside the door, although all she'd said since her arrival
was "Hello" and "Excuse me." She had been the last to arrive.

"The numbers . . . on the clock," she said now. No one answered her
and she added that the clock face showed everything backward.

"It's Hebrew," the caretaker said. "There are no numbers. Only letters,
and it goes backward."

"Yes," said the woman. "Yes."

There were two clock faces on the tower, the upper one normal, the
other with letters and hands that moved counterclockwise. The clocks had
been a part of the town hall for a few hundred years. The woman on the
chopping block was thinking about these clocks.

The caretaker had just announced that he was going upstairs to lock
up in order to keep anyone unwanted from coming to hide. He peered out
and up at both clocks before he locked the doors. They still kept time well.
They didn't need winding today. Mondays were always set aside for winding.

The doors were covered with thick sheet metal, and each had two
small windows at about the level of a man's head. Suddenly a barrage of
bullets hit the door near the caretaker's feet. The wooden paneling around

the door splintered, but the sheet metal which deflected the bullets saved him.

The woman on the chopping block jumped like a startled quail when the bullets exploded against the door. She was wearing a wrinkled beige suit, which made her look as if she were on her way to a meeting which for some reason had never taken place. Her forehead was finely lined, like an old woman's; the ripples looked like those on the surface of a pond. When the caretaker brought her down to the cellar to join the others, he noticed that she couldn't have been much older than his wife. The woman had told the caretaker that she was Jewish and had no place to live.

He looked out the window in the door. He saw a group of German soldiers leading two Czech policemen with raised hands toward the SS headquarters, located in the Law School building on the river bank. He felt relieved that neither of the clocks was ringing. There were no bells. It helped to make the place more inconspicuous.

The caretaker returned to the cellar. He sat between his wife and the woman on the chopping block; a stout woman sat opposite him, facing the children and the teenagers. He asked the two teenagers where they'd come from.

"Kelley Street, if that means anything to you," the older one growled. He made a wry face and turned away from the caretaker. Both of the boys were wearing jackets with rabbit fur on the outside. They could be concealing knives or weapons under those jackets—or at least it looked that way.

The woman in the crumpled suit on the chopping block seemed oblivious to what was going on around her. She was thinking about the clock that moved backward, perhaps because she had never seen anything like that. She thought she could feel the tension created by the two clocks, so near each other but in perpetual opposition.

In the twilight her skin looked pale, with unnatural spots of bright rouge on her cheekbones near the corners of her eyes. She looked like someone obsessed, or a person with a high fever. The woman sat on the chopping block as if she were dreaming. She made no spoken reply to questions; she would simply nod or shake her head. The caretaker didn't tell the others what she had confided to him upstairs.

"It's pretty boring here," said the younger teenager.

"Sit down here, if you don't mind," said the caretaker's wife. "It's only for a while."

It would be good for all of them to get ready for a long stay, the caretaker was thinking. He glanced around the room, saying lightly, "We haven't had so many people here since last Easter."

The German machine gun upstairs rattled again. The caretaker didn't mention the policemen he'd seen being taken away.

The chopping block had been cut from the trunk of an old, flattened oak. Near it lay an ax with a dull, jagged blade, covered with rust that looked strangely like blood.

"Thank heaven we cleaned up in here just a week ago," said the caretaker's wife.

"Thank you. You're very kind," the newcomer said shyly. "Please don't bother about me."

And then she whispered as if she were talking in a dream.

"Is anyone hurt?" the caretaker asked. He knew no one was; he only wanted to create an atmosphere of security and concern in the cellar. He pretended not to hear any of the sounds that penetrated from Maisel Street above.

The caretaker's wife seemed at home here; several times she had wanted to tell everybody her name was Olga, but the words didn't come. She gazed at the woman sitting on the chopping block as if she were trying to assess who she was and where she'd come from. Why was she so surprised that the lower clock turned backward?

"Here we're all as safe as if we were inside a great big granite boulder," she announced. "It's a good thing that none of our employees showed up. We wouldn't have had room for everybody. But, maybe. Yes," she contradicted herself.

"That's for sure," the caretaker joined in. He listened to the shooting down the street. "This cellar's a regular fortress. In a few hours we'll be able to go upstairs, just to make sure everything is OK. In the meantime, I suggest that you don't go near a window if you don't have to; it doesn't make sense to provoke them unnecessarily. After a while, I'll be able to go and take a look from the tower." He looked at the woman on the chopping block. "That's where the clocks are. You can see Paris Avenue and the Legion Bridge from there just as clear as can be."

"You don't think they'll go through every house?" the stout woman asked, heaving a sigh as if she really didn't doubt it. Her question emerged like a song from her heavy fleshy throat.

Both teenagers, looking like hunters or hoboes in their fur jackets, moved away from the window and retreated all the way back to the far corner.

"Consider yourselves guests, if you don't mind my putting it that way," the caretaker's wife said with a smile.

The children liked the way their mother spoke. They'd never seen her quite this way. She seemed pretty and resolute. Nevertheless, she was burdened with something she didn't wish to express. From time to time she turned away from the burning gaze of the newcomer's eyes. It occurred to her that it had been a long time since she'd last seen the sun. She sighed. As a child, she had imagined the sun to be an old man. In the garden of some mansion, she'd once seen a stone fountain engraved with an old man's face with the points of a sunburst radiating from it. The old man's face had been wide, cheerful, and beardless, with a carefully wrought smile.

Again, her eyes met those of the woman sitting silent on the chopping block. Life must be miserable for her, she thought.

"The Germans must thrust forward, break out, keep this street free for their sorties," the caretaker said. "When they get pushed back, they'll want to have free access to the bridge. It is pretty obvious that the bridge is of utmost importance to them—after all, the water's still cold." And then over the renewed stutter of the machine guns, he added, "Our people are doing all right. I'll hang out the flags when I get the chance."

"As luck would have it, I used up my wood sooner than the usual time this year," the caretaker's wife said. "Well, it was good for something. Every year we get a load or two of wood scraps from them."

"Who'd have guessed they'd wind up on our street?" the caretaker said. "They're always unpredictable. But what isn't, these days?"

The eyes of the newcomer remained indifferent to everything; nothing seemed to interest her.

The caretaker's children listened eagerly to everything said by the group. The caretaker's wife watched the teenagers in the corner. They seemed to be conspiring about something. They sounded raw and crass, but in spite of that, they had her sympathy.

"I noticed how many lilac bushes there are behind the walls of the cemetery across the street." In a conspiratorially low voice, the caretaker's wife added that she was fond of the smell of lilac, probably because it always reminded her of the forgotten sins of youth.

The stout woman laughed weakly. "My God, you're not going to talk about age, are you? How old can you be? Thirty? You can't even be that, Mrs. . . . ?"

"Belleles."

The caretaker coughed understandingly. "They wrote yesterday in the *Telegraf* that since the city is considered a military hospital zone, either today or tomorrow we should get food coupons for the next three months for sugar, bread, jam, and flour. They must have really had it."

"They can have my ration," the stout woman declared in her melodious singsong voice. The fleshy white folds of her throat trembled as she spoke.

"Hitler, yes, of course," said the caretaker, as if he were ashamed to pronounce the name of a man who, thank God, had been dead for five days. Was he really dead? Wasn't he still alive, in a certain sense, even after his death?

"Next time, I'd like to order wood from our old supplier," the caretaker's wife remarked, trying to keep the mood light. "I hope he comes back. The grocers and the carpenters will have their heyday yet. Some get frightfully rich off the war. And soon, after the war, they'll be getting richer. I wish they were getting rich already."

As the caretaker's wife spoke, the woman on the chopping block removed her gloves, one finger at a time. The leather stuck to her skin, making a disconcerting crackling sound as she slowly peeled them off.

"We couldn't have found anything better than this," the stout woman said. "We should meet again when it's all over and I'll bring my son." Then she turned to the woman on the chopping block. "No one should be so dumb as to take on this many women. But there's no need to worry."

"You should come at Easter—after the war—it's fun here," the caretaker said.

The initial tension had eased and he felt a wave of satisfaction. Everyone was more relaxed, notwithstanding the shooting which moved from the street closer to the river; only the woman on the chopping block still acted tense. The terse "yes" and "I wouldn't know" replies she offered to the stout woman and to the caretaker's wife seemed detached, offered so she wouldn't be considered rude. Her face looked sad and grave, as though she were being pulled in two, tearing in the middle.

The older teenager pulled the fur collar of his coat around his neck as if he were cold. "Is the policeman walking or isn't he?" he grunted to the younger one.

"There's no point in drawing attention to our house," the caretaker said, demonstrating that the situation was well within his grasp and he was able to keep track of what everyone in the cellar was doing.

There was a silence. The teenagers exchanged looks. The caretaker's children became restless and his wife scolded them; yet as she spoke, a vague expression of concern crossed the face of the woman on the chopping block.

By now, everyone knew that the six-year-old boy with the brown curls was named Toni; his seven-year-old brother was Oldrich; and the four-year-old was Olga. Little Olga wore long, almost new white stockings.

The caretaker glanced over toward the two teenagers who were whispering again.

"The paint always comes off the walls," the caretaker's wife said. "The rain leaks down here, and the cellar never gets a chance to dry out."

"We'd have to heat the place to dry it and that would be too difficult," the caretaker replied. "Where's the cat?"

Just before the newcomer entered, the stout lady had said that she was the mother of a pilot in the RAF. Shortly before her announcement, the two teenagers had appeared; the little one with the squeaky voice sounded as if he were too weak to speak louder, or just didn't want to expend the energy. The taller one's voice was changing. His Adam's apple looked almost like a man's but he still had the body of a boy. He watched little Olga constantly, as if reminded of someone.

The woman who came in last now whispered, "What kind of people are they? . . . What moves them? . . . I still don't know . . . maybe I'll never know . . ."

The caretaker lit a candle to break the tension that followed her words. The gray eyes of the woman on the chopping block stared into the small flame at the tip of the candle, absorbing it.

The older teenager yawned loudly and stretched. He exhaled, a long hissing sound, and then addressed his smaller companion, not paying attention to the shooting at the riverside. "So, have you made yourself comfortable here, you old Methuselah?"

His tone implied that no one in the cellar had said anything relevant, as if the others had been choking on the silence. He squinted into the dim, bluish glow of the candle.

"We're not getting back to Kelley Street anytime soon this way," he added.

"Mr. Belleles doesn't seem to mind having us here—so don't panic." The other one took pleasure in bundling up his fur collar as he spoke. "What's wrong with this place, anyway?"

A glint of light shone from the dim little window that was at street level facing Maisel Street. The waning day flowed in through the dusty glass, which was covered by a torn, rusted wire netting. The street could no longer be seen, even when the caretaker had put his eyes close to the netting to look out. It was hard to discern the facade of the house across the street with the balcony that hung away from the wall like a torn pocket. Half of the flagpole had burned down, and the other half was wrapped in a red banner. Before the caretaker had descended the stairs, it had become quite dark.

"I think they're still walking," the taller teenager murmured to the little one.

"They're walking, all right," the little one agreed, unceremoniously relieving himself.

The caretaker looked at his wife in silent consultation. She stood and went upstairs, passing through the hallway that opened at a right angle to the staircase. She returned three-quarters of an hour later with a kettle of soup, half a dozen plates, and her heavy, festive silver spoons. She gave the first serving to the woman sitting on the chopping block. The thought came to her that those eyes above the vivid artificial blush across the woman's cheeks seemed like two smoldering hearths; maybe she wore rouge to disguise her fears. She seemed to age right before their eyes.

"Eat hearty," she said to the woman.

She didn't even ask the woman's name. She'd probably made a mistake when she hadn't clearly introduced herself at once when the woman had first come; then at least she would know her name. But no one else had bothered to do so either. She wasn't going to now.

"It will warm you up," she said. "A cellar is a cellar . . . it's cold down here, after all . . . and warm food under any circumstances . . . it's the foundation of everything."

"No one will dream of searching this cellar," the caretaker reassured everyone again.

"What do you mean by that?" asked the stout woman.

"This is a town hall; nobody will need it anymore. The people whose names are registered here left a long time ago and no one has heard of them since. I trust you understand what I'm trying to say?"

"Are they still walking?" the taller teenager asked, his voice cracking. He kept buttoning and unbuttoning his rabbit jacket.

"They're walking all right," the little one answered as weakly as before. "So what?"

"They'll be walking till kingdom come," the taller teenager grunted roughly. He caressed the rabbit fur on his jacket.

The caretaker coughed in the direction of the teenagers.

"Eat carefully," he cautioned the woman on the chopping block. "It would be a pity to ruin your dress. Before you go, I'll lend you our iron. We have an electric iron and also a charcoal-heated iron I inherited from my mother."

Suddenly the caretaker's wife saw that the woman on the chopping block was exactly the person who'd been revealed to her through those smoldering eyes. She felt as though she'd known the newcomer much longer. She continued to serve the others.

"It's a bit chilly here because we're so close to the river." She told them she'd made the soup mostly to warm them.

The taller teenager turned abruptly to the little one. "They're not walking anymore, but don't get any ideas. They haven't been through here for at least an hour."

Without asking anyone's leave, the boys went upstairs to look through the peepholes in the entrance door to see whether the street was safe or if there were any German patrols on the prowl. They found a better lookout in the lower clockwork cabin in the tower. The turning gears smelled of oil.

Then they returned. The people in the cellar watched them crawl back into their distant corner like timid little pups.

"The landlord from across the street was opposed to hanging out the red flag," the caretaker's wife said after a pause. "The Germans shot the concierge and someone threw a grenade onto the balcony. It exploded and the entire balcony fell. Now the flag hangs down from the steel beams like a rag; so you can see it would be senseless to do anything like that now. She was too premature."

The stout woman listened carefully. She remarked, "That's bad. Maybe the woman had children at home."

"It's better not to talk about it," the caretaker said quickly. He turned to his wife. "I had no intention of doing anything now."

The teenagers could sense what part of the statement was meant for them.

The caretaker's wife caressed the children while she sat there musing. When children are too quiet, it's like an illness. She caressed them again. They seemed like small wolf cubs.

"So, you were a tailor?" the stout woman asked the caretaker, finally breaking the silence that had fallen over the cellar.

"Wouldn't that be something—you ironing our clothes?"

Nobody said anything.

The caretaker's wife glanced at her bigger son. He avoided her look and she again remembered the time when she imagined the son as an old man. She was sorry that it had been her husband's idea and not her own to bring down soup for everyone, even if he only conveyed it through his eyes. He always thought of things a little faster.

"Time is dragging on so terribly," the stout woman said. "Let's hope our patience is rewarded in the end. Here we are—stuck like nuts on a bolt—and up above, on the street, things must be coming to an end. This German horse isn't going to run very far." Her soft face puffed up when she smiled; her neck quivered.

Later in the evening, the caretaker took a second candle out of the box and replaced the one that had melted down to nothing more than a little stub.

"What are we going to do?" the woman on the chopping block asked suddenly. "What time is it?" She was trying to imagine the clock turning backward. Her voice sounded choked.

"We'll stay here—what else? What would you want to do? What could you do outside?" the caretaker asked. "You can hear the patrol walking right above us. And they're shooting all the time. The Germans won't surrender, and our side won't retreat. This is a revolution. It's either going to destroy us or them."

Upon hearing her husband's words, the caretaker's wife stopped feeling ashamed.

"A few bullets . . . you call this a revolution?" the older teenager said. His voice cracked and it sounded hollow and gruff, like it came from the shadow of the thick, damp walls themselves, condemned to darkness. He reached over and picked up the ax from the floor. "Whoever wants to can take this ax and go upstairs and try man-to-man revolution."

"They're still walking," said the little one, as if trying to temper the other's outburst. Walking soldiers meant passing danger. Their march kept time, and when the walking stopped, lives as well as time stopped.

It crossed the minds of both the caretaker and his wife that the two teenagers considered all of the inhabitants of the cellar—the caretaker included—cowards, even though the two of them were also hiding. The taller one constantly looked at little Olga. Then he'd spit or mumble in his low, cracking voice. Something was irking him. There was something dangerous in a voice like that, the caretaker thought. He'd never liked such voices. They were rough; you never knew what to expect of a person with such a voice. For a fleeting moment the caretaker felt he should get rid of the teenagers, kick them out of the cellar. Then he felt ashamed of the feeling.

"The doors are solid, there's no doubt about that," the taller teenager said to the little one, "a mass of metal plate nailed as tight as a coffin."

"Did you see the inscription?" the caretaker asked, intending his remark for everyone.

The taller teenager recalled the black metal sheet on the door of the building with the plate which read, in both Czech and German, "Prague Council of Jewish Elders."

"Jews," the little one said. "So what?"

"That's why, you idiot," the taller one answered.

"Who's an idiot?"

The children's eyes were riveted on the taller teenager. He looked secretive in his fur jacket. The rabbit fur was sewn inside out. The caretaker was sure the older teenager's sneer was meant for him.

"For all our bad luck, we've struck it pretty good," said the taller teenager to his friend. "I guess whatever isn't bad luck has got to be good luck, you old prophet."

The caretaker became annoyed. "It doesn't make any difference what you call it. The important thing is that without weapons—and we'd better not count on that rusty ax—it's better not to stick your head out. We wouldn't be helping anybody."

"They're walking," squeaked the little one.

Artillery fire could be heard outside.

The caretaker's wife turned and whispered to her husband that the woman in the beige suit was probably sick.

The caretaker wondered what it was going to be like when everyone tried to save his own skin. He coughed dryly, as if he had something important to say. But he didn't speak. The woman on the chopping block turned to him.

"I thought it might be safe to leave, now that it's dark outside."

"Possibly," the caretaker answered slowly. "But we'd be taking a risk since we have no idea what's going on upstairs. You can hear it yourself. Wait until I go up to the tower. From the tower gallery I'll be able to see everything."

They could still hear the chatter of the guns clearly; they'd just become used to the sound and were no longer aware of it as before.

"We can't eat up all your supplies," the woman on the chopping block said. Then she held her head cocked, listening. The German cannon was shooting at the Old Town Hall. "There are five of you including your children; we're strangers and I . . . "

She was interrupted by a loud crash. Apparently, a house nearby was tumbling down.

They could all picture the dust, the smoke, the roof fallen to the pavement. And then they listened, as if expecting ambulances and fire engines to pull up with their sirens shrieking. But everything was quiet, except for the rumbling.

"Don't mention it," the caretaker suddenly said to the woman on the chopping block. "The war is about to end, no matter how we end up down here. Those who will survive will have to learn how to live differently and to manage their affairs in a new way."

He spoke fast to make them forget the crashing sound. All of a sudden, he got the idea that he should tell them what he'd heard at the Black Hound Tavern on Soul Street—that bread could have been free in the East, if the Germans hadn't burned and devastated all the land from Nemen to the Volga. He felt they were ready to listen to him: He was gathering up all that was best in him, beyond himself, themselves, beyond Germany. But he only stammered, "Too much to explain at once. But it will be different for our children. I'm sure of that . . . "

The caretaker's wife wondered what he meant by all that; she was waiting for the crashing sound of the wreckage to stop. Suddenly she remembered that her husband once took his ration of bread to the Black Horse Tavern, claiming he'd get some unroasted coffee for it. She never got the coffee and he never mentioned the bread.

"Don't they have even a little bit of feeling—enough at least to show their better face before the end?" she asked.

"The sky's falling," the taller teenager broke in contemptuously.

He was caressing his fur jacket with obvious pleasure. It clearly wasn't made by a tailor.

The crashing stopped and it became silent again. Everyone wondered where it had happened, which house it had been. It could have been on Paris Avenue or on Soul Street. Or it could have happened in the small Market Square where the hardware store was. In the silence, all the imagined distances flowed together.

After a pause, the silence was again broken by the stout woman. She wore a camel hair coat and turned up its stuart collar to keep warm. "Oh God, oh God," she repeated over again. "To be caught so unaware."

The caretaker expected her to start talking about her son in England again. Her son was in some famous squadron with the word "Mandalay" in its name. She did begin to speak about him, and she told them that when her son came back as an officer, marching down National Avenue, she'd be there on the mothers' stand waving. They listened, but nobody had any idea what "Mandalay" meant.

She added a question unrelated to what she was saying before. "And how many of them fall into the sea? La Manche is there, you know.

How many were downed over Germany? What kind of people are we? Do we really deserve this?" And then, suddenly, "I have a bright apartment. All the windows are on the sunny side."

The woman on the chopping block looked up fearfully and then dropped her glance again, extinguished by the gray stone floor, the coldness of the cellar, and the shadows that covered everything in darkness.

"It's quiet now," the caretaker's wife said. "I'll go up and make some more soup. I'll thicken it a little; I've got enough. If you have any trouble going to sleep it's just the thing."

The caretaker turned to the woman on the chopping block. "You can't leave yet. You'll manage through the night, and in the morning we'll all go our separate ways."

He immediately realized that this might be interpreted as meaning he was turning them out.

"But only if it's quite safe. I won't let you out otherwise. Not now, not even in the morning. Not even in a week."

He didn't mention anything about going up to the tower to see what was happening and which house had been hit. Then he turned to his wife.

"Yes, go, you're right. If you have enough flour and margarine, thicken it up. Like when Oldrich came home from the hospital."

The two teenagers suddenly started conversing.

"They're walking. You can't stop it," the older one said. Walking soldiers could also mean approaching danger.

"Why stop it?" the little one replied. "Let them walk."

The taller teenager with the gruff voice looked about until his eyes rested upon the caretaker.

"Are there rats here?" he asked. "When I fall asleep, I prefer to be without rats."

The caretaker could always recognize the taller teenager in the darkness by his idiosyncratic voice. The caretaker answered, angry at the teenager for bringing up the rats.

"We used to have traps here, but recently the mice moved toward the river."

"The rats probably didn't have anything to eat here," wheezed the younger teenager. His head was completely shaven, but the hair was beginning to grow back in a semicircle that looked like a lawn sprayed with india ink. A gray stripe ran down the middle of his head.

"Where I'm from, it's the other way around," the taller one said, correcting the younger one. "So much the better."

"For crying out loud, how much longer are you two going to talk about this?" the stout woman with the son in the RAF protested.

The teenagers in their fur jackets paid no attention to her. In the meantime, the caretaker's wife had gone upstairs. The caretaker arranged the jute bags for the children and added canvas bags to the blankets so everyone could stay warm. "Well, here you are, like little Rockefellers. You couldn't sleep more comfortably."

He was wondering where the teenagers had come from. The story about the hospital on Kelley Street seemed strange. He listened to their muffled conversation, to the breaking voice, and to the voice that squeaked like a mouse. He felt that they were poking fun at one another. Yet somewhere in the noise of their words he could feel something else. They talked loudly, almost without a sense of the present danger, and the caretaker didn't want to ask them any unnecessary questions. Here today—and tomorrow, maybe at the end of the world. The second candle was burning out. Just as the caretaker was planning to light a third, his wife returned with the soup. He felt the presence of the city around him in the cold babbling of the river and in the wind and pervading darkness.

"They're walking," the taller teenager said.

"Well, is that something new?" squeaked the little one.

The caretaker was about to tell the female guests to lie down beside the children, if they didn't mind the bags; but the stout woman said, as though talking to herself, "My son is twenty-four. Maybe he's taking off just now on some mission, or maybe he's landing. And he doesn't have an inkling ... "

The caretaker's wife returned with silver tablespoons for everyone. It was pea soup, thickened with white sauce she'd been saving for Olga. She had to wake the children. Throughout the war she'd been saving things, depriving herself for Olga's sake. She felt that if something happened to Olga, she'd hang herself. She'd improved the soup by dropping golden brown croutons into each plate. Again she served the woman on the chopping block first.

"Here," she said, "when I found the bread I was so happy I burst into tears. It's just nerves."

"Thank you," the woman responded in a low whisper. There was so much gratitude in her eyes that the caretaker's wife was embarrassed.

The caretaker again covered the wire netting on the window with a piece of rag. He removed the shade from the candle and they could see relatively well once again.

The woman on the chopping block squinted from the light. Her light complexion seemed more pallid than before and the blush on her cheekbones darker; her face had aged considerably, as if years had passed since it got dark and she began to eat. She placed her gloves on the floor and held the soup plate between her small red hands. In front of her she imagined the lower clock. She saw it as a windmill turning against the wind. The propellers of the windmill turned in a direction opposite that of man—not from life to death, but backward.

"It would be better backward," she whispered.

"This could be silver," the taller teenager said knowledgeably, holding his spoon in the light.

"It was a wedding present," the caretaker's wife told him. "It's all clean; you don't have to be afraid."

"I could tell by the weight." His Adam's apple suddenly jerked up and down. With a grin he said, "There's nothing I'm afraid of, Mrs. Belleles."

"Why don't you tell them that you had silverware at home, too?" the smaller teenager said with a smirk.

"It's easy to tell by the weight and taste."

"God," the stout woman sighed. "It really isn't just. We don't deserve to have to listen to this bickering."

"Please eat," the caretaker encouraged, trying to put an end to the conversation.

He wanted to say that this was wedding silver, reserved for special occasions. They had two dozen pieces, but after the war they'd never again be able to gather that many friends and relatives together, even if they counted both his family and his wife's.

Everyone thanked him and complimented him on the food, even the woman with smoldering eyes on the chopping block. She had eyes like a smoldering hearth, he thought. But in her thoughts were the turning clocks, both the lower and upper one, and she saw the way they opposed each other like beginning and end, or life and death. The stout woman with the son in England was nervously clutching a clipping from an underground newspaper. It was five years old. The article contained excerpts from a speech made by the British Prime Minister at a time when it seemed the Germans would conquer England just as they'd overrun Poland, France, and Holland. "Pea soup . . . that may lead to air pollution," the taller teenager remarked with a grin. "Well," he said to everyone, "at least it will be warm here."

The little one was grinning. "I'm always the one who gets the blame," he squeaked.

"Are there any more blankets upstairs?" the caretaker asked his wife.

"Only jute bags, most likely," she replied.

A volley of shots upstairs cut off her words. The shooting was on Maisel Street, not on Paris Avenue. It was followed immediately by another volley or two. It wasn't the revolutionary's machine gun from the corner house. The caretaker would have recognized that. He knew it wasn't a German cannon, either. The sound came from above, muffled by something. It sounded as though there was only a wall or a house between the person who shot and those who were listening.

"Oh, my God," the stout woman screamed, "it's the Germans."

"Put out that torch," said the taller teenager. "We don't want to get in the middle of any fireworks right away. So the gravedigger's after us," he added. "Mr. Belleles might as well prepare our shrouds since he's so good at tailoring."

The taller one laughed gruffly at his own remarks while the little one peeped, "Where was it?"

His friend's voice was cracking again. "It sounds close by." His sharp Adam's apple bobbed up and down.

The caretaker immediately put out the light. They could smell the smoke as the wick dipped into the yellow pool of melted wax. The cellar was riddled with the sound of crackling and sizzling. The acrid smoke filled their nostrils.

"I don't think it was the Germans," the caretaker said.

As he said this the cellar rumbled. They'd all become very familiar with the sound, the sound that had come before the roar of the house crashing down on Paris Avenue or somewhere close by. But they didn't know exactly where the house was because the caretaker lacked the courage to go up to the tower. Now everything trembled. The caretaker was glad it was dark in the cellar so no one could see him raise his arms suddenly, as if in surrender. He stuffed his fingers in his ears, which were buzzing.

"It didn't go our way," he said, listening to his own voice. "It's over for us."

"You might as well take measurements for my shroud," the taller teenager said. "If we luck out, I can always have it dyed another color."

Little Olga burst into tears. Her sobs came in spasms, as if she knew she wasn't supposed to cry aloud.

Her mother tried to stretch her arms around all three children— little Olga, blue-eyed Toni, her oldest, Oldrich—as if she could protect them in some way. She was no longer thinking of the things that could shame her. She felt something was coming—some sort of shame after all. She kept pressing the children to her. The caretaker was listening intently. He waited for the sound of the crashing wall. But it didn't come.

"It must have passed over us," he said after a while.

"I won't let anything spoil that silver spoon for me," the taller teenager mumbled. "'Cause if you can hear it and it ain't entered your flesh yet, then it must have gone over you."

The caretaker was suddenly grateful for the coarse tone of the teenager's words.

"Well, enjoy your food, you old Garden of Gethsemane," the taller one taunted the smaller one.

The children thought this very funny. The taller teenager grinned contentedly, glad he could quiet the little girl's tears.

"As I was telling you, my twelfth apostle, no matter how scared I am, I won't let anyone take this warm pea soup from me. Over my dead body."

"It's all over," the caretaker announced.

"What'll we do with the plates when we're finished?" the taller teenager asked calmly.

"Should I tell you?" the little one squeaked.

Then, in the darkness of the cellar, the group listened to the sound of their own breathing and to the warmth of human bodies around them. The caretaker wondered whether someone had managed to enter the town hall attic through the roof on Paris Avenue or on Red Street or maybe even Josefovska Street and, if someone did, had he set up his shooting gallery in the window above the clock running backward? There he could take aim at the German cannoneers across the street. He was suddenly sure you could take the best aim at the German cannon from precisely that window. It was no more than two hundred yards, straight across, over the crowns of the silver spruce in the nearby park and over the broken black statue of an angel. The caretaker imagined the yellow side wall of the town hall as it looked from Red Street and pictured the clock tower with the Hebrew characters instead of figures— everything reversed on the face. He imagined the window and the second clock above the balcony with brass ornaments that looked golden against the black of the old Hebrew clock. Again he imagined the fallen marble statue—the black angel—with its broken limbs and heavy pedestal. He could go upstairs to tell the sniper that there were women and children here; he imagined all of Paris Avenue and the adjoining streets, the sidewalks lined with the bodies of wounded men. You couldn't walk the street for fear of stumbling over the bodies.

Little Olga was still crying softly. He could tell where the others were by the sounds they made when they shifted places. He could hear the brushing of skin. The caretaker heard his heart beat. He was ashamed that it beat so loudly. He really should go upstairs, he told himself, before the cannon's single direct hit razed the town hall. Again he recalled the black marble angel in the park. The angel's head and the left side of its chest were missing.

He remained sitting, his head in his hands, pressing his temples. The upstairs clock made a sound like a whip thrashing his head. Olga was now only sniffling, "Mommy, mommy . . ."

"We should have left while it was still light," the stout woman said when all was quiet.

The caretaker was glad he'd suppressed his earlier desire to go upstairs. It was better that he remained sitting and hadn't been hasty. But he couldn't rid his mind of the image of the sniper inside the lower clock, firing, drawing attention to the tower. He imagined the next volley from the German cannon would bury them in the cellar, which had only one entrance; bury them under thick walls over five hundred years old, enormous foundations below, and a mountain of masonry above. Inside all of this were three children, three women, two teenagers, and himself—nine pairs of human eyes trying not to betray their knowledge of what lay beyond the walls around them. He tried to take his thoughts elsewhere. He'd been a tailor and had made suits and coats for people in this quarter. Then he'd improved his situation by becoming a caretaker. Maybe this thing about the sniper in the lower or upper clock was just an idea fixed in his mind.

The silence was broken by the voice of little Toni, who was whispering in the dark, "Kitty, Kitty . . . Fina . . . where have you been for so long? Come, Fina, warm us up." And finally, after a long pause, "Well, at last we're all here . . . the whole family's together."

The cat stayed with the children only for a moment. They could hear her meow and they heard the rustle of her paws as she slipped by them and disappeared.

"Cats are too tough for me," the taller teenager said in his gruff voice to his smaller partner. "Kids, does someone want my rabbit vest?"

"Take mine, too," the smaller one peeped, but no one answered.

The caretaker had to say something before he choked. He didn't want to lie, not even to himself. He was waiting for the sniper's shot above him and for the rumble that would follow. He heard the crashing in his temples. And then he imagined he'd hidden a flag under the mechanisms of the tower clocks.

"I want to go up for the remaining jute bags," the caretaker said at last.

"No," his wife replied quickly. "Don't go anywhere. At least not yet."

The caretaker felt her hot fingers as she clutched his.

"No," she repeated. "Not now." And then there was all the shame in her voice she'd wanted to hide, but she didn't release her clutch.

"Should I light the candle?" the caretaker asked.

Suddenly he knew the deep voice of the one with the sharp Adam's apple wasn't dangerous. He wanted to look into the eyes of the stout woman who clung so comically to the glorious feats of her son, the pilot with the squadron named "Mandalay;" and he wanted to look at the woman with the eyes like a smoldering hearth. He never thought it would happen like this.

He imagined himself still alive at the time when everything would be covered with rubble, when the cannon would have avenged the sniper's shots in the upper portion of the lower clock. He knew he didn't want to survive at the ugly price of failure, of making the unknown sniper lose his aim. He knew he couldn't control his thoughts, and he was ashamed of them; he couldn't prevent them and they persisted.

To his wife he said, "Don't be afraid; I won't go yet. Don't worry."

It grew silent, and the stillness of the guns above offered a fleeting feeling of security.

"If anybody touches that candle or those matches, I won't hesitate to give him a smack with the ax that's by the block," the taller teenager said calmly. He wrapped himself in his fur and looked like a hunter.

The little one squeaked, "As far as I'm concerned, I'd prefer to sit in the dark for a while, even with the rats."

The woman who came last whispered, "Isn't it all backward? Didn't they know what they were doing was wrong? They deceived him . . . they lied to him . . . to the end . . . could they have believed their own lies? Can they so easily swallow their murders?"

She looked at the children, then turned to the caretaker, keeping her eyes on the two teenage boys.

The voice of the taller teenager again cranked out in confidence. "With an ax. What do you say to that, you Mount of Zion?"

The children didn't understand this and didn't laugh.

"Let's see what happens if we close our eyes and try to sleep," the smaller teenager squeaked. "It can't do any harm. Anyone against that idea?"

Again, no one answered, but everyone was silent for what seemed like a long time.

The breathing of the children and the snoring of the teenagers intermingled. At times the caretaker thought the woman with the smoldering eyes was crying, although she hadn't made a sound. He could only make assumptions in the darkness. The taller teenager mumbled something. He tossed and turned from side to side, emitting a sound like a low howl. The little one calmed him.

"Nothing's happening, so let me sleep."

The caretaker tried to answer the puzzle that tormented him: the sound of a pistol upstairs, strangely close—where had it come from? He was expecting two sounds: first the pistol, then the avenging cannon. At the same time, he listened to his children's breathing. He placed his fingers in his ears to stop the sounds from entering his head; he still had to think. There was time to run upstairs, to get into the space with the lower clock, the hands which moved counterclockwise. His eyes felt as though they were popping out of the darkness. Finally, he closed them again.

"Aren't you going to sleep?" asked his wife, Olga.

"No. I don't have to. I'll sleep later."

She said quietly, "I'm going to try to close my eyes for a bit."

He felt this was both the beginning and the end. They were caught in between, pulled by the opposing forces. The last night of the war? For them, for the city, for the world? In this dark cellar? And so his thoughts continued to drift, moving forward and then coming back.

Early in the morning, they heard pounding on the door. The outer doors of the town hall were old; the wide gate and the small doorway for the servants and pedestrians creaked because the dry wood had rotted. The sheets of metal that covered the door and the quiet of the hall at daybreak made the noise seem much louder.

"They're coming for us," the woman on the chopping block managed to say with effort.

"Wait," the caretaker said quietly. "Maybe somebody else wants to hide here."

At the moment he said it, he meant that the person who was in the window behind the tower clock had perhaps climbed down and couldn't go anywhere else.

"I knew it," said the stout woman.

"Don't turn on the lights," the caretaker's wife pleaded.

The night continued on toward morning like a border that had to be crossed. The caretaker waited for the dry sound of the pistol to come from the gallery of the tower. All his thoughts were mixed with the vision of the broken black marble angel and the man in the clock.

"Get up, you old battle-ax," the taller teenager ordered the little one. "Move back into the darkness."

"All right," the little one peeped.

The two teenagers moved their jute bags to the edge of the chimney where the shadows were still deep.

"He's using the butt of his gun," the taller teenager said, demonstrating the motion with his hands. "I'll bet anything it's the butt of a gun."

"They'll knock the doors in," the caretaker said. "It will be better if I go and open up for them."

"They'll think we're all Jews," the stout woman blurted out. Behind the chimney, the teenagers silently noted how the stout woman was shouting that they weren't Jews, while the caretaker's wife repeated one word over and over: "Children, children . . ."

The taller teenager spat. The spittle landed on the jute bag.

"You pig," the little one exclaimed.

"You know I don't like it when officers are mentioned." The taller teenager muttered. "As long as I live, I never want to hear that word."

That was all he said and only the little one understood, but he didn't make a sound. The taller one was lost in his thoughts. In his mind he could see the officer in the old camp pick up his sister, taking her into his arms as if to fondle her. She was so little she could still take only a few steps. Then he had lifted her above his head and held her fast by the hands and feet as if he wanted to whirl her around. But he hadn't. The taller one couldn't forget how he had lost his sister, what the officer had done to her with only one pull.

The taller teenager was now stroking the rabbit fur diligently. "Don't be a fool, little one," he said to Olga. "You don't want to cry now, wait until it's daylight. I'd like to be standing by the wall with your cat, that Finis, Fina, whatever you call it. I'd like to wrap her around my neck like a muffler. And then I'd teach her how to dance on her tail to make you happy."

Little Olga listened to him, crinkling her nose and pouting. She took in the taller teenager's stares. Upstairs, the pounding grew stronger. "You're a real nursemaid, you know?" the smaller teenager squeaked. "Why don't you try comforting me a little?"

"Sure, you're the one who needs it," the taller one muttered. Now his voice wasn't cracking.

Suddenly the little one changed his expression. He peered into the corner of the cellar closet nearest to him. In a crevice that widened from the edge to the inside of the wall was a rat, staring into the darkened room with its bright eyes.

Both of them began to laugh, but only for an instant; the rat backed up and disappeared into its crevice. The little one felt lucky. His eyes held the assurance that where rats weren't afraid, neither he nor his companions had anything to fear.

"I know we're all right," the little one answered, as if he could see the wheel of fate begin to spin in the right direction.

The sound of the caretaker's footsteps as he walked upstairs mixed with the pounding on the door. Finally they heard the clinking of the lock and the doors opening. The hobnailed boots of soldiers clanked on the stone floor, which was made of big tiles in the shape of six-cornered stars. They could hear it all as clearly as if they were upstairs alongside the caretaker. The sound was quickly drowned out by another volley of gunfire which stiffened them with fear.

The woman with the eyes like a smoldering hearth covered her mouth with her hands, as though she'd been struck. She grabbed the hand of the caretaker's wife and breathed heavily.

"I should have been the one to go," the wife whispered. "I should have gone alone."

She looked across at the two teenagers.

"Germans," the stout woman pronounced.

"Germans," the caretaker's wife echoed.

"We shouldn't have let them wait so long...God...my poor son..." the stout woman said.

A heavy step, followed by the echo of another, was heard descending from the dawn. And then—in the glare of a lantern covered by protective wire netting resembling a dog's muzzle—the group discerned the figure of a soldier in a German battle jacket.

The soldier stopped by the dusty lattice doors, looked around, and said, "Pack of swine." This was his introduction. "Is anyone else here?" he added.

This wasn't said in the same threatening tone he'd used before, but he wasn't waiting for an answer. He took a long, sharp, skeptical look at everything the arc of his lantern revealed: little redheaded Olga and her two brothers lying on the jute bags, the two women holding hands, the kettle with the remains of the pea soup, the mess of the scattered plates, the heavy silver spoons. The light revealed a deep scar on his forehead. It looked like two scars that had run together, dividing his skull and his forehead.

The stout woman was shaking. The more she thought of her son, the more she shook.

"You . . . shaking like that," the soldier said gruffly. "Cut it out! We're human like you."

The scar on the soldier's forehead was furrowed by several wrinkles, as though he were in deep thought. He stared at the gleam of the German silver spoons and at the same time at the woman whose son was in England and who couldn't stop shaking, even after he told her to stop.

The soldier sighed. "Well, are we the ones who started the war? I'm not playing this game of my own free will."

His stare moved from one to the other, as if he were expecting a reply.

Hidden by the shadows, the teenagers watched him. The taller one still had the idea fixed in his head that if they got out of this one they would be home safe. He saw the man standing with legs spread in handsome leather boots. He kept staring at the soldier's epaulets, for the twelfth time reassuring himself that this was just a simple soldier, not an officer. At the same time, he stared a little at Olga; he couldn't help thinking that she was a redhead like his sister had been. He was clenching the little teenager's shoulder.

The smaller one studied the soldier's forehead. He was trying to decide what made the soldier tick and what could be expected of him. Words were only words, and so he was on his guard, watching the soldier's face, his every move. The soldier's helmet was set low on his forehead, covering as much of the scar as possible. He was well armed. He even had a grenade under his left thumb in the hand with the lantern. He had a double belt of grenades strung like beads across his chest and back; in his right hand, he held a tommy gun at the ready, and on his hip were revolvers in open cases. All he had to do was move and he clattered like an ammunition warehouse. It was obvious that he weighed less than the arms he was carrying. His green eyes glimmered like a cat's.

The taller teenager knew that with just one of the soldier's weapons he could gain more confidence. He crouched involuntarily, ready to spring. He bit his lower lip until it began to bleed. Hidden behind the soldier stood his three companions.

"How many times do I have to ask you who's here?" the first soldier roared. His scar immediately swelled and turned purple and red. He turned to the woman who was sitting on the chopping block, closest to the entrance. "Get up!" he bellowed.

The fourth soldier was armed with a bayonet instead of a tommy gun. He stepped forward and prodded the woman, aiming the blade at her back and pushing her toward the wall.

"It looks as though they've been feeding their faces here all the while," he said in German with a Saxon accent as he kicked the kettle and the block. Both rolled away noisily behind the woman.

"Everybody against the wall," shouted the third armed man as he, too, stepped forward. He was holding a grenade under his thumb like the first man.

"We're not Jews," the stout woman started. Her fleshy throat vibrated like a mass of white jelly, pushed and prodded by an invisible hand.

"Against the wall, I said," the third soldier repeated. "No exceptions. Against the wall."

The caretaker's wife grabbed little Olga and quickly dragged her across the floor toward the wall until her knees became bloodied.

"I'm not going to say it three times, you can bet. Down. *Dalli, Dalli . . .* "

The teenagers hadn't moved, although the order had been given twice.

"Officers," the stout woman's insistent voice cried out. The taller teenager bit his lip hard at the sound of this word. "It must be a mistake . . . we're not Jews, even if we are here."

"Face the wall," the third soldier said. His voice was a young man's. He couldn't have been more than eighteen, perhaps twenty. But he sounded coarse—much different from the days when he'd sung in the choir of the little town of Wolfen, not far from the city of Halle.

The stout woman whose son was in the RAF didn't have the chance to tell the soldiers that it would be a terrible mistake if they shot them now because they weren't Jews—or at least she wasn't one.

"Can't you hurry it up?" the second soldier asked.

"Down," was the immediate order from the first soldier, the one with the cleft and swollen scar.

"Down you scum," the third one suddenly roared, aiming his gun, as he discovered the teenagers by the chimney.

"And you think we don't mean you?" the first one said to the teenagers, swinging his lantern around. "Everybody against the wall. I'm not going to say it three times, the third time we shoot."

"You obey or you've had it," the third one said in an amazingly clear and sonorous voice.

"Hands up above your heads," the other soldier with a gun insisted.

The taller teenager continued biting his lower lip. The tips of his fingers almost touched the ceiling and he knew he wouldn't be able to get hold of any weapons, although he knew where some were.

The shorter teenager's hands reached only slightly above the taller one's shoulders with his arms extended, although they were now bent at the elbows. The teenagers quickly moved close to one another, not wanting to separate. The taller one rested his palms against the wall, and his companion also found a way to rest. The wall was pleasantly cool, and the little one was in the seventh day of fever. It had been with him for a week, yet he paid little attention to it, indifferent but at the same time confident that the fever wouldn't kill him. But now, he would have liked to overcome it.

The cellar became very quiet again. The first soldier coughed in a friendly sort of way, as if he were sitting in a German pub drinking beer. He kept looking at the silver spoons. Then he wiped his lips with the back of his hand. It was an effort for him to raise the hand with the tommy gun so he could perform this function.

Suddenly there was a rustle in the empty corner. The first soldier immediately loosed a volley of shots in that direction. The third soldier started shooting in that direction as well, while the second stood aside for them. When the first one let the lantern shine in that direction, they saw the cat, Fina, mashed to a pulp on the wall, just a big, black, bloody spot.

"A cat," the soldier with the beautiful voice said, sounding somewhat relieved.

And the first soldier, the one whose purple swollen scar divided his forehead from the rest of his face, said, "Tough luck."

The smell of the shots filled the cellar. The caretaker's wife, stepping from one foot to the other, stepped on one of the spoons. It made a clinking noise. "Where's my husband? What did you do to him?"

"Shut up," said the third one quietly. "Shut your dirty trap now."

"Mommy, mommy..." Little Olga was squeaking as though she were in pain.

"They're children..." the caretaker's wife said in a lowered voice.

The soldier with the scar repeated, "Shut your mouth, woman. Or you'll be sorry. No one is to speak unless I ask you a question."

His gaze wandered to the spot where the remains of the cat lay, then to the spoons.

"Keep standing," the third said in disgust. "And keep your mouths shut. We're the ones giving the orders here, and we hope you know it."

"Who else is here? What's in the back?" the first soldier asked lazily, as if it were some sort of great effort to speak. "Is there some kind of hole back there?"

"Oh, officers..." the stout woman started. The taller teenager squirmed in pain.

The soldiers paid no attention to her and were not flattered that she'd mistaken their ranks. They started whispering among themselves. Then the one with the scar said louder to the second one, "Search the house and the main staircase—take Heinz with you. There is nothing more back here. This dump is as old as Babylon. I can take care of things here myself."

"But if need be . . ." the second one answered.

They knew that the young one with the voice fit for a choir was named Heinz.

They heard the soldiers run through the house. All the doors in the town hall had been opened. They heard different kinds of steps returning noisily downstairs. Suddenly there was an explosion. The soldier with the beautiful voice, Heinz, had thrown a grenade into the wooden outhouse in the courtyard. He threw another grenade onto the staircase, shattering the white statuettes and the golden, bronze, and brass candelabras on the walls—and all this was mixed with the laughter and voices of the two men as they approached the cellar. The soldier with the scar was constantly whistling the theme from *Alte Kamaraden*. Since he was quite alone, he didn't scold anyone any more. His eyes were searching for more silver spoons; he spotted six of them lying on the used plates. Whenever he moved, his weapons clattered.

"Well," he said when the other two rejoined him. "If anyone's got anything, raise your hands—you won't be hurt." He was addressing his prisoners. "You two," he said to the teenagers, "put your hands down. Well, is anyone going to raise his hand?" He turned to the man with the bayonet and said lazily, "Search them."

The second soldier searched all of them rapidly with his free hand. He took just a little longer with the women, as if they could have weapons concealed in the inner side of their thighs, between their legs, or around their hips. When he touched the breasts of the woman with the smoldering gray eyes, he did it as if he were picking an apple or pear off a branch, and he held his hand there much longer than was necessary.

"Who are you?" asked the soldier.

"No one who could interest you," she replied in German. Her smoldering gray eyes stared at the soldier. The soldier spat.

"What kind of nonsense is this?"

"Do you want to be the first to get a bullet in the head, woman?" the third solider asked. "This ax is a weapon, too, and we're not used to playing around, you know. Give me your name and date and place of birth. And hurry before I stick this bayonet in your grease." He ran his finger slowly down the blade of the bayonet carried by his partner.

The stout woman kept repeating "Mandalay," as if it were some sort of mantra or charm.

"Agnes Kant, typist, born in Prague on April 20, 1910," the woman with the smoldering eyes replied.

The third soldier looked at her in surprise. "Kant. I've heard that name somewhere."

He made the end of his gun whistle by bringing the barrel close to his lips and exhaling abruptly.

"School in East Prussia—*Ding an sich*—does that mean anything to you? 'The starry sky above me, the moral law within me?'"

Finally, he said with a sigh, "The same birthday as our Führer."

"Tell them we're not Jews," the stout woman again insisted.

"What is this place, anyway, that you can be sitting here and having a party like this?" the first soldier asked.

"Stuffing their bellies," the second one roared.

"These are my children and we've been living here for eleven years," the caretaker's wife said, embracing all three children. "When will my husband be back?"

"It was a Jewish town hall," the woman with the smoldering eyes said.

"Did you know there was a shooting above?" the first soldier asked.

"Of course they did," the soldier with the bayonet answered for the prisoners. "Unless they've lost their hearing or their brains."

"There was no shooting here," the woman with the ashen gray eyes said quietly. "If you shoot, you'll be the first."

"How dare she..." the second soldier with the bayonet asked.

"Yeah, a Jewish town hall," the third soldier said in his beautiful singsong voice. Then he added very matter-of-factly, "Every floor has at least a dozen typewriters. What for? What else could they want to write? Names? They can write them on the walls." And he hissed confidentially to the second one, "Hurry it up, we haven't got this much time." His voice was childishly clear. "There can be a few more names—do you get me?" He laughed almost guilelessly.

The second soldier couldn't stand the stare of the woman with the eyes like a smoldering hearth. He moved the gun into his left hand and hit the woman's face with his right. He muttered hoarsely, "Look at the wall..." The eyes that stared back at him were dead. "And you, too! All of you! Stare at the wall..."

The third soldier added more calmly, "Light the candle."

And the first one, whose forehead was scarred and who constantly watched the scattered silver spoons, added, "Heinz, light the candle for them."

"Wait, I'll do it myself," said the second. He held the gun's barrel under his arm, its butt rested on the floor; he struck the match twice; to the other two he said something in his Saxon German. It sounded like, "Don't fool around with them too long. There was an ax here."

He finally managed to light the wick. The woman with the eyes like a smoldering hearth didn't turn; she kept staring at the soldiers, as if she were looking for something in their eyes that she couldn't find. Finally, she searched the face of the younger soldier with the beautiful voice who might not have been twenty.

The cellar was now burning with the bright yellow light. The first soldier started to collect the silver spoons and was stuffing them into his pocket where, apparently, he also had grenades, which he removed and held by their chain in the hand in which he held the tommy gun. He held the last grenade in his left hand. The woman saw that it looked like an iron pear in a wooden holder, as if the grenade wasn't a weapon at all, rather a treat to be put into the oven to bake. The first soldier's helmet slid back to his nape and his cleft scar became more noticeable. The other two whispered to each other and moved back. The woman constantly stared at the youngest one; no one could tell why. There was no reasoning with her.

When all three soldiers reached the far end of the hall where it broke off into right angles, and where the fourth soldier stood waiting, they walked backward a few steps like crayfish. Then the first one with the awful scar on his forehead threw his grenade. There was an immediate explosion, similar to the preceding ones, but this time close at hand. The waves of fire and noise and the sharp blast of air prostrated the people in the cellar in front of the wall. The walls in the bend of the hall cracked and fell. The woman with the gray eyes staggered and fell over the back of the stout woman. More grenades exploded—probably because the first one with the kindly voice needed to free his hands and pockets. There were more waves of fire and blasts of air, followed by sounds of breaking and shattering bricks. The hall reverberated with the echo, magnifying the sound. The candle went out. The window right under the ceiling shattered and the light fell in. A red flag shot full of holes was flying from a burned mast on the distended balcony across the street.

"Children!" the caretaker's wife cried.

"What are you shouting like that for?" the taller teenager asked, and his Adam's apple went up and down. "Is anyone here still alive? It looked for a while as if we were all ready for the undertaker."

Upstairs, the doors slammed shut and someone was closing them from the inside with a bar. The caretaker's wife raised her head as if sniffing. "My husband is alive. Children."

"We're buried here," the stout woman said.

The taller teenager turned to the little one. "Rest your dumb head on my shoulder, you thrice-crucified Son of God. Let me feel if they haven't made a sieve of you. Boy, is your head hot! It feels like it's been boiling in a kettle all this time. Thank God these boys weren't from the Waffen or Allgemeine SS or die Herren Waffe. They would have taken everything, even our underwear. This one was satisfied with spoons."

The woman whose eyes looked like a smoldering hearth finally straightened up and remained standing.

"Oh, God," said the stout woman who had a son in England. "How well you told them. They thought we were all Jews. There's an ax here and it could have been suspicious to them. They thought we were Jews and had no weapons. If they hadn't thought that, we wouldn't be here. The Jews can't hurt them, even if there is a revolution." And then she added: "How can anyone refer to these people as 'boys'? What was it the young one said—about the names on the walls?"

"It's too bad about the cat," squeaked the smaller teenager.

"Oh, what are you saying?" the stout woman said. "My God, we should be rejoicing."

The taller teenager spat loudly and the stout woman sighed. "Why must people be like that?"

The skinny teenager stroked the top of his friend's head. The caretaker was just entering. They could hear him climb over the scattered bricks in the rubble where the hallway had caved in. His wife fell on his neck and felt him all over, as if she believed she saw a specter instead of her husband, as if she had to convince herself. She cried softly.

"Are you all OK here?" asked the caretaker, brushing himself off. He was covered with dust like a bricklayer. He went on, "I had to stand upstairs all the time because the fourth one wouldn't leave me. He poked me in the ribs with the barrel of his gun. He told me right from the start that if they found a single Jew in this house they would make a windmill out of the double clocks on the side of the town hall. I had to give them the keys. They cut all the telephone wires, as if they were still connected. They were suspicious of a wooden box with clips from some Portuguese sardines and of a rubber stamp bearing the name of the Central Agency for the Jews . . . I showed them that the stamp was on almost everything in the former reception hall."

"Why are people so evil?" the stout woman who had a son in England asked slowly.

"You don't have to look very far for an answer," the caretaker said. His words seemed to give some relief.

The taller teenager looked at the caretaker and asked, "You're a Jew, too, aren't you?"

The caretaker looked at him with surprise. "Why?"

And the teenager said, "Well, I asked if you weren't Jewish too— just curious. But your wife isn't Jewish and the children are mixed?"

The caretaker said only, "Let me catch my breath." Then he understood and smiled.

"It's only because of her," the teenager said. He tossed his head toward the stout woman. "Every Gypsy tells fortunes according to his own stars . . . some are full of courage and goodness when it's over . . ."

The taller one turned to the woman with the smoldering eyes. She straightened the chopping block and sat down. Her suit was crumpled.

"Why were you staring so long at that German? There must be something wrong."

"Nothing's wrong," she said defensively. She was quiet then, but at last the woman said softly, "My husband is a soldier like those three that threw the grenades and took the spoons."

The taller teenager stood up and opened his eyes wide. His Adam's apple went up and down several times. "And you?" he asked.

"My son renounced his father," said the woman. "If he had said his father was a soldier, he wouldn't have ended up where he did." And she added, "My son never said a word. He never owned up to his father. His name was Heinz. He had blue eyes and blond hair. Like golden fleece. He went to the gas chamber. He was there where you were."

"How do you know where we were?" the taller teenager asked. His Adam's apple moved even when he fell silent. "Just because we came from Kelley Street?" He was choking on his saliva.

The woman sighed and closed her eyelids, blinking several times. They were almost transparent, as if she hadn't eaten in a long time. She wept. The stout woman kept repeating to herself that a word couldn't be a talisman, even if it was "Mandalay" and it stood for a country or a city or some famous squadron whose number she'd forgotten. She had only been half listening. All she could think about was what she'd said before, "Why are people so evil?"

"I had a little sister and she went, too," the teenager said before the caretaker could put in a word. "She was just learning to walk. She could just take her first few steps. She waddled like a duck, but she could keep her balance." He wanted to say it as gruffly as possible. "She didn't make it; I would have been glad if she had."

It struck him as strange that he'd tell these things to her, that he'd tell these things to someone from the other side. "Don't think about it all the time. It turns a person into a walking cemetery." His insides turned upside down; he didn't even ask her if her husband was an officer.

The caretaker stroked his children's heads. Suddenly the machine gun from the house on the corner rattled unexpectedly, firing on Paris Avenue. Once again it was followed by the old sound, so very close that the caretaker turned pale. They could hear it more easily than the previous day because the grenades had shattered the windows. The machine gun became silent for a moment. Even now, he said nothing.

All the caretaker said was, "The house is locked. I won't open it again. I won't open it unless it is our men."

"Well, you could have started sewing our shrouds," the older teenager said.

He removed his fur jacket and placed it around little Olga.

Everything began all over again, but now it was different for the taller teenager, who watched the woman on the chopping block and who never took his eyes from hers. The caretaker just watched a cobweb under the corner of the ceiling. A hundred times he told himself he'd taken it down and a hundred times he'd left it there. He knew what would happen if the machine gun in the corner house continued to rattle. He looked at his children, at his wife Olga, at the two teenagers, at the stout woman, at the woman on the chopping block. His thoughts were interrupted by a blast from the German cannon which came to avenge the machine gun in the corner house. The charge from the cannon knocked down the weather vane on the town hall, which was thin and shaped like a star. The blast also hit the mast with its seven-armed candelabrum, and the mast fell crashing down. It sounded like the roof was caving in. Just at this moment, the caretaker's wife was joyfully saying to herself, although she lacked the courage to say it out loud, that the sun was rising and it looked like a cheerful, beardless old man. She was saying to herself that the war would be over, that they were still young enough, even though they had these big sensible children, and they could have been buried alive down here but they weren't, that everything was beginning over again. And she felt she understood what peace would be like.

Both of them were thinking that there would be a new beginning, yet it was actually quite otherwise. The second charge from the cannon hit lower, as the barrels of the German cannons were lowered. The path of the shell shattered even the pedestal of the stone angel in the park between Red Street and the house on the corner with the dead machine gun. Fist-sized pieces of schrapnel knocked down the mast.

The woman with the eyes like a smoldering hearth grabbed the two teenagers by their dirty and bony wrists and held them fast, sobbing. The caretaker's wife held her children, but her stare circled around the other woman's eyes; each an ember that glowed like a hot sun, warping the air around it into a half smile, then a frown.

At that moment, the German cannon was aimed precisely at the tower which housed the clock that turned backward.

RED OLEANDERS

Things remain only what they are.
———From an old song

Only man looks like a fortress that surrenders when it has stood its ground.
———A saying

Only in human eyes can loyalty seem faithless and love look like betrayal.
———From an old song

ONE

1

I n Acre, between Nahariyya and Haifa, next to the cannery and close to the police station, they built an insane asylum. In one of the cells lived a man who had escaped from Auschwitz-Birkenau in the summer of 1944. He brought with him all sorts of documents and plans that detailed the fate of the Family Camp in B-II where six thousand people from Bohemia died in the ovens in a single night—most of them children and their parents. Among those killed were his wife, his brother, and the smaller of his two sons. He made it to Lake Constance on the Bodensee and sent his testimony to America.

The old man never spoke or wrote to anyone, nor did he receive any letters or visitors. He lost all power of speech, but not because the Germans ripped out his tongue in the experimental barracks of the prison infirmary as they had done to his other son who had survived the war. The last thing that the sick man said was that after his escape from Auschwitz-Birkenau the Germans still managed to kill over a million people there, and that some people tend to forgive and forget in order to get on with their lives.

It was reported that he watched the sea constantly, as if waiting for someone's return. He had a biblical name no one remembered and became a legend in the area for his silence.

Before the sick man died, he watched from the window of his cell how they loaded old freighters with wheat, engines, and coal. It was known that in the winter of 1945 and the spring and summer of 1946 the old man had, with the assistance of the Hagana, organized transports into the Promised Land for displaced persons waiting in the camps in West Germany. His eyes always held unanswered questions: Where did all the lost people go? Where are the words for that? Why are the words not important anymore? There wasn't time before his death to tell him that his mute son had hung himself.

The asylum stood at the edge of the bay and was clearly visible even from Nahariyya. Mountains rose from either side of the shore and a desert spread to the east. On the western side loomed oil refineries resembling silver rings on the fingers of Mother Earth. In the distance, where the hilltops and the lowlands of the Nahariyya converged like two rivers, each day was filled with the sounds of people, horses, dogs, cats, wild birds on the cliffs, and music from the restaurants, Raveh's and the Pinguin, and from the garden of the Pension Popper.

At nightfall the songs and music from Raveh's would hover over the seashore and the water tower, which looked like a lighthouse, even with its seven-branched candelabra on the roof. The sounds floated among the clouds which had given no rain for the last eight months. An hour before dusk, a one-engined fighter plane that had been flying along the shore, from Rosh Haniqra, over Nahariyya to Acre, turned above the insane asylum and flew back. The wind carried off the sounds, smells, and songs.

The gulls screamed *Tee ooo terrr . . . Tee eee terrr . . .* from the tops of the cliffs, and the sea roared below.

2

"I'm much more practical now," said Daniela. "I wouldn't trade this for anything. Here I've found everything that I'd lost in Prague—all that no longer exists there for people like me."

"I guess I know what you mean," Kamil Dreisler answered.

She was thinking of the man who, in 1945—six weeks after World War II had ended—spat in the street when he saw her black hair and wondered whether Hitler had not failed in his job. Kamil Dreisler watched the flocks of seagulls. The seashore seemed drowsy as the darkness fell on the water like a thin veil that slowly became thicker as the earth and sky became one.

"No you don't," said Daniela.

"You're pretty." Kamil Dreisler looked at her.

"Why are we what we are?" she asked. "Never two and never one? It's so easy to accept now."

"Everything seems easy," Kamil Dreisler said. "Coming, staying, going."

"When you weren't here and I was alone, I watched the sea. The white caps of waves remind me of men kneeling behind cannons. And the foam sometimes looks like a man approaching. Do we really have to leave? Who or what is telling you to leave?"

"We've discussed that already."

"I won't leave you anymore."

"You left me once."

"Only to come here."

She felt a shiver she did not know, an energy she did not understand. It changed every day, hour, and second of her nineteen years. She now measured this time differently, along with all the places she'd known: Prague, Auschwitz-Birkenau, the big fortress Theresienstadt, Bergen-Belsen, the military camp in which she had trained the Voluntary Jewish Brigade in 1948, and on board the S.S. *Casserta* from Genoa to Nahariyya. They all melted into one. And all languages merged into a single comprehensible language, and many feelings of many countries into a single country. Confused feelings gave way to feelings of new self-confidence, many questions found a single answer, and desire bore closeness. This was her new secret strength. For the first time in her life she felt that the world was at her fingertips, that her dreams, forebodings, and desires were tangible. It was like creating from chaos her own world where she could be happy. But the word happiness scared her a little.

She watched the expression on Kamil Dreisler's face and thought of her own expression. She surrendered to her forthcoming existence like a bird resting its wings on air, like a fish breaking water, or horses running along the shore. Can one forget—even momentarily—that which was, that which one does not want? Maybe. Can one forget humiliations and past worries so easily? Maybe. She smiled.

She felt the pounding of her heart. She smoothed her dress, yellow with big green leaves.

"I would do anything for you to stay," she said.

Her smile denied the anxiety in her alto voice. Daniela's eyes were hazel. She was tanned from the summer sun. As she watched the cradles of the sea, the movements of the waves flowed into one another.

"We'll leave together, as agreed," Kamil Dreisler said.

One of the seagulls dove into the water and grabbed a fish. He flew up with his prey.

"I'll leave but I won't like it. I wouldn't leave with anyone else."

Then she said, "How can Pharaoh Blumen say that family is everything, perhaps more than love, when he's been living all alone as far as anyone can remember? He'll end up in the asylum one day. There are soldiers living in the Pension Popper. The army pays for their lodgings. Most of them are only slightly wounded." Then she said, "Isn't it strange? Since the morning we've been thinking about the same things, but we talk about something else."

"Did they let you keep the gun when you left the army?"

"I had to give it back. But I did it reluctantly."

Kamil Dreisler watched the bay. The wind blew. It mixed with the cries of the birds, the waves, and the music from Raveh's. It was the third time they played "Kiss me, Harry, kiss me . . ." They were lying but now sat up halfway. The sand underneath accommodated them. They leaned on a rock that lay there, like an anchor, smoothed by the waves and covered with mosses and seaweed. The shoreline was long and curved and smelled of dead fish, salt water, and tar. Some pieces of wood drifted ashore; polished like marble by the water, they looked like sculptures of men and women, or children or demons, or water nymphs—crossbreeds of men and animals, water sprites and sea horses, mysterious and innocent, tossed out on the sand.

"Here at the dock, the people from kibbutz Sasa wash their horses. You'll see in the morning. I wouldn't mind working there. I like the horses. They range in colors, all deep, rich as the shades of the sea, the sky or fruit. They're like the color of soil when they run on the shore, in the sand, over the dunes. Mahogany skin, the color of the sand, or blue-black like my hair. Sometimes they have a prettier brash red which the rose cannot approach, the chestnut horses with shoulders the color of sorrel. I like when the sun shines on them and you can still see the ridge of mountains across the waterside." She added, "I already know what I've learned from the horses. A horse wants you to respect him. He's patient. He's big and powerful enough to harm you. The people at the kibbutz told me that a horse will always try you. You must control the horse. Never let him turn his rear to you. Make him turn his head to you, smack his ass. If he turns his head to you, he can't kick you. Anyone who knows horses a little understands this."

"Do they have a lot of horses?"

"I didn't count them. Maybe twenty. Fifty, maybe. The men in charge of the horses claim that the best horse is the one who gets used to one man. For that man the horse will perform. He knows what you expect from him because it is always the one person. That kind of horse is considered best."

She smiled, as if for a hidden reason. "Horses have taught me many things, too. How good it is to give something to someone. With horses it's a cube of sugar or a crisp carrot. There are also horses that will do everything even when they're not being spoiled because they like what they're doing. Horses like that like to please you as a rider. There is generosity in them, kindness; they take their lot as a gift rather than a punishment. These horses tickle your imagination. They're more fun."

"What could they teach me?" asked Kamil Dreisler.

"You can set up a relationship by understanding what he likes, what he wants." She smiled and her eyes smiled also. "You comprehend his nature, his abilities, or his potential. For example, when a horse sheds his coat year round, but more in the spring, he rubs against trees and fence posts to help the shedding, and this feels good to him. You could scratch places where he couldn't get to. There's a fold of skin under his chin that's hard for him to rub. It must be like a caress to a person. As he comes to know you and understand you, he waits for you, whinnying and wondering where you've been."

"How do you know so much about horses?"

"I don't know as much as I know about you," she said, smiling. "But maybe not."

"I have secrets."

"I hope so."

The sea took away their words and reverberations. More pieces of wood floated up.

"Why did old Pharaoh say that ruby is your stone, and that it means passion?" he asked.

"He brought a lot of superstition with him from Poland and from the wars. He also claims that December's stone is turquoise and means unselfishness."

"Which stone means courage? And which one honor?"

Daniela felt his breath.

"Here and now everyone," she answered.

"There is salt in the air," said Kamil Dreisler.

"Wait until it gets completely dark," Daniela said.

"The moon and stars are shining so bright here. How come? It's strange, it's so dark and white."

Daniela also looked at the sea. "It's strange," she said. "Somewhere far away there is a land, a city, or a house and we will be there together. All oaths are useless. All words. I swore that I would stay here and now I know that I won't. Pharaoh Blumen says that will is stronger than love, but that's not true. Why does everybody want to be happy in his own way?

"Hold me," she said. "Just hold me like this."

"Your heart's pounding as if you'd been running," said Kamil Dreisler.

"You know . . ." she whispered. "You must know why."

She kissed him on the lips. Her lips seemed to wince when she let him kiss her back. She didn't want to appear nervous. She clung to him. She let him touch her breasts. The rim of the sun dissolved into the sea. The fiery pillar of the sun reflected in the sea got shorter and sank into the water, and the darkness fell. The moon lit up the sky. Stars shattered and perished into the sea.

"Everything . . . everywhere . . ." she said. And then, "So many stars . . . and each is forever."

On the sandy ridge near Nahariyya grew green oleander bushes covered with red blossoms. Magnolias bloomed beside some of the houses and clumps of grass pushed skyward in the shade. There were tunnels of trodden paths between the bushes. The fences stood shoulder-high, most made of empty gasoline canisters, bleached by the sun and dented, stacked one on top of another with the holders turned inward. In the daytime dogs and cats would lie next to the fence in the sun at a distance from each other; at night the fences were visited by rats in search of food. Occasionally a jackal would turn up.

"Wait until it's dark," said Daniela.

"The moon and the stars are out."

"A little longer," Daniela added. "This is the first place on earth I've come to where I'm not scared of darkness."

"Maybe it wasn't fear, but being careful," he said.

"As a child I feared a lot."

"You're not a child anymore."

Daniela stretched and pulled her hands behind her head. She had shoulder-length shiny black hair.

"My friend Eva was supposed to come," said Daniela. "You can never depend on her. Whenever someone close to her was killed, she went and slept with the first man she met. She has a reputation already. Lying to protect herself from being hurt. Sometimes she lied to herself without realizing it."

Then she said, "The watchman at Solel Boné—his name is Alexander Hermansdorf—promised me that he would let you work his watch in the tool warehouse occasionally, if we'd want. We wouldn't have to be afraid, he'd let you have his revolver for the night. We could use the money while I'm waiting for my papers to be processed."

She turned to him. "Wait. Let me button you up."

She held the edge of his cotton army shirt between her fingers.

"You don't think that I know how to button you up? You think there's something that I don't know or can't fix? I've been too long on my own."

Then her voice changed and her expression changed, and she looked at the sea as if it were a great big window into the world which they would now enter together.

Her heart was pounding so loudly that she knew Kamil Dreisler had to hear it, and she held him tightly around the neck.

Kamil Dreisler carried her in his arms down the sandy path past the oleanders to the small house that was loaned to them by a couple who had been interned by the British on Mauritius for the duration of World War II. It was a wooden shack made out of a crate for moving furniture—they called them lift-vans. Empty yellow ammunition cartridges lay flattened in the sand. Some had been run over by trucks and tractors, and they were still hot from the sun like the white sand the wind swept over them. Kamil Dreisler walked slowly and carefully toward the wooden wall that had the color of baked clay. The moon shed its light on the sea, on the waves of sand, and on the walls of Acre.

Daniela smiled. "I don't understand why my heart is pounding like this. I don't know what's the matter."

Kamil Dreisler stepped in front of the lift-van, which now emerged from the darkness opposite the oleanders, which seemed lighter than before. The packing crate stood there like a hut, a nine-by-twelve-foot structure, supported on two beams. You could see cats prowling between the floor of the lift-van and the beams. On the ocean side the original owner had cut a window. The mover's name had already been obliterated by the salt, last winter's rains, and the beating sun. The window looked out into the darkness through white fringes of a curtain.

Kamil Dreisler opened the door with his shoulder. He put Daniela down on the bed. It was stifling hot. The windblown curtain pressed against the window frame. Old newspapers, belonging to the innkeeper with the Napoleonic bangs, lay on the floor. The innkeeper had also lent them some pans and a mirror. The plates and silverware belonged to the woman from Mauritius.

"If my father were alive, if he'd managed to get here in time, we would have had a better house," said Daniela.

Kamil Dreisler fastened the door with a leather peg made from a belt that old Pharaoh Blumen had given Daniela when she left the army. The pale green leaves of the oleanders gleamed in the moonlight.

He lay on his side next to her, his cheek and eyes next to hers. Daniela yielded to the quiver that told her what would come, although she did not feel ready. Or was she? She had a feeling of closeness as never before.

She looked at the interior of the lift-van and at the oleanders, as if seeing them for the first time. Her expression changed, as had her voice. Her eyes no longer held visions of ravines, funerals, electric barbed-wire fences, trenches, and exploded hand grenades that she had learned to throw. Nor were they filled with strange people, distant lands and foreign tongues, dust, rocks, and sand. In her eyes there was a question and a promise of what she sometimes felt in the evenings looking at Mount Carmel, at the walls of Acre or the refineries of Haifa. She was ready to share her world with Kamil Dreisler, and with it those things she had never experienced before. She touched his soul as Kamil touched her soul with his breathing, looking, and wishing. What was it that was so close, warm, and unknown. For Kamil's sake, she was willing to leave her world and accept and embrace Kamil Dreisler's world, his party, all of his images. All that was far away, yesterday, a year ago, now approached fast, as when you mistakenly look through the wrong end of a telescope.

"Everything," she said.

"Everything," he answered.

She felt his body next to hers. She let him caress her for a long time and then she caressed him. Her lips touched his lips; her palms touched his arms, his palms, his body. She felt his breath. The sparks of an invisible sun ignited her. She felt this fire coming from outside and inside at the same time, and everything was quiet and fast. She thought about a lot of things that had happened. She thought about the innkeeper with the Napoleonic bangs who never had a woman for more than one night. She thought about the members of the Sasa kibbutz and what land and horses meant to them. She thought about people who fought here only a year ago against the British and then fought with the Arabs, with whom they wanted to live in peace, and they had to learn to fight because they'd forgotten how, and they learned to be strong after they had been weak for a long time. And she thought of her nineteen years which had brought her here to this moment, of all the things in life that were connected with killing. She thought about going back to Prague with Kamil to fulfill his devotion to communism, and about how fast her heart was beating. She felt all this disappearing from her mind without really leaving, just stepping behind her and freeing a huge space where something else might enter.

Feeling Kamil's embrace, she embraced him in return. She felt all of her body and all of his body and no longer thought about anything but the meaning of man and woman, about the innkeeper saying that people were like animals entering the ark in pairs, and she thought how different it was for her and why—why it would always be different.

"Everything." She mouthed the word but could no longer whisper. She lay there with half-open lips, eyes closed, and waited.

"Forgive me," Kamil Dreisler said then. "I'm sorry."

The sound of the sea and the wind from the hills, the sand and the night birds on the rocks, mixed with the sultry air. The wood of the crate had a dry smell. Some of the knots in the wood were covered with dried, amber-colored resin that was still fragrant. Their bodies were beaded with perspiration. Although her eyes were closed, something blinded her, diminished her hearing, took away her power of speech. She could no longer find words, even in feigned whispers. Did he hear the pounding of her heart? "Everything" repeated in the back of her mind.

"There's nothing to forgive," she managed hoarsely.

She felt the tension in her throat, her chest, and her hips. She felt the twitching in her underbelly and on the inside of her thighs. She forgot who and where he had been. Everything will start anew, again. Something was coming that reminded her of fire and clear water. All the quivers concentrated in one place, in her blood and in his blood, like light focusing into a cone. With all her awareness she felt his will; it joined with her desire, and she felt the dissolving between slow and fast, between yes and no, between perhaps, maybe, sometime, never. Everything was in her mind. Everything.

"Yes, yes," she said.

She opened her eyes for a second. She saw Kamil Dreisler's shoulders, his throat, his arms, his chest. His hair touched her forehead. She let him do anything he wanted to with her dress. Her naked skin, where the clothes protected her from the sun, was white as milk, and the color contrasted with the wood of the hut.

She whispered, "I waited for you. Come to me."

She caught a glimpse of the curtain, the white sheet, and the sliver of an oleander blossom that the wind had blown in. She saw an earwig crawling across the ceiling near the acetylene lamp and followed it until it reached the edge of the ceiling and touched the white curtain. She felt—and feared—that her blood was on the sheet. Not far from the lift-van, a cat screamed. She felt a movement that came from the depths of the sea, from the warm stream of wind which enveloped the hut, from the friction of sand grains against each other. This stream moved her soul, her legs, her belly, and her hands until she felt she was caught up in a whirlpool that also swallowed up her fear. She heard the echo of the voices of her mother and father, her sister and the dead—who now seemed alive—and she heard their weeping and their song. And then Daniela Klaus heard her own moan mix with the roar of the sea and their bodies. The earth around them wrapped itself in the sky, which was covered with night and the night with stars. She heard the moan of the sea, the pounding of her heart, the crashing of the waves, and the beating of Kamil Dreisler's heart. They heard the birds on the rocks as if far away in the sea: *Tee ooo terr . . . Tee eee terr . . .*

"Is it as you expected?" Daniela whispered. "Are you disappointed?"

Words that she never would have brought herself to say now flowed from her lips like waves of wind, like the hum of the sea and sunlight streaming down.

"Everything? Was it everything?"

It was like horses galloping and churning up sand with their hooves, or birds in flight, or children playing and shouting on the beach. As when she first pulled the trigger and learned to shoot in the army; she was the same as before, yet different, just a minute older, and so much more experienced.

"It's beautiful," whispered Kamil Dreisler.

"It's pain," said Daniela. "Beautiful pain."

"It's everything," he said. "It's for a long time. It's forever."

She kissed him on the lips, full of an unknown passion which was both new and full of self-confidence she could share without losing anything. This passion was different, unlike what her letters revealed or what his answers to her letters revealed. She left the smile on her lips and this smile seemed to turn inward as well.

"Everything," she said again, and let the word echo in her mind.

3

Patches of azure on the horizon seemed to split the sky and change darkness into light. At dawn the sea became brighter. The wilderness and the mountains, beyond which lay the deserts, broke through the twilight in the distance and mixed with the fog. It made the daybreak look like a veil that the day would pull off to reveal its face. The innkeeper at Raveh's turned on the gramophone. Daniela let Kamil kiss her and then she said, "Why aren't we carpenters? We could be hammering nails and singing away and we could be rich and never have to worry."

She had a pleasant, deep alto voice. She looked like a lovely flower that had just bloomed. What she said sounded like the songs taught to her by her grandmother and mother, songs about brides and bridegrooms, about meadows and rivers and about the good and bad fortunes that people are bound to encounter. Life was like a bridge, crossing unbelievable gaps and abysses between men and between lands. Why do we sometimes fear that we might betray something that could actually betray us?

She didn't want to say that it was strange that he hadn't received his papers yet. She was still thinking about what it is that makes the sun warm, what causes the sea to swell in waves, what raises the white wings of the gulls, whose white plumage seems dirty when you see them up close as they fly low. She thought how good it would be if they didn't get the papers and could stay here—it wouldn't be her fault, but it would satisfy her desire to live out her life here and she wouldn't have to say it.

She knew that people love their ideas as if the ideas were people; and that every idea had its own overcoat and cap, its own disguise. Every idea had a personification in someone or some place. This she already knew to be true.

It occurred to her that there is nothing stronger than the idea that old and new sufferings can be healed. An idea that could change the damned world into an acceptable place. An idea that could encompass everything, the whole world, from equator to the pole and from the pole to the equator on the other side, across the starry sky as seen here and by the antipodes, on the surface of oceans and at the foothills of the mountains on the other side of the planet. Is there in every idea a grain of a dream from which one will never wake up?

Kamil Dreisler built a fire in front of the lift-van and boiled water for tea in a cast-iron kettle.

"Burn the letters," said Daniela, handing Kamil Dreisler a bundle of papers and envelopes. She laughed as Kamil stoked the fire with her old correspondence. She was now more self-confident than when he arrived. She felt close to the mountains, the sea, people, including Pharaoh Blumen and the innkeeper with the Napoleonic bangs, the couple from Mauritius and her friends from the army who tried to talk her into joining the nursing corps. Even in the morning the sun looked like a glowing brass gong. Kamil Dreisler threw the letters into the flames. He probably wanted to convince himself that everything was going as planned, even though there were delays. He hadn't been to Raveh's or at the Pinguin for the last two days because his money had run out. Pharaoh Blumen had given Daniela a briefcase for the trip. It was made from the skin of a polar moose and was only a little rotted in some places. Kamil made no comments about that. It was too hot for moose skins.

"Everything you want is good," Daniela said suddenly. "All I want is good. Then why isn't it good if we put it together? I wonder why it isn't good for anyone but ourselves."

"You can't reconcile fire with water," said Kamil Dreisler after a while.

Some dead fish lay in the sand behind the lift-van. The cats must have dragged them there. The wind came in with the tide and carried the ashes from the burned letters into the sea. There the first wave licked them and the returning wave carried them off. The sand was glued together with the tar and the debris. Daniela had removed a ribbon from one of the letters. As the water in the kettle started to boil, she tied her hair with the ribbon.

"It's better now than it was," Daniela said with a smile. "Sometimes I wasn't even sure that I was made of flesh and bones. I felt I was made of ink, distance, promises, and unfulfilled hopes—and absences, too. I felt like a stranger to myself, as though I did not exist."

Then, when they ate, she asked, "Won't you have another piece of fish?"

"That's for you."

"I might think you're afraid I'm going to poison you." She smiled and he looked at her. Her eyes spoke of everything that was good and could be good.

Daniela watched the waves running up the shore and dissolving in the sand. She sat on the orange crates, swinging her legs.

"In the army they issued me size fourteen boots. And the first pants I got were five sizes too big, and the new ones cut me in the crotch. I was given the heaviest German rifle—a Mauser."

"What did that sailor want with Eva?"

"She provokes men, that's all. But otherwise she has a sweet nature. She's different with men. She told the sailor that the salesman in the lingerie shop wanted to sell her a muslin nightgown when she came to buy something with her last lover. She explained that she's not used to going away empty-handed. First she was just playing with them, but now I think it's for real."

"So what did he give her?"

"Don't even ask. We celebrated her twenty-second birthday recently. She doesn't have a lover anymore."

Daniela examined the calluses on her hands and the scratches that had healed. She touched the hot sand with her soles. She liked talking about her friends. It was like giving a vivid picture of them and bringing them close, even when they were far away.

"She dated the captain of a commercial vessel. He was married and wouldn't get a divorce. On Saturdays he stayed with his family. It's hard to live off men here. She told me that the mystery of love is that when a man gets what he wants, he's not interested in the next time. But that's not love. It's only need. Desire to be close to someone. She prefers soldiers. Sometimes to scare men away she tells them she's sick. She had a mailman, but he got locked up for throwing mail into the Gaaton creek so he wouldn't have to deliver it. They won't let him out to do it again."

Where did the two of you meet?"

"In the fortress Theresienstadt. In 1945 just after the war, she stayed in Germany. We were together in Auschwitz-Birkenau in the *Frauen-konzentrazionslager* with Slavs and Hungarian women. She didn't hurry to get home from Bergen-Belsen. She hoped to find an Englishman. She was afraid to return to Prague and not find anyone there. In Germany she learned how to eat, drink, and dance. How to distinguish trees, flowers, and birds. She lied, saying that she was looking for some girl— both of us knew that the girl died a long time ago."

Kamil watched the fire consume a letter that read, "They fell here. There was no place to withdraw." The breeze carried off the slivers of ash.

"Do you like my cooking?" Daniela asked.

"I sure do."

"It's going to be hot."

"It's been hot every day."

"This hot weather will drive people crazy."

"What do you mean?"

"Well, everything just slows down and seems sleepier. It's ninety-nine degrees in Jerusalem today. Here by the seashore it's only ninety-three or ninety-five. Sometimes it gets to a hundred and four degrees. It's like a beautiful hell."

"Even in the mountains?"

"Everywhere."

"And it never rains?"

"When there are clouds there's a storm with thunder and lightning, but it doesn't rain."

The longest letter that Daniela had ever mailed was now burning, all three pages of it. She had written him about her father who went to Auschwitz-Birkenau with the transport in September 1944, in spite of the fact that he worked in the Theresienstadt Jewish Administration with people who had become legends and who had monuments built to them here, whose names appeared on streets, gardens, museums, and some military installations. That way he had hoped to save the lives of her and her sister. Everyone who survived could do so because someone else was killed instead, and she often thought about those who had to go in her place—her father among them. She thought about this once when she was shooting and had become nervous because she did not want to tell anyone about it. She felt proud that her father did not let anyone go in his place, as some of the others in the Council of the Eldest had done. When it is a matter of life and death, man is an absolute egoist. With a few exceptions. Only the very best value their own lives the same way they value the lives of others around them. Her father was one of them. But she sometimes wondered if she wouldn't really have preferred that he wasn't one of them.

She didn't mail the letter because she didn't want to complain, to feel sorry for herself, and she didn't want compassion. But there were moments when she still wasn't sure. As a result, he suspected that she had forgotten him, that she had someone else; because prior to that she had made some remarks about people with whom she spent her nights.

She was almost happy to leave the fortress Theresienstadt. She had lived in an attic next to the fire station. Mice scampered around her head at night. This was the letter in which she wrote, "Come. You will understand why I don't want to go away. I have weighed everything, all the things I want and all that I don't want. I can be happy only if I am free. We were never free, you, I, or the people around us. And I have no illusions about the easy existence of freedom.

I entered the army because I wanted to live, not to die. My father's parents were killed and so were my mother's. Then they killed my father. Mother is dead.... This morning I dreamed that you were a sliver of daybreak, a dream spun of lonely nights, dawns, and memories. Your image floats to me across the sea." She was afraid that such a letter would repudiate him.

"What are you thinking about?"

"The same as you," she answered.

He thought about the letters she would get from here and how she would answer them. He wished it would come soon. But it couldn't be done without the papers. She was close to him and he smelled her hair, a fragrance that reminded him of vanilla wine, or maybe just vanilla, but it all mixed with the idea of wine and intoxicated him. He thought about her and the cities where everybody will eat when it's time to eat, and drink when they are thirsty. He thought about sunlit houses for people who come home from work, and about the equal share of silence and noise, smoke and hills for everyone. You don't have to be crazy to have such dreams. It's enough to have experienced three years in concentration camps for having been born of a Jewish mother. It was a dream about a land without fear, where no human cheek will be bruised by barbed wire.

"How do you feel?"

He smiled. He didn't want to say that not having received the papers made him feel like a man on board a ship moving away from the shore it wanted to reach. The members of the Sasa kibbutz washed horses on the dock. The trucks in which the horses were brought stood at the side of the road. They must have gotten up very early, he thought. He drew in the fragrance of Daniela's hair, the smell of vanilla and wine.

"Wouldn't you like to wash first?" Daniela asked.

"I did," said Kamil Dreisler.

"But not with soap. I don't want to get sick like Eva."

And then she added, "Once you told me when we were still in Prague and going to the Wolf Mountain that some woman had compared you to a young horse. Can you tell me why?"

"I was sixteen and you know where it was and why we did it. None of us wanted to leave the fortress Theresienstadt for Auschwitz-Birkenau naive."

"Did it help you in anything?"

"It gave us self-confidence."

"It's simple for men."

"Not in everything."

"I always found it strange that from the beginning you wanted to live with me like an adult, when I wasn't one, although I may have looked it. I can't blame you. Nobody will tell you what a girl should share first—her body or her soul. Aren't you ashamed?" She kept smiling but her eyes were serious.

"No, I may be ashamed that people better than me did not make it."

"Someone else should be ashamed."

"It's always the innocent who feel the most shame."

"I don't want to talk about it."

"Then why do you?"

"And I know who it was," Daniela said and smiled. "You and Eva will get along just fine when she shows up."

Later she said, "For God's sake, bolt the door. You want other things now. Nobody's ever done them with me. But you have done them, haven't you? All right," she whispered, "but wait a little. Only if you do it with me only."

Kamil Dreisler bolted the door of the lift-van with a peg. The tooth of a scavenger fish swung from the end of a rope. It was an amulet given to them by Pharaoh Blumen, the owner of the boat rental place and a small fishing vessel.

Daniela spoke in a whisper then, as if someone could hear them at the dock where the Sasa kibbutzniks washed their horses. "I'll do it to you now," she said.

And later she added, "Why talk about it? ... Yes, yes, anything you want. Everything. But keep quiet ... "

TWO

1

The resort town of Nahariyya, which can be seen from Haifa and Acre in the south, and from Rosh Haniqra in the north, grew in the 1930s when people started leaving Germany. The oldest structure in Nahariyya is the cemetery for Austrian soldiers who took part in the first world war and died here before the first immigrant wave arrived. There are white crosses and well-kept graves in that cemetery.

"How many breakfasts have I served you?" Daniela asked.

"Who'd bother counting?" said Kamil Dreisler.

Daniela smiled like someone who is learning patience, but she was anything but patient.

In the morning and in the evening Daniela set the table for them on the tomato crates. The heat wave had lasted for weeks and the radio meteorologists foretold more of the same. In the lowlands by the sea the temperature had reached ninety-nine; in the hills and in Jerusalem it was over a hundred. In Raveh's someone said that such temperatures occur only at the beginning or end of the summer. The local newspapers mentioned that a similar heat wave had occurred only once before, at the end of August 1881, when the temperature in Jerusalem had reached a hundred and eleven, and in Jaffa a hundred and six. It was hard to breathe.

"You can't eat?" Daniela asked.

"It must be the heat," Kamil Dreisler replied.

"You have to drink a lot."

"I drink like a fish."

"You're supposed to drink at least eight times a day."

"Yeah."

"A quart and a half," Daniela added. "I drink almost constantly."

In the morning Pharoah Blumen gave them some fish that he could not sell or eat himself. Letting it spoil would be a sin. He probably thought they would die of hunger without him, so he went fishing more often. Daniela watched the long blue ship with the orange stripe along the hull. It floated on the sea like a resting woman. She was thinking about herself, what it means to be a woman, by day and by night. The innkeeper with the Napoleonic bangs from Raveh's played some European and American pop tunes and then the *Kineret*.

"Why do you think the papers haven't come yet?" Daniela asked.

"I don't want to talk about it all the time," Kamil Dreisler said.

"Do you think I want to?"

"There could be a thousand reasons. The world looks like it's about to fall apart, on the brink of war, and not only here, but from pole to pole, under the sea and in space. Sometimes our personal concerns seem smaller than pinheads to the powers that be and about as important. I realize that for us they are about as important as those from pole to pole. But as I've said, we have to be patient and must not worry so much."

"We don't have to lie to each other," said Daniela. "And certainly not because of someone else who . . . " She did not finish the sentence because he would be on pins and needles after such a remark. But she knew words didn't really mean much. The heart of the matter was not communication—people speak only to assure themselves, or sometimes others. Daniela looked at him the way the innkeeper with the Napoleonic bangs looked at her, as at an idiot.

"Will you take the job that Alexander Hermansdorf offered you? He wants a few days off so he can finally go to the immigrant camp in Hadera to pick out a bride. He has a hard time choosing or finding one quickly enough. He's tried on several occasions. Or maybe none of them want him. He will never tell. He had a girl with him for a couple of days, but she moved out because he counted every slice of salami she ate, told her to close the refrigerator quickly because it uses up too much ice, and finally he just left her salami skins because things had become expensive. I wouldn't stay with such a person. We won't have to feel sorry for him. No one has to feel sorry for anyone here. It's still better than the *Frauenkonzentrazionslager*."

"What did old Pharoah Blumen tell you?"

"The usual: When you have no shoes, think of those who have no feet. The innkeeper from Raveh's offered me a job. And the old lady from the Pension Popper wanted to find me a job in the kitchen. She apologized for the bitter tea—it's not that she's stingy. Once she prepared crayfish for the English naval officers and didn't charge them anything. During the war against the Arabs she cooked potato soup for the soldiers—for free. She used dried mushrooms she'd brought from Europe and had been saving for five years."

"Is that all Pharoah Blumen told you?"

"He wanted to buy sugar from her older sister, who's the mayor's wife, but she didn't want to sell it at black market prices, and she didn't want to lose money either." She was silent for a while. The old man told her that it was always the same story. First utopia, then disappointment; first dreams, then betrayal; first promise, then killing.

Daniela handed Kamil Dreisler a piece of paper that the innkeeper from the Raveh used to charge his guests for food and drink. It read, "Haven't you gone through hell once already, and do you need to make life hell again? There can be no agreement between two dogs and a bone."

"But that isn't the handwriting of Pharoah Blumen."

"No, I just wanted him to advise me on what to do."

"What did he advise you?"

"To throw it away and not make you needlessly mad. To be patient and wait. He said everything will turn out all right, that you will get the papers for me too and that we will be able to leave."

"Can you swear that he did not say anything else?"

"You have to trust somebody," said Daniela.

"Some people maybe, some people never," said Kamil Dreisler. "Who gave it to you? Who wrote it?"

Kamil Dreisler turned red. It was easier to think about the world whose shadow would cover their worries, except for the fact that it was from that world that his papers were not forthcoming. He could guess who had given her that note and who had written those words.

"Did you get it last night?"

"I've been getting them for three weeks. It's not the first one. I've been throwing them away."

Now Daniela turned red, too. A seagull with white wings and a dirty belly circled above the lift-van.

2

The end of July brought hot winds from the East and no one felt any respite from the layer of cold air that had come for the last three days from the Mediterranean and southern Europe. The sultry heat continued. The sun looked like a mirror reflecting broken silver splinters. It was impossible to breathe in the lift-van during the day and unbearable to sleep at night. During the third sleepless night, Daniela sat on the bed, wiped the perspiration from her forehead and neck, and said that staying here was also a revolution. She knew that Kamil Dreisler was not sleeping. He seemed to be on duty, killing cockroaches. Twice a day they had to spray the van, sometimes even at night. The sky gleamed like dark blue porcelain. Daniela wrapped a wet rag around her forehead. The wind brought smells of stale beer, onions, garlic, and garbage from the inn. The innkeeper did not sleep either; he took the chairs out on to the beach and hosed down the dance floor to remove cigarette butts. The stars shone brightly.

Daniela had lost weight. Even Kamil Dreisler had become thinner. They both had tanned.

"Don't think about it," said Kamil Dreisler. "Sleep. You'll be weak as a fly in the morning."

"I've learned how to lose the dead, but I haven't yet learned how to lose the living. It gets on my nerves that someone is constantly making decisions about me. I don't feel like sleeping while you're not sleeping. Aren't you hot? It's hell."

The innkeeper had started playing songs from the time of Palmach. He probably played them just for himself, but they could hear them in the lift-van quite well. Under the stars gleamed the lighted and colored boats, and in the darkness they all seemed the same, like sisters. The boats would go out at night and come back during the day. Kamil Dreisler had been working on the road for three days, and at night he kept watch for Alexander Hermansdorf, who guarded the warehouse highway equipment owned by the Solel Boné company. The boats with their lamps looked like will-o'-the-wisps on the sea. Kamil Dreisler smelled of the asphalt which he and two other men helped spread over the road. He did not sleep long. He dreamed about greyhounds and dachshunds moving in space between heaven and earth. The dogs changed into fish; then into a moth. The moth changed into an aquarium fish, almost an embryo. It streamed down like a capillary or a disappearing meteor.

"My commander once explained to me how to throw a hand grenade, what you have to do so you don't kill your people and yourself. He told me what thoughts are helpful and what thoughts are not. For him a thought was like a parachute when you bail out of a plane. It makes sense only when it opens up, not when you fly and the parachute remains shut. Everybody knows how that ends."

In the middle of the night they heard a warning on the radio that bathers, trying to cool off, should be careful in the water and watch for anything that looks suspicious, including dead fish. Mines sometimes look like beer or soda bottles.

"Do you want to go swimming?" Daniela suggested.

"Well, if you can't sleep," replied Kamil Dreisler.

"How about you?"

"What's the farthest you've ever swum?"

"I only swim as far as I can still see the shore. I don't like jellyfish and I'm afraid of big fish. If I just touch them it sends me into a panic. I swell if I touch a jellyfish or even a bit of one. In the Hachotrim kibbutz there is a man who goes swimming only twice a year, when the khamsin comes. He swims toward the horizon, but never at night."

Then she added, "You don't have to worry about me wanting to drown. I hope you'll never want to drown next to me. Or drown me."

"I dreamed about Eva," Kamil Dreisler said. "She had an affair with an American. They walked arm in arm; they kissed every now and then, but that was all. Then he suggested that they take a shower together. She said why not, but she'd already had an experience with a man who considered showering with a woman to be the maximum he could do with a woman. He preferred to have men in the shower. He watched her, fascinated, and she felt relieved. But he didn't even touch her. He only asked her to marry him. She said that she would have to think it over. At night she dreamed that they were in a meadow with two of his friends. Suddenly all three changed—the American into a grasshopper, the second into a cricket, and the third into a dung beetle. He didn't understand why she gave him the cold shoulder. She needed a man, not a child."

Kamil Dreisler borrowed old Pharaoh Blumen's boat.

"There's a khamsin. In Arabic that means fifty. Fifty times a year the hot wind blows from the desert, carrying with it small grains of sand, like the seeds of a pomegranate. It gives people a headache."

The sea was transparent. The bottom of the sea, when you stood at the shore, looked like a clenched hand—the tissues, the blood vessels and veins, which looked like a body and a plant. Kamil Dreisler rowed the boat alongside cast fishing rods and went past the more remote ones, until they were almost alone in the sea. He already knew about the local goldsmith who was a head shorter than Daniela and whose mother tried to get them to move into their house. He gave Daniela an alarm clock and a business card that read, "Small but yours." Daniela gave the alarm clock to Kamil. When she helped out at the Pension Popper she was accosted on the staircase by a guest who offered to take her with him to Jerusalem. Lying on the dry grass after a night out, an officer of the infantry offered her marriage and was willing to leave his wife and three-year-old daughter. There was also a Piper pilot who was a confectioner by trade, and whose mother liked Daniela very much. He crashed while on a training flight. Now Daniela earned money by stringing beads for the lady from Mauritius. They gave her a copy of the French novel, *La rue du chat qui peche* (The Street of the Fisherman's

Cat). On the cover was a picture of a seated girl who seemed to be about the same age as Daniela when she left Prague with the Voluntary Brigade, wearing a coat that was hurriedly made for her from an American army blanket. Kamil Dreisler wanted Daniela to explain to him why immigrant stories are always so sad. She told him they were only sad in the beginning. She began to undress and folded her dress, placing it in the bottom of the boat. She had on the yellow dress with green leaves. The sides of the boat were cushioned with split tires. She kept only her underwear on.

"I had a dream about you," Daniela said. "They recruited you as a pilot here. You'd like that, wouldn't you? And then the assignment was changed to long-distance transport. They let you drive a truck with a trailer at the Hachotrim kibbutz. The truck was worth a hundred thousand."

"A hundred thousand what?"

"What does it matter? It was only a dream. Wouldn't you like to do that? I mean if it weren't here?"

"You said that once before."

"What have I said before? I don't think you're paying attention to me. You're preoccupied with other things."

The boat was green on the inside, with two oars and a box containing fishing rods and tin cans. On the bottom were hooks and tackle and fishing line wound around big spools. The sky lay on top of the sea and the two were joined in the darkness. The boat had brown sides and a red line around the trim. The old man called her "Freedom." He had christened her with beer and painted the name in big white letters, both in Hebrew and in Latin script. In the box he kept old newspapers and his collection of Dutch beer bottles with a patent seal.

With a quick movement Daniela removed her underwear and jumped into the water. She swam close to the boat. As Kamil Dreisler rowed toward her, she held on the edge of the boat and let the water run out of her hair. Kamil Dreisler gave her a hand and she climbed back into the boat, lay on her back in the bottom, and watched the stars. They were bright and looked like the signals she had known in the army.

"Do you want to tell me something I should know?" Kamil Dreisler asked.

"Maybe the man who is processing our papers doesn't like it that you came to get me. Maybe it isn't just a mistake or a delay. For some people revolution is what they have declared it to be, not what you or I wish for. When they lie to people like you and me, they don't even consider it a lie."

She didn't tell him that he should stay with her if the papers didn't come.

The waves splashed against the boat; the drops of water fell back into the sea and on Daniela, who did not resist them. She no longer showed Kamil Dreisler the anonymous slips of warning that she kept receiving. They opened one of the letters addressed to him at the post office. He was being summoned to get his papers processed himself. She remembered that in the army one noncommissioned officer spoiled her belief in the astrological charts by reminding her that they were not there for admiration but for orientation. The water sprayed against the side of the boat.

Daniela dried herself with a towel and reached for the yellow dress.

"I hope you're not going to get dressed yet," Kamil Dreisler said.

"Why?"

"So that I won't have to undress you again."

"I don't want you to think it's the only thing I can give you."

Night fell toward the earth and into the water. The waves gleamed. Here and there a fish flashed on the surface as the prow of the boat cut lightly through the water.

"You shouldn't spoil it—for me, or for yourself," Daniela added.

He felt that both wanted more, but it eluded them. Her body was the only attainable thing. He suddenly felt incomplete, even though yesterday everything still looked good. He had it and he didn't have it at the same time because it was not connected to the rest of what he wanted. An echo of what Daniela felt, also something unfinished, a sense of incomplete bliss. And again they both felt like a wave in the ocean. Joy and pain. Pleasure with pain. Ambiguity of desire. Desire to possess, yet knowing it could not be.

The warm wind, floating through the night, caressed the sea.

3

Kamil Dreisler and Daniela walked barefoot toward the barrels on the deserted shore, where there was nothing but rocks and sand. Kamil Dreisler pulled the boat up on the dry sand where he could keep it in sight. They spread their clothes on the sand so that they could put their heads on them. There was a black shimmer on the water and the foam looked like scales, like fins, like melted silver coins. The taste of stale beer blew in from Raveh's as cats fought behind the docks. The night floated away like an undiscovered tale of time that had no beginning and no end. From the darkness of the night emerged a ship. It approached slowly and sailed past them like a luminous mirage. As the night and the sea made way for the ship and closed behind it, all that you could see were the lights of the staterooms and the decks. The ship was sharply and softly delineated from the space of the night.

"It's lovely here," said Daniela.

"Why are you crying?" asked Kamil Dreisler.

"We could live here together."

The ship sailed into the night, carrying away its lights, far into the distance, until it became smaller and finally disappeared.

"Don't cry," Kamil Dreisler said again.

"What is the meaning of love, loving, promising and commitment?" asked Daniela. "I have never said this to anyone. I love you for the rest of my life. Just as I wrote it on the wall of our little house. It will still be true even after I'm gone."

Five minutes later she asked, "Give me your hand."

For a few seconds she held Kamil Dreisler's palm on her belly. He immediately understood.

"No one in the world knows it—only you and I."

"How do you know? Did you see a doctor?"

"I don't have to go to a doctor." And then she added, "So it happened. That first Sunday evening. On the twenty-fourth, when you carried me into the house. It only takes a fraction of a second."

He looked at her. There was a question in her eyes, and a reply, together with tears and a smile. Her expression changed. Her eyes, clear and somewhat nervous, reflected yesterday's and tomorrow's truth. Her truth, that she had to make him see. Her eyes explained why she didn't have to ask anyone, and it was as clear as the turning earth, the rising and setting of the sun, the seagulls sitting on their nests. It was as clear as night following day and day following night, like the flight of seagulls from the rocks behind Rosh Haniqra and as clear as their crimes. She smelled of the sea and of vanilla wine.

Kamil Dreisler suddenly felt older and more mature. He felt very proud but also tricked. His throat was dry. He caressed Daniela's temples, her hair, her lips.

The feathery tall grasses waved in the warm breeze.

"The second week in September we'll have better weather," said Daniela. "According to Pharaoh Blumen, the weather always gets better when the Nile floods. Very few people lie about the weather, even at Raveh's."

THREE

1

As Pharaoh Blumen left the shack and brought the evening mail, he watched the old freighter. Kamil Dreisler threw a paper back into the garbage can. It contained his hair—Daniela had just given him a haircut. Pharaoh Blumen stood there in the light of the full moon. His tanned and wrinkled cheeks looked like pulp, like the bottom of the boat, like a layer of tar, hardened and baked by the sun and scarred by the sand and pebbles on the shore. He pulled out the boat over land every day, and the sun had burned his skin.

Pharaoh Blumen brought Daniela a fishing line so she could hang her laundry, along with a monster of a fish that could last them until New Year's. He told them that some new immigrants arrived in Nahariyya on the freighter, but these were not nervous millionaires from Borneo.

"Maybe in this life I'm not supposed to have what normal people everywhere can have," Daniela said. "I can only dream of having my own bed."

Kamil Dreisler turned to the sea and watched the tall waves.

When no one said anything, Pharaoh Blumen volunteered, "Strong waves can split a freighter in two. The waves create a sort of cavern into which the ships fall. If the ship hits a wall of water in a certain place, it will split in two and sink. Of course, it's usually the wind that turns a wave into a strong one."

And then he added, "But it has to be between the tides. From low tide to high tide early in the afternoon, between noon and one o'clock, and from high tide to low tide early in the evening, between five and six. But I'd better be off now. Good night."

The wind made the door creak. One could feel the saturated breeze of late summer. Leather rotted and wood dried up.

"Good night," said Kamil Dreisler.

"There's life everywhere," said Daniela. "You can live everywhere if you want to and have two healthy arms. For God's sake, it's not a jungle here either."

Pharaoh Blumen took one last look at the two of them as he turned to the old freighter. He walked away slowly, barefoot, in cut-off corduroy pants, the calves of his legs covered with a web of blue varicose veins. Sailing above the sea, the seagulls flapped their wings.

"Good night," Kamil Dreisler said again.

Daniela was silent. At night, Kamil Dreisler had a dream that he threw himself into the sea and swam behind the dock, where they occasionally fished out an unexploded mine. He swam in the direction of the night waves, beyond the Pension Popper, all the way to the rock at Rosh Haniqra where the seagulls came from. He probably had a fever. He dreamed that someone was looking for the water that was spilled by the oxen in the children's rhyme, which every little kid in Bohemia knows. Then he dreamed about Eva. He was lying under a dirty blanket when she came to tell him she got a job at the Pension Popper and that she made the blind and wounded happy. She was slight, flat-chested, and had uneven teeth, and wore a gaudy green dress and white sandals and a very large vinyl bag over her arm in which she carried all of her belongings. As she removed the blanket, he suddenly felt her lips, shuddered, and thrust his fingers into her greasy hair, which was full of sand.

"You're not sleeping?" Daniela asked. "What should one do when the best things become the worst? Why do you want me to feel like a widow?"

Kamil Dreisler had given the money that he had received that evening at last from Solel Boné to Daniela. He had been keeping nightwatch for Alexander Hermansdorf, who came empty-handed from Hadera for the third time. When Kamil Dreisler returned the pistol to him, he did not even wait for Kamil to be far enough away before he shot himself. Nobody blinked. The innkeeper with the Napoleonic bangs served beer on tap and said that in the cemetery in Godera a big chunk of clay was reserved for suicides.

"Are you so cold that you are shaking?" asked Daniela.

"Something probably bit me."

"Don't you want to undress? Shall I undress you?"

2

On the beach, last season's hit, "Kiss me, Harry, kiss me..." blared out from Raveh's. It seemed to catch on in the last days of summer and in the last days of fall. The experts at the Pinguin and the Pension Popper predicted that the tune would keep its popularity at least until the next season. The gramophone needle got dull over the summer. The innkeeper with the Napoleonic bangs decided to add some wicker chairs and tables, and also introduced two brands of beer.

In the autumn the beach was deserted as the summer guests departed and the children went back to school. Only the die-hard swimmers showed up for a dip in the sea during the afternoon and evening. Someone had thrown a hand grenade into the water in hopes of quickly catching a lot of fish. Now thousands of dead fish floated on the surface, and the sand smelled of the dead fish that the sea churned up every day. There was a stone sidewalk leading from the mouth of the Gaston, and because of the construction there everybody had to make detours around piles of stone, cement, and wood. This went on until November. On Friday the eighteenth, it finally sprinkled a little. For the last two nights, Wednesday and Thursday, Kamil Dreisler could walk to the barrels buried in the sand without disturbing the surveyors who spearheaded the mayor's plans. He watched the seaweed, the morning sky, the horizon, and the stars at dawn.

The sparse sand grasses, the clumps spit out by the sea, and the sun-bleached stones, even at night and in the silver dusk and mist, resembled anything he wanted. They reminded him of the skeletons of big ships, wrecks of vessels washed up on shore, or exhausted swimmers whom the waters had thrown high on the beach. In the morning the tide carried most of it all back into the sea. Yesterday, Pharaoh Blumen had said that those who make decisions must suffer. Toward morning, the hours between night and dawn became silent. The light dissolved the nights more slowly, like the sea melts salt. At dawn, Kamil Dreisler would look toward the rocks at Rosh Haniqra or at the walls by the insane asylum in Acre and at the oil refinery. The morning arrived slowly, although sooner than the shadows and the sunrise, and wrapped the landscape, the sea, the sand, and the hills in gentler colors. Beads of dew glistened on the reeds. Between the stones covered with mosses and slime teemed aquatic life: newly born aphids replacing those that died yesterday, crabs, worms, and crayfish. The light dispersed the phantoms of the night and the mists; and the dock and the two barrels in the sand resumed their previous forms.

Kamil Dreisler watched the boat rental and the stalls where they had begun selling turkey cutlets. It occurred to him that a man can be good for the world but bad for himself, good for one person but bad for another, that he can be both good and bad, and that only some things are within his power. All the wise sayings of Pharaoh Blumen were short. Is a man tougher for having gone through what Daniela, or he himself, went through, or is it just the opposite? If a man has two dreams, can he give up one and lose both of them? Kamil Dreisler watched the morning buses at the stop in front of Pension Popper. When they carried wounded soldiers you could hear singing, and the buses would stand there with their lights on.

Finally Kamil Dreisler went to see if Daniela was up yet. He walked by the sea that spewed out all sorts of sediment, oil slicks, and splinters, as in the film about the destroyed submarine. The smell of tar filled the air. A white horse from the Sasa kibbutz stared with large eyes at the sea. The horse stood listlessly in the shallow water by the jetty near the dock. It was a little gray and moldy on the hips. The motions of the man who brushed the horse showed both carelessness and strength. The animal waited patiently for the kibbutznik to finish. The man was in no hurry. Kamil Dreisler presented his cheek to the morning wind. The air was humid and cool, the sand wet from the rain. Kamil Dreisler wore the red sweater with a rolled collar that Daniela had knitted for him.

3

"How did you sleep?"

"Good, and you?"

"I went to look at the sea."

"What is this future you are preparing for us? An empty crate in which you can hide everything? Do you still think that a person can do it like turning a light switch on and off?"

The clouds became heavy and again it looked like rain. The waves gathered at the line of the horizon and found their way through tides to make the shore. Again they looked to her like men bent over cannons, or sprinters on their marks before dashing out. Soon the waves began running in the opposite direction. Daniela looked at her tracks in the sand. The sky stretched away from the land and the sea, and they were replaced by fog, clouds, and a wave of cold air. Flocks of egrets found refuge on the other side of the dock which was protected by the wind. She thought about courage, about shame, about strength; as an echo came the reverberations of hope and hopelessness.

"You're bound to reproach yourself," said Daniela. "You will disappoint so many people, not only here. You're making me ashamed."

She felt that she couldn't breathe, as if it were only a second since the end of World War II and she were still in Germany, in Bergen-Belsen, in Auschwitz-Birkenau. She could not speak. Or did she not want to? Why? So many other things happened. It was the same face, faces. What is it, what makes life a lie? Old Pharaoh Blumen once said that the biggest lie of man was pride. Or, maybe love is the biggest lie? People do lie to life and life lies back to people. She could not speak, nor did she want to speak, for a long while. Now she restrained a voice that was ready to say, Why? Why? Why? She covered her mouth with her hand. She only wanted to add that she would be happy knowing that only the sea lay between his conscience and his will. She felt her heart pounding as if she'd been running.

"I never wanted anything from you," she said at last. "But now I do. Don't go. Write to them that you do not have a passport, that I threw it into the sea. Tell them that I'm sick and that you can't leave me here. Or throw your shirt and passport into the sea so they'll think you've drowned. We can begin a new life."

As the wind chased the gray waves toward the shore, they broke against the rocks, covered the sand, and then silently returned to the sea from which they again came roaring back. The sea made sounds like the crashing of crumbling rocks. The rocks at Rosh Haniqra loomed white as though they had come bubbling out of the water.

Farther away in the sand, a dying cat lay with its belly up and its legs outstretched near the pile of driftwood, tar stuck to its wet fur. A dried blot of blood on its side was covered with sand. The seagulls took no notice of the cat. Again trucks came from the Sasa kibbutz with the rest of the horses that were driven to the sea and run across the road and the railroad tracks. A colt ran alongside the gray mare.

Daniela watched the manes of the running horses. In the distance she saw the outlines of Haifa, the refinery, and the hills of Carmel. When she was nervous or depressed she would look toward the asylum at Acre and close her eyes until an image of the legendary, silent old man came to her. But now, she would force a better mood and think, instead, of the child. She wanted a boy, but she wasn't sure why. Perhaps because boys can protect their mothers. She would consider names. All those that occurred to her were biblical, names of fighting people with great devotion.

She turned to the sea. Why did old Pharaoh Blumen speak of love and endurance in the same breath? Why didn't he say that they were only rarely found together? She thought about the superior forces that make a woman give in, even if she had the right and the strength of ten men. Is it love? Maybe. God? She felt the absurdity of her life, of their lives: The feeling that comes when life is miserable; that she didn't know what to do, what not to do; that life had become a mockery of everything entrusted to man between his birth and his death, such as beauty, meaning, and endurance; the feeling that her life was a lie; that the abnormal had become normal; that life had become sheer punishment, and harbored no rewards. Yes? Maybe? No? Why? She could project phantoms of herself, backward and forward. Everything. What should a woman do to be happy?

She looked at the horses, at the lift-van, and at the sea.

Sometimes the world seems to be a place for fools, some in asylums, some almost free.

"It's raining," she said.

4

The echo of the ship's horn mixed with the low, almost animallike mooing sound of the wind. On the other side, at the entrance to Nahariyya, the November wind lashed at the signs which on one side read, "We welcome you and wish you success," and on the other side "Bon voyage and better hopes."

Whole islands of seaweed floated on the surface, all intertwined, forming sorts of families. The water close to the shore smelled, as it always did in the fall, probably because of the dead fish.

"There was a brief shower at five this morning," said Kamil Dreisler.

Daniela looked at him the way she did yesterday before she'd asked him if he'd at least enjoyed himself a little. But she said something else. "That woman from Mauritius who loaned us the lift-van told me that her husband wants to cover the roof with linoleum so the sand and mud won't leak inside over the winter. . . . I think the innkeeper from Raveh's had a woman in the house last night. I saw her leaving at six o'clock. Maybe he will love her from a distance," Daniela said. "I don't think she turned once, she just smiled."

Daniela said nothing more. She thought about the woman from Mauritius. She and her husband had left Germany and wanted to get here during World War II, but the British wouldn't let them in, as if this place belonged to them. They separated wives from husbands and children from parents. They were like the Germans. They sank their ships and beat them. When the woman bit the boatman they knocked her teeth out. Some people lost their teeth in Dachau, some here. How can one come to terms with such a world? Daniela felt ashamed to appeal to the testimony of the woman from Mauritius with the knocked-out teeth. She should have known all this beforehand.

The sun slipped out from behind the clouds and the light changed. It seemed to Kamil Dreisler that Daniela had a strand of gray hair at the temple.

"I'm sick to my stomach," she said.

"You should squeeze an orange for yourself."

"My belly aches. As if someone were ripping me apart."

She already knew what he wanted to do.

"You'll come and join me," said Kamil Dreisler. "I'll send you tickets for the boat or plane."

"What will you do if you don't succeed? If you don't get it even after a year?"

"Everything." It was a different "everything" than her thoughts remembered.

"Everything?" she echoed.

"Yes. Everything," he answered.

She tried not to look nervous. She remembered that the Nazis sold the living and the dead abroad, sold them truth and lies, took away people's jobs and citizenship, closed the borders and made people behave like scurvy dogs. Pharaoh Blumen knew that it all came from somewhere and did not evaporate like morning vapors over the sea. It was in the air. Should she remind Kamil Dreisler of that and make him mad again? Does he want to exchange an idea for himself, himself for her, her for an idea? She looked at the water touching her ankles and realized that it was thick and salty, like phlegm. She looked sideways at the white crosses blistered from the summer's heat.

"Does it hurt that much?" asked Kamil Dreisler.

He half closed his gray-green eyes. It started to rain. The land became quiet, and the silvery gray meadow of the sea heaved up and down. The water along the shore became muddy. Further out the waves broke in small hillocks with white foamy caps.

"Maybe you'll come back before I'm old, and not only to me," Daniela said. "While I'm still young and unwrinkled."

Grains of sandy dust and drops of rain settled on her eyebrows. The crystals of sand and the rain looked like needle points. Kamil Dreisler saw her watching his lips to see if his reply would be better or worse than she expected. The innkeeper from Raveh's played the gramophone as he always did when a ship left. He played the *Kineret*.

A little while later, all that remained was the content of her words and the dusk of her alto voice. The ship rocked on the open sea. Kamil Dreisler looked toward the shore. Did he see clearly? There was Daniela Klaus, beautiful and proud like a dark red gladiola, walking toward the barrels in the sand. The wind tousled her hair. She stopped and looked at the sea, her eyes following the ship.

She stood with her back to the red oleanders. The flowers were cuddled inside the tufts of leaves, silent and hidden from the sea. Daniela used to believe that the oleanders, in the morning, looked like cradled children; at noon like young, blushing women; and at night like brides and grooms. But that was before the winds began blowing through the bushes on those sleepless nights. The sea's breath flowed through the bush, creating a pleasant hum that blossomed into a gentle voice. It was a beautiful voice that spoke to her, telling her good things; but bad things, too, and the terrible things it came to say made her afraid of the red blossoms.

She stood between the oleander bush and the sea; her lips parted as if to speak, as if to interrupt the wind.

Kamil Dreisler imagined the questions that could not be answered. The sea, the sky, and the wind now spoke their language, as did the birds and the waves. The voice of the earth and the voice of the sea joined with the wind that carried them away. He heard questions for which he had no answers.

At the other end of the shore, but not clearly visible from the ship, stood old Pharaoh Blumen with his yellow straw panama hat. He leaned on his boat, which had been pulled out of the water and looked like a rotting seashell, turned over on its side, with the oars lying in the sand. Somebody else was coming: the woman from Mauritius. For her, land was like a flask and the rest of the world the place where one gets mail.

As long as the shore could be seen from the ship, Daniela stood there alone. Kamil Dreisler could still see the edge of the white bay at Rosh Haniqra toward the bay in Acre, and saw the long boat with the orange trim. Nahariyya became smaller and smaller. From the distance, the land at the edge of the sea and the sky looked like a bluish memory somewhere in the future, seeming clearer and clearer, and already lost at the same time. The oleanders looked desolate. Only the rocks jutted into the sky, and then they began to disappear, too.

Occasionally a flash of lightning cleaved the waters, and in the darkness at midday the drops of seawater glistened like tears. The white precipices would open for a moment, over and over, like a chasm, and then everything closed again like the ravines of all times, and the surface of the water was joined again by the golden rays of the sun. The depths of the sea, where everything was blind, would show up for a second.

At times the sea, the waves, and the land resembled eyes. And the eyes of the sea, the eyes of the land, and the eyes of the waves resembled the eyes of the madman from the asylum in Acre, who watched the sea and the world from his cell before dying, and this world floated away even though it was near at hand. He saw things that had already been forgotten or would be remembered differently by the next generation.

From the northern border, guarded by the old fighter plane, to the bay at Acre, the sea formed an alternate line of straight shore and shallow inlets, except for the deeper bay at Haifa. In the evening the sea rose with the tide and fell again through the night and morning. In autumn and winter, when the storm and rains came, the sea turned gray and black. When the days were calmer at the beginning of spring and in the summer, the waters would become quiet, and the surface would have a blue-gray tinge. In summer the sea had a calming effect, but in winter it was deadening.

During all seasons, little wild birds would leave their nests on the rocks deep in the sea. They would sail past the hulls of ships with hungry eyes, competing only with seagulls, ospreys, or cormorants. They waited for the live prey appearing in the rays on the foamy water, and they cried, *Tee ooo terrr . . . Tee eee terrr . . .*

The sea roared on.

DITA SAXOVA

Everything is possible given the will.
We will join hands,
and on the ruins of the ghetto, we will laugh.
—Song of an unknown singer, Theresienstadt,
1942–43

If a bear chases you, you will be troubled by an
enemy. If you kill the bear or elude it, it is a sign
that you will overcome your troubles.
—*Book of Dreams*, 1948

They'll listen, and they won't understand.
—*Jewish Gazette*

The best weapon against a submarine is still a
submarine.
—*Jewish Gazette*

I

1 Sometimes Dita Saxova dreamed she was naked, and other times, that she was going mad. The dream was like a windblown fog: it departed and then returned. After waking, to convince herself that it was only a dream, she tried to smile. To those who saw her, she looked happy. She was only afraid that somebody would ask her, "What are you laughing at?" And she would answer, "Life is not what we want but what we have."

Sometimes she was drawn to the depths and sat dizzy and still. Other times she dreamed of kissing on the lips a fair-skinned, blue-eyed German soldier with a straight nose. How could she kiss her archenemy in her dreams? Where did that come from?

It was pleasant to keep a diary, but only in her mind, occasionally, and selectively. "Fortunately and unfortunately," as the caretaker of the girls' home in Lubliana Street, Lev Goldblat, liked to say, "thoughts too are like fog and wind."

The camps where Dita Saxova had spent three years were related through distance. Sometimes she recalled how in those camps she had stood naked in front of the soldiers of the Waffen SS who fed on her body with despising eyes. Outwardly, a person at least could look normal. It was enough to hold herself in check and dress nicely. About that she knew. And what she didn't know she could imagine.

She could enjoy her fresh skin and unscarred body, which not everyone else could boast. (She could imagine how she would someday stand against a man—with her smooth belly and narrow waist, her wide, forgiving hips, willing to go wherever was necessary when her time came.)

She dreamed that her father's face was before her. His blue-gray eyes looked right at her the way they did when he was troubled, when they became watery and red at the corners. She said, "How can I know what is true?" But he began to fade away, like smoke, bit by bit, and the image got thinner and wispier, and she screamed, "Wait!" and he was gone. All the while a Strauss waltz played. Then she saw another man's face and recognized it as her boyfriend's father.

2 Isabelle Goldblat's seven cats prowled through the girls' home at 53 Lubliana Street, and the caretaker, Lev Goldblat, nicknamed For-Better-for-Worse, had not even noticed. That afternoon, among the messages he had picked up in the cupboard was an accusation. It referred indirectly to one of the girls, Dita Saxova. Dita Saxova was one of the oldest. Eighteen years of age, she had been living there for two years, from the time of '45 after the end of World War II, when she learned definitively about the death of both her parents and all of her other relatives. Dita Saxova was alone here.

Lev Goldblat was startled by the details in the note. The informer (and it did not occur to him to doubt that it was one of the girls) reported everything heard through the door of Room 16, at a time when the only person at home there had been Dita Saxova. According to the note, nineteen-year-old Alfred Neugeborn, of Krakovska Street (where the boys' home was) had designs on the Jewish Religious Community's safe. Apparently he planned, either today or tomorrow, to break into the hall through the cellar in Maislova Street in the Old Town, climb the steps past the ritual kitchen and the elevator, and get into the room facing the records, where the cashier's office was located. The caretaker first visualized Dita Saxova, then Neugeborn, and then the cashier's counter with the wire grill. There was no signature at the bottom of the page, which had been torn from a school exercise book. There was, however, yesterday's date: February 27, 1947.

Dita Saxova, the caretaker thought, was one of many, and the "lucky one"—or so he had referred to her until today. In his mind he could see Dita Saxova's smiling face, with her teeth all white except for one irregular tooth on the lower side. He thought about her fair hair and blue eyes and her tall, adolescent body with long legs and about her occasionally unfashionable shoes. They were all hungry, for better and for worse, for everything. Their bodies demanded more than pleasure—hidden appetites with anxiety—thought the caretaker about Dita Saxova and all the others. Everything in them was crippled, and Dita Saxova was no exception to prove the rule. One after another and then all together. There were many reasons why.

Maybe the whole world was deformed and distorted after the war—disgraced, defiled, and desecrated—and what people suffered from was not only some blind lack of appreciation but also a failure to acknowledge or a misunderstanding, an echo of abuse, neglected merits of some past virtues, or an immorality in the air, an old plague eating the soul little by little or all at once. Everybody is touched by corruption and shortcuts, fed up, sick or tired, nervous and disturbed, unsettled—you name it— by the sellout of values that were fair before the war but no longer applied in a world where the echo of an indifferent silence had up to this time penetrated from the outside into every corner of this house, and a silent cry spread from here to the outside. What can happen to a girl who, like all the others, again had to deal with laws without justice and with injustices based on laws? For girls like Dita Saxova, the world, as their now-dead parents knew it, ended in the gas chambers of Auschwitz-Birkenau and Treblinka or in some other camp. And the new world with its redemptions came too slowly. The original trust between them and the world was gone, and the new one was budding like a fragile flower.

Anyway, the caretaker thought, for better and for worse, he had full responsibility for this house, and he wouldn't let anyone spoil that even if the entire town became corrupted.

Yesterday a younger girl asked Dita Saxova to let her try on her green jacket just for a moment—just to have a glimpse in the mirror—and then she disappeared with it into the streets. Dita met her downtown three hours later. She took her jacket back. "She who dresses from another's closet gets undressed," she said.

The caretaker could not think about Dita Saxova apart from all the others. Six years of war melted them all together. It made something in them, including Dita Saxova, decrepit. She was thirsty, maybe impatient, for the vanities of life, but it was only a matter of time before the tides would turn for her.

Would Dita Saxova become a puzzle for him? Everybody here was a puzzle. Was she wise enough with her eighteen years to do what would be expected of her? Dita Saxova was one of the prettiest in the house, and not just because she was tall and blond, or because she had lovely blue eyes. People like that can afford to be as confident as Dita Saxova appeared to be. How strong was she? Maybe she was strong. She had survived. They all had. Did it harden them or make them more vulnerable? Or maybe both?

Dita Saxova smiled most of the time, and the caretaker concluded that she had enough reasons to be happy. She did not have to think every minute about the shadows of the three camps she had been in, just like the other girls here and like the boys from the dormitory on Krakovska Street. Some of them had been in seven camps. The caretaker always suspected that Dita Saxova, in spite of her face and her eyes and her smile, was not exactly as she appeared to be. She wanted to have choices. To choose, if not among many, at least one that was her own. Sometimes, the caretaker thought, she had the expression of being naked, completely naked. Her questions were endless. Yes and no. What kind of experience did she crave? He felt the mystery of everyone. The inability to see through her. When he'd seen Dita Saxova yesterday, she was in her white dress and was trying on her long cotton gloves. Was she vain? Innocent? Yes, to a degree. How do you deal with young people like Dita Saxova or Neugeborn, who had witnessed killing the way others watched birds in the air or tightrope walkers in a circus or rain or sunshine or fish in a pond?

Dita Saxova had told him long ago her theory about killing or being killed, and of her suspicion that man is gifted with the ability to kill even without reason. She always smiled. "None of us is in one piece, dear Mr. Goldblat. There is, in all of us, a bit of a con man who returned from the camps. Isn't that so? Maybe we are all con artists."

Another time she told him, "Everybody who lives after the camps lives in place of someone else. They did not kill me because they were busy killing others: Dutch, German, Polish, and Italian Jews—and non-Jews. But don't worry. I refuse to feel guilty about that. Just a little awkward." And Dita gave him her lovely, clever smile, as if her innocence would become a license not to be so innocent.

But even what she disapproved of, what disappointed her, the inability to change the past, impropriety, the inconvenience of her own past, of the past of other girls and boys, unfortunately for better and for worse—it was not just a little game with words. "There is no redemption for the punishment of death, for instance. And anyway, life is not what we want but what we have."

Maybe, the caretaker thought. "Dita Saxova, choice is not what we need or want but what we can do." Perhaps. Did Dita Saxova indulge in debates about killing with or without reason? Did she see herself being killed in her mind as one hears an old and aging echo? How much did she believe that the war was definitely over? Or what kind of war was she led by now? What game did she play with the boys from Krakovska Street?

The caretaker had just passed through the school kitchen, which, after the war, had been converted into an apartment. Like most of the houses in Lubliana Street, it was old, built around the turn of the century. It had four floors, an attic, and extensive cellars that had been connected with Legerova Street during the period of the air-raid warnings. Before the war the house had belonged to the religious community. During the war the Nazis had used it to store prayer books and other forbidden literature, as well as musical instruments—harps, pianos, clarinets, and so on. The house had served as a hostel for German Red Cross nurses passing through Prague in military convoys on their way to the eastern front and back.

"Has anyone been asking for Dita?" Lev Goldblat asked his wife.

"Someone from the office of statistics. I suppose she had put in an application for something, and the guy came to follow up on it."

"Didn't you ask what he wanted?"

Isabelle raised her head in surprise. She had deep brown eyes and a long face, like a horse. "You look terrible, Lev. Have you dropped in for a chat or something?"

The anonymous letter pointed out that Alfred Neugeborn, otherwise known as Fitzi, a third-year locksmith's apprentice, might ruin his whole future if he went through with the theft. The letter added that Dita Saxova was not what she seemed, in spite of her grown-up smile and the guise she wore. Was she really such a rock of Gibraltar? If anyone bothered to calculate her record of absenteeism in the Community Records Office when she had worked there, and at the School of Applied Arts, where she had enrolled after quitting Records, it would be obvious that Dita Saxova was nothing but an out-and-out parasite.

Between the soup and the main dish (as usual in winter, Isabelle served carp on Fridays), the caretaker mentally ran through the list of girls while he pretended to watch carefully for bones. He thought to himself that he could not let it pass as if nothing had happened. The girls here had seen death in too many forms—and many things worse than death. Their whole attitude toward life had been changed. They could not believe anything really belonged to them, as if they had bought an expensive watch and then had taken no interest in whether it kept proper time, just kept it so they could have something nice to look at.

"The water's come on again at last," said Isabelle Goldblat. "It's been some time since I've heard it. You must have nerves of steel. Listen to that awful racket."

"For better, for worse," answered the caretaker.

"Nobody's an angel here."

"Everyone here is a saint," objected the caretaker.

"After what they left behind?"

He could think of nothing but Dita Saxova. A week ago at a meeting of the Cultural and Educational Committee (she did not belong to the Religious Committee), she had proposed that the community purchase an original Chagall for the big room downstairs where there occasionally was dancing on Saturday afternoon or evening. She had a reputation for stinging remarks. When Mr. A.F. had talked about the efforts of the Czech government in exile in London, instead of a question she handed him a note with a Chinese proverb: The more you say, the less people remember. In response to her disarming smile, Mr. A.F. had answered with a French proverb, saying that a smiling face is no proof of happiness. "Chère amie," he added, "Ce n'est pas être bien aisé que de rire." In the end, he invited her to lunch. She ordered roast duck. Then, at home, she said, "After all is said and done, no restaurant can put together dinner like a good cook can herself. It's not even the cost of someone else's work. It's that creating food is an act of love. Letting someone else make your dinner is sort of like letting someone embrace a lover in your place. Even if you ultimately get the credit for it, it's not the same as having done it yourself."

She had her bad jokes. "Dying is easy," she said. "It's only the last few seconds, and then it's over. If you don't have to work too hard for it, who cares?" She actually seemed convinced that dying swiftly and effortlessly was a tremendous entertainment and advantage. Did she really think she could get away with anything and everything just because she was so pretty, tall, and alive? Once she'd said, "There is always someone who would be glad to kill you without needing a reason. People love killing without reasons."

Yesterday she said to old Munk, "I guess maybe we all need people to tell us how wonderful we are and then act as if they believe it. I must be starved for love. I always seem to need so much of it and always feel I get less than my fair share. I think I expect too much. I think I am appreciated, but love—I really feel that only once in my life was anyone ever really devoted to me through no doing of my own. Not because of how wonderful I was or because of what I did or thought. Just because, that's all. When you love your parents, everything is simple. Somewhere along the line I changed roles from the served to the server. It's time to get some self-confidence and self-worth back and let the pendulum return to neutral. I'm worth it. I just have to feel it in my heart, and then maybe it will be true." And then she sighed, "My freckles have come out—but of course, what can I do about it anyway? Men have always told me that they like freckles. But after all, what else are they going to say to a girl who has them if they like the girl?"

Before the war ended none of them anticipated what would happen to them or what would come about, and they were coddled because they had survived at the expense of others who had not. The caretaker wouldn't like to see what they might have had in front of their eyes, whether they closed them or kept them wide open. But he wanted them to know what he himself knew, that no past offers a justification: the most it can do is explain. Last year in early spring Dita disappeared for three days. She went to visit Theresienstadt, where she had spent two years during the war with her mother and father until, in 1943, they were separated, and each had traveled independently in a transport of five thousand people to Auschwitz-Birkenau bei Neuberun. From her recent visit she brought back some shoes with cardboard soles, picked up as a talisman. One day she even wore them on a trip to City in Wenceslas Square, where young people gathered together as they had done at the beginning of the war. She seemed to be very indiscriminate in her choice of company there.

Besides that, it was said she'd had an affair with a gigolo from the local Jewish bar—more precisely, from the bar that had been open in wartime only to the "inferior races," the Café Ascherman in Dlouhá Street. After the war for some reason it had continued to maintain a predominantly Jewish clientele. The gigolo was an Austrian who earned his living as a ski instructor. Someone said that when Dita had come into the bar with Mr. A.F., the gigolo had made eyes at her. When she went to the bathroom he accosted her and invited her to spend three days in the mountains. He would teach her to ski if she didn't know how or perfect her style if she had skied before.

If one judged on the basis of who talked most about it, Linda Huppert was the one most likely to know the details. But that was the very reason why the caretaker doubted the story.

The gigolo was said to be a former Austrian champion in slalom and downhill racing, although it seemed doubtful. Apparently he had taken Dita to a mountain lodge and had fed her sumptuously every evening. He had also promised to reveal to her the difference between a boy and a man. According to Linda Huppert, his age was somewhere between twenty-one and thirty-one. Afterward he allegedly tried to get money out of Dita for the skiing lessons, but because she didn't have any, she declined to pay, and so he taught her for nothing. They say he skied down steep slopes like a dancer. By his skiing expertise he had won Dita's heart. When she declined to go to bed with him, he asked her at least to spend the evening with him. The gigolo had drunk heavily, which was presumably why Dita returned a day early. Apparently he was reticent at first, but eventually he admitted that he lived with older women and taught them to ski or just kept them company, and let them pay for it.

The whole story was laced with hints, innuendos, and assumptions. But it occurred to the caretaker that things had not really been like that. It *could* have happened, even though he knew the reason for Dita's absence. During the visit to Theresienstadt she had caught cold and had almost developed pneumonia. Usually she seemed happy, but there was something in her that seemed to make her afraid.

For a moment he imagined Dita Saxova on the mountains with the unknown man. Her spunk might have been mistaken for strength, and her smile for self-possession, or maturity. Following the unwritten law of the house, the caretaker did not ask needless questions. (One thing leads to another.)

Immediately after the war Dita had been employed under Professor Erich Munk (spats, tie askew, and myopic eyes behind glasses perched halfway down his nose). She constantly complained that slaving among old documents was not her idea of fun. To Munk she confided that sketching was what she most wished to do. But she admitted that she had more inclination for it than talent. She was eighteen then but often spoke or acted like twenty-five. Once someone—also anonymous—gave the caretaker her secret letters. He let old Munk read them. They were strange letters, mostly about her dreams. About men. About nonexistent love affairs—very open. Then he put all of them back in her room one day when she was out. Maybe it would have been better if he had burned them. Who knows?

Her roommates in number 16 were Brigitta Mannerheim and Liza Vagner. Brigitta—also known as Brita, Holy Virgin, or sometimes Great Britain—had acne and stout arms and legs. She used to spend two days in bed every month as if she were really ill, blaming it on her cramps, backache, skin problems, and a monthly change of personality that she couldn't control. The caretaker imagined Liza, with a nose like the blade of a fireman's ax and a wide mouth with thin, blue-tinted lips. In the first autumn after the war she had had an affair with the local doctor, who had since been relieved.

Next door, in Room 15, was Linda Huppert, the stepsister of D. E. Huppert. She was a second-year apprentice at Schiller, a dressmaking salon on the corner of Lubliana and Legerova streets. Some time ago Miss Huppert had taken a box of clothing from Andy Lebovitch, one of Neugeborn's friends, and sold it to a used clothing shop before he came home that evening. She was quite capable of selling off the whole street. One day she had an argument with Dita, who ended it by retorting that even a gigolo (who was, incidentally, neither a murderer nor a thief) might still be elegant and daring, even if his morals were a bit flexible—unlike a certain person, who lacked the first two qualities but went in for the third in a big way. Anyway, what was wrong with a pragmatic approach, where you adjust the rule to fit the situation?

Linda's roommate was Tonitschka Blau, nicknamed the Mummy, owing to her inclination to become speechless when faced with delicate topics. Beside each other she and Dita looked like a feminine version of the comedians, the tall and short Pat and Patachon. Toni Blau was the smallest of the girls. During the war she had been raped. Sometimes she screamed in her sleep, uttering incomprehensible phrases into the darkness.

Apart from that, the caretaker recalled some other incidents. One day Dita Saxova lost a letter from an unsealed envelope. Someone tacked it up in the shower room. She had written that it was a mistake to confide in people who were in trouble themselves. A different quality flowed in every one of her veins. You couldn't tell in advance what she might do. They were all developing like children, despite the fact that they hadn't been children for a long time.

And Alfred Neugeborn? What did the caretaker know about him? The caretaker of the home at 27 Krakovska Street, Mr. Traxler, used to send him on all kinds of errands, so that he earned more than the others. He had repaired the water pipes and stair piling in the Lubliana house, though both really needed to be replaced. That job could not be postponed indefinitely.

The caretaker could not recall anyone's having to pay Neugeborn, nor had he asked for payment. As they say, For advice, go to an older person, but to get anything done, young people are a better prospect.

It was only possible to hazard a guess at where their ideas came from and what exactly those ideas were. Did they think that they would get away with everything tomorrow because of where they had been yesterday? They recalled the past and how the world had been ready to forget more quickly, or even to deny what had happened. Yes and no.

The caretaker opened the window. He could hear voices coming from the street, the stairway, the showers, and the rooms. He would have preferred the noise to be confined to the usual gramophone records, games, musical chairs, pillow fights, and forfeits. He tried to distinguish the voices. He thought he detected Dita's singsong voice: "I've never heard of tears for no reason. There are reasons that people can't see, because they lie below the surface, like water or oil. There are genuine reasons: it's just that you can't put your finger on them. Women's reasons, delicate or even doubtful inner reasons." Then he heard something he could not make out, and then again Dita: "Whenever he looked at me, I always used to smile as mysteriously as I could. Or else I'd burst into laughter. I couldn't stop myself. I can't explain it. Then I died. Only then did I wake up." Another voice said, "You're *really* off the deep end."

"For better, for worse," the caretaker said, and he shut the window. He imagined Dita Saxova in her room with a lace cloth over her head and around her shoulders, moving in slow motion to some protest song, with her hands folded under her chin like a young sorceress. "We're all mad," he thought, "for better, for worse. Nobody loses his sense of self-esteem, even if he goes to jail for forgery."

"Patience," he rebuked himself. It took three times as much effort to understand what was expected and appropriate, perhaps because up to that time they had managed to survive by inappropriate behavior. They had their own yardstick and rules, but for them the meaning of words had changed. They spoke with one language, listened with another, and conversed in codes and abbreviations, in what was almost a secret language.

They didn't have an ounce of forgiveness for the past. They could always find someone else who was for them the symbol of that past. They behaved like gamblers, who know how much depends on the skill of the player and how much on luck, chance, and circumstances. They divided people into a few basic categories and did not waste time on details. Not yet twenty years old, they behaved like veterans. For them the world was like a casino where you needed a lucky break and had to arrange it yourself, in spite of everything, every time you sat down to play. Did they expect generous treatment in return for all they had gone through? Did they expect to collect not only for themselves but also for those who, by no fault of their own, could no longer collect? But they had no intention of discussing it openly. They appreciated life and accepted its alternative, death, as casually as breakfast or dinner. But only in their own way, among themselves. They were tense, and sometimes they acted out of friendship greater than they were capable of giving, and sometimes in a way more hostile than they really felt.

"What should I do about them?"

"Shut one eye. Don't look through the other. And next time close your ears to what you don't want to hear," replied Mrs. Goldblat. Yesterday she told Munk that the house needed not only critics but models: that's the only way to do things. She reflected that some doors can only be opened from the inside.

After supper Lev Goldblat played on his battered old mandolin. As they used to say on the river Piave: You can't carve saints out of any old wood. "Non di ogni legno si fanno i santi." He never ceased to wonder how he could have imagined that once the war was over everything would be wonderful, as he did when he and Isabelle had taken down the wartime blackout curtains from the windows and the light had come flooding in.

Isabelle washed the dishes. Then she polished the cutlery she had hidden during the war.

Things got lost somehow, she thought to herself. She did not ask questions. There's no fool like an old fool. Behind the frosted glass of the kitchen cupboard she kept the photographs of her three sons, who had never returned. They occupied her thoughts during the day and her dreams at night. Knives and forks are about the only things a person can ever get back. Even the fried fish they ate on Fridays was not the same as before the war. But what was? The bigger the promise, the smaller the fulfillment.

Later the caretaker hung the mandolin over the trunk where the reserve quilts were stored. He imagined himself back in Trieste, where he had served in the First World War. He had risen each day to the call of reveille and lain down each night to the mournful strains of taps.

The informer's note had spoiled Goldblat's dinner. The denunciation had been successful, and he blamed himself. The whole thing was like a large shoe for a small foot. Some people are old among children, and others seem like children among adults. The caretaker thought of Dita Saxova and Alfred Neugeborn and what was between them.

3 On the day preceding Friday night snow had threatened since early morning. With this in mind, Dita looked out at the sky, the pinkish brown haze of clouds, and the smoke lying low over the rooftops. She went downstairs to pick up the portable gramophone the girls on the second floor had borrowed the day before to play some new records. She carried it up the stairs like a piece of luggage for a journey, then stretched out on the Chinese mat that she and her roommates used as a carpet on the floor in Room 16. She liked to stretch out catlike before taking a shower.

Propping her chin on her hands, she began to glance through Brita's magazine. Elegantly dressed ladies smiled up at her from the glossy paper. There were full-page advertisements for cigarettes and wristwatches by firms with impressive foreign names. It was a different world than that of the *Gazette* that lay on Liza's bed.

She already knew that the danger that threatened her came from the past—that she no longer had to be suspicious of everyone, that she didn't have to withdraw into herself like an emigrant departing for Australia or America. She wanted to shake off the fear that getting attached to somebody meant having to say good-bye. She looked into the communal wardrobe. It amused her to dress up like an actress, in a new role every day—a red dress with a V-neck, like a lady vampire; a green costume from *Rusalka*, like a combination mermaid and merman; for evening wear, a black sleeveless blouse and a black skirt; office clothes, a gray blouse and skirt; a schoolteacher's uniform, respectable, ridiculous, light—to confuse people with a profusion of faces and possibilities. Though sometimes it wasn't so advantageous to let people assume that she was mature and capable of anything: sometimes it would have been better and more bearable if they gave her time to grow out of her child's costumes spiritually, even if she had grown out of them physically a long time ago. She found it ridiculous that the worth of some people was only measurable in public. Privately they weren't worth the blink of an eye. The mirror also was a source of amusement. She could make a wise and benign or a willful and sulky face. She could look greedy, questioning, bored, distrustful, and then smile broadly, confusing even herself, and wipe the rest away. It was a shame that she didn't look as nice in photographs as she did in the mirror. Only some of this was logical; the rest was an inexplicable game. She wished that she were stronger like Liza or Brita and that the boys were interested in something more than the kind of dress she would wear to the party, how quickly it could come off, and what was underneath. On the other hand, it would bother her if they saw her as an ice princess.

She sighed. It was a shame that nobody was made in one piece. Or maybe it was better that way? Yesterday at home they argued about the meaning of civilization. Dr. Fitz resolved it. "Civilization means not oppressing the weak or obeying the strong. For us and the immediate future, that will have to do." The doctor was also heard saying, "You can emigrate from one country to another in body. You cannot emigrate from your soul."

Everybody and everything was obsessed with bodies. She did and did not understand why.

It would all fit on the head of a pin, she thought to herself. She liked advertisements without knowing why. Maybe because, like the record player, they satisfied a need in her life for entertainment and wealth, and she could imagine herself stocking up on all the lavish goodies they offered. The advertisements in Brita's magazine, decked with the coats of arms reminiscent of royalty, came from Switzerland. She sighed involuntarily.

She knew only too well what hunger was, and cold humiliation, what pain and submission were. And she also knew satiety and security, stability and pride. She knew how much courage she wrung out of her past fears, and how she would conceal and deny this fear. She wanted to turn her experience in the camps into something she could lean on. She knew that opportunity waits and that chance runs away. And at the same time she wanted to prove, in a different way, that both of them belonged to her because she deserved them, even if she didn't know yet exactly how. She wanted to give the best of herself. In the meantime it was easier to dream about it. She dreamed about what she was capable of doing. The study of languages? The theater? Marriage? The more ambiguous the dream, the more attainable it seemed to her. She felt like the ground in spring that has endured the frosts of winter, like a tree whose fortifying sap rises upward from the roots.

It's always been a mystery to me, she thought, how other

women find love and why I'm not like them. A sense of being different that some men will not respect? There was ambiguity in a man's mind about whether it was right or wrong to pressure a woman when she seemed half wrong, or in some way teasing. Men who become resentful tend to speak as if women are sure of what they want but conceal their desires as a game. Yes and no. Men never seem to realize that women are unclear about what they want and have a right to want. It's their vague feelings that create the mixed signals. It's possible that I could have meant what I said Monday night and also what I said afterward, and it's an unpleasant thing to be torn between these two different feelings. Why bother yourself about things you cannot control? It's a waste of time. What is expected of me? If I'm the hottest thing on two legs, why can't I do anything worthwhile?

In the *Gazette* she found the speech of Julius Schwarz, a community storeman and a former sergeant in an eastern front unit during the Second World War. The speech turned out to be his last will and testament, but it was never delivered to the committee because he had not lived to attend the meeting. He jumped from a window after being accused of joining the army only at the eleventh hour. It spoiled all those glamorous Swiss advertisements for her. She skipped articles titled "Warning against Pollution" and "Before the Day of Reconciliation" and a claim by Rabbi Jakov that one hour of blessedness on this earth was more than the whole of this world and that one hour of atonement and good deeds was worth more than a whole life. Further on, someone had started a legal goose chase about whether an old man from Varnsdorf, who spent the war years in England, had any right to his factory when similar enterprises were being nationalized.

Anger against the dead storeman rose within her. Why feel sorry for someone who by now didn't even have fingernails to scratch himself with? As For-Better-for-Worse would say, those who live in glass houses shouldn't throw stones. No need to envy the dead.

Once more she took up Brita's magazine, but the spell was broken. Fates had combined to decide that her place of birth was 7 Josefovska Street—no noblesse, as Dr. Fitz would say. Life abroad, lived by alien people in foreign lands, both attracted and eluded her. Men say that thirsty people are secret drinkers and that hunger is a great teacher. One day her father told her that there was an American actress named Marion Davies who had fifty bathrooms in her house, each one a different color. What Pied Piper had lured Marion there? When, how, and why? Erich Munk would know the answers. But castes and classes did exist, and entwined in their fabric was an evil fate condemning so many to isolation.

She thought of the girls in the hostel and how they regarded each other. Sometimes it occurred to her what a pretty girl Tonitschka was and what might have become of her if not for the war. Perhaps that was why she kept having her picture taken and why she secretly studied her reflection, as if she did not really believe in her beauty.

In the showers someone shouted: "One and one make two. Don't you have somewhere else to go? Something else to do? Are you hungry? For warm water? You want a piece of me? Don't you want anything else? Take my second blanket—my spare sheets."

Dita Saxova remembered the children she had taken care of in Theresienstadt. She had put them to bed and told them how the world would be someday. The future is always a tunnel into which no one can see, while memory is more like a funnel through which everything pours onto the head of a pin. Men used to hang around her in those days. She did not yet understand why. At Auschwitz-Birkenau, on the road between the camps, she had carried stones with a man who bore the heavier ones for her.

She thought about what Linda Huppert had said, along with the rest of the gossip, about the awful things that had happened to Dita's gigolo. According to Linda, the gigolo had lived with an older woman for three years. She took him to Italy first class on the liner *Andrea Doria.* (As the rumor spread, it became the *Leonardo da Vinci,* and even later on, some other famous or nonexistent ship.) One day he told her that he wanted to end the affair and did not seem very concerned. That evening they went to bed. The next morning the gigolo awoke, but his partner slept on and on. He called the doctor. There was a scandal that involved the captain. The woman had left behind a bottle of sleeping tablets and a farewell note. But the captain put the note in his pocket, so no one ever even knew what she had written. Fortunately she recovered, but the gigolo nearly found himself in jail, and the rest of the cruise was a disaster. Everyone pointed a finger at him: "There goes the gigolo." The captain withheld the note from the police. That, at least, had been a stroke of good fortune. As For-Better-for-Worse would say, what's the use of locking the door when everyone else has the key?

Dita thought about the other girls and their mothers. She wondered where they had died. Which had wanted children? Which had not? What had they expected? She thought about her mind and her body. How far could she go in using them for an end that would inevitably lead to further complications? If she felt she could not do that, would she depend entirely on her own resources? "How much can I rely on myself? How much on men? How fastidious can I afford to be? How much do I really need to be content?"

She had her own secret theory of happiness. She imagined an invisible constellation in which stars revolve in undetermined circles. It was possible to be drawn by sheer chance into the orbit of one of them but impossible to stay in it for good. Stars and people were in constant motion. One might miss one orbit but, with patience, catch another. It depended on how long and where you lived.

She wondered how they were all alike. As an animal senses its own ancestral core, and man reverts to it through instinct or experience or intelligence, so she discerned in herself a dynamo emitting a new energy. It was enough to be alive. Life was at the beginning and end of everything. She had already managed to understand that. There was in her, as in others, an unsatisfied appetite, a curious avidity, a disappointed wariness. In her soul she carried the invisible scars of a life without dignity. Conscience was that modest, inexplicable component of man, the weakest and at the same time the strongest, which succumbed to and yet overcame everything. At least I have something to lean on, she thought.

She thought of the selections she had survived in the camp, of mothers who had died because they had chosen to stay with their children, and of the children who had survived because they relinquished their parents. She reflected that people who escaped the net now were living in Argentina, Brazil and Paraguay, or the Andes. Somebody in the shower room hummed a tune by Gershwin. Dita stretched her back. There is beauty, meaning, and balance.

To how many dreams should she yield? How many times could she give of herself unconditionally? Must she surrender her reservations? All the girls were filled with these feelings. They toyed with them as though they were fire eaters standing in an oil spill. How close—or how far away—was it to every woman? It was easy to tell lies from a distance, as the caretaker used to say. Was it so much more difficult up close?

It was just a step from what yesterday had been an unknown quantity, more or less nothing, and now suddenly it meant so much. Heavens, she thought to herself, surely I am not going to be like one of those girls who endure a new moral crisis every few seconds. The melody of Gershwin got lost.

She stretched out her long legs and slipped her feet back into her red slippers. Forbidden fruit? Is it true that all foxes meet at the furrier's?

She was proud of her record player. It was English, and everything made in England was good. In spite of the exorbitant price, and without knowing its real value, she'd bought it last summer at a one-day-only sale using the money from the Repatriation Office on Hybernia Street. She suffered, with more caution, from the same obsession that plagued Tonitschka Blau and Linda Huppert—whether to save carefully for a nest egg or to spend everything on food, like the others. She wanted, and did not want, to own everything that a savings account promised. But at the same time she felt repelled by living as though catastrophe could strike tomorrow.

She thought about what had happened with Liza, what Liza had admitted about the first time a woman stands naked before a man.

She had her own code of law whereby she decided, according to circumstances, which represented a greater injustice: the letter of the law or her inner voice, instinct, and experiences. She wondered how much they were all the same.

Room 16 was a haven for Isabelle Goldblat's cats. The landlord next door at 51 Lubliana Street declared they took care of his mice. Dita was the only girl who could distinguish Mrs. Goldblat's seven feline beauties by name. She would stroke them with the palm of her hand, rub their fur gently with open fingers, and scratch them under their chins and on their stomachs. Liza Vagner did not like them at all. They pulled threads out of the rug and played with them. She complained that all the clothing would be overrun by fleas. But apart from one case—and that was caused by a dog, brought in by Neugeborn, that subsequently ran away again—nothing of the sort happened, though the whole house had been turned upside down for that one flea. As for Brita Mannerheim, cats were of no interest to her.

4 In the shower room the bath was still occupied. Dita began to comb her hair. One hundred fifty times on each side. She was thinking about what she would wear to the party tomorrow night: a pin-striped skirt with lace at the hem, a belt, a navy blue crepe de chine blouse with a bow, and a red sleeveless vest. (She had sacrificed almost three-quarters of a month's salary for this outfit.)

There were two records that she played when she was alone: "Ti-pi-tin," with "Mack the Knife" from *The Beggar's Opera* on the flip side, and dance music, which recalled for her the world in which her father had met her mother. She regarded her records as her first inalienable property (What a laugh!) and had decided to extend her collection appreciably as soon as circumstances permitted.

She would have liked to own "When They Begin the Beguine" and "Dinah, You Are My Heart's Delight." Then she thought of the songs of Voskovec and Werich, "Farewell Till Better Times" and "Dawn," "The Hangman and the Fool." She only needed to find a new needle (supplied by Fitzi Neugeborn, who could get almost any metal object from his workshop), wind up the portable machine, put "Ti-pi-tin" on the turntable, and lower the tone arm. Wouldn't it be nice to have a life like that song? As a German officer used to say in Auschwitz, more people drown in wine than in the Rhine. He also used to say to mothers who asked if he knew where their children were or to girls who searched for their mothers: "Was ich nicht weiss, Macht mir nicht heiss." What I don't know doesn't worry me. In Auschwitz-Birkenau, when he struck one of the women out of boredom, or

from annoyance that it was against regulations to commit
Rassenschade, he would accompany the blow with the well-
known saying: "Weiber und Pferde wollen geschlagen sein."
Women and horses like being beaten. Yesterday caretaker
Goldblat had pointed out that they had been saying that in Italy
for years.

"We do not matter to anybody," Avi Fischer said at the meeting of the International Blue and White Union of Jewish Students. "Even those who now consider us friends had plenty of
acquaintances and friends among the Nazis. Was it different
outside Prague? What about what's happening today in England? It is enough to throw a bomb at a British automobile in
Palestine for them to stop trying war criminals in London. It's
OK for them to hibernate in Argentina or Brazil for a couple of
seasons. I can hear the Nazis complaining of witch hunts in
America." And then: "Nobody cares for the victims of the past.
Every justice—other than mine—only looks forward, toward the
living."

Into the sound of "Ti-pi-tin" merged noises from the shower
room, the stairway, and from Room 15 next door. It sounded as
though Linda Huppert was rummaging through Tonitschka's
things. For no good reason everybody thought Tonitschka concealed some treasures under the mattress. (Eight months after
the war she still kept a stash of bread, sugar, and margarine in
her bed.) Crista, the black cat, looked down from the scratched
top of the chest of drawers. She spat and mewed. From her myr-
tle green eyes shone feigned or genuine devotion. Was it true
that cats, only faithful to their environment, not to man, could
never be trained like dogs, lions, or circus monkeys? Some
detergent, not yet swept up and put back in the box, showed
white beneath the trunk. Dita gazed at the cat and began to
brush her hair again.

Outside the snow was very white. Looking at the snow, Dita

was overcome with the calm and resignation that older people feel. Fleetingly, she felt a pang of conscience for the morning of class she had missed at the School of Applied Arts. Evidently the word *applied* evoked in her some association that she could not yet identify. She regretted that she could plunge into all kinds of things with a verve worthy of better causes, and then later drop them and deceive herself. The fervor with which she had gone to school in autumn, because it meant getting away from the Community Records Office, had melted away.

Standing in the window, she saw her reflection. A snowflake brushed against the glass. In a moment it would be warmed from the indoors and disappear. Dita did not need to close her eyes to see, in her imagination, "The road from somewhere to somewhere," the "green lake surface," and to hear the tune to which she improvised at will. She might steal Munk's book on ancient Rome. Why did old Munk talk so much about victims of illusion? When she stepped back, the reflection in the window vanished, replaced by a white space to be filled with that part of herself she would share with another, one whom she had not yet met and could not imagine.

If she went out now, the man who ran the bar across the street would invite her to have a glass of tea with rum to show that he regarded her as a grown-up woman. She rewound the gramophone. Music took the place of breakfast for her. She would make up for it that evening. She was pleased with her hair. She wondered whether she had slipped through the net in the camp because she was young and pretty and could work. Perhaps she had been luckier than she could judge. But she knew that for everyone who saved himself, someone else must have vanished. The machine had to work day and night, year after year.

She saw behind her in the mirror the slitted eyes of the cat. Fortunately, Fatty Munk had enough tact not to remind her of the books he had lent her. Thanks to his reading matter, she was able to expand her supply of pocket money. That morning Liza had observed: "If a bar of chocolate was thrown into the deal, somebody might get suspicious about you and Fatty. When it's only books, it's still platonic. Even with a dinner invitation it is still pure."

Whenever Munk came to Room 16, he knocked repeatedly on the door, lacking the courage to march in, as if the girls were in the habit of strolling around in their undies.

"Cut the noise, for goodness sake!" echoed Linda's piercing voice though the wall. Dita paused for a moment and then turned down the phonograph.

5 Half an hour later a small man in a business suit stood outside the door of Room 16. He had snow on his overcoat. He explained that he had come on business concerning Dita's uncle. She asked which uncle.

"Uncle Carl," answered the man. "You've got a nice place here." He looked around the room. "An interesting house."

"A better sort of orphanage," smiled Dita. She flushed. She recalled that in Auschwitz-Birkenau, her uncle Carl had worked in a Sonderkommando, as a dentist, in a labor squad that began work where others left off. ("Remove clothing and shoes. Fold all garments and underwear. Tie the shoes together with the laces. Remove all rings and other jewelry. Those with glasses, put them on top.") On the doors to which the victims were ushered was written the word "Disinfection." There were arrows: "To the Showers." The prisoners were responsible for all the arrangements. They were detailed to conduct other prisoners into the underground chambers and to organize them so that everyone went through as quickly as possible. After all, there were more people waiting behind them, and still more behind them, six million altogether. Sometimes everything went smoothly; other times they had to hustle them, until they closed the airtight doors. Outside, up on the roof, a German soldier poured into a funnel-shaped pipe cans of Zyklon B, which then fell from the sprinklers and turned into gas. After that, the people in the Sonderkommando would open the doors, drag the bodies out into the light, and wash them in cold water. It was the job of the dentist to extract all gold teeth, bridges, and usable dental equipment from the corpses. Dita also remembered the officer in the women's camp. He would call out: "Aus nichts wird nichts. Wo kein Holz ist, geht das Feuer aus. Fettes Fleish gibt fette Brühe." (Nothing comes from nothing. No wood, and the fire dies. Fat meat gives good gravy.)

The people who entered the chambers directly from the ramp were hungry and thirsty. The Germans promised them that as soon as they had had their bath, they would get food and drink.

Rarely did the people in the Sonderkommando offer an argument. What was the point, when those hungry and thirsty prisoners kept pushing the slower ones on, increasing the pace of everything? "Was man wünscht, das glaubt man gern." (People believe what they want to believe.) When someone asked what was behind the red brick wall, they would reply: "The hygiene facilities. Over there, by the chimney, they exterminate lice from hair and clothing."

"Won't you sit down?"

"I have been waiting all this time in case some member of your family contacted me. In the end, I got your address. I am about to enter the Civil Service. Your uncle and I were the best of friends even during the hardest times." The man sat down carefully. "There were heavy penalties for looking after Jewish property." When he was seated, the difference in their heights disappeared. "May I ask you a few questions for the record?" He wanted to know when she had last seen her uncle.

"He wrote to us in 1943 from Heidebreck," she said. "He used a code name. The date was wrong as well. By the time Mother got his postcard, they had all gone up the chimney. It was a so-called Family Camp."

"They weren't there anymore?"

"No."

"They had all been killed then? I understand."

"May I switch the light on?" asked Dita.

"Were you all at the same place?"

"For a while. But we didn't meet. There were 250,000 people there."

"I heard it was only 120,000." Then he said: "What were they told?"

Dita smiled for a moment. "That they were about to begin a new life, to settle wastelands. The men would cut down trees and fertilize the land, build houses and work in factories under German supervision. The women were to cook, do the washing, and look after the children. On the ramp they told them that before their journey, they would have to be disinfected."

From Room 15 came Linda's voice: "He shows up, and I ask him what he wants for supper. Dates, he answered. I don't even buy dates for myself, I told him." Another voice said: "Isn't that a lovely idea, to ask for dates and nuts for supper?" Then Linda said: "What good is love, when two out of every three affairs in this house ends in a fight?"

"Did you say a Family Camp? Did he work there in his profession?"

The man studied Dita's oval face, her complexion like an unripe peach, sharply etched blue eyes, the forehead with tiny wrinkles. When she smiled, she revealed two rows of white teeth. One tooth, the color of ivory, protruded a bit from the regular arc. She ran her fingers through her hair.

"I had the impression you consulted your legal adviser," the man said suddenly. He noticed the record player, the red carnation on the milk bottle, and the Mobil Oil maps on the wall. "A lot of positions have been opening up for folks like you," he said after a while.

She smiled. She recalled how Olga, her grandmother on her mother's side, had once owned a tract of land. Dita had never gone to claim it, needless to say. As far as that field was concerned, it seemed dangerous to her to get involved with something she might subsequently lose again.

Then there was her other grandmother, Louise. According to Father, she never owned a thing. When she was asked about anything, she would say, "A fool has more questions than seven wise men could answer," and that it was better to be envied than to be pitied. Up until the beginning of the war Dita's parents had had a laundry at 7 Josefovska Street. Father had sold it in 1939, although close scrutiny might suggest that "sale" was a pretense, just as in those days there were pretend marriages and divorces.

The man looked up at her. "The danger has passed," he said. "Don't get yourself mixed up in anything. There's no need to feel you are under a magnifying glass. People who bet on the wrong horse during the war are still getting fired from their jobs." He added: "Does the community pay your electricity bill as well?" He fingered the lock on his briefcase. "We have all learned how to survive. We here. You there."

Involuntarily, Dita remembered an officer in Auschwitz-Birkenau who used to say: "Frische Wunden sind gut heilen. Alte Schäden heilen schwer. Andre Zeiten, andre Sitten." (Fresh wounds heal well, but not old pains. Other times, other manners.) And thirdly: "Zufriendenheit macht Glücklich." (Satisfaction brings happiness.)

She smiled at the man. Once she had asked her father: "Why is Uncle Carl so sad?"

"Don't you know? Nobody likes dentists. Most people are afraid of them." She wondered why, in that case, Uncle Carl hadn't become a chimney sweep instead.

She conjured up a vision of her father. During the war he had looked like a caricature from the *Stürmer*—tiny, shabby, and threadbare. Mother had been a handsome blond. Maybe she had married beneath her station. Perhaps Dita had inherited her fear of the past, and of the future, an anxiety veiled by a desire to live in a nice white house. But if Daddy hadn't lost all hope that they would survive, he would have learned to be a cobbler in his old age.

She looked across at the man. Like Fitzi, Andy, or D.E., she had learned to make quick judgments during the war, by faces, eyes, scars, wrinkles, or voices. You had to judge a person by a word, a gesture, a breath. The distinction between guessing and knowing disappeared. One man's life depended on the wink of another. You could tell by a single gesture what a person had gone through or what lay ahead of him. Speech and silence blended into one another.

"Not a bad idea to put you together like this," the man said again. "I guess everything's easier when you're together." He took a packet out of his briefcase. "Miss Saxova, these are sheets of gold foil. Here is your half. It is twenty-two-carat gold. To give you an idea—nowadays they make rings from ten-carat."

He put the pack on Brita's bed.

Dita's throat tightened. She tried to hide it by saying, "Excuse me." She did not wish to betray her surprise. That morning she had cut out an ad for Tonitschka from an old paper: "Aches and pains? Use Feller's fluid under the brand name Elasafluid. Try our rhubarb pill."

"My luck is still holding," she said to herself.

"What did you do there? Is it true everyone had to work until he dropped?"

"For a while I took care of children."

"Wasn't it the same everywhere?"

"It depended. That was a long time ago."

"Did any of them come back?"

"Yeah," she said. "About 1 percent, they say."

The man took one more look at the packet with the foil before he said: "Perhaps everything is relative. There is no absolute moral code." Dita lowered her chin. She watched him almost casually. "Ninety-nine percent of everything in this life revolves around money," the man said.

"At one time I carried stones."

"Really?"

"Thank you," Dita said, and she blushed.

"Not at all. I thank you, too. It was my duty. My way of resisting. There was not one of us who was totally with them. The Gestapo had more than five thousand men in Bohemia. Their answer to everything was a noose or a bullet. I expected you to get in touch with me yourself. I hope I haven't given you too much of a surprise."

"Not too much," she lied. She smiled. She had grown accustomed to people taking her smile as a sign of self-confidence.

"Any bank will take it as a deposit."

"Could I do something for you in return?" The man eyed her for a moment. "A cup of tea?" she asked.

"Thank you, no. I really must be going."

"No receipt?"

"Can't we consider the deal closed by a handshake?"

"It's still snowing," she said.

"Fortunately I don't have far to go," the man answered.

6 For about ten minutes Dita stared at the packet. She no longer felt compelled to think about how many of her relatives could have lived for a day or two longer on the contents of that package. Sad that the man misunderstood her when she looked as if she found the idea of gold teeth distasteful, in spite of her gratitude for the gift. She sighed. That's life, Uncle Carl— the privilege when one survives. Women to the left, men to the right, children in the middle. ("For the last six thousand years no one has discovered a better substance," the man had said earlier. "Who knows what they will do when all the gold in the world is gone?")

It was property. And she had achieved it easily, like everything else so far. She turned on the gramophone again and looked at the package. He had gone to a lot of trouble wrapping it up. What should she do with all the twine? In the autumn of 1944 she had stood before a soldier who was supervising the distribution of underwear. He wore polished leather riding boots and a green leather vest. With a jerk of his thumb he motioned for her mother to move on. Dita knelt in front of him and begged him to reconsider. He had hollow eyes and all the power in the world. He kicked her. She was almost glad when she fell, face down in the mud.

At a little party the previous Friday, the talk had gotten around to Switzerland. D. E. Huppert voiced the suspicion that Swiss banks were stuffed with gold teeth, the property of German soldiers, officials, and judges who had deposited the stuff into numbered accounts. D.E. urged her not to let herself be put off by that, or by crazy Munk. ("Switzerland must be a marvelous country.") D.E. believed the cleaner and more orderly a country was, the more our people would like it. Avi Fischer said they ought to set up a center for tracing war criminals, somewhere on neutral ground. Maybe with certain people they might also find the key to the Jewish-German-Swiss dental gold.

The snow tumbled down on the other side of the window. The sky was overcast. The record droned on in English about how yesterday a maiden rejected her lover under a full yellow moon. "The voices around here echo off walls like in the mountains. At night I hear hooting; in the daytime, this." Linda entered without knocking.

"Well, they could have bought a better house," said Dita. She knew the pleasure it gave Linda to eavesdrop. "You've got blood on your lips, kid. Don't you want to wipe it off before it trickles down your chin?"

Linda wiped her lips. Dita turned down the gramophone. She sat down on the windowsill. The snow fell thickly and reflected a soft light.

"When you tell Dr. Fitz you've got peritonitis and your teeth are crumbling, don't forget to attach a properly stamped application," said Linda.

A shoe with a cardboard sole lay next to the pack of foil. Linda picked it up by the lace. "Surely you're not going to wear this cardboard to the party tomorrow?"

"What do you suggest?"

Linda was in no hurry to reply. She couldn't understand why Dita had not first asked the fellow his name and address.

"War turns people into pigs," remarked Dita. She put on the shoe and began to tie the laces. Linda did not dare touch the packet. She had also not gone to work, for the same reasons as Dita Saxova. It seemed to her that Dita sported a rather aristocratic air.

Last Friday Dita had invited some people over, students and acquaintances, including Linda's stepbrother, David Egon Huppert. They sang and laughed loudly. They had eaten potato pancakes with garlic, prepared by Dita with the help of Isabelle Goldblat and served with tea. They had been listening to her "Tipi-tin":

One night when the moon was so mellow,
Rosita met young Manuello . . .

When the food ran out, Andy Lebovitch began to complain that the Promised Land (in capital letters) was still far away, as if someone there were responsible. To change the subject, Avi Fischer, a law graduate of Charles University in Prague, began to speak highly of the monarchy in Denmark. It did not occur to D. E. Huppert to knock on Linda's door. Dita quoted to him from the story of Agnes, in *The Rat Catcher*, Viktor Dyk's version of *The Pied Piper of Hamlin*. To Dita, the Pied Piper was Mr. R. (A person should not take for himself the measure of love intended for two.) She fired more quotations at him: There is only a fixed measure of love, limited and unalterable. Do not love too much, if you want to be loved. Fischer said that the quotation was lifted from the Apocrypha, at least the "Beware of loving too much" part. The excess love you give destroys the possibility of love you should receive—and so on.

They regarded "Ti-pi-tin" as their theme song. To complete the picture, Dita, according to Linda, had the big blue eyes, the smile, and the support or crutches of the Pied Piper's survivor. Dita felt no compunction at misquoting him. (No one should consume himself the amount of love intended for two.)

She knew the book almost by heart and found in it mystery and deep meaning, promise and inspiration, an unfathomable beauty of content and language. That was what really bugged Linda. With her laughter, Dita Saxova washed away all the unpleasant things about 53 Lubliana, not all of them the fault of its cautious caretaker and his wife, Isabelle. It did not even occur to them to invite Linda. When Dita laughed, she gave the impression of being mature.

Ever since Linda had lived in Room 15, for twenty-one months, there had been no fixed routine to all these Friday parties. Sometimes they ended with dancing, sometimes with silence. Such silences always puzzled Linda.

"Don't you think every girl ought to get an unexpected inheritance now and then? No well-heeled welfare organization wants to pay me an extra monthly salary anymore."

Linda regarded her as the kind of person whose life is so filled with sunshine that she hardly notices the stars, or someone who gets the best of everything just by sleeping.

"Are you going to be there tomorrow?" Linda thought that in Dita's place she would have squeezed more than half a share out of the fellow who had concealed the foil. She tossed the other shoe over, so Dita could put it on. The little packet of gold bounced.

"Because of my elegant shoes, you mean?"

Linda rolled her green eyes and stretched her turtlelike neck. Tossing back her wisps of reddish hair, she glanced at Dita's bed. The expression on her face was of a person whose spirit has been crippled beyond recognition by past experiences.

"Is Herbert Lagus still running after you?" Linda said Herbert but meant Neugeborn.

"As far as I'm concerned, you can have him," said Dita. "Have you noticed that living here is like living in a fishbowl? Everybody watches everybody else."

"I am much obliged," Linda said, answering only the first part of Dita's words. She glanced into the open chest of drawers where Dita kept her underwear. She bit her nails, as usual, and eyed the lingerie, imagining Dita as a little girl walking beside Daddy and Mommy in a broad-brimmed hat with a ribbon, a lace dress, and patent leather shoes. Sometimes she imagined Dita as a nightclub dancer, the kind of girl men of questionable reputation wait for at the entrance, flowers in one hand, a bottle of wine in the other, always courteous, with well-combed hair and clean fingernails. "What are your plans?" she asked Dita.

"For today or tomorrow?"

"Oh, in general."

"I suppose I've still got a little time before I'm driven out onto the streets."

"Not girls like you." Linda knew how reluctant Dita was to talk about her future. How can somebody, Linda asked herself, who is lucky most of the time, pretty all the time, appreciate less than more? It helps to be pretty, that is for sure. It makes her strong and happy, so she can afford to smile so often. For a girl like that, everything is much easier. That's unfair. Who distributes justice? "You've been getting a lot of invitations lately," she said. "You will soon know everything about the best places in Prague."

Dita weighed her answer. "The mark of a really fine restaurant is that the service is attentive but not obsequious. They never ask you how everything is because they know it is perfect, watching to make sure it is. No one ever interrupts your conversation to ask you if you want anything." She watched Linda to see if she still listened. Linda didn't know exactly how to stop her. "You are never actually aware when wine is being poured, water glasses are being refilled, or other items on the table are being brought, taken, or replenished," Dita added. "The food is beautiful to the eye. The light is subdued, and the noise is only a pleasant hum."

Linda kept silent. She swallowed saliva. Suddenly Dita changed the tone. "You are not so inexperienced yourself from what I recall. Maybe you don't even remember them all."

"I even remember when I saw a man naked for the first time," Linda said matter-of-factly in order to sound experienced.

"Who knows what I'll have to do once I find I haven't a single duke in my family?" Dita said.

Linda raised her eyebrows. She thought that Dita talked more to herself than to her. She was sometimes accused of doing that herself at work.

"Do you know that song?" asked Dita. "'Now I'm going to sleep, and tomorrow I'll wake up and won't be so sad.'"

"Is that what's on the other side?"

"No. It's 'You believe that?' And 'Don't know. Maybe.'"

To Linda, it seemed as if Dita's eyes and voice were full of restlessness, fantasy, something mysterious that irritated her. It was not envy that devoured Linda; it was envy mixed with admiration, a bit of jealousy, and an endeavor to imitate it. She did not know what all was involved in it. She would drop comments: "Other people would like to idle away time in the showers or have a bath, only it's occupied." "Whoever goes without a shower, as I read in Mr. Langer, must resign himself to having demons turn his spirit into a waterfall. I can just see my soul washed by Niagara."

"Your worries are on my head," said Dita. "Postage has gone up again, but as far as I know, you don't write to anybody, do you?" Dita thought, "It's funny. I am here physically but in my spirit who knows where? Nature urges us to kill. Education helps us to repress the desire. The Germans knew that long before I did. Education teaches you not how to protect yourself, just how to keep it secret."

Offended, Linda drew in her turtlelike neck. Dita tied the sash of her kimono with its fake Japanese design. Linda's expression hardened. The phonograph slowed down, and the record limped to an end. In place of the record, Dita began to hum: "'Gentlemen, come to us every day.'"

The door of Linda's own room was ajar. A minute later she saw Alfred Neugeborn walk by. His hand passed over the rickety banisters he had only recently repaired. Before he knocked on the door of Room 16 and grasped the handle, he unwrapped the tissue paper from a bouquet of snowdrops. (Linda assessed their value as at least five crowns.) Friday afternoon was Visitor's Day. Neugeborn had passed by Linda's room unaware of her disappointment. He did not know she watched him, nor how glad she would have been if he had chosen another door. At meetings of the hostel, Linda Huppert was fond of boasting, in her whispered voice, that she had almost finished her apprenticeship and would soon be able to support herself. At 53 Lubliana Street she had the reputation of being a gossip. At unguarded moments she was able to dig out all kinds of information that was not her business. Her primary victim was Tonitschka Blau. Very little escaped Linda's eyes. (For instance, Doris Levit, who nine months after the war became pregnant, decided she could get rid of it if she let as many boys as possible sleep in her bed. She was forced to leave, although they found her a nice little place.) Linda knew that Dita had taken care of children at Theresienstadt for a short time and that Liza Vagner had worked in the Delousing Station at Auschwitz. She disinfected clothing with Zyklon B at the women's camp. Whereas fifteen minutes was enough for humans, lice and fleas could resist for twelve hours, if only because the Germans had cut down the entitlement of the Delousing Station to increase that of the chambers. Liza picked up the cans from the German Red Cross ambulance, whose third stop on the way to crematorium number 4 was the Delousing Station. Sometimes Liza used to argue with the man in charge of the cans. As she used to say, you can't kill lice just by blowing on them. Occasionally Linda asked Liza which clothes she had disinfected when the new transports came in. Liza had had all the European fashions from 1940 to 1944 within her reach. Linda also knew about Kitty Borger, who, before she went to Australia, used to pose as a paid model for painters, who overestimated her age. Linda also seemed to be well informed about Doris Levit's two aunts, and the connection between their long spinsterhood and her pregnancy. She knew that in December, Isabelle Goldblat had discovered Liza Vagner in bed with the community doctor, who was later relieved by the incoming Dr. Fitz.

A voice sang out, "Come in," as it had already done once this afternoon. Linda could hear irritation in Dita's voice from a visit she herself would have been only too glad to receive and dismiss. Through the crack between the door and the frame, she looked out at Fitzi Neugeborn. She even whispered his name. She imagined his lips, the touch of his hands, as she told him she would like him to be free for her, to give and receive, or even do more. She appreciated and condemned his lankiness, all arms and legs. Leaning her forehead against the door, she wept for a moment.

7 "All by yourself?" asked Fitzi Neugeborn by way of greeting. "For a while," Dita replied.

"What's up?"

"Nothing. Apart from the fact that the shower is out of order. I'm waiting for spring. Andy believes that when girls cry, it spoils the weather, Fitzi. And if so, once it starts raining, it rains on everyone." She smiled. "What would you like to happen?"

Fitzi glanced around. He put his hand in his pocket and returned her smile. He had come in a freshly ironed white shirt with blue stripes and a plain, wine-colored ascot. His well-brushed hair was wavy, bleached at the ends by the summer sun, and parted on the left. Since he had been going to the gym in the Medical House to box with Andy Lebovitch, he had acquired a flattened nose and movable cartilage. Liza declared that his little snout had been like that long before he had even thought of boxing.

"How are you?"

"My luck is beginning to turn, Fitzi. Yesterday, on Munk's recommendation, I attended a lecture on the nationalization of factories and the rights of the propertyless classes. And on the advice of Dr. Fitz, I found a way to address envelopes on the typewriter at the Emigration Office at the speed of twelve words an hour."

There were about four inches of snow on the windowsill. The cats prowled silently about the room, their eyes like revolving wheels. Now and then Dita rubbed Crista's black fur with half-closed fingers, as if allowing the animal to feel her dormant gentleness. She felt Fitzi's eyes on her. How come everybody looked at her as if she could be naked in the blink of an eye? For a split second Fitzi had her flesh in his sights. Do I look like I'm standing naked, talking, half hiding behind my clothes? Funny, for a moment she did feel naked.

"I dreamed that I was lying on something spongy that smelled like pound cake, probably because I was wearing vanilla perfume yesterday," she said. "I'd forgotten that when you said the room smelled like cakes, but it was firm enough to hold me. I had my hands up over my head, holding on to the end of this fragrant mattress. A man without a shirt—I think he was wearing pants—was touching me, but he never got past my breasts, and he was rubbing some sort of oil on them. At least I think that is what it was. Even with my head up and my arms over my head, I could still see that they glistened as he rubbed. I couldn't see his face, just his upper body. It was very muscular and tanned."

Fitzi waited for what would come next.

"Then you were there, standing at the foot of this cakelike mattress, and you had a bowl of whipped cream and a large artist's paintbrush," Dita said. "When I saw you, your body also glistened. You looked at me, you studied me for a while, paintbrush poised in the air, and then you got down next to me on the spongy bed and spread my legs apart with your knee. You studied me again for a little while and began to paint with the cream, starting with my throat and making your way down my entire body. I felt the soft strokes of the paintbrush and the cool, smooth cream. I felt hot and was afraid that I would melt the cream. And maybe I did, because I could feel it running down and mixing with my own wetness, and I remember that I was embarrassed by that. I was also beyond caring.

"You put the bowl down but held the paintbrush in your mouth. Then you bent down, and while I was wondering about this, the man from before reappeared and began rubbing the whipped cream into my skin as he had the other stuff before. When I woke up I was completely tangled up in my sheets and blanket, and I was clutching handfuls between my legs."

"That's all?" Fitzi asked.

"I also dreamed about the worm tree . . . That I was a sparrow and had found a spreading chestnut tree. But instead of leaves and chestnuts, it was full of wriggling little earthworms. I was hungry, but I didn't go up to the tree because I didn't know if I was supposed to or what would happen if I did. Then another little bird who saw me there told me that I was looking at the famous worm tree and that any little bird was allowed to take as many earthworms as he could eat. But he could not take any away. They had to be eaten right there. I ate and ate until I was so full that I couldn't fly away. So I sat in a birdbath and cooled my tail feathers until I felt better. Then I flew away."

"I have two tickets for the movies this evening," said Neugeborn.

"What if my eyes ache or I have got other problems?"

Neugeborn took Munk's books down from the shelf one by one. They were destined for the secondhand book shop—Hermann Hesse, Tolstoy, and Turgenev.

"How can you be so sure I don't have other plans this evening?"

"If your eyes ache, it's from all these books. What are they all about?"

"This and that. A sort of private Emigration Office."

Fitzi grimaced. Under Brita's bed he saw some of her lingerie.

She usually put intimate attire for the laundry into a case, but sometimes she just threw them on the top of the trunk or under her bed. The presence of Brita's underwear and Dita's pretty face aroused conflicting feelings.

"The first book is about a tramp who despised everything conventional. He refused to believe he had grown old along with everything else around him. The others felt sorry for him but at the same time envied him. He was free, but he didn't have a thing to his name."

"At least he could move around easily," remarked Fitzi.

"The other is the tale of a horse. Written by Leon the Fat . . . Listen, Fitzi, couldn't you by any chance get us a stronger bulb? And a pair of earmuffs for me before winter is over?"

"Would you wear them? Does Munk already know about horses, too?" he wondered.

"Only draft horses, I suppose. In any case, he gives the stuff to me. And I pass it on. There's this old nag who moved like a dancer when he was young, but as time went by no one could recognize the former beauty. They end up driving him out of the stables for being worn out."

"What's the third one about?"

"How people die in comparatively civilized countries. A little idyll for adults. A beautiful woman appears in the dreams of a man in his prime. She carries him off to places he had once seen but had forgotten. He wasn't very grateful about it, I suppose. He just expected what happened. It's already my third story, where the Grim Reaper appears as a naked woman and offers to men something he doesn't usually have in stock."

Fitzi laughed. "We've both had one foot in the other world. We know which world is better, don't we?" He spoke in a deep voice that echoed for a long time.

"Munk always keeps me supplied with fresh fodder. Do you want something to read?"

"I would prefer it if you told me the stories." He shifted his weight from one foot to the other. He took the snowdrops from his pocket, let them revive, and put the little bunch into a glass by the washbasin. From the other pocket he took out the cinema tickets. To Dita's surprise, he began to tear them into pieces.

"Was it a Russian film, Fitzi? Warm corpses, revolution?"

"An American comedy. Technicolor."

"Six of one, half dozen of another." She tossed back her hair. "What's the difference?"

Fitzi sat down on Brita's bed. "What kind of shoes do you have on?"

"You're the third person to ask me that today."

Black-haired Crista turned her green eyes to Fitzi and dug her claws into the cuff of his trousers. Neugeborn kicked her away.

Dita sat down beside him. "Do you think it's an advantage, Fitzi, when suddenly there are fewer of us than before? It ought to be an advantage, considering the cost, shouldn't it?" She wondered why there were different rules for men and women. Why were some boys so easy to annoy, and then to calm down again? Why did boys and girls lie so much to achieve something doubtful or of fleeting value? What was it that suddenly swept away whole groups of people, nations, classes, to make room for others? And how long did it take before the next lot came?

"You can't kill two birds with one stone." Neugeborn breathed Dita's scent. Her hair reminded him of the vanilla his mother used to bake cookies. It seemed to him he could almost hear the little sighs of her body. He tried to understand it. He watched the snow on the window, packing itself tightly, embracing everything he wanted, everything that gave meaning to life. "I came by yesterday afternoon. There was nobody home."

"I was out sitting on a bench near the bridge tower. When the sun shines I try to believe the world can be as good a place as the best people, according to Munk, or contrary to him, have wanted it to be. I was reading the poems of a Croatian Partisan, shot by Serbian Chetniks in 1943. It was about the Partisans, how the Fascists gouged out their eyes, threw them into a pit, and urinated on them, until finally the Fascists magnanimously threw a couple of hand grenades on them. It was called *The Pit*. As I read, a boy from school sat next to me, opened a packet of chocolate, and offered me a piece. It melted on my tongue like cream."

He looked up at her. "I'm tired of girls for one afternoon," he sighed.

"I've heard the opposite, that you and Andy have your hands full."

Fitzi was silent. Through the wall with the Mobil Oil maps came a hollow sound. Outside the snow began to fall again. There was a muffled, rustling sound, barely audible to Fitzi. At times the window shuddered. Flakes lifted before settling on the glass, melting, and trickling down, before they spread out and finally disappeared.

"What did you do last Friday that you didn't call, Fitzi?"

"Played poker with Andy."

Fitzi glanced across the room, at the rest of Brita's wardrobe.

"Do you play for real money?"

"Otherwise it wouldn't be any fun for me."

"Why?"

"Andy plays down to the last penny. One of his seven principles. You can't play poker for anything other than cash."

"I see you both like playing risky games," she said ambiguously. "Both of you want to win. How many losses count for one win?"

Fitzi Neugeborn picked up Munk's books once more, upside down, like packs of cards.

Their eyes met. In that second Dita sensed Neugeborn's question. She was at a loss, wondering how to respond, until she said: "You're like a cat, Fitzi. They can throw you off the roof, but you always land on all fours."

"You have blue eyes," said Fitzi.

"You're always in too much of a hurry, Fitzi. Are you like that with other girls?" She smiled to conceal a combination of embarrassment, fear, distaste, and encouragement.

Neugeborn looked smartly dressed, as if he had just stepped out of a window display. Well-pressed slacks, tweed light green jacket, polished brown shoes. Generally he went about in a ragged pilot's shirt that Andy Lebovitch wanted to buy from him.

"Gifts from the postwar Mrs. Lagus." He guessed Dita's thoughts.

She pulled the sides of her Japanese kimono close together up to her neck, which made Neugeborn's thoughts move in the opposite direction. She tightened her sash. That, too, she must have undone earlier.

"Who is she? Is she a redhead like Lagus? I thought it was because of him that you didn't come Friday."

"She's a prewar social worker in the Jewish Community. When I was a kid I used to go there with my mother at the end of each season for discarded clothing."

"I was almost tempted to believe that the prewar Mrs. Lagus had survived. Will you stay for supper?"

"For a little while," answered Fitzi. He picked up a copy of the *Gazette* from Liza's bedside table.

"Liza's latest love, Mr. Maximilian Gotlob, ordered it for her. No one's raped her for some time. No duels on the horizon. She's got her dinner lined up for three months in advance." Then she said: "He has us all read and classified like new species of animals inhabiting the globe."

"Some people can do that."

"What?"

"Get it spread around that they've got a good reputation."

"Do you think he was in the army?"

"Does it matter? Some were, some weren't."

"I hope you're not going to hold it against your little sister for not shooting at the German army, Fitzi."

"According to Andy, Gotlob had all the best mistresses."

"Do you mean Liza?"

"I don't know whether he had the brains, as they say, but I do know Huppert fell for him."

Fitzi withheld a sigh. Dita reflected on how it had begun to snow again, on the time, and on what it is that transforms life's meaningless days into good ones and vice versa. During the years that had passed, for Liza, Fitzi, Andy, Tonitschka, had there been some change in the character of everything that turned bad things into good, and ugly into beautiful? Aside from the detergent on the floor, the room was clean. The snow fell steadily. Winter, if nothing else, was still reliable. It was late afternoon, still not dark enough to make them turn on the light, that is, unless Neugeborn wanted something more. Only caretaker Goldblat believed that under cover of darkness conspiracies were hatched. "Il buio favorisce i segreti."

Fitzi began to read the *Gazette* from the back page. "Legal advice. Unregistered inheritance freed from taxes, property and interest. Rates lowered."

"Further down, Fitzi, by the notice about the bedbugs. I underlined it for Liza."

There it was in heavy type: "Bugs and pests with larvae guaranteed exterminated with cyanic acid (Zyklon B) DEPURA. Officially licensed disinfection center." Next to it was another classified: "Learn a trade—the cornerstone of life. For information write to ORT, G Prague I, 6 Hastalska St." To think what some houses used to harbor and continue to harbor.

"Does it matter?" asked Fitzi.

Dita smiled. Fitzi ripped the ad out. He spat on it and stuck it over the Dostoevsky quotation. He wanted to tear out another one as well: "In Prague, Lodz, and back again in Prague, your friendly optician Jan Haim. Health insurance honored."

"You can spit on that one if you like, Fitzi, since you are so keen on spitting. But don't stick it up there."

"Her name was Hermina Lagus," Fitzi said hoarsely. "They were looking for undernourished children. They sent three of them to the mountains. I sucked in my cheeks so they would take me."

"Did they?"

"No."

"Bad luck, wasn't it?"

"Depends on how you look at it." All of a sudden, Fitzi Neugeborn's Adam's apple began to bob up and down. His voice became thicker. His breath came quickly. His Adam's apple dropped, grazing his collar, so he unfastened the top button and loosened his tie.

"What a joke," remarked Dita. "Nice of them to note in parentheses that *cyanide* is another word for Zyklon B. Apparently in Germany now they call it Uragan. We will stick to the good old terms. Forgive but don't forget, as the French say. Man—that word has a noble ring."

Fitzi Neugeborn finally got up the courage to put his hand on Dita's knee. Outside the flakes fell on the windowsill.

"And now you're going to tell me you love me, Fitzi. Is that it?"

Fitzi's breath was audible. "I wanted to ask you something, Dita."

"Is it something I've read somewhere?"

"I meant something that lasts longer than one evening, Dita."

Neugeborn's lips were pressed tightly together. They were not the soft lips Linda Huppert next door imagined to herself, along with the touch of his hand and her saying how she wished he would do more, what a good lover he must be. Dita moved his hand away.

"Isn't it strange, Fitzi?" Dita stood up, and she carried the little packet to place in the chest of drawers. "The longer I live, the more I find people talking to me as a sort of Salvation Army. It's easy not to lie and not to tell the truth. As Dr. Fitz says of us girls in the house, we have no dowry, so if we're not wonderful, he'll at least keep us healthy. If you hadn't torn up those tickets, we wouldn't have missed more than the newsreel." Neugeborn said nothing. "Not even a soft-boiled egg, Fitzi?"

"I'm not hungry now." Dita was silent. "I wish I could understand you."

"I'm just not a good-time girl. That's all, Fitzi." The scratchy sound of "Ti-pi-tin" filled the room. "As a matter of fact, I've seen it once, but it's worth seeing again. A girl in the park resists the advances of a man who wants to kiss her, telling him she wants only a lasting relationship. She has been married once before, and divorced. On the whole, she's not much fun in bed."

Fitzi had a question on the tip of his tongue, but he suppressed it.

"He forgot a T-shirt at her place. The next day his friends found out and teased him terribly. He couldn't explain that nothing had happened. What had happened was just that nothing had happened. In that regard, women's problems are more complex, Fitzi. Different red cells in the blood, different heartbeat, pulse, different skin. And different pelvis, Fitzi, different hormones too. Your 'I must' is only maybe for me." In her singsong voice she added: "When the girls come, you'll be able to dance."

Fitzi stretched. His puzzled expression made him look as if he sought a key to open her like a door or a window. He no longer had the nerve to tell her Andy's theory about the fountain pen: It dries up, whether you write with it or not. Before he lowered his eyes, he looked at her as if he were trying to cross a bridge and had suddenly come face to face with a wall.

"People think I'm a butterfly," Dita said. "It's a delusion. I'm not like that. Maybe I need something like the Salvation Army myself. In the Palestine bureau or the Emigration Office they would have put us all on some liner like the *Exodus II* and sent us off to the Promised Land. Last week, on that bed you're sitting on, Herbert Lagus was trying to talk me into going to El Salvador with him. His Uncle Solly has gone ahead to find a house. Who doesn't hear the Pied Piper's music without rushing after it toward his own Land of the Seven Mountains?"

Fitzi found her words defensive, apologetic, and even truthful. What worried him more was what he did not hear.

"I had a dream that I was walking in a field with you on a beautifully clear and sunny day. I stepped on what seemed like scraps of a blanket, but actually it was the tail of a kite. I called you over to look at it, and then I picked it up in my hands. It was heavy and soft, but smooth like silk, and it was bright green like the grass. All of a sudden there was a gust of wind, and then we could see the massive, multicolored box kite. The tail we held seemed attached to it from far away. The wind blew harder, and unexpectedly we were lifted into the air, holding on to the tail. The kite climbed higher and higher, and we flew. Only it wasn't scary, but a lot of fun. We flew over the field and a lake and above the tops of trees, each holding on to the tail of that kite. And because it was silky, it didn't hurt our hands as it pulled us along in the air, you on one side and me on the other. We laughed and watched the scenery below us with great delight. The wind whistled between us, and we were moved quickly. After a while, the wind died down, and the tail dropped with us back into the field. We lay in the grass, still laughing, and watched the kite floating in the sky without us. Eventually it disappeared, or I fell asleep. I forget which."

"I like your dreams, but I wonder . . ."

"I also dreamed that I was in a dress shop trying on pretty gowns, one after the other. The dress shop had royal blue velvet walls and twinkling lights and mirrors everywhere. You were

there, sitting in a huge blue velvet chair, and I modeled the
dresses for you, spinning slowly around in the mirrors and
reflecting lights. I don't know what I was buying this dress for—
what occasion—but you must have known, because you had definite ideas about the one you liked and the ones you didn't.
Finally I tried on a dress of black silk organza—my favorite
material!—a real ball gown with a tight bodice, off the shoulder
with long, tight sleeves. It had a full skirt and an asymmetrical
garland of red and pink silk flowers and leaves that ran from the
top of one shoulder down to the bottom of the skirt. I remember
now that my mother once had a similar dress that I liked to play
in when I was little girl, only it wasn't a gown. You asked me to
come closer so you could inspect the dress, but when I did, you
laughed, grabbed me, and pulled the skirts of the gown up over
my head."

"That's all?"

"No. Are you interested in hearing more?"

"Yeah."

"I dreamed that I was in a beach house on a jetty overlooking
a rocky shore. The waves rolled in a long line from far off the
shore and broke thunderously at what seemed like inches from
the house. The landscape was clifflike, almost desolate. The
house had a stone fireplace with a long mantelpiece that was
covered with shells someone had collected. The pine logs in the
cavernous fireplace kept popping and spraying sparks because
of the sap. I was alone, drinking from a large glass and warming
myself by the fire. I wore a thick, navy blue wool sweater that
came down to my knees with nothing under it, but somehow I
wasn't really cold. I sat on a rug made of a leopard skin until it
got quite dark. The fire sparkled and burned brightly. It was
completely quiet except for the fire and the waves pounding the
shore and the rocks. Suddenly I heard the door open and slam
shut, and then you were there, standing before me, wet and cold.

My heart leaped because you were ready to take off your clothes and lead me to the fireplace. We didn't talk, but after a while you put down the glass. I remember looking out at what should have been the sea, but it was too dark to see anything at all. The waves still thundered, and the fire snapped and crackled, but it was as if you and I were completely alone—really, really alone. No one and nothing was going to intrude or rescue us."

"Will you go?" Fitzi asked.

"To produce a couple of baby Jewish Indians as my contribution to humanity?" The record droned on. The needle wandered among the cracks in the words about a stolen kiss. "I'd just be a decoration there." She put the kettle on for tea. "Maybe Herbert will call later to say how far they've gotten. In San Salvador they're going to have a big house with a private zoo and a two-story tower, like Mr. Hemingway in Havana."

"Did you ever hear what I did during the war?" Neugeborn looked at her face, eyes, hands, and her long fingers.

"Would you be very annoyed, Fitzi, if I had not heard about it and did not want to hear about it, or even if I decided to forget it? Or would you only be surprised?"

"It would be as if I said 'Open sesame' before every lock and they all opened."

"Last Thursday you told me you were going to buy a dog and call him Hitler." Then she smiled. "A woman who accepts, sells herself; a girl who gives, surrenders. Dress slowly when you are in a hurry."

"The International Red Cross or some support agency in Switzerland sent some money to the Welfare Department. I wouldn't take all of it."

She thought, to make a virtue of necessity? Castles in the air? A great boaster, like a great talker or a great liar, does very little. But she said, "Do you still have trouble resisting offers? Maybe instead of my love you want my applause?" Dita took a

piece of bread in one hand and adjusted her kimono with the
other. "Giving something is not the same thing as allowing it to
be taken."

Fitzi gave her a calculating look. "Do you need money?" He put
his hand on his pocket.

"What do I have to do in return?"

"Just take it!"

"Do you win at cards?"

"Sometimes."

She was tall, as tall as Neugeborn. "You think I'm a whore,
don't you, Fitzi?"

"Why do you say that?" Fitzi blushed.

"Because that's what you think about all of us, don't you?"

"You can't really mean that?"

"No. I'm only pulling your leg." Dita smiled. She spread margarine on the bread and took a bite. She ate standing up. To Fitzi
it seemed as if she took a step back every time he took a step
forward. Was it simply caution? What didn't she trust about him?
He looked at her. Dita had her own three circles of caution that
Fitzi didn't know about and that he ran up against like invisible
barriers. The widest circle encompassed her social acquaintances, the second her friends. So far she had allowed no one
into the third. The third circle extended only to her fingertips.
She was in the third circle, all by herself. The first circle was
general mistrust, which could be dispersed; the second was
youthful self-reliance, commensurate with repeated experience,
which she was willing to share and communicate with people
she had already assessed and from whom she had no fear of disappointment, betrayal, or worse. The third circle, the innermost
one, was a dream, and caution went along with the dream, and
with caution the instinct of all women, reaching far back in time.
There was a difference between giving yourself and being taken.
She was tall and pretty, and at that moment she didn't look so
proud.

"Why so quiet?" asked Fitzi.

"When anyone asks me a question quickly, I answer slowly. And as Brita says, listening is half of the conversation. Didn't you have your past? Or don't you have a future?"

"I don't owe anyone anything."

"What do you want from me?"

"I wish you would say something."

"I have nothing to say, Fitzi."

"Are you afraid?"

"I no longer have to fear the Germans, or even myself. Why should I be afraid of you, Fitzi? Should I jump from the third floor to prove it?"

She chewed the bread slowly, giving herself time. Liza and Brita would be coming soon. Fitzi's offer of money had startled her but at the same time made her feel good. She appreciated feeling as common as those who bathe, comb their hair, and dress just to stay home. She smiled. A shower is a good investment, after all.

That morning Tonitschka had told them how, night after night and sometimes during the day, she dreamed she would be saved by a man lying wounded in a jungle or desert camp, how she wanted to marry him but would not go to bed with him before their wedding night. But, for God's sake, the sooner the better . . .

Dita displayed her white teeth. "You already told me. A man is two things: his word and what he becomes in the eyes of a woman he is interested in, right? And also that he is never sorry for anyone who is sorry for himself, because that uses up all the available pity. And what he thinks about himself is his own business. Even if he makes one mistake after another, at least it's proof that he's doing something. It's a pity you aren't a sailor and I am only a saint. Though I know you wanted to be a pilot."

"My own mother couldn't talk me out of it, Dita."

"How could she?"

"Are you capable of making a decision?"

"Can I still say no?" She spoke slowly between mouthfuls.

"Once you get a reputation for being indecisive, people don't think much of you."

"That's all the same to me, Fitzi." She took another bite.

Neugeborn handed her a crumpled copy of the letter about the bank draft from Switzerland. It occurred to her that he must have gotten it from someone. Who could it have been?

"Isn't it funny, Fitzi? Even if there were crates of books like this, people like you and me would still insist there's a deluge coming." She laughed at the thought.

"One day Andy and I caught an Angora cat in Theresienstadt. Andy gave it to a Dutch girl from Leeuwarden whom he was fond of."

"How old was she?"

"Fourteen, like Andy."

"What was her name?"

"Mary Ann. They kissed once. The cat slept with her. She tied it to her wrist with a strap."

"Was she afraid of the rats?"

He didn't answer.

"Do you mind if I go on eating, Fitzi? I hope that from then on she slept like a log."

"The following Monday she left for the East."

"Don't you think it's funny, Fitzi, how easy it is to find an explanation for everything that happens?"

"I don't have to explain anything to anybody, if I don't want to."

Dita handed back the note with her left hand.

"There's no guarantee that you won't regret it."

She had scarcely bothered to read the heading.

"Will you be at the party tomorrow?"

"I'm certainly not trying to talk you out of it," she said finally. "But it really would be burglary. And I'm not even sure if I am a good-senough friend to bring you a bowl of tripe soup in jail. You had better buy that dog, Fitzi. I would rather see *The King Doesn't Like Beef* in the theater with you tomorrow, instead of Sunday."

8 On Friday night Lev Goldblat just missed Alfred Neugeborn. He had told Isabelle that he was going out late to lay poison baits in the rat traps. Isabelle held her hand to the ill side of her breast. The only certainty is uncertainty, the caretaker thought. Why do people deceive themselves that they see a swan when looking at a goose? He wondered where Dita Saxova had gotten the white knitted coat of Australian wool. It would be more at home in a fashionable spa.

At the hall the caretaker looked around him like someone condemned to wasting his time. His chest was shaped like an emptied washbasin. As long as he was in Lubliana Street chasing mice in his steel-rimmed spectacles and showing his prey to small girls to frighten them and to toughen them up, that was OK. He did not enjoy the role of man hunter. Rats never forget that they are rats. Better late than never, he repeated to himself. "Meglio tardi che mai."

He circled the synagogue. It loomed up through the dusk of the snow-covered street like a listing ship. He knew from experience that when rats are not hungry, they would rather peer out of their holes than eat more than they need. Rats eat each other only when they are starving. The caretaker thought of the difference between hunger and insatiability. Hunger, as they used to say in Italy, is a great teacher. Hunger forces strongholds to surrender. A stomach has no ears to hear, and an empty stomach does not sing. But he did not have to go to Italy to know that a man who steals once will never lose the habit. "Chi una volta e sempre ladro." Young delinquents, old criminals.

Less than an hour later Neugeborn slipped into the room on the first floor of the Jewish Hall, pulled up the blackout curtain,

opened the safe, and inspected the loot. After a moment he
tossed the bundle of notes back. He pictured Dita Saxova in
Theresienstadt. She was fifteen years old, she had blue eyes,
and she passed herself off as a nanny. She wore blue shorts with
elastic in the legs and a white T-shirt with a light blue six-point-
ed star. She was tall and slim, but with developing breasts.

In those days Fitzi Neugeborn led a gang of the Knights of the
Empty Table. His pals would greet him: "What did you steal for
supper?" Using a stick fitted with a scoop and a hook, they used
to take their pick of freshly baked meat pies from a Nazi bakery
under the nose of the German guard. If the guard had awakened,
he would have blasted away at the thieves behind the bars with
his automatic. They were German pies, meant for the casino, the
garrison, and a few Jewish leaders.

Fitzi stood there, his knees and buttocks pressed tightly
together. His will, his dream, and his conscience all pulled in
different directions. He wiped his sweaty forehead and touched
the wrinkle that reminded him of a bridge he had once crossed.
"Ti-pi-tin" still rang in his ears as echoes from the world of boys
and girls for whom Dita Saxova was the little fish everyone
longed to catch. The English words of the song, which he knew
by heart without understanding their meaning, haunted him like
a prayer for entrance into that world where they belonged.

Fitzi stood there, transfixed by the words of the song, as if he
drew from them some new message, or even more, an invitation,
a chance to exchange the names of the two lovers for others. He
imagined himself tossing Dita the packet of notes, held together
by a red elastic band from a jam jar. "Take this: it's for you." And
then, with a casual air: "Forget about Fatty Munk and the wise
sayings of Dr. Fitz. Or don't. Do as you wish. And go to theaters,
concerts, and exhibitions with D.E., if that's what you want. But
as you can see, my intentions are serious." And finally: "Go and
buy whatever you want." That would be better than the books

Herbert Lagus carried around to show off, or the house for the future emigrants in El Salvador, quite different from when Dita went with D.E. to *Eine kleine Nachtmusik* when he himself had been unable to take her. Dita had smiled, sitting next to Huppert, like the wife of Thomas Alva Edison after he had invented the light bulb.

Fitzi felt as though, in spite of everything, he had become a pilot, had gone into a tailspin, and, even as he righted the aircraft, was plummeting headfirst toward the ground. Once he had boxed with Andy, who thought he was going at him too hard and so knocked him down. When Fitzi came to, he was still dizzy. That was enough for Andy, who retreated to his own corner. Fitzi Neugeborn valued strong arms and a clear head. He thought of people who easily managed to have things other people had to attain the hard way. He regarded them with an envy devoid of vindictiveness, anger, or sour grapes. Only he kept asking himself why he chose to prove his mettle by filling up his cellar with the records of people who had ceased to exist. Had his own relatives survived? He thought of the boy in the sailor suit that he had seen in the park. Dita had once told him that as a little girl she used to wear a dress with a sailor's collar. In that moment he saw all the world's darkness, which had enveloped Theresienstadt when he, like Dita, was just fourteen, darkness over the chimneys at Auschwitz-Birkenau dissolving only in flames, blackening again with ash, first hot, then cold. And the darkness within the gas chambers into which they shoved the living and from which they pulled the dead. The darkness no longer seemed threatening or friendly, this darkness that lay upon Prague, Maislova Street, the Jewish Hall, the room in the Welfare Department. All the darkness in his soul echoed, so that he saw and heard when, where, what, how, and even from whom he had done wrong, whether intentionally or even against his will. He saw distant places, strange faces, and always himself next to the action. Chills ran up his spine. Goosebumps jumped over his entire body.

Neugeborn was not impressed by the vaulted cellar where he sat among the old records. They invoked in him the specter of the slaughtered people, as if he walked on top of them. He did not like buildings that had escaped demolition through the Ministry of Architectural Monuments. To a locksmith, they meant a great deal more work. The corridors here reminded him of old people. He pushed aside the thought of how much effort it had taken to return to the workbench after the war. He knew that a much easier way led to the top. And when you pay in a store, who examines the money anyway?

Sometimes there were evening socials in the great hall of the Jewish Religious Community building. There was a piano in the ballroom upstairs. In December about five hundred people had attended the Jewish Community's celebration for the Feast of Lights. It was like a stock exchange of people who had outlived Hitler. With capital like that, they could join in any revolution without fear of being devoured. They expressed their mutual congratulations with a glance of the right eye, condolences with the left. To be a Jew in the twentieth century is a privilege when you look behind yourself, a catastrophe when you see what lies before you. Or vice versa?

Usually everyone was satisfied with the functioning of the kitchen and the service, not that anyone put a high demand upon ritualistic cooking or preparation. The chief offender was Andy, bane of all waiters. Nobody worried much about details, such as how sandwiches, cake, and hot sausages were prepared. Everyone had his own views on that. According to Jewish regulations dating back to the time of the desert and the caves, the souls of animals, even those intended for slaughter, are located in their blood, and that is why the blood had to be removed before the meat could be prepared for human consumption. The young people had facilities, as usual, in the assembly hall on the third floor. Brother Otto Sattler from the Barberina Bar performed on the violin, to Mr. Havranek's accompaniment on piano.

Jews do not like blood, whatever people say, thought Neugeborn. But the blood is there on the plate for them, even when they speak about trees, as when the chief rabbi told how they plant them out of gratitude, a cedar for a son, a cypress for a daughter. What about the legend of how people may not eat from the tree of life and thereby live forever? By now they had eaten from the trees of paradise the fruit of every possible perversity.

Fitzi stood up and stretched his back. His backbone cracked. "I'll tell you one thing," he addressed Dita, as though they had not parted. "I don't care what you think. I've been at the bottom of the heap a long time. Now I'd like to have it good for a while. Wouldn't you?"

In his mind he heard the singsong, carefree voice of Dita: "Good, Fitzi? I want it to be even better than good. But I guess it's no use telling you that a wise son makes his father happy and a crazy one makes his mother miserable?"

Fitzi felt as though the distance between them had grown. Dita wore a pink blouse and a blue scarf tied around her head. She smiled like a grown-up woman. She smelled of soap. He wished she would ask him if he would share his days and nights with her, and he wished he could answer yes. In that single moment Fitzi exchanged the insecurity of adolescence for the loneliness of adulthood, without realizing what had happened. He stretched out his hands toward unselfish love and attained only jealousy, as though it were the fruit of an unknown tree. He wished Dita would either give or deny him everything. Why? He did not understand that love and hatred are like sisters who walk hand in hand. The idea of a pair, man and woman, was linked in his mind with the image of the pairs that Noah had taken into the ark—lion and lioness, male and female eagles, ram and ewe—as well as the image of Adam and Eve. It was as if he instinctively felt the millions of years that preceded his evolution, from tree, bush, or fish, into Fitzi Neugeborn. At the same time he felt like the first human being who had ever found himself in that position, completely alone, the first and the last person on earth.

His thoughts moved to a vision of a harbor, a ship, and a voyage. He longed to touch the face, breast, and belly of Dita Saxova. At that moment, for the first time, he touched her inner spirit. He stepped out of himself and felt the lightness and weight of his existence. Surrounded by the darkness of the cellar, he no longer had the strength to recognize what was emerging from the old husk. Here he was alone. He had no fear of being caught. The long outline of his shadow did not disturb him. He realized that Dita Saxova wanted nothing to do with his mission. Even in his old pilot's shirt, zipped up to the neck, he felt cold.

He recalled how he had been with Dita last July at a lecture at the International Blue and White Union, titled "The Promised Land and You." She had worn a white dress with a blue beret. She had told him that her dreams for the last few nights had been about children, blue-eyed and black-eyed babies. She asked him what he dreamed about. Money? His career? His abilities? He had a dream about an open door in an unexpected place in a wall, where no door had been before, and there was no city there either. And once he dreamed he rode a horse on a long journey. The horse was always fresh, although riders lay all along the road. Before the war his father had a dream of horse riding; later they received an order to enter the transport. He told Dita how often in the war he had calculated the distance between Theresienstadt and Prague. That was where his home was. He couldn't feel at home anywhere else, nor did he wish to. And for God's sake, why should he?

In the cellar, to avoid leaving empty-handed, Fitzi Neugeborn picked up a bunch of pencils emblazoned with blue postal trumpets, which had been made in the Third Reich in 1941, as well as a dusty box of rulers, donated to Prague for the schoolchildren in June 1945 by the American organization JOINT and stamped "U.S. Army, Made in Belgium" (thirty centimeters, twelve inches). Originally fifteen thousand children had lived there; fewer than a hundred had returned, not one below the age of fifteen. In four years the Germans had succeeded in killing off 1.5 million Jewish children. Dita was one of them. She was no longer a child. Fitzi Neugeborn felt he was treading on his shadow. He sat back down on the heap of files. In the darkness he composed a report, never delivered, on the state of his soul: "Dita. I love you as no one has ever loved anyone before. I would like to write it in capital letters so it would shout. I can offer you nothing." Below that he wanted to write: "I swear."

9 By the time Lev Goldblat returned to Maislova Street in the Old Town, Fitzi Neugeborn was already huddled under his blanket, which was entered as an item in the inventory in Lubliana Street. The boys' and girls' hostels helped each other out. The war had not been over long, and there was still a shortage of things that meant warmth, and peace of mind for caretakers.

Andy Lebovitch asked Fitzi: "Were you at her place? Did she give you something?" To be on the safe side, he mumbled his second question. He knew how adept Fitzi was with his fists.

Fitzi imagined Dita hiding in the tall wheat, being shot at by a squad of *Einsatzgruppen* in Poland. The bullets made small holes in the girl's white skin, edged by a ribbon of ruby-red blood. The snow on the windowsill reflected light into the room. Dreamily, Fitzi ruffled his shiny golden hair. A deep wrinkle ran across his forehead. His handsome, worried face under the

blanket melted into the darkness along with everything but
Andy's last words. They hung in the air for a long time, until the
gray-blue flush from above and the white dazzle from below
melted into the pink light of dawn.

When the caretaker finally climbed into bed, he clumsily
stroked Isabelle's fleshy arm. His days as a lover were over. He
muttered something about a wolf changing its fur but not its skin
underneath. Lev Goldblat knew what the official verdict would
be if the informer's note turned out to be correct. No law corresponded to justice. Why? Because law was a stick for beating
them, a rope for hanging them, and a poison for killing them.
The significance of things was buried in the past, like an echo.
These young people very much disliked being told what they
ought to be doing. They grabbed the good things in life, like
apartments with bathrooms, with no regard for the class to
which they had belonged. They elbowed their way into courses
for which they were sometimes unqualified, trips abroad, things
they had once never even dreamed of, and their eyes said: "Well,
so what? Who is going to judge us? And by what right?" They bit
the hands that fed them, readily exchanging yesterday's scars
for the sweeter and fresher wounds of today. They waited with
barely veiled impatience and a secret passion for all the vio-
lence and intensity that had become part of their beings to fade
into history—the sooner, the better. The disorder accompanying
revolution was their chance. But there was another side to it, a
sort of fourth dimension, the spiritual essence contained in a
glance, a voice, a silence, a shadow, or the effect of time. Their
barometers did not measure the pressure yet to come, only the
pressure that had been. They did not believe that a future with
fifty years of peace would make up for the last fifty years of war.
They sought neither treasure nor love from the world. They were
satisfied with a few mouthfuls from any source, but it had to be
immediate. By their ways they had become a living reproach,
and a burden, to the surviving remnants of the Jewish Commu-

nity, and from this stemmed a mutual lack of understanding. It was predictable. The majority would fail to attain much or never live to see much, and this helped to drive them apart.

Even if it was not written across their faces that the rest of the world owed them a debt, it had in fact (at least in the view of Maximilian Gotlob) sunk into their marrow. The palms of their hands were widely extended, their pockets bottomless, their senses of gratitude dulled. They expected every form of aid while at the same time they disliked anyone who helped them, as if every offer of assistance was both good and evil. And even as they felt themselves grow stronger, it reminded them of their real weakness. Like the Arabs, they believed that for every murder there is a murderer. They felt the same sense of superiority that war veterans and invalids feel. They allowed themselves to be fed by international organizations yet acted as if they scorned their officials because they had not gone through a fraction of what they themselves had endured. As if they were trying to say: "Just go for at least an hour, a minute, or a second where we have been for weeks, months, years! If by chance you survive, we'll ask you bluntly how you managed to survive. What was the price? And who paid the bill? Why is it that you came back and not somebody else—your mother, father, brother, or sister, your friend or enemy? Then we shall see how you react." They carried around with them an impenetrable sense of guilt because the best had died. It had been blind fate, an accident, very rarely any personal quality or service that preserved them from catastrophe. They did not believe that only the strong, stronger, strongest survive. Occasionally, perhaps. They saw in the situation an additional element that the world had not known until then. But next to their guilt they wore their pride, and the belief that it was their destiny, a sign of some very unusual human qualities.

The caretaker avoided looking at Isabelle. "As my grandma used to say, "Man wird alt wie ein haus und lehrt nie aus." (One can be as old as a house and know less than a horse.)

"Do you think I'm an idiot?" whispered Isabelle. "It's true what they say: The older the man, the bigger the fool."

The next morning the caretaker showed the note to Isabelle. She swept the snow from the sidewalk in front of the house.

"Good morning," she greeted him, frowning. "In the pan by the window there's a piece of fish left over from yesterday. But sunset and sunrise don't come at the normal times for you, do they?"

"No thanks, I'm not hungry. Give the fish to your cats. That's all you think about anyway. Shall I cut up the bacon for the traps?"

The fish stayed untouched in the pan, covered by a plate, behind the window. The black and ginger cats crouched motionless, like a double shadow. The third cat, striped like a leopard, rubbed herself against Isabelle's cold, swollen legs in their brown cotton stockings.

Lev Goldblat's eyes dropped to his wife's ankles. "Why don't you sit down and have a rest?"

"Am I supposed to start the day with a rest?" smiled Isabelle. "You need to go to the barber. You look awful. Anyway, I feel funny, Lev, to tell you the truth. The best thing would be if you would tear up that stupid note."

She stopped to catch her breath. She had large breasts and a thick neck. Wrinkles furrowed her low forehead, and coarse black hairs grew in twin arcs across her temples, almost down to her eyebrows. "Fortunately, things never turn out as bad as they seem, Lev. Even the best-made clothes attract moths."

The caretaker felt despair mingled with affection, anger with resignation. "If anybody wants me, I'll be in the yard." He set his glasses more firmly on his nose, which was small, like his ears.

"As I said, Lev, tear it up," she repeated. "There's plenty of time for our cloak of shame. I can't stand informers, any more than I like cleaning silver."

"Who's talking about cleaning silver? Or about things going bad?" He asked his wife if she had read in the *Gazette* about the community store owner, Schwarz. "He used to look like Max Baer, the world heavyweight boxing champion. Why did he ever do it? He could have lived to be a hundred."

"I suppose he had nothing left to look forward to," Dita Saxova said, coming out of the house. The snow was dazzling. She narrowed her eyes. "Or maybe living just wore him out?"

"For better, for worse," said Lev Goldblat.

Isabelle again began to sweep up the snow. Half the sidewalk in front of the house was already cleared. Dita had to wait for a moment. "What are our Jewish kittens up to?" she asked.

"I'm afraid they are more normal than people," replied Isabelle. She knew that the girls and boys were children and grown-ups at the same time. Grown-ups are no more than over-grown children. Dita rewarded her with a smile, as if she were speaking, disagreeing, and confirming all at once. She wore a brown tweed jacket with three buttons, a peach-colored blouse cut like a dirndl, together with one of her silk scarves and a jumper. She smiled at Isabelle the way people do when they feel safe. It occurred to her later that Isabelle's smile in return seemed rather forced.

The remains of the fish behind the window were gobbled up by black Crista and ginger Sarah. They licked their furry noses with their small pink tongues. With full bellies, which grazed the white window frame like inflated bladders, they crept to the edge and jumped onto a branch of a lilac tree.

"Look," said Isabelle suddenly, "in case you hadn't noticed, the war with Hitler is over."

"Who won?" asked Dita.

"You can ask Neugeborn when you see him."

"Why?" said Dita. "As I see it, owning a dog named Hitler isn't such a bad idea after all."

I hate ugliness. Ugly people are the first to die.
— Diary of a girl who left Prague for Israel

As long as you have a mother, she will tell you
fairy tales, and then later you will go on telling
them to yourself.
— A girl from the Lubliana Street hostel

II

 The jeweler looked up at Dita Saxova, appraising her. "A bracelet?" Perhaps he thought that she needed a new spring coat. "What price range?"

"I don't know how much they cost."

The man behind the counter wore a gray three-piece suit. Suddenly Dita felt like an acrobat preparing to step out on the high wire. She chose a bracelet at the end of a row in the black satin-lined drawer. The jeweler held up the clasp in his fingers.

"I saw it in the window last week."

"It costs five thousand. A beautiful piece. Shall we try some others?"

"I think I'll take it." When she began to unwrap the packet of foil on the counter, she sensed the jeweler's surprise. She laid her identity card down beside it. "I inherited it from my uncle, who was a dentist before the war. They told me it is twenty-two-carat gold. I would like the bracelet if I can pay with this."

The jeweler bowed politely to her. "In the meantime I'll polish it up for you, if you don't mind. It doesn't happen every day that . . ." He pressed a button under the counter. "This is the first case, madame."

A lady emerged from the workshop behind the showroom, and he whispered a number to her, evidently a code.

"May we inspect your foil?" he asked. The lady took it over to a microscope fitted with a light. From time to time she glanced at Dita through the safety glass.

Since early morning Dita had wondered how she could join the excursion being run by the International Blue and White Union that summer. According to the *Gazette,* students would get top priority. She planned to get rid of the gold over the next four weeks and then fall back on her own resources in the same hunt for prey as the rest of the girls at 53 Lubliana.

The lady got up from the microscope, brought back the foil, and left again. She had attached a record of the weight and the number of carats with strong thread. It crossed Dita's mind that the use of code numbers by the jeweler and the lady was like Cabala.

"You may take the bracelet. There is money left over. Ten foils would be enough. If you like we can pay you the rest in cash."

"Give me six pieces of foil and the rest in cash."

"You have lovely blue eyes," observed the man behind the counter.

"I would like to have something engraved on the inside. A motto of mine. It's very short."

The jeweler took out a writing pad and unscrewed the top of his fountain pen. "Luckily our engraver is here today."

"D.S. 21 III 1947," Dita dictated. "Life is not what we want but what we have."

On National Street men turned around to eye her. Dita thought about Brita's saying: Woman is an elegant creature. She rejects men before they can reject her. Brita never blames herself when a boy lets her down. She doesn't keep calling him; she just lets go. Brita isn't dazzled by the arrogance of boys. (Of course, she told Andy yesterday evening, "I like it, even when I'm not with you. I like mashed potatoes even more.") My goodness, I'm not so innocent myself. A pair of lovers passed her. They walked with their arms around each other's waists. Some things need no explanation. In her mind she played her secret game; which one might walk by her side—D. E. Huppert or Fitzi Neugeborn—equally close to her? But neither of them, like their predecessor Herbert Lagus, yet represented for her that "green lake" or "the path from somewhere to somewhere else." She thought about them as girls think about boys before there is any "consuming passion," when one boy is as good as another. Fitzi cared for her. But how deep did his inner urge go? How long would it last? What would be the payoff? And where would it lead her? That reminded her of being fed with the crumbs of others, maybe luckier ones, and she wanted to get her portion independently of theirs. It's humiliating, inconvenient. Very inconvenient.

It was a sunny March day. The winter had been unusually long, but last Saturday the sun had melted the snow, the wind had turned warm, and suddenly it was spring. The wind had brought rain, and just as quickly the mud had disappeared from the sidewalks. On such days—and sometimes on Sundays—she felt something she couldn't express. She thought of Andy Lebovitch. Andy was like a bitch: he could do it with anybody. He belonged to that category of person who thinks that because he has survived, nothing can ever happen to him. If the world should accidentally and suddenly come to an end, people like him would be the last to go. The way she thought about Andy was like peeling away the layers of an onion. Andy remembered only the good things that happened to him. (Maybe Andy's memory was like a piece of Swiss cheese.) The way he told it, Auschwitz-Birkenau might have seemed, in retrospect and at a proper distance, like a holiday camp for Jewish volunteers from Europe. He would relate to the uninitiated how he stood on the ramp, or by the concrete posts of the fence—electrified to stop wolves and foxes from getting in—and listened to the *Horst Wessel Lied* alternately played by a female or male Jewish orchestra in front of the entrance to the barracks showers, as if he had been a few steps from a garden restaurant, or how he used to play soccer against a team of German noncoms serving there. Or how he once slipped across the tracks at Auschwitz-Birkenau into the orderlies' quarters, where there was a film of bombers over Louvain. Needless to say, he failed to mention that the orchestra played for people who were about to receive their ration of Zyklon B instead of water. And that among them were people with injuries from being kicked in the shins before the German referee blew his whistle at the end of the soccer match. If Andy had not forgotten the worst things, he did not bother people with them.

In Theresienstadt, when Andy had been two months short of sixteen, he had been initiated into the secrets of physical love by a twenty-year-old half-Jewish prostitute from a German circus, who had worked alternately as a bareback rider and a cashier. Andy claimed that an artist, brought to Theresienstadt with a Dutch transport, had painted her picture in oils. He had lost track of her somewhere in Poland. The portrait had, of course, disappeared, along with the artist.

For Andy, she was the most beautiful of all the women he had ever known. He claimed that she looked like Mata Hari. Later she put on weight; still later she became terribly shrunken. In retrospect, he still loved her, he said, not only for being kind to him and for teaching him but also because she foresaw that he would be successful with girls.

Dita smiled. There was warmth in the sunshine. Could you really believe people who were recounting their pasts? Was it true that peace joins what war divides? Andy's carefree nature, his manners and behavior—a mixture midway between brashness and shyness—brought her closer to him every day. It was a pleasure to listen to him chat with Brita. "Is it true that when you get excited all the blood rushes from your head to your waist? And that's why it's impossible to talk to you normally?

And isn't that what happens to girls later, when the boy's blood has all gone back to his head, and all his senses are operating again? Doesn't your blood all collect between your legs?"

He combined incisiveness with roughness and unfailing impoliteness, plus goodwill and lack of continence. She appreciated Andy's friendly manner. But it was more a kind of appreciation than an interest in one of the available boys. It occurred to her that she measured the first one by the second by the third.

Andy Lebovitch figured that he had risen from the dead, and he claimed the right to do anything, as far as the feminine half of humanity was concerned. During the selection of old people and children in Birkenau in the fall of 1944, Lebovitch had gotten as far as the showers. (Selection took place mostly on Mondays.) They were ordered to undress quickly and go forward into disinfection. There was a German officer with them, drunk on vodka. He amused himself with them: Although during the flood they had learned how to breathe for forty days under water, he was curious to know how they would survive the next five minutes. "Der Teufel ist nicht so schwarz, wie man ihn hält. Von zwei Übeln soll man das Kleinste wählen. Besser das Kind weint, als die Eltern." (The devil is not as black as he is painted. One should choose the lesser of two evils. Better that the child should cry than the parents.) Later he would confine himself to sharing his proverbs with the Sonderkommando.

But something had gone wrong. The officer ordered the airtight doors opened. He told them to get dressed again, and the people in the Sonderkommando were sure they would be shot, though they did not say so. No one yet had come out of the chambers alive. They used to say that when the floor was wet, the pellets of gas did not dissolve properly and the quality of the Zyklon B was beneath criticism. Sometimes there was not enough of it, and not only because during the last year of war the Nazis economized on gas cones.

On such a sunny day as this the crystals would have dissolved beautifully, thought Dita. A postman with his bag smiled at her. Before he disappeared into a house, she returned his smile—the kind girls use to signal that they are not married. Friday evening at Room 16 Andy had described what happened.

That Monday, in the silence before the roar, a noise came from the shower heads in the ceiling, like mice scratching, and instead of water, crystals of cyanide began to fall through the sprinklers. That Monday it had been raining from dawn to dusk, and water had gotten into the showers. There were big pools on the concrete, and outside the rain poured down. After a while, Andy said, it sounded like rocks crumbling. Or sand poured into the wind. Or the tide coming in an invisible sea. In the remaining light, they could see the concrete ceiling that had been scratched out by the fingernails of people before them—married couples, families with children, whole clans, villages, towns, the whole of Jewish Europe. Rarely did the supply of gas cylinders from the Degesch Company fail, as it did that Monday. The scratches and marks were like stars or burned-out suns, someone portraying the birth or death of stars, strange writings or indecipherable hieroglyphics. According to Andy, they were the marks left by those who had climbed up to the ceiling on the backs of the smaller and weaker ones. From them you could read only screams, dying twitches, the gasping for air of dumb, futile mouths, the dribbling of saliva. The densest cluster of corpses lay by the door. When everything was quiet, and the people from the Sonderkommando had removed the belongings of the dead, the greediest among the Germans would begin to count the gold, cash, and precious stones, the valuable papers and the pearls of rich men and great ladies, jewels hidden in the cigar cases of men and the lockets of women, gold teeth, concealed and discovered treasures in linings, padding, dress shields, and hems sewn into underwear and other garments in better times.

The most callous of the Jewish Sonderkommando, together with selected prisoners from the Red Army, first dragged the dead away to the furnaces. Only then did they begin to count their much smaller loot. As the Germans used to say: "Der Tod hat keinen Kalender. Alte Mauern fallen leicht." (Death works to no calendar. Old walls fall easily.) There were clothes and shoes earmarked for the sweethearts and friends of the men in the Sonderkommando in the Frauen Koncentration Lager, or sometimes for mothers and sisters or fathers and brothers. They had just helped to push the others into the underground structure. Sometimes they had tried to calm them down, maybe by offering a drink of water. When it was all over, they would say a prayer for them. One shift ran from five in the morning until five in the evening; the other, from five in the evening to five in the morning. They ate eggs and bacon and washed it down with vodka.

Andy Lebovitch divided the people in the Sonderkommando into three categories: cynics, bastards, and saints. They had tough luck. He did not forgive them, nor did he blame them. They never volunteered. He conceded that a crime is a crime, even if extenuating circumstances rise above Mount Everest. They did nothing of their own volition. They were not even allowed to smuggle themselves into the ranks of the condemned, which would endanger the operation and, with it, their fellow prisoners. They were replaced only on German orders, sometimes after a few days, sometimes after five weeks or, in some cases, two years, just as they had earlier replaced their slaughtered predecessors. ("Whenever I try to remember anything, my imagination conjures up things I'd rather forget." Dita replied that for her it was the other way around.) It is impossible to be just and to acquit any of them. Andy acquitted no one.

Andy counted it as his greatest stroke of luck during the war that he didn't go into the Sonderkommando. *Even if* and *even though* were the words most commonly used by Andy in connection with the Sonderkommando. "Who knows what it was really like?" Hundreds of people apparently survived the Sonderkommando—those the Germans didn't manage to kill—and they scattered all over the world. Mostly they were unwilling to talk about it, at least not yet. Andy knew one of them in Prague; he used to come to see Andy when he was boxing with Neugeborn at the Medical House. This man used to say that to turn a man into a beast is not difficult. It is enough to deny him food for three weeks. He becomes deadened and behaves like an animal. Period! They alone know what *period* means. Like a split atom, an unquenchable sense of guilt, a helpless anger, resentment that fate should have drawn into its game men already marked in advance as losers and winners, guilty and innocent, just and unjust. (Had they really been marked in advance?)

Ever since that time Andy Lebovitch treated everything as if he were going to lose it again within five minutes. Including himself. His frankness allowed him not to bother with anything he wanted to get rid of. It was a pleasure to watch him eat at the meals on Friday evening, or Sunday, when the people from Krakovska and Lubliana streets dined together. He quickly devoured his meal, as if afraid that what he didn't swallow all at once would be taken from him. He ate a lot, with gusto, and often. The result was that he stayed slim. Andy was still a pagan: every meal was a celebration. He appreciated every day and every night for what they were and for the very fact that they were. For what he knew might not be. He bathed three times a day (sometimes with soap). Afterward he would ask her, "Dita, are you really still a virgin?" Or, "Do you know how to waltz?" Or he would say, "Rats and mice are everywhere—six million rats."

He described to her a drunk German officer in crematorium number 2 who used to say: "Arm und Reich, der Tod macht alles gleich." (Death spares neither small nor great.) Andy had been fifteen going on sixteen, and in the camp he used to divide the

German soldiers into two categories: OK—which meant that they did not kill on sight, wantonly, or for fun—and Beware—dangerous. At the beginning the others did not take him seriously, but when he proved right in ten, twenty, and then fifty cases and risked his own skin, they stopped grimacing, as if Andy were an expert on people, a born judge of character.

Dita imagined herself saying to Andy: "Do you remember, Andy, how we looked at each other the first time you shook my hand? Like when old people feel someone is watching them. Although there is no one there, they wonder whether they will still be there in an hour, tomorrow evening, or next Friday—like when you feel the grip of some fear, like being buried alive."

Andy would reply: "Well, you won't get me in on that, kid. Do you know what Neugeborn and I had for dinner last night? We each had two large Wiener schnitzels. And for a good price." Had they escaped from the restaurant?

One Sunday afternoon he told her that there had been more clever and better educated people than him in the camp. His gift of second sight, or clairvoyance, or whatever it was, had given him particular satisfaction, because it never let him down. He used to bet on people in SS or army uniforms, just like betting on horses before a race, or like buying tickets in a lottery. He went on living, proof that for three years he never went wrong.

"You have to live like an animal," Andy claimed. "Listen to your instincts, whatever they tell you."

Dita reflected that people see themselves one way, yet show people another face, to change the truth. Why? Who knows? At a community social, the man from the Sonderkommando asked Andy: "Was our greatest mistake deciding to stay alive in spite of everything? How many people here know that we were the only ones to resist? We didn't wait until some Allied forces arrived, like they did in the other camps. Don't look at me as though I were a grave digger, or a hangman's assistant."

Andy chose to excuse himself. In fact, that was just how he did look at that man. Now he could hear them playing his favorite, "Amour." Had it been that Monday when he had met that man? Certainly it was here and now that they had met, between the bar and the buffet, two people whom neither the most artful nor the most naive German could have imagined escaping from the walls of the crematorium alive.

Over afternoon tea in the Café Phoenix, Andy had said to her: "When it was dark we were all like blind rats. We lived and died like rats." He was obsessed with rats, but he did not act that way. "As long as there's breath in your body, there is fear." To this Liza would reply, "Our Sampson."

Now Andy had an elegant thirty-eight-year-old mistress who wanted "to make up for those dreadful years." He had spent the preceding afternoon in bed with her, and in the evening he had described it to them. Suddenly she had burst into tears; he did not know why. She was blond like a Viking and looked a bit German or British. It gave Andy great pleasure to look at her. Once she had put on a silk nightie with lace, which, as she said, she had only worn once before, on her wedding night. She apologized for the fact that the nightie had faded. Of course, she paid for him with her husband's money. She made some shirts for Andy and promised to knit him a blue sailor sweater with an anchor as a birthday present by the twenty-first of December. He had actually gotten a knee-length gown of cashmere wool, a tie, and gold cuff links with the monogram A.L. What pleased Andy most was when she assured him that he was better than her husband. Andy thought that unbelievable, coming from a married woman. After that he slept with her one whole night, and in the morning she said to him, "At this moment my youngest child is just going off to school."

He liked to watch her when she slept, undressed or dressed, or when she ate. Once he had gone out to lunch with her wearing a white silk ascot from Italy. She invited him to the restaurant, The Two Swans, where you had to book three days ahead to get a table. She told him that in his white scarf he looked like a prince. She had, he said, eaten slowly, her elbows pressed to her sides, with long fingers and clean fingernails. He did not know what to concentrate on first—the perfect order of courses—snails cooked with garlic in butter, served with toast, onion soup with melted cheese on a slice of bread just firm enough for the spoon to penetrate, grilled frogs' legs with lemon, filet mignon, with a glass of wine, then burgundy, strawberries floating in a sweet liqueur, followed by the kind of coffee only to be found in Italy—or her telling him that he looked like a prince. He almost felt as if he were. "She kept trying to show me that she is no whore, as though I didn't have to show her likewise."

Like Boccaccio, of whose existence Andy was oblivious, he could declare that it is better to experience a thing and regret it than not to have experienced it at all. When he was depressed, all he needed to do was ride for one or two stops on the streetcar without paying and tell himself that he had gotten away with it again. Sometimes he would steal a flower in the park and give it to the first old lady he met. He felt better right away.

Dita walked slowly. The sun was shining. The street was quiet. From an open window not very high above the sidewalk came the sound of a radio playing a familiar melody: "My sweetheart is wonderful and turns all heads as he walks by."

Fitzi was not as easily satisfied as Andy. Lebovitch enjoyed living. Just as the sun's rays give out warmth, some kind of invisible sunshine radiated from Andy, a relish of life. He was superstitious. He believed that some girls bring misfortune, some good luck, and that some women seem to be born to wait in the house until their husbands come home from work—which did not, on the other hand, diminish their attraction in the least. At

Auschwitz-Birkenau the rule was: Everything that was not explicitly permitted was forbidden. Andy turned this rule on its head. He agreed with Dita's rat catcher that "whoever waits patiently and submissively will wait forever." He took everything as just a down payment on what was still to come. He had the reputation of being a six-week boyfriend. Two months was his record for an amour. He had his own definitions for virtue and sin. According to him, girls always promise more than they deliver. That made him raise the threshold of his promises to women when he wanted them to give him his chief aim.

"When you pretend a girl is pretty, the devil himself helps you to convince her."

He would facetiously remark that his skin was still as supple as when he was at Buchenwald near Weimar. It was still suitable for the manufacture of lampshades or suitcase covers. He lived as though he were trying to pack five hundred years into a week. He was helped by his beautiful, innocent, chestnut-brown Jewish eyes, like the center of night, like stars, sometimes cheerful, other times sad. He had shaved his head to avoid having to comb his hair, and he knew it suited him. His clothes sometimes looked as if he had deliberately creased them, unless, that is, he had made them himself.

Andy summed up the world with a formula: "To kill or not to kill; to kill or be killed. I'm glad when my dreams at night are about racehorses."

For a moment Dita pictured Liza's father and sister. She could imagine what Liza's father had shouted when the Germans shot him against the wall of the crematorium after he'd done a week's work in the Sonderkommando.

In her mind she heard Liza's experience of being naked for the first time in front of a man—how it was coupled with anticipation and anxiety. How is it going to be with me? Dita wondered.

Finally, she put a smaller question mark beside the name of D. E. Huppert. She had the feeling, as she did so, that she was giving David Egon a present. She smiled. We are just as crazy, not one bit more advanced, than our ancestors in their leopard skins.

On the way to 53 Lubliana Street, Dita bought pastries, cookies, and wine for her eighteenth birthday party. Bread, butter, and ham. Paper napkins. She hoped she had not forgotten anything. In the Feurop flower shop on the 28th of October Street she bought a rubber plant. She was very choosy, and she irritated the salesgirl.

She struggled with her load, to which she had added a phonograph record of "Sentimental Journey," with "Brazil" on the flip side. She smiled. The more her legs seemed about to buckle under, the more radiant she was. She was glad that she had almost gotten rid of the gold foils.

"There," she puffed when she reached the house and put her packages down on the pavement for a moment. She was less preoccupied with her new possessions than with the prospect of the trip to Switzerland with the International Blue and White Union and the promise it held out to her.

She suppressed the pleasure of owning her new bracelet. It's only a matter of time. Every day one is still alive is a victory. I am the master of my time. I am winning just by living. Bad? Explicitly good. And she knew that if she thought of anyone before she fell asleep that night, it would be D.E.

 Dita turned toward the door and opened it abruptly. She and Tonitschka saw only Linda's back.

"That's the kind of thing that makes you feel like murdering," she said. "If you had a life of your own, maybe you wouldn't hang around outside my door." Linda disappeared.

"Eavesdroppers hear the truth about themselves," said Tonitschka.

"She was born at 3:30 A.M. on a Thursday at the hour between the dog and the wolf. What do you expect? I'm beginning to believe that some people are born at a lucky time, others the reverse. I suppose Munk would beat me over the head with Karl Marx to refute the idea. Do you think that Munk dreams of *Das Kapital* at night, or of *Dialectical Materialism*, as I dream of Satan every time I see a uniform in the daytime?"

Dita asked her to stay for tea and bread and butter. "I've been trying to find out what happened to our laundry in Josefovska Street, and Grandma Olga's block of land. For better or for worse, the honeymoon won't last much longer. Too bad my ancestors didn't give me the opportunity to learn what poetry lurks in the smell of manure. That reminds me, I'm going to need a new bathing suit."

"Do you like the spring?"

"I like the warmth."

"You're terrible," Tonitschka said. "You spoke to the doctor about me to send me to Karlsbad, without telling me."

"Sorry, I hadn't had time to inform you. They have to buy you a new outfit."

Dita put on the record of "Brazil." She noticed that Brita had again stretched her shoes. Dita's foot was as long as Brita's was wide. Sometimes the Holy Virgin also borrowed her skirt. When she couldn't fasten it, she'd use a safety pin. How can one choose her company? Sometimes she gave the air of someone not knowing whether she is coming or going. Or whether she is fighting her monthly cramps or searching for her identity.

She danced from one corner of the room to another. She felt her own body, her long legs, and the lightness of it.

"How much do you tip the hairdresser?" Tonitschka asked.

"Why? Don't you have any money?"

But Tonitschka thought that Dita looked pale, with circles under her eyes, like girls who lead too active a nightlife.

Dita danced, with her hands above her head. She felt giddy and stopped.

"You speak a little German, don't you?"

Instead of answering, Dita said, "I read in the papers about an actress. They asked her what her greatest wish was. 'To bring someone a little bit of happiness every day.' So they asked her what she meant by happiness. She merely smiled. She has a husband and child. She is beautiful and famous. She seems to be a decent person, too. At one time there was talk about a lover who was happy with her. She used to bring roses to him every day. Maybe he got scared by her devotion. It isn't only the petty, miserable things that scare people. The big things do as well as those that aren't equated with money: perhaps a painting, a fairy tale, or a song. I don't know. As far as bread is concerned, love comes in a close second, as my Grandma Louise used to say. In Palestine, they say that when hunger comes in the door, love flies out the window."

"Do you often think about them?"

"Not really."

"I wouldn't think about them so much either, if it weren't for the way the people at work look at me, like a wild beast that's about to wake up."

"Nobody really knows. Very few are interested. So much is happening every day. In Argentina they throw people into the sea. In Palestine there's fighting. In Malaya there's shooting."

"I'm almost glad."

"Glad, why?"

"That there's nobody left alive."

"Are you serious?"

"At least no one can find out what I don't want them to know about me."

"Don't exaggerate. What does it amount to, to let yourself be raped? I'd have done the same thing in your place."

"It's easy to say that."

"They say that children, girls, and fools speak the truth."

"You aren't a fool."

"Don't they also say that where there's no prosecutor there's no judge?"

"So they say. There's an awful lot of things that people say!"

"Except that some of them are true. For instance: that a burned child is afraid of fire. And that it's better to let sleeping dogs lie."

"You are like my mother."

Tonitschka reflected that Dita had gotten away with a lot and always because she was pretty. Then Dita remarked, "People say that the father of that actress was shot because he sided with the Germans during the war. She was in love with a Jewish boy. I'd give anything to know what it is that draws people together. I suppose we'll never know why anybody does what he does."

Dita slipped two sheets of foil each under Liza's and Brita's pillows. They usually went to bed late and didn't have time to make their beds, nor did they bother about it. There were colored papers hanging in the windows. In the corner where the boys had been sitting on the floor lay pillows. Newspaper cuttings, like lace, adorned the walls and windows. Melted candles peeped out from the candlestick. Dita handed Tonitschka a small packet of gold foil. She felt subdued and guilty.

"Surely you're not going to give away gold?"

"Haven't you heard that money makes you feel better?" She remembered what her father used to say: that an evil that can be paid off is really not so terrible. In Tonitschka's surprise, Dita heard an echo of her own fear that had made her wait a month to decide whether the foil was really hers.

"As Dr. Fitz says, if you'd been born a century ago, you'd have been a baroness," Tonitschka said.

"If I'd been born fifty years earlier I would not, I hope, have gotten mixed up with the Gestapo."

"Are you crazy?"

"What do you mean?"

"Nothing. I'm probably crazy too."

"That actress was raped when she was fourteen, with a pistol at her head, and in the end she did everything they wanted."

"Did she tell people about it?"

"Not everybody she met. But she told him."

"What did he do?"

"He didn't want to make matters worse. He knew she was innocent. Purer than if it had never happened. I suppose it's true that if you love someone you accept them entirely, just as they are. She was still a child when it happened. She tried to find some person she could believe in. To bring matters back to some order. No one ever heard her utter a word of complaint or regret. She never pitied herself, and she refused to worry about herself. What concerned her was being reliable to those who seemed reliable to her. She didn't allow herself to be changed by a world she couldn't change. Maybe she's crazy too. For some people, what is distant is most present. Or the reverse."

After a moment she added: "Apparently she used to write to her lover about how she loved him more than she loved herself, and always would, as long as she lived. Things like: 'My darling, I'll love you all my life. I wish you happiness and peace.' And so on. About how her heart stopped beating when she thought of him or when she walked through places where they had walked together. In one letter she sent him a wooden ring. She gave him a locket with a picture in which she appeared beautiful, and a little sad. She gave him a bottle of perfume, which she used when they could still be together. Her letters had the scent of roses. She wrote that it would be wonderful to die for him, if it would make him happy in return. And that it meant as much to her to give to him as to receive. She wrote that he had become the sense in her life. And that he had no need to ask why. In short, that's how it was. But she never understood why he didn't answer her letters. If I had been in her shoes, I would have understood."

"Maybe it drove him crazy too," said Tonitschka. Suddenly she blushed, as though she had been caught in the act of doing something wrong. Who could tell what was going on in her head? Sometimes Tonitschka blushed without reason, and because it embarrassed her to blush, she went on blushing. Once she went red because they talked about how little girls mess the bed. Other times it was because something was missing on the floor she lived on, or because the toilet was clogged. "Do you think that love is madness because nobody knows what can happen or when it will end or when it may kill someone?"

"I haven't yet gotten in the habit of measuring everything by the standards of the camp," Dita answered.

Tonitschka bit into the bread and butter with her tiny mouse-like teeth. Dita looked up at the newspaper cutouts, columns of newsprint glued together in star patterns, and at the Mobil Oil maps.

People fear involvement. Who knows, maybe from cowardice. Balzac wrote about a cautious lover who never wrote a single love letter for fear of being found out. Dita said the letters she received were at the bottom of the drawer where she kept her lingerie, then later she burned them to make sure. "People in love are afraid of being betrayed. Or else of deluding the other person. Not that they wouldn't like to start something, but because they can't do what they really want."

"That reminds me of Andy Lebovitch."

On the other wall were posters and pictures from illustrated magazines. Women in them posed provocatively with their legs outstretched, and behind them were smiling, sunburned men. Behind everything were brand-new cars.

"You've got everything a girl could wish for," said Tonitschka.

"Thanks, Tonitschka. And when I'm old, people on Lubliana Street will say what I must have been like before I ran down." Dita laughed. It cheered her up just to look at Tonitschka. It was an upside-down confession.

"When I was little," Dita continued, "my mother told me that she had expected me to be dark, with black eyes and hair. When she took me home from the red brick maternity home, she saw that my eyes were black and that I had some dark fuzz on my head. But my eyes turned blue, and when my hair grew it was blond. And so with every birthday it became more obvious that I was going to be tall and fair. At first sight of me, Hitler would have been delighted."

Tonitschka was seized by a fit of coughing. On the floor below, For-Better-for-Worse was making a clatter with his mousetraps.

"I have been feeling that I am still just as I was when I came from my mother," Dita said.

"The original thing?"

"At school I always had to sit in the back row, so that the others could see. Apparently in the first grade I cried and asked the school doctor if there was some operation they could do to shorten people. Tall girls were expected to be able to cope better. It wasn't very pleasant when boys my age ignored me. I envied girls like you, because they had more luck with the boys." Then she added, "A girl at school told me that her parents didn't like her boyfriend because he wore tight pants. Her mother said that in such pants, nothing was left to the imagination."

"And what did the girl think?"

"She said her parents were right. He was too old for her."

"Fitzi was at Linda's again. She didn't get anywhere. She asked him over, saying she'd cut his fingernails. He snapped at her that only corpses get their fingernails and toenails cut."

"Nice to hear that they have such charming conversations. Both unfortunately and fortunately, no one stole anything on account of me. Even if he wanted to. If I were a real femme fatale, I'd have fun seducing him. I'm a bit short in that department." And then: "For Fitzi, it's like that British writer said, that danger is a cure for boredom. He always misses the point. It doesn't test my soul, don't worry."

Tonitschka was small. Dr. Fitz's repeated course of hormone treatment had no effect. Tonitschka had spent her vital years in the camps. She tried to compensate, through cheap feminine tricks, for what nature and the Gestapo had deprived her of. She slept with an advertisement from an old copy of the *Women and Girls' Companion:* "I Am Beautiful. I attained the shape of my bosom, an imposing embellishment of my beauty, solely by the use of Professor Larry's balsam." She used to do exercises. She felt guilty because she was so scrawny—like when people refer to someone by saying that he's got a brother in jail, his grand-dad's gone to America, or he won fifty thousand in the lottery.

Tonitschka had a boyfriend who was a typesetter at a printing firm in Legerova Street, not far away. She confided in Dita that the typesetter played the guitar and kissed the number tattooed on her right arm.

"He probably believes in the number eight, as you've got it there twice," said Dita.

After a while the conversation turned to the inevitable daily topic. Tonitschka declared: "If you don't do what they've come for right away, they get back at you by telling everybody that you're not a proper woman, that you lie in bed like a corpse and have the body of a girl with the mentality of a man. Andy, for instance."

"I don't want to be one of those people who ruin their lives by always asking themselves what other people might say. I can see right through Andy: he sees women like items on a menu in an eatery. He only wants fast food. He's not interested in what goes on in the kitchen, who does the shopping, peels the pota-toes, and does the cooking, or who washes the dishes. He just wants to have a meal, pay, and leave, or else, preferably, to get out without paying."

She thought to herself that it was wrong to keep anyone wait-ing so long, in addition to the fact that Andy had nothing to learn about the art of avoiding loneliness and boredom. Was it really? What was certain was that he wanted everything to be straightforward. Without problems. According to Andy and Fitzi, it was harmful for a girl to be a virgin for long. "They think sex is like swimming. The sooner you learn, the better, so you don't drown. For Andy, sex is a religion. For every occasion he has some little god or goddess." Dita laughed.

Tonitschka pointed out that Fitzi had survived eighteen transports, Andy sixty. They had helped each other like two young wolves in a pack. Each had contributed to the best of his ability. Dita wondered when the best means the worst and vice versa, and of the few people she had known, who had worked for the Gestapo. How should one think of unsettled accounts? Andy joked that it was always harder to live than to die. "Apparently vixen are the most faithful of all beasts," Dita said. "But they also say that in case of emergency, the pack turns on the injured or the weakest. I'm not sure why. Is it to save themselves? Or to save him? Apparently they are by no means as savage as people say."

"I've heard the same about wild geese."

Dita looked at Tonitschka's mouth. She thought that to some people life must seem like a bet at long odds, but from another point of view the problem is the fear of losing. Anxiety is the equivalent of hope; hope is anxiety.

There was something inexplicably open about Tonitschka. It was hard to say whether it was strength or weakness. Dita stroked the arm of her chair. Tonitschka's eyes were clouded with thought. They reminded Dita of grass. For a moment Tonitschka's eyes looked aged.

"You don't need to be so anxious, Tonitschka," Dita said. "They found some treatment for my lungs, too, after the war."

She wondered why old people say that life is short. It would be more sensible to ask why it is that when a girl matures—and everything that follows depends on that—then even a person who's done nothing wrong still feels guilty and ashamed.

"For Andy, a girl is like a well to a thirsty man," Dita said. "If he can't drink at one, he goes to the next to quench his thirst. Yesterday he actually held the door open for me. I asked him why he was being so polite."

"Andy?" Tonitschka said, "When I was little, I used to make a birthday wish to be a millionaire. I'd build myself a house with a school in it, for my children to have everything they needed."

Dita smiled. She reflected on why a girl's body changes from a promise into a burden. Why is everything dominated by the laws of exchange, A for B, giving for receiving, meals for marriage? To have the figure of a full-grown woman was like a double-edged sword. Boys took it as a signal that they could step through an open door, only to find out that it was the wrong door.

Tonitschka looked at the sheets of gold. She held them to her ears, waved them like a fan, and listened to their golden rustle. "Would you like me to wash your hair?" she asked Dita.

"Do you feel like it?"

"Fitzi told Munk that during the war you saved 105 children."

"I did look after a few children in Theresienstadt. That's all. First I worked in a gardening squad. Sometimes I used to put a bandage over my eyes to get out of going to work every day. Many people there used to stare blankly at me. I like sleeping, so I offered to take care of the children."

"Close your eyes, so the soap won't get into them."

Dita lowered her chin as she always did when she remembered how tall she was, so that she might appear smaller. "What we have now is a different sort of competition. Tomorrow I'll take you to lunch in a restaurant, nothing expensive. Roast duck—the large portions. And we'll wash it down with beer."

Tonitschka kissed Dita on her wet cheek. "Isn't it nice how popular you become when you have money?"

Tonitschka returned to the topic they had been discussing when they had caught Linda Huppert behind the door. "Who knows what he was thinking. Since I was so grown up, he was afraid somebody would pick me out for what, in Birkenau, they called 'the massage department.' They selected actresses, dancers, and singers, or just good-looking girls."

"What happened to him?"

"One day he didn't come."

"You don't look all that Jewish."

"You don't look all that Jewish either." Tonitschka wiped her hands on the towel around Dita's shoulders. She looked at Dita in the mirror, and at the same time she looked at herself.

"Isn't that some body?" Dita said in English.

Tonitschka blushed. She suppressed a cough. The room smelled, as usual, of the shampoo they used, the odor of DDT and the eau de cologne, mixed with the flavor of the food locker, made from a container for a foreign radio with the trademark Philips. Under the container lay a rag, together with the cleaning powder. Brita had brought the packing case, the trunk, and the case she kept under the bed from England after the war. By a stroke of unusual luck, her parents had sent her there just in time.

Isabelle Goldblat shooed away the cats on the stairs. The day drew on. She shouted at somebody on the second floor to go easy with the water.

"Think what you like," said Dita, drying her hair. "'Life goes on' means the day as well as the night, and everything has its magic. I think I would be just as impressed if someone thought I was a nun as I would be if they thought the reverse—that I had no other interests anymore."

"I have to go," said Tonitschka. "I'm going to see *First after God*. It's a French film about a captain who sails around the world with a cargo of Jewish refugees without visas. They don't

allow him to land anywhere, until he loses patience and sets fire
to his ship, so they will have to let him get out."
"I hope it worked. Being decent is as good as being beautiful.
Enjoy yourself. And come back in time. We won't start without
you."
"What are you going to do?"
"Tattoo my other arm," smiled Dita.

3 When Tonitschka Blau had gone, Dita Saxova ran a bath.
She sprinkled a handful of chamomile into the water and
placed the soap on the edge of the bath. She unfastened her
kimono and stepped out of her clothes like a stork. My bath is
my castle. Chase three hares and you won't catch one. You can't
kill two birds with one stone. Even a hair casts a shadow. The
rising steam smelled fragrant.

She lowered herself into the water. She was aware of her body
as one is aware of a secret, or of something that is alien but at
the same time is part of oneself.

She examined herself in the water. Her skin, the slightly
raised breasts, the soft, whiter flesh of her long legs and firm
thighs turned pink in the bath. Two supple pads of muscle lay
below her belly. Was she her own labyrinth, in which she
explored how far she must provide from her own resources
everything she wanted in life? At the same time she looked at
herself as if she were nothing but eyes, each of which, merely by
squinting, had the gift of seeing all the images accumulated
within herself over the last eighteen years.

She thought about what Liza had said yesterday: "I remember
him telling me that he could feel me trembling, and not to be
afraid. That trembling might have been fear, but the sensation of
flesh on flesh—I guess I felt excitement, because even now,
when I think about our bodies touching for the very first time, I

get that same sensation." But that had been Liza's experience, not hers.

I am fighting my private war, like Tonitschka with her TB, and it is nobody's business. She looked at her breasts and thought of the Aufseherin, the German wardress, who came for the selection to the Frauen Koncentration Lager carrying a riding whip with a lead weight at the end, looking as if she had just left her horse at the gate. She amused herself by picking out the weak and ill and by testing the firmness of the skin of the healthy ones. She stood in front of her victim and struck her with a hard, sharp blow. She repeated this until the beaten woman's breasts were ripped open and bloody.

The Frauen Koncentration Lager also witnessed a few love affairs. But more frequently it was mothers without children, women without lovers, wives without husbands. Sisters without brothers, daughters without fathers. Except they had, as everywhere, a house of ill repute, on the second floor of Block 4 in Auschwitz, the *mein,* or mother camp.

It was said that just before the end of the war, before the evacuation, the same Aufseherin issued salami and bread to some of the girls, like Liza Vagner.

Dita looked at her groin, the place where even a woman felt herself to be mysterious. She thought of a deep sea, of sailing ships that glide quietly over blue water under a blinding sky, and of vast meadowlands, full of flowers, and of thick, fragrant forests. She thought of brightly colored fish at the bottom of the sea, of birds in tropical jungles. Everything was connected to her skin, her body. What caused people to feel love? What did it mean to give birth? How would I feel if I were a man? How will I feel when I begin to age? It was like being an iceberg, sailing through a dark night, with nothing visible except the tip rising above the surface. As if she had become conscious of her strength and at the same time of that which she feared.

What did it feel like for those people who fled into the woods in wartime, or hid in towns, like submarines, with forged papers, at the mercy of others? Sometimes they ended up different than they had begun. She thought of the stars and, in the same breath, of the slaughtered. From where do they arise, those secret suns in the night sky, and to where do they depart? She thought of the light that falls upon the earth from nowhere, for the stars from which it was born have long since passed away, like the dead planets. She spread the soap with the palm of her hand, and with her fingers, she smoothed her skin until she was entirely clean, without lather, but still wet.

For a long time she looked at herself, until her eyes closed. There had been times when her mother had warned her to take care. But what her mother had in mind were precautions other than those needed between the years 1939 and 1945. During that time no caution could have helped. People were killed simply for having been born. The Germans smothered and extinguished their lives as if they were the embodiment of some hideous cosmic force—like remnants of gas explosions in the universe, survivals of something from before the two-thousand-year-old molding of laws against killing, some demonic spark that gnawed and threatened the flickering Nordic or Aryan light. Dita's hand held her breast. In the case of Serbs, Russians, or the French, the Germans had merely put out their eyes, nailed them to barn doors, or wrung their necks like chickens, in order to bring their fellow citizens to subjection and obedience. But in the case of the Jews no such German benevolence had been extended. It was enough to be born from a Jewish mother. They had less space on the face of the earth than fleas, lice, and cockroaches. They had less value than the hounds of ancient Rome to whom, as Dr. Fitz used to tell, men used to give their masters' food for tasting. Fitz liked to add that as a result of the way the meal was served, the hounds also ate poisoned food, like the people. On the other hand, the hounds were buried with full honors. Only that morning Fitz had recommended to her a writer who had dealt with the subject.

Had the Germans turned the world so far back? Even beyond the point when people believed that the human brain was in the heart? Was it really any worse in their days because it was so long ago? Mother used to warn her to be careful in choosing her friends. It is human nature to betray others, and that includes, above all, one's own friends. The end result is that people reject their good friends and cultivate their enemies, simply because friends are not threatening but enemies are. Don't let anyone get too intimate, and don't let anyone get you into his pocket. The ideal is for your best friends not to be sure of you. In the end, the strongest drop their friends and requite their enemies. A broken friendship can never be repaired. That's human nature, and who is any different?

It was not only her body that Dita gazed at and listened to. She listened to a voice within her, compounded of many voices and echoes. She felt like a person who walks across thin ice over a frozen river, with spring already in the air. She had the impression that she could hear her own words, as a person hears the sound of ice cracking beneath his feet.

Several times she had caught herself judging people by whether or not she would have chosen to be with them in Auschwitz-Birkenau. How would they behave? What would it be like to be with them? Was it just the impossibility of escaping from memories and, with them, from responsibilities? Sometimes she had the feeling that a cloud rose up above her, floating above oceans and continents after a volcanic eruption and modifying the power of the sun and the weather for years to come. Later, when the volcanic cloud would fall, it would form a lake. (Apparently that really happened in 1912.) She imagined a cloud as a monster circling the globe. Ten million tons of ash and fragments. The blue of the sky turns milky, like a shadow. Henceforth, neither sunrise nor sunset would be the same.

At school, her career had been far from brilliant. Why? I suppose I have no interest in pretending I'm something I'm not. I've got no interest in momentary success, as though it might cause me to miss the thing that everyone wants, as though a new war were about to break out tomorrow. It occurred to her how often she had come close to dying, like people locked in cells, waiting for a sentence to be carried out. She smiled to herself. Yes and no, not anymore. Why was it that she was never willing to answer the question of why she had not died, when so many others had been killed? She thought of the extraordinary thread binding everything that a person has seen, heard, and experienced with what that person expected from life. And how bizarre and presumably futile to try to cut all those threads at once— that which is known and binds one to one's past, and that which stretches somewhere into the unfathomable space that lies ahead.

What was it that joined the past and the present with what was still to come? It was only a fraction of a second. Less than the movement of a finger to a throat. She looked forward to the party. She would make it very special. How many times in her life would she be eighteen? She felt her blood pulsing under her skin, maybe just as flowers feel water and sun, birds height, and a girl's heart spring.

The water became cold. Sometimes, like Andy, she bathed three times a day. Why? Is lasting friendship possible between a man and a woman? Would she have liked to be a man, at least for a little while? She thought about the International Blue and White Union of Jewish Students, of the parties, meetings, and Saturday dances. Or how she had danced with David Egon Huppert, and with Herbert Lagus, and with Neugeborn. Or how she had taught Andy the tango. Her life now was a little tough, close, warm, and sad, all at the same time. Someone was reputed to say that the tango is a sad or melancholy idea you can dance to. The tango was something familiar and worldly, old yet fresh, a puzzle of the body and soul, of the melody. The tango is the beauty of sadness, she said to herself. She returned in her mind to Andy and then passed from Lebovitch to D. E. Huppert. He waddled like a bear and took advantage of his own clumsiness. She sank down into the water up to her chin. Life is not what we want but what we have.

4 Toward morning, during the night in which she celebrated her coming of age and which had begun with her birthday party, Dita Saxova dreamed that she was at a country hotel with D.E. He was at the bar, serving beer, tea, and coffee with rum to the laborers, drymen, and farmhands. He wore a white apron and checkered slacks. Outside, darkness had settled on the windows, and inside, streams of yellow light poured onto the glass. It was getting late, and the guests began to leave. In the end, only one man was left at the table. He was tall, with a shock of brownish hair. D.E. coughed to indicate that it was time for the man to go. When there was no response, he grabbed the lapels of the fellow's stout cotton jacket, picked him up from the chair, dragged him a few steps from the door, and prepared to throw him out into the darkness.

Suddenly in the hands of the tall man there appeared a kitchen knife with a well-sharpened blade. He held the knife shaft like children do when they throw darts. The knife handle, with its greenish brass inlay, shaped at the end like the prow of an ancient ship, sailed through the air. D.E. ducked behind a chair.

When Dita looked into the face of the tall man, she jumped, as when someone forgets he is eating fish and swallows a bone and can neither breathe nor call for help. Both tall figures were one and the same being.

She glanced around the bar. Deserted oak tables were stained with spilled beer froth. There was a keg of Moravian wine with a clock on top. From it glared the glass eyes of the cuckoo with a raised beak.

Dita tried to scream but could not. She had no choice but to keep watching until she awoke.

The dream clung to her like a crumpled dress. Outside, the rain fell. She was in her own bed, presented to her as one of the longest occupants of 53 Lubliana Street at the end of 1945 by the Community Welfare Department. At that time For-Better-for-Worse had said that only when the well runs dry do you appreciate the value of water. He informed Munk that dogs bite only the slowest straggler.

She leaned her head back on the end of the bed. The night was flooded with darkness and water. Raindrops drummed against the windows, tapping out signals, like someone throwing crumbs at the windows, or like sand, or tiny coins too small to buy anything with. At times the wind moaned like a catch in the throat, like an ancient, unspoken grief.

For heaven's sake. It had been a lovely party. Munk had seemed forty years younger in their company. He had been gentle with them, as he would have been with his Sonia, whom he could not be with again, for she disappeared into the chimneys at Auschwitz-Birkenau, straight from the ramp, as did all those who wore spectacles. "Always think what you are doing, girls. Just think what you are doing." Munk had danced with her. He had fallen out of step and trampled on her feet. "You have your whole life before you, Dita. One day you will look back with longing and envy at your courage today, at all that you are living through now." And he said: "Lack of faith is forbidden today. That's the right of revolution. Only hope is permitted. We don't understand it all yet, but this we do know: to outlaw despair is a great thing, even if ridiculous."

Andy laughed. "Doesn't one plus nothing still make one plus nothing? Isn't it true that every tale lasts only until someone else comes along with another?" Andy and Munk always fought like cats and dogs.

Liza stirred in her sleep. "Let me sleep." Dita waited to hear what else she would say. But Liza was silent. Dita groped about. The sheet beneath her was as crumpled as if she had wrung it out. Her nightgown was hitched up to her neck. In the dim light she looked down at her body. Across the room, the bracelet glittered in its case on top of a pile of her underwear. Next to it lay the record that Munk had given her as a birthday present, "I Love Life." She straightened her nightie and closed her eyes. She felt how her heart raced and ran her hands over her body, wishing they were a man's hands.

On other nights, as soon as darkness fell and screened out everything that kept people in a state of alertness, she was able to dream of a white house, of D. E. Huppert and other boys, or about the fisherman in *The Rat Catcher* who "always said today what he ought to have said yesterday."

She knew that she had reached a point where she could no longer be satisfied with what she saw and how she saw it, what she heard and how she heard it, what she perceived and how she perceived it. She felt she could no longer live for herself alone.

She knew that somewhere there was a person linked to her by fate, even though he remained unknown. Did she own two bodies, one her own and the other the one that she would share with someone else? She felt an energy she didn't yet understand. She felt giddy. The room was silent apart from the sounds of the sleeping girls.

Peace and school teach you how to hide things—but not how to hide from the feeling of being naked. Why do I feel so naked?

As Dr. Fitz says, "The hardest fight, my girl, is the fight against illusions."

She ran the tip of her tongue across her lip. Very far away, as if there was something separating her from herself and at the same time drawing her together, was the thought of the connection between parents and the fate of their children. It was a small room. Even in the darkness she could see across it, from wall to wall, and feel the closeness of the two girls next to her. She had an impulse to touch them, as a mother has for caressing her sleeping child. For a moment she caught sight of her outstretched arms and fingers through the dimness.

Time passed, as if the rain were washing it away. Low in the sky, the clouds floated past her window. The sky was like a heavy weight above her. The rain poured down.

She had a strange feeling, as if she were drinking lukewarm milk and lying on the bed of a warm blue ocean with open arms, watching transparent blue and purple fish go by, and flowers that enveloped her in their heavy scent. She got warmer and warmer. It was a strange feeling, pleasant, almost frightening, and at the same time natural, as if long expected. Her arms, legs, and face became tense, as though she were preparing to take a deep breath, hold it, and dive. Then her heartbeat and her breath came faster. Before her she saw a blue, red, and white light. Then suddenly everything went black. It was a fine, lukewarm darkness, like a wave that washed over, then gently ebbed, full of white foam, like the sea. Still it touched her gently, her fingertips, her whole body. Finally, like an echo of that blackout that had now melted away, shame crept in. She waited for the morning.

Liza slept with her blanket thrown back, like a deer, arms and legs curled up below her almost bosomless body. Brita slept huddled in her blanket in the shadow of the new rubber plant. A stout leg protruded in three places, at her ankle, knee, and thigh. The dawn's light crept in through the rain.

"Heavens," Liza woke up. "Has someone sold the alarm clock, or has it disappeared? It didn't go off."

"There must be some butter left over from Wednesday," said Dita. Great Britain turned to her.

"Are you really missing a pair of red panties, you Communist?" Brita's garments, peeled off at a snail's pace late at night after the party and thrown down haphazardly on the chairs, floor, and table, were mixed up with Liza's. The Holy Virgin began to sneeze—seven times. "Justice," she said. "Why is it that all brides are described as beautiful?" Her flesh shook like jelly.

"I went somewhere last night," said Liza.

"So did Dita. Didn't she?" asked Brita.

Dita went red. But she decided not to fight back. Everybody knew that when Brita went out on Saturday with one of her boyfriends, she wore, as a sort of insurance policy, a pair of less than immaculately laundered panties. Sometimes she limited herself to saying, untruthfully, that she had to be home by ten.

Dita finally pulled herself together. "My, you look beautiful. How much weight have you put on again that all your clothes look too small on you?" She walked over to the dresser where they kept their clothes and pulled a pair of blue lace-trimmed panties from Brita's pile. "I reckon that, thanks to my blond hair, I'll still find some benefactor."

"They'd be too small for you." Brita grabbed the panties from her. "You can have them, Liza."

"I'm afraid they'd make me look too alluring."

"It's only after the first disappointing experience that princesses like you two are afraid of it," Brita observed knowingly. "Fortunately, in some circles, introductions are unnecessary."

That was the end of the panties episode. Liza began to make

her bed and found her two sheets of foil beneath the pillow. The same thing happened to the Holy Virgin.

"Somebody around here must be stealing." Liza looked at Dita. She kicked away the black cat, as Fitzi had done. "And I thought there was honor among thieves."

"That cat has outlived Hitler," said Dita in her singsong voice.

"Where did you get it?" Liza asked. The hostel was awake. Noise came from all quarters.

"A real lady never asks such a question." Dita threw a towel over her shoulder. "Do I ask you or Britannia how it tastes?"

"It tastes exquisite," announced the Holy Virgin. She imitated Munk. "I know, Dita, I know. You would like to find what you are looking for."

Noise came from the showers. They were already occupied.

"Is it someone I don't know?" asked Liza. "Is he circumcised? Do you think it's the advantage they pretend it is?"

"Do you have a date with D.E.?" asked Great Britain.

"Don't you realize that I can't stand him these days?" said Dita. "I've got all three of them after me now, David Egon, Fitzi, and Herbert Lagus. I think I prefer Andy. And by the way, I don't let anyone feed me with the crumbs left at the table after the lucky others are through feasting on their whims. I want to be fed according to my own taste and will."

"Listen to how it was with my first serious boyfriend," Brita then said.

"People complain endlessly about how unhappy their lives are, yet no one wants to die, and people will fight against all odds for survival," said Tonitschka, who had come in quietly.

"Everyone else's lot in life looks more appealing than our own. But if given the choice, no one would really want to trade places with anyone else," Dita said.

The circles beneath Dita's eyes deepened. Her mouth curved into a smile. It was another day made for daydreaming. The sky had cleared after the gloomy, rainy night. Dita strode into the bathroom like Lysistrata of old.

5 "What do you think?" asked D.E.

"'Your heart is your trouble, friend,'" quoted Dita. "Is this thing really all yours?"

To the admiration of the local chapter of the International Blue and White Union, David Egon Huppert had bought himself a KDF, a German amphibious car from the loot store of General Patton's Third American Army at Pilsen. The price was absurdly low. It had cost him the equivalent of one month's scholarship money.

Dita leaned back on the cracked oilcloth upholstery of the seat, repressing thoughts of who had sat there before her. "With you, this ride will be very short or very long," she said at last.

While Linda, his stepsister, was mean, boring, and goodness knows what else, Huppert himself resembled a voracious little fish, elegantly equipped to swim in a variety of waters. At school and in social life, he stood for diplomacy. In the International Blue and White Union of Jewish Students he promptly put into practice all he had learned. He did not believe that the first step is the most difficult, nor that what is postponed is half lost. One term's study of the American constitution had won him the reputation for being a likely coarchitect of the IBW, and maybe one day of a new constitution for the World Jewish Congress.

He liked talking about his interests, whereby he supported the idea. He had already had free trips to Belgium, France, and Switzerland. On all sides, he reinforced the impression of his competence and the view that with his organizing ability he was destined to serve the International Blue and White, and later the World Congress. He was the embodiment of Dita's vow: "Don't let anyone feed you the crumbs from the lucky man's table. Be

well fed on your own." He could hear the ring in his ears of her:
"I feed myself only with the very best." He whistled "Stormy
Weather." Yesterday he had been introduced to the president of
the World Congress, Mr. G., who traveled through Prague from
Turkey, Moscow, and Bucharest. Huppert had been allowed to
join the group, which had been invited to after-dinner coffee at
the Hotel Alcron.

Dita turned her face to the wind, savoring once more the pleasure of being asked out on a date. D.E. had invited her for the
trip with suitable tact. She felt the wind on her face. It ruffled
her hair. She tied a red scarf around her head.

As D.E. drove past, up to the corner of Lubliana and Legerova
streets, Dita firmly pushed aside the feeling that she had
absolutely no one to rely on but herself. ("Come in the car to
make sure no one sees you," D.E. had nodded in his man-of-the-
world style.) She could not help wondering how far she might be
willing to submit, in case D.E. treated her as he did other girls
like Doris or Kitty or Liza, who suddenly, to the surprise of 53
Lubliana Street, seemed to have become indifferent to their
flesh.

Before D.E. called for her, Dita had let Tonitschka do her hair
and had tried out her own charms on the tavern keeper across
the street. Fortunately his wife was not home.

"Nothing wrong with my heart," said D.E., grinning. "What
about yours?"

An hour later they stood at the window of a little resort hotel,
decorated with fresh flowers. Spring had brought wet snow. Far
away were the silhouettes of slag heaps from the coal and silver
mines. There was a smell of clay in the air. In the temporary
parking lot stood the amphibious car, the shabby, wartime run-
about that had chalked up so much mileage that it looked as if it
had gone around the world three times already.

6 D.E. stood behind her, chewing peppermint drops. His ten commandments included a ban on smoking, heavy drinking, and late nights. Only his closest friends knew how much he liked sleeping in. Most of the numerous hours he spent poring over his books for the good of the world were in fact spent between the sheets. Even by midday he was capable of appearing as if he had been cheated of a good night's sleep.

"Shall we stay here?" he asked.

"I don't like the way they check on you in hotels at night," answered Dita, in a way that indicated how important it was for her to show D.E. that she was experienced.

"Don't worry," said D.E., startled. To cover his surprise he began to whistle the Jewish anthem.

"Maybe you won't get away with it this time." The words came out of her mouth like a song.

"I'd like to figure you out."

"It's never as they say." Should she tell him that she was sometimes happy without knowing why, and unhappy for no reason at all? She thought back to when she was thirteen and had experienced her first flow of blood.

D.E. swallowed a mint. He stroked her hair and ran his fingertips across her cheek. She felt the warmth of his hand.

"Do you still believe that the stork brings babies?"

She lowered her eyes and looked out of the window. She had large blue eyes that looked a little sad or anxious, even when she smiled her grown-up smile. The moonlight shone upon her.

They sat down on the edge of the bed. She lay back, and D.E. remained sitting for a while. Then he put his head in her lap. He ran his fingertips over her eyelashes, the arches of her closed eyes, her lips, the corners of her mouth. Dita responded to his touch the way the cats responded to hers. "The spring is lovely this year," she said.

"It took its time."

"It was a long winter."

"I don't like long winters."

"I want you to like it here."

"I know you do."

D.E. was silent. In the air between them lay an unspoken question, whether it was within his power, and also how far it was within her power. Instead of asking, however, she said: "When I'm in the country like this, when I lie in the pine needles or the grass or the moss, I feel time in a different way. As if everything that has been, stretching far back, and everything that is, and everything that will be could last forever."

D.E. laughed. His eyes shone. He felt something more than just the implications in her words, and the feelings grew stronger the more softly she spoke.

"It is as if every place, even the tiniest place, like this room, is a whole world."

Instead of answering, D.E. stroked her.

"Yesterday I went to buy a scarf. A tall, well-dressed lady came into the shop with her mother. The salesgirl asked if she could help them. 'Yes,' said the lady. 'I'd like to buy a hat for my mother here. OK, Mommy?'"

"Was that all?" D.E. asked.

She worried that she might smell too much of soap, but at the same time she felt proud of it. His hand warmed her. He laid his arm upon her brow and stroked her temples and the roots of her hair.

"It's true when they say life's beautiful." She half closed her eyes. Actually he was the first boy to caress her. She felt his hand on her temples, her lips, her chin and throat. It seemed protective of her. "You can be glad you're not a girl," she whispered.

But for a moment she thought of Herbert Lagus's and Fitzi Neugeborn's hands, how their nails were always dirty. She surrendered to the caressing hand of D.E. like the cats in Room 16 when she petted them. His hands stripped something away from her and at the same time added something. Layer upon layer. "Night is more dangerous than daytime," she said.

"Why do you think so?" asked D.E.

"I don't know. Maybe because of the darkness."

"I hope you don't believe in demons."

"They come from the North." Dita smiled. "Are you afraid of falling? Tonitschka is afraid of her own fear of what people say."

"Tonitschka? Or you?" D.E. asked cautiously.

"Who wants to be with a person who's afraid of everything?" It sounded as if she were putting the question to herself. Suddenly she was surprised by the sound of her own laugh, her voice. "Could you always be so considerate?"

Several times later she had to shift D.E.'s hand up higher, toward her throat. Twilight came pouring in through the window. D.E. caressed her wherever he wanted to. "You must not laugh at me," she said. And when he did not answer: "And you must not pity me."

She looked up at the moon. It was suspended in the upper half of the window. The stars shone brightly. D.E. was silent. She could hear the thumping of his heart, his breathing. "You must not do that, D.E."

She knew he would not answer her and was grateful for his silence. Within her mind she saw herself. And suddenly she also accepted him as part of herself. "I have no one to protect me. All I have is myself."

Several times D.E. kissed her on her temples and her face, her lips and her forehead. His lips and hands were warm. All at once they were everywhere. She let herself be kissed and caressed but did not reciprocate.

In June 1945, right after the war, she had gone for a ride in a jeep with two Russian soldiers. They had smiled at her as if the world had survived unscarred. They invited her to a forest camp. She had seemed rather grown-up to them. They sat on the hood of the jeep the Americans had brought to Murmansk by ship, their feet planted in the leather. Dita felt like hugging the whole world. Sometimes the problem is that you have to have something to believe in.

Then the two Russians talked something over between themselves, and she felt their eyes upon her as if they were undressing her. It flashed through her mind that she was about to join the masses of girls who had taken on more than they had bargained for. She jumped up from the groundsheet and ran through the woods. Their laughter followed her. Maybe she had been right, maybe not.

"You shouldn't do that," she heard her own voice say again. It sounded different somehow. It was no longer the turtle's shell.

"Yes, I should," answered D.E. firmly, as if there was nothing more to be said. "So should you."

"But just a little. Just a little bit. I'm not used to it. Maybe I'll learn—to get used to it."

She suddenly felt like an island that no one had set foot on for a long time. She stopped reproaching herself. The brightness of the moon gathered in her big blue eyes. The moon was ripe, very white. Her eyes, at some moments still impatient and tense, grew soft. The window hung like a rectangle of light on the darkness and silence. From somewhere nearby came the cry of a child. Then a fresh silence fell, but the baby's cry had not quite faded. It's always a test of the soul, even when it's also a test of the body, she kept telling herself, her lips slightly parted.

D.E. undressed her, then got undressed himself. She was conscious of her own body, her thumping heart, her moist eyes. She trembled all over. It was a delightful kind of tension, which she had never known before. She felt a twitching in her abdomen. A delicious shiver ran along her body. She helped D.E. to find what

he searched for as a compensation for all that she could not yet
help him with. Through her head flitted the thought that she
would never have been able to act like this if her father and
mother had been at her back, if she feared them. A kind of awe
and shyness came over her as she realized this. Dita had put on
her best underwear, realizing what D.E. had in mind and what
she had in mind herself. (She had made a feeble pretense that it
was accidental.) She felt the aroma of his breath and his body,
mixing with her breath and flesh, the scent of his arms and legs,
of the furniture, bedsheets, and whitewash on the walls. She
was glad that D.E. knew what he was doing. She refused to think
of his past, of how many other girls he had had. But now she had
taken their place, and that canceled everything out, even though
in some ways nothing had changed. Or had it? (Once D.E. had
mentioned Linda's name in a context involving Linda and his
father, which instead of drawing them together had permanent-
ly alienated them. Of course there were a lot of prejudices, and
some other factor too.)

"This is the first time in my life I have been like this, David."
He kissed her mouth. "I'm not scared," she whispered. "Only just
a bit."

"Don't be."

"It's a nice kind of fear. I've never been scared before like this.
Only everything is happening so fast."

He could feel her trembling. He had the feeling that it was her
secret strength that drew him to her. As though her weakness
had been transformed into its opposite. But he did not tell her he
could wait no longer. He did not speak.

"I don't want to be alone anymore," she whispered. "I don't
want to go on dreaming at night about things I don't have and
wake up sweating. I don't want to be like other people who have
been dead for a long time, even though they are still living."

"You're not alone," he answered.

"And don't tell me this is all I'm good for, David. Never tell me that."

They whispered to each other from only a few inches away. She ran her hands down his back. Again he told her there was nothing to fear, that everything would be all right. As he embraced her, she remembered how they used to cling to each other at Auschwitz-Birkenau to keep warm. It was their only source of warmth—animal warmth. She pressed herself to him. Outside, she heard the wind, bringing a thaw with it.

"It's as if you were taking me to some other place where I've wanted to go for a long time, David," she said. She felt her head spinning, as if her consciousness was ebbing, to be replaced by something else. She felt his firm, taut skin, the muscles beneath it. It wasn't obvious when he was dressed how strong he was. He lay on his side next to her and turned her face to him.

"No, David, no," she whispered, but her voice was all acquiescence. Even as she whispered she touched his body. She fell silent and arched her body as she felt a sudden stab of pain. She took his body within her as if it were bread and she was dying of hunger. He opened her with his body, as only a man can open a woman. D.E. went deep inside her. She tried to draw back, but he held her firmly. She writhed closer to him as though she were pierced with an arrow that drew her toward it. "David," she whispered, and trembled. "My love." In her voice there was a sound she had never heard before.

"My love," she repeated, still trembling. "I never called anyone that before." Then she whispered: "No need to say you're sorry, David. There's nothing to forgive you for. Or to forgive myself for."

It was like an undeveloped photograph, emerging from the darkness suddenly, at a single glance, revealing limitless, undreamed-of things, changing darkness into light, softening the harsh outlines of cliffs, so that one sees what he has never before seen. As if everything suddenly attained a new meaning.

It was like the reward that everyone gets who surrenders what will never be had again—when giving is the same as receiving.

She heard the echo of her own cry, a voice in her throat, a crumb of pain or astonishment, as if the sound were trapped in a narrow passage through which a voice came like a sob—a half insane joy, a muffled crack, the fragment of a second in which her voice broke within her. It seemed to her like an echo, as if she were experiencing some pleasant epileptic fit. Is that how life began? Or how it ended? She smiled. She felt a new sense of fullness. A fullness that balanced the emptiness. It reminded her of what Andy Lebovitch, who had come close to death, had said: that a person who is dying experiences a sweet, almost dizzy sensation, a feeling of vertigo, of spinning, of nearly fainting— and also a feeling of regret, or of drifting off to sleep, as if life were like the air escaping from a balloon.

Pain inspires a feeling of lightness, of weight dissolving like breath. A moment when even dying would seem easy.

D.E. kissed her. With the palm of his hand he wiped her cheeks and eyes. He told her things no one had ever said to her before.

She longed for him to feel happy next to her, happier than anyone had ever felt before. And she knew that in response she too should be happy, happier than she had ever been. She longed for him to ask her if she would be willing to die for his happiness, and she knew how she would answer. She heard the voice of shadows, the voice of the void, the sound of that which has no existence. She felt and saw what had blinded her. The eyes of the shadows watched her. She felt space, and confinement. The self-renewing state of life. As though she had histories, two parts, the crumbs of others, a feast of herself and with herself. Or rite. Yes, man and woman, woman and man. She let both live side by side. As if she had shed every encumbrance, every speck of dust and dirt.

She looked up at the curtains and at the ceiling, and she felt a

vague sense of peace and movement outside of herself. It was
something outside of the present, the past, and the future, and
at the same time it was connected to all of them. She suddenly
felt as if she were bigger than all three, connected to all that
time ever was or would be. She felt within herself the silent
forces by which man is linked to trees, rocks, the sea, the entire
universe. It was deeper than her consciousness. It had only a
tenuous link with her earliest experiences. She felt a warmth on
her thigh, a trickle of blood. Her body, his body, the strength
from his body.

"Now I know, David," she said. And then: "I know who I am.
And I know that I am. There is no pain, only beauty. From this
moment everything will be different. I don't care what has happened to me."

"None of us wants to miss out on anything," D.E. said quietly.

"It is beautiful. It hurts just a little."

7 But not long afterward she felt as if a tide were slowly
ebbing. It was almost eight-thirty. Her thoughts seemed
far away—as if she were someone else, or as if she had two sets
of brains. She thought of certain qualities of D.E.'s with which
she could not come to terms. It was only a fleeting idea, perhaps
merely a way to control her thoughts. Or else it was what Andy
Lebovitch called instinct, what Herbert Lagus called common
sense and Neugeborn called truth. That which joins people
together, and divides them. Whereas she had been thinking of
D.E. as an extension of herself, now it was the other way
around—man and woman, woman and man. She was pleasantly
tired. She thought of herself as potentially a part of D.E.'s life,
as when two people who are acquaintances suddenly enter each
other's lives and encounter new questions before the former
ones have been answered.

She wished he would reach out and touch her again. She hoped he would notice the bloodstains on the sheet. But she hoped he would not turn on the light. The moon was still low. It seemed very large. She wished D.E. would do certain things so that she would not have to think of others. D.E. handed her a towel for her to dry herself.

"I can imagine girls all over the world smiling at you, maybe all at the same time," she said.

The sky was beautiful. The darkness, heavy and veined with silver, was like the breath of many scarcely glimpsed shades of blue, green, and black. The stars sailed across in silence, like distant airy ships, full of fire, as one eternity succeeded another, and a second succeeded a third, and so on forever, in a way she could not understand and suddenly felt no need to. The feelings of nearness and distance for her suddenly merged. It was as if a curtain between darkness and life were drawn aside in a different way.

The buildings of the hotel and the outlines of the garden and fences looked like an old castle shrouded in gloom.

"I didn't know that you could touch immortality without moving a finger," laughed Dita.

"I took precautions," said D.E. carefully. He was not sure that he understood what she had meant.

In one of the rooms a door opened. You could hear what they played: "April in Portugal." In a moment the door closed, and the melody was lost.

The shadows on the moon looked like canyons and oceans, white deserts and silvery rocks. She thought of the ocean, without knowing why. The moon looked like a pearly landscape, as if the whole sky were a stream gushing forth from another sky that lay deep beneath it, or next to it. The stars around the moon looked like pearls too. At times the moon looked almost reddish. She asked herself whether she had changed into someone she had not been an hour ago. "I have never seen the sea," she said. D.E. looked at her questioningly.

"Do you think I'm crazy, David, for not telling you before?" It occurred to her that some girls were ashamed of having done it before. On the other hand, another girl might be ashamed of not having done it. She smiled, and D.E. had no idea what her smile meant. D.E. remained silenced by something that she had said earlier: that maybe she was here on behalf of her own mother, or of both her grandmothers, on behalf of the many women whom she had known and also whom she had never met, so that she might reap a share of happiness on their behalf.

"Time does strange things to what has happened, what is happening, and what is still to come," she said. "In spite of everything, some things become clearer at a distance."

Was she talking about wartime only because she felt the advent of peace? Or about faraway distances because at this moment she had a feeling of immediate closeness that she could not yet understand? Was it the first impulse in her not caused by war? Did the presence of a man in her life signify the opening of her soul? All the myths about women and men. She recalled what Brita had said: "When you wake up on your birthday, you don't feel you are a year older. And losing your virginity doesn't turn you into a woman, either." According to Brita, friendship between a boy and a girl comes to an end at the moment of sexual intercourse. They had talked about myths—for instance, the one that a nursing mother becomes pregnant easily, and other kinds of myths, like the one that no one knew what was going on in Auschwitz-Birkenau, or that Hitler didn't know about it either.

For goodness sake, surely she was not going to lie in bed thinking that every engine driver had known where the eastbound trains headed, and what for, and what would happen to the people in the carriages—to the last baby, the last old woman. But are we all inclined to shut our eyes to reality?

Suddenly she remembered a German phrase that always made her flesh creep: worthless lives.

She lay motionless. She felt the movement of D.E.'s hand, the rotation of the earth, the motion of the sun around the night, the impulse that had moved her body toward its first experience, all the things that were still to come and for which she was still young. She had always known that there was still time for everything, to solve how other girls seek and find love, the act that would become easier and less mysterious as she grew older. She wished to win the respect of men, no less than that of women, and to be rid of the fear of being exposed, as if she really had some unshared secret that drew together the bodies of all the women in the world into one gigantic body, the fertile heart of humanity.

She sensed the body next to her own, the aspect of her own self, the eclipse of pity, of everything that had filled her with fear, the joy that may arise from a woman's danger. How strange that a woman should have a sharper sense of her womanhood in one second with a man than in a whole lifetime spent alone. A smile appeared on her lips. She felt like one who rejoiced to give, because by giving she also received. She felt within herself a wildness, a savage, somewhat muted pride in the hunt. She felt rebellious and at the same time devoted to an extent that she had never before experienced. She felt both tolerance and conviction, and a sense of that kinship that can flourish between people. She had discarded all that girlish spite that diminishes both man and woman. It was as if, after being lost in the shady groves of her inner thoughts, she had come upon a mist that shrouded all that remained of her feelings.

Outside the window, the breeze gathered strength. She breathed the air of spring and the sound of the wind.

"Maybe," D.E. answered. "I don't know."

"I suppose I'm choosy. I'd like it all to stay just as it is now."

"I guess we both are," he smiled. He gazed at his own body next to hers. He looked satisfied. He knew what it meant for her to appear naked before him. He knew everything it meant.

"Sometimes it's enough to know there's somebody next to you who understands it all, and you don't need to say a word," Dita said.

She began to tell him how some of the girls she had been with in Poland in 1944 had been shipped off to the Arctic that summer. It was as if she wanted to share something with them now, retrospectively, in some kind of reversed cycle.

"In the end, I've always been better off than people that I once envied." It was then, too, that she learned not to overestimate or underestimate anybody. And that you have to be able to replace yesterday's values with those of today, and be ready to do it again tomorrow, as conditions change.

"I know that, Dita." There was a note of dismissal in his voice. He made it clear it was something he preferred not to discuss.

"No. Nobody knows who they are going to need, or when or who it is that can pull them out of the mud. And what the most important things in life are—like friendship, food, and health. To know what's coming tomorrow. The meaning of it all. I guess it can't just be unspoiled joy." And it shouldn't be color blindness either, she added to herself.

D.E. waited a moment. She continued, as he had feared she would. "People said that the girls were in luck. They'd be attached to some fishing crew. They were hand-picked girls. The prettiest and the strongest. In a factory over there they had made fishing nets out of female hair. They worked wonders really—children's clothing, insulation for German army barracks, and outer walls for electric ovens. They turned out riding whips, horsewhips, and whips for lion tamers in the Busch circus. And of course, nice little whips for the women SS guards. Quilts and sleeping bags and overalls for the German submarine crews. A few of those girls still had long hair when they came to Auschwitz-Birkenau. The Germans fancied the idea of having their mattresses stuffed with blond hair. I guess it gave them a better night's rest. Others preferred children's hair—black, ginger, curly, straight. Children's hair is finer and softer. Still others wanted the 'Jewish mixture.'"

"I can imagine what you looked like without hair," said D.E. "Must have been fun. I worked in a place where they made corsets from the bones they brought to the workshop from crematorium number 2 at Auschwitz-Birkenau. Who knows who's wearing those corsets to spring balls today? Somewhere I heard that there were also corsets for the German wounded."

"I had to go twice a month to the Delousing Station for disinfection, before Liza Vagner began to work there. After that, I was issued better clothing. We had to wash our hair with a mixture of some kind of disinfectant and tar. It stank. And it burned like hell. You can visualize where. At least you could feel sure that you'd been deloused."

"Was it far from our barracks?"

"Where exactly were you?"

"Should I draw you a map?"

"No need."

"Did you work in any of those hair factories?"

She laughed. "No. I try to avoid work whenever possible. Even though I know Munk's whole repertoire of sayings about why you ought to work so you won't see yourself as a thief."

"Arbeit macht frei."

"I used to carry stones for the building site at the Buna Werke. There and back again. Like the idiot who tied knots and untied them. I used to be afraid I'd be sent to work in the soap factory or the candle works. To collect fat into barrels. I could never get used to the idea that my grandma Olga might turn up in a cake of soap or a candle. A girl I knew worked there, in a factory near

Danzig. They were under the Reich Ministry of Railways. She
used to work in the accounting department—she had the quali-
fications—and she saw how the German firms competed for the
contracts. Topf and Sons won the biggest contract for ovens in
the crematorium. In their advertising brochure they claimed
that their ovens had the capacity to incinerate five hundred bodies in an hour."

"Well, don't you like 'Stille Nacht, Heilige Nacht'? Would you
want them to sit about in the dark while the air raids destroyed
Dresden and the power station?"

"Some of the girls produced tolerable perfumes and colognes.
If you didn't know what they were made of, it wouldn't occur to
you. The stuff was for women in the German homeland. The soldiers and officers didn't care. One Feldwebel used to stand at
the entrance to the women's showers and taunt the girls who
looked shy. I can remember two girls, twins, who were used by
the doctor for experiments on comparative reflexes, until he was
transferred. I heard that the Nazis shot him, not for the experiments but because he had stolen the twins' golden wisdom
teeth. That sergeant major used to send perfume home to his
wife, mother, and grandmother. In the end, you have to get used
to anything."

The deep blue sky, scattered with stars, streamed through the
window. It was a luminous, sweet-smelling evening. There was
still no sound except for the fire. The night smelled of the earth,
snow, and wind.

"I can imagine it," repeated D.E. after a while. "I try to see the
situation the other way. I think I'm done with all that. What an
upside-down world."

"'He who is merciful to the cruel will be cruel to the merciful,'
as the rabbis say."

"Of course. And, 'It is forbidden to sympathize with a fool.'"

"Why don't you like to talk about it?"

"Maybe I'm ashamed of it," said D.E.

"Maybe we're all ashamed."

"It's not much fun to dwell on it."

"Are you that strong?"

"There are a lot of things I've thrown overboard. I guess I'm not the only one." He did not need to specify the kind of things he had in mind. She could guess. He thought that telling something to a fool was like beating the air with a rod, as his father used to say. A rock of Gibraltar. Dita smiled.

"I guess I'm spoiled and upside down. There's something missing in everything for me. I wish I could be at least half as contented as I look."

"They say that false prophets are chopped up for kindling in hell, while frauds merely fry in melted pitch, and infidels and heretics lie in graves of fire. I guess all that's left for me is ice, as a traitor to my country, king, and office." It was evident that he had at least peeked at Dante.

She stretched herself, and she looked good, with her fresh, rosy, peachlike complexion, the smile lighting her oval face, and the placid light in her blue eyes.

"The worst punishment is for betraying hospitality." She was reciprocating well. "I'm going to be careful not to burn myself on the ice." Perhaps she also wanted to hint that she had read the same books. "Is it possible that when the Germans see pictures of ruins, they feel it is Berlin, Munich, or Dresden after the air raids? People say that now they think of Dresden and Auschwitz-Birkenau as six of one and half a dozen of the other. They are getting to the stage of forgetting who actually started the war and broke every rule. Maybe they were afraid that they would get back gas for gas? Andy read that German scientists, engineers, and industrialists invented Zyklon B as an insect spray, to kill two thousand people in less than half an hour at a cost of less than five pfennigs per body. What will they think of next?"

When D.E. looked at her quizzically, she said: "At the party, Munk was telling about a Chinese opera in which there was a prince whose father had been murdered. He hired two servants who had one sole duty: to remind him, every morning, as soon as he woke, of who had killed his father, and how."

"I hope he hired two more servants for a good-night chat. You are always looking back two years. Try to look ahead two years."

Dita smiled. Was D.E. going to ask her for more? Or should she ask? "Two years? A hundred years ahead, David. Who can forget faster than me, and better? Of course, we can only live once." She had an inviting voice, a little hesitant. Did he understand? Or not? "Have you seen the latest copy of the *Gazette?* The community is looking for someone to run the kitchen, even part-time. And a waitress for the kosher restaurant. Attractive conditions. Married couple considered."

"I don't want to tell you any lies," D.E. said slowly.

"You can, just a little," Dita answered. "Do you remember how they made a film in Theresienstadt? In the spring of 1943 a German crew came to make a film of my marvelous life. They selected me at the girls' home on L419. The director was Kurt Geron, who made *The Blue Angel,* with Marlene Dietrich. They assembled three thousand of us in J Block 4. They wanted us to laugh. I vowed to myself that I would not laugh even if they tickled me in all the places where I'm ticklish. Geron stood up high on the battlements. Cameras were all around us. I made the mistake of looking at him for just a moment. In five minutes he managed to make three thousand people laugh, including me. I laughed until my belly ached. I think we laughed for a quarter of an hour. In the end—and this I still don't understand—I didn't mind laughing."

"There are some people you just shouldn't look in the eye, that's all."

"The Germans relied on my sense of humor."

"The Germans also had a sense of humor," D.E. added. "They

rewarded Geron with a trip to the East. He went straight from the ramp into the Hygiene Center."

For a moment they both imagined the laughter to which people had been forced at an actor's command, just as easily as they had been forced to embark on the transport.

"Did they ever show that film?" D.E. asked.

"I didn't watch for the posters," Dita smiled.

Her eyes shone with a fantasy, both light and serious. She savored a man's company. It gave a new taste to everything, including a greater meaning to words. With her eyes she asked, What is love? What must one do to make the subject of one's love happy? How could she obtain what she had never had? What was it that put God and man on the same wavelength? She had always been a mixture of freedom, responsibility, and thoughtlessness, between consent and rebellion.

"Munk has a terrible influence on you." He thought how strong she was beside him, and how she made him feel weak. He had chosen a good place. The room was not too expensive. She wondered what it was that made certain words beautiful, for at the same time her thoughts were the reverse. Is it possible for a person to coincide with the words he says, perceives, prefers?

From the woods, the smell of old pine needles and damp roses floated toward them. Frogs croaked in the fields far away from the hotel. Night fell on the woods and meadows and on the roofs. One moment the stars were silver, and the next they were white. Some moved, others disappeared. The door was locked, the high window covered by long white curtains.

"At the same time you were there I was working at the DAW, Deutsche Ausrüstungwerke," said D.E. suddenly, as though he were apologizing for something that had just occurred to him, or as if he wanted to pick up somewhere that he had interrupted her. As if he were repaying a debt, reluctantly. "Old wounds heal slowly," he added.

D.E. was pleasantly self-possessed. She could not judge him as the kind of person who matures early and decays early too. There was something in him that made her uneasy.

"I probably wouldn't have talked about it with anyone else, D.E."

A train whistled in the distance. She thought of the girls who had sailed away to the Arctic Ocean and had acted as if they were going to a seaside resort. Some of them had worked in other establishments than those that processed hair or bones. They used to call them masseuses. They had a great assortment of experiences with the Poles and with the German soldiers and officers, not to mention prominent Jewish prisoners, who, in return for proven service of various kinds, had access to more substantial rations and the highest privileges available to prisoners. After a full day's work with their own people, they also wanted some relaxation. Among the girls were violinists, singers, and pianists who sometimes also helped in the massage parlors. They soon wore out. The place was nonstop, twenty-four hours a day. The turnover was faster than among the men in the Sonderkommando. They were a pitiful sight when they were loaded on the trucks, like broken-down hags, eighteen- and twenty-year-old girls, taken away, ostensibly to other work sites. When the windows were open in the summer, you could hear the sound of arias from *Die Fledermaus* and *Madame Butterfly* or *Carmen*. Polish and French stars played Chopin, Mozart, or Bach on the piano or accordion for selected German officers. If it were not for the haze of black smoke and dust from the chimneys of all four crematoriums, floating like clouds over the camp, summer and winter, you might almost think you were somewhere else at that moment. But as soon as they loaded the girls into the trucks, taking them to the fishing boats, they started to get nervous. In the end they didn't need to ask where they were going, only who sent them there. The train continued to whistle. Then there was silence.

"In 1944 people would probably have found it difficult to go to paradise if Germans were the ones escorting them."

Was D.E. listening? Probably. She thought how nobody wanted to make it more difficult for them in those days. She imagined how an animal must feel when forests are on fire, the land is flooded, or a storm is brewing.

"It's all just like delirium," D.E. observed. His eyes showed disgust, almost contempt, even if it was not directed at her. "I never knew you were such an unremitting authority in the field. You have a very developed sense of humor."

"It never occurred to me, either," Dita answered. She ignored his barb.

"Somebody told me that you were raped—or nearly raped—in the woods at the end of the war, or soon after it," D.E. said, suddenly, in the same tone he had used to tell her where he had worked during the war.

"You must know that nobody raped me," Dita smiled. "The things they say about people when they survive . . . and even if it had happened, David?"

D.E. returned her smile. She had surprised him by the mildness of her reply. He was pleased that he had been able to confirm what he had thought, even though he did not overestimate its importance. To be the first? Or the last? He would have come here with her anyway.

"I know what they say about me. It would surprise me if they didn't. They say it about every one of us. Always the same old story. It happened so often, and to so many girls. I know a version of the story involving an actress, not a Jewess. Two men, one with a pistol aimed at her head, his finger on the trigger, the other one holding her down. You can imagine the rest—according to taste, hunger, army unit, and goodness knows what else. They did whatever they fancied. If a girl doesn't get herself shot, they always manage to pin some guilt on her, whatever the circumstances."

Once again she wondered what it is that transforms the best into the worst, or the most beautiful into the ugliest. She shrugged. She heard the voices of ghosts—ghosts of voices and eyes.

"That isn't the worst that can happen to you, D.E. Things like sickness and death. There are heavier burdens than 'the burden of honor.' What about when your dearest wish is just to cease to exist? What's that in comparison with rape? What does it matter if there were two, or three, or ten at once, one after another? You just open and close your eyes. The world is full of perversity, D.E. It has as many faces as there are people in the world. Maybe more. As if every person had more than one face. It's just one aspect of the way we live."

She thought of what Liza had said. On her sixteenth birthday she had asked whether all women in the world only made love with the darling of their hearts. She also remembered the secret Tonitschka had persistently kept to herself.

She laughed as mildly as she spoke. She was happy that D.E. was silent, stroking her hip. He touched her as if reminding himself that she really was the same girl he had slept with a short while ago. Her big blue eyes closed. She thought how far away his thoughts were, and that he did not trust her with them. Someone opened a window in the kitchen below. The clatter of dishes, pots, and saucepan lids came through. They began to serve dinner.

"You're probably the first person I would have said that to." She smiled. "I suppose you think I've been lying." The words sounded as if they came out of nowhere. She realized she was capable of lying to him. She tried to stretch out on the bed as comfortably as possible.

"You don't owe me anything," he said, implying at the same time that he too owed her nothing. She picked up on this immediately.

"Do you know the tale of the man who came home from work and received a telegram? He opened it and read that his wife, who had gone away for a cure at a resort, had died. He put the telegram back in the envelope, set the alarm clock, and thought: 'That'll be a surprise when I wake up in the morning.'"

It sounded wrong. D.E. looked at her almost with gratitude. From down below came the noise of cups and glasses, the rushing, bubbling, and splashing of dishwater. For a moment it seemed that someone had dropped a whole stack of glasses and plates.

"As For-Better-for-Worse says, there's many a slip between cup and lip."

She laid her hands on the sheet and looked at the curtains and out the window. It suddenly occurred to her why she had always liked windows so much. The twilight and the noise from the kitchen felt pleasant. She had thrown back the sheet and lay naked on the bed. D.E. looked at her. She wondered how he saw her. Dita had always been careful to show only those parts of herself that she regarded as attractive. She was quite pleased with her own body, the way it looked on the clean bed, and with the idea that she could measure its quality through the eyes of the boy she had chosen. She breathed in the smell of the evening, and of his body and hers. With it came the scent of pine needles from outside. She experienced it all like caressing music. She thought about what she had said to D.E. and what she had long ago wanted to express but had never dared to say to anyone. She lifted the corners of her lips, as if she were smiling to herself without opening her mouth.

A train whistled in the distance. Apparently the trains did not travel very quickly here. From the sound you could follow how it turned and traversed the area between fields, woods, and clay pits, on its way into the spring night. The whistling of the train went on for a long time. Only gradually did it begin to die away, each finale covering the next, until the sound of the whistling merged with that of the wind. It was no longer possible to tell the sound of the wind from that of the train and the whistling.

The sound of running water from the kitchen became a noisy laugh. An older woman's voice could be heard among the cooks.

"Now I know the difference between us, D.E. You want to live fast, and I don't want anything fast, except a quick death, if it has to be. But right now I would like to live slowly."

"I know exactly what you want. But apart from the fact that I want to live fast, I want to live long. I think we understand each other, Dita. I'm also in favor of anything that lessens a person's suffering."

"Tell me what the sea looks like."

She thought that an echo might be louder than the original sound. But she was not the only one to behave as if the barrier between the Second and a Third World War was weak and uncertain. She glanced into the mirror beside the bed. In the failing light, she saw her body, her face, teeth, and eyes. Her ultimate weapon was her smile.

"There's a seaside town, something like a spa, Biarritz. We made a short stopover there, at a meeting of the International Blue and White." He looked at her body, face, and watchful eyes. "We had great weather. We stayed at a lovely hotel. In fact, we lived like pigs in clover. I don't ever expect to live like that again. But I don't mind. I'd probably soon get tired of it anyway."

"Did you go sailing?"

"Why? How did you know?"

"You can't keep a secret for five minutes here."

"Once. I had to pay for it."

"What was it like?"

"Like battling with the wind. Or with eternity. It dragged on into the night. The stars looked as if they were circling around each other. It made our heads spin. At night the moon was like gold. You can feel a sort of basic untiring strength. Only *you* get tired. I had the boat for eight hours. I sure collected a few bruises."

"Do you think I'd have enjoyed it?"

"It's made just for you, Dita."

"Were there lovely suntanned women in alluring bathing suits?" She did not add what Fatty Munk had told her at her birthday party, about the ninety-three girls from a school in the Warsaw ghetto in 1943 who had chosen to take poison rather than be sent, after disinfection and hot baths, to the German brothels.

"There were women there, without their husbands. But there was a shortage of the kind who don't scare me."

"I thought you were through with fear, David." Then she asked: "What kind of women scare you most?" In reality she thought about those he sought after most. It was almost as if she were saying "next time" to someone who answered her that there would be no next time. As Munk always said, it isn't what you say about yourself, it's what other people say about you. But is it true? Sometimes it is, sometimes not. She stretched herself and hugged her knees.

"It's the most accessible women who scare me."

"Does that include me?"

"Present company excepted," D.E. smiled. He touched the sheet and white pillow. "These sheets smell good!"

"Am I weak or strong, D.E.?"

"Maybe both. Why do you ask?"

"You know, when those girls were shipped off to the Arctic Ocean, everybody said how lucky they were—not everybody could be so lucky. No one ever saw them again, not one of them."

D.E. held her head in his lap. He stroked her eyelashes, her eyelids, the corners of her mouth.

"The Arctic Ocean, the fishing unit, fishing nets—why don't you leave it alone, Dita? As far as that goes, the Baltic Sea is not going to have the pleasure of my company for a while either, though it's not the sea's fault." He laughed. He kept her head in his lap. She wondered to herself what he expected.

"What's wrong?" he asked after a while. He had the impression that whatever had happened to her, perhaps he should not have asked her so bluntly.

"It's fine. It's fine. Believe me."

"It'll be great when you can speak English, French, and Spanish," said D.E. "I'll be glad to know you. I can just imagine how you'll be the center of attention, and how proud you'll be." D.E. listened to the music. They played an overture.

"Dr. Fitz says that the most difficult fight is against your own illusions."

"Yeah."

"You know, D.E., when those girls went off to the Arctic Ocean, they were loaded into Mercedes and Renault trucks—the best trucks in Auschwitz-Birkenau. Trucks always reminded me of horses. All at once the girls began to sing. We thought our ears were deceiving us. Perhaps the girls were happy because they were leaving, and maybe they sang as people do when they are afraid of being alone. It was a beautiful song. About ash trees and mountains, about life and love, about everything that lasts for only a brief time. It was awful, because it could have been so lovely. It was as if they were saying to the Germans that *this* was their world—not the camp—that the camp was the Germans' world. And that they were glad to be leaving, whatever the price. We were permitted to sing only when the Germans ordered us to. For unauthorized singing you got beaten, sometimes shot. And suddenly I saw that I was crying. I prided myself on how tough I'd become, how all the humiliations, beatings, hunger and cold, had hardened me. All at once the tears were running down my face because I heard a beautiful song and saw who was singing it. All around us there was fire, pots where people were frying in their own fat, hot ash like a volcano, stoked with people whom the Germans had crippled and eliminated so that their own Aryan world might seem bigger, at least in their own eyes.

"Then the trucks began to move. Across the sky wild geese flew, higher than the pits, chimneys, smoke, higher than the barbed wire and the silos above the showers where I had seen the German technician tossing the green crystal Zyklon B from the containers, and higher and farther than all the mess we had to live with. The birds flew in wedge formations southward, just as they will do ten times ten thousand years from now.

"Somebody pointed them out as an omen of good weather for the journey. I couldn't hear the sound of the engines running anymore. I only saw the birds getting smaller and smaller, like white dots in the sky, and as they got tinier and tinier they darkened in color until they were gray spots, and then even that faded away, and finally the geese were gone. I wept, because people I had been with were always leaving me, and I was left alone, just as I had left so many people, and left them alone too. In spite of everything, this world seemed beautiful to me. Even though we were in Auschwitz-Birkenau. Or perhaps just because we were there. I don't know. We always wished that at least one of us might survive and be able to testify what was wrong with us that we lived like that, and why they beat us for no other reason than because we had been born, without regard for what each of us might have become, what talent each had, what contribution to the world each might have made. I could never explain it to myself. You know, I don't talk so much about those dreadful things. What can you say about them? And whom can you tell it to? Yourself? What secret does life hide within itself? It was like a magnet drawing you toward anything that was alive. And suddenly I felt again that there is no secret. I knew that life is just that which we all have in common, and that, just beyond the chimneys, the sky is blue, and soft, and so beautiful that it hurts. And that no one should take possession of another's life, because when you do, you kill your own life too. And because just as no one can have two hearts, no one can bear the weight of any other life than his own. And I saw that people could live like animals but that they could be good. I felt able to forgive everything and begin again. Including forgiveness for the Germans. I know how you feel about that. Draw a line and make a fresh start. Stop thinking about your own interests. End the spiral that runs through people, from nowhere to nowhere, even though I knew in advance that I can and may forgive only on my own account, not on behalf of a single one of those innocent people they murdered. And I said to myself that if I had to die—and every second we were as close to it as the sound of your breath—I would like to die at a moment like that, when the song of the girls and the sound of the motors died away, and the wild geese were flying across the sky."

A shadow of helplessness passed before D.E.'s eyes. He refrained from saying that it is best not to open the eyes of the dead or the blind. Or that, given the right circumstances, you have to be grateful if it is your brother's head that falls instead of your own. "I really don't want to think that just because my own horse has been killed the grass doesn't need to grow anymore, Dita."

He had heard a note in her voice he had heard at the very beginning, not a dynamo that recharges itself without the energy it generates. While she whispered, with her head in his lap and her words floating through the dimness, he had wondered what had been opening up within her like a softly rumbling volcano, as if she released her words into the current of a stream and the stream carried them away, as if she followed her own words, walking behind them on the water's surface toward some unknown sea into which everything disappeared. He sensed an echo of the fears they shared, whether long forgotten or recently suppressed, that could not be kept from surfacing again and appearing in words not yet spoken and in actions that had not yet even happened. Simultaneously, she inspired in him a feeling of recognition, and admiration, and regret. He sighed, knowing that it was a thing each could only settle alone, though not, perhaps, from start to finish, completely alone. There were still many things that he knew only as long-vanished echoes, and other things he didn't even wish to know.

He was not sure whether it was sadness that he felt in her, at the time, or a will to live, some haunting myth about what the joined wills of human beings can build—the kind of myth that holds people and their world together, as opposed to myths that divide and destroy. He sensed a longing in her to come to terms with it all, to penetrate the bottom, the end of things that lie in the recesses of the brain, like the sediment in mines or fallen rocks on a path. Something inexplicable. He touched her eyes with one hand and left the other on her hips. He wished she wouldn't look backward or forward.

Down below the overture had ended.

"It smells like apples here," D.E. said. "I bet there are lots of apple trees around. You can smell honey, too. Do you like apples and honey?"

Dita's complexion was soft and smooth.

"I'd rather listen more and talk less, too," Dita said, smiling. "And if I've got nothing nice to say, nothing pleasant, then I won't say anything at all." Then she said: "Mother used to give us apples for Jewish New Year when she wanted the whole year to be sweet for us."

"My parents used to eat them too. Each one of us had to take at least a little bite. The whole family used to get together— uncles, aunts, cousins. I had about forty cousins."

"My uncle was in the Sonderkommando. His job was with teeth!"

"One of my cousins was in it too," said D.E.

"Do you know anything about it?"

"To tell you the truth, I don't really want to." He did not say what he had learned from Mr. Gotlob: to separate things into categories—interesting and important, for everybody or for him. What was important for him was to keep his fate as much as possible under his own control, to separate himself from the past.

"Actually, we were all in the Sonderkommando in one way or another—Liza with her cans for the Delousing Station,and you and I—the fact that we were there, and survived. Except at the expense of someone else? Even if it isn't anybody's fault, they're not entirely without guilt either."

She felt like children when they build a house of sand or snow, or from fleeting moments. She had no proper word for it. She looked at her bracelet.

"For me, memories are another country, far away," D.E. said. "I'm here now. I never go back."

"Sometimes I dream of Theresienstadt. I'm doing well— enough food, clothes, entertainment, occasionally a lecture by a world authority, trips to the mountains—at least in my imagination."

He glanced at her. She smiled back at him. Her eyes were soft and deep blue. It occurred to him that for Dita the past was like a gorilla, every movement a threat, dangerous at every point where its bared claws reached outside the cage.

"Do you think everything that's beautiful is also dangerous?" she asked.

"The past hurts. That's all I know just now. They say an elephant never forgets." D.E. smiled. She returned his smile and looked into the darkness to find his face, but she found his hands.

The music began again, playing for the diners. She wondered what she actually wanted to convince D.E. of. What was it she wanted to reassure herself of? Was a lost virginity enough to open the door to all she wanted? Enough to enable her to understand everything that had baffled her? So that she could come to terms, once and for all, with everything that she did not need to or must not take into her future?

She listened to the music from below—the melody, rhythm, and words. Perhaps what she really sought was to give it to someone else, like the ferryman in the fairy tale who had to jump out of the boat and leave the oar to his passenger—as though by words she could jettison her burden, like the oar in the tale. Did she seek to master all of life's secrets, all those things she had waited for, all the quiet, yet hidden mysteries? Could anyone attain all that in a single stroke?

She listened to the song coming from below, the words, the tune. She smiled in the darkness, but the smile was forced, and D.E. noticed it, recalling his own remark about the elephant's memory. The music drifted up to the windows, and the wind carried the melody away toward the woods.

"You don't have to lie to me," Dita said. "Though I'm aware that it doesn't bother men to lie to girls."

D.E. laughed too, without knowing exactly why. He had an urge to hand her a knife or scissors, so she might try to cut herself off from the Arctic Ocean. He took her hand and kissed her fingertips. Then he breathed on her, as if trying to warm her, because she had come from the Arctic.

8 The window was half open, and from the outside they heard the clatter of trotting horses. Invisible under the veil of the evening, the horses ran across the meadow, quiet, alert, with neighing and snorting, distinguished from the darkness by their bodily sounds and hooves. Then the clatter of the hooves on the grass ceased. They could guess what was going on in the other parts of the hotel. From the nearby village they heard the sound of the bell announcing vespers. The wind carried the sound closer and mingled it with the sound of cars on the road leading to the hotel between the castle and the monastery. They were only twelve miles from Prague.

The bells swung in the darkness, sending all kinds of messages on the wind, as well as the message that night was falling—time passing and receding through the present, further away into the past, like the echo of the music from the garden restaurant. The music stopped.

Nothing moved on the road now. For a moment the sound of bells lay in the air as if, by their ringing, they had reached out like fingers to touch the space of the world. Then they saw two gypsy wagons lit by Aladdin lamps. Fragments of voices, screams, a wild melody, the neighing of a draft horse.

"Gypsies," Dita said.

"Yeah," D.E. sighed. Once when Dita was still a child, she heard the sound of gypsies playing and singing from far away. She had been afraid to go nearer to their camp. She drew near only once, almost up to their camp—three wagons with awnings and five horses grazing in the wood. The gypsy children harassed her and demanded that she give them something. She gave them everything she had in her pocket, including her handkerchief, but they wanted her shoes and skirt too. One of the horses was fat; four were emaciated. After that she was afraid of gypsies until in later years her fear was supplanted by the gypsy songs or just the echo of their songs, charming from a distance. In Auschwitz-Birkenau she met gypsy women brought there before the Germans recalled their husbands from the front. They served in military detachments on the railways and as engineers, building bridges. Surprised by who their families were, the Germans loaded them on trucks, brought them to Auschwitz-Birkenau, stripped them of their uniforms, and gassed them. The German guards chatted with them, even on the way to the crematorium, for the gypsies knew the Germans well. Some of them had distinguished themselves at the front. Some of them, when given the chance at Auschwitz-Birkenau, behaved worse than Germans. The Germans had only racial objections against them, but for the Germans an order was an order—no appeal permitted. In Auschwitz-Birkenau it was said that in the underground chamber, before the Zyklon B crystals were dropped through the shower heads and dissolved into gas, the gypsy women made love to their husbands and the old men, to make up for all they were losing.

In Dita's mind, gypsies were connected with freedom, beautiful singing, and how the children had robbed her and pushed her around. The last thing they were able to grab from life before they were choked by the Zyklon B was what they, like Andy, regarded as the very substance of life.

The voice of a voice, the eyes of eyes, shadow of shadows. It was like a river that had eyes and could gaze back. Now it coalesced with the sound of the cicadas, the sight of the stars, and lost itself among them. She thought of the strange laws of memory that can rarely be controlled. The gypsy wagons were swallowed by the night.

The sound of vespers rang out above the spring earth for about ten minutes. It seemed to her a bit childish, perhaps as old people are childish, and it implied a certain clarity and comprehensibility of death, organized into the earthy ground. She thought of the gypsy men, women, and children. All had disappeared; their camps had vanished. The gypsy wagons, horses, and pots had become German wagons, horses, and pots. Few had survived. But there were always a few survivors. It was said that after the revolution many of the gypsies who had survived the Nazis emigrated to America, where their king lived. Who could tell? She remained silent until D.E. said, "According to Mr.

Gotlob, there is something that outlives all revolutions."

"Do you mean horses or gypsies or Jews? Churches? Mr. Gotlob?"

"Banks," D.E. said, smiling.

"He should talk to Munk. Munk believes that man rises above himself only because he creates something that lives longer than man, whatever that may be."

It seemed strange to D.E. that Dita discovered, heard, or saw three or five things where others found only one. Or ten? A connection of thought escaped him. Was she able to leave the landscape of the past, throw off from herself all that made life uncomfortable?

"Give me five years, Dita, to look after myself and put the past behind me, as if it had never been. Then I will invite the grandeur and nobility into my life, like when you have plenty of food and space, so you can invite guests. We both know the generosity of the satiated."

"That reminds me of the joke about the magician on the *Titanic*," Dita said, smiling. "I would be surprised if you hadn't heard it. Evening after evening he quarreled with the parrot, who objected to the way he made rabbits, pigeons, and handkerchiefs disappear into his hat. Then they ran into the iceberg of ill renown. The magician and the parrot were holding on to a spar. It was night; the water was icy. The angry parrot asked the magician: 'And now tell me, Mr. Smarty Pants, what have you done with the ship?'"

"Have you heard the one about the rabbi and the priest? They were eating and drinking together, and all of a sudden the priest asked, 'Rabbi, we're alone here, no witnesses. Tell me truthfully, have you ever eaten pork?' The rabbi looked up with lovely, deep chocolate eyes and nodded, 'Once.' They went on eating and drinking, and all of a sudden the rabbi asked, 'Father, we are all alone here, no witnesses. Tell me—but the truth now.

Have you ever been with a woman?' The priest gazed at him with his beautiful innocent eyes and nodded, 'Once.' Then the rabbi gave him a friendly pat on the shoulder: 'Better than pork, isn't it?'"

"I'm still young," Dita smiled.

"Lonely people age faster."

"I can almost believe it."

"Your eyes are hot."

"Old winds blew away the cold. Like last year's snow." The smile, half sophisticated and half helpless, remained on her lips. "Do you know how I see myself with you, David? Like I felt before we went to Theresienstadt, on the last night of the holidays. Like when I was taking care of children, and I thought to myself how good life was, in spite of everything. Or like when I grabbed something from the German storage rooms stolen from the Jewish transports—warm underwear, gloves, thermoses. Once I took a beautiful rosy bathrobe with a sash and horn buckle." She drew in the night air deeply.

9 "Your eyes are really blue," said D.E.

"Arctic-ice blue?"

"Blue and gentle eyes," D.E. repeated.

Dita took his hand into hers and laid it near her heart. He left his hand limp. She didn't feel him responding.

To him the sound came like an insistent voice that she had built around him as one builds a bastion, and he suddenly realized that behind that wall was her secret. Maybe she did not even realize it. Perhaps it was better for her not to know. It was only a fleeting thought. But the abyss was no less frightening just because those blue eyes into which he had been gazing held certainty beside uncertainty, maturity together with derision. He recalled, without quite knowing why, the old saying that the wolf never swallows its prey in front of its own den. He breathed in the moist air at the window and the scent of fresh construction in the annex.

Calm flooded into the room, like deep water that seems dark only because it goes so far down from the surface, and because the sun has set long ago. Within the deep water was an unknown, still unfathomed life that she had until now barely touched. A dream of a man, of dependability and equilibrium. Pictures of life that she could not drown in the water like pebbles, and that the wind did not carry away like the sound of evening bells.

In Dita there was a toughness that D. E. Huppert had noticed the first time he ever saw her, and at the same time a frailty, with no boundary between. He let his hand lie there. Her breasts were supple and cold. Finally David Egon Huppert regretted what he had done.

"Is it as you imagined it, D.E.? Is it worse than you expected, or better?"

D.E. laughed. He could not tell her that it takes more than one brick to build a wall. Nor that a wolf is never happier than during a storm. Nor that he would rather have one egg today than the promise of roast chicken tomorrow. For him it was better to remain silent.

It was not his words she longed for. She just wanted to hear his voice. She thought of the courage a girl looks for in a boy, of the past frontiers she would be willing to cross by his side, and of the strange path that runs between inner servitude and inner freedom. Didn't she know him? Didn't he know her?

"Do you feel all right?" asked D.E.

"How about you?"

She got to her feet, walked to the window, and looked out at the stars. She was conscious of a depth that, in her fear, she would never be able to compass. She wanted to tell him a nursery rhyme about the stars, one that she remembered from when she was a little girl and longed for something she could not comprehend. She feared loneliness, even in his presence. Instead, she said, "I know exactly what I want to do with my life, D.E. First English, French, and then Spanish and maybe Italian. I have already picked up a few words of Russian. In spite of everything, I like German. I can't understand why. Maybe because my mother spoke it fluently. When I was little, she used to read Heine aloud to me—the passage where he says that, however brightly the sun may shine, it must sink in the end."

Then she recalled that Hitler had ordered Heine's tomb in Paris to be removed. It struck her that the game she played was a constant struggle between restraint and fantasy, the curb and the free rein, between bitter and sweet. Down below they were playing a medley from Gershwin.

"I'd like to stay here overnight," said Dita suddenly. "I suppose that time's more important for a girl than for a boy. Or else it's just different. Maybe that's the real difference between a man and a woman?" She did not want to talk about what she had missed in life anymore, or about anything that reminded her of it. She wanted to ask D.E. what he valued most. At the same time she caught herself in the realization that she was putting into his mouth the replies she wanted to hear, fearing the replies she did not want.

"You are asking too much of me."

"You know, D.E., when life is as wonderful as it is just now, I'm not afraid at all." She failed to add "of dying." Maybe love is also a form of death, like babies falling asleep, not like people dying bit by bit, aware of it or not, in the camps.

"You don't have to fear anything."

"Everything that goes quickly is fine with me." She started laughing. "If it would go first I might be able to decide to die. In style, of course. In my best outfit, on some nudist beach, like when you start to waltz. But without any effort. Just like swallowing some cherry stone. Or yet even easier. It must be the easiest for people like me. You need to have a gift for that. Don't worry. I'm dying to be alive."

D.E. smiled. He closed his eyes for a while. She saw how he lay naked on the white bedding, with one arm stretched out toward the warmth of the glowing stove and the other over himself as if in modesty. She was not surprised that he did not reply.

"Once I was very close to the place where you, Neugeborn, and Andy Lebovitch were, when you were staying in the gypsy camp. I was in the women's camp, separated from you only by a few rows of barbed wire. From where we were, we could see into your place. There used to be gypsies there before they sent them up the chimney and before your group came. On the other side we had a view of the chimneys and the ovens, the brothel and the concert hall, and the massage parlor at the other end of the tracks. There was a sixteen-year-old girl and her mother with her in our barracks. Lots of people envied them for being able to stay together. And how they understood each other. During those seven to ten days the mother aged. It was certain that they would pick her. They had no one to protect them and couldn't send anyone else in their place. I slept just across the aisle from their bunk, and every night I heard the girl trying to prepare her mother for it, talking to her as if it were going to be the other way around, and the mother telling her that we were all born and must die, and that when life is so dreadful, dying is a relief, a gift, that it is not just false comfort. They didn't talk about justice and the ways of the world. Not a word about God, though sometimes I thought I heard the old woman—she was forty-five—repeating the words over and over again, like when you say prayers. Occasionally somebody would shout at them to shut up and not prevent the others from getting a few hours of sleep. One night, in fact, one of the women hit them because that same evening the German wardress had beaten her. 'My child,' the mother said once, 'children and fools speak the truth.'

"Then came the selection on Monday. The girl assured her mother that there was nothing to be afraid of, that she would go with her, if she wished. I knew it was not true. Both of them knew it. She did not want to die. She was just sixteen. Then, afterward, I was not so sure. She repeated to her mother that it would soon be over. She promised to walk up there with her, when it came time. She even struck up an acquaintance with a man in the Sonderkommando who had a sweetheart in our barracks, and she begged him to ask the German executioner-technician to throw as many crystals of Zyklon B as possible into the shower heads, so she would know she had done the absolute maximum for her mother that could be done. Generally no one could accompany anyone there, unless you wanted to run the risk of being included in the party, in case there happened to be one missing, to make up the number.

"They looked at the chimneys as one might look at the end of the world. That wall was the end of the world. The offer was genuine. Not like when people say something and in the same breath pray to be rid of the other before the shadow of danger falls on themselves. We all used to breathe again once the selection was over. Out of sight, out of mind. When the truck had driven away with the people they'd selected for the chimneys, we could look forward to one night. It was all part of our general routine, like morning and evening, Monday, every day in the week. Nobody was surprised at anything.

"The worst thing—and in some ways the best—was that they picked the mother. It could have been the other way around. They could have taken the girl and left the mother to stew in her own juices for a few days and nights, filled with guilt, as if she had been responsible for picking her daughter and sending her off to the gas. Sometimes the German soldiers used to kill them

by doing that sort of thing. They took pleasure in proving to us
that nothing was quite as we thought. They were bored. Life
around the ramp, transport, selection every Monday, and ovens
was boring. However, the block deputy in our barracks was a
decent French Jewess, and the girl was allowed to go and
accompany her mother to the gate where the truck was standing. It was dangerous, but she went. Maybe she hoped that
someone might decide to put her on board and take her with
them. Sometimes our own people ordered such things, when the
number was one short and they wanted to avoid any misunderstanding with the Germans. Both of them were aware of that, of
course.

"And so they walked away together. You should have seen
them, the skinny mother and her scrawny young daughter. Both
with eyes sunken from lack of sleep, because they had spent
every night explaining that there's no art in dying. Both of them
knew that twenty paces from there it all came to an end and that
Mother would never see the sun go down or rise again, the grass
growing, or the stream running. It all looked so peaceful, maybe
like when a plague comes, carried on the wind. They were reconciled to it.

"The girl escorted her to the covered truck. She had her arm
around her mother's neck. Now and then she tried to press her
cheek to her mother's. They were not crying; they just walked
side by side. It was as dreadful, and as dignified, as any person
could be. The girl did not hurry to get it over. She didn't dawdle
either. I wonder what she thought about during those twenty
paces. Behind the gate, by the fence, the German truck was
waiting. Suddenly they stopped. I think it was the mother who
stopped first. The daughter took a step backward. The mother
touched her arm gently and told her she didn't want her to go
any further. The girl caressed her in return. She did not say a
word. Her mother also didn't want to make it harder for her. To

go on living was not much easier than to die. We watched them as they stood there, as if, without words, merely with their eyes, they were saying all that they had never been able to say to each other before. As if they were chatting together about all those things people chat about when they are not going to see each other again for some time. After that the mother said no. Just one word. No? No what? We could only guess.

"The girl was just able to kiss her on the lips, stroke her hair, face, and arm. The mother smiled and winked. Her eyes were terribly sunken. But even now they did not cry. The old woman even had a faint smile on her lips, as if to comfort her daughter that there was nothing to be done and this was the best way. And at the same time tears were streaming down her cheeks. She kept whispering, just a few words. I couldn't hear what she said, and I suppose I didn't even want to. Maybe she was saying that dying is not such a terrible thing and that they would meet again somewhere. It looked just as if the girl had taken her mother to a bus station but couldn't go any further with her. The way people know that they live and will die one day, and it isn't always fair when, how, and whose turn it is now. But there are certainly worse things in the world than dying. For example, living."

"What is done is done," said D.E. "As a matter of fact, didn't we say that forgetting means living?"

"Forgetting means dying, D.E.," Dita said. The words came pouring out from between her lips like a choking wave. "Isn't it true that a fool only glimpses what the wise man already has?" She did not tell D.E. what had happened to the girl a few days before, in front of the hut, when they were forming a line for food. She had wanted to make a place for her mother in front of her. A noncom of the SS struck her in the face with a dog collar. The buckle knocked out her two front teeth. She had to go back to the end of the line. Another SS man who was dishing out the food had noticed the incident and put an extra piece of pork pasty into her hand. She didn't want to eat it herself, so she closed her fist and took it over to her mother. The pasty began to warm up in her hand and run down between her fingers. The other women mobbed her and began to lick her fingers. In the end there was only a tiny scrap left to give her mother.

D.E. was silent. Then he asked her, "What would you like me to do to you?"

She knew what he had, and most certainly did not have, in mind, but she answered: "I don't want to be as afraid as I was then, D.E., even if life wouldn't be as sweet as it is now. Could you caress me like that some more?"

She walked across from the curtain back to the bed and lay down in the same position as before, with her hip next to D.E. Through the dim light she looked into his eyes. Then quietly she asked him, "Do you think we can learn how to die? Learn to accept what comes, what is inevitable and inescapable, whatever it may be?"

The way she was lying on the bed, naked and pretty, seemed incongruous with her questions.

"It's like a work of art, but there are no rehearsals. Or are there?" She stretched out. "Everybody does their show only once. Maybe you need to have a talent for it, like for music. I don't know. But it also takes courage, and a kind of dignity. I really don't know. I've known many people who knew how to die, and plenty too who were very inexperienced."

It sounded almost flirtatious, for she had soft skin, healthy and young. At the same time there was something that went deeper than the defiance with which young people sometimes speak, as if they were challenging death to a duel in the expectation that it is still so far away. Her voice was like a ship on a deep ocean, like a spark flying above an open volcano, like a cloud that has swallowed up all the water it intends to drop in the form of rain.

It struck him that one could say that death, too, is not what we want but what we have. Only the dead are spared envy. As old For-Better-for-Worse says, after the death of many, even more of the living breathe a sigh of relief.

She smiled to herself. Again D.E. did not reply. She felt his hand on her hip. It reminded her of a role in a play she had heard of only from the accounts of others and was now playing herself. Playing herself. She smiled at the thought.

"I would like to be able to view the world as you do, D.E. Do you think I've become insensitive?"

"Maybe you've grown tougher."

"Is it in self-defense?"

"It's as if you were standing on a bridge."

"Is that taboo now?"

"What do you mean?"

The curtains were ruffled by the wind. The white lace, weighted at the bottom, swung in the draft.

She thought of the kind of memory that flowers, trees, and rivers have or that of animals, birds, and fish, scorched fields, hills, forests, and rocks crushed into dust. She thought of extinct volcanoes, lifeless deserts, dried-up seas. She stroked the surface of the blanket.

D.E. looked at her as though, for a moment, he did not see her body, face, and eyes. He stared as though he saw through her, something else far removed from her, linked by an invisible chain.

She drew in her breath sharply and held it in as though she were swallowing a thought. She recalled how she had dreamed about him, how for a fragment of the night he had seemed like a mirror image of himself.

A new melody and voices came through the window from the garden restaurant below. The song was soft, full of promise, and the human voices gave it meaning that emphasized, and at the

same time challenged, the feeling of loss arising from the songs
and happiness that no one would ever claim. Dita listened as if
they were playing for her. The song filled her with fear and hope.
She listened to it as if she were reading a letter from an
unknown sender, and she thought of Fatty Munk. The clay earth,
the distant hills and woods, and the stars and moon in the sky
brought that song about songs, journeys, and happiness to life.
Or else it was the other way around: the song gave life to them.
Although it was soon over, it lingered on in her memory together with its melody, and it distilled its meaning into her as a
flower head drops its seed into the ground, corn its grains, or
music its melody. It struck her that things are not as unfair as
they sometimes appear to be. A world opened up before her that
she had perhaps never noticed before. She smiled faintly, with
raised lips. D.E. looked at her.

"The music here is not bad," he said.

"It isn't."

"They sing very well."

"I hadn't heard that tune before."

"Songs travel faster than people. One country steals from
another. But what do we care? As long as they go on playing and
singing."

"Should they really punish song stealing?"

"If they catch them?"

"Even if they do."

He caught his breath as if he were angry, though not merely
with her. "Apart from the art of remembering, there's the art of
forgetting, Dita. The art of thinking of oneself. I don't need to
take two steps backward so that I can take one step forward like
Fatty Munk."

The voices from the kitchen died down and then grew louder
again, according to how many guests came into the restaurant
or departed. She leaned back comfortably. She summoned a

secret world to the surface of her mind, as if trying to sort herself out—a kind of spring cleaning—a world that put a weapon into her hands or disarmed her by jettisoning excess baggage, both a gain and a loss. Fortunately, only the inhabitants had any conception of this world.

Wrapped in the gathering dusk, the outside silence deepened. The stars grew brighter, until they appeared so near that you could reach out and touch them. Upon their world lay the shadow of a war that had changed into peace.

Down below two fishermen deliberated what the night would bring, and in which spot the eels would be in two hours. One of them was talking about worms he had collected in the clay. The other observed that they had five bottles of beer apiece. They had to wade through the marshy ground. You could hear them sloshing along. They cursed and then roared with laughter. In the end they were lost along with their fishing gear in the darkness and the mud.

A telephone rang across the corridor. It rang seven times before anyone lifted the receiver. It occurred to Dita that seven is a lucky number. Somebody slammed a door twice. They could hear an airplane in the sky. For a brief time the engine throbbed high above them. A party of five ordered dinner—asparagus, onion soup, fried trout, beer, and black coffee. The band played a march. Then they saw the lights of an aircraft through the window. It looked like a star, slowly losing height, until it changed into one of the many pinpoints in the far distance.

Dita feared that D.E. was getting bored with her. The stars increased in number and faded, and again she began to wonder about the life of the stars.

D.E., on the other hand, was thinking that Dita was not so naked as she had seemed to him when he had first undressed her and later, when they had been lying next to each other with nothing on.

"You know, D.E.," she said, "I think all those people are wrong who say that since Auschwitz-Birkenau the nature of all things has changed, from the core of the Earth to the farthest star, from the trees that were growing before we were born to the babies who are not yet born. Nothing has changed. Only something has been added—something we must learn to live with."

She realized it was time to stop talking, unless she wanted to spoil the evening for both of them. Again she looked up at the stars.

"I don't worry about the stars, and they don't worry about me," said D.E. He smiled as if sure that he had led her away from a topic on which he did not wish to dwell.

"Tell me some more about your trip to the sea."

"We left Paris at night. The train looked like a rocket, something between a sleeping car and a synagogue. It was marvelous, apart from the fact that it cost so much money. But the International Blue and White paid for everything, down to the toothpicks—except for the booze, that is."

"What does it feel like, to cross the frontier?"

"As if everything had returned to normal. As if you belonged to the chosen people, and everyone was chosen. Traveling with a valid passport was the best thing that had happened to me since Hitler. Like traveling with your former shadow, in broad daylight."

"Did you think about what it would have been like with a different passport?"

"I knew which passport that would be."

"I'd love to travel with you one day on an express train like that."

"Do you want me to turn on the light?"

When she did not answer, because she had expected a different reply, D.E. was silent, like one who knows when it is best to say nothing. If everything is erased with time, she should feel like a winner, she said to herself. Maybe. I must still try harder. "Everything's naked here, D.E. Does it seem naked to you too?"

"There's only the two of us," he said with a smile.

"You're handsome and tall," said Dita. "You know, when I'm with certain people I like myself more, and when I like myself I like the other people too. Funny, isn't it?"

"I really can't recall when I did not like myself."

The band below took a break. Now they could hear the sound of the wind, the movement of spring in the trees, the rustling in the branches, the hunger, and the call of the nearby forest. Dita did not understand what it was that both attracted her to D.E. and also repelled her. It was as though she were surrounded by an impenetrable mist. Why can't the hearts of people be reached, especially when they need it most and there is no lying? "You are very grown-up in every respect, I see, D.E." She noted his body, shoulders, face, legs. "How many times have you been as grown-up as that?"

She did not wait for a reply. "I guess I'd like to have a baby, D.E. But only with someone who understood all that has happened. Do you remember, David, one Friday you were at our place and you brushed against me with your shoulder, and I warned you not to confuse me with somebody else. Were you really offended that time?"

"A bit. Not really."

"Is it always 'a bit, not really,' with you?"

He looked at her. "The best is still to come," he said.

Her lips were moist. Suddenly she seemed to him defenseless, particularly from the way in which she had attacked him. He did not ask why she turned everything on its head. The effect was intensified by the fact that she had been naked the whole time he had been lying next to her. It struck him that she had been inexperienced and yet at the same time bold, as though she balanced one thing against the other. He looked at her, at the stars, and at the curtains but said nothing. She wanted to ask him whether he also thought about gratitude. What should we be grateful for, and to whom? What was sin? How long could people go on without greed and selfishness? She remembered the people who had come back after the war, the remnant, left over from the dispersal. They had been satisfied just to be alive.

"I can feel one of my crazy spells coming on. It's what Liza, Brita, and I call my spiritual diarrhea."

"Where did you get that bracelet?"

"Well, I'm not so poor, and sometimes I like to prove it. At least you can't say you've seen me with nothing on."

She could tell D.E. was laughing in the darkness. He felt that she had made a breakthrough, as if she had crossed a frontier. She could feel his abdomen, his muscles and thighs. He had powerful legs. She enjoyed touching him.

"What do you mean by your spiritual diarrhea?"

"Can I tell you later? Go on caressing me, D.E. Actually, no one has ever known how to caress me like you do. Maybe you were born for me. And I for you. But I won't ask how long it's supposed to last, D.E."

"Why do you keep on using my initials?"

"I'm not exactly fond of your stepsister, and I don't want to be reminded of her now."

D.E. sighed.

"Your sister's boss is one of the people we were talking about. A hopeless case. The girls call her Gestapo because she hires mostly Jewish girls and is mean to them. She is a German Jewess herself."

For a moment the room was flooded with silence, like a stream flowing on toward an unknown destination. It was once more as it had been in the beginning. She was reminded of the green lake and the path. She drew in the scent of pine needles and dark forests. Merely by breathing in and out she felt the movement of spring upon her like the onrush of night. Her breasts were swelling. She changed places with David Egon. He seemed calm and clean. She realized what he expected. She did for him everything he had done for her. Suddenly it seemed certain. After all, at 53 Lubliana Street there was no topic you didn't hear about. She no longer wondered whether her mother had done it, and her grandmother, and if she ever had a daughter, she would do it too. She took him into her mouth.

Later she whispered: "D.E., do you know how to say *blood* in Italian? *Sangue*. I learned that from Liza, as a symbol of all that we girls have in common."

There was a hint of something that he could not understand. A hint she still had on her mind and had always sought and never attained, or the question of whether it was possible for anyone to offer one's own life to another, as a sunbeam that a child tries to catch in his hands. Wasn't she asking too much in wanting everything right from the start?

Afterward, D. E. Huppert fell asleep for a while, pleasantly tired, and kept his hand in her hair as he slept, as if he wanted her to leave her head where she had had it at first. He had the other hand on her neck, with one leg thrown over her legs. She watched him, and she realized that she was discovering something that she would keep for the rest of her life. She watched him the whole time while he slept. She breathed in his breath, the scent of his body, his arms and hair. She could feel his body. She grasped something that perhaps no one can grasp until he has it and is in actual contact with it. She discovered a new patience within herself, a new surrender—a feeling that she had something more than she had before, more than she had expected, an inexhaustible source of giving. Is it true that a woman gives more than she receives? She felt the sleep of D.E. and her own taste in his mouth. She took a deep breath of the sweet air.

But when D.E. opened his eyes, she said: "It was my body, D.E., and it still is. I guess it's always a struggle between body and spirit. The darkest and the loveliest of all temptations. Maybe like everything you pay for with blood, War and peace. You're afraid of getting close, and at the same time you want to be." And finally: "Isn't my head too heavy, David?" And before he could or wanted to reply: "I wouldn't be here, David, if I didn't want to be."

Slowly, so that she would not misinterpret it, he rose and went over to the sink.

"You are nice not to turn on the light," said Dita.

In the moonlight her eyes remained wide open. Her face and mouth were smiling, but her eyes were grave, lost already from her words. D.E. washed himself. When he turned, it was to smile at her.

10 The resort had been built before the war, of brick and stone. Apart from the well-surrounded main building and its large garden and restaurant were several offices and residential buildings, set amid bushes, trees, and a fence. Downstairs, cars honked as they came and went, chickens clucked, dogs barked from a distance, and the sound of horses came from a nearby farm—a mixture of town and country noises, with interludes of silence. D.E. opened the window, letting in a breeze that carried the smell of forests, fields, and clay and the tang of whitewash from the annex behind the barn, where the owner was building garages. It was a homey atmosphere. From the distance the whinnying of horses could be heard again.

"We could come back tomorrow and go riding," D.E. suggested.

"Can you ride?"

"A little. Can you?"

"I learned last summer."

"It's not much fun falling off."

"Fortunately, I never have. If we could stay here, I'd like to go riding, David."

The hotel signboard was propped up on scaffolding: "HOTEL ASTORIA/NOVAK, FORMERLY YELLOW STONE INN." The garden stretched off toward the fields and woods. There were rows of apple, pear, and cherry trees. Gooseberry bushes grew along the fence, now invisible in the darkness. On the other side birch trees tossed in the wind. The trees in the garden had been treated with a white-washed mixture halfway up the trunks.

The room was warm. David Egon Huppert piled more wood on the fire—cherry, oak, and birch. Among the roughly hewn firewood lay old broken roof shingles, which caught fire immediately in the stove. Flashes of reddish light flooded the room. Next to the logs, away from the hot stove, lay sticks for kindling and newspapers. A bead of resin oozed out of a knot in the wood. "NUCLEAR STORM OVER NEW YORK. END OF AMERICAN ATOMIC MONOPOLY. ALARM IN THE WHITE HOUSE." The yellowed edge of the newspaper looked like old parchment.

"D.E.? I don't mind if you turn on the light, but you don't have to."

"Silly," breathed D.E. He was tending the fire. "Awfully silly."

"Do you think that child will start crying again?" And when D.E. glanced at her: "Whenever I shut my eyes or stare into the fire, I can imagine that child crying next door."

D.E. held her in his arms for a while. She savored it as if it were a foretaste of all that she dared to imagine for herself. She suddenly seemed alert, an impression reinforced by the way he watched the stove as well as her. To her he appeared more open than before, even though perhaps only temporarily. In her mind she heard the voices that belonged to him and to her. It was no longer in the here and now, nor did it come from the depths of recollection. It was as if a year had flashed by—twenty, fifty years? Suddenly she smiled uncertainly. The smile encompassed a whole new alphabet, forgotten symbols, a lost language. She read into it whatever she fancied—joy, sorrow, home, or the loss of home, fire, floods, earthquakes, hailstorms, war. Everything that people fear.

She breathed in the evening air that came flooding into the room and felt the fire's warmth. In her imagination she saw children who are born, people who create families, construct homes, and work the fields, a vision of the annual seasons that go on in spite of tempests or droughts, snowstorms, explosions on the sun that Brita called "the wind of the sun." She thought of what a man can submit to, what he can rid himself of, what he can permit to grow within himself. She allowed herself to be embraced, and she tried to take D.E. into her arms even as he had embraced her. She sought from him words she did not, and could not, find.

"I try to believe that each of us is of equal importance, David."

"Come close to me."

"I am close to you."

"Closer."

"Are you insatiable?"

"Aren't you?" He kissed her lips and caressed her. The outlines of buildings, garages, and scaffolding merged into the darkness beyond the window, along with the piles of sand, the concrete mixer, and the bags of cement. Nails were scattered among the dark-shadowed mud and snow. Some of the rooms of the annex were almost finished. Only the glass was missing. As long as the light remained, window frames and doors could be seen lying on the ground. Darkness enveloped it all now, like water flooding over the future entrances and exits. The raw smell of fresh construction, the work of human hands, aspirations, something that can be fulfilled. Only for a second did it flash through her mind that with those who had been killed, energy had left the world, just as with every newborn person energy enters it.

"What are you thinking about?" D.E. asked.

"I'd prefer to be like those people who don't talk about what they are going to do but do it."

In the restaurant they still served dinner, but there were fewer people there now. The orchestra played "You Belong to My Heart." A trio of musicians accompanied it with a vocal: "For now and forever."

"I know that from Hagibór, in 1942: 'You belong to my heart, for now and forever,'" said Dita.

D.E. began to whistle to the sound of the saxophones, trumpets, and the English lyrics below. Dita sang in Czech: "Your heart will call, and I shall come back. From that distance forlorn I shall return."

There were picnic tables and wooden chairs in the restaurant below. In the interval between the songs D.E. whistled: "You are my sunshine, my only sunshine," and "You make me happy when skies are gray."

"Thank you," said Dita in English.

There was a gently puzzled look in D.E.'s eyes. His forehead creased. It was more a questioning than a worried look, she thought. He split a shingle and tossed it on the fire. A red glow flooded the room. He looked different as he stood naked by the fire.

Dita lay down on the bed. She stayed as she was, crouched on her side to watch what D.E. did with the fire. When he looked up at her, she said: "The girls say that everything looks good on me, but only you know what I look like when I'm wearing nothing but a bracelet."

"You look great like that."

"I don't want to jump off the ship until it starts to burn or sink."

"Good."

"When we were digging trenches, as the Russians were coming near, I was shoveling earth with a spade, and suddenly it began to pour. We took shelter under the truck's tarpaulin. Up came the Scharführer and shouted that we would have to work naked as punishment. That wasn't so bad. It was worse when they first shaved my head bare, and that it was a man who did it. The next day he brought me some clothes. Those clothes probably saved my life later. I survived three selections."

She thought differently now. How she'd come here because she had wanted to, that everything had happened by her own choice. Her eyes wandered over the furniture and around the room.

"Are you trying to learn this room by heart?" asked D.E.

"Do you want me to lie to you?"

Down below they were playing "Dinah," and afterward, "Love Doesn't Come Every Day."

"It can never be more wonderful than it is today, even if I never come back again, except in memory," said Dita.

She looked around the room as if she had crossed the Alps or reached the North Pole. "Why is it that everybody who's had some wonderful experience immediately starts wondering how it will seem a year from now, how they'll recall it in fifty years? People are terribly sentimental. Everybody clutches his past as if it were a pocket souvenir album."

The music floated up from below.

"Your memory's like a house where no one else lives," said D.E.

"Or, rather, a house where nobody else lives."

"What do you mean?"

"I was just thinking of the saying that once you get used to being naked, you feel embarrassed to wear clothes."

He looked at Dita.

"Do I have a nice body?" she asked.

"What do you mean?"

"Just what I said, David."

"Of course." He did not hesitate for a second.

"All of it?"

"Absolutely all of it."

"I'm glad you say that."

"Did you expect me to say something else?"

"Nobody ever told me before."

"Well, I'm telling you now. What made you ask that?"

"I was never quite sure."

"Do you seriously expect me to believe that?"

"I would like you to, David."

"Well, from now on, you can be sure."

"In everything?"

"In absolutely everything. In every way that matters. One hundred percent," D.E. smiled. "A thousand percent," he corrected himself.

"Have you always been sure of yourself?"

"A boy has other worries. Normally nobody tells him they like him only for his body."

"Girls hear it all the time."

"But it's a fact that a girl's body is beautiful."

"Like bread? Or like wine?"

"It depends, as with a hundred things. Including bread and butter."

"A man's body can be beautiful too. I never knew it before."

"Everywhere?"

"At certain moments, everywhere."

She wondered what was going on in his mind. And she remembered how she had sometimes gotten what she wanted when it was almost too late, and in a form she had not originally intended. She sensed how close she was to provoking, if not exactly offending, D.E. She didn't know why. Maybe it was a survival of some lost, nameless instinct. Who knows? She had no reason for it.

"Boys worry more about being ready, about being able to last, and sometimes about their size. They get upset when they fail. And sometimes they don't make it just because they are trying to create the best possible impression in the shortest time. It looks as though they are rejecting the woman just because they want her so desperately. They feel guilty. The more they think about it, the worse they feel. And then they get depressed and irritable. With boys you can see it all right away."

"That doesn't sound like you, David, does it?"

She expected he would smile back at her, but instead he suddenly asked, "Are you afraid of something?"

"Sometimes," she answered. "But you needn't worry."

He did not ask about what, so she wouldn't have to explain.

She had told him everything—once and for all. Even the most important thing, that with him she was different. Something surrounded her like a fog, as if she couldn't see herself so poignantly. She felt as if they were on their way here again.

To his surprise she again said, "I didn't know a sin could be so beautiful. And for so long you acted as though you hardly noticed my existence." That was not entirely true, but she was giving him back something he'd been hesitating about.

She glanced at her dress, shoes, and underwear. She could hear the wind outside sweeping through the trees and grass, gliding over the marshes, stirring the leaves that remained on the tops of the fruit trees from last year.

She rose, went to the window, and wrapped the curtain around her. D.E. went into the bathroom.

"Everybody sees it differently, David. In Theresienstadt I looked after children. I think about that now more than ever. Nobody asked what would happen tomorrow or what had happened yesterday. There was only now. Now, of course, there's only now too, but nobody believes it. Maybe there's more abundance than before, but something is missing. I don't know what, or why it is, and I don't want to be greedy. It reminds me of what the rabbis used to say in the days of the caves: 'A low roof that's standing is better than a high one that's crumbling.' The present now ought to be the nicest of them all. Every now comes only once."

D.E. turned on the shower. Down below they played "Begin the Beguine." The music rose up to them as if from a great distance, a melody full of echoes, implications, and signals, promises carried on words, like ships on the ocean between distant shores.

The noise from the shower interrupted it. She felt something restless within her, a new life that would touch everything that had existed before. The furniture in the room was old. Paint was peeling off the mirror frame. Dita thought of her own now as if it were an apple ripe for plucking, the pollen of all the bees that had touched it when it was still a flower—even if the little apple had worms.

She smiled to herself. For goodness sake, she was not right out of boarding school or the convent.

"The present now ought to be the nicest ever, David. I'm saying I always feel it is. But I'm glad you brought me here. Honest. And that you told me that I am well developed. And that you didn't hesitate."

"You look like a will-o'-the-wisp." D.E. looked out from the shower. He was wiping himself dry. He had a big bath towel. He toweled himself thoroughly and with enjoyment. "There's more to you than I can take in all at once."

"Maybe in fifty years I'll think back to this evening, and how the child was crying next door." She let go of the curtains. Although he had said nothing, she added, "You shouldn't repeat yourself, David. I don't want to spoil anything, or lose it either."

He looked around the room, as Dita had done before him, at the double bed, the white tiled stove, the chestnut furniture. The bed's headboard was high and adorned with carved wood, two snakes' heads and a dove above them, a snake-dove fraternity carved in wood.

"One day little Munk was telling me about his own consciousness. He discovers things, new stars, like an astronomer. I am happy, David. You can think what you like. I have to keep reminding myself, as though I can't believe it. Recently I've been longing for at least a few hours like this. Making a virtue out of necessity."

"I know you have a lot of plans."

"To finish the course in applied arts, then languages. Some traveling. What about you?"

"To finish my law courses. In the meantime to keep making contacts. To find a way to get to the people running the World Congress."

"I presume you've heard of those miraculous Jewish boys."

"I've heard of miraculous rabbis, but I don't believe in them. There aren't any miraculous rabbis or boys left among us anymore. Why not take the chances you have?"

"I'm glad that you're so honest with me."

"Don't exaggerate!" Then D.E. asked her, "Do you want me to lie to you?" But in that moment they were as close as they could be.

Fig leaves, carved into the wood, ran in a regular pattern from one side of the bedstead to the other. A piece of French furniture stood by the window. Dita's grandmother Olga had had a similar chaise lounge. Dita lay the other towel on it and sat down.

"You've got a nice-looking rear," said D.E.

"Thanks."

"And everything else, too."

"For goodness sake," said Dita in her singsong voice. "After all, we're all eighteen once." She refrained from saying that Doris Levit boasted about what she had gotten in return for it. Dinner always ranked lowest. Instead, Dita added: "Last time Linda allowed Andy to sleep with her she pinched the margarine carton he keeps his out-of-season coats in."

"If you're hungry," said D.E., "you can say it right out." He preferred to avoid discussing his half sister. She had no place in his scheme of things, and he did not want to be reminded of her by Dita.

"I'm quite happy to be in this world," said Dita, smiling, "but there's still plenty of things I'd be ashamed to do and probably never will do."

D.E. looked at her. The wind moved the curtains. A spider crawled up on the outside of the glass. It reached the frame and the wall, then disappeared.

"After it happened to Liza, with that bald-headed doctor who came before Dr. Fitz, she changed and started not to give a damn."

It took D.E. a moment to grasp the connection. Dita understood why Liza was hanging on to Mr. Gotlob. She was very good at pretending, like the ones who hadn't experienced it yet. Was that why some Jewish girls, like Tonitschka Blau, were willing to go with men who had never been there? Or the reverse? Was it something like rape? The best thing was that it could happen to anybody. Ugliness wasn't the worst of it.

D.E. dressed. There was something in her eyes that pulled him nearer to her and at the same time kept him at arm's length. It was only later—and in a different place—that he saw the significance and drew conclusions from it.

"They say that in hell witches look backward and walk backward like crabs, while suicides sit on thorns and practice usury in burning sand," Dita said casually. "Get it?"

"No," said D.E. She looked up at him as he pulled on his socks and stood silently, as if everything had now been said between them. David Egon Huppert had the impression that she was looking right through him to her own reflection in the mirror. Was it a mirror in which she saw something other than her own pretty, oval face? She reminded him of girls who needlessly find fault with themselves, as if they were warning a man in advance that sooner or later they would let him down. Was she an odd one out? Was she something of a strange fish?

She asked herself whether she was just one of the many women who opened their doors because they did not want to be left on the shelf. The feeling of blood flowing through her veins beneath the flesh passed away. "I would like to be a grown-up," Dita said suddenly and wrapped herself in the towel. "And at the same time I'd still like to be a child, so someone would take care of me like I took care of the children in Theresienstadt."

"You're not asking for very much." He said the reverse of what he meant.

"I haven't given that to anybody, or gotten it from anybody."

D.E. did not answer.

"I certainly don't want to behave like a leech, clinging on to somebody, the kind of woman that frightens people off."

D.E. was by now almost fully dressed. He adjusted his tie. Dita made no move to begin dressing. He fastened his cuff links, then the buckle on his belt.

"Brita is probably returning to England. She'll polish her squire's riding boots in the evenings and ask him, 'How are you, husband?' and ask how his thoroughbreds are getting along." Dita turned her face toward the warmth of the stove. She felt like one of Isabelle Goldblat's cats. Monks and cats love fish. Married women like to kiss, and girls love to smooch. A cat chases mice, and the body goes after what nature wills, as Lebovitch says. Presumably Isabelle Goldblat would no longer put her hand in the fire for her. "According to my Aunt Mimi's dream book, white lilac means a rich bridegroom, a happy marriage, and at least three successful children. Roses mean love. But love, as the book says, is like a rose that blooms and fades. Still, nobody can deny that even a faded rose was once beautiful."

"Don't speak badly of relatives."

"Guilt and desire, D.E. I'm glad it was you who did it to me, David."

"You are pretty."

"A girl doesn't always see herself that way."

She felt almost shameless saying it. There was something about him—maybe his expression as he dressed, while she remained with only a towel over her shoulder—that made her say it. The thought came to her that no one in the world can order, compel, or induce any other person to feel what the other feels, be it joy, anguish, expectation, or anything at all.

"I'll tell you what," said D.E. "I'll go ahead and order dinner." He was showing his diplomatic talent. He had understood barely half of what was going on in Dita's head.

11 In the garden restaurant D.E. chose a corner table. He looked very masculine as he sat there. When Dita came in, he rose to his feet and held out a chair for her. She wore a dark-colored dress with the skirt gathered at the waist.

"It didn't take you very long," said D.E., exactly the opposite of what she had expected him to say.

They were served by a quiet, gray-eyed waiter. D.E. ordered him around, but the waiter took it in stride, as if his mind were far away. He brought the menu and waited for them to order. He wrote the order down, passed it to the kitchen, then went over to the other corner, where a girl in a black jumper, about nineteen years old, was sitting. She sat with her feet tucked under and her hands folded in her lap. When the girl looked up at the waiter, a smile broke out on her lips.

Dita felt herself blushing. Suddenly she realized that the child she had heard upstairs crying belonged to the girl and the waiter. Maybe they had been lying in the same kind of double bed, with carved snakes and doves on it. Apart from the chaise lounge, there had also been a child's crib, and something had happened that brought an echo of happiness to the girl's lips.

After a while the girl rose and went off into the hotel. The waiter went into the kitchen. A chain with an old pendant watch hung down at the girl's breast. She walked slowly between the tables. When she returned, she carried a child with big eyes and shiny, freshly combed hair. She smiled at the waiter as he bent down to the child.

Dita looked at the tree and at the musicians' instruments. She stroked D.E.'s hand. The rustling of trees was around them. The fields stretched into the distance, and the forest receded like waves amid the darkness.

The waiter laid out cutlery for them on the tablecloth, then brought the food and finally a flagon of red Melnik wine. He wrapped the bottle up to the neck in a white damask napkin, uncorked it, and poured. While D.E. tasted the wine, the waiter paused for a moment. Then he bowed to Dita and filled her glass. He wished them an enjoyable dinner and a pleasant evening.

"This should be the best time in our life, David. Perhaps I'm bad, I tell lies—to myself and to you. I cheat—myself and you. Maybe I go about things the wrong way. But there isn't a bit of deception in what I feel now. Cross my heart, David."

"I'm as hungry as a wolf." D.E. raised his glass to Dita. When he looked in her eyes, it seemed to him, for a brief moment, as if she were somehow confused. He took a few sips and began to eat.

Dita raised her glass slowly and then put it down again on the table. She began to eat no less slowly. D.E. had made up his mind not to let things get too serious if he could avoid it. During the meal he observed that in ten days a lion eats nearly its own weight in food. He smiled.

"Look at the girl in the corner, D.E."

He glanced at the girl in the corner. Without opening his mouth, he nodded, then went on eating.

The moon high in the sky shone down upon them. Its rays glanced back from the white tablecloth. The wind brought the smell of freshly plowed fields.

Later D.E. paid the bill with the air of a man who has been to Belgium, France, and Switzerland. She was glad that the tip he left in the saucer was a handsome one.

The road was narrow, and D.E. drove carefully. The darkness was filled with noises of the night. Dita listened to the sound of the motor, cats mewing, crickets chirping. It was a clear night. They could hear a distant honking and the broken sounds of human voices, The croaking of frogs came from the marshlands and the thickets. The train that they had heard whistling at the beginning of the evening was now apparently on its return trip. It whistled again for a long time, almost as if in jest. For a while they kept ahead of the train, just in earshot. Dita wore D.E.'s scarf wrapped around her neck.

"Some Frenchman once said that loving means understanding," said Dita. She had uttered the one word that D.E. never used. Then she said, "Munk once explained to me why, in his view, it's more correct to use the word *we* than *I*. The word *we* includes all the *I*'s, according to Fatty."

D.E. wore goggles like the Italian racing driver Caraciolla.

"I'd be interested to know what the fat man really thinks, and what he actually believes," Dita said.

D.E. seemed only interested in himself.

"It runs well, doesn't it, considering it's such a piece of German junk?" Dita asked.

She also asked him if he was glad he had his own car. D.E. did not answer, and she didn't try to tease him anymore.

"I'd like to do something for you, if you'd tell me what you want, and what you like," he said.

In his voice she heard a slightly veiled attempt to show off. She could no longer ask him whether it wouldn't be fairer for her to help pay for the room and dinner, or at least to chip in for gas. But apart from the fact that D.E. ignored her questions several times, he gave her little excuse to criticize him.

They turned into Lubliana Street. D.E. stopped a block away from number 53.

"Thank you, Dita. I don't know about you, but for me it was lovely."

"That sounds like a Japanese poem."

D.E. vaulted over the door, as Dita did not open hers for herself. He walked around the car, picked her up, carried her to the sidewalk, and put her down. It was paved in blue and white squares, illuminated by the high street lamp. Dita returned his scarf. They said good night. D.E. began to whistle: "You Belong to My Heart." It suddenly occurred to him that she had behaved neither as a virgin nor as a whore. "For now and forever."

As D.E. drove away, very slowly during the few steps that Dita took to reach the entrance, he whistled, "And the melody under the bamboo tree, my dream . . ."

How is it that life is not so exciting as in
wartime?
—A girl from Lubliana Street, on a postcard from
Australia

When I stop in a street to watch children playing
and go nearer, the mothers look at me
suspiciously.
—A girl from 53 Lubliana Street

Why is everything so provisional?
—Letter of a girl from Lubliana Street

III

 After her trip with D.E., Dita Saxova wrote him a letter. It was not exactly a love letter, as she noted, and not exactly the truth, but she stuck it into an envelope, wrote the address, and put a stamp on it. On the stamp was a deer, colored green, which figured in her dreams the following night. When should a girl fight for a man she wants neither to lose to another person nor to fight to the death for? Then she dreamed about D.E. In her dream they spoke of love, of marriage and children, and about what makes lovers happy. At the end of her dream Fitzi surprised them, and she told D.E. what a rat he was, seducing her just to abandon her. But Fitzi whispered to her that she was a rat too, and a traitor. "I don't trust you, Fitzi," she said to him in her dream. "I trust only D.E. You don't know about love, only about war." Then she woke up, wet as a sponge. She wrote D.E. a letter about her dream, but D.E., as she expected, ignored her letter, including the dream.

Every Saturday afternoon Dr. Fitz examined the girls at 53 Lubliana Street. His growing paunch showed under his blue poplin shirt. Nudity didn't mean the same thing here as it might have meant otherwise. Except with some of the girls, Dita thought.

It was almost 6:00 P.M. The house was noisy. The voices of Lev and Isabelle Goldblat rose up from below. Saturday was cleaning, recreation, and visiting day.

"Three more," the doctor said. He had a deep, hoarse voice. He looked at Dita. This was the first man to look at her without her imagining he was seeing her naked body.

The sun was going down outside the window. It was the beginning of April. The sunny days grew longer, as the rains diminished and the evenings warmed up. After a while the doctor was left with only Dita.

"You should eat, sleep, and exercise—if possible, all three at once. In a year and a day we could make a real Rita Hayworth out of you. That's what I'd like to see."

"What's wrong with Tonitschka?" Dita asked.

"Look here, Miss Saxova, medicine is my business."

"Is she as afraid to tell you as she is everyone else?"

Dr. Fitz did not appear anxious to talk about Tonitschka Blau. He drank water from a tall glass. "Somebody mistook the famous tenor Benjamin for Leonardo Gigli, a famous Italian brain surgeon and gynecologist of the nineteenth century. He knew that the only way to help some brains was to drill a hole in the head. The brain of an average man weighs 1,500 grams. Ninety percent is water. Except for some small mysteries, we know almost everything about the human brain—about the right and the left hemispheres and what they control. Much of this was already known at the time of the old Babylonians. In the twentieth century we advanced mainly because of wars. After each war we see a little bit more about how to deal with that mushy, ovoid mass that houses most of the secrets of men and life. During wars they make larger, more frequent holes in men's heads. That explains everything. Ridiculous, isn't it? And great, too. Like everything that's happening to us."

"Did Tonitschka gain weight at least?"

"And you? Do you realize that we still don't know even elementary things about what happens when we sleep? Or why we dream what we dream?"

She thought what it was like when she, like all the others in the women's camp, had been made to undress in front of the Waffen SS officer, and how humiliating it had been. Now she coughed.

"If anything happened to Tonitschka, I wouldn't stay on here." The doctor noted the circles under Dita's eyes, just as he had earlier noted Tonitschka Blau's transparent skin. In her eyes Tonitschka bore the vision of the men who had raped her, maybe of the place, too. The doctor looked at Dita. She wondered what he had been concerned about. Last time he had said the same to Tonitschka, Liza, and company, that they should stop brooding over the worst and try to make the best of things. She smiled. The doctor asked Dita to remove her clothes. He waited, and as he smoked, he observed the bracelet. Dita wore a jumper. She had three jumpers—white, light blue, and pink.

"You've got quite a nice back, blondie. What do you intend to do with that handsome tall body of yours, woman? A grown man feels almost ashamed to be peeping at you nowadays."

"I'd like to join that summer excursion the International Blue and White are organizing. They are looking for people to escort the children."

"Why don't you have some of your own?"

She rewarded him with her grown-up smile.

"How's school going? What are you studying now?"

"The architecture of ancient Babylon. Brown towers made of wood and terra-cotta."

"Don't breathe."

He pressed the stethoscope to her chest. It struck her that his reference to school had not been entirely innocent. I suppose I'm not so innocent either, she smiled to herself. She thought of D.E. During the war the doctor had been in the so-called I. G. Auschwitz, a branch of I. G. Farben attached to Auschwitz-Birkenau, where they perfected the manufacture of fertilizer

from the ashes of Jewish workers. For this Farben paid a nomi-
nal fee to the finance department of the SS and in return was
permitted to use gold taken from the dead bodies for the war
fund as well as hair for textiles, mattresses, rope ladders for
submarines, and overalls for sailors.

"I suppose you are really studying it. I can still remember as a
young man how impressed I was at the way they transported the
stone when the laborers had no machines but their legs, hands,
and muscles. See, a prototype of Dachau! From building pyra-
mids to building dams. The statues of the best-developed models
actually represent the working class of those days. Yesterday
Professor Munk spoke to me about you. He expounded the scientific basis of your frivolous ways. According to him, frivolity is
very important to a young lady like you. In his view, it was this
that enabled you to survive even in the toughest times, against
ordeals that would have probably crushed anyone in normal circumstances. The circumstances no longer exist, but the frivolity
persists." He cleared his throat and lit another cigar. "As if we
weren't familiar with free love in Prague."

He tested her lungs, listened to her heart, measured her
pulse. He always looked for some hidden tones—if not in the
head, then in the soul—some fixed idea, something more complex than her carefree smile and friendly manners, as if everyone had at least two portraits in his pockets.

"We must all resign ourselves to our meatless Thursday,
child."

The preceding Saturday the doctor had told Dita about the girl
who had been in a car accident. She had crashed into the wind-
shield, and he had done his best to repair her face so that after
the operation she would look like before. The results were good.
Except that she didn't believe it. Her face did not seem to her
what he had made it, but what she herself saw in it. Men paid
her compliments, but she interpreted them as rejections of her-

self. She was afraid that what they admired was her mask. She believed, apparently, that a decent man is still the exception rather than the rule.

The doctor put a band around Dita's arm to test her blood pressure. "It's all right," he said. "You are not as enigmatic as you look. These things can be measured, weighed, and tested." Then he muttered, "We have all begun to believe that the best is still to come, haven't we?" He looked at her questioningly, from head to foot. "Last year at this time I asked you whether you really trusted people. You answered that you did, but only in the daytime, because there is a threatening criminal in every person you see in the night. Well, do you remember the answer I gave you?"

Suddenly he looked closely into her eyes. "Aren't you, by any chance, also thinking of emigrating, Miss Saxova? Jewish girls make an ideology out of everything. Especially if they are running away from something. Sometimes they see the impossibility but go ahead anyway. Half a climax is still a climax, isn't it?"

"Sometimes it's the other way around," Dita said. "Ideology can make Jews of everybody. How I spend my time is my business, isn't it?"

She thought of why Kitty Borger had gone to Australia, the farthest and most mysterious land. Suddenly she smiled at the doctor. It's best to be a clown. People enjoy it, and it's the easiest way to manipulate them.

In the pub across the street the music had started up. In the corridor a voice shouted: "Men are different with girls who give them self-confidence. So what?" And another voice: "Would you rather not go with any man so that when you're fifty you'll know that you didn't catch it? Don't pretend you're so cautious. Boys prefer less-complicated girls. Where can girls get self-confidence?" And finally, Great Britain said, "I know forever is not such a long time."

Dita was glad that the doctor had found nothing wrong with her. She breathed a sigh of relief and felt his gaze upon her like a touch.

"Do you know what you actually are?" Dr. Fitz asked.

"What?"

"Innocence with experience."

"Are you serious?"

"Why not? None of us remains as we were born."

"Thanks a lot."

"Hear me out."

"I'm listening."

"Only desperate people do desperate things."

"And I look desperate to you?"

"Certainly not."

"When something is rightfully yours, it eludes you. When it's not, you can still take it," Dita said. There was something missing, something she didn't say. Dr. Fitz tried to find out what it was.

"And you really believe that?" he asked.

"Of course. It's part of my main principle."

"Which is?"

"Never despair."

Dita's girlish blue eyes met the doctor's gray-green, molelike ones.

"I wish I had such a maxim, a single rule that I could apply to everything. Now what do you mean by that, Miss Saxova?"

"I have another. You cannot communicate with anyone who is a stranger to the truth."

Dita began to dress. "Do I take myself too seriously?"

The doctor lit a cigar and turned from Dita to the window. "That's not for me to say. Hurry if you like, but I urge you to go slowly. If you are never in a rush, you will never be surprised."

"Yeah," she answered. "I'm relying on my sense of humor."

"You're really becoming a woman now," he said ambiguously. "A woman's happiness is unusually friendly and unusually fickle." She laughed, waiting for some further comment. "So how's your love life? I hope you aren't afraid."

"I'm afraid of sharks. I've had dreams about them, but they have nothing to do with the sea. And it is no use telling Herbert Lagus that I've given up dreams of splashing about in the ocean surf in El Salvador." She laughed.

"Do you like cold melon?"

"Sometimes."

"Even in winter?"

Shouting came from the showers. Dita could recognize Liza's voice, then Linda's. "Don't you dare touch me, you slut." Then immediately: "She's got cancer. They cut her breast open. Ask Dr. Fitz, if you don't believe me."

Dita got up and unlocked the door. She went straight into the showers and smacked Linda across the face. She was dripping wet. The marks of Dita's five fingers stood out on Linda's face.

Even if she had been deaf, Isabelle would have heard it. She stood outside the washroom with her hand on the knob. She nodded her long horselike head, and her eyes glinted. "What's going on?" Isabelle asked. "Are you cold in there?"

Brita said, "Andy is having an affair with an unhappily married woman, for a change. One day her husband will kill him." She explained that the most reliable test in the art of kissing was to take into your mouth a cherry with a stem. "You carefully chew up the cherry, discarding only the stone. Then you have to tie a knot in the stem with your tongue. When you can do that, you are a real woman, with a capital *W*."

In the silence, steps could be heard in the corridor, and a door banged in the surgery. They could hear the noise of the water pipes in the cellar below.

Then came the voice of Lev Goldblat: "Bella, for goodness

sake, where are you?" And then: "Would you kindly tell me? What suit shall I put on for the party? The one with the waist-coat?"

Isabelle Goldblat, thinner than she had been even a week ago, glanced at the girls from face to face. She seemed to be getting more and more gaunt before their eyes. Then she called through the open door, as if nothing had happened, just like Brita a moment ago: "The black suit, Lev."

She turned to Dita. "Excuses only make things worse. Aren't you going to dry yourself? Do you want to catch a cold, silly goose?"

2 The first spring dance was organized by the management of the Lubliana and Krakovska street hostels and held at the SIA Academic Café in Paris Street. It began at 8:00 P.M. At 8:30 Alfred Neugeborn got up from the table where a few of the community leaders already sat, and he sauntered over to the bar.

That afternoon a rumor had gone around the Krakovska hostel that Mr. Jakub Steinman, "a one-time ambassador and great friend of the younger generation," would attend. The same thing had been said in reference to the February dance, in spite of the fact that nobody had ever actually seen Mr. Steinman at such a function. Usually it was said afterward that he had suffered an attack of rheumatism or a toothache. Even that was stated with a air of importance denied to common mortals. At the dance there were also people from the International Blue and White Union of Jewish Students, the World Jewish Congress, and the ORT central organization for youth industrial training.

"Balzac warned against women dressed in violet," the cloak-room attendant said to Dita and Tonitschka about Holy Virgin. Dita laughed. Again she had had dreams about D.E. and the devil. Satan had asked her, "Do you think you can love someone you hate?"

Fitzi looked at her from the bar. Linda watched Fitzi. At the entrance to the cloakroom Andy tied a shoelace in the way of about five people. He looked up at Brita. "Everything's as it should be, isn't it?"

"Perhaps you could finish doing that job tomorrow." Britannia shooed him out of the way.

"Suppose there is no tomorrow?" Andy gave her a toothy grin.

"Oh, by the way, it's Hitler's posthumous birthday today. I hereby wish him all the best, and especially that he'd never been born," said Dita. She felt on top of the world, surrounded by friends.

The bartender chatted with Maximilian Gotlob, who waited for Liza. They talked as if the decorated table between them was the English Channel and they were still retreating to Dunkirk. "I left my whole platoon behind," Mr. Gotlob announced. The sound carried as far as the cloakroom. "Bravery and cowardice? Before, at the time, or after? An hour after the medical orderlies leave, a battlefield looks just like plowed land again. When the whole thing's going up in flames under your feet, there isn't even time to tell the difference."

"Oh dear," sighed Dita as she winked at Fitzi. She knew they shared a view on this. She also realized she had put a run in her stocking and would have to do something about it. Should she go to the bathroom and remove her stockings? She decided to do so at once. She disappeared from Fitzi's view and returned with bare legs. Where was D.E.? She hadn't seen him in three weeks. Maybe a man doesn't want a woman if he doesn't need her, but what woman wants a man who only needs her?

"If I don't have to think about it, I don't," the bartender answered, "My memories of that bit of coastline are nasty." He declared that the French had looked forward to a quick defeat, so they would not lose as many young men as they had in the First World War at Verdun. And that the British did not trust the French to keep the secret of radar out of German hands, thanks to the French love of money.

From the end of the bar Fitzi watched the bartender and Mr. Gotlob, and he remembered how they used to sing "The Boys from Zborov" at school, and the teacher had almost wept. To this day, Fitzi still didn't know where Zborov was. Somewhere in the Polish Ukraine? He wondered what Dita Saxova had meant by that smile. He looked at her naked legs. He knew she was waiting for D.E. "Nobody can serve two masters," judged Mr. Gotlob. "Nul ne peut servir deux maîtres à la faire."

Fitzi did not mind the meaning of the words. He too had come to the dance mainly to chat with people. The way they talked and clinked glasses disturbed and nettled him, but it attracted him as well. It was a pretty adroit style of swaggering in the face of death, now that they felt safe again.

"Haven't you got something to drink with a bite to it?" Mr. Gotlob asked.

"For you, captain, we can always find something."

"Have you read about the business at Varnsdorf? How can they possibly accuse *anybody* who was in England during the war of being pro-German, and then nationalize his factory? Not to mention the people who shed their blood for this country, while over here they grumbled about weak beer."

Fitzi listened with only one ear. He returned Dita's grimace at the expense of the bartender and Mr. Gotlob, glad that he had her again in his sight. He watched the musicians as they sat down again and set up their instruments. He wondered if the bartender and Mr. Gotlob had gone through it all just so they could stand up and drink and call each other "Captain," "Doctor," "Sergeant." At the same time he couldn't say that they had done nothing to earn it. True, he hadn't had to tremble like they had done because their lives were in danger. But they had not been sentenced to death, like Fitzi or Dita. Beyond the French coast lay Britain, and beyond the British shores lay the coasts of America and Australia. Beyond the chimney at Birkenau lay only the chimney of the Birkenau crematorium. There was the chance of living a bit longer while the chimney was not actually smoking, or while they burned the Jewish populations of Hungary or Germany or Poland, and so owing to the shortage of German time, they might prolong the life of a prisoner from Prague, Athens, or Milan. There were still incinerator pits waiting there, and everyone knew that once the Germans had the time, everybody's turn would come.

With a smile, Mr. Gotlob explained to Dita the difference between *Blitzkrieg* and *Sitzkrieg*. Then he announced: "Les rois ont les mains. Kings have long arms." He knew what he was talking about, and he was aware that Dita and a few other people listened. He advised Dita Saxova to read Arthur Schnitzler. He had clever, alert gray eyes.

The waiters had to bring extra chairs for the latecomers. Before each short break, the band played three numbers. The dance floor was always full. Dita sparkled in her new short-sleeved, champagne-colored dress. Her long white arms were aglow.

"What have you stolen for supper?" she asked Fitzi.

She smiled on all sides. At last she could hear the voice of D.E. In the entrance, a boy from the Krakovska hostel said to him, "On the first floor they're playing 'Up from the cliff sailed the fleeting dove, awaking from slumber the eyes of blue.' On the second floor they're talking about sex, or washing clothes, to the last virgin. On the third floor they've begun kissing."

Dita observed Fitzi, while watching D.E. approach. "There are Prague Jews. Then Jews from Brno or Bratislava. And third on the scale come the Jews from Czechoslovakia."

"No one in my family was born east of Komárno," Fitzi observed, "except in Budapest."

"What classy people you are!" Brita interrupted both of them. She looked at Dita as if she were something the cat had dragged in. "It reminds me of people who can't bear the thought of being heard in the toilet. When they flush, they call for a band to play music."

Mr. Gotlob watched Liza offer Tonitschka wine from her glass at the bar. She even poured her a drink from Mr. Gotlob's glass when he turned his head in Dita's direction. He picked up his own glass. "You've got a generous heart, my girl. Ami de table est variable. Friendship in a bar is gone overnight."

Herbert Lagus led Dita onto the dance floor. He wore a checkered suit, a brown knitted tie, and shoes of African Zebu leather. He would try to win her favor with his devoted eyes. You have no chance, replied Dita with her own eyes. It was almost embarrassing. Finally she broke the tension by smiling one of her long smiles. In the middle of the dance, Fitzi Neugeborn accosted her. "May I?" he bowed. Herbert Lagus retreated with some reluctance. D.E. came for her before the third number finished. He looked as if they had parted just yesterday. Neugeborn watched them as they moved among the dancers. The band played Cole Porter's "I Love You." Dita savored the music, the soft harmony of the saxophones, muted trumpets, syncopation accompanied by lyrics. They played "Express" and "Quiet, Please."

Dita danced with almost all the boys from the Krakovska hostel, moving from arm to arm. She danced with Dr. Fitz and with Munk. They played her favorite tunes. She could have drawn a map of her feelings and desires for them: "Brazil," "Bei mir bist du schön," "April in Portugal." D.E. came for her again. She felt like asking him, "How many more times will you steal the essence of a woman's soul and then disappear?"

They played "In the Mood." D.E. gazed closely into her eyes. His navy blue jacket and the tie he had chosen went well with her dress. They matched like puzzle pieces before they are fit together. He felt her warmth. They danced to "Mexican Rose," then to "Poinciana," and lastly to "Amour." Dita cuddled up in his arms. The band played for all it was worth, and the guests applauded.

Dita let herself be carried along by the music. In the melody of the dance she felt everything that had happened and that was still to come—that one side of herself. She loved parties. As time went on she learned to like them more and more. And thanks to this party she met D.E. again.

"Are you just a good starter, or can you manage the long haul?" Dita asked.

"Why?"

"I wanted to invite you to the Astoria/Novak and pay for it this time."

"Where would you get that much money?"

"Why should anybody die rich?" She smiled. He returned it.

"Thank you," said D.E. "Dancing with you is almost as good as eating strawberries in a garden restaurant."

"Meeting of the eyes, meeting of the minds?"

"Certainly. True love can never be forgotten."

"What turns a man into a rat?" Dita asked. "Is it when he promises something to a woman and, because it wasn't all that important to him, forgets about it and then expects her just to forgive him and forget about it too? And then makes her feel bad about it when he doesn't?"

"A man is a rat when he knows he is a rat and doesn't care. In fact, he is kind of proud of it," D.E. said.

D.E. knew himself. She was not, and who knew if she would ever be, capable of giving herself to another person. Not only in body, but in soul. Every day, as she had said in the Astoria/Novak, was a ticket in the lottery for her, and she would rather not be concerned with the list of winners. He knew how to translate her code into words. After those years in the camps she had learned never to trust anyone, never to love without holding something back, because for her everyone was marked by the dead whom she had loved, to whom she had always had to say good-bye—as if she couldn't, even now, say "so long" to anyone without an unspoken "until the next selection." But he couldn't tell her. He thought of himself that way too. Perhaps it would disappear with time. But what man wanted to wait for a girl to be cured before he could get her into bed, as if every new lover were a sanatorium free of charge? He didn't want to be cynical, uncharitable, or unfeeling, not even toward himself. He had offered her a friendship of the body and soul, but so far nothing more. Perhaps she had interpreted it as much more. Should he tell her, to make her want to recover?

She danced well. He looked at the tip of her nose, at her mouth and throat, and then glanced away toward the musicians. He felt her press against him.

They heard Andy telling Fitzi, "I have my own idea of faithfulness." Lebovitch continued to express himself: "What I don't get on the left, I get on the right. What I don't find here, I look for there. I know girls who are a thousand miles away from here. Nothing I desire here touches them there, and even having known them for so long I never contact them. Who is cheating whom? First they let you get cold, and then they complain how cold you are."

"It's nice here," Dita asserted.

"A bit too hot," D.E. responded.

"The heat doesn't bother me. I'm dressed for it."

He took a minute to decide whether she had in mind getting undressed as well. "This is great fun," D.E. said.

"Who doesn't want to have fun?"

"I should introduce you to someone who's come back from England. He claims that what Hitler did had already been tried on a smaller scale everywhere."

"Where's everywhere?" she asked, but D.E. had guessed from her voice that her mind was elsewhere. What she looked for in his eyes confused him. And so he acted wisely and didn't answer. D.E. took her over to the bar. He did not say a word that she could latch on to, nothing she could interpret as a sign of any future or past involvement. He did not refer to her letter.

"Is it just an illusion?" asked Dita.

"How should I know?" D.E. responded.

Linda looked reproachfully at Fitzi, not too far from Dita Saxova at the bar. "You are putting your trust in someone who doesn't deserve it. It's as if you're deaf and blind. Heaven only knows where Dita got that dress. It is far beyond her means. Like the bracelet."

She gazed at Dita's back. "And she's having an affair with my stepbrother."

Neugeborn frowned. The long wrinkle in the middle of his forehead deepened. He too, like Linda, saw Dita's back and her long, bare legs with golden slippers. And how she looked at D. E. Huppert.

"What's wrong with your voice?" Neugeborn asked Linda. "You sound like a croaking old bird."

Linda smoothed her skirt. She wasn't wearing any underwear. The idea of being near Fitzi and not wearing underwear excited her. She would have liked to put her hand on his thigh. Instead, she took his hand, as though she was at her wit's end, and tugged at him. Linda was pale. Her glance flew across to D.E., who was just ordering a wine shandy for Dita and a Napoleon brandy for himself.

"Some people really believe that by putting a few kids to bed at night and telling them fairy tales for six weeks they probably saved their lives, or prolonged them," Linda said. "There's someone who thinks that just because by some chance she survived Theresienstadt, Auschwitz-Birkenau, and Belsen, in return she'll be served the world on a plate, as though by a waiter in an expensive restaurant. I suppose she thinks it's just a matter of time until they come running after her with a slice of the world and ask her kindly to help herself to as much as she wants."

Fitzi felt he could bet his life that Linda was provoking him, and he saw she was trying to wreck his chances with Dita. The band played a medley from Gershwin.

There was a notice above Dita's head: "Never get between the bar and a thirsty man." And below that: "If you feel that the bar is swaying, please remain in your seats."

Two youths from the Krakovska hostel were trying to convince her that originally, millions of years ago, horses were as small as foxes and already had hooves. Dolphins too were not yet fishes. They lived on dry land and looked like dogs, with tails and a dog's mouth. What had happened was that they had moved from dry land into the sea, and water had done the rest. They also argued that the Milky Way, of four hundred thousand stars, moves toward and away from Earth at a speed of thirty thousand miles a second. A girl's voice behind Fitzi objected, asking, "Why could the world be discovered only by going backward? Why was life like a river running through the night?" Both the youths claimed that sixty million years ago the world had suffered an accident that had changed the weather and devastated the globe. As a result of this, pterodactyls had died out and had been replaced by pigeons, nightingales, and larks. If by any chance she didn't believe it, she should go and look it up in the university library. And that people who, like those three, look part Jewish and part non-Jewish have been on the Earth for only about fifty thousand years. The band continued playing Gershwin.

"If you want to know what I mean, Fitzi, it's about the cash box in the Welfare Department on Maislova Street that you were talking about in February." It was out now. Linda laid her hand on Fitzi's knee.

"Couldn't you just once get pleasure out of something that isn't at the expense of others?" He looked at her as if to say that he had never liked for people to attack him with his own weapons.

"I don't want you to rush into something and find that the person you'd do anything for won't lift a finger for you when you're in jail." She looked as if she were trying to teach Fitzi how to swim, and he was trying to drown her. Or as if she had done him a favor just by trying, and he hadn't even batted an eyelash in response.

There were tears in her eyes. At the request of Maximilian Gotlob, the band played an old wartime hit, "Don't Sit under the Apple Tree." Andy Lebovitch sauntered across the room toward the bar. It did not take him long to sum up the situation.

"Don't you think, my young Jewish friend, that you're making a bit too much noise for the price of one ticket?" He grinned at Linda. "Look here, little darling, if you've lost something from your handbag—and you're always losing something—just cross the room, and over there is a microphone in front of the band-leader's beefy face. You can ask some honest finder to hand it in at the cloakroom for a 10-percent reward." Now Linda cried out loud. She must have known that she broadcast information to people who didn't have the slightest idea what she was talking about. Dita Saxova blushed. She couldn't believe what she had heard and seen.

The bartender exchanged glances with Mr. Gotlob and D. E. Huppert. "Biting the hand that feeds you." Behind Fitzi was the corridor leading to the bathrooms. The cloakroom was just opposite. Dita's head was bent over her drink as if she expected to find a ring at the bottom of her wineglass.

"Excuse me," David Egon Huppert said to Dita as he got down from his stool at the bar. "Don't stray too far." He adjusted his tie and stopped at the table where Linda was crying. "Give it a rest. You're not the only people here, you know. We're not at the circus."

The bandleader had the musicians run through the score for"Besame Mucho," "Little Field," and "Ti-pi-tin." Neugeborn rose to his feet slowly. It looked as if D.E. blocked the way to the bathroom. Both were about the same height.

They stared at each other for a moment. Not a word was said. Suddenly Neugeborn drove his fist into Huppert's mouth. Andy Lebovitch began to whistle the beginning of the "Internationale" in Dita's direction. Blood ran down Huppert's lips. He would have fallen if he had not crashed into the bar. He straightened up. Then the fight began, and with every blow that landed on Neugeborn's chest there was the sound of cracking wood. It was the breastplate that Fitzi had unwittingly obtained in the form of rulers from the community. Then Linda screamed. She took a blow from her stepbrother. D.E. didn't even apologize.

The throng of bodies on the dance floor packed close and watched in silence. The whole of SIA was suddenly quiet. Dita went red, then pale. Should she be proud that men fought over her? Maybe. This wasn't her greatest victory. Why? She suddenly didn't feel like the master of her destiny. Why? Why? Why had this happened?

"We're not in Chicago," remarked Munk.

"For better, for worse," Lev Goldblat added.

Dita felt the eyes of Munk, Isabelle Goldblat, and Neugeborn all fixed on her. She blushed again. What should I do? she asked herself.

The caretaker said: "Il cavallo che meglio tira tocca le peggio scudisciate." (Only the willing horse gets a bigger load than it can carry.) Only Dita heard him. He placed the open palm of his hand on his sunken chest. Dita concentrated on her glass of wine.

Neugeborn and Huppert were separated by Dr. Fitz, who then brought on the star attraction of the evening, one of Andy Lebovitch's discoveries. It was a double act, a man and a woman dressed in bathing suits for the number "Bronze Statue—Immobile Beauty." Dita glanced at Fitzi.

The members of the band took the advice of Mr. Traxler, the caretaker of the Krakovska hostel, and began to play. The beefy-faced vocalist sang in English:

> *One night when the moon was so mellow,*
> *Rosita met young Manuello.*

There was applause and laughter. Dita was silent. She raised herself up on her narrow golden slippers. The vocalist had made a name for himself at the Baroque, which had been closed after the war because of the narrow sidewalk. They had demolished the whole building, together with the café. Now the vocalist performed in the Café Vltava, where Dita had been once on Saturday afternoon with D.E. before they visited the Hotel Astoria/Novak.

D.E. accepted a glass of mineral water from the bartender.

Andy Lebovitch led Alfred Neugeborn away to the cloakroom. They took their coats. Andy bowed to Dita. "As far as I can see," he remarked to Fitzi, "we're through for tonight."

Five minutes later Andy Lebovitch watched uncomprehendingly while Fitzi Neugeborn, still deep in thought, threw a bundle of rulers and pencils into the gray ripples of the river. Their trademark was indecipherable in the darkness. They floated on the surface like torpedoes next to cruisers. Lebovitch put his arm around Fitzi's neck.

"You nearly knocked him down with your first punch, but he managed to pull himself together. He's not such a weakling, Fitzi." He did not ask whether Alfred Neugeborn had done it on account of Dita Saxova or to teach D.E. a lesson. "You're not in the best shape when you drink. And you didn't move fast enough either. What do you say, let's go over to the Rumania Bar. The best way to spend money is to waste it."

Neugeborn did not budge from his rest on the handrail. "Some girls want the whole world to love them, just because a little while ago they were almost devoured by hate."

Both knew whom he meant. On the nighttime haze of the river floated the reflection of Dita Saxova, her slim legs, her small waist, and her pretty mouth with a smile for all seasons. Lebovitch, like Dita Saxova, believed that above all else what people needed was happiness and then, come what may, to take everything as it comes, even the most outrageous and unexpected things. That was the secret of success, not to be surprised by anything—people, circumstances, human nature. If he was asked what it was above all that he could sympathize with and understand, he would without hesitation give one answer.

"There's a kind of girl who imagines that every day is Sunday and that the world will carry her on its shoulders. Everybody owes her something, but she doesn't owe anybody anything." His brown eyes shone in the dusk.

Neugeborn looked dejected. For him, the evening had ended like a period at the end of a sentence that he could not, would not, or did not feel able to express in words. He knew that there were some kinds of rejection that did not even have to be expressed in words but were valid just the same. Dita Saxova was present in him, a sweet prison, something he couldn't explain.

"If you like, Fitzi, you can borrow my blond for a day or two. She'll go along with whatever you want." He thought to himself that it was easier to stir Fitzi up than to calm him down. "Sometimes the medicine is worse than the disease. That's how it is, Fitzi." And finally: "Why should we deceive ourselves, Neugeborn?"

The city breathed its multicolored glow. The stars in the sky shone blue and silver. Moonlight swam on the river, and little boats tossed on the water. Prague was a quiet and peaceful city. For the community of Jewish kids in 1947, the words *home* and *land* were equivalent to the word *Prague*. It was not their fault that the water was to carry it all away.

The SIA Academic Café was only a few steps away. The music filtered through the ventilators and the open windows and doors—trumpets, trombones, the triumphant drums. They could hear the beefy-faced vocalist pouring out the vague and appealing lyrics.

3 During the night following the dance, Isabelle Goldblat, née Steinitz, died. Three days later the residents of the Lubliana and Krakovska street hostels went to the cemetery in a group, straight from a meeting with a black-haired, sunburned young man who recruited for the Promised Land.

Brita asked Dita reproachfully why she didn't try to start something with the black-haired fellow.

"I'm not developed enough erotically. Apart from that, he's got forty admirers already, and I've got things to do here. One leaf on my tree is sick, and another one has just been born," Dita said.

"As if you didn't know that with girls it's the other way around," Liza said. "The sooner they start, the sooner they finish." After a while she added: "It's possible to do a great job of pretending, I can assure you of that. And you don't have to pray for a drop of gypsy blood in your veins to make you look passionate."

Tonitschka wondered why people put pebbles on Jewish graves.

"So you can rot away in peace and not be gnawed by vultures, worms, and hens," Liza observed. She had heard all about it from Mr. Gotlob. They could have embroidered on it further by quoting his erotic theory of the three circles, as he had expounded it to David Egon Huppert at the dance. In the first circle were women from all over the world, provided they weren't sick, hunchbacks, or the like. The second took in the wives of his best acquaintances, and in the third circle were the wives and daughters of his nearest and dearest. He wouldn't go with those even if they wanted to. With the rest of them, including women from all over the world, he was entitled to go to bed, without prejudice, and keep his self-respect.

He watched Liza as if she were a botanical garden. She enhanced his reputation by saying that he could see in a second things that it took other people years to see.

Tonitschka was also concerned about knowing whether there was anything more to come. She looked at Dita. Tonitschka reminded her of the washhouse back home, putting embroidered curtains through the wringer, even the voices of her mother and father, a memory of a table and three chairs. Tonitschka probably still thought that all you needed was a straight nose, breasts, and long legs to get by in the world.

"Maybe an honor guard from the Hitler Youth," Andy remarked. "Just look out."

"Body and soul," Dita said. "They're all mixed together. Do you believe that the manna that fell from heaven to the desert was really lichen blown over from Arabia? And that Pharaoh's army was swallowed by a tidal wave thrown up by an underwater volcano on Greece or somewhere in Sicily?"

A while ago the young man with black hair and a complexion like sifting sand had been distributing the books of Herzl. Dita had asked for a copy of one, and before she returned it, she had written on the flyleaf: "To the champion shadow-catcher for the

Promised Land, from Theodor Herzl, via Dita Saxova, Prague, June 1947."

"Ever since I learned that the burning bush was a photonyide plant, I have been in favor of a regional branch in Prague." She wore her gala smile, as she always did when the room was full of people. She told him that she had been in Theresienstadt with Theodor Herzl's daughter before she had been dispatched to Auschwitz-Birkenau with a party of feeble-minded people.

A summer breeze blew. The path narrowed, and Dita had to walk ahead with Tonitschka. The sun poured down through the branches of the trees. Dita took smaller steps for Tonitschka's sake. Her tiny chin shook. She wore tight slippers, like the Chinese girls who cripple their toes in order to make their feet smaller.

"I take a size five shoe," Tonitschka said. "I could play the part of a boy in amateur dramas."

"Have you heard that in America, or England, they feed cats, dogs, and white mice special canned food? They say that in wartime women painted their legs, because the factories were turning out ammunition instead of stockings." Why did she never confide in anyone about what had happened with D.E.? She was not sure herself. At least it was easy to pretend. She smiled. "I can imagine it. Our little darlings who have tried, and will always try, to get rich by selling pickled herrings, regardless of the direction or the speed with which the world rushes on, toward its destruction. Not to mention their distant cousins, like you and me, who are at the end of their tether."

"It's not in my power to change it, nor in yours," Tonitschka said.

"I like wandering through Prague," Dita said. "I suppose it's because during the war we looked forward to it so much, and at the same time nobody really believed we'd ever come back." She smiled. "Whenever I talk to the people from school, in spite of myself, I feel like a foreigner here. I've given up trying to explain it to myself or to others. People loathe misfortune. They are terribly settled. They accept me without question as one of them, but really they have no conception. Last Wednesday I was invited to dinner at the home of a boy from my class, whose father is a technician. After the meal I pretended to be interested in how their holidays had been washed out by rain, and how they had to take a dozen umbrellas with them. It was nice and clean there. I told him what it was like in Theresienstadt—about the parties, the amateur plays, lectures by various European celebrities who were in trouble because they were born. About how the boys had played soccer and how many women's orchestras we'd had. It just occurred to me incidentally that with other people I never recall the grayness of the days that passed, one after another, although most of them were like that. Like when you only remember Sunday and not the rest of the days. They were surprised to hear me talk about a cake I enjoyed, because I never talked about the slop that I didn't. And now, hold your breath. Do you know what that boy dreamed about the night after my visit? That he had to go to the concentration camp because of me. Somehow I upset him."

Roots of the chestnut trees grew along the path. "And don't worry about your chest measurements either," Dita said. "I had the same problem, because in those days it was better to have none at all. In September 1944 I lived in a fairly decent prefab with Italian women. From bits and pieces they fixed me a bra that even the Technical Museum wouldn't exhibit nowadays."

Trees from the neighboring Catholic cemetery hung over the wall. Higher up, above the bricks, the branches and leaves were all intertwined. For a while the two girls walked together in silence. Dita thought of D.E. Tonitschka knew that no matter what Dita spoke about, she thought of D. E. Huppert.

Suddenly Dita said: "I am a murderer of feelings, of hope. I know very well what I'm doing, even when I'm not really doing anything. Sometimes a person can be a liar, thief, or killer, even if it's only of feelings and relationships. Sometimes I pretend so much that you can hardly call it pretending anymore. I don't want to envy anybody, like a beggar peering into another beggar's pack."

"I know it's already happened to you," Tonitschka said.

"I don't want to think badly of Isabelle. I don't know what makes me like that. You keep meeting it in some form or another, a sort of perverted echo. I still dislike the blind or sick instead of hating the disease. In the same way I'm afraid of the weakness in weak people. There's some devil in me. Maybe it's because the Germans kept on trying to convince us of our Jewish or Slavic inferiority. Perhaps there is such a feeling in us—the one they put into us, that makes us believe in it." She didn't say a word about D.E. How was her experience so vast, or so rich, in spite of everything? Again she felt as if she were naked, waiting humbly for love, joy, fun, and maybe stability—for some deeper meaning, an all-encompassing beauty.

Then she said, "Sometimes I feel like ending it all—jumping from some low, one-story building. Like when people in the camps got hold of morphine or cyanide and laughed at all those who wanted to kill them anyway and before killing to humiliate them."

"Are you mad?" Tonitschka asked. But then she sighed, "I get this idea, too. But not from a low, one-story building. Maybe my turn is next. Maybe everybody carries that inside him like an infection. It's funny. Would you be able to do it, really?"

"No. Only if somebody or something would humiliate me. What about you?"

"I don't think so either," Tonitschka said.

Dita thought about the contradictions surrounding love: when a man is not good for a woman, and she knows it but can't stay

away from him; when a man isn't worthy of a woman and takes
advantage of her, yet she fears she will lose him and wonders if
she is worthy of him; when people who hate lies and hate to lie
do so with impunity when it comes to love; when a man knows he
is in love with an unattractive woman, who in his eyes is a goddess; when you love someone so much you hate yourself for it;
when a man knows (or at least suspects) that a woman is faking,
but he asks her if she is and she says no, and he is happy to
believe her; that something tastes better when beautifully displayed—or is that when a meal tastes like a feast when someone
has prepared it with love? Or that in many cases men like food
better than anything else, but they will never admit it? Does that
also apply to women? Or is it true that even when they didn't
think much of it in the first place, women will appreciate something more if another woman admires it? (The same for men: a
man tends to appreciate his woman a lot more if another man
wants her too.) When a woman says no but means yes . . . but
the person she says no to knows that the more she protests
without resisting, the more aggressive she really wants him to
be.

Liza and Brita caught up with them at the memorial to those
killed in both world wars. Mr. Gotlob and D.E. were already
standing there. Dita blushed. Mr. Gotlob wore a gray flannel suit
with blue stripes. He wiped his sweating brow with a white
handkerchief. Dita joined D.E. Everything was suddenly as
before.

"What's wrong with you?" D.E. asked.

"Neither anger nor pity nor sympathy," Dita said.

He didn't look at her like the other boys, who could strip off a
girl's dress without touching it. But she would like to stand
naked in front of him, her flesh, her heart, her willingness and
friendship revealed—out of hiding once and for all, forever.

D.E. looked at her. "Do you think a Jewish girl from Prague

could ever be something else if she were in a different place?"

She closed her eyes. "What's so wrong with being Jewish? Why should I be ashamed? Is everybody who survived?"

He suspected that Dita Saxova's chief problem right now was herself. He had no idea what she was filled with. Tall and slim, leaning, with one knee bent for comfort, on one of the white memorial stones on the edge of the path, she looked like a different person, in another place. Had the graveyard stolen her customary balance? Smiling was not appropriate here. She wore a springtime traveling suit with a beige-colored blouse. She had a black ribbon around her neck and another ribbon instead of a belt to gather in her skirt. She had thrust her right hand into a pocket as though she were palming something she wished to conceal. Her body and face were lean. There were questions in her blue eyes, and something about them suggested a song. In them he saw time, not running through fingers like sand, but as illusions, people and memories and forgiveness, something that made her pleasant company and too much for him at the same time. There was irony and alienation in her eyes, too. He glanced down at her skirt. It was rather long for her. She had no desire to adapt her clothes to her tall figure.

Dita said, "In thinking about my dream, I realize that the men hurrying about were like those men in the Jewish cemetery who used to run after us when we took Grandma during the Jewish holidays. I hated that part of the visit to the cemetery more than anything else, though I also hated it when Grandma got so upset and my mother became nervous and flustered. I didn't know the dead people, not really. They had died before I was born or when I was very little, so I wasn't upset. But those men—all that shouting and waving of prayer books and flapping of black coats! I dreaded those cemetery visits so much. Why did my mother insist on putting us through that every year?"

"I never go to funerals if I can avoid it," Brita said. "Since the dead are dead and you can no longer change the situation or say good-bye, you ought to be able to find a way to let go and express your grief in a more personal way. Funerals have too much ritual and are too religious for me. But maybe it is true that funerals are for the living and not the dead."

Dita stood there with her ankles touching. What could she hear in the air? A melody, coming from far away, or from nowhere. A virtuoso from a private play not yet staged, separated from real life by a memory whose thick or thin wall hid the dance of invisible illusions?

She refrained from saying that the cemetery had no real attraction for her. She felt alive but did not understand her life and still did not know why. Life was, and was not, as straightforward as it seemed. She felt ashamed, without knowing why. She looked at D.E. as if she were standing at a window and watching people in the street, close and far away. D.E. returned to her eyes, but he had no answer for her, just as she had no answer for him. There was too much about her that was beyond his comprehension, and too much he understood too well. He finally gave her a smile. She felt his uneasiness.

Later, when they each threw three spadefuls of earth into the grave, Dita remembered that D.E. was going away. What was that song, what echo, what silence did she hear within him? Not to mention her fear of soiling her white gloves?

She said to him, "Long time no see. It seems like yesterday when I last saw you, and it seems like an eternity. Nothing has changed here—nothing is different—life just sort of goes on and on. Same routines, same way of doing things. Same irritations and happiness and sorrow, same as always. Life is like an old shoe, not necessarily pretty or even all that comfortable anymore, but at least you know that it fits. I'm having anxious dreams. They aren't frightening, but they are very unpleasant. I had lots of them when I was trying to decide, D.E."

In her mind, she spoke to him in her mind, asking him to understand.

"You don't owe me anything except your friendship, or your love, D.E., if you choose to give it. I've never asked you for anything personal, but I hate to think of myself as a toy, or less—a mere diversion you find convenient. I may be of little real significance to you, but I am not a toy. I am a woman . . . and I guess you already know that women can be fragile playmates . . . and they sometimes come with unpleasant side effects such as tears and falling in love with you. I will never ask you for anything more than your honesty and allegiance—never for more than you can or will give to me—but I will not be a toy. Since I really don't know what I mean to you—I don't think that I ever have asked or probably ever would ask you that question—I guess my feelings are mostly conjecture, conjured up by my own insecurities. But they are not unreasonable either. At least I know we are friends . . . I feel responsible for my part in that friendship, and I do try to give you what you want and need . . . but I have to know that it matters to you. If not, heck, we'll just have a good time, but we won't really be friends. Life is so unusual. People surprise you. A decade is coming to an end."

Munk bowed low over the grave. He was dressed just as in winter, in a dark coat with a woolen scarf and a dandruff-covered collar. Sweat stood out on his forehead. He was short and fat. His eyes were on Dita.

"Will there be a bugle call?" Dita asked.

"Isabelle Goldblat has died," Munk said at last.

"The mountain has brought fate its mouse," Brita muttered.

Dita nudged her with her elbow. The Holy Virgin had never liked Munk. It was probably a reaction to his statement that "people are born to be equal" or "history will bring about equality, sooner or later, all over the world." Apparently Brita felt obliged to protest on behalf of the British royal family.

Munk pulled a piece of paper from his pocket. He did not take his eyes off Dita. He spoke of how an echo springs from Isabelle Goldblat's three sons, Ignac, Arthur, and Arnošt, who had become dust carried by the wind across the fields, and from them sprang weeds or corn, bushes or moss. He is speaking to me, thought Dita. But I am not speaking to him. Is this my new problem? Her thoughts slipped again to D.E.

Anyone who did not know how Munk had been deported during the war might well have thought he had not changed at all since 1939. His face was bloated. The skin beneath his neck quivered like a rooster's. Wrinkles covered his throat and chin, webbed with bluish tendons and veins like an old dog's. His complexion was the color of parched clay. It wasn't until the next day that Dita wondered what he had thought about when he had stared at her. Actually, Munk thought that if death came to one of the boys and girls and said, "It is your turn," then he wouldn't hesitate to ask to take the place of that person. Or he might ask only that it could happen during the night, while he slept. On the yellowed newsprint of the *Gazette* there was in fact not a word of what he went on to say:

"I should like to say a few words, as a veteran with overseas service. I did not join the army at a late stage. My service number is 272. I fought at the battle of Sokolov and in all the subsequent battles, until I finally entered Prague with General Svoboda. I graduated from light machine guns to the Maxim. With me were three brothers, also Jewish. Two of them were killed in action. The youngest, age sixteen, also served at the front. The general gave a personal order that he should be withdrawn from the firing line and spared for his mother's sake, after his two brothers had been killed. I myself was wounded," he said as he pointed to his left side, "and lost a pound of flesh. Before I had recovered, I volunteered for the front. I did so in spite of the fact that I no longer had any chance of defending any of my own people. My parents had been killed, my brothers and my wife murdered, my child murdered. I regret what is happening today and that people talk as if we had entered the fighting only at the last minute."

It was the letter that former sergeant major Julius Schwartz had intended to read to the committee of the Jewish Religious Community in Prague before he jumped out of the window on New Year's Day. He was one of the first to discover that what counts is not whether anyone is against the Jews, whether there are large numbers of them living in a country, only a few, or none at all. And that it has nothing to do with whether they are courageous in battle or energetic in the workplace. What dismayed Munk was the realization that yesterday still had an impact on tomorrow. How much longer could he believe that it was not true, that a miracle had happened, that he was not living in a utopia?

"We are burying a brave Jewish mother," Munk said. "She witnessed, and lived through, many trials. Her sons lived and died like three trees. She was born to endure." He felt cold sweat running down his head and spine. At that moment Dita felt a similar chill run through her own back.

"There is much that is strong and clean in nature," Dita said.

The trees prepared for the coming summer. Someone spoke of Doris Levit. D.E. stood next to Mr. Gotlob.

"When I was at Grandma Olga's place," Dita said, "I used to love it there, like today. If I had a piece of land, I'd certainly grow something on it."

Andy looked around a bit further on, where Franz Kafka and the workhouse attendant, Julius Schwartz, were buried. "I see that we still manage to turn a blind eye to suicide," he said.

"Would you prefer to leave him lying in the street?" Dita asked, turning toward him. "Or do you think he really should have jumped into Etna, to be more sophisticated?"

"Well, if anybody wants to do himself in, why not? That's his own affair. Myself, I'd settle a few accounts first. That's all." From the look in Andy's eyes it was evident that he most certainly would not do such a thing as long as he thought there was still something in life to look forward to. He would probably never be driven to it by suffering—more likely by exhilaration. He'd said on Friday that when he was twelve years old and Hitler had come to Prague, he felt willing to die, because he thought he'd already had all the fun there was to have.

Before the funeral, Andy had come over to Dita's for a cup of tea. He kept helping himself to sugar until Dita asked him if he was trying to develop sugar diabetes. That reminded him of how they used to dump people out of cattle trucks at Auschwitz-Birkenau (and that he always had a smile on his lips). A doctor in an SS uniform asked an eight-year-old boy whom he liked better—his mom or his dad. He would have to make up his mind by the time the doctor had counted to three: "Eins, zwei, drei." The boy looked first at his father, then at his mother, then once more at his father. The doctor sent the mother to the chimney. Dita had grown used to Andy. She felt close to him, except when he confused her body with meat or public transportation.

"From roast lamb to roast people and back again," Dita said as if announcing the arrivals and departures of trains at a railway station. "To die 'quietly and unbroken,' as they write in the *Gazette* every day on the first. Or perhaps 'silently, humbly, and patiently.'"

"I would like to know what lies beyond the stars," Tonitschka whispered. She looked like someone who had just had a choice morsel snatched from her lips, or like someone in a hurry who keeps falling over her feet. Was her mother responsible for the fact that her chest resembled her father's?

"There's a notice here that the cemetery keys should be picked up at the community office," Dita said. "I've found that everyone is a kind of prostitute. Some more than others. Everything is business, whether or not it's moral. I suppose the question of ethics must be separated from that of prostitution, but maybe not always." At once she realized she was no longer on the wrong track. She nearly bit out her tongue.

Brita pierced Lebovitch with her glance. "It's only fear of Andy that guarantees my sound health, and I assure you that I'm not the only one." She looked at Dita Saxova.

Andy was unable to answer her because Lev Goldblat and Mr. Gotlob, with D.E. next to him, walked toward them. For-Better-for-Worse smiled, as if to say that when earthly remains pass away, not everything departs with them. His expression showed peaceful resignation. He took Dita's hand, as children do. He smiled as if wishing for each of his three sons—and not only for them—a farewell ritual such as this, one that does not bring the dead back to life but provides a fitting recognition of their life's end, like an assurance to the living that they will not perish like the beasts, recognizes that people need one another, and not merely for company at the cemetery.

The gasoline pump by the train stop at the corner reminded Dita of a German machine used for pulverizing bone. She had worked it herself at one time. She used to fill sacks with bone dust that was not needed for soap or glue. It was subsequently used for fertilizer in the German homeland. Evidently Andy had forgotten Brita's remark, or else he thought that it was safer to give her a wide berth. She had forgotten to tell D.E. about that in the Hotel Astoria/Novak, formerly the Yellow Stone Inn. Didn't it occur to him that she only wanted to let go with him?

Maybe the world, to be fair, belongs to people like Lebovitch. He did not burden others with his moods, as Brita or Linda Huppert did. But neither did D.E. When Andy woke up in the morning and saw that he could see, heard that he could hear, felt that he still had arms and legs and was without pain, that sufficed to make him feel humble and grateful that he was alive. Am I the same? I might be.

Dita listened to the rustling of the leaves. Andy was telling Liza that an old she-cat prefers young mice, that a dead bee brings no honey. His hints were hardly obscure. Dita wondered why she could not stop examining herself. She thought of Munk, only to return to D.E. She wondered if she could rely on him to arrange the approval of her application for the trip to Switzerland.

Some time later Dita left the cemetery and walked with Munk.

"Maybe you are growing up too quickly," Munk said.

"Is that good or bad?" asked Dita.

They walked slowly through the Old Town, toward the Charles Bridge. Munk knew that this was the first time Dita had been at the cemetery since the war. As far as he knew, none of them went to the cemetery except Andy Lebovitch, who used it as a hideout, or a free hotel. None of them had relatives buried here.

"What are you applying to Mr. Gotlob for?" Munk asked Dita.

"I'm only asking for a reference."

"Do you have any unsettled legal problems?"

"No, none. I guess he'd soon realize that I don't have a very high opinion of lawyers."

"Books are not your worst friends."

She walked slowly on Munk's account, but even so she got a step or two ahead of him. She could imagine what he wanted to talk to her about. He said nothing about responsibility and innocence, as he had after the party at SIA, or about the road that leads from insecurity to danger. Munk thought of that immortal English pound of flesh from *The Merchant of Venice*, which had become common knowledge in many lands east and west of the Elbe. Although it was only an offspring of a vision inspired by all sorts of things, this actual, bloody piece of flesh of the soldier in the eastern army would be forgotten as quickly and completely as the first one would be universally recalled.

"You are failing in almost all your subjects, Dita."

Above the river the sea gulls performed their unpaid acrobatics. "One can see disaster approaching, but cannot stop it." That, too, was a quotation she had learned from Munk's Turgenev (already sold to the secondhand book dealer). Did he hope to talk her out of it, if she got permission for the trip? Or just to give her a bit of consolation if she did not get it? "Why can no one ever know what will become of him?" Turgenev, again . . . She smiled.

Munk waited for her reply. In spite of all that had happened, he found it hard to accept that all values were only relative and that there was no absolute morality. He had to live with a contradiction that he had developed during the war that had swept away all his relatives, family, and friends and the world he had known until 1938. It was a contradiction between old principles and a new era that pronounced them absurd and inadequate— almost irrelevant, because they had betrayed men, and men had betrayed them. He had no wish to be guide or adviser. He was afraid of seeming blind to her, or alien, or perhaps like someone who walks into a wall in the darkness and proclaims that it is the end of the world. Did he not inadvertently ask that from her?

She explained how she had made clay pitchers last week and baked them in the school kiln (three of them had been stolen), and how she had broken up the ones that had not turned out right. She felt glad she was able to speak about a different kind of breakage. She had offered him one of the pitchers. Munk was as nervous as he'd been the previous week when he had given her a hundred-crown note. She had learned to accept gifts now and was surprised that there wasn't a wolf on the bank notes instead of a picture of a naked woman. Munk refused to admit that friendship had disappeared since the wars. Did he know something about her trip with D.E.?

For a while they walked along the paved riverbank. On the other side was a hill with a park. On the surface of the water little boats stirred. Anglers landed their Friday night catch—whitebait, loach, and little carp.

"I heard you have a gold bracelet."

She did not answer.

"I don't want to interrogate you like a magistrate, or like a guardian, Dita. You don't need to tell me."

"I think I should go now."

They looked like an unmatched couple. The June wind pressed against her. Suddenly Munk stopped. For heaven's sake, maybe he thought she got presents from men of doubtful reputation. Why did he avoid her eyes? Would he be capable of wanting to go out with her himself? Or she with him? She knew it was nonsense. But it flashed across her mind that in the last few days her voice had changed.

She left Munk standing on the bridge and ran down the steps to Kampa Island. "You're growing up fast" was code for "you are depraved." "You are failing in nearly all your subjects" implied some doubt about her chances of going on the Swiss trip. "Where are you going? With whom? When will you be back? What will you do?" They were the sort of questions he would ask his daughter Sonia, if she were still alive. The things that parents say to their daughters differ from those they say to their sons. And the things that daughters and sons without any parents or relatives say are different again. Munk had looked at her as if asking what sort of future she imagined for herself, when she was so careless about her present. "What will become of you, Dita? When you begin like this, what do you expect it will be like in a year's time?" All he needed to add was "The best people always manage to do what has to be done, even if they wait until the very last minute."

All things change: only numbers stay the same. Yesterday he

had slipped Aristotle in among the new books he had given her. She had already sold his Plutarch, both volumes. "Those who wish to participate in life, Dita, must realize that a new era has begun. New questions, new answers. What will be the new meaning of *people?* Perhaps we are into something previously unknown." His utter seriousness was absurd. He invited her to have faith in life and feared that his own faith was faltering.

Even without Munk's admonition she felt how wretched her life had become and that she ought to do something about it. She would have been happy to believe that the fat man was at least helped by the truths of his old heart. Here I am, alive. I am the master of my destiny. I can do whatever I want. Life is not what we want but what we have, and I still have a couple of tricks up my sleeve.

Dita watched the sea gulls. They floated, immobile, in the air. They flew in higher and higher circles, then fell, and rose again in their flight.

 "You look well, child."

"Thank you, Mr. Gotlob."

"Don't you like pleasant surprises?"

Maximilian Gotlob had presented himself that evening in his soft black hat in front of the International Blue and White's library in Little Charles Street. He looked like a British member of Parliament. He wore the smile of a man who knows what's what, had always known it, and always would. He kissed Dita's hand through her glove and proposed that they talk "inside." He recommended the Sophocles Bar.

The manager of the nightclub came forward to greet them. Mr. Gotlob ordered a table for two.

"We must try to take the rough with the smooth, my dear. You can't blot out the sun with your hand, you know." Then he added,

"I've been in the world long enough to have learned that. Personally, I prefer the evening to the morning. One day I'll tell you why."

They were given a small table next to a square pillar, inlaid with mirrors as high as a man. A gypsy orchestra, led by Egon Levit, of the Jewish Religious Community, played "Sentimental Journey."

Mr. Gotlob sat at a right angle to Dita. He turned toward her. "What kind of a day have you had? After all, the weather was nice. How do you feel, child?"

"I think I have recently left that category behind."

"By the way, Dita, Liza sends her apologies. You can probably imagine why." Mr. Gotlob smiled with all his chins, just like Uncle Carl, thought Dita. Was he trying to suggest that we only live once? Or that it would be an evening with no horrors on the menu? Not necessarily, in my case.

The Sophocles Bar was built in an old style. She had never been there before. It looked a cut above what she had expected. But she could not answer the question of why she had come here with him at all. Which of them had misjudged the other?

She rewarded him with her brief, grown-up smile that said nothing. Was it such a sin to sell yourself for one evening, when others sell themselves for 365 days a year, which, as Avi Fischer had once calculated, came to 8,760 hours, 525,600 minutes? I am an irredeemable fool, thought Dita. Why, for goodness sake, do I always have to keep resurrecting phantoms from the past? She had been prepared to enjoy herself and humor Mr. Gotlob, at least to the extent of getting a bit tipsy. Liza was not present, and although neither Dita Saxova nor Mr. Gotlob had mentioned her previously, they thought of her now, and she created doubt in both their minds. The time was a quarter to eight.

"I hope you are as hungry as a wolf, child."

"I hope so."

"A hundred percent."

Mr. Gotlob took a drink. He watched her through his wineglass. The mirrors enhanced the effect of light, as did her eyes, the ceiling, curtains, pillars, and the music. Her dress looked as if it were too tight.

"The body of a woman is like the profile of a beautiful slim fish," said Mr. Gotlob. He ran his eyes down to her waist. She threw back her head as if to toss her hair from her forehead. Mr. Gotlob lifted his glass with one hand, and with the other he stroked her hand. His palm was heavy and meaty.

"I think I must be drunk already, Mr. Gotlob."

"For heaven's sake, after those few drops?"

"It's terribly hot in here, Mr. Gotlob. It's been a long day."

"We haven't yet drunk a toast to Grindelwald, child."

"Really, I thank you very much, Mr. Gotlob. You are really very kind, Mr. Gotlob."

"Here's to your grown-up loveliness, Dita. You are no longer a child. You have certainly left that category behind."

He sensed in her and in himself, too, an insatiable impatience, something forgiven only in young women. He sat, still holding his glass near her face, and nodded to the waiter to bring another bottle. Meanwhile he said, "You know, Dita, when this wine was bottled, Otto von Bismarck was still alive. Except that when you say the name Bismarck you hear the name Hitler. Tell me, is it true that one of your admirers has bought a dog and named him Hitler? You must have a man for every finger, child."

"You know more about it than I do, Mr. Gotlob."

"You have to believe in yourself."

"I try. I do." She smiled. "But what can I do about things that are beyond my control, like the wind?"

The waiter wiped their table. Mr. Gotlob leaned over closer to her. She felt his hand, eyes, and breath, like a hot wind tearing off her clothes. At the same time she could see herself in the mirror, smiling at everything. She could always count on her appearance.

"Petit à petit, à chacun son nid," Mr. Gotlob said.

"What does it mean?"

"Little by little a bird builds its nest. Tell me about yourself, child. The story of your life interests me. You are too modest. Liza often speaks of you. Mr. Huppert has talked about you too. You are very popular. I'm glad that we've found the chance." He smiled. "When I'm with you, I feel about eighteen too." He raised his glass: "To a closer friendship, perhaps?"

She smiled. It struck her that the prize for this contest had been devalued in advance. She felt the wine in her cheeks.

"As a soldier in the army abroad, you were probably in worse situations, Mr. Gotlob."

"You have lovely blue eyes, child." It sounded like an echo.

"It's funny how easily your reservations melt away."

"For goodness sake, child. Why a guilty conscience? The best healer is time. And this." He lifted his glass. Then he said, "Man does not live in isolation. And for a flower to bloom tomorrow it must be planted now. You believe in your now, at the moment, don't you? That you can race against time and win? That you can beat the clock?"

"I hope so. Maybe. They say that telling lies means stealing another's truth. And that a little patience in a moment of anger helps a man to avoid a hundred days of sorrow." She smiled. Mr. Gotlob drank.

The band played "Don't Leave Me Lonesome This Evening." Dita noticed that everything conjured up echoes of D.E., or of Munk's hoarse voice: "Red is the color of hope, children," or "Every slice of bread has two sides." One day the fat man had left a note for her in the basement, in For-Better-for-Worse's cupboard: "I'm sure that everything we do for our people, near or far, we do for ourselves. The fate of every person is to a certain extent my own fate too. No matter to what extent I am conscious of it, now, or later, or never at all. At your age, knowledge of the goal is just as important as the goal itself. As the rabbis say: 'If anyone claims that he has sought and not found, do not believe him.'" And so on and so on. Everything seemed as full of truth as her feeling from the wine and, at the same time, as empty as her glass was becoming. But was it half empty or half full? Both at once. She smiled.

For only a moment she caught sight of herself reflected in the wineglass: a tall slim girl. It was as if she had donned seven-mile boots and was able to leap across time. Her father washed his hands before his lunch of a piece of bread and a cup of milk. It was the best meal provided at their home on ordinary days, apart from Saturday, and sometimes on Saturday too. In the mirror she saw how the blood had rushed to her face. Did people still live like that every day? For fifty-two weeks in the year? The back of Mr. Gotlob's neck was the color of furrowed red timber. She held the glass in the palm of her hand and played with it. She looked around at the people. Am I one of them?

"I wanted to ask your advice about the summer excursion, Mr. Gotlob."

"Of course, my child. If someone has to go, why not the prettiest?"

"Thank you, Mr. Gotlob."

"This afternoon we decided to include you. Hasn't Mr. David Egon Huppert told you yet? You'll either go with the children or on a study grant to Grindelwald, Dita. I didn't know that you had not been told yet." He smiled pensively. "You don't need anyone to keep his eye on you any longer. As they say in England, girls and dead fish need no protection." Then he added, "I'm sure you agree that it's wrong to keep anyone waiting too long for something he really wants."

"Thank you, Mr. Gotlob." She felt herself blushing. "How can I repay you, Mr. Gotlob?"

"What could a person want from a girl like you, Dita?"

"I don't want to disappoint you, Mr. Gotlob."

"I saw you when you went away on holiday last year, still just a child, Dita. Almost a year has passed now, and you've really grown up."

He laughed. "Relatively speaking, child, everything in the jungle is coordinated." He explained how the leopard fears the lioness and lets her chase him up a tree and looks more like a wet hen in the rain than a leopard.

"It's interesting listening to you," Dita said. She saw her reflection in the mirrors.

"I have lived enough to be able to say this, as a man who has been through fighting, child: If you and I stood up now and ran forward and missed each other and went on running, we would have to run around the whole globe to meet again. And even that is not certain. But by the time we did, if we did, this place would have changed. It would belong to someone else. Where they welcomed us like victors two years ago, now they would say, 'Sorry, ladies and gentlemen, this place is occupied. Comrades, you've come too late.'"

The band struck up "The Rose-Red Crinoline," followed by "The Old Mill." Mr. Gotlob waited until the waiter had filled their glasses. Dita smiled.

"I would be quite happy if the law of the jungle applied here, not merely because I have such unstinted admiration for the jungle."

"They play very well."

He was smoothly shaven. Dita knew from Liza that sometimes Gotlob shaved twice a day. Occasionally he got invitations to the embassies. He had a bald pate with a bulging forehead. He wore the same dark three-piece suit as he had that morning, and a white shirt with a silver-gray tie. He looked like a man of letters.

"I support all good causes anywhere in the world," he said. "Now in England, I could show you a dozen places superior to this. I would love you to see the Four Hundred or the Caprice. We should begin with oysters and end with dessert. Or the other way around—dessert first and oysters to finish?"

The wine had a green tint, like the surface of a deep lake. She thought of how her shabbily dressed father used to take her to a restaurant and order a Grenadier March for both of them, one and a half portions of noodles with potatoes and onions.

"I see that you really like strawberries. Why?"

"I like the way they slip into your mouth." Her face grew rosier. "They taste wonderful."

"How did you spend the rest of the day, child?"

"I went for a walk with Professor Munk."

She realized that this was the third time her dark dress had come in handy that day. There was a pause, and she could see that Munk's name had hit a sour note for Maximilian Gotlob. He raised his thick eyebrows.

"Did he by any chance start shouting 'Death to your class' at you, like he did yesterday when he was discussing social policy at a community board meeting?"

"We talked about school. And plans for the summer. The possibilities of excursions. And about how you get alienated from things, even with the best intentions in the world."

"He'd be a regular bleeding heart if anyone paid attention to him. He has proposed to sell off the community's property and hand the money over to the Welfare Department. An old man, a young fool. A second Prague edition of Karl Marx. It's a pity everyone wants to right the world at other people's expense. You know what we call that sort of thing, child?"

Bleeding heart and *child* were evidently his favorite terms. Dita looked around her. The mirrors helped. Soft music and champagne, white tablecloths and red-tinted lights, attentive waiters. She thought how much gypsies and Jews have in common: both look almost indistinguishable from everybody else in the country they live in, and yet at the same time they feel alien.

"You are both connoisseurs of the arts," Mr. Gotlob said. "How do you like the wine?"

She wanted to tell him that it was a little sour and a little sweet. (Liza would say: "Honey on the tongue, poison on the heart.") Mr. Gotlob sipped his wine slowly. He gazed at her with an interest she sought to interpret.

"We live on a savage planet, child. We fought and bled and died, and now others are slicing up our victory cake. Everything's been divided up, even the family table."

From the little basket, he helped himself to a roll, wrapped in a damask napkin. He broke the roll into several pieces and slowly sank his teeth into one of them. He remarked that on the way to the cemetery he had talked to D. E. Huppert about the law of the jungle. There, in his view, the stronger does not always devour the weaker, but only when driven by hunger. Live and let live. "Il faut vivre et laisser vivre. Leben und leben lassen."

"Sometimes our people kill each other in business negotiations, as cruelly as with a knife or pistol. It can be just as dangerous," he said.

In the mirror the reflected and deflected light shone more softly.

"I have a favorite saying, Dita. We can get away with anything, as long as we're not caught." He sensed her hunger and thirst, a kind she would never be able to satisfy.

He studied the menu and the wine list. He counted on the effect a good dinner would have on her. For just a moment, when they had sat down, it had looked as though they might have nothing to say to each other.

"Will you allow me to order? Do you have any particular preference?"

She felt the blood rush to her head.

"I know you like strawberries," Mr. Gotlob said.

As an entrée Mr. Gotlob ordered a spiked-flesh fish cooked à la Greque. This was followed by American canned soup, supplied by the UN Relief and Rehabilitation Administration, with delicious, if somewhat fatty, bits of meat. After that, Holstein schnitzel that melted in the mouth, together with golden fried potatoes. The cheese strudel, straight from the oven, was as fragrant as the strawberries covered with whipped cream. The soup reminded her of the sea. The strawberries showed blood-red under the cream.

"Are you still such an active supporter of the International Blue and White, Mr. Gotlob?" She ate and drank slowly. She felt rather sticky, as if she had taken a bath in ice cream and dried herself in the afternoon sun.

"It's something you get into as a youngster." Mr. Gotlob drained his glass. "Men you served with in the platoon got killed, not all of them raw recruits either. And when you stayed alive yourself, you couldn't help thinking that something was wrong. There's no fairness in the way luck is distributed. It doesn't change anything: I personally am not doing badly, with a good job and money in the bank. But when you get up in the morning and go to work in the streetcar with all the other workers, you have certain regrets."

"What did you do in the army, Mr. Gotlob?"

"I beg your pardon?"

"What was your job?"

"I was an accountant. First I served as an accountant, then in a fighting unit, and finally in my old job again."

"I should really be getting back to Lubliana Street."

"Here's to your ripe beauty, Dita. And to those who don't have it anymore." He gazed at her and had admiration in his eyes. "You are a lucky child, Dita."

He had to stop talking for a while, as the Italian belly dancer had come on. She did her act to the accompaniment of Indian music. In Dita's look there was some new element that Mr. Gotlob had not taken into account. It struck him that it was the gap between what she had offered and what she was really prepared to give, though he realized how much she had drunk. He knew that she could have had only an approximate idea of his thoughts. Just as he had been teasing and irritating her, she had been teasing him and making him nervous. Thinking of the other girls, he came to the conclusion that they couldn't identify with Dita because they did not like what they saw in her and did not want to admit that they were like her.

He touched her glass with his and peered keenly into her pretty oval face, with its slightly bitter smile. He thought to himself how clever her generation was and, contrary to logic, how carefree. They were both weak and strong. For them life no longer concerned being on the right or the wrong side, but being in a place where it was possible to survive. They were not afraid of the unknown, but of what they had come to know. They were like a patch of unburned grass standing in the middle of a blackened field. They were closer to the jungle than they were willing to admit. Was that so? Maybe.

Mr. Gotlob watched the dancer, with her half-naked body, the gold sheath, and her bare brown legs.

"All the way, Dita," he said. "Everything." He saw her sitting before him, and also reflected in several mirrors.

They had the same goals as his generation, but not the same ambitions. Had they lost their judgment and capacity for extended self-denial? They were modest in their demands, but it was the modesty of the very strong, who can afford it. They were modest like one who has scaled the sheerest Himalayan peak and does not bother to broadcast it, because he knows the whole world is already aware of his feat.

Patience was on the last rung of their ladder of virtues. They were neither extravagant nor merely carefree, but neither were they thrifty or restrained. They wore their best things and never waited for a so-called better deal. Unless they saw some definite gain, they concealed their weaknesses, ills, or mistakes like a burden that might cost them dearly. It was as if they stood with one foot still in Auschwitz-Birkenau, waiting for selection. They had their own ten commandments, which they kept to themselves. To them the world was a volcano that explodes, hurling streams of burning lava on all sides, and destroys everything in its path—a world to which only those who had fled in time or survived could return. But they would never again see the old style of life, the old weather. Nothing. They had looked upon the world like children who knew that they were no longer children. Sometimes they saw, as a horse sees, things magnified in size; other times they saw things reduced in size and multiplied, as a fly sees them.

"All the way, Dita, *all the way.*"

He looked at her and at the row of mirrors that reflected her head, back, shoulder, neck and breasts, her long white arms, her hair, and her ironic, smiling blue eyes. Mr. Gotlob looked at Dita and thought of Liza before returning to Dita as he saw her. He sighed and drained his glass. War had awakened in them a new source of animal energy. Yes and no. With his gray, knowledgeable eyes he gazed at her neck, breasts, and arms, as if he were reading them. "Everything, Dita. Absolutely everything."

Their Pied Piper was Munk, and Munk followed his own rat catcher. For them the old world did not deserve to survive, from the gas chambers to the pits in which people had been burned in their own fat and had their flesh and bones and hair become the raw materials of production, to the forced labor and extermination camps and extermination centers where not a pin was mislaid. Both East and West were their pipes. Actually both were only an excuse for finding a more comfortable seat for their behinds, a roof over their heads, and something in their stom-

achs. Only then did they ask themselves about its name, its
source, and its owner.

To them the world was only a fruit tree in an autumn garden
that they would forget at the first fall of snow. It was the ripe
fruit that interested them, more than gardens and how things
grow. Things they sought, they demanded at once. The deluge
was not before them, nor behind, but within them. It was in their
blood. It suddenly struck him that there was a bit of Dita Saxova, Liza Vagner, and David Egon Huppert in every one of them.
"Maybe," he thought, "in all of us." He watched the Italian belly
dancer perform. The only question was how it surfaced in each
of them.

Sometimes he objected to their manners. They never got up
from the table until they had finished everything on their plates.
They were never in a hurry (to put it mildly) to answer letters.
From the way they treated their possessions, you might think
they had stolen them, no matter what they cost. There was never
any need to remind them that a mouse with only one hole has a
slim chance.

He gazed with appreciation at the performance of the dancer
and the music. "Fol est qui se fait brebis entre les loups." And at
Dita's inquiring look, he gave an English equivalent: "Cover
yourself with honey, and you will never want for flies."

They behave like cats who fuss over those nearby and forget
about them when they are with somebody else. He felt that Dita
Saxova, like Liza, sometimes felt guilty, thinking about life
instead of living it. There was more than one "why." Every why,
as in a house of mirrors, had hundreds of reflections. He sensed
that she was on the track of something, as a hunter scents the
presence of an animal, or a poet reaches out for the truth, or an
astronomer glimpses a star that rarely appears.

He smiled. "Gardez-vous des gens oui font pattee de velours.
Isn't it said that while a cat will smile to your face it will claw

you behind your back?" He added: "Malheur des uns fait bonheur autres. One man's meat is another man's poison."

"Mr. Gotlob . . ."

"What is it, child?" And when she was silent: "You are still innocent."

"I'm not so sure. Maybe not, Mr. Gotlob."

"You are like a dream. Partly real, partly imaginary."

"I don't know, Mr. Gotlob."

He could see that she was on edge. She avoided his gaze. Her eyes dropped to her waist. There was something missing.

Sometimes he had an almost perverse desire to have spent at least one day in Auschwitz-Birkenau, Theresienstadt, or Belsen, if only to understand it. As if it were the key to their future, and not to their past. He looked at her as a soldier looks, when one man after another falls around him and he still hangs on to the hope that he will be the one to survive. Mr. Gotlob felt somewhat guilty and a little cheated, but he understood. He was old enough to know the rules of the game. He could not go around shouting that your experience won't protect you from what still lies ahead.

Like Dita, Maximilian Gotlob observed the orchestra as it tried to accompany the belly dancer. He looked at the nearby tables and the people sitting there, and at the waiters on duty. The more girls he had gone out with, the more democratic he felt. Whenever they became pregnant, they almost always did something about it. All except Doris Levit—the exception that proved the rule. Questions of marriage, family and adultery, or blood relationship held only a distant interest for them. They were reluctant participants in all the mysteries of bodily contact, simply because, in their view, he did not deserve them. He could testify that this was a generation that had abandoned all taboos, at least in physical relationships. They were more open, to say the least. What their fathers and mothers had considered to be prohibited and perverse, they performed so naturally that they restored their innocence.

Dita noticed the way he looked at her, at her throat, at her teeth, at her hunger. She smiled encouragingly, as if the difference in age had moved from one chair to the other. Did he think she was already unredeemable, beyond shame? Would he claim for himself what didn't belong to anyone?

But gazing at her peachlike complexion, Mr. Gotlob returned to his first interest. The dancer finished and bowed. She supplemented her nudity with a few glittering garments. The diners applauded. Mr. Gotlob wiped his mouth with a napkin and said, "Bravo, bravo . . ." He put the napkin down. "I'm seriously intrigued by you, Dita. Tell me, what interests you most?"

"Antiques," she answered and waited for Mr. Gotlob to get up and slap her face. Contrary to her expectation, he kissed her hand.

"Anything you want, Dita."

"I've had too much to drink. I can't stand this heat."

"You're as fresh as grass, child. You can count on it. I'm 100-percent sure."

"I'm drunk, believe me. I'm 100-percent drunk."

"I'll tell you something, child. Nobody can take away what we have and enjoy. Unless they take us with it, as you say." He smiled. "Listen, Dita. You're a grown-up, sensible person. You know how briefly some things last. We can speak on equal terms. After all, I too know secrets binding both parties. That momentary pleasure is only momentary pleasure—and not only at my age, Dita. Nothing before, nothing after. No aftermath, Dita. After all, that's an advantage. Certainly not a drawback."

Dita leaned back against the plush chair. For a split second the spinning stopped and then multiplied. Sophocles. The name of the nightclub shone above the bandstand where the musicians sat, or at times stood, playing. In all the mirrors she could see the show that she put on for Mr. Gotlob's benefit. A fish, a dear little fish. A trip to Switzerland. The road was open.

She could count one point in her favor. D.E. should have seen her. Or maybe not? She had already learned to win. Or at least not to lose. She smiled. Surely she looked happy, or at least pretty.

Mr. Gotlob's eyes, heavy with wine, feasted on her white neck. Her hips were slim, and her hands aroused in him the imagination of touch. He looked closely into her already reddened eyes and at her mouth, moist and slightly parted with weariness. "May I ask you for a dance, Dita?"

"I am really drunk, Mr. Gotlob. I am already 100-percent drunk."

Mr. Gotlob rose and took her arm to help her rise. He held her for a moment. Automatically she bent down so as not to emphasize her height. She smiled. Someone requested that Egon Levit and the gypsies play "Jericho." Dita felt she had entered a contest where a woman could only lose. The gypsies rose to their feet and sang as they played. Mr. Levit smiled. The trumpets took over and prolonged the lingering melody. The lights of the nightclub were dimmed, as if the tune touched everything with its coarse fingers. The drums. "Jericho, Jericho, Jericho."

Dita smoothed her dress. Red silk curtains, white tablecloths. The smoke-filled dimness. Music. The bar in the background. She felt as if she were stepping onto the deck of a ship. The sea rolled, along with the harbor. Was it true, as D.E. alleged, that millions of years ago humans had been fishes, had crept onto the shore, and had turned into what she now saw as herself in the mirror? She smiled again. Perhaps in every one of them (for instance, Mr. Gotlob) there was still a little bit of that cold fishy soul? A bit of the crocodile's double chin? The teeth with which the tiger had defended itself, before its descendant found itself on the dance floor of the Sophocles nightclub? The people at the next table laughed uproariously. Someone boasted how he sold refrigerators even to households where there was no electricity. They asked him how much he weighed. One hundred sixty-three pounds, of which 150 were all brain, as he was so clever. The same as his brother. Perhaps they expected his mother to produce one in green and the other in red? More laughter.

"I can't stand on my feet," she whispered.

"I knew you wouldn't let me down, Dita."

"The whole room is rocking."

"When an older man is with a woman as young as you are, child, he feels half his age." She recalled how Isabelle Goldblat used to say that when an older man is in the company of a young woman, he is younger, and the girl older. She finally stopped thinking of D.E.

"What would you like, Dita? Anything at all."

"I would like to go bathing. If not into a yellow swimming pool, at least in the dew."

Mr. Gotlob led her to the dance floor. Pinpoints of light rained down upon her. She still felt as if she were on a ship, on the slippery floor of the deck, or on ice. She saw herself reflected in ten mirrors simultaneously. She glanced at the battery of colored bottles behind the bar. The gypsies played, sang, and laughed. Their dark skin gleamed as if freshly oiled. They had white teeth and deep voices. She felt Mr. Gotlob's right hand holding her, his palm moving over her to touch her hip and breast each time they turned in the dance. Now the gypsies sang in a deep voice: "Jericho, Jericho, Jericho." Dita caught her breath. She felt as if she were walking underwater. Were there lights shining below the surface? She felt the pressure of waters, like a fish belly up, unable to swim. The leader, Levit, drained a pint of beer in one draft. Or had she imagined it?

"You are really a mature woman, Dita. If you'd let me, I'd drink you up like a peach. To the last drop." And then he said again, "All the way, Dita, everything."

She avoided his eyes as he brought his face close to hers, but she could not avoid his hand. She felt as if two echoes closed in on her, one from each side of the room. They joined together and brought a new meaning to it all. Then she laughed, perhaps more loudly than she had wanted and more than Mr. Gotlob might have wished. The room streched far into the distance. She could still see the staircase and the cloakrooms.

"I would tell you, if you'd let me, what a beautiful figure you've got—even if you were wearing nothing but a bracelet . . ."

It lasted only a few seconds. She smiled. The lights spun like falling stars. She felt as if the ceiling breathed down upon her. And the lights—as if they stood for something else. Water. She was stained with sweat. Her stomach felt heavy. Everything seemed to be swimming about her. The colors began to run together. She was afraid she might be sick. Then instantly she was sober. She brought into focus the dance floor, staircase, cloakrooms, tables. She used the orchestra for orientation. Where did the gypsies stand? Mr. Egon Levit smiled, as if he had stars in his eyes. What had he done with his drink?

"I'm very fond of you, Dita." Mr. Gotlob touched her. "I waited as long as I could to meet you . . ."

"I think I hate you both," she said slowly. "Even though you have been so kind and fixed the trip for me. Even if I still need you both."

She felt as if she were standing on shaky legs, dependent on Mr. Gotlob's guiding hand.

She left Liza Vagner's bridegroom-to-be standing in the middle of the dance floor. The name of the nightclub, Sophocles, shone above the entrance where the fat gypsies stood. She did not hear Mr. Gotlob venting his feelings: "Worse than a whore . . ."

5 In the bathroom back at Lubliana Street Dita slipped out of her clothes. She looked at her panties. Not a drop. She felt sticky. The water tumbled noisily into the porcelain tub. Down below, Liza looked after the caretaker. Dita slid into the water. Her teeth chattered. She waited in vain for the feeling of refreshment to come. The water was like ice. It made her body feel lighter, but her head felt like lead. Her eyes burned, and the lids felt heavy. "Something has to happen," she thought. She had to be punished. She shivered. Would Munk find out about it tomorrow? Or Liza? Anybody? Nobody? D.E.? She was shaking. Why? Had she piled a new sin on top of the old? Why? A hangover? What was it that kept forcing her in a direction she did not want to go? Why did simple things become complicated, and complicated things become impossible? Why did even the harshest past appear in the end like a lost paradise? There was a puzzle. Did she understand less than she had two years ago? Why? Perhaps it would be better in a while. She would award herself a point for another of her victories. She closed her eyes.

Out of nowhere Dita suddenly remembered the girl in the black jumper in the Hotel Astoria/Novak. She wished she could drop everything and make a fresh start. She sank down to her chin in the water. She might do more sketching or try to write. To break up a routine that had become nothing but a struggle between memory and apathy. Like Neugeborn and Herbert Lagus. She knew it was only a transitory feeling. Soon it would pass. She had lots of friends—some very good friends, and a few very close to her. I'm a fool, a silly fool, as Andy says. Lebovitch was particularly observant and, in his own way, sensitive. He took everything at face value, never wasting his time or strength on pointless surprise. I have to learn, and I will learn.

She heard a creaking noise and realized that she had not bolted the door. I'm too full of myself, she thought. She raised her eyes. Liza cast a knowing glance at her damp clothes and wet body.

"Are you so rich already?" She began to pick up Dita's things and hang them on hooks.

"I'm on my way. Like you."

"Let me know if you get there first. You can't push a rope, but you can pull it. And morning is wiser than evening. As if you didn't know that you can never please everyone."

"Yeah, and time changes all things." Dita switched on her smile for all occasions. Liza sighed knowingly. "It was not one of my best days."

"No kidding."

Dita was silent.

"Getting anything out of you is like pulling teeth. Munk has been here at least eight times looking for you. I hope you're not starting something with him. Apparently he's arranged your supplementary examination. All you have to do is fill in the form."

Dita did not answer. Liza asked her, "What have you been talking about to D.E. for so long? Do you still have a lot to say to each other?"

"About ships. About where the International Blue and White are going."

"I've had a few discussions of that kind with Mr. Gotlob."

"Did he also tell you about the unsinkable ones?"

"For Maximilian Gotlob there's no such thing as an unsinkable ship."

"Let him take you to see the film about the *Titanic*."

"I doubt if he would go and see it again just for my sake. I thought it was great when the ship goes down and the ship's orchestra keeps on playing."

"And playing . . ."

"What was it you wanted to ask me in the cemetery?"

"Why do they say that rats are the first thing to leave a sinking ship?"

"I expect they know where the holes are, because they made them themselves."

Dita replied with a question: "Isn't it absurd when children survive their parents?"

Liza glanced around the bathroom. She did not want to keep staring too curiously at Dita's body and face. She paused at the chipped porcelain of the tub. Plaster was peeling off the ceiling. The wooden mat smelled. From the bath Dita said, "Do you know, sometimes the whole world reminds me of one concentration camp. Or a network of camps. You can get transferred from a worse camp into a better one, or the other way around. But you can never get out."

"You shouldn't blaspheme. At least you've had your dinner, haven't you?"

Dita got out of the bath. Again she had thoughts of D.E. She looked like a swan and a stork at the same time. She clutched Liza's skinny shoulder. She felt Liza's body and her own damp skin. She threw her arms around Liza's neck.

They lay down side by side in Room 16.

"Remember how you went with that old doctor, Liza? Are you really going to marry Mr. Gotlob?"

Liza sat up and leaned on her elbow. "Why do you ask me just now? What do you think about him?"

"He could play the part of the bald footman in a farce, when he brings you a letter on a tray and says, 'Your lordship, there is a corpse outside.'"

"I don't think of it as a kind of retirement. I've been with younger and with older men. It all amounts to the same thing."

"It must be revolting, letting yourself be touched by a soft belly. I don't mean just *him*." She was wearing light blue pajamas.

Liza giggled. "There are worse things than that. They all do it. Some women choose to marry the oldest men they can find for that very reason." She tried to whisper. "I guess it turns my stomach even now—all sensuality, even the so-called healthy kind you get from young boys. That's all they think about, anyway. Doesn't it turn you off, the way they're all after it? How can anybody put up with it? It's bitter. There's rarely any life or joy in it, unless I can say, 'Yes, that's exactly how I want it.' Ever since spring I'm just glad to get it over with. I've learned to pretend I'm satisfied in bed, with the result that I feel even more annoyed. I'd hardly call that a victory. How do you expect anything else, than it's a contest where one party tries to win at any cost, and victory for one means defeat for the other? How is it that only the whores have rules that everybody respects, and the ones that don't try to cheat in the middle of the game? I'd be a rotten *fille de joie,* as Brita calls them. I might as well get married." She tried to find a more comfortable position on the bed. "All wrinkles and neuroses. Do you know what Lebovitch says to me? 'I only wish you could be the man, at least for a fraction of a second.' Oh, it's so incredible how many people still don't realize that women own their own bodies 100 percent."

"It doesn't make that much difference." Dita looked up at the ceiling. "Doesn't it sometimes seem perverse to you?"

"Why should I blame myself?"

"Then why do you do it?"

"It makes him happy, that's all," Liza said in English.

"You told me once that young boys don't want it like that."

"They do want it, but not all the way. You're still inexperienced in some ways. People do all sorts of things without knowing why. That's only one of them. What I'm afraid of isn't just a pair of raw eggs. It's ugliness. Or that I might find myself back in Auschwitz-Birkenau one fine day. Sickness, or being as poor as a church mouse. Going batty. I think that more or less sums up what I want to avoid."

Dita did not reply. She wondered whether that was the sacrifice that women make. It included something she had never been clear about, and it went very deep. D.E. was only a small part of it. It was more than the shadows she saw, more than the maps on which she had found or lost her way. Were Tonitschka, Liza, Brita, and the others in a similar plight? Or did it go back to their mothers, their mothers' mothers, far away into the past? Something that brought disgrace and guilt instead of happiness? The feeling that you're hauling heavy baggage, when all the time your hands are empty? Had they used up so much energy during the war that they were exhausted now that peace had come? Was it possible to change it? Could they ever recover from it? They looked all right.

"It's something else," Liza whispered. "Have you heard of opera singers who drink raw eggs before they perform? Or Japanese fishermen who eat raw fish at sea, like their wives and children at home? Roe and juices, everything—just like that."

The room was filled with the scent of lingerie, perfume, and damp towels. Darkness had settled in. A summer breeze stirred the street lamp outside the window. It swayed like a pendulum, casting strips of light within the room. At times the sounds reminded them of the bar across the street when the doors were opened.

"There's a mystery about it, even when you've gotten used to it," Liza said. "It's as if you've gotten used to it long before you actually do it. As if you were born with it. Or as if it had been born a long time before you were."

Dita still did not reply. Liza added, "I always wonder, when I'm doing it—or afterward—whether I'd want it too, if I were a man. Once a boy told me that maybe he likes it because he was not breast-fed by his mother." Liza almost burst out laughing. "Fortunately, things remind you of other things."

As she listened, Dita felt as though she had crossed a new frontier. She wondered what carried the two of them, or all girls, across an invisible line. She could not understand what made her keep her own experience secret. What had happened with D.E.? Did it show her lack of frankness? Or something else?

Her propensity for being cautious?

"Don't you feel like an animal forced to submit to some stronger beast?" said Liza.

Dita felt sorry for Liza but didn't know why. She did not want to feel sorry for herself, and she did not. She never would. He who wants to be with wolves must eat with them. Why is it that when a girl is ready to offer her nakedness unselfishly, only expecting to be loved, it's not enough? Have we all passed beyond shame? Beyond longing? Are we condemned to remain waiting?

"People have always done it," whispered Liza, speaking as if she were judge and defendant at the same time. "Only they don't talk about it. And it's not the only thing that people secretly do. Have you ever heard of an artist who used to paint one kind of picture for popes and cardinals and another kind for himself? One of those pictures shows a man's head and what he's dreaming of. Sixty-nine? And so what? One artist painted a picture of a woman, just her top and her middle. Head, mouth, eyes—and then just the groin. For one person it's a ravine where he loses himself; for another it's a cradle and a grave. Heaven knows, what can I do about it? That's how lots of boys see you, and that's how lots of girls see themselves. Kings, rabbis, and priests forbid it, but people still go on doing it. It's like a taste. You can't describe it; you have to experience it. Nobody can do it for you."

"I don't know," Dita answered matter-of-factly. She felt guilty. "I thought that once the war was over, many things would be different. Isn't it like someone offering you a choice between food and poison?" She smiled. She thought of the story of the apple, the tree, and the serpent. The story of Medusa, the story of the shadow and the spirit, dusk and dawn, and how far it all went back, and where it would all end. She was still puzzled that even the Germans with first-class educations were able to kill, with or without reason, just like the most primitive soldiers, police, or civilians. She thought of the grounds on which they had killed women in the past, and why they had killed them just yesterday. She thought of her own blood. And about D.E. all the time. There were always good and bad things, but it was difficult to tell them apart. "In order to maintain peace, you have to fight today and tomorrow the way you did yesterday," she said.

"It's not much of a relief," Liza said. "At the Delousing Station in Auschwitz-Birkenau I worked with a small guy. When we were opening the cans of Zyklon B, I used to wonder how the fleas and lice could resist it for twelve or fourteen hours. 'Don't ask why. Some things just happen like that.' He used to open the cans for me. Once he explained the law of gravity, why a heavier stone does not fall to the ground more quickly than a smaller one, but I could never understand it. I learned to accept certain things just as they are. You shouldn't ask why. They happen. That's all.

"I have a bad formula for joy and happiness," Liza continued. "If during the war I was 90-percent unhappy, for obvious reasons, the opposite must or should be true in peacetime. Right? Just the reverse, only 10-percent sorrow and the rest bliss? Of course not. Whoever could explain why my grief has not ended with the war would surely get the Nobel Prize. It isn't enough for people to think I am happy because I smile more than I cry and because I'm not the ugliest, and of course, how strong. I do all I can. I am not hungry, and I have no real catastrophes anywhere close to home. That should be sufficient, right? So why is it not enough for me? Maybe my formula—I want to and must be happy—is wrong. You should at least be satisfied with what you deserve. That's enough. Or should be. So why isn't it?"

Dita smiled. She had a feeling it didn't work that way. "I don't believe for a second that the rest of the people in the world are going out of their minds with happiness, but as for me, I'm better off half closing my eyes." This was far from her original formula of happiness, resembling the stars and their circles in the universe, kind of cosmic, a personal Russian roulette. Suddenly Dita asked matter-of-factly, "If Dr. Mengele were standing in front of you now, like on the ramp at Auschwitz-Birkenau, and gave you the choice to go to the chimney yourself or send someone else in your place—maybe your mother, sister, or a friend— what would you do? Or if he asked you whether you were willing to go to the chimney instead of them? Bearing in mind that there would be no witnesses, and that everybody had to choose, unless they were just bundled off and relieved you of any choice."

"I always knew you were crazy," Liza said, but the question stayed within her, together with the darkness, as it did with Dita, and with it the expected answer, implied in the question itself, and her own assent or denial. "I feel good," Liza said. "So it must be good. I don't give myself time enough to deny that."

There was more between them than the secrecy of adolescence or adulthood as they lay side by side facing the window that was alternately illuminated and darkened.

"It all goes deep down within, never high above, never far away," Liza whispered. "It's like when you're giddy for a while, like dying. The best sleep is always the deepest. Sleep is like sinking down. It never raises you up—like when Toni screams out in the night. What can you do about it?"

"Somebody once said that a woman is emptiness and that it's a man who fills it. But then, it's not man but woman that represents fullness. Woman is emptiness and fullness at the same time. Not bad, huh? I'd like to meet whoever said that first."

For a while they lay together quietly. It was like the ring of a subconsciously registered and never-ending song. It was no use to ask about its source. It was compounded of fragments of words, or echoes, pictures, and images. With the passage of time, instead of fading away, it all seemed to gather force. It occurred to Dita that the night that lay around them enveloped her with a force that was stronger and more ruthless than darkness. Dita remembered how her grandma Olga had gotten out of the truck at Auschwitz-Birkenau and taken her first steps on the ramp. Before she reached the baths, her whole body had turned gray.

"Sometimes I almost wish I were an old woman already," Dita whispered with a smile. "Just so my life would be over, and I knew that nothing like that would ever happen to me." All the tension escaped from her, like a river flowing in the night. Dita turned to face Liza. The old gaiety and irony had returned to Dita's voice, as when she told the swarthy man that she took three showers a day so that at least some tears would fall for her, and that her desire for travel had been satisfied by just one visit from the kind of man who came from an Israeli kibbutz in a pilot's leather jacket.

"As Great Britain says, you have to do everything perfectly but, at the same time, beware of appearing too experienced, or they may get suspicious and lose respect for you," Liza said. In her voice there was a mixture of ambition, helplessness, and need, a need to desire and to be desired. "You've got to be a magician," Liza said. "But at least with our boys, if nothing else, you can be sure they're clean." Her voice contained an undertone of something that she did not put into words: A girl can never be quite sure.

"Aren't you afraid he might die, maybe in the very act?" Dita asked. There was an unexpressed laughter in her words.

"Sometimes," Liza responded. "Once when we were at it, he told me not to move an inch or he'd never recover. For a second my heart stopped. But he meant something else." Liza smiled into the darkness. "For goodness sake—men. Sometimes you sit for an hour, drink and have fun, then suddenly out of the blue he starts peering at you with glassy eyes, as grave as hell. As if he's gone nuts. Absolutely idiotic. And then suddenly his eyes get fixed in a stare. In high society that's what they call desire or longing."

Dita thought that not only Liza's children but also her children's children, and so on, many years ahead, would still hear the echo of what had happened to the grandmothers they would never see. And then she began to think that perhaps people had invented an Almighty God to protect them and later put the blame on him for failing to do so, when in reality it was they who had failed. She also thought of dignity, and how much of it had been killed in the war. Dita listened for the note of sincerity in her voice, but her question was also addressed to herself. "At night, everything is different," she said. "It's easier to tell lies. Do you think Hitler is still alive?"

Liza felt sleepy in Dita's presence and had to force herself to stay awake. She yawned. The night seemed to stretch on endlessly, and the dawn was still far away. Brita could be heard snoring. From time to time she turned over, and the sound of her breath and sleep changed.

"No, I'm thinking about what it means to be a woman," said Liza. But she was really thinking about something impossible to explain.

It was an inexpressible mystery, as tiny as the head of a pin. Dita remembered how they used to carry the stones at Auschwitz-Birkenau, one day there, the next day back. Or sometimes there and back in one day. In that she felt lay the key to understanding the world. In a year, in ten years, children would ask their parents how they could have allowed it to happen. But at the same time she realized that even now the memory of her father and mother, uncles, aunts, and cousins had faded, as if their faces had been changed or lost, together with the record she carried in her memory.

"The best thing is just to accept it, as you accept the weather," Liza said. "And incidentally, for some people a night in bed brings out the best, and for some people it brings out the worst. In my case either it reveals nothing or it brings out both."

"My Aunt Mimi committed suicide when the Germans came to Prague in 1939," Dita said. "She jumped out of a window into a skylight. She was ashamed. To her, people seemed either greedy or apathetic. And the German bands were playing as they marched past—drums, fifes, songs about faraway countries. Her grandmother also took her own life. I can't tell you why she did it; nobody knew. Whenever she saw anything nice, she would say that nothing ever seemed so much fun as when she was young. Nothing would have brought her greater pleasure than to take a match and set fire to everything. Whenever anyone wanted to give her a present, she used to say, 'Don't give me anything. I'll throw it all out of the window.' She would sit for days on end, looking out of the window without a word. She could hear the German soldiers marching over the cobblestones and singing a song that today Germany belonged to them, tomorrow the whole world. She drew her own conclusions. Life had lost all its dignity for those people. They could see no sense in living. My father carried Aunt Mimi upstairs in his arms. He was ashamed. Grandma remembered a lot, but she forgot a lot too. The experiences she had gathered were lost to her in the end. For them the world had ceased to be the world they had known. They knew there was no going back."

Then she said: "Maybe everybody carries the date of his own demise around with him from the start. Once I asked Mimi where her earrings were. 'Where? Hitler took them from me.' My father said, 'Never mind, Mimi. When the war's over, I'll buy you some nicer ones.' She did not have her ears pierced until she was eighteen. She never married. She kept saying she had to hand over the earrings when all Jewish gold—engagement rings, jewelry, and wristwatches—had to be surrendered to the Prague branch of the Bank of Germany. Mimi used to think that my dad had gotten everything he wanted in life and that she had hardly gained a single thing she had wished for."

"Why don't you forget all these things? It's funny. You look so happy."

Dita continued: "She was sad, guilty, and tired. All at once everything seemed hopeless to her. She lost her appetite. Every time the sun went down she was afraid. She would look out the window and cry. She never said what she was crying for, or what was wrong with her. She couldn't concentrate on anything, though I had the feeling that she did concentrate on something she kept to herself. She showed no interest in our visits. My dad used to go there so she wouldn't be all by herself after Grandma was gone. To Mimi it seemed immoral to cling to life. There was nothing worthwhile left in it. She couldn't sleep, didn't eat. A few weeks later she began to think it was not only immoral but impossible, I suppose. Everything she had in the kitchen cupboard, including the cups, disappeared—things she still owned from her grandmothers, the kind of things that people collect all their lives and then prepare to leave to their children so they'll be remembered—a sort of innocent attempt at a bit of immortality. She was a very tidy person. Everything in her home had its proper place. Then what had been so permanent was suddenly gone. It was like a cellar being flooded, or a deluge carrying away the riverbanks. It seemed to her that justice was dying before her eyes, like a sick person. Her energy flowed from her like tiny ripples outward from a stone thrown in deep water. She was afraid of the dark, of ghosts and dreams. She was afraid to go on living. It wasn't only that she had to hand the things over but also that the Germans went on taking them. She didn't even leave a note behind, just her broken body. Did she want to present the Germans with her final offering? They had gotten what they wanted from the start, to the last ounce of gold, to the last drop of blood, to the last shadow and the last thought. Stealing is just as evil as rape."

"I would put it off until another time," Liza said.

A little later Dita whispered, "Neither my father nor my mother ever talked to me about it. But in time I came to realize what had happened. Mimi had felt rejected by the world, and in return she rejected it." She imagined her aunt Mimi, tall and bony, with blue eyes. She had longed for peace and quiet. Sometimes she would tell them about the lands where nature does not die. Dita could imagine how the world must look to a person who sees everything dying before her eyes. Circles flowing from a stone thrown into the water, ripples, and then nothing. Suddenly she smiled. "The best thing that happened to me during the war was taking care of the children at Theresienstadt. Who would have imagined it?"

Both the girls were now almost invisible in the darkness. They had both been children themselves when they went away, but when they returned they were children no longer. Dita recalled how Aunt Mimi tried to catch chimeras—distant lands, justice, equally binding laws. Her visions had always eluded her, as they had her grandmother, until at last she jumped down after them, the skylight below so far away.

"I don't know whether it was the world that ruined Hitler, or Hitler the world," she said, still smiling. "I agree with Andy Lebovitch that if we had done nothing but weep in the camps, as people do today, it wouldn't have been a mere six million, but eight or nine million of us."

"We'll be half dead tomorrow," Liza sighed. "You have a terrible sense of humor, to tell the truth."

"Do you know what's really strange? The best people I ever met in my life were among those I saw in the camps. The longer I live, the more sure I am of it. In fifty years' time, when I try to recall the highlights of my life, I guarantee that the most important years will have been at Theresienstadt, Auschwitz-Birkenau, and Belsen. I rarely feel sorry for myself. Or for the living. I feel it for those dead. That there is nothing you can do about it.

It's even impossible to transfer, or communicate it. It's the border of some wasteland."

"No tears, no memories. That's my motto," Liza said. "Leave it alone. Put it aside."

"People see themselves as different from the way that others see them, and as different from what their words and actions make them out to be. In the end we accept only what we can bear and what suits us, not the things we're powerless to change, whether they're true or not."

In the dim light Liza looked like something between a nymph and a badger. She kept pulling the sleeves of her batiste nightgown down to her wrists. "I'm tired of regrets and bored with memories." Liza observed that it was better to see herself as it suited her and not other people. She felt sleepy.

Dita kept silent. Liza whispered, "Do you know what I've found out? That even memory is crippled when my present is invalid, and that you can't get relief through memories. In the end, my future and my hopes and wishes are crippled, too. We'd better pack it up and go to sleep. Aren't you sleepy?"

Dita thought how unreliable memory is, and how it plays down or exaggerates what has happened. "Possibly." But she recalled how she had lain beside D.E. in the hotel room. Just for a few seconds she would almost have given her life to make him happier with her. It had not been a lie. He opened her lips with his, gently, as no one else in her life ever had. She couldn't forget that. She felt the mystery of all mysteries. It was the highest level of unselfishness that she had ever attained.

Ripples of warmth passed through her body and mind. She thought of D.E., including the fact that she had not received a single letter from him. Once he had told her that before his family received the summons to the Exhibition Palace in Prague and for Theresienstadt in the cattle truck, his father had dreamed about it night after night. It was not surprising, since there was so much talk about it. They were all afraid. When at last the message came from the Jewish Religious Community, they stayed for three days at the exhibition building on filthy mattresses. Then they left. By that time it did not seem so dreadful to them. Fear and dreams had prepared his father for it.

"What are you thinking about?" asked Liza.

"About three women who changed their fate and controlled it. One was pretty, another wise, and the third was strong."

"They were able to say no when they were expected to say yes and yes when they were expected to say no?"

Dita was silent again.

"Sometimes I remember my father," Liza whispered. "Somebody said that he last worked in the Jewish Sonderkommando at crematorium number 4 in Auschwitz during the uprising in October 1944. But who knows if there's any truth to it? Or whether someone just hopes she'll feel better because I feel worse. I questioned everybody I could who served at that time in the mortuary or the ovens or the stores, but no one knew for sure."

She spoke like a fly whose wings had been torn off. As if she knew that now nothing could be proved or disproved, and she didn't know which she would prefer.

"My father was the first man I saw naked," Liza said. "He was taking a bath, and I was sitting in his room, just next to the kitchen, and reading. He didn't realize I was there. He walked out of the bathroom with nothing but a towel in his hand and a surprised look. He turned around and secured the towel around his waist, but not before I had seen that dark patch between his legs—so different than me. At that time I didn't even have pubic hair of my own. His embarrassment embarrassed me, too."

Her father had still believed that a man who did not claim his rights was as good as dead, and that it was better to live for one hour as a free man than a century in chains, and that a lark cannot live in a cage. They had shot him against the wall, like the father of Dita's mysterious actress, about whom she was fond of talking, as if she was her ideal. If a child does not cry, it does not get fed. A poor man may praise his hovel, but it still crumbles on top of him. Liza just wanted to close her eyes and sleep it off. Then she said, "Now I feel naked as if I have forgotten something. I am aware of the warm air kissing and touching my skin. I feel as though I am remembering something. As an infant I probably spent a great deal of time naked, except for a diaper. Little children look for any excuse to take their clothes off and run around, and when I was younger I did this too."

"I don't agree with people who think that there are no words to describe it," Dita said again. It was clear that she refused to accept the idea that anything people did, even the most wicked things, ought to remain beyond comprehension. But—who knows? She felt the difference between the words "I could not" and "I would not." "Every reality can be described in words. The best things and the worst."

Dita refused to believe that even reality evaporates like mist, one darkness into another. She recalled the transports of Hungarian women, waiting, in the summer of 1944, among the birch trees near the gas chambers. They had no idea that in an hour, or two hours, or three, they could be on their way, thirsty and weary, toward the showers. And instead of showers and a rest, they would be gassed. She remembered how they had stood up when they were told it was their turn, and she remembered the children who had come with them. What a relief it had been for the rest of the women in the Frauen Koncentration Lager. As long as the Germans were busy with the Hungarian women, the Czech, Polish, Rumanian, or Russian women's barracks were safe. "I'm like Andy," Dita said. "I've got no word for guilt or hope, because when they combine they become something else."

Then she thought of how the Czech Jewish women were told

that their children were lost anyway. They might as well go to work with their husbands, as long as their health lasted. And their husbands had persuaded them to accept it. If they survived, they might still be able to have more children. Those were the two realities to which she returned more than any others. Why? She did not know. One person burns down a house and blames another for it. She thought of how much the women had accepted. What would she have done in their place?

As night drew on, the darkness in the room became transparent. It lay upon them like a quilt. Through the open window came the sounds of the sleeping city. The light reflected from the glass was crossed by shadows, like outstretched fingers. Liza was silent, apparently asleep. But she did not sleep. She was too cold. In the end Liza said, "I think I'll buy a new nightgown with lace, gathered in at the hips, since I keep losing weight. I noticed you've got one like that."

Dita said, "It isn't true that after Auschwitz-Birkenau there can be nothing but ugliness among the memories of what happened to us. That would be oversimplified and unjust. Even if it were true, it would still be a lie. It would be like closing your eyes to the truth to make it easier. Or doing something even worse." But she was not quite sure. She thought of D.E. She could not understand it. How could she have forgiven him everything? Or had she? Is anger such a poor adviser?

It was almost midnight. The doors opened in the bar across the street. The strains of drinking songs penetrated the darkness. Into the room drifted snatches of lyrics, together with the sounds of a harmonica:

> *The first love is the best of all.*
> *The rest's not worth a dime.*
> *Then love the rest, my pretty lass,*
> *several at a time.*

Dita whispered, almost to herself, "I believe that one day, for every one of those people who were killed, for every one who deserves it, there'll be a poem, a song, or a statue. Or maybe a book. Others will be born who will take their place. Six million children." She caught herself speaking as if to David Egon Huppert. Why only to him all the time?

"They're more likely to make a statue of Hitler first," Liza whispered.

Dita did not reply. Rock of Gibraltar? She closed her eyes. She felt the night stretching far away and her voice and breath coming to her from a great distance, as if from a different world, from a different person. In her imagination she once more saw the little girls from the Hungarian transport waiting among the trees near crematorium number 5. They carried their coats over their arms, still wearing the clothes in which their mothers had dressed them at home. They waited impatiently. No one had told them what they waited for. Dita did not know whether she had seen it in a photograph given to Andy Lebovitch by his friend from the Medical House who had been in the Sonderkommando, or whether it had been a tale that had reached the Frauen Koncentration Lager. It had become confused, as when someone standing at a great height loses his balance, or something attracts his attention and he feels as if he is falling.

Once more she heard the voice of a voice, the voice of something that has no existence, and the voice of reality, the beginning and end of all that is. But it was only an echo, something that blinded her so that she could not see what had blinded her. Eyes of ghosts, and ghosts of eyes. Space and limitation. Togetherness, unison, differentiation. Fullness and void. Her own two selves, her two sets of experience that had to go on living next to each other. Everything she had wished to shed, to rid herself of for good. As if her burden of horror, by some invisible, internal process, were multiplying within her, as she sometimes felt at night in dreams. That element by which life is renewed, and without which it withers, like grass, trees, and flowers, in drought and darkness, deprived of air.

Liza again made a face in the darkness. "Considering that Hitler is in his grave, he is not doing too badly."

Dita refrained from saying that they should be the finest songs, poems, or statues. The kind of thing that would be sung in the bar opposite, like the familiar tunes of workers and people who had survived ten Hitlers. She felt in her very bones that from all that had happened something as fine as songs should remain. Sometimes the men and women from a punishment squad used to get the order to sing. They would sing a German song about a lovely maid. On another occasion Slovak volunteers at Auschwitz sang it, SS Freidwillinge Schutzstaffel, Hauptscharführers, and Hauptsturmführers, all the way from Trenčín to Bratislava. But she thought of what she, just as Tonitschka or Liza, had never said to anybody because of shame, and because a person's self-confidence and self-respect can be lost both inside and out. She knew there were things that she, and people like her, would never tell a soul, in an effort to deny the truth even to herself.

"Do you believe in fate?" Liza asked.

"Wouldn't it be a waste of time?" Dita asked, with irony in her voice.

Liza remembered the question that Dita had asked her in the bathroom a while ago and how her father had been when they shot him. Like Dita, Liza never told the whole story. The true significance of words lies in what is passed over in silence. But there was also everything they were ashamed of. Nobody could erase that.

Dita imagined the Aufseherin who had known what had happened to her mother. Once the Aufseherin had also given Dita an extra piece of bread. All that was beyond her. Why did she remember that now? It was not enough just to survive now. And it was not enough just to dream endlessly. But she dreamed about her plans of language courses: of Spanish, French, Italian, and, certainly, English; of skills for which one needs lots of time, gifts, and luck; of travels—alone, with somebody, somewhere.

Apparently Liza read her thoughts. She laughed and whispered, "While we're on the subject of boys, remember how they hug you to death when they're dancing. They bellow at you and dance as if they're wiping their feet on a doormat. One offers it to you as if it were an injection to clear up your skin and stop blackheads. Another regards it as the proof that you really care for him and all that goes with it. Yesterday Andy asked me why a man can have three lovers at once and a woman can't. 'Because the man has no vagina,' I told him. What do you think?" She sighed.

"I'm almost asleep." Dita wondered how it could have happened. Would D.E. be enough to explain it? Brita snored intermittently. "Do you think you'll ever have children?" Dita touched Liza's hand. Liza was skinny; her skin was cold and coarse. Dita did not wait for a reply. "We're still young," she whispered.

It crossed her mind that on the last night before Mimi had jumped, she had had a dream. She dreamed that the name of her favorite cookies, Orion, was the place where she wanted to go, but nobody knew where it was. It was not on any map, nor in any timetable. In her dream, so they said, she had asked in vain where it was.

When Dita touched her, Liza whispered, "My breasts don't amount to much. But I don't mind."

Suddenly Dita felt a clutching pain in her abdomen. The cramps came late, as a punishment. After that she felt a dull heaviness below her stomach, as if her blood circulation was undergoing change. She began, like the last Eve cast out of her garden, to describe in detail the building and the room at the

Astoria/Novak, formerly the Yellow Stone Inn. She described the flowers in the wooden window boxes, the double bed, the chaise lounge, the curtains, and the white tiled stove with sticks of kindling beside it.

But she did not mention D.E. She described her companion of the past day almost precisely: gold teeth, double chin, white cuffs with golden cuff links. She subtracted twenty years from his age and went into the most intimate details, the sequence of events, her own thoughts, both hostile and calm, and how the atmosphere had changed from moment to moment. A snap of the fingers, and a friendly chat—if that. And finally, the cry of the child from the next room.

"It was laughing or crying," Dita whispered. "Then later I saw its mother downstairs in the outdoor restaurant. She was a nineteen-year-old girl wearing a black jumper up to her neck. She was sitting with the waiter. The girl was pretty, healthy, and contented, and so was the child. I can't describe it. Never in my life has anyone given me such a blissful look." She thought about being naked and feeling not exposed but redeemed—full of beauty both inside and out—of the meaning life has for a woman and man, for all people, at least sometimes.

Dita mixed truth with lies. She could not herself understand how she did it, but she felt better for it. She considered playing the clown. Wasn't the girl at all afraid of what she might dream? Didn't she ever fear falling asleep, in case she allowed her dreams to surface? Dita wondered whether the girl feared what the future might bring. What was the significance of her present, of her past? Did she think of who needed her, and whom she herself needed? Or how to arrange her life? Did she ever feel like an uprooted tree? Was her love for her husband the simplest, or the most complex, of her problems? Did she face life as if she were a dying tree or star? And was life for her a well that war had filled? Or emptied? Dita remained awake late into the night and

early into the morning haunted with exchanges, giving, receiving, and returning.

Brita was awake, first an audible, then a visible, figure.

Tonitschka, who had come over from Room 15 to escape the
formidable Linda, huddled next to the Holy Virgin, who had not
lifted an eyebrow the whole time. "It's all right if he loves you,"
Brita said huskily. "But don't expect anyone to take you to a
hotel the next time for ten minutes of business and two hours of
crazy talk." She added sleepily, "Every one of us ought to try an
affair with a married man from time to time. Though I really
think that married men have an aura of mystery that they don't
deserve. I don't know whether they deserve it or not, but the fact
is that there is some such mystery about them." She yawned and
said, "Do you know that the male of the butterfly impregnates
the female with a sack of fluid, and not only fertilizes the eggs
but at the same time provides her with a food supply? I guess
that's not so in the case of humans, but it often looks like that."

Tonitschka added, "The last time it happened to me during the
war was with two soldiers from the Wehrmacht. They took me
into a compartment where there were about twenty women and
pushed them out into the corridor. It was the first passenger
train I traveled on in wartime. Then they shut the door and
began to take off their uniforms. I didn't know what to do. They
had long winter underwear. I was scared but afraid to cry. One
of them couldn't unfasten the string on the leg of his underpants.
He gave me some ground coffee in a can with an enormous
swastika on it. He treated me like he'd picked me up on the
streets. Suddenly I burst out laughing, like I was crazy. They got
angry and went away. At the door, one of them slapped my face
and ridiculed me: he said I had teeth spaced out like a mouse.
Maybe it's a good idea to laugh when worst comes to worst."

"Our little lady of the night," Dita said.

"They also say you shouldn't spit on the hand that feeds you,"

Brita said. "I hope they let you keep the can."

"We had no water to make the coffee with," answered Tonitschka. "We ate it as it was. There was sugar and chicory in it."

"The next time Andy talks to me about meat or pastries, I think I'll knock him right on the head," Brita said.

Their words contained weariness and a desire for sleep, and something that supplemented their physical life, what they sought but could not explain, express, or account for—like the vacuum left when a person misses out on childhood and crosses straight over into middle age. Like children with some rare disease that makes them age quickly, so that their skin wrinkles, they go gray or their hair falls out, and they look like aged people but are not. Yet like old people, they die, even though they are still children. They rarely live to see twenty.

"Well, good-bye, ladies, and sweet dreams," Dita said. "There are still a couple of reasons left why we should be satisfied."

"It just occurred to me that we should let our young gentlemen try it for a change, at least for once," Brita said with laughter in her voice. She had a sleepy, husky, and lazy voice, like Andy. "Let them taste it, like when they give you a sip of cognac, from one mouth into the other, if you know what I mean. The first time I really enjoyed it. He took a sip but didn't swallow it, and when he kissed me he passed it over. I mean, just do the same to them."

After a while they were all asleep. Dita wished it were already morning. The bar across the street had closed. Somewhere a train could be heard honking and braking, hissing to a halt. The street lamp swung. The wind had picked it up. The summer night came pouring through the open window like the wind blowing from one place to another, from the unseen to the unknown, across the surface of a green lake, with a path along the bank.

6 On Monday, June 30, the day of his marriage to Liza Vagner, Mr. Gotlob looked twenty years younger. He wore his suit of Italian cloth, a snow-white shirt, and a light gray tie. In one hand he carried his borsalino hat and calfskin gloves.

"He looks like a waiter on Sunday," Dita observed to Tonitschka. "He thinks he's the ultimate, because his pockets are filled with money. But what can you expect? Imagine waking up in the morning with a bald head beside you?"

At 11:55 A.M. the official car of the International Blue and White Union picked up Liza Vagner and brought her to the city hall.

Everyone from the commissioner's office had collected around Zoltan Traubman, Liza's boss, including the accountant, his female assistant, his secretary, the legal officer with Austrian nationality (certain laws and protocols did not apply to him), and the tax specialist, whose services Mr. Traubman would not have been able to afford anywhere else. Perla Traubman stood a short distance away, like the wife of a Turkish vizier. She came from Rumania, where Mr. Traubman had done business in cattle and horses.

"He's giving Liza a present. He's a rich man," Tonitschka commented.

"I hope he doesn't expect to draw interest on it," Dita replied, matter-of-factly.

"When a man's tightfisted with money, that's the first sign for me to call it a day," the Holy Virgin said. Dita thought about the fact that Liza was marrying someone who had not been in the camps. She wondered if it was a good move. She was indifferent. Perhaps it was neither good nor bad. She called out to wish Liza the best in her marriage, and all the rest. Liza did not try to elucidate her meaning.

Dita wore her smile reserved for gala occasions. Brita had put on Dita's scarf. Dita could hardly believe her eyes. "A scarf like this has to be worn, hasn't it? To get your money's worth," Great Britain said defensively.

The grown-ups stood in little groups. Munk wore his overcoat, as usual. Fitzi wore a bow tie that hung askew like a slanting propeller. The whisper went around the room that the bent-over man in glasses was Mr. Jakub Steinman, "one-time ambassador and great friend of the younger generation." He had reportedly taken over the job of general trustee for orphans from a man who had migrated to Australia. D.E. joined Dita in front of the stained glass window.

"Next week you're off to Grindelwald. Did they tell you? It's a summer study grant."

"Thanks, D.E. I know you did your best for me."

"No gambling debts to be collected." He smiled exactly as he had when leaving the Hotel Astoria/Novak, formerly Yellow Stone Inn.

Dita smiled back, lifting the corners of her mouth. She felt fine, as she always did in the midst of people, gossip, laughter, and talk about world problem number one. It made her feel good to be seen next to D.E., with him smiling at her and her returning her smile to him.

Dita had managed to get Liza a taffeta dress with lace in front. Liza's hair was tinted auburn, thanks to a touch of peroxide, and fashioned into a pageboy. A white lace veil fell from her pillbox hat over her forehead and sharp nose down to her thin lips.

"Everything that is beautiful is probably moral, I suppose," Dita said.

"On Thursday I'm leaving for Paris," D.E said.

"It's worthwhile to take risks for a good cause." Dita took care to sound carefree. Was it possible to love and hate someone at the same time? Was she feeling something else?

D.E. observed Maximilian Gotlob. Dita smiled. D.E. preferred happy girls. She did too. Suddenly she was happier, inside and outside, than she had been in the last two years altogether. "They say you should never feel sorry for a young person who can't sleep or for an old person who sleeps all the time," she said.

"I think they told me a different version."

"May I ask what?"

"If you wish. Where there's an old woman, there's mischief brewing."

"Where there's an old man, there's trouble."

D.E. gave up.

"I'm sure that even if you consulted Mr. Gotlob twenty times a day, in the end you'd make up your own mind," said Dita.

"I hope so," D.E. answered. "You don't know why I don't like weddings?"

Suddenly she felt D.E.'s hand on her back. Who needs a wedding, she wanted to say. Life is not what we want but what we have. That's all.

The clerk ushered them into the hall, where they formed two loose triangles. The place had begun to feel like a steam bath. A fly was buzzing while two photographers clicked away. Mr. Gotlob had invited only one. The fly beat its tiny wings. It was blue-gray, a very visible little creature. Dita wished D.E. would once more lay the palm of his hand on her back, as he had done before. But she did it instead of him.

"You're lucky I'm not ticklish," he whispered.

The bride and groom exchanged rings. The clerk gave an address in which he spoke of the revolution that now assured a peaceful existence to them and their children and an even more peaceful one to their children's children. The times were over "when the rich man paraded his wealth, the poor only his children; when the poor could only buy what they could afford, while the rich bought anything they wanted." No longer would the rich break the law with impunity while the poor went to jail for the same offense. Money would no longer be the measure of all things. Revolution had removed the vipers from the sunny side of life. Man would no longer prey upon man. And so on. It would no longer be the rule that the oldest daughter had to have money and the youngest beauty. Every bride deserved admiration. Now nobody needed to make his life harder for the sake of appearance or to look more handsome.

Mr. Gotlob had apparently commanded an honor guard for Lord Beaverbrook. He had snapped to attention and roared out like a lion. "Honor guard! Attention!" Then he had escorted his lordship. Now it looked as if the clerk had replaced his lordship and Liza the honor guard. The wedding guests played the part of the general public, and Mr. Gotlob threw out his chest as if standing in front of a parade, with his back to Liza and facing the lord, while he took a deep breath for the "Present arms" and "Eyes right."

"Life is not what we want but what we have," Dita said again. "You need common sense to pursue happiness. The two qualities are indirectly proportional. After all, every army needs its accountants, even the Germans."

Dita looked at herself in the windows of the wedding hall. She and David Egon Huppert made a handsome pair, both a head taller than the rest of the wedding guests. Everything inside her smiled.

"In this world anyone who pretends to be objective is a crook," she said. And then: "I've also heard that people with high blood pressure lose interest in bed."

"What about you?"

"What do you think?"

"I don't."

"Think? Is it better?"

"Occasionally. With someone."

"It's relaxing with you."

"Thanks."

It was time to congratulate the bride and groom. Mr. Traubman, who had sought the job of general manager and had failed in competition with Jakub Steinman, pretended that old Steinman was absent. He leaned over to Liza: "Dear Mrs. Vagner-Gotlob, take it while it's there to be taken. It seems that the time is coming when the state is going to take an interest in Rumanian cattle, imports and exports, business practice, and taxes."

"It's hard to keep it up," Dita said to D.E. She felt more confident next to him. But did he know this? Should she tell him?

Zoltan Traubman looked like Nostradamus four hundred years ago, predicting the end of the world led by idiots.

"This is better than scrubbing floors in some Israeli kibbutz," Dita remarked. "Marriage, like pregnancy, transforms every woman. I wish I could understand why they say that a weeping bride soon becomes a smiling wife. Perhaps he knows more than all of us together know about ourselves. He's always yes-yes, when the woman is no-no."

"Sour grapes," the Holy Virgin commented.

"At least he won't be unfaithful," Dita said. "And with her marriage certificate she won't feel exploited." And after a moment: "Then too, you learn from your mistakes. What's the use of spending every hour, like a detective, tracing the difference between a mistake and love? It always goes from passion and desire to relaxing after a good dinner." Finally she said, "When it ceases to amuse me, I'll get married too. What about you, Tonitschka? Everything is going well, not to mention the relatives. Who are we to say that the bride isn't worth all the costs involved in a marriage?"

Dita then said to the bride, "Happiness is in the cards for you unless you expect to get something for nothing. You'll discover what has eluded you for a long time. They say that experience is the best teacher, and some men can never be satisfied." She sighed. "No one should be entrusted with everything. We have to learn to help each other in times of need." Liza's eyes asked, "How?"

Zoltan Traubman claimed that happiness, like wind, soon passes. "Who says that not all flies can fly?" Dita asked Tonitschka. "Or that a fly sits only on fat women?" Everybody laughed. Being a clown was not bad at all, she thought. Dita said to Liza, "You have to tell us all about it later."

"I hope that from now on I won't need anything," Liza said.

The wedding reception was at the Grand Hotel Europe.

"Ladies and gentlemen," Mr. Gotlob began, after a small drink. He lifted his plump white hand. "When I lost my platoon in France in 1940, I never imagined that my lifeline would lead me to the harbor that we still call matrimony. It seems like only a year or two ago."

"Hear, hear," Mr. Traubman cried. "Bravo, bravo."

Mrs. Traubman wore black mesh gloves, which reminded Dita of the doctor at the Delousing Station at Theresienstadt. Dita took the opportunity of asking Liza if she had worn them at Auschwitz-Birkenau. Mr. Gotlob ostentatiously offered to spend more than enough. The tables began to sag under the weight of the food on them. Mr. Gotlob had invited most of the guests, and he did his best to ensure that they enjoyed themselves as much as he did. Liza didn't seem to want to be the center of attention. Could she remain silent now, as long as she was prohibited from her new marriage bed? The honor of words was left to her marital partner alone. Mr. Gotlob almost outdrank the guests.

Mr. Traubman sang, in Hungarian, "There's Only One Girl in the World for Me." Spurred on by the applause, he added a Transylvanian wedding song and made faces like Dracula, with teeth enhanced by gold fillings. At the request of the guests, Egon Levit's gypsies began to play the antediluvian "Dark Eyes." It became apparent that the gypsies and Mr. Levit had become acquainted at Auschwitz-Birkenau, where they had played in a band, sometimes for the prisoners on their way to work. Next, the gypsy orchestra played for the bridegroom "There Are No Sunsets over Grenada," and for his bride, "Songs My Mother Taught Me," sung by the gypsy leader in a Hungarian accent.

"You can't beat a czardas and goulash," acknowledged Dita.

The waiters wore white Transylvanian dress, specially ordered by Mr. Traubman. Lebovitch had had to promise Liza, before she invited him, that he would not get into a fight with the waiters.

Dita asked D.E. if he knew a Japanese poem: "We two are in love, they say, but we hide our love away. I wonder if you care or not. What hurts me most of all is this: that there's no truth in what they say."

D.E. laughed. "Verses written on the water?"

After the hors d'oeuvres and the soup with liver dumplings and noodles, there were golden chicken legs to nibble.

Mr. Gotlob selected the best for Liza. He broke a cup, then gave everyone a piece for good luck.

"How is it that every wedding reminds me of a funeral?" Andy asked with a grin, when they brought him strawberries and cream.

Brita announced, "This is how you eat strawberries. First you take a little strawberry on a spoon, then you add a bit of cream. You lick it until not a drop is left. You open your mouth as wide as it will go. OK? Then you push the strawberry in. Get it?"

Mr. Gotlob looked at her, and then at Dita and Liza. It occurred to Dita that a lot of things don't make sense. Everything in my life that has been true and good has always happened only once. Was D.E. frightened by what she had told him in bed, that he was the first man in her life but that she would by no means be the last woman in his?

After lunch was over they began to trade stories. Liza spoke about the nicest thing that had happened to her at Auschwitz-Birkenau. She had been with her older sister in the women's camp. One day her sister, who collected the rations for the whole family, sliced the bread. The first slice was slightly thicker, and she offered it to Liza because she was the skinniest. Liza began to shout at her, "What is the difference if anyone here is skinnier or older, when we are all cold and hungry?" Her sister lost her temper and smacked Liza. "And now eat it up," she shouted. "You've got to grow." With tears streaming down her face, Liza had eaten the thicker slice so that she would "be able to grow."

For a few seconds Tonitschka daydreamed about being slapped by her relatives. Mr. Traubman gave his opinion that a man who goes hungry in order to get rich will stay hungry. The band began to play "Ti-pi-tin." Mrs. Perla Traubman was forced to listen to Mr. Gotlob saying that everyone ought to be sleepy before he goes to bed and hungry before he goes to eat. It was fortunate she only understood Rumanian, not Italian. "A hungry bear will not dance," Mr. Levit said. Today he played the violin. He conducted his gypsy band with the help of his instrument. His wrinkled and handsome face indicated that hunger had taught him many things. Dita asked herself, Isn't that so with all of us?

Neugeborn said it was great fun to talk about hunger when hunger was far away. Around Mr. Gotlob, the talk was about the last war and the English Channel in 1940.

Dr. Fitz put his arms around Dita's and Tonitschka's shoulders. "Either of you could be the queen of England if you'd put your minds to it." Then: "Do you know the disadvantage lovely women have? Nobody believes them."

"Only the first hundred years of marriage are difficult," Lev Goldblat said to Mr. Gotlob, but he wished him happiness anyway.

Andy called across the table, "Tonitschka, you don't have to worry about life after death. You'll certainly be dead a lot longer than you'll be alive."

Andy told Neugeborn that nobody managed to survive by strength or cleverness alone, but by luck; he pointed out that Fitzi was blond and had blue eyes. Maybe that helped, didn't it? Fitzi observed that Andy's head was shaved, so that nobody could see what color his hair was, and also that Hitler hadn't had time to finish the job.

"Nobody survived only because of his lovely eyes," Dita said. "Instead of sending him up the chimney, the Germans chose someone else. That goes for all of us who are here today. Pity we are not as good as we look." She smiled. "Luck is as useful as a bad joke, isn't it?"

Brita reserved her ammunition for Andy. She suggested that boys like him basically prefer girls with whom they can have a good time, rather than so-called decent women. Munk looked shocked.

"With people like you," Dita put in, "prostitutes always have an edge, don't they?"

"Not at all," Lebovitch protested. "If I'd been born a girl, you'd never find me on the streets more than twice a week."

"I suppose you'd be in the kitchen for the other five days?"

It was obvious that Andy relished having been born a boy. Not that he would have necessarily felt suicidal at the thought of being female, but even so, he'd gotten used to maleness. In the same sense, he believed that nature and the elements are related to the soul as a form of energy. The energy that creates winds, rains, and earthquakes is the same one that creates life. To ignore the elements is to ignore life. And to waste something—food, lust, desire—was for Andy a drain of energy in the sense that the energy was harvested and not returned to the cycle of life.

"Are you so quiet because you agree with me, or not?" Brita asked.

"You'd have to let me get a word in first," Andy responded.

"Do you know the proverb that frankness is a killer?" Dita asked, smiling. "We all know the advice given to young gentlemen like you by Balzac, who, incidentally, you have forgotten to return. He said they should treat a woman as a slave, while assuring her that she is a queen."

"Thanks. I hope I won't forget that."

"You forget about everything—except about yourself. Where is my Balzac?"

"As a matter of fact, I use it to press my red scarf when it gets wrinkled."

Andy never indulged in self-flagellation. He never spoiled anybody else's fun if he could help it. He let Brita go on telling him that people like him proposition women every day and would sleep with anyone, preferably on the floor in the cloakroom, the kitchen, or the lavatory. And that he didn't care how many children he had, or with whom. By now she had drunk rather a lot of 1946 and 1947 Riesling. It was well known that Andy used to press his trousers under the mattress, and that he kept his scarf pressed between Dita's Balzac and the 1946 bound annual of the *Jewish Gazette.*

"Holy Virgin, are you by any chance pregnant by me?" Lebovitch switched to the counterattack. It amused him to show off.

"I'm not one of those slow trains that stops at every station," Brita answered. "And you most certainly are not a luxury express."

Dita made the point that a blood sample does not prove who the father is. Somebody capped this with a joke about Mr. Gotlob, that he took four hours, thirty minutes, and one second to do it. Thirty minutes of preparation, one second in action, and four hours to recover consciousness.

"There's an awful lot of cowardice in the whole situation," Dita said. "The two things that I find most reprehensible in people are an inability to be happy and the habit of offering praise for no reason. I think that no matter how awful or difficult life is for a person, he can still find a simple thing in other people or in nature that is valuable. Those who cannot find happiness in the vast world that surrounds them are lost souls and should be pitied."

Nobody understood why she had said that. "Why?" Andy asked.

"False praise is a quality I find difficult to deal with. I feel that those who flatter extensively tend to want praise themselves. Vanity is the downfall of many, and false praise is the Achilles' heel of people susceptible to it. Praising people who don't deserve it makes them believe that they are more capable than they are." Dita smiled. "I also feel that every person has a soul. Not to say that I believe that animals also have souls."

"Yeah," Andy said. "And it's recycled from one lifetime to the next, right? And dealing with others, you find that a silent pride is more than a person's desire for his own gain or benefit, isn't that so? And creativity is the most important quality you try to extract from others in conversation—the thing you hope to find in people, right? You enjoy the process just as much as the finished project, if I am not mistaken, right? Only one question: Is shameless behavior cowardice too?" Andy demanded.

"The inability to say yes or no," Brita insisted, rather tipsily. "A lack of courage."

"Sex isn't like mathematics," Dita said. "One and one is two, and two and two are four, never five. With women it is not so predictable."

"Yeah," Andy said.

"Tell me something, Mummy." Lebovitch turned to Tonitschka.

"Help us with a bit of your girlish wisdom to guide my steps when I get off the track again, Tonitschka."

Dita leaned over the table confidentially. "Of all the girls, prostitutes are the best, aren't they, Andy? The same light that falls on the feet of madonnas, mothers, or little sisters also illuminates the feet of whores. There's no difference between them. You're absolutely right, Andy."

When Andy had been at Auschwitz-Birkenau in 1944, they came to tell him that his grandma had arrived at the ramp. He had friends among the Polish prisoners and the loading squad that was known as Kanada, and they enabled him to contact her. He wanted to spare her the selection process and the revelation that followed it. So he went with her almost all the way. The mothers would either push their children away from them, so they would survive, or else they would link hands, so they might go to the gas together. The SS guards used to take pleasure in frustrating this. They would send them through one by one, sometimes only the mother to the chimney and the child to the camp, or the other way around. They did this over and over again, hundreds of times, thousands of times, times without number, whereas the mothers with children did it for the first and the last time.

His grandmother asked about the chimneys. Andy replied that it was the Delousing Station and that he had friends there. "Wherever could I have picked up lice, for goodness sake?" Grandma asked.

"It's the normal routine here," he told her. "Children below fifteen and adults over forty-five have to be deloused, whether they've got lice or not. They all have to wash their heads." He tried to calm her down. "It's all in a day's work here, as normal as a fish swimming or a butterfly flying. The Germans organize the arrival and disposal of each transport as quickly as possible, to make room for others." Luckily she did not notice much of what went on at the ramp. She did not even hear the machine guns or pistols firing. She was glad to be out in the fresh air after the overcrowding in the truck. They were thirsty, and the SS had promised to give them water if they obeyed orders and did as quickly as possible what they were told and went where they were sent. Faster. Faster. She had probably forgotten for the time being what she had heard in Poland. She shut her eyes to keep out the dust. She was amazed at how much ash was in the air. The locomotive was already waiting.

"See you soon," Andy said.

"I believe you, son. Look after yourself."

"You too."

The wind was blowing. Grandma held on to her hair. She turned around. Then she went on, confused, walking with small steps.

Immediately after the war, in Prague, a French circus came with a twenty-year-old female acrobat on the flying trapeze, and with animals and sixty trained rats. Andy Lebovitch took care not to miss a single one of sixteen shows. He claimed that the artiste on the trapeze looked exactly like his former girlfriend in Theresienstadt. He cut out of the newspaper photographs of her lying on the trapeze, like a slim fish with floating hair, a big smile and staring eyes, under the dome of the red and white striped tent. He never spoke to her; he could not speak French. He even went to the shows with the trained rats. The object of Andy's love had no name. He used to say that the trick of surviving consists of not allowing yourself to be annihilated. The enemy might be an SS officer, or it might be some crazy rabbi driven by hunger to take anything he sees—bread, a shoe, a glove—so that you can lose your last morsel and be finished. He also said that whatever you begrudge or deny yourself, even though you can afford it, you will finally lose. If anyone pretends to be worse off than he really is, it's a sure bet that that is how he will end up. Why? Because times have changed. Life is not a well. Life is an express train. Whoever doesn't believe it should ask Dita. He was sure that some people's obsession with winning was just an inverted fear of losing. He was prepared to concede that fate was stronger than man, but if he had to compare it to something, it was like flying through the air between two trapezes. The only way is to let go and to catch hold at the right moment. Every mistake was simultaneously the first and the last.

Andy possessed a rare quality. He could be happy without always thinking about his needs. He made quick decisions, as if still in the war. Nobody knew how he felt by himself. But there was no doubt about it when he felt on top of the world. And when things went wrong, he would retreat into his own den and not worry anyone else. Except that even his hideouts could get him into fights.

What do I have in common with Andy? Dita wondered. Everything and nothing? Would she be able to live with him? No. No. Three times no. She smiled at him. He didn't have the slightest idea. Dita looked across at Andy as though she knew in advance how he would reply. It was good to know how easily Brita's attacks bounced off him.

"No one is perfect," Andy defended himself. "What are you afraid of? Noah, too, forgot to take fish into the ark."

"Who is it that you really love, as you pretend to, Andy dear?" Dita inquired. Why did she ask? She almost flushed. But she covered it with her long smile.

"Apart from you? Myself."

"And what about true love, like to your circus cashier whom we've never seen?"

"I've got a woman nowadays, and that's enough for me."

"How long have you been confusing glands with love?"

"How do I know what will happen tomorrow?"

"And what about responsibility, Andy dear?"

"What's that?"

"You certainly won't see it when you look into the mirror."

"Everybody's only responsible for the present. Surely you don't expect me to take responsibility for things that don't exist anymore, or haven't happened yet?"

"What if I don't like it?"

"The secret lies in at least putting on a good show." Andy grinned. "Somebody hands you a hammer and shows you a nail and where to put it. You just bang it in. That's the main thing you have to do."

"How do you judge it, so you don't make a mistake and hit your thumb?"

"Like you judge the weather. You take it as it comes. Sunshine, wind, mud. Sometimes you run to shelter, or remember not to leave your umbrella at home. You're not responsible for the whole thing, are you? It also depends on the weather."

"Certainly," Brita hissed. "As my English landlady used to say in London, one man's ceiling is another man's floor. She didn't bother to translate. When there's no wood for the stove, the fire goes out. Thanks for putting women in their little cages. As if you weren't in a cage yourself. I don't understand Dita's patience. How long can you go on, you clowns?"

Andy tried to swat a fly on his napkin. He was capable of seeing to it that none of the girls would twist him around their finger. He glanced at Dita. Not long ago Mr. Gotlob had told Liza that Dita was like a badly timed bomb. So what? We're all time bombs, thought Andy. He had a look in his eyes that reflected something he had discovered for himself. Sometimes a person is satisfied if no one is beating him and he is neither cold nor dying of hunger. Also he thought about what he had in common with Dita. He suddenly glanced at Brita and said, "Come and have a drink. I know very well that when you were a child, you pulled the wings off flies."

"I pulled off their legs, like you." The rash on Brita's forehead

itched. She began to scratch herself. "Look, scratch it, hormon-
al changes are here in me—now."

The party was at its height. Mr. Gotlob winked. Something
brewed within him. Nobody had to tell an old cat what mice were
or what to do with them. He looked around, at D.E. and Dita Saxova. His leg had gone to sleep. He secretly glanced at Dita's
face. He compared Liza with Dita, and both of them with Holy
Virgin and company. He felt what he had lost with Dita and realized at what point he had been defeated. Perhaps he still felt
that she was more important than she was or could be. Suddenly he linked her face and expression with the thought she had
inspired in him. And he smiled at D. E. Huppert. Then he avoided looking at Dita.

Like him, they had all learned one thing, a discovery they had
paid for with blood—in their case with the blood of their nearest
and dearest—that civilization is a thin veneer that does not protect the weaker victims and is not a compelling enough incentive
for the stronger, who don't waste their strength in trying to save
themselves. So they had become not only victims of their
enemy—nazism and fascism in Europe—but also victims of
human weakness. At every period of violent change, weakness
forms a vacuum in which many others die without anyone to
save them—as if it were in the interest of those who were a bit
stronger than others, but not quite strong, to keep the machin-
ery of slaughter going, so it will feed itself on the flesh, bones,
and blood of others. The skin that divided nature from civilization had grown thin, weak, and it was beginning to wear out.

For Mr. Gotlob the just man was a myth, possible in legend,
fairy tale, or prayer, but not in real life. But even that thought
only occupied his mind for a fraction of a second. He knew that
the clock had turned them back to the age of paganism, when
God did not yet exist, whether they called it that or even realized
it, so that they did not condemn him as he had condemned them,

or try to kill him, as he had allowed their nearest ones to be killed, by the hands of those whom he had created as he had created them. The impulse toward the process, the result of which had been the civilization of the man of our times, as Mr. Gotlob thought, had given them more freedom, and maybe more possibilities. It occurred to Mr. Gotlob again to wonder what would happen, what time and fate had in store still for this generation. There can be disputes about the definition of strength. What is indisputable is that only the stronger, or the strongest, survives, even if it means that nobody survives at all.

He stood beside his young wife and looked at Dita and Tonitschka, then again at Dita. For a further fraction of a second he compared them with all those he had known at Lubliana and Krakovska streets, and he felt closer to the impulse that had drawn him toward them: Dita, Neugeborn and Lebovitch, Huppert, Liza and Linda, Kitty Borger, Doris Levit, and Brigitta Mannerheim. What common factor grouped them into a sort of community and made them what they were proud to call basic, or natural, or revolutionary people?

He lifted his glass, as if for a toast to them all, but he changed his mind and merely drank. There was something in them that made him hesitant to speak. He felt that he stood, as he had so often, face to face with his bride and her friends, including Dita Saxova, numb. Fortunately no one expected any toast or further speech from him, so no one noticed—not Munk, Dr. Fitz, or Lev Goldblat. Egon Levit's gypsies went on playing, eating, and drinking, sometimes all at once. Someone warned Liza that the lady of the household was nothing more than a well-dressed servant and that Lebovitch didn't believe in anything except his own physical prowess. Brita claimed that half the boys in Krakovska Street opened their mouths wide while kissing, as if they were opening the door to the gymnasium. The band kept lengthening the intervals between numbers, until Mr. Gotlob referred to

them as the most expensive intervals he had ever paid for and
Dita compared them to the holes in Ementhaler cheese. After
two hours the first few guests began to leave. Everyone
exchanged kisses. Twice Mr. Gotlob saw Dita duck when someone tried to kiss her on the lips. She offered them all her cheek,
except for D.E., who only shook her hand when he left.

Mr. Traubman praised the food, the taste, and the manners of
the "younger generation." Sitting next to his snow-white wife, he
had been eating busily. She kept suggesting, "Won't you have
another piece of cheese, Zoltan?" Zoltan Traubman had put
away enough cheese to last him a month. He insisted that
"accountants were, are, and always will be the backbone of
every army and of the world. Business is the salt of life, and
whoever denies it is a barbarian. What you do, doctor—it the
noblest trade in the world."

"It is time to express our thanks to the parents of our dear
bride," Mr. Gotlob said.

Suddenly Liza began to cry, and Dita felt embarrassed and
smiled at her. The tears stood out in Liza's small eyes. They
were the color of the empty green beer bottles scattered about
on the tables. Mr. Gotlob tried to comfort her. "Come on, Liza.
Now then, darling. No . . ."

7 Mr. Gotlob did not have a record player in the apartment,
and so Liza brought back Dita's wedding gift, the record
of "Jericho," to 53 Lubliana. Among the books, cosmetics, and
remnants of fabric and food were the things that Brita had
packed for her journey.

The Holy Virgin had dragged up from the cellar the two cabin
trunks that she had brought from England in 1945. Through the
hostel, and the room, together with the smell of the whitewash,
floated the strains of "Meadowland," "The March of the Red

Army," and "Ti-pi-tin." "One night when the moon was so mellow . . ." For three days there had barely been space to move. "Perhaps I didn't even originate on earth but somewhere in the stardust, as Hitler said," she said. "As if Hitler himself were not also just a piece of heavenly dust. Ho, ho, they just seated me in the house of Julius and Louise Mannerheim."

"By mistake you've created a personality that no longer impresses me," Dita said.

"It goes right past me, like a train on another track. I stepped into my conscious life on the wrong foot. I began in a rhythm that turned out to be a mistake."

Dita checked off the list. "Butter, milk, documents. How do you remember where you live when you're always moving?"

"I've got one problem." Brita turned her gaze on Dita. "The missing dimension that tells you when you're living to the fullest. Like that black-haired fellow from the kibbutz said, 'Life is a four-engine airplane that is flying on only one engine.'"

"Things in this world are sometimes well arranged," Dita conceded.

"How on earth am I ever going to carry all this?" Brita said plaintively.

"You're going by train and ship. You'll have a compartment to yourself. How many people still travel like that?" Tonitschka said with a sigh.

The Holy Virgin had vainly tried to spend the last two out of three days in bed. But they could all see it wasn't working. While Dita and Tonitschka tried to cram her clothes into the trunks, Brita watched them with sore eyes set in her pasty face. Dita hummed, "And the flag of Askalona will fly over my grave for ages . . ."

The packing presented the cats with an opportunity to tear up whatever they wanted. When she had finally gotten everything packed in the trunks, Brita began to pull things out again and offer them to the two girls as avidly as she had been trying to ensure that not even a tie should get lost.

"Apparently suicides are always giving things away," Tonitschka said.

"How do you know?" Brita asked.

Apart from the fact that the girls were not inclined to strip Brita of her possessions, most of them were in less than first-class condition.

"It feels about as warm and cozy as Siberia in here," Dita grumbled.

"Look here, girls, don't hurt my feelings. After all, I'm going to England." Brita had to watch helplessly while everything, except for a rubber hot water bottle and some blue lace underwear, was tossed back into the womb of the trunks, in the same arc as before when she'd pitched it out. Finally she gave up and lay back with her hands under her chin, looking like a beetle. Dita picked up one of Munk's books. She wrote on the flyleaf: "To Brita Mannerheim, from the seashores and steppes. Maxi Peshkov. 'Man—that word has a noble ring.' Prague, 4 July 1947."

Brita said, "You know, girls, we all have to do it sometimes, and it's probably better to do *it* now and then than to do nothing at all. But you know that I've never done it for money."

Dita yawned. "According to Balzac, God punishes the man who tries to buy for money what can only be given away." She wanted to feel naked, with all that it meant for her, but she could not. It wasn't as much fun the other way around.

"The most important thing in the world is not love, truth, or money, but something else," Brita said. "Ask Munk."

"There is certainly much more to wish for than to need," Dita said. "Or less?" Then: "I can't discuss this with you. You were definitely the smartest child."

"Of course. I was the only child." Lying down, Brita looked

across at Tonitschka's underwear. Tonitschka had brought it over, as she intended to move into Liza's place.

"Our little baby doll, Tonitschka," Dita sighed.

They started laughing. They remembered how Brita looked in the early spring, as if she had just been dragged out of the wardrobe, as if she hadn't changed clothes—not to mention underwear—since the start of winter. Sometimes she looked as if she had just been taken out of mothballs. Brita compared Tonitschka's petite lingerie with her own.

"Who are you leaving behind you?" Dita wanted to know.

"For a couple of weeks I've been going around with a nice boy whom I made into a man," said Brita. "He understands me a little too well. I guess that's the first thing that puts a girl like me off. It's a sure sign that my romance is drawing to a close."

"'Loving too much?'" Dita quoted.

"You know how I like to jump from one to another. It's a kind of struggle of my hormones against the remnants of a good upbringing. The beginning and the end are always the same. Except that your body is constantly changing."

"Yeah. We wear it out," Dita interjected, and they laughed again. Behind her smile she wondered why life seemed like a slow-moving avalanche, and why what made sense in nature made no sense at all in human life. Did she feel she had the ability to understand, forgive, and forget? Or did she lack that ability? She thought of the cats in the house and their ability to go on sleeping forever. Then to wake up and run, disappear, and get lost all over the place. And how it was with Britannia, who was away from here the entire war and escaped what her parents did not.

"Is it really your theory?" Tonitschka asked.

"Do you really want to know my theory? That we are not prepared for anything. The fact that our parents went through hard times and that more things disgusted them than not, and that they wanted to shield me—all that doesn't explain anything. I remember how they used to drill the rules into me: 'Virtue, honor, honesty.' And all the rest. But when I really tried to be like that, they nearly went crazy. They shouted at me and asked me whether I'd lost my mind."

"Why do you always throw your boyfriends away so soon?" Dita inquired.

"I haven't got the energy to waste."

"Nothing more?"

"Instinct," Brita assessed herself. "Anyway, you can't hold them for long. Either they get tired of it, or else they meet somebody better." She spoke as if she were talking about a bubble. It reminded them of early in the summer, when Brita had read a book by a Turk, Italian, or maybe a Persian author. This author wrote that a woman will forgive a man even murder from lust, provided that it happens because of her, but on no account if it's because he is tired of her and he's lost interest.

"Sometimes people don't know what they want," Dita said, "but they simply want, whether or not they deserve to. Is it possible that everything has to be earned?"

Brita sighed deeply. "At the beginning sometimes you seek and find happiness, the things that bring you together. In the end you only see what drives you apart." And then: "At a good show you can tell it's the end even before the curtain falls."

They exchanged glances. It sounded as if Brita was anxious to move on before she lost her position as head of her male harem, not yet entirely extinct, but that she couldn't take with her like her trunks. It also sounded like an echo of what the Holy Virgin used to say in the spring: "For me, too good is too bad. Men abandon their principles much more easily than women. They sell themselves at a price no woman would ever consider, except in a critical emergency and for the sake of others." But she also admitted that amorous affairs kept her going. In her eyes there was always something between memory and anticipation. Once she confessed that men had appealed to her even before she learned to walk. For her sex had a secret that nobody had yet discovered. Eroticism was a dynamo, exuding more energy than everything else combined.

"Don't you do it just so they can't do it to you first?" Dita asked. "According to Rabbi Loew, a girl who's been brought up right admits when she doesn't know something. And answers first the first and last the last question she was asked. What you need is not reason but luck."

"You have to take everything lightly. That's the whole secret of living when you're a woman. Because you probably find more lies and deceit and cunning in relations between men and women than anywhere else, even though each alone might be a perfect angel," Brita replied.

"How's that?" Tonitschka inquired. "Don't two and two angels make four?"

"If I could answer that, I'd get the Nobel Prize for mathematics, and I wouldn't be going to England third class," Brita answered.

"Aren't you afraid of fooling around with married men?" Tonitschka asked.

"Why should I be afraid? The commandment doesn't say, 'Thou shalt not covet thy neighbor's husband.' Only 'thy neighbor's wife,'" Great Britain answered.

Once Tonitschka had asked Brita why she didn't like Munk.

"Because he's a know-it-all," Brita had said. "And in the end, a know-it-all doesn't know anything about himself or anyone else. He knows nothing. So don't ask me about him."

"He's a dreamer," Tonitschka had said.

"A dreamer? What does that mean? Wasn't Hitler a dreamer, too? Didn't he dream of some world with a thousand-year-old *Reich?* A world without circumcised boys and dark hair and dark eyes?"

Tonitschka had looked hurt.

"I know," Brita had said. "But you know what I'm talking about." She expressed in her eyes things she rarely put into words. Her complexion was deteriorating.

The Holy Virgin sighed as though averting Dita's gaze, as if to say she would need some of her things. "Justice, girls. Who knows where that lives? But before I leave, I want to tell you what worries me more than anything else. In order to survive everything, you've got to be a chameleon."

The procession to the railroad station set out at 9:00 A.M. Dita looked as if she had not slept, her blond hair combed at the last moment. She had put on her best clothes. For three days now she had struggled over a letter to D. E. Huppert, telling him what conclusions she had come to about their relationship. They all set out from 53 Lubliana Street, across Washington Street, around the Hotel Esplanade and the park. Mr. Goldblat led the procession. "Women and chickens are easily led," he chuckled. "A man destined to drown can never be hanged. And a pretty face is only chosen after a good name." On the off-chance that someone might be interested, he began to recite the wisdom of the infantrymen of the Piave: "Dove la voglia e pronta, le gambe sono leggiere." Desire and purpose make light shoes.

Doris Levit, who had moved in with the caretaker, stayed behind to look after her daughter, little Sonia, and to help out around the hostel, while Neugeborn repaired the railing, the water pipes, and the gutters in the yard. Apart from them, the entire population of Lubliana and Krakovska streets had assembled at the station. Andy Lebovitch led the combo organized by Mr. Traxler, who pushed about in excitement and kept shouting, "More drinks for the band!"

"Sure," Dita said. "You musicians are always thirsty."

Mr. Jakub Steinman, general overseer of young people, crouched in the corner of the waiting room. He had only one middle tooth and tried not to speak, to avoid lisping.

The others helped to improve the mood. The station attendants must have thought it was a college outing, but there were only two pieces of luggage. The third, which Brita used to keep under her bed, she had thrown into the garbage. The people from the Palestinian and Emigration departments arrived, Avi Fischer in front. Lebovitch shouted over the noise of the band:

> *They used to be so proud of him*
> *But now they claim he was a beast . . .*

The railway coaches shifted noisily along the platform, and a cloud of white, sweetish smoke settled over the crowd. Dita watched the belly of the locomotive. Tonitschka coughed. There were signs painted on the coaches: "Prague-Nuremberg," "Prague-Paris," "Dining Car," and "Sleeping Car."

Mr. Gotlob had the same attitude in his eyes as Great Britain. He shouted, "See you at Marble Arch—that was my wartime stomping ground—or at Finchley Road, where the underground comes up. Don't forget to give my regards to my friend Winston."

He was rewarded by a burst of laughter, which swallowed his additional comment that the best time to leave is when you're thoroughly fed up. Lev Goldblat repeated to Munk, "Della pienezza del cuore parla la bocca," which meant that God helps those who help themselves. Munk steadfastly maintained that the world was one—a wretched one perhaps, but still one. He looked on, as Brita was lifted up to the steps of her compartment. He watched Dita, observing her smile.

"We'll meet at St. Wenceslas's tail," Dita promised. "Or at City."

"They're planning to close it down," Andy called out. "There'll be a Soviet bookshop there instead."

Brita stood at the window of her compartment with her pimply face. She rested her bosom on the windowsill.

"Let's hope there's an international express like this in store for every one of us," Dita called, smiling.

Lebovitch grimaced. "Prague, Belsen, Prague, all change! All aboard for London."

"I'll send you a lovely lace bra, Mummy," Great Britain said.

"Don't forget me," Dita cried.

The male contingent smirked. Mr. Traxler signaled to Lebovitch, and the band, well known for the soirées at 53 Lubliana Street and 27 Krakovska Street, where it played in the gymnasium, broke into the "Radetsky March," which would have been long forgotten but for Dr. Fitz, Munk, and Lev Goldblat, and also "La Trieste": "Lieutenant, oh Lieutenant, just put it there for me . . . Your carnation, your carnation . . ."

Once upon a time they had sung it in Italy, when they stood near the Piave, up to their knees in water and bathed in "the blood of their enemies." They knew it in Czech and Italian. It rang through the station as if a unit of army veterans was on its way.

The Holy Virgin kept her arms folded across her chest. A moment later the train began to move. Her suitcases were lodged securely on the rack, labeled with the return address 53 Lubliana Street, and destination Parkeville, Madelay, Lelford, Shropshire County.

"So long, sweetie," Lebovitch called. "Bust out."

"But look out for the pillars," Dita shouted beside him. Laughter didn't leave her face. "You look as though you seriously believe that when the *Titanic* sunk, the orchestra went on playing a hymn in the first-class lounge," Dita observed. "Smile at me."

The wheels of the cars rolled. Brita's bust, her pimply face, her velvet dress, and her newly washed white collar were still in sight. They could hear the sound of steel clanging on steel.

Dita ran alongside the moving train for a little way. "Just don't die of it," she called, referring to a time when Brita, in Room 16, had complained how complicated it was to be born a woman. Liza had countered with the comment that, on the other hand, her man had to shave twice a day.

The hollow sound of the whistle echoed through the station. The station was old and had lived through many name changes—from Franz Joseph, through Woodrow Wilson, and goodness knows how many labels it carried under Adolf Hitler, until it had ended as Prague, Main Station.

Dita smiled. She had circles under her eyes. The wind ruffled her hair. She wore her raincoat open, and as she ran, the collar tossed in the air. Tonitschka coughed loudly. She stopped at the luggage trolley and rested her head on the back of it. The wheels of the train had begun to gather speed.

The choir from Krakovska Street, supported by the girls and other people from the community and friends, began to chant in unison, "Brita, Brita, Brita." Dita finally gave up and stopped. She thrust her hands into her pockets. The locomotive disappeared into a tunnel. The train was gone. Within one minute Brigitta Mannerheim, Andy's bit of flesh for one rainy afternoon, who was known as Brita, Holy Virgin, or Great Britain, was gone. And to those who did not know that she had lived here since the end of the war, it was as if she had never existed.

Not far from the newsstand, Herbert Lagus turned to Dita. It was enough for him to be in her presence for everything in him to melt. He kept a step behind her. Twice she turned around. Behind their backs Lebovitch told Mr. Steinman confidentially that Linda Huppert was in some international Irgun Zwa Leumi camp near Košice, where she was learning to handle hand grenades and an automatic rifle.

"Shooting to kill," Andy added. "Aim, fire, and don't miss."
Then: "Who needs a three-engine plane to fly on one propeller?
I bet you that down there among the oranges things are going to
get real hot for someone." He capped his words by saying that
99 percent of people thought that our lot were on the gravy
train. And the remaining 1 percent? "You can forget about them.
It's only us." Andy carried his new accordion slung over his
shoulder. He talked to Mr. Steinman as if they were old buddies.
"You can bet your life that anybody who married her would
either run away or commit suicide within a year and a day."

Linda Huppert had left a note in the caretaker's cupboard. He
did not need to be a handwriting expert to see the connection
between the February informer's note and this lined paper, torn
out of a school exercise book. She wrote that she was not going
to stand by and watch "unfair discrimination shrieking to high
heaven."

"There's a difference between slapping somebody else's face
and getting slapped yourself, isn't there?" Lebovitch said. That
distinction expressed his profound idea of Zionism almost perfectly. The place where Andy was going to meet Neugeborn was
the World War I beer joint. They had switched from a place
called By the Thirty-Six Just.

"This reminds me of how Mr. Rosenblatt and Mr. Cohen were
traveling by train," Dita said. "As they left the dining car, Mr.
Rosenblatt complained: 'God should punish them for charging
such prices.' 'He already has,' Mr. Cohen answered and pulled
two silver spoons from his pocket."

"My family simply doesn't believe there's any future for us in
Europe," Herbert said, "after all our experiences. Both world
wars started here. If anything happens again, we think it'll start
here first. It's worth it for us to bet on El Salvador."

He smoothed his hair, although it was already carefully
combed. When he talked about things he could put into words,

he expressed himself very clearly.

"People head for the big city just because they know how to use a comb?" Dita smiled. She felt the excitement pulsing through Herbert Lagus. He walked close to her, tall, with a thick mop of wavy red hair. She certainly didn't need to feel ashamed to be seen with him.

"I like you, rat catcher. You must have been loved. You must have been loved by many women. And now you should reply, 'I don't know. I can't remember.' Or words to that effect."

"I suppose Brita will be better off there than here," Herbert Lagus said. His nervousness made him awkward in her presence. She felt him inhale. She knew what he wanted to ask.

She got in first. "Do you really mean it, Herbert, or are you really questioning yourself instead of me?"

He looked into her eyes.

"They say that rich girls are practical, Herbert." And then: "I don't know if you're right about how strong I am. Not everybody gets around like the Holy Virgin, you know." She smiled at him. He looked as Neugeborn had once looked, as if he were willing to go to war for her, to build a house, to nurse children. From one man a girl wants everything, from another nothing. Why? No reason. And it is the same reversed. "How could I ever find my local train to bring me back, Herbert?" Finally she said, "Maybe you don't care for me as much as you kid yourself you do. I'm beginning to think that people imagine lots of things about me."

She did not point out that it was a certain type, and only about certain things. Generally, different types, and different, incongruous, undesirable things, turning sweet into bitter. It is not, as Isabelle used to say, that a pretty face is the bane of innocence, or that a boy begins to live when he is born, and a girl when she marries. Those days have gone for good. She smiled.

"I want to keep in touch with you," he said.

"When are you leaving?"

"Next Wednesday."

"I see you're not wasting any time."

"It would not make sense to."

"You're sure to find pleasant company."

"As soon as you let me know, I'll send you a boat or a plane ticket."

"Don't you like it here, Herbert?" Then she said, "There are so many myths, Herbert. Like the myths about safe or dangerous continents. Myths about changing the worst into something better and the better into something best. Only because you want them to. Myths about where the next war will start, and where it won't. Where you will be free, or where you won't be. Where you can and can't choose for yourself. I've just read about Mata Hari. Apparently they shot her through the ear with a mercy bullet. It's said that she was as innocent as the well-paid whore of three centuries. I'm confused. She blamed everything on her extravagant tastes." Dita smiled again.

"Isn't it true that the greatest racist slaughterhouse of all time was here in Europe?"

"It's true. But didn't it all happen as a culmination of those myths? Or at least with considerable help from them?"

Herbert walked on in silence by her side. Dita continued, "The myth of Jewish omnipotence on the one hand, and of Jewish helplessness on the other. According to one myth they are weaker than lice, and about as clean. According to another myth, the same people are trying to gain control of the whole world. One and the same person is simultaneously the weakest of the weak and capable of surviving against inconceivable odds. But of all the myths, the one that disturbs me most is the myth of Jewish solidarity. One people, one destiny. Or Jewish destiny in Jewish hands. The urge to wander from place to place. As Mr. Steinman says, we are not as powerful as our enemies imagine and our friends would wish. There's a similar myth about the Germans.

They are either all-powerful, or else they are demons."

But all this was not what Herbert Lagus was anxious to hear. He asked himself who Dita's real friends were, and what she meant to them. How and with whom did she really want to live? Whose song did she wish to sing? And who was good enough to share her journey? He liked her smile. Maybe she was able to make people besides herself feel that things are better than they could have been. He admired her and at the same time felt sorry for her. He sensed her courage and lack of courage, strength and lack of strength, independence and lack of independence. She felt his secret questions. Had she accepted even things irreconcilable with her feelings? Was her desire for freedom satisfied merely by clarifying the alternatives to herself—like at the selection in Auschwitz-Birkenau? Right or left? And that was all?

Dita smiled. She was not sure that Herbert could see what she meant. Why did he prefer to be color-blind on his own? "Just imagine, Herbert. People are crossing frontiers and don't need a false passport now, only a good tailor." And she smiled again.

"Why are you so much against leaving?"

"I haven't yet made up my mind."

"I hope you don't believe, like Munk, that it would be the end of idealism? I would like you to feel that you can count on me."

Dita smiled. "Thanks, Herbert, that sounds encouraging." She laughed. "Maybe you're going to tell me that I carry my life around as if it were a stillborn child. Don't."

Herbert hesitated. She could see that some of her words were lost on him and that he was impressed with others. He saw in them a meaning she had not intended. Suddenly she realized that she had made the right decision, at least as far as he was concerned. She smiled again. She knew that in his mind's eye he saw a blue-water bay, sea, sunshine, and the valleys and hills wrapped in a silver haze. Perhaps he visualized himself standing next to her with his arm thrown around her neck. She would not be an ideal wife for him. Nothing he could do would satisfy her. Not because it would not be good enough, but because she would be no good there. The world of El Salvador? She did not say that she would be afraid of a place where she had no one and would have to start all over again.

They left the station yard and stepped out into the street. Last Friday in Room 16 Herbert had proclaimed that what had happened once could happen again and again, and that it would happen. "What is the point of leaving, if we wish to return?" The Rat Catcher.

"What sort of suitcases have you got?" she asked him.

"Like Brita's."

"She should be somewhere near Dvůr Králové by now. But maybe I'm getting mixed up. Geography was never my strong point. I love grass. And when I try to decide what I like best, it's cactus that loses."

"It's a lovely day."

"It's been a long time since we had such a lovely summer. It's my second good summer. No, the third one."

He wiped a bead of sweat from his forehead. She smiled. Everybody tried to look further into the future than only tomorrow. Nothing wrong with that. But something got lost that might have been enjoyed here and now. She knew that she had only one thing to offer Herbert. But how long could she sustain his self-image? Some things she would be unwilling to do under any circumstances. But she could not really tell him that she felt with him, at best, as if he were her younger brother. So she just kept smiling.

"Isn't it funny, Herbert, how people like you and me always find some use for suitcases, no matter how long they've been keeping company with the mice in the cellar?"

She could imagine the type of letters they would exchange before the summer was over. She decided to go to join Lebovitch and Neugeborn for a beer. Where on earth was D.E.? Brita maintained that a person had to love himself before he could love anyone else. Maybe that alone was not enough. To give? To receive? Did it ever occur to D.E. to ask if it is any different for a woman? When a girl is pretty, it's just her looks that the boys are after. So what?

She parted from Herbert with a handshake, lifting the corners of her mouth and tossing back her hair. Just to be on the safe side, she did not permit him even to kiss her cheek. On the way back home Dita stopped at Josefovska Street. She could still hear what the landlady had said to her immediately after the end of the war: "So you've come back, Dita. Oh well. It doesn't matter." At least I've gotten that over with. Her mother had kept a few towels and dish cloths hidden at the lady's house at the beginning of the war.

That day Dita had taken a streetcar, and three boys from the English Brigade had gotten on. One fellow had looked at her and said, "I bet you couldn't wait for these black-haired characters to come back, could you?" And on her first evening in the girls' hostel, she walked down Lubliana Street on the other side, and people spilled out of the bar at number 52. One of them spat in front of her, as though the sight of her had turned his stomach. Who knows what she might have heard if she didn't look like a Scandinavian blond?

A coincidence? Perhaps. Three times over? Why not. At times it seemed strange to people that they hadn't all been burned in the German ovens and pits and made into cakes of soap, corsets, or hammocks for submarines, as the newspapers had reported. The people felt as if they had been deceived. As For-Better-for-Worse said, people who live in glass houses shouldn't throw stones. How would she become the source of her own happiness, as Herbert Lagus imagined? The Germans has stabled horses in some synagogues. After the war the poor horses

were turned out into the rain. That ``was probably the only reason some of the holy places had survived the war. They should
put a notice up on them: "The Jewish Religious Community is
sincerely grateful to the horses." Andy did not like people in the
bar at number 52 asking him, "You are still alive?"

The enterprising landlady had converted the laundry into living quarters. It never occurred to Dita that those people ought
to move out because she had come back. She remembered the
well-pressed curtains, the lace, and the tablecloths that she
used to wrap herself up in so she could dress like an actress.

It was a sunny day. The entrance to the laundry that had
belonged to Josef Sax and Vera Saxova was now bricked up. In a
sense the same thing had happened to the academic year their
daughter had spent at the School for Applied Arts, and also to
their dream of a beautiful white house and the life that might
have made it possible. Was it the price they had to pay so that
their daughter could sail on safe, deep water? "I am not going
anywhere," Dita Saxova said. "Why should I go? What would I
find there?"

The river was heavy with the smell of summer. It really had
been a lovely spring and summer, and she knew why. She was so
superstitious that as soon as she had said it she told herself it
probably wouldn't last. She recalled her favorite songs from
Lubliana Street. The trees were not yet weary; the leaves had
kept their color. She looked across at the river. The wild ducks
swam against the current, ruffling the water. They headed away
from the weir, where the transparent green water tumbled down
into white foam as the current carried it along. There was no
point in going away. She stopped and leaned on one of the street
lamps. Then she sat down on a bench and began to write a letter to D.E.

Dear D.E.

I think I am still in love with you. It took me some time to understand that when a man wants to go to bed with me it does not necessarily mean that he wants to marry me, and that I've no reason to be angry with him on that account. And I have just discovered another secret: that not everybody who seeks my company wants to take me to bed—which is not so much his loss as mine. But I refuse to admit to myself that what was the most wonderful sin in my life could turn into disappointment, humiliation, or both.

I would like to do many things. And I ask myself why I am afraid that it will all go wrong and end in a mess, and I'll finish up as a washerwoman. Otherwise things are going well. I have made plans, and there are a few people who can, and will, help me. But I feel as though within me there is some gap through which all my endeavors escape to nothing, and that in the end I'm capable of caring for myself, and nobody else will care for me.

Last night I dreamed of you—the third time this week. A thick envelope from you had reached me. (There was a green stag on the stamp—I had already had one dream about a stag. I'm afraid that when I dream about a stamp with a stag on it, it's very likely that I'll have to wait a long time for your reply—assuming that you ever do reply.) I undid the string and kept unwrapping more and more paper, and I could not get to the inside to read what you had written.

I don't know why I feel so uncomfortable writing love letters. I suppose I should have taken Balzac

or Stendhal as a model. Like Andy (although he's
not your idea of what a man should be), I know
that love—the kind of love I'm capable of and the
kind I need—can only be paid for by love. You like
strong people who don't feel sorry for themselves.
I hope that one day I will be strong enough. I do
not want to live on my knees, or beg. I am still convinced that the best is still ahead of me. (I try to
convince others of it too.) I carry around a vision
of a world where no one goes away. A vision of
visions that do not melt, with a hope that does not
collapse like a house of cards into fragments, into
illusions that turn into lies? Some lasting inspiration. It is not just a room with a white stove,
books, windows with white curtains. A bathrobe
that smells of apples, pure water, and you. Full of
light. And your first love waiting for you. You see,
then, that my stars are kind to me, and that hard
upon the heels of the fat nights come the nights of
hunger.

I know now, too, that the less I say to you, the
more willingly you listen, and that the closer I
seek to hold you, the further you back away from
me. Would I be the same if I were a man? Would
you try to make me laugh again if I broke down and
wept in front of you? You know I don't cry.

I suppose that your bags are already unpacked.
You are like an iceberg, D.E. With other people I
only need to know a little to imagine the rest. It is
different with you: in spite of the fact that I know
so much about you, I know only a little. Are you
afraid of me? I've heard that men do fear women.

I can guess why, and also what it is they are afraid of. The worst of all prejudices is that everyone has gotten what he deserves. The second worst is that there is always, somewhere, someone who knows why. Finally, I am bothered by the question: How come one can manage a thousand times to part with people, and then the one thousand and first time, it knocks you down?

I hope that things go well for you and the tempo is right. Every day brings what it is here to bring. I force myself to accept it, without getting too excited over it. As the rabbi would say, in Prague XII, where my mother used to go: Life is a mystery and is poetry, and what an old melody needs is a new cadence.

I will miss you when I am away, but I promise you that I will think of lying next to you while I am lying in the warm sand, and dream of bringing you pleasure as I swim in the blue water and feel the coolness swirling against my body. I will remember how you look by candlelight as I look out over the rail of the ship at night and see the vastness of the ocean and the night littered with stars, and I will hear your voice in my ears as I listen to the soft whirring of the engines and the rush of waves against the bow. I'll remember how things taste and smell and feel so I can tell you about them when I return, and I will pretend that you will escort me when I am dressed in my favorite satin gown and sparkling jewelry for the evening. So, in your words, "You will be with me." And I hope wherever you are and whomever you are with, I

will be with you, too. (By the way, I will be back
and will be there also.) I hope that we can manage
to see each other to celebrate your birthday,
Hanukkah, and the New Year together. What a celebration that should be.

I'm sorry that I won't be with you on your birthday, but I will drink champagne in your honor on
that day and love you so much that you are sure to
feel it wherever you are. Then when you or I get
back and we can be together, I'll make it up to you.

Either I am ruthless myself, or I find the ruthlessness of others hard to bear. Sensitivity should
be the most important thing in the world. Sensitivity, and the ability to listen to others—at least, for
a while. So speak to me.

Dita

She knew the letter was wrong. She tore it up and threw it into
the stream. In her castles in the air she thought about a letter to
Herbert Lagus in El Salvador. But she wrote a new letter to D.E.
instead, as if already from San Salvador. She decided to throw
this letter away too.

In the early summer she looked pretty, young, and fresh.
Spoiled and unspoiled at the same time. Nobody should make his
way over corpses, she thought. Not even over one's own corpse.
She smiled to herself and stood up. How to fight for a man? Isn't
it humiliating, too? At least I can be decent. I would like to
receive and to give back, that's all. Or is it? For a split second
she could have sworn she saw D.E. in his white cap. (Maybe it's
my mistake, to sleep with only one man? She knew others were
attracted to her, even though she didn't feel it. But should I use
what I have instead of what I want?)

The gulls, she thought, are like life. They hovered in the air and suddenly swooped down, only to soar again. The thought that lay deepest in her mind, and against which she could find no defense, would not leave her. For a long time she stood there, watching the water.

Pass judgment on no one, and consider nothing
impossible, for everyone has his own potential,
and anything can happen.
—Chief Rabbi of Prague, February 1948

Do not expect an answer to everything.
—Delousing Station advertisement, *Jewish
Gazette*

I still have a few trumps in my hand, and some up
my sleeve,
The cards are still in play,
and what is not today may be tomorrow.
All is as it should be.
Do not worry.
—A girl from Lubliana Street

IV

 Nine months later Dita Saxova sent her first letter from Switzerland. She enclosed a postcard showing the three-pronged peaks of the Matterhorn together with the glacier, with ice on the mountainsides and bare spurs on the peaks. She imagined how Lev Goldblat would display it on the china cupboard. Her letter was to Munk.

I can just hear you saying: The most unfaithful of all women, even to her own ambitions. You must be wondering why I went away. The longer I am here, the more attractive home seems. And at home, as I'm sure Mr. Goldblat says, every dog is like a lion. There are lots of people here who have nothing in common with me and perhaps even more whom I want nothing to do with. It's important to have money here, and people want to know what sort of family you come from. The mortgage on the house I live in is for a hundred years. For heaven's sake, that's ten times ten years, a hundred times a year. Some people plan a hundred years ahead. They already know where their yet-unborn children will live. Nobody seems to bother as much as I do about what's about to happen right now. My now must

seem absurd to people whose nerves are so good
that they arrange loans for a hundred years to
come. But if anyone asked whether I envy them,
and would be willing to exchange my now for their
property and faith in the future, I wouldn't hesitate
for a moment. I suppose it's true what the Italians
say, that people who move from one place to
another change only the stars over their heads, but
not their nature. Once a house is built, death
enters. "Niddo fatto, gazza morto." They also say
that only what's new is lovely. And that it's better
to fall out of a window than off the roof. And every
affair, as Brita says, must come to an end.

Don't worry, I haven't accommodated a brick. On
Monday I met a fellow who had some Polish-Amer-
ican connections. During the war he managed to
escape from Germany to Switzerland, only to have
the Swiss return him to the German frontier. They
refused to accept refugees. They told them, "The
lifeboat is full." Poor things, they even had chocolate rationed. Now they are here, the children who
never in their lives saw chocolate candies, ate a
banana, or saw a puppet show. They made him pay
for the journey. He was not even aware they were
turning him over to the Gestapo. He had believed
that he was on his way to some job.

My fast has just ended. I have put on five and a
half pounds, not, unfortunately, on my face, but on
the other end. I go for long walks and to the theater. I eat à la carte. I sit at the table in accordance
with the set rules, and I dress in the latest fashions. I ruined my chances by telling Andy's joke
about Mr. Novak's boasting that he had been hiding

Mr. Baum in the cellar. "How's that? The war's been over three years." "He doesn't know yet," explains Mr. Novak.

It is the end of idealism. When I wake up and find that the end of the world is upon us, I'll stay in bed, and by lunchtime the situation will more or less have cleared up. Emigrants are like virgins in a dancing class: they have to pretend to be newborn. Forget everything you've ever learned or experienced. Fortunately it doesn't worry me. The greatest mistake you can make is to tell people straight out what you were before. It makes no difference in the way they treat you. I just can't be sure to what extent it's good for me. I don't irritate anyone, because I have nothing. I get by. You would be proud of me. I know how to take care of myself.

The Swiss are a dissatisfied, unimaginative bunch. They work like donkeys and skimp on everything they touch. They rush off to the bank with every centime. Hence the wealth of this beautiful but disgruntled land. There are coins in circulation here dating back to 1830 that are still accepted. Emigrants have had a hard time of it here and still do. It's worse to be a foreigner here than to be a Jew anywhere. There is no appeal against it, nor moral support. What's more, when a Swiss moves to a different canton, he's a foreigner just the same. If you think that's unfair, you are probably right.

Dita had no idea that Munk had sent her a card from Prague at the same time that she wrote to him. He wrote that he missed her and wished her all the best for her nineteenth birthday,

although he said he was a bit concerned about her without really knowing why. He had the kind of faith in her that he had in
grown-ups. He went on to say that her life reminded him of a
person who starts a fire but refuses to begin with kindling. He
wrote about the dignity of life, and that he could not believe that
the world they had known could melt away like the mist. He did
not write that he was afraid that nothing would ever be the same
as it had been before Hitler came. "It is the fate of our children
that is closest of all to our hearts," he wrote. "The world cannot
be so big that we should lose one another."

Through the window in front of Dita ran the white surface of
the valley, all the way up to the mountain. She did not mention
in her letter the behavior of Mr. Zoltan Traubman at the Austri-
an-Czech border when, with his wife, he acted as escort to the
undernourished Jewish children. In České Velenice, when he
discovered that his luggage had not arrived, he lost his nerve
and whispered, "I knew it all the time." Then he went off to hang
himself in the lavatory. She also did not mention that he was cut
down in time and continued his journey in the best of spirits.

On the Swiss side of the border, the quarantine doctor complained about the unruly behavior of the Jewish children. They
refused to be vaccinated or to take the showers they were supposed to have before being admitted to Basel. The doctor shouted, "If they don't stop playing around, take them back to Prague,
and we'll take German children instead." Meanwhile, one of the
Jewish children had asked a German boy, "War dein Vater bei
der Gestapo?" (Did your father serve in the Gestapo?) "Jawohl,"
he said and got his face slapped. In Basel, the group had been
welcomed like long-lost relatives. A reporter from the local Jewish paper had taken charge of Dita. She had worn a travel suit of
gray flannel with a chiffon blouse. The reporter asked whether
there were still Russian troops living in the Prague Castle. Later
he published a three-thousand-word article about her.

"You're very pretty," the reporter told her. "Blue eyes, fair hair, a Slavic type. Almost Swedish." She had refrained from pointing out that a Slavic type was more likely to be dark-haired. In her replies, she had stressed the future—how to protect herself *now*. She remembered how her mother used to say that only a fool tells his entire story; a normal person sticks to the essentials. But her mother also used to say that a human being is like a tree with visible strength and beauty, like a trunk, branches, and leaves, and invisible strength, the roots.

She told the reporter how strange it had felt in 1945 to walk around Jerusalem Street, in the synagogue that the Nazis had not demolished during the war, and to find it empty, without people, like a lamp that had gone out. It had seemed to her that you only had to cross the border to find yourself somehow transported back a hundred years in time. He commented that her eyes were like the fresh wind, the falling snow. She told him that only a cat has nine lives. A human being has to make do with one. She confided in him her vision of "green lakes" and "a path that leads from the unseen to the unknown," from "somewhere to somewhere else." He was interested in whether it was possible to buy objects from the dissolved synagogues, as it was apparently possible to buy people from certain lands. What was important for her? "To be able to come to a decision. To find stability and beauty. To feel the meaning of things. To see and hear as much as possible." She said she would like to believe, if not immediately in God, at least in decency, in a sense in which all people are the same. To believe that tomorrow will be better than yesterday, just as she too would be. She wished to be old, in a hurry. Did she believe that she would live until she was twenty-eight? "Until a hundred and twenty." How did she account for high spirits? She must have been well-bred.

The meadows were fresh and luxurious The colors of the grass and flowers were incomparable. Golden bees, glittering dragonflies, knee-high wet grass, frogs in the fields, and mountains. Her photograph, with the smile she had borrowed from the girl at the Hotel Astoria/Novak, was printed with the article. In the photograph she wore a white blouse with embroidered flowers and leaves, white on white, giving it the effect of lace. She received two copies of the article at Grindelwald, together with a request to acknowledge receipt. Not a word about any fee. "I'm still learning," she said to herself with a smile. After an hour or two of this, she thought, even a smile may be hard to keep up. What does one have to do to live to be twenty-eight? Was she lying, to people, to herself? A little. She had her drums to play.

Outside, the snow fell. Snow made her sleepy. Maybe I was a bear or a badger in a former life, and when I see snow, the air and cold ground weigh on me. I must do something about all this, she told herself. As Isabelle used to say, in a strange environment, people lose their confidence. According to her, three kinds of dreams come true: those you dream early in the morning, those a friend dreams about you, and those you understand in the midst of dreaming them. You shouldn't be afraid even if they tell you you'll be dead tomorrow.

Next time she would write to Lubliana Street that she was opening a bank account and that she would spend the money with D.E. in Paris, or on a trip around the world. She laughed at the thought of all the things she would leave out. The world is turning, so that even by standing still, you still get somewhere.

Through the window Dita could see how the snow had closed in on the three peaks of the mountain, and on the fourth, which soared above them. Perhaps, billions of years ago she had been a lizard, and now she longed for the warmth. In the glacier something cracked. Signals from the center of earth? From somewhere where it was also cold? Several times she had thought of climbing up the glacier, preferably in her shoes with the cardboard soles. These shoes, and the shaved head of Andy Lebovitch, reminded her of Lubliana Street. When would the barbers in Prague stop pointing their fingers at him? Like an Indian, he rarely shaved his face. On the other hand, he shaved his head. Even if she were on Mars or Jupiter, she would remember Lubliana Street. Even if she were gazing at one of Jupiter's moons, she would be reminded of a couple of the bricks, the fallen plaster, the mice—sometimes as large as squirrels. It was a pity she had not brought her shoes with her, and her gramophone, and a few records. For goodness sake, what a thing to worry about at such an hour. As always when she felt herself standing at a parting of the ways, she said to herself, "My girl, you must *do* something about it."

Everyone measures the world with his own yardstick. Why do they say that sometimes one second is more momentous than a whole year? She could visualize Fatty Munk walking about in the house at Lubliana Street with his book, like a traveling salesman of lukewarm water. "I know, Dita. The disease of distrust and isolation is strongest in that handful of you who came back from the war and the camps, too young to be left to your own resources and too grown-up to be looked after." As For-Better-for-Worse always says, the real worry is not that you might drown yourself, but the social stigma of doing so. Those who clutch at hope will be carried off by the wind. Hope is like a tightrope walker who carries a thin pole to maintain his balance.

That's Munk for you. No one can teach an old dog new tricks. Actually, she felt flattered by the fear that her carefree attitude might be genuine. "I must *do* something about it." Why did Munk suppose she was obsessed with the past? D.E. thought so too. Once more she had the feeling that a gigantic cloud circled the earth—fragments of dust, but not from any active volcano, only a silent echo. In her imagination, she saw the dust, and every cubic inch of that multitudinous cloud and every grain of that dust had its name, face, and voice. It was a strange and invisible nebula with two eyes representing six million pairs. She felt her heart beat faster.

There was a motto hanging on the wall: "Ask your parents for their blessing, and climb as far as you can to the top of the mountain." And below it: "A horse fell down from the precipice, but the owner wept." A third, which someone had written with indelible ink: "The best way to deal with anger, grief, and empty pockets is to sleep it off."

She remembered the roots and grass beneath the snow. They say that the best horses come from the plains, but the best riders come from the hills. She felt cheered that beneath the snow lay the awakening earth, life that does not die.

The snowflakes glittered like stardust. It reminded her of when she came to Prague by train in May 1945. Looking out of the compartment window somewhere near the border where the station was crowded with gypsies, she saw the German military units being bombed from the air, so far away that you couldn't hear. You could only see the explosion. It was almost a beautiful sight. The Germans retreated in a hurry. They still held out successfully against the Russians but preferred to be defeated by the Americans. Dita thought to herself: I've got everything wrong. To build a mill you have to have two millstones, as my mother used to say. It's the bottom stone that takes the greater weight. You'll soon find out why it's not turning as it should.

In winter she loved to look at the trees. Now they were quite bare. In the wind and snow they reminded her of women's bodies. Naked, unprotected, exposed to the cold and ice, they stood like the women at Auschwitz-Birkenau, with bare arms, legs, and bodies, silent and isolated in the midst of others. Dita could never admit to herself that the trees could be nothing but trees. No gust of wind, no storm uproots them. Even though no mortal eye may perceive it, no matter how steadily it watches, they grow. And within a year or two the tree is stronger and taller and casts a greater shadow. In Auschwitz-Birkenau she had envied the trees. She wished she could be born and grow like a tree. Or die as they die. Last of all she remembered Dr. Fitz. "Some girls are mysterious," he used to say, "but only until they open their mouths. Please don't pretend to be a sphinx just because you happen to be studying them at school, madame."

"Yes, of course, certainly, doctor."

She thought of Aunt Mimi, almost more often than she had in Prague. Everything temporary holds hands with its older sister: yesterday's transience. Perhaps I should have made my career in the theater, Dita thought to herself. I like acting out my life as if it were a stage where I simultaneously perform and watch my own productions.

Where could Herbert Lagus be now? Everything seemed straightforward to him. Civilization and human consciousness constantly improve. Words express all meanings clearly. Freedom is the easiest existence. Thinking things through from start to finish is better than following instinct. Everything begins and ends. Human beings are the best of all living creatures. Yes, of course, certainly. Should only logical things have priority? Why? Just because!

One Saturday, at a dance at the Café Phoenix, Herbert had been talking about earthquakes shaking the bottom of the Pacific Ocean, far away from the shores, and endangering ships at sea and buildings and people on the mainland. He took pains to emphasize the threat as total, menacing everyone and everything equally. They had chatted as twelve-year-olds do at Hagibór. He had spoken of tidal waves as high as the *Titanic*. Why was everything in Prague finally reduced to the *Titanic*? When the *Titanic* went down, there were probably few people left on deck singing "Nearer My God to Thee" while the people who failed to secure life preservers or places in the lifeboats demonstrated their belief in the findings of the past, present, and future Darwins. They should really ask Mr. Sattler of the Barberina Bar what it was like when he played the violin to "Bei mir bist du schön" on the ramp at Auschwitz-Birkenau for the people on their way to work at the auto works or the Buna Werke, while the rest of them were being carted off in the opposite direction by the Mercedes Benz trucks. (There was a man in Paris with whom he corresponded. He complained to Mr. Sattler that nobody believed him when he told what he'd performed for the elegant and music-loving German SS officers.)

Earlier she had awakened, rubbed her eyes, and looked into the mirror. She felt as if she had disintegrated into a thousand pieces overnight. But the mirror assured her that her face looked rested, with no circles under her eyes. Her looks were fortunate. They had helped her often. She began to comb her hair again. Isn't it true that you see in the mirror what the mirror sees in you? Another little bit of Herbert Lagus's traditional wisdom.

The room was empty; the girls had gone out. She felt only partially satisfied. Did she still expect to be at the center of the universe, as if she were at 53 Lubliana Street or at Theresienstadt, and before that at Hagibór?

She remembered that night when she returned from the evening excursion with David Egon and had run into Fitzi Neugeborn in his pilot's gear. (She had felt naked in front of each man, but in each case it felt different.) Fitzi stood smoking in the corridor, as if by chance. In an offhand manner, he commented that he had just fixed the water pipes, in case she wanted to take a bath. For a while she didn't answer. Then she told him that she didn't owe him anything. She hated false hopes more than she hated her detestable overseer at Auschwitz-Birkenau. Wasn't it more rational to live without hope, as Andy Lebovitch used to say? Everywhere west of the Elbe you had to. The days for imaginative utopia with Munk were over. Instead of replying, Fitzi had begun to whistle the tango tune about the whore and the virgin. She quoted to him a noted writer who said that the tango is the end of capitalism. Why in Prague did boys always think that to dance the tango with a girl for three minutes was enough to make her a whore? With whom had she danced the tango for more than an hour? With D.E. and with Mr. Gotlob.

It was quiet in the house, except for the squeaking of the doors in the changing room below. The language course just now ending had also been attended by female emigrants from Poland, Rumania, and Hungary. It was just like at Theresienstadt between 1942 and 1945, when former cabinet ministers and secret councillors had boasted about how distinguished they had been, the more so as their old glory faded. The more insistently they tried to demonstrate their former distinction, now removed to the world of shadows, the more fervently they came to believe in it. Many of them felt miserable, homesick like fish out of water, and were ill two days out of every three. Those were the days when, as For-Better-for-Worse used to say, the pessimists had departed, and the optimists were dead. This was a favorite saying in the Café Ascherman in Dlouhá Street in the autumn of 1945, after which Andy Lebovitch misnamed For-Better-for-Worse "Fuckluck."

She could hear old Munk speaking. (Of course, yes, certainly, tango and capitalism are dead, and people will discover new dances.) He assured her that she had nothing to lose. Life offers everyone a chance, even if not to the same degree. (Yes, of course, certainly.) What is it? It is like a great boulder: people must strive with all their might and hang on to it. A pity that through distance Munk could not glue together what refused to stick as he wanted, for time passed quickly. What a shame that you cannot get ahead of yourself for a year, for ten years. We just look back at certain things, while others we only dare to imagine. You must be strong, Dita. You are strong, aren't you? Yes, of course, certainly.

Even if she was not strong, at least she was tall. She thought of the houses, streets, and places that had not changed, merely because she herself was now somewhere else. She had a vision of Prague, down on Kampa Island, of the seat where she had written a letter to D.E. Mentally she glimpsed a stretch of the river, of the mills with the steam baths, like a mother gazing at her child, or a child at its mother. She herself had never had a child and no longer had a mother. But it was there that she'd learned whatever those mysteries are that turn a small animal into a human being. All she had was a vivid imagination. Apparently she remembered too well.

D.E. took care not to be cheated out of his sleep. No doubt he got plenty of it in Paris, just as he had done in Prague. For-Better-for-Worse was sorry for children who could not sleep and for old people who slept too much.

In her mind, the recollection of childhood was mixed up with that of war, and the liberation, with all the various armies taking part, together with uniforms, types of currency, pop songs. Then afterward came school, parties, gossip, the boys she had been interested in, and those who had been interested in her. Brita knew what she was talking about when she said sleeping was better than eating. A pity Brigitta hadn't taken her own advice. Avi Fischer used to quote someone who said that legends are outdated gossip. In a few hundred years the juiciest slander becomes history.

The immortality of the individual, of one female soul. One Monday, Andy Lebovitch had tried to seduce her by telling her he felt like a lonely animal in the jungle and by offering to teach her how to play poker. He had his own seven principles: number one, Never show your cards before it's your turn. Dita had asked him whether he wouldn't rather teach her how to box. He put on an exhibition bout before her and knocked himself out in a minute. She recalled the look in his beady eyes under the brow and the gleaming skull when she told him why that wasn't good enough for her. Some days, Room 16 was transformed into a makeshift café within ten minutes, when the boys who regarded themselves as the elite of the young Jewish students would drop in.

She recalled the remarks of that dark-haired kibbutz man who had come from "down there" to recruit new people for the Promised Land (the land with the capital letters). He had talked about the camp for displaced persons in West Germany and about his journey through other camps across Austria and Italy. In conclusion he announced: "The next Jewish government will give every new settler a bed, his first wages, and unlimited residence in one of the tented camps in Palestine," until he can "stand on his own two feet." Dita had been a little disturbed at the thought of so many kinds of camps still waiting for people all over the world, but she didn't want to trifle with mere words. To this the young man replied, "Show me one other country in the world where the grocer stops selling potatoes and begins to argue about Plutarch." The man had strong shoulders and sad chocolate eyes. She could bet her right hand that he was a poet. He said he was a paratrooper. The sun radiated from him. There was something in him she didn't understand.

As Dr. Fitz put it, you just have to keep up the pressure, morning, noon, and night, and so on. That's how it is, and against the wind you can't . . . what? "People soon forget what they don't want to remember." Perhaps the ability to forget is the only form of immortality of which we are capable. Philosophy is no help at this point in time.

Dita said in a low voice to the empty room, "I live here, but I wake up over there." She could have included in her letter that she was fond of waking up to Bachalpsee below the Faulhorn, where the water is as cold as ice, even in the summer. Instead she added:

By the way, I heard about two brothers from Lublin. They had gone to America to join relatives after losing their wives and children. They started a new family in America, except that the younger brother would not speak to the elder. The rabbi called on them to settle whatever it was they had against each other. One day during the war the younger brother returned from work in the quarries to find his wife and three children gone from their quarters. The Germans, in default of a promise not to break up families, had transported them to Sobibór. The younger brother knew that the elder had bought rat poison from the Poles after selling them the family silver for practically nothing. He asked his brother to give him half. "Why?" asked the elder. "Why not?" replied the younger. He sold him half the poison for a golden rouble. The younger brother suffered nothing more than a stomach cramp. He couldn't get up to go to work. The Germans and the Kapo laughed at him. They beat him up for trying to dispose of himself, as if he still held the rights of taking his own life. The other brother admitted he had bought the poison for himself. He did not realize that it was so old.

I don't know anymore about them, though I have heard of two brothers who survived Auschwitz-Birkenau and are now in Canada and are not on speaking terms either. They quarreled over some business matter.

And finally, I've come across a rabbi who collected money for orphans in Palestine and built himself a house with a swimming pool in America. On the other hand, I've met a boy who was promised a trip to Stockholm with the Swedish Red Cross, and he went. Originally, his younger brother had been chosen to go, but his brother refused to believe it. He struggled with the officer. They shot him on the spot. His elder brother went in his place.

It's been snowing all week nonstop. It may be the last of the snow for the season. I am looking forward to the spring, when everything melts. I will stop now, so you don't have to pay extra postage.

Yours,

Dita

Grindelwald, 22 March 1948

2 An hour later it had stopped snowing. The radio blared out from the Bort Restaurant. Dita shrugged her shoulders. She was taking the letter, with the enclosed postcard, to the post office. The pointed Gothic lettering reminded her that the Oberland would still welcome her.

The air smelled of snow. More than ever the mountains looked like a woman. Dita thought about the quantity of rocks up there that had never been measured, and of the evening ahead. There was to be a farewell party at the home of Mr. Jakob Alfred Wehrli, the man who had financed the language course.

She dropped the envelope into the box with a flourish. An American tourist with fair hair and a crew cut came up and spoke to her. "Are you all alone here? I'm very much alone myself."

"I don't think I'm the person you're looking for," she replied.
"When I came out, it was still snowing. It's cleared up now.
There's a nice smell to snow, don't you agree?"
She felt like saying that she was waiting for the thaw. She
walked away from him with her eyes fixed on the rocks and
woods above them. From out of nowhere the American said,
"Good luck to you."
There were two letters waiting for her at the hostel. The first,
decorated with huge stamps, was from El Salvador. Inside were
some snapshots of a new house with a flat roof, suitable for sun-
bathing, or for mounting a machine gun, as in the news shots
from Palestine. (The poet-paratrooper with chocolate eyes must
have his hands full.) The letter contained a renewed invitation.
The other letter was from D.E. in Paris. (It reminded her of the
correspondence between two former Auschwitz-Birkenau musicians, Mr. Sattler and his French colleague.) Inside was a fifty-
franc bank note, folded twice. He wrote about his new aims, why
he had said farewell to the old life, and that he saw "no reason
to exchange one ghetto for another." Dita blushed. Her fingers
trembled. In opening the letter she tore the envelope with the
return address. Heavens, she thought to herself, as if hearing an
echo. I am not. I know I'm not. But it's the "in between the lines"
that gets you. Ten days before she had written a long letter to
D.E. with a postscript. It included her dreams about him. (Sometimes I have dreams about warm sand. I sink deeper and deeper. The waves just roll over us, so that our bodies are wet and we
stick together.)
   She could imagine herself naked. To a girl, being naked means
waiting, giving and expecting. To offer her soul and skin and
flesh. To advance forward after her retreat from hiding.

   Life is such a circle. There are no really defined
   beginnings and no real endings (at least, so far).

Am I ready for something new? Yes, I think so, but what? For a rock of Gibraltar?

I expect that I'll be seeing you. I am looking forward to that meeting with a mixed sense of anticipation and fear. What will be, will be, I guess. I always do hope for the best but prepare for the worst, so I won't be shocked when and if it happens. A whole nine months apart—but it's a long time. The semester is over. The year is new. Now the month is over. You've been away—and I still love you.

I had a dream last night that you came back and didn't bother to call me. Then I ran into you, and you hurried away with promises to call me when you found the time, but of course you didn't. Then I had another dream that you came back and came to see me right away and told me how much you'd missed me—much more than I knew and more than you thought you would yourself. Then we kissed. In the light I don't feel so alone.

The clouds looked like drifts of plowed snow—uneven, tufted, white, and lumpy—dark on the bottom.

I have a cold and keep sneezing. All I want to do this week is to sit in the sun and feel the warm sand. I hope the sun will clear up my cold and give me inner peace. I long for that.

I've just had a vision of you asking me to enter. How is it you feel so real to me at this moment that I feel I could touch you, and yet you are no more available to me than the clouds drifting by outside this window?

In the end she sent only the postscript. She asked him why it was that she had been happier in Theresienstadt than she was now. She didn't want to think that it was because in the camp she could still, in spite of everything, look forward to seeing one of her own people again, as though it was easier to maintain than her present certainty that no one would come. She wrote him that to this very day she still didn't know the answer he had wanted to hear, if he wanted an answer at all, when they had returned from the Hotel Astoria/Novak, and she had gotten out of the amphibious car at Lubliana Street. His last words had lingered in her mind. She had finally accepted it as a courtly gesture in an interrupted game that was destined to end anyway. She thought of how the next time he'd acted as if they had seen each other only yesterday and had oceans of time before them. He had awakened something within her that had long been dormant and of which she did not want to be reminded. Of course she had felt like every woman who gets brushed aside, especially since she had actually not asked for all that much. It had gone so far that she had almost gone out of her way to insult him. She had done things that she had not counted on, acted almost against her will. After he had left, her departure had been something between a defeat and an escape. Or was it the other way around?

As much as I feel like a frequent part of the society around me, I think that I am overly sensitive to people's feelings. Allowing someone to maintain his dignity is more important than drawing attention to his weaknesses and failures.

Had David Egon Huppert been a kind of mirror in which she saw herself as different from the way she appeared elsewhere, and in which she also saw her possibilities, the woman she might become? Tall, pretty, confident. She could repeat by heart those few moments, minutes, and hours when she felt what love is—how far it can carry you, and what it does to you. Yes and no.

A moment when it was possible to believe in any miracle. The new "I" that discarded the old. No more selfishness. No more discretion. Just the good in life. The voice of shadows, the voice of a voice, the voice of something that does not exist, and the voice of reality—space, closeness. The possibility of a new life. She did not ask him how anyone could reject a person and at the same time want him. "I was so disappointed, but the good-byes aren't supposed to be pleasant. Certainly not. Hellos are for that." Those who throw stones should think of the consequences. She always knew that she had a place to go.

In the postscript that she sent, Dita wrote that she still wanted to believe that the world is good, even for her. It was good. She had known worse times. Italian girls say that a stone is a stone. And a man is a stone. Woman is neither wood nor stone. She had to laugh. Neither grass, nor moss, nor money grows on a stone. There are some things that a person cannot get from himself alone. Nor can he get them only from others.

"I am not," she repeated to herself. "Maybe I look that way, but I'm not."

And then she had a final dream about D.E. He smiled at her and twirled a scarf around his index fingers—first one, then the other. In French, he asked her how she was feeling. She answered, "Fine," also in French. Then in English she asked, "Where are we?"

"At sea," he replied.

"Will we be there long?" she asked.

"Do you have some place you need to go?" he asked her.

"No," she replied.

"Then stay with me," he said. "I won't hurt you."

"All right," she said. "But I don't have any other clothes."

"What you're wearing is fine," he said. "But out here you don't need any clothes."

"But how will I fly?" she asked. She felt anxious.

"You don't need this dress to fly," he said to her. "Take it off and give it to me."

"All right," she said.

Then he tugged at the scarf, and the dress fell away. He took off his clothes, and they lay together on the deck in the sun and the breeze. He fell asleep holding on to her ankles while resting his head on her legs. (Is that even possible?) She woke up curled into a ball.

In another, unsent letter, she wrote:

> Fragments do not a story make. I am missing you lately, D.E. In many ways I have been proud of myself for my overall ability to cope without you this time. I am not breathless with yearning for you as I was last summer. Of course much has happened since last summer to strengthen my defenses against you and the agony I so often have felt because of you. But this isn't to say that I don't miss you. Because I do. I think I miss you on a more profound level now. I suppose because I love you on a deeper level, the lines of my experience with loving you have deepened; hence, so too have the levels on which I feel for you.
>
> I am reading much poetry these days. You said you went to Chinese poetry in your darkest moments and that it helped save you. I too went to Chinese poetry and now on to Greek and neo-Latin. I am reading all about you in whatever form the poetry takes. White-haired old Chinese men rekindling the fires of youth with a young woman or a young wife. Young Greek and Roman lovers, sequestering their passions until the holy wedding night and the rites of passage from virgin to world-

ly lover. You are in all of it. For me it is all about you.

I suffer slightly when I read about the fire of youthful desire and how this young man calmed his youthful passions with that young lady. I am not with you when you are a young and hungry man searching to soothe your own fires in the fresh dew of young and breathy women.

There is much sexual frustration in poetry. But for me personally there is not much poetry in my sexual frustration. A frustrated lover often turns to poetry for love. As a poet turns to a lover for poetry. Without you here I'm neither a poet nor a lover.

I don't think I've recorded any decent dreams lately. But I've had rich daydreams. One was that when I'm an older woman, I'll be so rich that every year I will put an addition on my house, and from all the carpenters and workmen who work on the addition, I will seduce the handsomest. Then I day-dreamed that I was one of the deceptively inno-cent-looking girls next door who had all the sexiest boys in the neighborhood as dedicated lovers by the time I went away to college. I would make love to them in the toolsheds, behind the wood chip piles, and in their hideouts in the woods.

I have to dream this way because as a woman almost nineteen I come home to an empty house and an empty bed. There are no children to squeal with glee as I walk in the door, no men waiting in my bed. I have only me, and imagination, and a few places that when stroked can ignite the hottest thoughts to warm the coldest of beds.

And then she wrote:

> I've been fighting with this dream, fighting not to
> make it a letter to you. But that's what it is really,
> another of my materializations of the constant dia-
> logue I have with you in my head. And if I'm not
> talking with you, I'm just feeling you. Around me, in
> me, above and below me. Some of the dreams I've
> had lately have really saddened me. So desperate
> have I felt in them, desperate for and without you.
> In the last couple of days, they have settled down. I
> am not waking up from dreaming feeling complete-
> ly despondent. I'm even able to laugh at the latest
> dreams. They always have so many things to do in
> them, so many stories, but lately at least they don't
> break my heart.
>
> I've been staying up late at night. I find some
> inexplicable energy and complete lack of fatigue,
> the way I used to feel when our love was just dis-
> covered. Or rediscovered, as it felt to me after
> years, maybe millennia, of having been cobwebbed
> and lost. Late last night, after having spent the
> entire day alone with only a brief trip to the gro-
> cery store, I was in the bathroom, and the only
> light in the apartment came from the dim bulb next
> to my bed. It cast a weak shimmer on the wood
> floor in the hall. I thought of a pond at sunset, or
> the shore on autumn evenings. I thought of what
> my life feels like without you: Sometimes the dark
> rushes in and fills everything up like the first rush
> of high tide. A dark murkiness gushes in and fills
> every hole, every crevice, so powerfully, so pro-
> foundly, until it feels like it will always be this dark,

this murky. Even when some vacuum from beneath the shore sucks it all back out until it looks as dry as if there hadn't been any water there at all, I still feel the possibility of it rushing in again, the possibility of there being only two ways of living—flooded either with murky darkness or with the dread of waiting for it to return.

I had another observation. If I can call it that. It occurred to me that life is but a battle between the practical and the romantic, the real and the surreal. The clash is when they butt into each other and are forced to blend, to coexist inclusively. Most people keep their romantic life, if they are lucky enough to have one, in the closet where they go when no one is around and pull it out of its oaken box and fondle it. As soon as they hear someone coming, they shove it back in the box, which they close and lock and then push under a pile of unused sweaters or handkerchiefs or socks. I can't do that. I can't hide my soul in a closet and pretend that it is wrong or bad or at least undesirable. I carry it inside me, sometimes even outside me, where it slips into sight and causes a furor, where people scorn and condemn me, some overtly, some tacitly, but the effect is the same. I retreat deeper into my soul, my bulletproof soul, which I told you about once, about how I had picked its essences from the many potpourri jars of the soul-conjuring alchemist. And my soul takes me to those places deep within me and far far away from me where I find myself and lose myself at once, and I become part of the greater me in balance with whatever is even greater than that, where no practicality exists, where it doesn't even have meaning and where the only real part of being is that I know that even this bliss is only bliss because I will have to move on and on. And that on and on will sometimes take me to the reality where again the romantic is not revered, not prized, and rarely even given place to exist. And that is what I have to deal with with you. For you are my everywhere and my nowhere, and I love you beyond any and all its boundaries. But I don't enjoy it when life slips in between us and pulls the romance out of you and tears the romance from me and makes us people we are supposed to be by convention. And I wonder how it is that convention hasn't killed me yet. And I remember that that is the battle of my life, not to let it kill me but to fight it until its death and not mine. And then, and probably only then, will I go on to the next level and all the levels beyond that. And I will never fight these battles again.

3 Dita Saxova appeared at the party wearing a light blue taffeta gown with white accessories. Lately she dressed in Zionist white and blue, except for the black lizard handbag she had bought with the last of her pocket money. (Easy come, easy go, is my main asset.) It was a pretty dress. The girl who, among other things, cleaned the language school had helped her to make it. Dita was able to talk with her in broken Italian. For-Better-for-Worse would have been delighted. A white line on a white stone. She told the girls that at Auschwitz-Birkenau in 1944 she had managed to get a piece of material that had meant a great deal more to her then. "Figlie a ventri son sempre pericolo." Girls and widows are always in danger.

She smiled and greeted people she did not know. The ballroom was already filling up. She heard snatches of conversation: "Never? *Never* is a big word." And an Italian boy: "A fiume turbido guadagna il pescatore." (The best fishing is in troubled waters.) Someone answered him: "Città che vai ragazza che trovi." (Different cities, different girls.) Then she heard someone speaking in German: "Wer zwei Hasen auf einmal jagt, fangt keinen." (Chase two hares, and you'll catch none.)

A fair-haired young man in gray trousers and an English blue blazer with gold buttons reminded her of Neugeborn. "Somewhere they unearthed a prehistoric flea that had been petrified for millions of years. And in New Zealand, or Patagonia, they've found dead whales that had swum into shallow water, though they must have known they would die. Up to a few hundred years ago they had never been caught. Whales seem to do that from time to time." He had childishly large blue eyes; his hair lay in shining waves; instead of a tie he wore a red cravat. Dita looked at herself in the mirror.

"Nobody knows why," added the young man. "Once they found a parasite in the ear of the leader of a pack of whales. It was an inch-long worm that may have impaired its navigational ability. Whales also apparently call to each other playfully at a distance of six thousand miles under water. Nowadays, they probably disturb the communications of submarines, passenger liners, tramp steamers, and warships, which sometimes outnumber the whales. And some children drink a fatal disease with their mother's milk. There's no way of preventing it." He glanced around the room. "Why is it that some people, when they arrive, immediately look as if they've been dead since last Tuesday?" He had a pleasant masculine smell of eau de cologne.

A couple of people of Dita's own age stood in the corner. Dita heard a name and turned toward the voice that had spoken it.

"Andy," a girl said, "I thought you were in Australia."

"I'm not. I stayed here. Things got better for me after the races," the youth answered. He had a chestnut-colored mustache and looked like an oaf.

"You found a woman?"

"Yeah."

"No. How old?"

"Forty."

"Rich? Married?"

"Yeah."

"How many kids does she have?"

"Four."

"But Andreas, why are you starting that all over again?" It reminded Dita at once of the things Linda Huppert used to say about her last winter at 53 Lubliana Street, including the rumor about her affair with the gigolo at the Jewish bar.

Later the girl said, "I like her, but I don't trust her." It seemed to Dita a comical remark. She glanced at the girl's companion. The girl still talked to the boy with the mustache. "A wolf never allows his running mate to eat a lamb, Andy. Even two fish frying in the pan don't trust each other."

"How far would you go in my place?"

The girl hesitated, searching for a reply. "About as far as I'd go in believing every word a beggar told me, or somebody I met on the sidewalk, Andy."

"Seeing is one thing. Hearing is another," the youth said.

"Now I can understand why people are so frightened of going crazy," Dita observed.

"It's not as sudden as it looks," said the young man who looked like Neugeborn.

"I suppose not," Dita agreed, and she watched as the girl facing the fellow with the mustache crouched like a tigress preparing to leap and scratch out the fellow's eyes. Instead, she saw tears in the girl's eyes. The boy with the mustache threw his arm around her shoulders and led her off to the cloakroom. Slim in the hips and broad-shouldered, he looked like a skier. He changed steps twice to accommodate his walk to the girl's short steps.

"Are you superstitious?" the young man who looked like Neugeborn asked.

"More and more all the time."

"How do you account for it?"

"How about you?" Dita Saxova tried to imagine what she was so unsure of. Her eyes reflected her watchfulness, nervousness, laughter. She felt something in the air. Something she had to do. The necessity for some basic change. Tomorrow "real life" would begin, "standing on my own two feet." She turned away from the mirror, gilt-framed and curved in the Venetian style.

The young man like Neugeborn commented, "Someone said that what is true doesn't always need to appear probable. Le vrai peut quelquefois n'être pas vraisemblable."

"Maybe," Dita said. She stayed by his side. "There must be at least ninety-three girls here, don't you think?" She glanced all around and behind her into the adjoining rooms.

Instead of answering, the young man asked, "Do you like clean things?"

"Do you like whales?" She favored him with her innocent smile.

"I'm crazy about them." The youth turned toward her. "But I wouldn't say no to Chinese shark-fin soup."

Laughter mingled with the reproach in Dita's eyes. "Isn't it strange that in a different language, you become a different person?" she said in French.

The young man also glanced around the room.

"In some languages, a person almost disappears." Dita added. "He begins like a human face, and then merges, let us say, in a picture. Everything becomes smoother, for the sake of the others."

"Don't you feel that this is like a luxury express train that has just stopped at a junction?"

"A junction? Where to?" She smiled.

"It all depends on how much money you've got. I know a nice song about money."

The young man's eyes swept over the small knots of people, and he said, "Fortunately, nothing is doomed to destruction from the very start. And only animals feel their isolation." He smiled. It sounded as if he'd said "criminals."

"I've read that only an animal has a soul that cannot make contact with another soul," she replied.

"Have you ever woken up in the middle of the night sweating all over and trembling with fear?"

"And now you'll ask me whether I get wet and dry all by myself. Do you want to know if I wring myself out too? Maybe you'll just ask me next whether I'm really speaking to you?"

The young man like Neugeborn took it all in. His eyes lit up. He looked at her in the way a sailor looks at a big ship, a great danger, or a raging storm. She was startled. She drowned his sudden interest with her own laughter.

A couple in evening dress danced nearby. Dita remembered the letters in her handbag. She caught herself thinking about how people try to win some lasting form of happiness, and maybe that's what makes them seem like lost souls.

The chandeliers glittered. There were flowers everywhere. Moonlight shone through the curtains. Chalky white snow covered the mountain peaks. Pines and fir trees grew near the house, and they swayed gently in the breeze.

At the front of the reception room someone made a speech. Suddenly Dita closed the gap between the echoes of 53 Lubliana Street and the speaker, a short fat man in a Sudeten German plaid waistcoat and a Bavarian tie. "We shall return to our places, ladies and gentlemen," the man said.

The young man next to Dita commented, "Too many captains

sink the ship. Only occasionally does the wind blow as the sailors wish."

Someone said to an exquisitely dressed girl, "You're so pretty." She answered, "What good is that to me? It won't feed me or pay my rent, electric, or heating bills." She smiled briefly. "I want happiness. Surely it must be possible for a person to be happy if they've never harmed anyone." And then, "Why is it that things are never as they seem? Or as people pretend them to be?"

The man said, "Do you know what it means to be rich? Freedom of choice." Then he went on, "Money makes it easier." And finally, "Shortage of money comes in waves. Everybody feels it, even the richest. It all works out in time. Either you pay out what you've got, or you don't pay. The problem goes away, until it starts all over again." They danced past, out of earshot.

Two middle-aged men in three-piece salt-and-pepper suits sat at a table with an Aladdin lamp and roses in a Chinese vase. They sipped whiskey. One of them said, "Every night her husband used to shout at her, 'Can't you get rid of her, for God's sake?' It took twelve years before she could shake her mother's ghost out of their bedroom and sit at the foot of the bed or the side where she slept. 'How can anybody concentrate on making love to you,' said her husband, 'when you bring into the bedroom everyone you remember?' She stared at him and asked, 'Doesn't everybody?'"

The young man who looked like Neugeborn turned to Dita. He sized her up for a moment. "Some people seem to have the basic instinct of migratory birds. They hardly touch the ground. Most of the time they are in the air."

"Even when dancing by themselves?"

"Even while jumping up to the ceiling."

"Life is short," Dita said. "And some birds have to fly halfway around the world to reach home."

"Even farther, if you want to know the truth. Some birds fly from north to south around the Cape of Good Hope, and in spring they fly back—not only to the land they came from but to the same tree, the same branch, the same nest."

"Who knows where a person feels most like himself?"

The young man like Neugeborn fastened the two gold buttons on his blue jacket. "Do you like fairy tales?"

"I do. But not the German ones with cruel endings."

"Doesn't everybody get what he deserves?"

The glare of the lights reflected in the darkened windows.

"What do you think of the weather?" she asked.

"Lots of people will never live to see the spring. When winter ends and spring is on the way, changes take place in the trees' sap and the people's bloodstream. There is a lot of sickness. Only the healthy and the strong survive. And so on, until the next spring comes around again." Then he said, "Old people believe that the value of human life sinks in proportion to aging."

"Are you such an expert?" Dita laughed.

The young man really did remind her of Neugeborn. This was just how Fitzi would have looked if he had been born here instead of on a small, narrow street in Prague. Now the fat man spoke about the purity of Western civilization and its flawless nature, which had to be guarded just as in the time of Torquemada. He spoke in French, and he acted like a man who knew what he was talking about, as if his warnings had several times been vindicated. The orchestra resumed playing.

"You have a nice bracelet," the young man said.

"Thanks."

"You are one of the prettiest girls here."

"Don't exaggerate."

It seemed as if she really had two souls. She could hear the voice of Munk saying that he too was getting ready for spring. Soon the snow will have melted, Dita. She smiled. The young man like Neugeborn presumably didn't understand why she smiled. D.E. had said to her, "You can be relied upon, because you don't need anyone." Andy had recommended that she only play the games she was sure of winning.

"I think it's my turn to have my feet stepped on by dancing, and to pardon it in advance," Dita said to the Neugeborn-like young man.

She had her eyes on her host's two sons. They were identical twins. Their mother was a platinum blond. The woman's escort said, "Both your children look marvelous, madame. It's a wonderful thing you are doing."

"Flattery will get you nowhere, my dear," the twins' mother said.

Dita waited for the introductions to end. It was different from the parties, theaters, and nightclubs in Prague. The two letters she carried in her handbag had a bearing on each other. D.E. had worked himself into a position at the office of the European headquarters of the International Blue and White Union. The bank note, enclosed like a bandage on her lamentations, served only as a soothing balm on his announcement that by the time the postman delivered her last letter, he had been "happily married" for all of two hours.

"Would you like some wine?" the waiter asked.

She strolled through the adjoining room, holding her crystal goblet. Another waiter addressed her, "Would you care for some dessert?"

"No, thank you," she replied.

She ran her hand down her hip. The Neugeborn-like young man winked at her. They gazed at each other as if they were looking into a mirror. She walked over to him with a swaying motion. He came to meet her.

Dancing had begun in the middle room. She put her handbag on a small table near the window, where brocade drapes were

held back by fringed gold cord. The young man led her into a
waltz and held her courteously. "You dance very well," he said.
She only smiled. Her long arms and tapered fingers appealed
to him.

"Is your head spinning around too?"

"I'm very dizzy," Dita answered. "It's like looking at one thing
and seeing another." She closed her eyes. "It's not a wheel. It's
a river, flowing gently, and I'm not sure where it's going."

When the dance ended, the young man escorted her to a table.
She picked up her handbag.

"Are you really so superstitious?" he asked.

"In the Middle Ages they would have burned me at the stake."

"At your own expense," he added.

"How do you mean?"

"You're looking at me as if you'd seen everything turned to
ashes several times over."

"I hope not."

"Your eyes are soft and warm. You've got very blue eyes."

"I hope you didn't mean what you said about the fire and ash."

"No," the Neugeborn-like young man said. "It's just a way of
leading you on, as you might say."

"Who told you I wanted you to lead me on?" She gazed into the
mirror and with her hand smoothed her hair. She looked at her
eyes in the mirror.

"Do you have your return ticket?" the young man asked.

"Yes. I have you."

In the intervals between music and dancing, the waiters carried around glass bowls of fruit salad made with almonds,
grapes, egg yolks, cottage cheese, and sugar. It was the first
time in nine months she had tasted it. She didn't feel like dancing with the boy like Neugeborn anymore and avoided him. He
pretended to look at something else.

As soon as she had read D.E.'s letter, Dita had mentally composed "a message filled with humility and love" to Herbert Lagus.

But the youth like Neugeborn soon returned to her side. "I hope you're not bored without me." As if he had come to prevent such a thing from happening, he went on, "Isn't it absurd when they say that the uniqueness of man solely determines the suffering of the soul? As a matter of fact, just this afternoon, I read about the capabilities of the chimpanzee and the dolphin."

Dita did not reply. She gazed at the older, still elegant ladies. They put on a face as though they wished for what had been theirs a long time ago. Isabelle Goldblat had once convinced her that even the oldest women still loved romance, but not their own bodies.

The young man added, "Do you know what monkeys and dolphins hate? Monkeys are crazy about bananas and chocolate, dolphins about herring. Once I stood in front of a monkey cage eating a banana and didn't give them any of my chocolate. I waited for one of them to start crying. They must be happier than people. Have you heard that skylarks descended from dinosaurs? All living things have to adapt."

"What, for instance?"

"I hope you've nothing against chameleons."

"Not at all." She recalled what Brita had said on her last day in Prague.

"It's said that just like all other creatures, they are quite all right until they begin to doubt the meaning of their own existence."

Dita reflected that from the start there had been two D.E.'s in her life. She too probably had two lives in D.E.'s eyes. (Once Tonitschka asked her why she didn't fight harder to get D.E. "I don't know," she answered. "It humiliates me. I want to, and I know I should. And at the same time I don't.")

A soprano from the Berne Opera sang a folk song about a path in summer. She stood in front of the microphone in her close-fitting dress of green silk and her golden slippers. The song reminded Dita of a print she had received from Munk on her eighteenth birthday, which Brita had used to light a fire. It was entitled "A Summer Morning." Dita could not decide which vision, each drawn from reality, to reject first. The wine had flushed her cheeks. Her eyes shone; her body swayed. She walked across a thick carpet patterned in the shapes of snakes, birds, and trees. On the walls hung tapestries embroidered with shepherds and sheep, hunting scenes, dogs, and horse riders.

Dita listened to the soprano. Whenever her thoughts strayed in the direction of D.E. and herself, she felt as if she were unconscious, listening to some secret refrain in which she had a part, but one of unequal importance to his part. To her, D.E. seemed to be just as guilty as he was innocent. Of course there were also two Dita Saxovas. What did they mean to D.E.? What had she spoiled that day in the hotel room? Was she also both guilty and guiltless?

The voices seemed so loud that she could hardly believe she was the only one who could hear them. They sounded like an explosion tearing through the earth and stars, sending a cold blast of air out into the universe. Each of the voices floated around her as though reverberating within the shell of a nut, or like some distant sun containing within it another sun, like something she had read about in one of her favorite books. Amid her own silence she heard her own voice and the echo of D.E.'s voice. It didn't matter what he was saying at all. There was fear in the song for something she thought would have no place in her future.

As Dita listened to the Swiss singer, she felt as if the woman were imposing on the aria some song of her own that was, for a moment, stripped of its own melody, just as a person strips before going to bed, as if nakedness suddenly had assumed the role of words and music.

She tried to laugh and found it easy. D.E. had bought a Renault sports car that, as he wrote, was not in the same class as his old KDF. He said, "Farewell to sentimental memories" that could only "get in the way of" the concentration that was "so vital to the tasks of the new generation." He had underlined the words *logic* and *reality* in his dictionary. He wrote that if ambition was like an arrow pointing the way ahead and giving a man no time to turn aside, then the further he went the more ambitious he was.

It was both sincere and pompous, just like D.E. himself. He hardly needed to mention that he had resolutely said good-bye to his past and broken off an already infrequent correspondence with his stepsister, and also that he felt much more mature than the French people of his generation. In the end, he wrote, all of them, regardless of what they said or pretended, were one-sided, prejudiced first by their own selves, then by their careers, and then by their possessions. It was human nature. It would be a lie to deny it and absurd to feel guilty about it.

"The end of idealism," she said below her breath. No one listened. "Life begins now."

The young man who looked like Neugeborn retreated behind her. "Do you know what Americans say? They used to say that it is better to wish you had not than to wish you had."

Dita smiled. The young man had disappeared.

D.E. assured her that, whatever happened, they would continue to be friends. She thought back on all the time she had spent with him. Each time they met she had varied her behavior, probably in a way that repelled rather than attracted him. Had she lacked the love that might have shamed him and made him afraid to betray her? Perhaps he had failed to find in her enough bravery. She had not inspired in him a state of mind that made life easier for him. At first she had been too patient—had waited for too long—until D.E. for the second time had been frightened off. Then she herself had seduced him, which may have led him to doubt her.

We forgive a friend everything: behavior, folly—what was the third? We are not ashamed of him, whatever he does. She could just imagine how he would behave if they were to meet here. Would she just act crazy, laugh aloud? Feign forgiveness and bitterness? To conceal her feelings, would she press his hand at least? To say good-bye to a man means to admit you have made a mistake. Between wounded vanity and a broken heart there is not a great deal of difference. Failure of magic. Trieste. We did not make it. You will not be the father of my children. You will not comfort me. We shall not grow old together. I shall not be the one to touch you when you are troubled.

Her eyes grew soft. Saying good-bye meant that there was nothing left to remember but the hand that had lain upon her hip as she closed her eyes. She knew that the same hand existed, but very far away, and that it comforted, teased, and caressed someone else. The letter she had written ten days ago expressed things D.E. would never know, because she had not sent it. Her heart raced. The palms of her hands sweated. She felt as if she were being carried away by a stream, far from the people she did not want to lose. D.E. had definitely cut her out of his future plans.

For a moment longer she thought of his presence, which would also mean the presence of his wife and her father. D.E. would pretend to watch her jealously, even if the poor creature could not take a step without the aid of a crutch. He would forgive her father anything, even if he were an armaments king.

It was all different from what the green-clad soprano from Berne sang about. A force flowed into her from D. E. Huppert, regardless of his character or their experiences of mutual contact. Perhaps the same force flowed from her into him. It was an invisible, intense energy that could not be expressed but that existed nevertheless.

Dita heard applause. The audience smiled, and the singer bowed.

Dr. Fitz had once told her the story of a farmer who plowed when a thunderstorm came along. Lightning struck the plow, and in an instant the farmer suffered all the horrors that she could well imagine. But he survived. The next time it happened he was ready for it.

The next act on the program after the singer was a band in evening dress. Dita reminded herself of the pointlessness of it all. Everything that had ever happened in her life had occurred only once. Attempts to repeat an experience never succeeded. There are two kinds of fidelity, as Brita used to say, physical dedication and spiritual attachment. Perhaps one should admit the first, in order to put a deposit on the second? Too many phrases from accountancy had entered her vocabulary. To hell with it! Liars have to expect to be lied to. She felt what everyone must discover individually, what is found neither in books nor in precepts. It was so hot in here. She felt the sweat on the palm of her hand.

She looked around her. She seemed surrounded by waves of heat. The mirrors on the walls reflected back to her all the varieties of smiles that she wore like armor. She felt as if she were touching herself. When you feel poor, does everyone else seem rich? When she was a little girl, her mother had taught her that she must always conduct herself as if someone were watching and learn to behave like a "young lady on every occasion."

The blue dress appreciably enhanced the blueness of her eyes. The arc of her smile was like a rainbow whose invisible half completes a circle.

A woman who looked very Jewish, wearing a cross on a golden chain, spoke in French to her dancing partner. "Maybe you were never home enough to see the charms of everyday things. You can't leave when you were never there in the first place." And later: "Il ne faut pas avoir deux poids et deux mesures." (One man's food is another man's poison.) Her companion said, "In five minutes we can talk in bed."

4 The fat man from the former Sudetenland asked her for a dance. They played an English waltz. When he asked her in French with a guttural German accent, "May I have the pleasure?" she could smell that he had swallowed the last of the smoked salmon. He kissed her hand. His cheeks were as pink as the sliced fish.

"My name is Kaiser," he introduced himself, "a sort of drill instructor in commercial practice with 150 employees. The only reliable criteria are based on military achievement: ex-officers are ideal. Analytical powers, singleness of purpose. But some people are always overly sensitive where our unspoiled and basically good little world is concerned." He added, "It's a lovely evening, young lady." He looked as if the full moon reminded him of yesterday and tomorrow. When Dita did not offer to give her name, he said, "Do you believe that the present is important? Your arms are like the necks of two swans, Fräulein."

"Are you here with your wife?" Dita asked.

He gave a conspiratorial smile. "As it happens, last Monday at a graduation dance in my hometown I met a girl I used to go to school with. Once we thought of getting married. It was a beautiful love affair, as the saying goes. She had the same blond hair and blue eyes that you have."

"You don't dance badly either."

"What do you think of America, young lady?"

"Why?"

"We can't let the Americans stab us in the back, as they did after the First World War."

"I think I'm immune by now."

"If we learn to lie well enough and don't leave all the lying to others, we shall all live to see better times. May I have the pleasure when they play a polka?"

Should she ask him whether he wore his old military medals under his jacket? *Für treue Dienste in der SS,* for instance.

He was quite a respectable dancer. The smell of his eau de cologne made her dizzy. She could visualize him in Auschwitz, directing her toward the showers. He wouldn't have wasted time then over the color of her eyes or the shape of her arms.

"You remind me of something," he said. "Spring 1945, when the Russians occupied Bismarck von Osten's castle in Pomerania. There wasn't a single German man there."

"Had they all run away?" Dita smiled.

"The castle was being looked after by Frau Hofeditz and her seventeen-year-old daughter, Gerda. An excellent future lay before her, irrespective of how the war went for Germany. One February night a couple of trucks with men drove into the courtyard. They raped Frau Hofeditz, her daughter, and anything in skirts. The name of the place was Plathe. No one could imagine how both those ladies must have felt when they learned that they had gotten a disease as old as the history of rape. They were treated by a Jewish doctor, a Mr. Arndt, who had spent six years living in hiding, like a German submarine. They have many people underground."

Dita watched as he patted his mat of hair. She could imagine him in some punishment camp, striding along, well fed and energetic, complacent with the vision of the next thousand years of the German world, wearing a uniform made for him by some Jewish subhuman and carrying a nine-millimeter Parabellum automatic and a riding crop with a little lead ball at the end of a whip braided of curly black hair. He probably wouldn't have been so fat in those days and wouldn't have complained about losing memory. Dita recalled the public execution of K. H. Frank

in Prague, an event to which Neugeborn and Andy had devoted
two seconds of their valuable time on their way to the Medical
House to arrange a boxing bout. Apparently K. H. Frank had spat
in the face of the executioner, and the hangman had punched
him in return. That was as much as Fitzi and Andy had been willing to tell, and only after a considerable lapse of time. It
occurred to her that the fat German might have spent the war in
Norway or Sweden. Who could tell? Should she ask him? He
might very well tell her himself.

The fat man smiled at Dita and added, "The young woman told
the doctor about her sleepless nights, and how she was covered
in cold sweat whenever she heard the sound of an army truck.
She described how her mother had tried to commit suicide.
Shame killed her in the end. They buried her in the castle cemetery."

Even now Dita did not reply. She lowered her chin and gazed
at the fat man's benevolent expression. It was a look like that of
a bull gazing at a toreador, or a dog preparing to bite. Was the
kind gentleman going to tell her next that what had happened
yesterday was no longer relevant to today? Or that, in the common interest, they shouldn't allow themselves to be weakened
by yesterday's definitions of good and bad, right and wrong,
because such categories were, to put it mildly, out of date? Was
it still just a question of one and one, us or them, yesterday or
tomorrow? Would what had happened one day eventually seem
like an innocent Sunday compared with what was still to come?

Sound, colors, and movement merged with the rhythm of the
dance. The rooms filled with music and light.

"After a while the doctor noticed a change in the girl's behavior. Even as she described how the soldiers had raped her
against the wall over and over again, she smiled and cut a notch
in the door. She infected seventy-five soldiers. In the courtyard
before she was killed, she said that it was for her mother's sake,

and that she did not want to go on living either."

"Who?"

The question took the fat man by surprise. What kind of punishment had he pronounced for the infection of the seventy-five soldiers and the weakening of the occupation army? Dita laughed. He reminded her of the German officer at Auschwitz-Birkenau who always had some apt comment for them. "Not bricht Eisen." Necessity breaks iron bars.

Then he said, "Last week one of your colleagues told me in the pub here what great times they had in the East. In Bucharest he had been entertained all night in the best hotel for three marks. He never had to dirty his own hands, as he put it. Antonescu insisted that nobody can touch his inferior race. He will attack their pockets, in the best tradition of striking an inferior race at its most sensitive point. In the Ukraine his friend had lived like a pasha on ten marks. The farther east, the better. In Lembeck he had an unforgettable time for fifteen marks: geese, ducks, chickens. White flesh less than nineteen years old—apparently dark-skinned girls mature by the age of twelve, thirteen at the most. (In the German brothels twenty-year-olds were regarded as too old.) Gypsy, Ukrainian, and Rumanian orchestras, violins and cymbals. Deer cooked in cream, mutton, wild boar, fish, meat, game. Apparently the girls were let out of the field brothels into the corn fields each morning, and they were allowed to shoot them like pheasants. They were finished anyway, after one night."

The fat man looked at her curiously, with a steady gaze. Or maybe he searched for something in himself? She stared straight back into his eyes. This was yet another thing she had not anticipated last year. Would such people continue to be her destiny? Or would she be theirs?

"I didn't ask for details," Dita said. "He just smiled. If I had the patience to wait, he told me, I would see some new perfor-

mances. And some new people in the camps that had been temporarily vacated. He warned me not to be surprised."

"You can't believe everything you hear, kid," the fat man said
benevolently. "War is war."

They danced past the tapestry with the hunting scene.

"Ladies and gentlemen," announced their hostess, "ladies'
choice." Her husband led her out onto the floor.

Dita looked toward the two brothers. She continued to smile,
and her eyes sparkled. She went out to the balcony. She looked
into the parquet and saw her own reflection upside down.

Above her head the stars shone brightly. She felt homesick for
the Slavic leisureliness, though she never missed German thor-
oughness. She asked herself what was so Jewish within her,
even though she was blond and did not pray.

It was not yet completely dark outside. The moon glittered like
a piece of ice. She imagined Slavic woods and meadows, gentle
slopes and rises, some fragment of the Slavic spirit that pervad-
ed her being and had mingled with whatever Jewishness was
within her, and what was German too—for she had lived too
long in Germany and occupied Poland during the war for that
not to have left its mark. What summary can explain a person?
Character? Date of birth? Career? All that he dreams about,
what he detests? All that he accomplishes? All the places visited
and still to be seen, ambitions, beliefs sometimes lurking deep
below the surface, things forgotten and memories preserved—
the entire package.

It struck her that the fat man was quite capable of blaming the
gasometer for the loss of all the people who had been swept off
the face of the earth. To him, everything that belonged to yesterday was dead. The earth is the dominion of the living alone.
To live means to win. For people like him, to get killed means to
lose. The gas of yesterday was for him a guarantee of cleaner air
today and of an unpolluted atmosphere tomorrow. He did not

bother to turn back, even in thought, to his yesterday; he marched on confidently toward his tomorrow. Was there any point to asking about the value of one human life? For many people the life of another person means less than last year's snow. Sometimes it does not even mean very much to the person involved. He has to be alone for a long time before he discovers it.

She watched the crests of the woods swaying in the wind. The branches were hung with snow. From the fire in the adjoining room, out of sight, light came flooding out into the night air. The stars looked like fishes washed up on the shore. They lay motionless. She imagined the voice of fire, which sounded like the gulping of water, or washing hung on the line to dry, creaking in the wind. The sounds of the flames devouring each other. She visualized the glowing ash dropping through the grating into the fireplace and turning black. As she gazed into the night at the snow and wood, she saw ash before her eyes. She remembered Kitty Borger and the people who had left for Australia after the war, how pregnancy had changed Doris Levit. There are other things too that bring about a change in girls. Not only Brita, with her two of three "horrible" days. She felt the breeze from the valley on her face. An icy wind blew off the glacier. With it came the indefinable scent of the spring and meadows. Before her eyes the world rolled on through the thin star-filled darkness illuminated by the snow. She experienced the strange tension felt by people who intuitively sense what may happen but at the same time feel as if it had nothing to do with them. The evening swam through the mountains, touching the night and etching faint patterns of light. Stars began to appear in circles around the moon.

That was how the spring came every year. People always longed for things to change for the better, when at the same time their minds were busy with thoughts of money and connections. It would be fine to have plenty of money. A hundred times, a thousand times greater than the bank note from D.E. And without the humiliation of asking for it. Or stealing it, as Neugeborn had thought of doing last year. Certainly, when you're rich there are plenty of friends, but with poverty comes loneliness. She stretched out her arms into the darkness. On her back she felt the warmth of the room. She drew into her lungs the cold breeze from the glacier, and she knew in her heart that she could stand there for an hour and finally be abandoned.

5 "Why did you go outside?" a voice came from behind her. "Aren't you cold?"

"There was a door here," she announced with a smile. Something had replaced the feeling of superiority in her voice when she had talked to the fat German, and the impatience with which she had last spoken to the young man who looked like Neugeborn. "A lioness doesn't feed herself on little herbs," she added.

They took her inside and showed her through the house, pointing out the pictures in the corridors and anterooms. She looked at one of the paintings.

"Salvador Dalí, father's pride," the second brother said. "This one is by Hieronymus Bosch. Four hundred thousand marks."

"Do you know Kafka?" the first of the brothers asked. His voice was deeper.

"As well as I know myself."

"There's never been anyone here from Prague before," the other said.

"Did you have any problems getting here?" the first brother asked.

"I only know that in Basel two Italians almost got into a fight over who was going to carry my suitcase."

"What shall we drink to?" the second brother asked. He nodded to the waiter, who brought three glasses and a bottle of champagne to the table.

"What were you talking about with fatty over there?"

"Nothing interesting."

"When the thaw comes, the path turns to mud, as the Chinese say," the first commented.

The Rumanian girls had asked the pianist to play a polka. Dita drew both brothers onto the dance floor. She could feel their interest and also her own, a feeling that enhances attraction at first sight. Next, the pianist played a polonaise for the Polish girl. The brothers once again called over the waiter to fill their glasses. They danced, all three, to the fast tempo. Dita was very happy to sit down. She was in high spirits, taking this as a good omen for the whole night, for tomorrow, for her whole life to come.

She drained her glass, throwing back her head and letting the wine slip down her throat—to the last drop. She tossed the empty glass into the curtains behind her, and she laughed out loud. When she had recovered her breath, and the brothers waited for what she had to say, she began:

"I met the brother of a wartime friend here. He hadn't heard a word from my friend. He met me by accident. He's a nice man, a painter, very well known now. He carries his whole past around with him. He's not happy, although he owns a white house in a part of the country that looks something like Bohemia. He spends his time in the garden. He has a studio, a gramophone, and records that he plays over and over again. Otherwise he says he wouldn't be able to work. He talks a lot about the Czech countryside and claims that he paints it. It's hard to tell: he paints abstracts. He owns two cars—three really, because he's just bought another for his nineteen-year-old son. He never leaves the house, except in the winter. He owns another house in the city. His wife is Swiss. She keeps worrying about what will happen to the children. They have no grandmother, grandfather, or aunt on his side. Nothing unpleasant has ever happened to her in her whole life, but she has no peace, just because nothing dreadful has happened to her yet. I guess she's the kind of person who can't help sharing in the misery of others. At the same time her husband has never wanted her to feel sorry for him, even if she never said a word. He wanted her to think of him as strong and to admire him, which she did. When I left them I had the feeling for the first time in my life that I envied someone. Not for the white house, or the cars, flowers, and garden, but because that man can do what he likes, and his wife has nothing to worry about except the future."

"That's about all we have to worry about too," the second brother said.

Dita suddenly burst into laughter. Somebody near the tapestry was saying that the wife of a hunter or mountaineer is sometimes alone, but a fisherman's wife or mother must expect loneliness as a matter of course. Does fear make people lose even the little that they have? And the one who has lost only a little—doesn't he weep as much as the one who has lost a great deal?

"They are going to America," Dita said. "People always try to solve their problems by going from place to place as if the solution is in a change of scenery. And maybe it is."

On the smaller tapestry the shepherds turned sideways toward the shepherdesses, who looked at them shyly, provocatively, and seductively. Sheep grazed nearby. The tapestry must have been several hundred years old. It occupied half of the wall between the window and the door. Dita applauded the Polish and Rumanian girls, who had been dancing together. She sat under the chandelier, in whose light her hair shone like gold.

"Don't you like it here?" the first asked.

"That's not quite the right word for it," Dita answered. "I liked it at home, too. I didn't want to leave as the others did, or to be disloyal in any way I'd regret later on. But when you add it up overall, the fact is that here I am, and it's rather pleasant."

6 The room belonging to the first of the brothers was arranged as a combination library and bedroom. He had a large number of paintings there—some standing on the floor unframed, leaning on the wall or the cupboard. A fire burned in the fireplace. On the mantlepiece above the hearth stood an oil lamp and an old French clock. In the corner a white stove reached almost to the ceiling. The floor was covered with carpets, a lion skin, and sheepskins. The furniture was walnut, very old, the work of some skilled cabinetmaker. The chairs' armrests were carved into the shape of crocodile jaws, into which fingers could be inserted.

Magnolias grew in the knee-high flowerpots. A few still lifes hung on the walls. There was a picture of the sea, with a light blue surface, almost yellow in the distance, and also a painting of a road by a lake with a green surface and a path strewn with sand.

"You've got a nice place here," said Dita.

"Please make yourself at home."

"Are you cold?"

"On the contrary," she answered.

"Too hot?"

"No. I'm fine, thanks."

"May I offer you something?"

"No, thank you." She laughed. Whenever people have a roof over their heads they call it home.

She inhaled the scent of the fire. The flames glowed dark red and white at the tips. The shining tongue of flame reminded her of the Hebrew script. She smiled to herself. Why can't a person get rid of this sentimental haze that binds him to the vision of his former home and only hinders his entry into the life ahead?

The thought of money had already left her, and along with it went any resistance she had felt when she entered the room. There was no sense teasing them for their coolness, fine clothes, and kind of patronage, even though the idea of money as the basis of it all had not entirely vanished from her mind. Even if, by chance, she were able to help herself to something there— she clung to the idea, almost like Neugeborn—she might still find a way of returning it later. The clock made a nice sound. She glanced at it and smiled.

"Did you want to say something?" the first of the brothers asked.

"I don't like the silence."

"Don't leave it all up to us," the second brother said.

"Here's looking at you," the first said.

"I like the rug. Is it lamb or sheepskin?"

"Sheepskin, I think," the first answered. "Or lambskin? I don't know. Can you tell?"

"A lion skin?"

"Maybe it is," the first said.

"Shouldn't we have a drink?" the second suggested.

"That's a lovely bracelet you've got," the first said.

"What shall we drink?"

"Whatever you like. Just name it."

The light thrown by the fire reflected in her eyes, and on her lips and teeth when she opened her mouth. She caught sight of herself in the mirror. It struck her what it was they expected of her, and what she expected of herself. Whores are at least pretty, she thought to herself, when they are lucky.

"You have a pretty smile," the first one said.

"Thank you."

"What are you thinking about?" the second asked.

"This afternoon somebody was saying that a child needs sleep, flowers need sunshine, and old people need wine and bread. But the young need money to get anywhere."

The night sky cast its light into the room through the window. The stars shone brightly. Behind the windowpane the wind was still, and the woods and mountains whispered. The snow-clad Alpine gorges and peaks rose sheer to the sky. The moon had become full.

"How do you feel?" the first brother asked.

"Like sitting by a nice fire."

"Are you homesick?"

"For what?"

"I don't know, for everything."

"No. My eyes are full of light."

"Don't look into the fire."

"Why not?"

"People who stare into the fire have dreams even while they're still awake."

The corners of her mouth rose, as if she were smiling at herself. She twirled the bracelet around her wrist. There was no use telling them that when you've been away from home for a long time you begin to miss things, places, and the sense of comfort that rises from remembering them suddenly, like steam above a cooking pot, and that you cling to what reminds you of it all.

The second brother uncorked a bottle. She gave him a smile. She waited until he placed the cork on the table, and then she picked it up. "Château Margaux." The second brother sniffed the aroma of the wine. He nodded approvingly and poured. She thought how lucky she was, how lucky she had always been. Luck is worth more than all the rest. Had her stars come together into the right constellation for her to meet these people almost at the eleventh hour? She burst into laughter once more. Those who are born lucky have nothing to fear. She gazed through the window at the moon.

"Home," she said, and almost felt a catch in her throat. But she did not say that when you are abroad, you are more grateful for everything. I must do something about it, she decided. Like when they had accumulated laundry for two weeks in Room 16, and somebody would say, "Come on then, let's get it done." But now I have to say it to myself. And why not?

"In the old days we used to play for stakes," she said. She thought of the words *determinism, fate, evening*—of the words *girl, courage, innocence. Whores, money, sin.* To hell with it all, she thought. If I start thinking that the word *whore* is as all-embracing as the word *god*, or the word *life, man, world*, we won't get anywhere, and I'll just spoil everything. What's the point? It was her voice again. A voice of a voice. The echo of a faintly familiar song. The shadow she carried with her everywhere. Things better left unsaid. Whoever had more than one love was in luck.

"I never expected an evening like this. Downstairs it didn't look so promising."

"You couldn't act like this with everybody," the second brother said. The first one threw a questioning glance. He didn't ask anything. Once more there was a brief interlude of silence in the room. The exchange of words between alien people—signals that carried other signals within them—had stopped. They could hear her breath. Her eyes betrayed excitement. The mountain ranges, gigantic rock formations, ice, and earth, formed and piled up over millions and millions of years, surrounded them, together with the night. The first of the brothers put a record on the gramophone. They waited to hear the opening chords.

"'Ti-pi-tin,'" she said in her surprised, singsong voice. "'One night when the moon was so mellow . . .'" She blushed.

"Ein Walzer . . ." the second brother said.

"Does it remind you of something?" the first brother asked.

"From time to time I meet people better than I am, I guess."

She recalled the sound of the night wind, carrying with it voices and music, the barking of hunting dogs, all fading away into the rosy-fingered morning light. She imagined the smell of the earth, covered with ash, as if she touched it with her lips, as in a kiss. Before her eyes rose the image of a pool and a road, a white hotel, a room with curtains and windows, looking out on the garden where she had been with D.E. A table, and dinner in the garden restaurant. The amphibious car in which he had brought her back to Lubliana Street.

"How do you mean?"

She did not reply.

"Did anybody ever tell you that you're a nice girl?" the first brother asked.

"Let's have a drink," the second one said.

"How do you feel?" the first one asked.

"Naked," she answered.

It was good wine, and it slid down the throat like velvet. The bottle was elegant, with an exquisitely decorative label. Through the window she could see a broad expanse of the night sky. It's best to take your time over good things, she thought to herself, but she did not say it. They exchanged smiles and fresh toasts. They clinked glasses. It was a pleasant ring. Half of her face was lit by the fire; the other side was in shadow. The first of the brothers looked at her.

"You've gone through a great deal. Certainly more than we have."

"I've just left that subject," she said. "Did you know that so many people would be coming?"

"We're completely alone here," the second brother assured her.

"No need to be scared," the first said.

"I'm not scared. There are few people to whom I feel responsible. I'm an adult now, very carefree. After all, we're not living in the last century." She smiled. "I suppose our grandmothers would have listened to some love poems or a song on the flute. But where are our grandmothers now?" She laughed again. "How is it that the road back always seems shorter than the road going?" And finally: "Sometimes I wonder what I would have been if I had been born a few years earlier."

"Maybe you would have collected stamps?" the second brother asked. She detected something in his voice that she had not noticed in the voice of the first.

To begin with, they danced. Dita left her handbag and letters lying on the floor next to the chair. With the unspoken consent of the brothers, she slipped off her shoes. She glided over the carpets and furry rugs. The occasional words that they exchanged meant very little compared with the force that joined all three together as they moved in the dance. The inside pane of the window shone, reflecting back the outside snow and the fire within, the silent tension, smiling lips, sadness in the eyes, all that attracted them. They savored the contrast between the noise and confusion on the floor below and the silent, extraordinary dance here. The window formed a transparent barrier between the light and the dark. Did it reflect back into the gloomy night the sense of regret for what was now over, and the fear of what would begin tomorrow?

Dita kept silent and danced on. She closed her eyes and could feel her own body and theirs, the warmth of the fire, and the house.

The first brother put the record of "Ti-pi-tin" back on the turntable. Dita pulled away from the second brother and put her ear to the door.

"You smell so clean."

"What would you say if I didn't?" she responded.

"Are you alone?"

"What's wrong with being alone?"

"Aren't you the one they say saved children during the war?"

The record of "Ti-pi-tin" was halfway through. The saxophones softly harmonized. The second brother took Dita by the hand and led her off to dance at the other end of the room. He put his arm around her waist. The palm of his hand touched her hip, and then her body, climbing higher. For a moment she pulled herself away. She took his hand in hers, and they danced together as they had done earlier in the room below. He laughed as if he'd asked about something and had replied instead of her. He looked into her eyes and wondered what about her irritated him.

Dita looked at him and around him, as if she were dipping her fingers into unknown water. She could feel a familiar tension. She searched through her memories. Now she too closed her eyes, as if memory were a stream into which she was sinking. With a smile the second brother found baffling, she wondered who could be lonelier than children without parents and parents without children, sisters without brothers and brothers without sisters, husbands without wives and wives without husbands. Her smile did not falter. Why did people believe that one period of time cannot anticipate another? Or that a person cannot cross the gulf in a single leap? Her memory felt like a high range of mountains where a person travels along deep gorges and sails on underground rivers, as though he could pass in a moment of time from one end of recollection to the other.

As they danced, she tried to guess which twin was which. She looked intently into the eyes of the first, as he looked at her. She pressed to him so closely, and his lips touched her neck, shoulders, and temples. It was a surrender to him that she would later make to both of them. She noticed that he really had the deeper voice and regarded it as her first discovery about him.

"You don't need to apologize," she whispered. "I won't either."

They both had the same large, hazel eyes, relaxed and without the dark mud-colored rings that little Munk had had. Their eyes were deep set, as if they came from southern stock.

Dancing, music, and warmth flooded the room. It lay in semi-darkness, so that no one was exposed to direct light. From time to time a brighter flame would leap up from the fire. Splinters of light danced across the room, touching walls and faces with a reddish glow.

Dita smiled. The first brother turned off the lights. The second locked the door.

"We only answer to ourselves," she whispered.

At first she felt a little afraid. She wondered what would happen if their father came in and surprised them. But the feeling passed. She didn't even know their names and wasn't sure whether they had picked up hers. She took the lead in their game of mutual seduction. She remembered Liza, who had proved to herself what a weapon it could be for a girl, what she could gain by it, or what she could do with it. Its limitations.

She kept her eyes on the dark lashes and brows of the two brothers and danced with both in turn, pressing her breast closely to theirs. Among the records they played were "Bei mir bist du schön," "Mama Inez," and "Sibony."

"I don't even know you yet," she whispered. "But then, talking only spoils everything." She fell silent, as if to say that life is not what we want but what we have, and that it is sometimes painful and is won with tears.

She had had a lovely year. She saw it as a snow-covered field. To live on friendly terms with herself, surely she must be at least as charitable to herself as one is to a friend. She could feel the texture of the rug with her bare feet. It was lamb on both sides, not lamb on the top and wolf underneath. She recalled the gypsy camp of her childhood, with its neighing horses. Why do they say that a clever lamb sucks milk from two mothers? Then she remembered how the gypsy women at Auschwitz-Birkenau had danced in the women's barracks at night as if they were trying to exorcise something—some echo, or the call of a lost past. They had danced like mutes without music or singing as if they could hear the wind whispering the echo of lost songs.

Without pausing in the dance, she continued observing the brothers' teeth, which were the color of ivory, like her own. She looked into their mouths as they gravely touched their lips to hers. Then she passed to their throats, until the moment came when she clung tightly to one, or the other, or to both.

All tension had dissolved. Hadn't she once said to Andy that he should dance either well or not at all? And Andy had replied that maidens and not mountains are haunted by madness. Dita looked into the fire, and at the poker hanging loosely by the wall. Fire and straw? Even crooked bars can be straightened by fire. The flames crackled quietly. She drew in a deep breath, and she could feel the pounding of both brothers' hearts. The dim light merged with the night outside and with the shape of the pine forests. Sometimes the fire caved inward; at times it exploded outward like a spark of pitch.

Enclosed within the dimness of the room, they played a game of opposites, as if forming a new beginning. The world emanated from each of them, all decisions once again waiting to be made.

It was just as before, when she felt their fingers upon her. She was very close to them. With her hands she touched their cheeks, arms, and bodies, and they caressed her cheeks, arms, and body with their hands. Then gradually the moment arrived when she danced free and unencumbered, as tall as they were, in the darkness. Hung on the bamboo that bent like a bow, the lantern glowed with the reflection of ice and snow, with the reflection of moonlight on the nearby glacier. At times the giant rock seemed like a woman with pointed breasts of ice, its slopes like a white underbelly and the mountain passes like rounded shoulders. Quietly the wind rustled in the snow-capped tree-tops. The clock's pendulum struck the hour and glowed through the darkness. They could hear the sound of departing cars and bits of conversation. But the room was bathed in silence, breathing, and the touch of hands.

"I have never been like this," she said. "Nothing like this has ever happened to me before. It's the first time. I swear it." She lay down on the floor.

Then she turned her cheek to the lambskin, while she touched the skin of the lioness with her body, legs, and arms. She was glad that through the window she could see the moon and the highest tips of the trees. Farther back, she could picture the clean edges, deep gorges filled with cold and darkness. The moon looked like a wide-open mouth that swallowed stars wider than itself. Dita drew up into her eyes and mouth the glow of the stars and the moonlight.

She suddenly saw before her eyes a vision of the Aufseherin at Auschwitz-Birkenau who had forced a woman to bite through the throat of a live chicken in front of her. Dita stretched out on the lambskin rugs, then turned on her side and drew up her knees. The ceiling appeared white in the starlight. She wished the next few minutes would pass quickly. Then the world closed in on her like a vision of darkness divided into heat and cold. Every act asked for self-justification. One moment, a thousand moments. A little while, a thousand years. Isn't there a price to be paid for everything on earth?

She knew that she would never reproach herself. Her breath came faster. She lay without stirring. She felt as if she were being stripped, even of her skin. She had never been so very naked. Again she felt the vessels of her body filling to the brim, like the earth after rain. The blood pulsated through her veins like a stream running in the night, but also like a dried-up stream. She imagined the dampness of the stream, the sticky mud between the two banks. Reality—nothing. She could picture herself, with her smile. She closed her eyes and saw D.E.

She tried to hold on to the sudden thrill that possessed her like a resource, the feeling that it had all happened before, a long time ago. It conjured up a scent of old pine needles, clay, the dampness of melting snow. For a moment she recalled feelings shared by women both young and old. As if she had severed the thread that connected them, if only to see where the two ends lie. Or as if she had lit a candle at both ends to see how quickly it would burn through. As if everything, even in retrospect, deserves to be beautiful.

She envisioned ships, the sea, and lights. She noticed the scent of a male body. She felt the sense of freedom that fish feel in the sea and birds in the air, and the sense of bondage that she had carried with her from far away, like the remains of leg irons on her feet. She glimpsed children watering shrubs and trees, as one offers water to weary travelers. She could hear the flight of birds, their wings beating like the ticking of clocks. And she saw trees as tall as the masts of sailing ships. She felt her eyes grow moist. She shuddered all over her body; her legs shook. She could hear the murmur of voices, unable or unwilling to comprehend. She felt darkness like sunshine upon her, and sunshine like darkness. Sweat covered her body.

Then there fell around her a silence that told her that black is black, and white is white—a silence more deafening than sound. Motionless, she fell, and apart from the beating of her heart and the movement of her blood she heard nothing. Her eyes too saw nothing, until, at the end of her fall, it was as if she lay in the bottom of a boat, and beneath it the water, like the darkness, slipped away.

Outside, the wind beat on the window. She opened her eyes and looked into the fire. Its base had become dark, like blackened wood set in the glowing ash like a cradle. Higher up, the fire was red; at the top, almost white. The colors of the fire merged. The shape of the flames were constantly dancing, growing ever smaller. They gave off, at times, the sound of old men whipping other old men.

Dita summoned up a feeling of peace, as in the early morning when she would call out toward the mountains, and they would send back to her a cry like the memory of a song. On the window the snowflakes lay clean, white, and young. The clock struck the third quarter. She remembered the man at Auschwitz-Birkenau with whom she used to carry stones and whose hair and whiskers had been clipped. Once, as they stood together by the heap of stones, he had said to her that there was no past and no future, no good and evil. Behind the windowpane the stars wheeled in the sky, as if revolving about each other, as once they had done.

She also thought of Andy. Once he had told her of how the Germans had stormed the last bunker in the Warsaw ghetto in 1943. They drove out the rebels with tear gas because they wanted the rebels to feel defeated before they were put to death. It was said that the first man in the bunker shot his own mother, then himself. They all committed suicide. The Germans had seen them defeated but not humiliated. The clock began to strike twelve. Had it really happened? D.E. had deliberately put it out of his mind, so that it would not disturb him in the life that was, or soon would be, his. Physical intimacy and friendship were for him two distinct things. In her mind she kept asking what she really was and was not, whether a person ever becomes what others believe him to be, even though he may still believe himself to be different. I am not, she repeated to herself. I am not. But maybe I am.

"No more," she heard herself saying.

"Why not?" the first brother asked.

"It is loving too much to die of love," she said. And: "Everyone has a joker up his sleeve."

"Are you ill?" the second wanted to know.

"It's late," she said. Her voice had an alien ring to her ears. Her eyes were moist. The fire crackled quietly. She smoothed her hair and leaned on the wall facing the fireplace. "The final moments of March the twenty-second, the beginning of March the twenty-third. I am nineteen years old." The drops of sweat on her face looked like grains of sand. They could hear the resin on the firewood on the hearth. It looked like a cave dug into a dark cliff. The walls of the fireplace were built of rough clay, bleached by traces of flames, heat, and extinguished fires.

"I guess I'm not the most appreciative person," Dita said slowly, as if to say that everyone more or less would like to spin out his life as long as possible, like children in a game. Was that part already over for her? She laughed, and her laughter became a kind of upside-down apology. Its echo was not an accusation, but a quiet sound that grew stronger and finally rose into a cry of pain. "I must *do* something about it," she said to herself. She remembered the actress she'd spoken to Tonitschka about, and her wish to bring happiness to someone every day.

The gramophone had stopped. Dita looked out at the trees and the snow, the mountains and stars. Then she looked at the door. It struck her that when she had begged for her mother's life, she had perhaps been begging for the right to go with her. She realized, too, that when she had been with D.E. in the hotel, it had been her wish to give him a piece of her own life, at least a few moments. That feeling had been as genuine as what had really taken place there. And also as genuine as that blinding revelation that she had seen so clearly just because it had blinded her. It had been as if every shadow within her had grown eyes—a feeling of self-renewing life. Perhaps it was for the last time?

"I hope you won't think too badly of me." Once more she wondered when the thaw would begin. She imagined it as the land drinking thirstily. A time when birds fly, horses gallop, and dogs bark. Her voice sounded distant. "And if you do, well, life is sometimes hard for a weakling." She tried to smirk. "It's easier to jump from a low, one-story building."

I am a whore, she said to herself. No doubt about it. As Andy had said to Neugeborn when they left that spring dance at SIA, "Every whore was once a virgin." Only whores buy themselves warmth, company, and prospects for tomorrow like that, and then in the middle of it they change the rules of the game. Should she carry on like this for another fifty years, day after day, night after night? And suppose she did it in the legitimate way, as a wife, for a slice of bread and a bit of security. Would she then come to know that sudden cry in the night that Tonitschka Blau knew so well?

She gave them both a smile, but they did not understand her smile. Then she smiled once more and dropped her eyes. She felt as if she were back on the train that rode away, and she could not get off. Was it because she had been where she had been? Or would it have been like this anyway? She imagined herself writing a letter to D.E. As usual, she began: I really don't know why I'm writing. This letter did not count, written in the mind or on paper, never sent, about a dream from which she was unable to wake and whose intoxication she could not shake off, because she was hopelessly, childishly, irretrievably credulous, and—maybe—faithful. She never wrote to him of her sleepless nights or how she lost or gained weight. Instead she told him what she wore at the time and her style of dress. Nothing to drive him further away or to frighten him. Maybe she should send him an infernal machine for a change. D.E. was smart. He suspected all those who searched for happiness, because this showed that they had lost it. In his yesterdays, D.E. found no guarantee for the future, only warnings. Only for Andy was the world reborn anew each day. Only for Andy was boundless weariness a material from which he could draw an unfailing encouragement. It seemed that Andy had been born with the mentality of a pirate who wins sea battles and dispenses with all honor and decorations, because the main, the only victory in his life was survival. The excitement left her. Her heartbeat became calmer. She breathed in and out slowly. She tidied her dress and covered her knees with her skirt. She stood with her toes and heels close together. The entire time her calm and grown-up smile had remained on her lovely oval face.

7 "Are you still here?" The voice of the first brother came out of the darkness.

"It's not your fault," Dita said.

"I've got to feed the fire," the second brother said.

"It's not very late," the first said.

"Of course, we're all from far away," the second said. "I'll put a bottle of champagne on ice, just to be on the safe side. It's Rhineland champagne."

"Shall I switch on the light?" the first brother said.

"Not for my sake," Dita said.

In her imagination she talked to Neugeborn: "That's the difference between you and me, Fitzi—the Neugeborn who is willing to have his nose broken so that he looks manly, though he's a dreamer underneath, and Dita the realist. You're happy just imagining what nice children we might have together, while I'm cautious even in the moments of so-called happiness." Her gaze was far away. She smiled. She hoped that the saying "Out of sight, out of mind" might prove advantageous to her now. She said, "I don't even know what I want. I guess I am never satisfied with anything. Maybe I want too much. Ah, well."

Before Dita's departure Fitzi had dreamed about riding a fresh horse. There were other horses, ridden to death, lying all along the roadside. In the dream he had been searching for a door. Everything was in its proper place—the wall and the town. He completed the journey on the last horse, which collapsed under him just as he reached his destination. He had awakened at that point and tried to explain the dream to Andy. She, on the other hand, had dreamed of the stamp with the green deer. She didn't need anyone to interpret that. It meant that D.E. did not write. Did he think it wasn't worth wasting money on a stamp? Had he perhaps been deterred when she had revealed to him in bed that he was her first lover, at a time when he intended her to be anything but the last? Would she want to marry such a woman if she were a man? Did the struggle for a career involve a battle with one's own memories?

The first brother stood up, and he took down from the wall the picture of the sand-strewn path around the dark green lake. "This is for you."

"No."

"Yes. Please."

"No more gifts."

"You should take it."

"Why?" The worst of it is, she thought, I haven't even behaved like a good whore—more like a bad one. "I'm beginning to think that the world is not the best place for me." The mood reminded her of a long sleep. She yawned.

She looked outside. The moon had changed its position and now had other stars around it. She kept the unreal smile upon her lips.

"In Auschwitz-Birkenau, before the selection, one girl told me that no one should ever give up her whole being to a person, a land, a relationship, hope, or wishes. It breaks you up into so many pieces that no one can ever put you back together again."

She thought of her mother and how her father probably had behaved during the final phase. It seemed almost indecent to think about it. Even the most forthright of people would never be able to tell the whole truth.

"I suppose that when you're ashamed, you're not in the best position to make judgments, are you?" She was anxious to avoid silence. But when she was not talking herself, she could only hear the sound of the fire.

"Everything is OK," the first brother said. "Everything is all right again, isn't it?"

"No problem."

"What do you mean?" the second brother asked.

"I'm thinking of the difference between when you look forward to something and when you're afraid of it." She laughed. She felt something like the onset of seasickness, like a person who had lost the compass that oriented him and did not mean to sail south in order to go north, or to try evil in order to know good. The shadows in the window reminded her of her own thoughts.

"I only believe in what I can see," the second brother said.

Dita leaned back, her hands supporting her, elbows locked against the floor. Her fingertips touched the end of the lion skin.

"You should give it a rest now," the first brother said.

"Next time I'll be more prepared."

"You should come again," the first brother said.

She substituted the word *go* for the word *come*. The second brother threw a piece of birch wood onto the fire. It hissed when it touched the hot ash. The treebark gave an almost human gasp. It threw light and the scent of pitch into the room as it flared up. The second brother tossed two more pieces onto the fire; the flames spread and lit up the room.

"Sometimes it's hard to be that carefree type of girl you would like me to be." She could feel an ache in her abdomen.

"What are you going to do?" the first brother asked.

"I still have my secret weapon," Dita said, smiling. Her smile had suddenly changed. She appeared more relaxed and comfortable. They did not ask, and she felt no need to explain. She smiled uncertainly. She was surprised how quickly she had convinced herself that all was well. Everything in the room suddenly seemed lighter and brighter. "I am waiting for the thaw," she said.

"I can see that you are all right," the second brother said.

"Why shouldn't I be?" she said, smiling.

"Are you really OK?" the first asked.

"I'm fine."

Once more in her mind she substituted the word *could* for *should*. She smiled vaguely, as if there was a radiance within her, but it came out a little fractured. They exchanged good-byes and smiled. The words they used were no longer of any importance.

The second brother turned on the light in the hall and in front of the house. She let them both kiss her lips. She asked them not to see her out. How long would it be before everything would be thawed, in the sun and wind? She felt she could see herself from the inside and outside at the same time, but a moment later she could sense herself only from without.

The stars were empty. She found it hard to believe that she had been in this world for nineteen years. Nineteen? A thousand? A two-way, fleeting, almost unreal bodily surrender.

With the dawn came the frost. The clusters of stars had melted away. It seemed to Dita Saxova that she could have said thank you to her hosts. I'm drunk, she thought, but not too much. The snow was hard. On the surface it shone like stardust, firm and exceedingly white. Somewhere an invisible rooster shattered the remainder of the night with his welcome to the morning. The sound of his crowing carried to the mountains and came reverberating back. A cold wind swept through the rocky fissures that cleft the mountains.

She suddenly saw a maze of ice and snow towering high above

her. She didn't feel tired at all. She set out along the mountain trail as if it were somewhere she'd been many times before. The overhanging walls of snow were firm and fairly safe. From time to time she paused to catch her breath. The remaining stars in the sky faded, then disappeared in the daylight. The tops of the pines and firs swayed gently in the wind. Along the track there were warning signs and safety chains. It was absurd to go on in the shoes she wore, and she realized how cold she would soon be. In the distance she glimpsed inaccessible mountain peaks that no one had ever climbed. She thought of a universe where everything is interconnected—memory and forgetfulness, nearness and distance, war and peace—things stronger than man, and the reverse: a journey that man sometimes takes into the most secret passages of his existence, into the first or the last state of his being, in order to join his own shadow for a fragment of a second, a day, a night, a morning. Things that cannot be expressed in words and that cannot be shared with any other person. It is not a question of self-denial. A person may do something that promises him happiness. To whom had she ever brought happiness? From whom had she taken it? "Why should I survive? Why should I attempt to escape?" She felt very tired. Maybe she was never so tired before. Her instinct whispered to her something she had never heard before. It came from her bones, from her hair and nails. This was the darker side. But there was a brighter part too. She felt in contact with the whole wide world, as if merging into infinity was like running into the blank wall of her own conscience. At the moment when the sun rose above the glacier she found herself at a point where she had many times before longed to be. She decided to wait for the new day.

Down in the valley life began with every sunrise. Here on the mountains the snow had not even begun to thaw. The whole expanse of virgin snow lay untouched by the sun's rays. She gazed at the scene before her, rejoicing. At her feet lay the valley, with its back to the mountains and its face to the sun, from one horizon to the other, the burden and treasure of the world. The whiteness of the snow blinded her, but instead of making her sleepy it sharpened her perception. She caught sight of the rock that, from a distance, looked like a dead bird in the snow.

"No," she said. "Not me, not yet."

Why are we born? Why had she been born the person she was? Where was the lasting haven, the security that could take from her that relentless questioning of what she would do tomorrow? How? How to reach that point at which no one can keep clean hands, and not feel like a beggar whose best trait is that he never gets lost?

She smiled to herself. Everything was all right. Everything was as it should be. Things might be much worse. It could not be long before the thaw would come, and in the end everything would thaw out. It was almost like the joke Andy used to tell in Prague, about how 99 percent of the people thought they had an easy life, without any effort. And the other 1 percent? "They don't matter. They're us."

She drew into her lungs the icy morning air. She could hear the wind and smell the sweetish scent of the pines. The taste of last night's wine still lingered on the roof of her mouth. She smoothed down her hair. She began to feel hungry but did not feel like hurrying. Again she felt naked, even though she was dressed. Her skin, her flesh, her soul, her hunger, her waiting, her hopes and her shame, her childishness and her maturity.

She wondered if her imagination had any firm base on which to lean. Among the numerous major and minor disasters through which she had passed, how had she prepared herself for the time when it would all be over? Why did one person know how to cope with life, while another moved from blunder to blunder? How was it that one person was tough and insensitive, while another in blindness imagined that everyone could see into the depths of his heart? How is it that one finds what one is seeking, while another is lost in the clouds—like herself, unfaithful to her dreams of yesterday, but somewhere inside true and trustworthy, free from the outside world? Why had she inherited a spirit hurt and humiliated by things to which the rest of the world was immune?

The frost tingled under her fingernails. She no longer wanted to ask: "Where shall I go, what shall I do, to be happy?" only to receive back, like an echo: "You have nowhere to go. Do what you wish." I'd never get anywhere like that, she said to herself. I cannot keep asking myself what I have achieved, what proof of myself I have given, except for eating, sleeping, and studying. Her teeth began to chatter. Suddenly everything came over her at once—hurt pride and vanity, fear of the future, and disappointment as deep as her expectations had been high, hatred and envy, helplessness and loneliness, one after another, splinters of emotions that coalesced into a deep pain. Why had she been able to bear the loss of her parents but unable to squat at the side of the road like a beggar?

She had made a long journey from the chimneys in Poland—from fire, smoke, and ashes, and from the longing in Prague—to this morning, to this place and this moment, and she knew it.

She gazed downward. The snow lay untouched. The whole scene shone crystal clear. In the morning light, vistas of white earth opened up through the passes. She turned up the collar of her coat. Could she still write and ask for that boat ticket to El Salvador? To write everything off and go? To nurse redheaded children and continue to yearn for some phantom vision that probably didn't exist? What would she gain by going? Comfort? Peace? That would not be enough. What about her inner self? What would she be over there? An immigrant, a foreigner without ties, except maybe to the colored maid who brought her

morning coffee in bed. There could be war, and her husband and
son would go. Why? To fight for what? For El Salvador? America?
On the side of the Germans?

She had to laugh at herself. She threw back her head to toss
the hair from her forehead, and she breathed in the raw air.
Things had never gone as she wanted, and she had never wanted things the way they had gone. Life is not what we want but
what we have. She was amazed at how simple the answer was.
It's all right, she repeated to herself. Soon everything will be
fine.

The memory of the past night returned to her in all its details.
Its symbol was no longer fire. It was more like a summing up of
her nineteen-year-old life. The trees stood like candles in the
snow. The wind-battered bushes were transformed into white
cupolas. The day had come, and the sun shone with increasing
power. Dita's eyes were tired. She stared defiantly. They were
suddenly no longer the eyes that had registered only passing
fears of a world that had been kind to her for so long. Now she
felt ready to embrace the world, her part of the world, to take all
its burdens on her shoulders, and to wear it like a veil. She
pulled tightly at her upturned collar. Who knew when the thaw
would begin?

She remembered a song they used to sing in the camp. The
cold wind blew off a hundred glaciers, and even while the echoes
of the song still lingered, she realized how irrevocably the cold
and lifeless gust carried away from her the melody, words, and
spirit of the song—all that it had meant and promised. The song
was called "Against the Wind." On the morning of New Year's
Day 1945, they had been singing on the way to the munitions
factory, which had formerly produced cooking pots. She had had
a toothache. It had been a good year. Perhaps the first half had
been hard. Within five months the war had ended. It had been
the best year of her life, except that none of her relatives had
come back, apart from one cousin who had been at El Alamein,

and he had avoided her. Everything had begun all over again. I must be strong, she said to herself. No one respects weaklings. It was as if she were reaching for something. No, she told herself, not this way. But why not? No, she repeated to herself. Something had changed, but she didn't know what. Somewhere deep inside her there was the silence. (It grew and lifted, then dropped in her insides like a downpour.) And all the time there was more and more quiet, as if it had many layers. Her only thought was that it is, was, and would be with her always. The same way. As if she had two minds for everything, even for the silence inside her, and they fought. There was something propelling her, and she couldn't control it. As if someone would tell her good day, and she would know for sure that it was not evening. Yes and no. She felt tired. The fatigue, as usual. Muscles, feet, heart, head. Were all her yeses and nos the same?

What was this silence in her that made her dizzy? She felt the echo of its stillness surrounding her. Inside and outside. Was it letting up? She began, in the middle of that quiet, to long for a fairy tale. Fairy tales had happy endings. And what was there at the end of her silence that almost lulled her to sleep while standing here in the wind? It's too cold for me, she said to herself. Too windy. Too unpleasant. Tomorrow, she said to herself, everything will start again. Yes, she added. So what?

She stretched out her arms as if to make contact with what was still ahead of her. Suddenly it was tangible and within her grasp. She saw her own hands before her, poised as if in fear of a collision. Slowly she took one step toward the edge, closer to the sun. She had the new day in front of her, like a gift waiting for her, and for which she herself waited, deeper and heavier and more incommunicable than all other mysteries put together. All the ifs and whys sank away from her. She spoke both question and answer in a cry that dissipated into silence. The morning was bright. She had never seen such radiance. The rising sun was deep red, with orange tints. The white mist melted away, and the sky became dazzling blue. Should she end it all? Yes? No. No. No.

A second later there was no edge. She slipped and fell. Her body collided with rocks, ice, and snow. Her hands tried to hold on to something, but a hard object struck and dazed her. She felt she had pulled down upon herself the rocks that she had tried to grasp and that had gotten in her way.

The snow she fell through whistled like an avalanche. She could hear the sound of rocks colliding with rocks. Some she left behind her; others struck her as if she were pelting herself with them. She drove them before her on her downward course. Her mind registered an echo of long sentences she could no longer utter. It was as if she had for a long time carried within her something waiting to be said. Was it a voice calling her? Was she calling out to someone? Silent? Screaming? She no longer asked: Who am I? What are people like? She felt naked, completely naked.

First there was darkness everywhere, then a flood of sharp light, as if she had reached the sun. Finally there was darkness again. She no longer knew up from down. There was nothing above or below her anymore.

Everything melted away as she lost consciousness, including the fear that she might cause difficulties for someone else and including the shock of the impact on her delicate skin that was the color of an unripe peach.

That same day the postman brought a letter addressed to Dita Saxova. The sender was Erich Munk, from Prague.

"Dita," he wrote, "you are a year older. How are you? What are your plans?" After that he wrote of his hopes and wishes for her, besides determination, happiness, and patience, and that he kissed her. He gave her all the news and wrote why he thought hope had a red color, and about freedom and justice, which were never married, as always. He also reminded her that she was nineteen, now an adult, and also that he hoped her life would be everything that she wished for herself, and everything that she has. "Every slice of bread we eat has two sides."

Also the date.

Since the addressee was no longer there, the letter was returned unopened.

INDECENT DREAMS

Novellas

Blue Day

1

INGE Linge was on the small side, but if you'd seen her early last spring, training on the sports fields reserved for the *Wehrmacht* and officers' wives, you'd have said she was muscular. Her calves were rather short, her thighs firm and round, as if made of white india rubber. She was a woman whom life had not yet overwhelmed, and her arms were plump and strong. There was no fire in her round face; its freckled pallor, low brow, and hair brushed carelessly across her temples all combined to rob it of expression. A soldier once scrawled on her door: "When a woman is pale, look out for wormy," followed by a nasty word. That was why she bothered with physical training.

There were times when she dreamed she was the owner of a thriving house, with young ladies wearing cornflower blue cotton dresses with white collars; she reigned over them all and occasionally took one of the customers for herself, for her own amusement or just to chat. At other times, she dreamed of a house in Prague where she entertained her former German friends, just to show them how well a woman could get on in life. And there were times when she dreamed she was tall and well built, with the long legs of a film star. Her eyes were snake-green with dark lashes, playful and demanding.

Originally, Inge Linge had come from Magdeburg to work in the Prague Labor Office as a secretary to one of the Reich's administrative officers. She turned out to be ill-suited for the role of office mouse because of her temperament and faulty spelling. Nor did she show any enthusiasm for the job. She was not very popular with the wives of her superiors, either, and so it had been fairly easy for her to strike out on her own at the beginning of February 1943. The German Reich was in trouble along the Don or the Volga just then, trying to cross the river and then proceed across the steppes to occupy Russia.

The four-story house, Number 14 Chestnut Street, where Inge Linge lived in her office days—she had refused to live in the Regulus Hotel with the other German girls—had two lower floors intended by the builder to be expensive bachelor apartments. With its front of Swedish marble, the building stood self-assured among decaying palaces which were collapsing one after the other. The apartments were taken over by post office workers, tailors and shop assistants with large families.

Inge Linge had been given an apartment here in May of 1942, and just as she did not have to stain her hands or her green overalls with black and red ink for long, she did not stay here long, either. This was the time of great military victories, except for brief delays here and there along one of the Russian rivers. All she had to do at the Housing Office was mention the name of her friend, Major Detleff von Fuchs. From the very beginning, the slim, dark-complexioned major with the pimply face and brow had been her mainstay; he always treated her like a lady. He liked her because she gave him what he wanted without beating around the bush, and as with his barber and his tailor, he set aside time for her.

She was given a larger apartment with a southern exposure. The sun filtered in almost all day, and she could watch the children playing in the street in front of the chemist's. They would lean over the gutter, which seemed to them to contain secrets waiting to be revealed. Children were her unfulfilled desire. Now, though, they were strangers and called each other Ivan and Jimmy and Friedrich and played and fought every day until the blood ran.

This apartment had belonged to a Jewess named Ida Geron, who suffered from tuberculosis and had been sent away in January of 1942. Inge Linge had watched her move slowly down the hallway, stooped with the weight of the two bags on her back. The old woman's greed had punished her, Inge Linge thought, for trying to take the entire allotted fifty kilograms with her to the east. Only ten kilograms were allowed for hand luggage, and the transport authorities issued a receipt for the rest. Everyone knew quite well what that meant.

Without a word of farewell, Ida Geron had gone, disgustingly thin, dragging her feet down the stairs, her shoulder blades sticking out, with her old-fashioned boots laced up over her ankles like a bareback rider in the circus.

Inge Linge told Major Detleff von Fuchs that Ida Geron's apartment was empty. Then she asked if she could trade her own small apartment for it, lowering her long chestnut lashes as she spoke. Even before he replied, she realized he wanted to take her to bed immediately. Then she enjoyed one of those lovely days that made up for having been born to a barber and a mother she never knew.

She was delighted whenever she thought of the girls in their corn-flower blue dresses with white collars, and of herself standing at the entrance where the door set in motion tinkling xylophone keys playing Christmas carols. She could hear herself singing with the chimes: *"O Tannenbaum, wie schöne sind deine Blätter . . ."*

Her life had been pleasant enough, like that of a grubworm warmly wrapped inside a leaf. And now—out of nowhere, it seemed to her—it was as if a gale on a savage river had blown that life away.

At this moment—it was May 6, 1945, the third spring she had spent in this apartment and the beginning of the second night of the insur-rection, although the German High Command had declared Prague an open city to spare it the sharp odor of gunpowder—Inge Linge wore widow's weeds and sat in an armchair covered with black crepe. She turned on the radio. Whenever the 415 meter band came on, the announcer said the Allies were bombing German airfields. He encour-aged the rebels to hold on.

The various news items were often contradictory. Sometimes they were so brief and terse that she shivered; other times they were so vague that she could interpret them any way she pleased. But the truth was clear: the city had taken up arms to fight the Germans, and Inge Linge was being forced to recognize that something had ended and something new had begun. Everything she'd lived through in Prague, everything she'd enjoyed and dreamed of, was now gone forever.

She turned the radio off. The bells of St. James's Church were ringing and ringing. The policeman who had been on duty had disappeared. Inge Linge's snake-green eyes were desolate. The women in the house had settled their accounts with her early that morning, before she had even managed to ask whether they were bringing her milk. In a few short moments she realized that Germany was no longer what it had been the day before.

The chemist, who not long before had looked longingly and vainly up at her, pulled down his shutters, had put on a yellow tropical helmet—the sort once worn by the German Afrika Korps—and came to tell the concierge that he was off to join the fighting in the streets. The concierge was only half-listening.

She slapped Inge Linge's face and said to her, while the chemist stood by, "You want to know what you are? A whore, that's what you are, stuffing your belly when we didn't have enough to keep body and soul together. You were drinking milk when our children had to drink cloudy, gray water. Sucking our blood, that's what you've been doing!" She thought more was needed and went on: "You go back where you came from, you know very well what for, you viper, you. Get back to your whore's nest and stay there."

"Leave her alone," the chemist said. "She wasn't the worst of them."

Inge Linge was still rubbing her unhealthy pale cheek; it no longer smarted from the slap. She didn't feel at all grateful to the chemist for standing up for her. The wonderful feeling of those quiet evenings filled with the ringing of bells disappeared; no longer would she be certain that someone would come. No longer would she have to open the door.

What happened to her now would be decided by the Regional Command and detailed in the circulars issued by the office of the Reich's Military Transport Inspector, with its headquarters in the Prague Subcommand in the Bohemian-Moravian territory. The generals with diamond crosses and orders pinned onto their chests ruled the fate of the soldiers moving across the Czech lands and, indirectly, also the fate of Inge Linge.

Inge Linge was sitting in the armchair with her playing cards spread across the table in front of her. She wondered what she would say to Father Hesmussen in the church of St. James if she were to go to confession. He had blessed the soldiers' arms while she was dreaming of her house and her business, and he had sprinkled holy water on the artificial limbs of soldiers coming and going.

She was frightened by her thoughts. Yet this was only the beginning. She thought of what she would say to tubercular Ida Geron—whose furniture had been taken away by the Reich secret police to the warehouse in New Town—if she were to appear at the door. Inge Linge had been disappointed when she'd seen Ida Geron's furniture: a wardrobe with shelves built over it, a glass-fronted pendulum clock, a table and chair, and a broken electric heater.

She had never even been to confession. She only went to church to listen to the music and consider which of the devout flock would be worth sinning with. Once she had heard Father Hesmussen preach.

He had said of a couple, "The two went forth together." Now it seemed as though she and that Jewish woman might have set out on the same journey.

Why had the other woman always been so alone? Inge Linge wondered. She thought of her several times, whenever she found something in the apartment to remind her. That spring day in 1942, for instance, when she'd been washing the glass panels in the door and had scraped off a tin container stuck to the paint. Inside she had found a scrap of mica bearing the Ten Commandments. Why were all the Jews she had ever known, like Ida Geron, bent over as though they were looking for something in the dirt and dust beneath their own and other people's feet?

Inge Linge got up and went over to the wardrobe: a double wardrobe with shelves for her linens. She was still attractive, despite the veins standing out high on her calves. Usually she swung her hips like a sailor, holding her head high and her chin in the air, her full lips parted and the wrinkles of her neck smoothed out. At this moment, however, she did not bother to straighten up, and her walk lost its charm.

Her eyes passed over the green overalls with the white stockings she had worn in the Labor Office. She turned to the shelf of cut glass bottles containing a sickly scent of violets, roses, and orchids to tickle her nostrils. She had never cared for the smell of men's perspiration as some women did. Only a day or two before she had taken an oil treatment for her soft, flax-colored hair. Her creams were arranged beneath a lid of walnut. She felt like a pharaoh's wife whenever she looked at her jars of fine Meissen china and chose "Astrid" for nights and "Flora" for the day from among the gifts brought to her by German soldiers passing through Prague on their way from Paris to Moscow. She preferred Helena Rubenstein, or the Argentine Elizabeth Arden from Madrid, or the English Max Factor 3, an almost theatrical makeup.

The blue-marbled shadows with the words "The two went forth together" took on the shape of the old maid Ida Geron. It was likely that no man had ever touched that woman's body. Even in fantasy, the idea filled Inge Linge with scorn; it was something she found hard to forgive.

There had been a time when, partly out of pride and partly out of caution, she would not say good morning to her. It would have looked too strange when she was wearing her green overalls and white stockings. But she had never done anything to annoy her either, although at that time she might have hurt her as she pleased, even killed her, without any unpleasant consequences.

Ferdinand Linge, her father, used to say that everybody on earth had one nose and two eyes; he had shaved whole regiments of faces and he'd seen plenty. He would add that it didn't necessarily mean that a German woman had to go marry a Jew or a Chinese coolie, but he didn't go along with those sharp divisions that got even sharper as the territory of the Reich grew larger. Once, an officer her father was shaving—a tinker from their street who had taken over a Jewish workshop—said to him: "There are eighty or ninety million of us, Kamerad Linge, and every one of us might know a decent Jew. But if we hadn't kept our eyes open and given them what-for, everything in Germany would be topsy-turvy before long. A Chinese coolie? We're from the same street, Mr. Linge; take my advice and hold your tongue and be glad your blood's as German as Magdeburg itself. Luckily your daughter's got a head on her shoulders and she'll choose the right man for herself."

She, too—dressed in these widow's weeds—had caressed many a face and knew that, roughly speaking, they all had a nose and two eyes, and one desire that took on many forms. Pure blood had nothing at all to do with it. What else could happen that hadn't already happened to her? Suddenly Inge Linge put her hands to her throat. So many people have died, she thought.

Inge Linge had always wanted children and now, for the first time in her life, she was glad she didn't have any.

It had been a long time since she'd had any coffee—not even on the A-1 German ration ticket she'd kept since her office days. Who could guess that the smell of it had helped to drown out the smell of poverty that clung to the old days? She could say: "I've made something of my life, haven't I?" She'd never worried about things before. She had learned to live with herself. She never sought revenge for the wrongs she had suffered.

Maybe that was strange; foreign women had felt better in the wastelands of the east. A sudden change was not always a bad thing—she had heard them say so more than once in the office and on the radio. A German soldier from a Halle dyeworks lost his duodenal ulcers when put on military rations. She had heard this from another solider who had served with the dyer in Odessa on the Black Sea. He talked of nothing else, as if there were nothing of interest in his own life. Before that, he said, the dyer hadn't even been able to eat minced veal; it reminded him of boiled babies. His family was glad in the end that he had joined up! Meat was rationed in Germany, too, and she supposed they didn't like his saying that it made him feel like a cannibal. In Odessa, on Revolution Square, which they had renamed Adolf Hitler Square, the dyer pushed Russian partisans into double cages and left them there until the flesh froze off their bones. Nobody had to bother about his diet anymore. Then, too, there was a soldier with asthma who joined the Afrika Korps under Marshal Rommel and started breathing as though he'd been given a new pair of lungs.

She herself would like to get as far away from Prague as she could just now, except maybe not to the wild Polish plains on the Russian border where the bogs shone with a copper light. The young Germans from Magdeburg told her about the light when they came through Prague, after getting her address from Jenny Burckhart. Even Major Detleff von Fuchs said something about it, as did many others who wanted to talk, no matter about what, and were afraid to talk to anybody else.

Ida Geron? Who did that woman have? Was she really quite alone? And then Major Detleff von Fuchs—she knew perfectly well that he had bought his "von" for thirteen hundred marks. The "von" made his racial origin sound safer, and nobody bothered to look into it too closely.

What Daddy used to say flashed through her mind, that some people are too proud of their conscience not to drown in it. She longed for something she couldn't express.

Sometimes she would receive food tickets from the soldiers, coupons for fifteen hundred grams of meat and artificial fats, and coupons for two hundred and fifty grams of butter. Once she had three years' worth of coal allocations. She exchanged two of them for vegetable and fresh egg coupons, which only German hospitals received in Prague. She recalled the smell of the Egyptian cigarettes smoked by Major Detleff von Fuchs. He liked the Spanish proverb that said that a man without money is better than money without a man.

One of the sergeants she'd had here, Gerhard Muller, could not get promoted to lieutenant because they said he not only behaved, but also looked, like a Jew. They claimed he looked like a rabbi. That was enough for him to remain a sergeant eternally. He had mentioned this once, rather casually, and after that had never talked about anything but the weather—as if there were no war going on. It seemed unreal to her, like something that had existed briefly and was no more.

She recalled the song Major Detleff von Fuchs sang when he drank and when he got what he wanted:

> *Wir versaufen unser Oma ihr klein Hauschen,*
> *ihr klein Hauschen*
> *Wir versaufen unser Oma ihr klein Hauschen,*
> *und die erste und die zweite Hypothek.*

Inge Linge wanted to know whether his grandmother really was a Mexican princess. Who knows? Fuchs would say with a smile. What was her name? Delfa. She had a seafood restaurant on a famous lagoon. Strangely enough—in Fuchs's case—everything agreed, at least on the map. Inge Linge didn't care if the major was a gypsy or a part-gypsy.

Detleff Fuchs was married, though not happily. She could tell when his wife had refused him; it darkened his mood, even with her. He had his own ideas of order, of his personal things, which he wouldn't change. He knew how to make her laugh.

To cheer herself up she turned on all the lights: the big chandelier in the middle of the ceiling—like three enormous ornamental chrome candelabras, upside-down—the table lamp in the hall, and the white bulb behind the aquarium. She stayed awake, hour after hour, prey to the anxiety she was trying to keep at bay with memories of all that had been pleasant in her life and all that belonged only to her own experience, which nobody could take away from her.

She rummaged through her memories as though they were a bowl of dried peas, and then she suddenly realized that what had once made her happy was no longer enough.

She trembled as if in a fever. Did that soldier who was cured make good use of his lungs? The night dragged on and the harsh light glared down on Inge Linge crouched in her chair, throwing a series of shadows, first sharp, then softer and softer. She was wandering along the corridors of the hour-by-hour Regulus Hotel or in one of the war-time nightclubs of Prague, the Berlin Bear perhaps, where Czechs were not allowed. Or she was in some apartment where a German officer had lived before making his way to the front. Or she imagined herself standing at the door, or sitting in this chair, opening letters from the front and reading words of gratitude. They nearly always began with the same words: "First, my warm greetings and fond memories," as if they had all been written by the same man.

Or she was watching the tubercular little Jewish woman, Ida Geron, with her hooked nose, and trying to run away all the way back to the time when she was a green-eyed little girl in the parlor behind the barber's shop. The shop and parlor were separated by a curtain, and she could hear everything that went on. Ferdinand Linge came in wearing his patched white barber's coat. "You're a Prussian on your grandfather's side and a Saxon on your grandmother's side, you little imp. You got that black and gold flash of Bavaria from me, but God only knows what you got from your mother! Those snake-green eyes, I suppose!"

Inge Linge had never known her mother. All she could get out of her father—before he fell as regimental barber in the lightning French attack on Paris—was that he himself had only seen her mother on the day she conceived, and again just after she gave birth. Then her mother had run away with a hussar. Her father never liked shaving Hungarian cavalrymen after that.

And then she saw herself running over the dry Polish plains and coming up against silver barbed wire. A German soldier had told her about the wire. He was barely twenty-one and he wept on her bosom. He said that out there in the east, in the General Government, there were chambers with showers which they called "baths of eternal oblivion." The people were driven in and then, instead of water, they were showered with gas. Soldiers were specially detailed to collect the clothes and shoes and underwear from the changing rooms, where the people had stripped naked, and to send the items to the *Winterhilfe* to be distributed. At first they used to gas and burn the people as they were, fully dressed, but then one of the big shots—Heinrich Himmler himself—had given special orders to strip the people first.

Her hands went to her thighs; her fingertips felt the texture of her supple muscles. It was better to get up and cross the room to the aquarium. Inge Linge believed that the little goldfish would bring her good luck. Most of her fish were yellow, red, and gold. Detleff von Fuchs would tell her that a goldfish was only a little carp with transparent skin. He told her that the Chinese had cultivated it already thousands of years ago. Gold was the blood of the fish. And it didn't bring good luck, but bad. Once he had brought her a Chinese silverfish. It was still swimming here. The only good thing about a goldfish, Fuchs claimed, was that one could predict the weather by it. When the fish lay or swam near the bottom, it would rain.

She touched her neck with her palms and the pads of her fingers. The throat is the first to betray age, or fatigue, or a woman's worries. She noticed that her ankles were swollen like those of a pregnant woman. Perhaps I look swollen all over, she thought. Who knows why? She turned all the lights off again, including the three big candelabras hanging down in the dark. She pulled up the blackout curtain, opened the window, and leaned out, breathing in the fresh night air. The bells were still ringing.

The sound of gunfire came from far away. She felt the pavement below draw her out and down. If she jumped now, perhaps she would suddenly solve the strange puzzle. At the same time, she was filled with the fear of what lay below. She closed the window and sat down to her cards again.

2

Later that night Inge Linge heard the doorbell ring, a single note. She was crouched in the chair. As the sound died away, the door opened softly. Only Major Detleff von Fuchs had a key. Once he had said there were snakes writhing in her eyes. Standing in the doorway now, under the blue gleam of the corridor nightlight, was an unknown German officer. His tired face bore long saber scars and his eyes were a steel blue. There was no sign of his rank on the epaulets of his tightly belted leather overcoat. It was the sort of coat the U-boat commanders wore in the newsreel she had seen only the Friday before. For a moment she was afraid he might be one of them. He had a large paper bag draped over his arm that made him look like a tailor's delivery boy.

Inge Linge felt as though her heart had begun to beat with a different rhythm, and her blood had begun to flow backwards through her veins, causing her pulse to flutter. Her fear quickly became expectation and she was prepared to accept the arrival of this unknown man as a sign of change for the better, although he had not yet said who he was, where he had come from, and why he had come to her, of all people. Maybe the rebels weren't doing as well as the concierge had pretended when she'd left her alone in the apartment, or as well as the 415 meter band announcer declared when he urged the rebels to fight on.

In the silence and darkness Inge Linge could hear the man's

breathing. Even if nothing happened, she thought to herself, the spell of her solitude had been broken. She smiled. The man carried, in addition to the paper bag, a small attaché case. He looked around the room nervously. Then he shrugged and sighed. She didn't understand. Before she could say anything, he spoke.

"You must excuse me if my visit is inconvenient," he said in a heavy voice. "Major Fuchs sent me here. My name is Paul Walter Manfred zu Loring-Stein. I was military observer at the People's Court in Prague. You seem to be alone here. I should like to stay with you for an hour or two."

Her mind was busy with his complicated name. Then she realized it wasn't wise for her to loiter, endangering them both if any of the tenants appeared.

"Please come in and close the door," she said quickly. And then, "I hope nobody saw you."

"I don't think anyone did."

When he spoke, the multicolored saber wound on his face moved as though it were following his words. There were three scars, side by side.

"You are courteous," he said in a low, serious voice. "Today a German woman is like an island in this city."

Her reply was a hesitant, forced laugh.

Then he said, "We sound as though we had met at a dance, but things are worse." He probed her uncertain smile carefully—thinking that the rebels had grown stronger in the past forty-eight hours, and the Germans weaker—and then went on. "I belonged to the Tribunal presided over by Counsellor Dr. Johannis Danziger. He was transferred to Wiedenbruck and took the last Mercedes. I myself was on my way to Germany and was taken by surprise when bandits captured the railway station. You can imagine the rest."

"I never thought judges looked like this."

"What do you mean, like this?"

"Like this. . . ." She wanted to say she had expected a monocle and a protruding stomach.

"Is there any danger that we'll be overheard?"

"I don't think so. On the left there's a separate building, and on the other side there's only an old woman who has lived alone for several years now. The rest of the family appeared before the People's Court in '42. I don't really know why."

"Are you a member of the National Socialist German Workers
Party?"

The question didn't surprise her too much. She realized at once that
the emotion she had felt in him that first moment in the dark, before
he had begun to speak and the saber scars had begun to quiver up
and down, had not been real. He was a German, filled with fears like
her own, a soldier, an officer, and a man. Wasn't that the most important thing?

Although her memory was not well trained to deal with names—this
had caused her some trouble at the Labor Office—his name stuck: Paul
Walter Manfred zu Loring-Stein. With the same horror she had felt
when she realized how alone she was, she remembered that she was
wearing ordinary cotton underwear. She had possessed the foresight,
however, to have sewn on the labels from more expensive underwear
she had bought in Paris. She was pleased, too, that Detleff von Fuchs
had sent her a judge. Recently her visitors had been soldiers from the
Hradcany Hospital.

"I'm all alone here and I was beginning to feel that it was more than
anyone could bear on his own." Now that this man had come, the
meaning of Father Hesmussen's words—"The two went forth together"—had changed.

The officer who stood looking at Inge Linge did not understand the
light in her green eyes. He had too many other things to worry about to
wonder why her nostrils were quivering and her eyelids fluttering. She
was thinking to herself that she would almost prefer his "zu Loring-
Stein" to have been bought like Major Fuchs's "von." Perhaps the
mere fact of his coming had saved her life, for she was no longer alone.
If that other woman, Ida Geron, had died, Inge Linge thought suddenly,
it would be better, if she were really and truly dead, with somebody who
could officially confirm the fact. People from the law courts could do
anything; they had laws and papers and rubber stamps for all purposes.

It was a silly idea. She realized at once how foolish it was, but
she still felt the wave of relief that had come over her when she
saw somebody else standing in the doorway. "The two went forth
together." Perhaps if there really were someone who could confirm
it, her fears might disappear, too. She looked at the military judge
as he walked past her with his right hand in his pocket and marched
slowly and deliberately around the entire apartment, examining the
kitchen and bedroom. When he returned to the hall, he looked into

the lavatory and out of the little window into the ventilating shaft, and into the bathroom as well.

"Which way do your windows face? Into the courtyard or out onto the street? Would you mind pulling the blackout curtains down?"

She responded to both his questions by pulling down the curtains; meanwhile, he put his things down. He waited until she had switched on the light.

He must have been surprised by something his words had not expressed, for he remained silent, first watching Inge Linge and then the fish in her aquarium. There were black fish, and tiny transparent fish swam gaily around them. The ripple of the water made the green plants sway. The military judge's lips were set. Now that she was no longer alone, Inge Linge was herself again.

"I'll put the kettle on for tea," she said comfortingly, and knew at once that she was going to behave differently. But her quiet, boyish alto voice sounded oddly hoarse. She asked herself why she still felt so frightened.

She said no more, and set out the teapot, cups and sugar bowl, gifts from a Russian town on the Don. Somewhere out there, on that day of national mourning, it had all begun. Or was it on the Volga? She had always confused the two.

"Thank you," Paul Walter Manfred zu Loring-Stein said, and then he thought for a moment. "If you would care for coffee, and would not feel hurt, I have some with me."

She was filled with joy and the hoarseness left her voice. "The two went forth together." Wasn't this a good sign? This high-ranking officer had what she had missed before. He was a German, a man, and not an emissary of the revolution.

She was looking at the door leading into the corridor. She had two kinds of doors. One was a heavy wooden door made from an ash tree, painted white, with two locks, top and bottom, and with a chain she'd bought in a hardware store with a German name at the Old Town square. And then the door into the bedroom: two white wings just a bit broader than a man's shoulders, the upper panels made of milk glass with a horn of plenty pattern. In the center, like a transparent moon, was a ball resembling the crystal balls old women stared into.

"What do things look like out there?" she asked.

"It's difficult to tell. What do they say on the radio?"

"I've only heard the rebel announcer. They seem to be holding out.

It sounded as if there was some shooting close to his microphone—a nasty crackly noise. Rifle fire, or a pistol. Quite close. The announcer said they were fighting the tyrants. He couldn't have meant us, could he? You . . . or even me?''
     "Can't you get one of our stations?''
     "They say they have surrounded the houses from the Czernin Palace down to Kepler Street where there was a German machine gun nest.''
     Her direct, rather frightened eyes were now focused on the officer. He was still in his early thirties, she guessed. His hair was soft and light, the kind that never turns gray, and his complexion was fair, too. He was tall and very slim. She watched him bend over his luggage, his back curving in a graceful arch, the gray leather of his overcoat stretched taut, smooth and gleaming like the sea. He took the tin of coffee out of his case and handed it to her with military certainty.
     She couldn't tell what he was thinking. The judge dropped his eyes and thought to himself that she might have suggested he take off his coat and make himself at home. He would have welcomed a proper apology for what she could and could not offer him if he had to spend the dangerous time here with this little Inge Linge after a hard day's work examining informers. She was only a whore who tried to look like a Niebelungen beauty; he would have to be blind in both eyes and deaf to the hoarse note in her voice, and would have to forget what Major Fuchs had hinted at when he'd sent him here, not to see that. Even on a desert island he wouldn't want to exchange more than a few words with this woman. But he tried to keep the smile on his face. He wondered what he'd do if she became too insistent.
     "Shouldn't you take your name off the front door?''
     "The people here know me, and they've settled their accounts with me already.''
     "Who lives in the house?''
     "There are only women at home now, and they won't bother me anymore. They slapped my face this morning when I went out to get the milk, and called me names. I don't think they really believe I was ever a tyrant. I've never done anyone any harm.''
     Then she added, "Why don't you take your things off? There's nothing to be afraid of. Major Fuchs never lets anyone down.''
     The military judge still didn't move to take off his coat. "Isn't there anybody in that chemist's shop?''
     "No, the owner got himself a gun and went off with the other men

this morning. He had one of our tropical helmets on his head."

"Fuchs said this was a quiet spot, but he didn't say anything about that shop. Won't you take your name off your door?"

"I don't want to open the door unless I have to. If you think I should, though. . . . They told me what they thought of me this morning, and they slapped my face, and that settles things between us. I suppose they've won, now, and there'll be courts set up to judge . . . but not me . . . I really never have done anybody any harm. I haven't got the heart to hurt anyone."

She saw his thoughtful metallic blue eyes in the network of saber scars, and she couldn't be sure whether or not he approved of what she had felt forced to say.

"I didn't look out of the window until now, in the dark," she went on. "There was shooting quite near. I expect it was near the Regulus Hotel, but that was this morning. They've got all the arms that were stored opposite the police headquarters in St. Bartholomew's Street. That's why I think the men who went away won't come anywhere near us."

Because the officer maintained his skeptical silence, her thoughts returned to that woman's hooked nose. And once again she asked herself whether it was possible to grant or withhold the right to live. Here, with an expert on questions of law, she could ask and receive the comfort of reply. Why should she go on worrying about something she couldn't help anyway? Wasn't it a great Reich, and wasn't it clear that the Reich had the right to use cruelty in order to prevent others from destroying it?

If only this military judge would take his coat off—she imagined him in the judge's cap they wore at the Special Courts—and if only he would bother to respond when she was making such efforts at conversation! It was easier to talk to people who were not so educated.

Now Paul Walter Manfred zu Loring-Stein saw that Inge Linge was by no means as calm as she pretended to be. His steel-blue eyes took in the droop of her mouth, the embittered expression.

"This should never have happened to us," he said. He was taking off his leather coat with its satin lining stitched in a diamond pattern. "It should not have happened at all. Europe was ours, from the Atlantic to the Urals. This should not have happened to us. It appears we put our affairs in the wrong hands. We couldn't be everywhere."

It seemed to Inge Linge that the tubercular Ida Geron had gotten into

her head, behind the snake-green of her eyes, that she was peeling the
tissue from them and saying something in a soft voice which no one else
could hear. The judge, too, was thinking of one thing as he said another,
in a low voice: "There's no need to lose hope. We still have an
untouched army a million strong. We'll still show them what's what,
German fashion."

"Let me hang up your coat by my uniform here." And when she had
put the coat away she said, "I have some rolls here, but they're left over
from Friday."

Perhaps it would disappear, after all: that ugly living ghost with its
hooked nose. The courts would need some confirmation. Paul Walter
Manfred zu Loring-Stein spoke to her as an equal even though his
"Madam" and his smile lacked the intimacy she anticipated. She was
an expert in different sorts of servicemen. She had given hospitality to
sappers, foot soldiers, gunners, signal corpsmen, and airmen.

She knew that gunners were hard of hearing, and that when the signal
corpsmen heard there was something in the air that might spoil their
leave, they would search the middle waves of the radio, since the Reich
secret police had all the short and long waves taken out of even German
radios. She knew how generous and yet how niggardly officers could
be, how impatient they could be, and how quickly their interest waned
once they had taken the edge off their appetites. Short gasps of
happiness were all that remained of her first boss at the Labor Office.
Their first task was to fight: soldiers fought and generals won battles.
But both lost something through this, and had less time for love. The
generals never came to her apartment. The soldiers were different. They
covered their feelings with rough talk and ridiculing themselves and her.

She had never had such an attractive and well-educated man with her
before. Soon she would be able to ask him where he'd seen service,
whether he'd been wounded, what battles he'd won. No man would
refuse to speak with ostentatious modesty of the risks he had run; no
man would refuse to reply to her questions. He would tell her all about
the law and the courts, crime and punishment, criminals and cases.

Everyone had something to be proud of. She had never learned to be
anything else. She had never been anything but a woman. She was
flattered by a visit like this, as well as uneasy and uncomfortable.

Paul Walter Manfred zu Loring-Stein had taken off his fine officer's
cap and put it on the crepe-covered armchair. His hair was as gold as the
sun, brushed smoothly and neatly over his narrow head. He did not

speak for a long time, and she imagined his scarred, gloomy brow full of deep thoughts; she took his mistrust for cleverness. He saw that after his few vague remarks the corners of her mouth were turning upwards again. She was smiling at the wardrobe, where his magnificent coat hung next to her green cotton overalls, and at his peaked military cap, lying on the crepe-covered chair.

"You must have suffered a great deal," she began.

"Lock the door and we'll block it so no one can get in. We can push this wardrobe against it." Paul Walter Manfred zu Loring-Stein took a broomstick and broke it awkwardly in half; he put the pieces down on the floor and managed to roll the wardrobe onto them towards the door. His fingers were strong and white, with ginger hairs at the first joint. He waited for Inge Linge to lock the door and slip past him—so close that he could smell the creams she used—and then he pushed the wardrobe up against the door.

"Do you see what I mean?" he asked. "Law is strength. That is the whole secret. Now I can make up for what I've missed the last three nights. We were sitting until the very last minute; there were about two thousand of them to be sentenced during April and May, their people and ours."

When Paul Walter Manfred zu Loring-Stein spoke his words seemed real, made of lead. Now his silence had the same quality. She imagined him standing in his judge's robes, passing sentence. It was strange that for no reason she imagined it all happening in a dark rocky ravine, and, instead of a black gown, he had on a bearskin. His tired eyes watched her. He really hasn't slept for a long time, she thought, and she felt sorry for him, as though there were no cruelty in what he said, in life, or anywhere in the world. The mess they were in had brought them all down to the same level after all.

3

The night passed slowly.

"You've got everything you need," Inge Linge assured him for at least the third time. "The men are certainly out of the building." The officer-judge's look brightened and in his eyes she thought she saw the one response that could touch a chord deep within her.

"Are you of pure German blood?" he asked.

"What do you mean, exactly?"

"Are you from Germany, or from around here?"

"From Germany. From Magdeburg."

She remembered the soldier who had made fun of the Russian armies: A single soldier puts a horse to a two-wheeled cart, loads the cart with as much munition as the little horse can pull, and rides for over forty kilometers on a road muddier than German fantasy can imagine. If nothing befalls the horse or the soldier along the way, what happens next? The soldier had laughed in his bed: They'll use up the munition, kill the horse, roast it over the wood from the cart and then eat it. She wondered how different this military judge would be from that soldier; they both had two eyes and a nose.

The officer-judge looked doubtfully at her for a moment. She turned on the radio, tuning the receiver in search of the 415 meter band. When she found it, the announcer declared that Prague was fighting well and that the battle had moved from the suburbs to the center of the city. She turned the volume as low as possible. Sections of the enemy army had surrendered. Whenever tanks were sent against rebel units, they were either disabled by Molotov cocktails or else they surrendered. "Attention, attention! Prague is fighting . . ." Then he said it all over again. She turned it off.

"What did they say?"

She tried to tell him briefly.

"Were your parents German?"

"Of course," she replied. "Do you feel rested now?"

"I am a lawyer and I like to have certain fundamental things quite clear. I am sure you understand. Where could I change?"

Inge Linge smiled. It occurred to her that whenever two people came together, it was always possible for something to happen between them.

"You can change here or in the next room." And then, "My grandmothers on both sides were quite in order."

"Naturally," he answered. "That was not what I meant."

"I was almost afraid," she began, and waited for him to ask of what, so she could answer that she was afraid he had really come to her apartment only to change clothes.

Paul Walter Manfred zu Loring-Stein assumed that it was his question that had startled her, and asked no more. "So they closed the chemist's.

That's a good thing.'' He looked at her with his gunmetal-blue eyes. Not a muscle moved in his face.

"The kettle's boiling," she announced.

He raised his pale, sun-bleached eyebrows. He was thinking how strange it was that he—a judge, an officer, and a historian—should have come here to this little creature of the streets to find a refuge where he could pause to consider his next move. They had not counted on this uprising.

Was it only a matter of days now, or even hours? Was it a question of which Allied army got to Prague first? He gritted his teeth. And if worse came to worst and the fighting drew closer to this quiet street where the half-gypsy Detleff Fuchs had sent him to hide, he'd stand at the window and fire until his ammunition was gone, as the Germans had done at Annaberg.

He looked around the apartment. The wardrobe stood against the door and there was a big empty space where it had been, with old cobwebs on the wall. Inge Linge slowly swept away a cobweb and squashed the spider.

Meanwhile, Paul Walter Manfred zu Loring-Stein had discovered all there was to know about the place. If things turned out as he was hoping they would, he'd be leaving as quickly as he had come. He wouldn't let this little whore, who kept rolling her eyes and trying to act like a widow, get in his way.

He followed the silent movements of the black fish in the dark green water. The tips of their dorsal fins broke the surface. The bright little neon fish swayed rapidly from one glass wall to the other.

Even if she'd saved his life—and maybe she had, who could tell?—still, he wouldn't burden himself with her. Nor could he give her any reason to think he might bother with her. At the same time, he wondered whether he could leave as easily as he'd come, and he began to worry about ensuring that he could. For the first time, it occurred to him that she might betray him. Should he make certain of his safe departure by performing as expected? A swine like Detleff Fuchs might saddle himself with her. Someone in the German High Command must have a cruel sense of humor to have put a man like that in charge of the Protection of the Reich German Women in Prague.

In 1941 Adolf Hitler had thought of turning Paris into a vast amusement park for the whole of the Third Reich, but it hadn't worked out. Nor had the floods that were meant to hold up the invading Allies.

Around Dieppe almost everything had drowned; beyond that, it wasn't so simple. Those were the great days when Hitler, the parvenu, still found favor with the German nobility, the army, and the High Command. A lot of things had happened during 1943 that might have turned out either way. The law had decided to wait and see and to serve in the meantime. The fact that all was not revealed before the putsch, but only afterwards, had confused things for everyone.

It occurred to him that he might be able to buy his security in advance. He suddenly wanted to win Inge Linge's trust; her look was bold and skeptical. He was well aware that a mistrustful person is never easily or completely deceived. If it meant she would have to do unpleasant things to get there, would she even try to escape to Germany?

The furniture was not new. He was looking at it with an appreciation he hoped she would notice. Probably Major Fuchs had had a hand in that, too. He was responsible for the confiscated furniture stores of Bohemia and Moravia, as well as for the Protection of the Reich German Women in Prague. He was grateful to the major for giving him this hiding place. But what if the fighting did spread to this part of the city? Had the swine sent him here deliberately to get rid of him? It might have been treachery, or it might have been the only way out.

He could, even today, have Major Fuchs shot without the slightest regret. He told himself that he must get some sleep.

"Are you sure the light can't be seen from the passage? Through a crack in the door, or the spyhole?"

"Yes, I'm sure."

"I have brought you a little present; I don't want something for nothing." He probably wasn't as sensual as she would have liked, and he wanted to make his intention quite clear while gaining her confidence in some other way.

"Oh, no, I wouldn't like you to think that of me." Inge Linge's reply was unexpected.

Paul Walter Manfred zu Loring-Stein took out a small jewel. She didn't see that his interest was elsewhere, and not on her soft white hands and this house with the black marble front. For a moment she forgot black-haired Ida Geron, but it was strange for how short a time. It occurred to her that that woman, too, had been young once. She, too, might have received a gift from a man. But the gifts given to people like her had always passed into the wrong hands.

"Does Detleff Fuchs come here often?"

"Thank you," Inge Linge managed to say at last. "No . . . I don't expect him . . . I haven't seen him in a long time."

"There would be no danger for him in this street," Paul Walter Manfred zu Loring-Stein said in a voice too detached for her not to hear another undertone as well. "This isn't quite the center of the city. Still, I don't think any insurance company worth its salt would cover us now. I doubt if we'd even find a judge to set us free. And if we get hurt, there's not even a bandage left in the chemist's across the way."

Inge Linge suddenly stopped wanting to calm his fears. "You said you wanted to get some sleep. You can go to bed."

For the second time he thought she might betray him. Were she and von Fuchs plotting against him? He didn't like her green eyes, reflecting, perhaps, her weakness. Every woman who was attracted to him wanted something. He had to resist her influence with every fiber of his will.

Inge Linge was silent. Had the jewel belonged to his family? Had he taken it from someone? He was a judge, after all. He dealt with the law and the courts.

In her mind, she saw again the inflamed eyes of the tearful soldier, and he was telling her how they sent everything home to Germany, even umbrellas, spectacles, artificial limbs, and gold teeth. He told her how they used coal shovels to pile up the heaps of children's shoes, and how glad he was that his little niece had been killed by a bomb. It must have been a mountain of children's shoes: white and blue and pink ones, with straggly laces.

But Paul Walter Manfred zu Loring-Stein was looking into the wardrobe again. It seemed rather too luxurious. He thought about how they had all been ready when the trough was filled to the brim with the loot of the special commandos.

The dresses were heavy with perfume. It made him feel a hundred times sleepier. Why should he restrain himself in front of this little whore? Why shouldn't he do what he wanted to?

He looked at Inge Linge. He took in her firm little figure, the knotted muscles of her legs, one crossed over the other. He looked at her calmly through his network of saber scars. She was a woman for hire, a saloon artist on whom all he said was wasted. Just as Detleff Fuchs would never stop stealing and whoring with anyone who came his way, so this creature would go on spreading her legs in the name of the Third

Reich—in the name of anything—for herself. His eyes had begun to smart. He was more tired than he had thought. He was thinking about the men he'd seen during the last several hours—the unstable characters, disintegrating people.

Did she have siblings? Was there illness in her family? He was thinking about hereditary diseases. He remembered the sleek, well-cared-for riding horses, and leaning on the fence to watch the slow, rhythmic movements of the grazing horses. Huge in the dense gray mist, they reminded him of the local farm wives, with broad buttocks and breasts and modest pride.

The military judge was reading her every motion, even though she hadn't batted an eyelash. He detested fat women and knew in the depths of his soul that if she were to appear before the court, she wouldn't have a chance. The way she was trying to seduce him, as if she were snaring him in a trap, insulted him. It reminded him of the scent of perfume that attaches itself to a man. He gave her a wry smile which Inge Linge immediately returned with one of her own.

She didn't know what the military judge wanted from her and turned it upside down: What would he not want? The judge's look slid down her neck.

He was feeling the tired energy of the woman before him. He didn't like people who had neither the ability to speak nor the strength to keep silent. Disgust and disdain were rising up inside him, forcing him to control himself.

"Do you think I could lie down without fear of perfidy, then?" he asked dryly.

"Of course." Inge Linge went to turn the bed covers down. She did not know what he meant by "perfidy."

"I want to be alone." It sounded like an order.

The corners of her mouth drooped. He was harsh. Why did he behave as though she were going to bite him, or as though he found her disgusting? Once more she felt guilty because of Ida Geron with her TB, and goodness only knew what had become of her. Now she doubted that sharp line of division which had once separated her from people like Ida Geron or Jenny Burckhart, who used to live in their street, or her father, Ferdinand Linge, as long as he had been alive and lathering the chins of all ranks and services except the Hungarian cavalry. She knew the woman had died long before; indeed, there was no need for anyone to give her confirmation of that fact. She still saw her as she had looked that day—with the two bags no one helped her to carry.

"Naturally," she said aloud. "Here's your bed. Sleep well. I'll be in the kitchen."

She walked out slowly, as though she'd given up the battle, hurt and surprised by herself. He did not create the diversion she'd hoped he would. She thought about the officer-judge, and Paul Walter Manfred zu Loring-Stein let his eyes rest on the wall where the picture was hanging.

"Is that a Prussian general?"

Inge Linge looked around and nodded. The figure was wearing a blue general's uniform with broad red cuffs and a high stiff yellow collar that made him hold his nose in the air.

She went out and shut the door behind her. Perhaps it was all due to his fatigue. She should have realized it sooner and saved herself the trouble. He wasn't a pear hanging on a tree waiting to be plucked. If only Paul Walter Manfred zu Loring-Stein had tried to overcome his anxiety, had tried to forget it all, things wouldn't have been too bad. Now she realized that the officer-judge who was so coldly dispassionate would stay or not stay according to his own judgment. The bells had finally stopped pealing. Neither Father Hesmussen nor Herr Haske was likely to be asleep, though. Germans in Prague would not be sleeping. She felt like someone who wonders what parts of herself had been lost along the way, someone who stops wanting to go on.

She tried to sleep on the sofa in the kitchen. She feared rejection. Was it rejection? But instead she lay on her back and gazed with open eyes at the dark ceiling. Where did it come from, this longing to be with someone, even though the other didn't feel it in the least? She listened to what was on the other side of the wall. Paul Walter Manfred zu Loring-Stein was lying in bed but he wasn't resting. She could hear him tossing and turning. The house was silent. Number 14 Chestnut Street was not part of the Prague uprising, and suddenly Inge Linge was not sure that she was really glad of that.

4

Later, the judge saw how depressed she was and knew he ought to cheer her up. His head ached as he watched her cross the room toward the radio.

"I thought I heard someone tapping," Inge Linge said to explain her entrance. It was clear that she was lying.

Paul Walter Manfred zu Loring-Stein crouched a little. "When? Now?" The saber scars seemed to be moving across his face.

"It's been quite a while now."

"Did you hear it a second time?"

"No."

"Are you sure?"

"No."

"Couldn't you have dreamed it?" He was listening carefully now.

"Yes," she answered, suddenly weary. "I think I must have dreamed it. I can't bear to be alone now."

"Pull yourself together."

"What's going to happen?"

"We have to wait. And anyone who doesn't know how will just have to learn, that's all."

"Are we going to lose?"

"Certainly not, not in the long run."

"I'm only afraid I may not live to see the day. That's why I'm so uneasy."

She twisted the radio dial and wondered whether she would be able to hold out until the very end.

Then the 415 meter band came on the air. The announcer quoted the Flensburg German transmitter, saying clearly: "Germany has surrendered. After five years and eight months of fighting, Germany has given up the struggle. This announcement was made by the German Minister of Foreign Affairs himself, in a speech broadcast from Flensburg, Germany, at 1430 hours. These were his words: 'Men and women of Germany! The German Supreme Command, on the orders of Admiral Doenitz, announced today that all German forces are to surrender unconditionally.' Reuters adds that it is not yet known whether these orders will be obeyed by all the German forces still actively fighting. In Norway the Germans have surrendered . . ."

She turned the radio down and half-closed her eyes.

"For God's sake . . . you heard it yourself . . ."

"Calm yourself. There must be something else on. It could be a trick."

She remained standing in the middle of the room. With her green eyes fixed on the scarred face of Paul Walter Manfred zu Loring-Stein, she remembered the very first time she had been with a man. She hadn't been very sure of what she was doing. She didn't even know as much as Jenny Burckhart, then. She had stroked his thighs and felt him tremble, waiting with bated breath for what would come next, for whatever she would do with her gentle, sensitive, caressing fingers. When she'd realized how happy she'd made him, she felt happy, too.

It was never the same after the first time. There were moments when it came back to her, like a distant reward for much hard work, but it was never more than a feeble reflection of what she remembered. When she woke up the next day she wanted to sing, she felt so happy.

She watched the steel-blue eyes of Paul Walter Manfred zu Loring-Stein. She felt sure she knew him. She might have forgiven him the insult of the night before. She really was what the concierge had called her.

The 415 meter band, which was now her weapon, spoke up again as her fingers turned the knob: "The Allies officially announced today that Germany has unconditionally surrendered. The act of surrender took place at 1441, French time, in the small school which houses Allied Headquarters. General Kurt Jodl signed for Germany. Although Admiral Doenitz has unconditionally surrendered, it is probable that at the last moment Field Marshal Schorner will order his forces in Bohemia—"

The broadcast was suddenly interrupted and Inge Linge turned away, as though even the radio had let her down.

"Can you get me a glass of water?"

She said nothing.

For a second his eyes—narrow, steel-blue, and cold—seemed almost dead.

Suddenly she had to leave the room before she did something inexplicable.

5

When she returned the officer-judge was not wearing pajamas or his uniform with its green and silver epaulets. He had changed into a dark gray civilian suit and was standing in front of her mirror. He looked like the representative of a German export firm. His blue eyes were nearly kind. Tall, neat, with a polite expression on his face, he was quite different. Only the saber scars did not fit his new image. The paper bag in which he'd carried his suit had been flung carelessly onto the bed. The sheet was turned back, and from the bed came the sickly fragrance of her own perfume mingled with his warmth.

As Inge Linge gazed with involuntary admiration at the man, the insult of the previous day dissolved and sank deep down to join the image of black-eyed Ida Geron. Paul Walter Manfred zu Loring-Stein was wearing a plain sea-blue tie. He looked serious but refreshed. The sight of him awoke in Inge Linge the same longing that had overwhelmed her the day before in the kitchen. The longing was memory, an echo of a feeling long past.

"I get silly ideas when I'm alone too long," she said. "It's no wonder. I'm ashamed of it, though. How did you sleep?"

Her last words were spoken in a low voice. Her hoarse alto rang with anxious appeal for the warmth of human companionship and a strange fear that sprang from the fate of that other woman who had walked about this same apartment. "And the two went forth together."

"Thank you, I really needed to sleep," replied Paul Walter Manfred zu Loring-Stein. He looked around and said, "I like your flowers. I like flowers."

She looked with appreciation at his fine, tall figure. She knew only too well that there were not many men like him left now. She understood the situation in her own way. She felt grateful to him for being more accessible. What did she expect from a man at a time like this? Understanding, coddling, the return of affection, or at least the sharing of it?

Inge Linge felt like going to him and stroking him. She trembled seeing the gleam in his blue eyes and the saber scars. She wanted to soften him for herself. She had misunderstood him.

Paul Walter Manfred zu Loring-Stein was thinking that nothing was sacred to a woman like Inge Linge. She did not share the concern that occupied the men and women of Germany at this dreadful moment—the loss of the rights and power of the great Reich. You whore, he thought to himself. He wanted to shout: Our great men are dying, and all you can think of is that?

"When the sun shines, as it does now, and the sky is so clear, there are wonderful blue days in Prague," she said. "I don't know why they seem so blue. Perhaps because of the bluish-colored roofs and the gardens."

"Blue days," Paul Walter Manfred zu Loring-Stein repeated thoughtfully. He wondered whether dark-skinned Detleff Fuchs made sure that women like Inge Linge were inspected thoroughly and often by an army doctor. Fuchs ought to hang, according to the canons of military law. The deep-set eyes darkened. The face with its mobile scars flushed. Maybe even her blood was bad for transfusions for wounded soldiers.

"Have you got someplace I can burn my things?"

"No," Inge Linge said. "Major Fuchs had everything wired for electricity. He was afraid of gas and open fires. I haven't got even a cellar here. I gave it up to the concierge. It's a big family, three men. They all work on the trolleys."

"Could you hide these for me then?"

"There's only the cupboard. I could put them way at the back."

He was reconciled to the fact that beneath that fair hair, carelessly loose about the temples, her head was empty and her snake-green eyes were without intelligence.

"Hide it somewhere," he said. "You know how important that is just now."

She felt the need to turn the light out. It was sudden and obvious. Everything was mixed up in her head—a head so round that German officers always said her mother must have come from Bohemia, or at any rate from Upper Silesia, where everything was so mixed. But certainly not from Germany. She turned the center light off and left on only the little white bulb behind the green aquarium. Flat-colored fish were swimming about, slowly and lazily. As long as she'd been able to buy fresh ants' eggs every day, they'd avoided the big black fish, but now they came out of hiding even during the daytime. They wanted to be as near the surface as possible when she sprinkled food for them. Now they were all starving and would be lucky to survive until dawn.

Once again Inge Linge saw the image of that woman floating there, the woman who once breathed the dry air of this apartment and then, as the young soldier had said, had been frightened by a final, bitter smell. Inge Linge reproached herself. She shouldn't think about it, if only because she was sitting here alive, with a well-built man, drinking tea. Because she existed at all, separate and apart, since there was no hope of union with anyone else.

She switched the radio on. It was her comfort, her weapon, and a challenge to him to stay with her.

"Who lives next door?"

"The men have all gone, and on that side there isn't a man, anyway.
I told you so. They were arrested and never came back. I'll keep the
sound low."

Sarah Leander was singing softly on one of the stations. Inge Linge
knew the words to the song. She half-closed her eyes and watched Paul
Walter Manfred zu Loring-Stein. How many men she had held in her
arms, good God! Even if they hadn't all been his sort exactly, with his
fancy name—as long as he hadn't stolen it, of course, or made it up.
Would he really be as well-bred as he pretended to be if they ever got
into a tight corner? She knew very well that his kind of breeding
encouraged generosity when there was plenty, but meanness when bad
times came. What sort of breeding was it, though, that required a man
to withhold himself when there were thousands of reasons not to? It was
a pity the major had not come. He wouldn't have left her comfortless at
a moment like this. The singer finished her song and the dance music
played on softly.

"Are the walls here so thick that you can be so lighthearted?"

"You can't hear through them. I've tried. You can believe me."

"Whether I believe you or not isn't the point."

Inge Linge was becoming more and more conscious of the silhouette
of the man facing her, as though her breathing helped her feel him more
clearly. She sat politely drinking her tea, watching his dark eyes with
their metallic gleam. She felt a new wave of excitement pass over her.
He really does have a fine figure, she told herself again, ready to devote
complete attention to careful scrutiny of his person, even his saber
scars. She wished simply to drown the fact that they were afraid of each
other, the two of them, like dogs and cats, or cats and rats. Then a new
fear swept over her, an anger, and a sense of expectation.

"It was a funny sort of day today. I couldn't sleep."

She couldn't help thinking again of the woman with the shriveled
breasts. Where was the Jewish woman's grave, if she had one at all?

For women such as this one, Paul Walter Manfred zu Loring-Stein
thought, for women who lived in hotels that had become dormitories in
the hostile, conquered territories, German soldiers had stolen. They stole
towels, silverware, lacy lingerie, napkins, pillows. Sometimes they
used ships, which became transport vessels for the stolen goods. Others
who had the opportunity and who couldn't withstand the temptation stole
diamonds and rings for them in camps. He had only to look around the

apartment to get the full picture. He grinned to himself. There was no need to reach deep into his memory to recall other such cases he'd judged. The war had become an opportunity for many. His eyes were cold and held a sense of distance.

"It's night," she said to fill the silence. "The morning will come." Didn't Detleff von Fuchs sometimes say that you should protect yourself from those for whom you'd done a favor? Had it been perhaps something other than kindness that led him to send this man to her place?

She thought of the spring, which she'd always liked better than the fall; she thought of the way spring changes so much, everything changes from the ground up. Daddy shaved men in the street and told them: The worms in the cheese are made out of the cheese itself. She wished her father were closer. She thought of fish and swallows. Of the church and prayers. She was afraid of the night, of all that she would hear in the darkness.

She remembered what two Italian soldiers who had come here together had told her right away, in order to give themselves courage: The secret sin is a sin halfway forgiven in advance. The Italian soldiers were different from the German soldiers. They acted like people who had come by mistake to a different coffeehouse and, since they were already there, would order coffee or wine; but one could see that they'd be more comfortable someplace else. Those two Italians had laughed and said that to pray and to sleep are the same thing.

"I want to be practical."

"Of course. We both have to be practical."

"I don't want to be obnoxious."

The military judge didn't answer that. In her eyes he caught flashes of the instinct for self-preservation.

The military judge looked at her. What did she know of the People's Court passing death sentences for everything, including so-called nothings? He had learned a long time ago to read with a sixth sense the slightest gesture and facial movement of every person. He had inside him a map of his own world that also measured time; he wanted to spend it as he wished, not according to other people's demands. His mind selected, identified, accounted and classified. He would weigh and measure the wind and the stillness if he could. He had in him a compass he retained and which he would never give up. He felt connected with something of a higher order than what was incarnated by this plump little whore, with whom he had to share his company. Innocence made his skin crawl.

"I'm glad you are here with me," she sighed. "I wanted to tell you last night that there was no need to give me anything. Maybe you have someone at home who could use the ring."

"It's out of the question. I know what I'm doing . . . assuming that I stay here, of course. It's dragging on and you didn't expect that it would."

"Thank you, thank you very much . . . that's not what I meant, though." Then she added resignedly, "That's not why I said it."

6

For supper Paul Walter Manfred zu Loring-Stein sacrificed two tins of Portuguese sardines. Inge Linge opened a jar of peaches and a jar of Italian apples. The officer-judge thought again that Detleff Fuchs, who had humbugged the Racial Office, had never had any use for military inspection. And undoubtedly he had sent doctors anywhere but here, where they were most needed.

"I've never been alone here for so long. I always try to be brave. In a little while they may start shooting again."

"What would you say if somebody did turn up?"

"I just wouldn't open the door. I couldn't, anyway, the wardrobe's in the way. But even if I could, I'd say you were a friend of mine, Colonel."

Then she watched him slip the safety catch on his pistol and put it back in his breast pocket.

"I like having visitors," she said. "Visitors from Italy were always the nicest." But that was not what she'd wanted to say. She thought of one flier who was killed in an aerial accident near Rome, where he was later buried. She recalled how the first time they had gone into her bedroom it had been dark except for light from the streetlamp that filtered in between the curtains. Though he had seemed passionate, he had taken the time to remove and fold his uniform carefully, draping his trousers on the chair. He had the legs of a girl. He began at her ankles and left a wet line along the length of her body. She had been told by a friend of his who'd later come to her about his remains, which were interred in the Christian cemetery. The other pilot had also been lost, in the Naples area; his body was never found. She looked at the military judge and wondered to herself: Are women more aggressive physically than men?

As she helped herself to more biscuits, her fingers brushed his. She felt him withdraw a little. She touched him again, and again she felt an almost imperceptible withdrawal. Where was it written that the man must be the aggressor? Women were better suited to that role. The old excitement rose inside her again.

Softly she began to sing in a hoarse voice that couldn't compare with the voice of Sarah Leander. What else was in the air? What did Sarah's song echo? Flensburg was silent now.

"Do you like sitting here like this?" she asked softly. Her lilac perfume was strong.

"Sometimes," he admitted. "Of course, I have a mission to fulfill, even if I am here with you. Yes, it really is nice here."

He spoke with cold brevity. And as his mouth opened to say something, anything at all, and the saber scars moved in their own way across his face, in his mind his voice was quite different. What an impudent little whore she was, indeed. Maybe she'd like it if he hit her. Adolf Hitler had been dead a week. And here he was, sitting somewhere in Prague, resisting this woman's solicitations. Maybe she would enjoy being beaten.

He would have to go on being careful. Inge Linge was persistent, and he could not push her away rudely, like a cow on a country lane. Nor could he sentence her for undermining military vigilance, particularly since he was wearing neither his judge's robes nor his officer's uniform. Perhaps she no longer felt herself tied to the German cause. After all, the concierge had considered the matter settled with a couple of slaps and a few curses. He needed this refuge for a while. If it had to be, he would just close his eyes.

"Shall I make the bed again?" Inge Linge asked. She knew for certain now that she would have her way, and she held her own with soft music and warm breezes.

"A little later," replied Paul Walter Manfred zu Loring-Stein, officer and judge. "I must finish my tea first."

7

Then Inge Linge was lying beside the officer-judge. She was still wearing a dressing gown, made of Japanese silk in a bright green floral design, the best her wardrobe had to offer.

"The bottles are all empty," she said apologetically. "I haven't got a single drop."

"It doesn't matter," he said.

He was looking at the empty bottle with complete indifference. They were strangers. She felt the urge to pick it up and fling it at his steel-blue eyes, which were full of disgust, and at his scars, to reduce the distance between them. She had before her the proud, tight-lipped mouth of an officer-judge, smelling faintly of aftershave lotion.

Yes, she thought, she was only a slut from whom anyone might turn in disgust.

Paul Walter Manfred zu Loring-Stein, although thinking more of himself than trying to fathom what was going on in Inge Linge's mind, nevertheless dimly realized what had happened. His scars were set in motion again. Her green eyes, full of distress at all the questions to which there were no answers, gazed at him, and her chestnut lashes were moist. Her complexion was pale, almost white, milky.

"I'll go and lie down in the other room."

"Why should you?" he asked. After a moment he said, "I would be better company, I suppose, if I had come to you under different circumstances."

As suddenly as she had decided to go into the next room, she now felt pity for him. Then that, too, passed away as he bit his lips, slashed and scarred in two places. Her old anxiety, driven by anger, threatened to return.

"Were you ever wounded?" she asked the military judge.

"No," he answered. "Why do you ask?" And then, "Do you think that's why . . .?" And he laughed deep and loud, as if he were laughing to himself about something else. It really meant nothing at all to this slut that the finest soldiers had been put to mending the streets. "No, I'm just preoccupied with other worries."

It was a lie. And yet what was worrying him most of all was how to get out of this lacuna of German law and order. It was taking longer than he had thought it would. For Paul Walter Manfred zu Loring-Stein would really not have enjoyed mending the streets of Prague, all dirty, his head shaved, dressed in rags.

Inge Linge felt somewhat relieved that her guess had been so near the mark. She felt a grain of superiority and the seed of a new cunning.

Paul Walter Manfred zu Loring-Stein, turning from his own thoughts, wanted to talk to her. Was he afraid even of this tramp? Was she capable of joining the bandits and betraying him? It was most unpleasant. His thoughts returned to mending streets.

"What are you thinking about?"

"Nothing in particular."

"What are we going to do?"

"We can only wait."

Could he take her with him if she asked him to? How would he get rid of her if he did? Inge Linge realized that the officer and judge Paul Walter Manfred zu Loring-Stein would never take her with him so that she could find Jenny Burckhart in Magdeburg, Number 29 Gotschal Street. He was afraid, just as fine ladies were afraid of everything that was rough, and as many of the men she knew were afraid. Again she was hurt. Under the metallic gaze of his eyes, she recoiled. Her warm breeze had chilled. She wondered whether it was really the way she thought, and she decided it was. Meanwhile, Paul Walter Manfred zu Loring-Stein lay at the very edge of the bed and felt that even that was enough to infect him.

"Would you like to go to the bathroom?" Inge Linge asked scornfully. She felt like a cat that had just spat. She realized she was being unkind but felt relieved that she had said something.

"Why? No, thank you."

Her first upsurge of anger receded, and with it the distant waves that had been rising and falling. Her green eyes, dulled and inflamed by lack of sleep, conjured up again the image of Ida Geron.

"Tell me something about yourself."

"That would be very boring," he said. "I was a soldier, a judge, I fought for Germany, and now I am a civilian."

"You will always be a soldier, even without a uniform, after the moths have eaten holes in it and it's become a dust rag."

"It will never become a dust rag!" he said sharply. He sat up on the bed. "Despondency does not become German women. Never, never dust rags."

"There was a soldier here once who did nothing but weep in my arms."

"What has that got to do with it?"

"He told me about a camp. I can't remember everything he said. I've got such a bad memory. He said there were showers, and men and women and children went in and nobody ever came out. All he had to do was open cans marked I. G. Farben. He checked every can off on a slip of paper and then he handed it in for them to send to Berlin. They were awfully strict about his checking every single can. Do you see? He had been a parachutist before, then he was demoted to the infantry. Perhaps his nerves weren't good enough for the parachutists. He didn't say exactly. Is it true what he said about those showers?"

He noticed her green buttons which looked like little rainbow flies in the faint light. The buckle on her bathrobe reminded him of a cobweb.

When she saw he would not answer, Inge Linge felt anxious. She wanted to relieve her feelings, to stop them from constantly whirling around in her mind. For the first time she thought that he might kill her. She no longer worried about what he might say next. He was still sitting up, leaning back on his elbows, the scars on his face twitching. Inge Linge lay quietly in the bright green Japanese kimono with her hands behind her head. The officer-judge watched her intently.

"A Jewess used to live in this apartment." Now it sounded terribly distant, the idea of the tubercular, dark-haired Ida Geron. "In 1942."

It must have been a long time ago, nineteen hundred and forty-two. Yes, she, Inge Linge, had the portrait of a Prussian general hanging here, nearly a hundred years old, and someone had given it to her, and his chin hadn't had been shot away. And the story ought to go on with more Czech heads, just as the judge had said so convincingly. Some shot-away chins her father had lathered with snow-white soap. Paul Walter Manfred zu Loring-Stein, Doctor of Law, was much more sure of his ground there than in bed; he must know what he was talking about. And somewhere, someone was smiling happily at it all. Inge Linge thought of the concierge's head, downstairs, and the heads of the three men of the family with the flat workmen's caps. And if that Jewess were ever to come back, her head, too.

Inge Linge looked at his gun.

"There's nothing to be frightened of. I will protect you."

"I told you I wasn't afraid anymore."

"We can only expect the worst from the people downstairs who tried to beat you up. Be glad you've got me here with you and that we aren't unarmed." Again he paused before saying, "Let me tell you something, my dear."

Inge Linge watched his lips and knew that Paul Walter Manfred zu Loring-Stein was talking to her only because he had no other audience. "Now listen," he said. "The rebels aren't likely to send dead men where I want to go, so we must do all that we can to get out alive. First I, then you." He fell silent again, disappointed that Inge Linge had not cried out enthusiastically.

Then he said dryly, "How long have you been living here—five years? A plague on this filthy city. The courts couldn't send more than a hundred to the wall each day. Don't you know what these Czechs are like? Only the most aged collaborated with us. Even though I hate them, they're like young trees full of sap and the juice of life. They were bent to the ground but they didn't break. You can stamp on them, but they spring up again, unless you shoot them in the head to make sure they're finished. It's a good thing these bandits aren't Germans, as we originally planned for the better specimens. They would have made bad Germans. But the time will come when they'll all be dead, anyway. Do you know how to use a Steyer?"

"What is it?"

"A pistol. My reserve weapon."

"No, I don't." And then: "I never bothered about such things. That's why I'm where I am, I told you."

There was a desolation within her, a graveyard in her heart. She was no longer listening to Paul Walter Manfred zu Loring-Stein. In her mind she was putting flowers on a grave, and the words of Father Hesmussen took on a new meaning. White lilies and hyacinths and red roses—not only for herself. The thousand perfumes in her bottles in that cupboard, and her underwear, artificial silk and real muslin, her beautiful dresses, and Ida Geron who had lived here before her. Inside of her, there was no trace of anxiety, nor of hate.

"They say we have done terrible things," she said.

"We only did what others would have done in our place. That, of course, is the legal way to look at it. Now we are sent to mend the streets. It's a good thing we did what we did. Fear inspires respect. They had to be shown who they were dealing with—that for each one

they killed, others would come, worse, more brutal, more ruthless.
Don't try to look innocent! Every child knows about the liquidation
squads. That was what your befuddled parachutist was talking about. I
would say he didn't deserve to be demoted to the infantry; he should
have been hanged outright. You can soothe your conscience, though.
We were never as thorough as the world would like to think.''
    "So it is the truth."
    "What do you mean, 'the truth'? Czech truth? Or even Jewish truth?"
    "I mean the baths and showers."
    "Have you seen them with your own eyes? You haven't? Everyone
should be asked that when he starts asking impertinent questions. What
you haven't seen doesn't exist, do you understand?" Then he laughed.
"My dear Inge Linge, perhaps this isn't the right moment for what I am
going to say to you. When those who survived our baths and showers
grow up, they will be astonished at how mild we were—as mild as
lambs. Relax. Where there is no evidence, there is no crime. And in a
few years . . ." He paused. "Our German lawyers will know what to do
and when and how to do it. There's no need to think about it all now,
if it makes you nervous. Things weren't as bad as people say. Our
camps were places of opportunity, after all, for our soldiers and the
undisciplined units. We gave the strong a chance and the weak a way
out. Everyone had an opportunity to show what he could do. Don't
listen to stories. There are far too many stories being told. The strong
will be grateful to us one day. The weak would have died anyway,
without our help. Life is like that. The criterion of selection."
    And he was thinking that no one would have any interest in glorifying
those who had gone to the gas chambers without resisting. He still held
his pistol in his hand. She noticed once more his strong white fingers
with the ginger hair.
    "Chin up, now! There's no need to be sad, Inge Linge."
    "They're still shooting."
    "Yes, I know."
    "I heard it while you were talking, but I'm not afraid now." She was
wondering if the rebels would do the same things that had been done
to them.
    "You were always kind to them. There's nothing for you to be afraid
of."
    His stern, metallic blue eyes searched her green eyes a third time for
signs of treachery.

"I'm living in a Jewish apartment," she replied.

"There are no Jewish apartments anymore, Miss Linge. It's as if, in addition to everything else, you let these people tie an iron ball to your legs."

It flashed through his mind how many people at this moment were begging for proofs that they had given to this or that Jew, communist, or lunatic, a ticket for a hundred grams of beef, a coupon for soap, or a train ticket to the countryside. Or trying to prove that they had paid a good price for Jewish furniture, dishes, or fur coats. The world was topsy-turvy, he thought to himself. People were confusing Germany with a whorehouse. He looked at her but was thinking about the German submarines. What are they doing now? Are they sinking enemy ships or taking their leaders to safety? German submarines, he thought: the best, the fastest, the deepest diving. What are they going to do tomorrow, the day after tomorrow, when the war is over? Are they going to surface? Where? Brazil? Canada? America?

8

She went into the kitchen, still filled with a feeling of desolation. She opened the window so that she could hear the men if they came back, and the shooting if it came into Chestnut Street. Night air filled the room. With strange deliberation Inge Linge set about her task. From a wicker hamper she took a little flag, a swastika embroidered on silk. She had been given this flag in return for her services by a nasty tank officer of the *Grossdeutschland* division, who had never dared to come and see her again. Leaning well out of the window, she attached the flag to a nail driven into the sill, left there from the days when Ida Geron had grown flowers in a windowbox. It took her some time to fasten it securely.

When at last Inge Linge finished, she stretched one hand through the window and felt a gentle breeze. She could smell gunpowder and spring and a new unsullied life. Perhaps the breeze carried the ashes of the black-eyed, black-haired, tubercular Ida Geron, and deposited them on the peeling paint of the window sill, so that the flat-breasted woman found a resting place at last. Inge Linge could smell it still. She guessed at a thousand scents when she laid the pistol on the sill by the curtains. She lay down in her Japanese kimono without a blanket to wait for daylight. The shooting came nearer, through Tyn Courtyard, where the Regulus Hotel was, and around St. James's Church. But Inge Linge no longer recalled Father Hesmussen or the pealing tones of the organ. The pistols and the Steyers and the grenades sounded closer and closer.

An hour or so before daylight, Paul Walter Manfred zu Loring-Stein looked in. She told him not to switch the light on because the window was open so that she could hear better. He looked suspicious.

"The two went forth together." It sounded like a slogan.

"I'm glad to see you are being sensible," he said. "Keep the pistol with you." The scars on his face looked almost purple.

She trembled with fear that he might go to the window.

Instead Paul Walter Manfred zu Loring-Stein left the room with the uneasy feeling that although he had managed to calm Inge Linge, his method had not been best suited to this time of anarchy.

Outside the night mist still hung in the air. As dawn broke, it began to thin. Inge Linge waited.

She looked toward the window. She felt a strange, quiet anxiety that rose within her like a wave in the sea and then fell off and began to dissolve almost into infinity. Suddenly she couldn't recall the way she looked. It was as if she saw in herself someone she'd never seen before.

Paul Walter Manfred zu Loring-Stein was waiting in the next room. At the moment of daybreak, when the steel grenades came through the windows of the apartment where once a stooping Jewish woman had lived, Inge Linge thought that at last the night had gone and day had come. She knew the sun would be shining brightly, first red, then yellow, and finally white. The blue day was there in her eyes, but nothing else now: not light, not the breeze, not even the gulping of dying fish from the shattered aquarium.

The Girl with the Scar

1

WARM, muggy air poured into the classroom. The pale girl suddenly gave a loud sigh, clearly audible in the total silence of the room. She was sitting near the teacher's desk, in the front by the window, where she could see only the tips of the magnolias on the Superintendent's house across the street; she could just glimpse the soft blue of the sky. Her sigh had somehow slipped through the barrier of the heat. She had a little face, a long, thin neck, and a small body with small breasts. It seemed as if the silence had taken her by surprise. The heat seemed to spread under her feet like an abyss, as if the tremor of an earthquake had opened up the ground. All morning it had been building up inside her, like a pressure that might erupt without the slightest warning.

She was fumbling, somewhat listlessly and absentmindedly, with a narrow-hemmed scrap of beige handkerchief which she'd made out of an old curtain in sewing class. A long, narrow scar ran across her forehead.

"Jenny Thelen," the teacher reprimanded.

"Yes, ma'am," responded the girl with the scar.

"Is that any way to behave?"

The girl said nothing, though in the reprimand there was also the promise of pardon. She languidly closed her large, green eyes; they were like sharply outlined little boats lodged in the rift beneath her scarred brow, bordered at the temples by shocks of light brown hair. She tried not to hear the teacher's throaty voice, but it rasped against her like a wire brush.

She tried to return, at least in spirit, to where she'd been before the sound of hobnailed boots, husky voices, and shrill whistles had called her back.

She let the sun caress her, its rays gently touching her like fingertips. She could feel her chest being warmed by the sun. She thought suddenly of hellfire.

On the wall, next to a picture of a scene from German history—Frederick the Great and Freiherr von Stein—there was a quotation from Immanuel Kant, lit now by the streaming sun. She tried to return to the daydream she'd begun while Elzie Mayerfeld was explaining the difference between the borders of the German Reich and those of the Great Germanic Empire.

Sunlight was playing on the magnolias. Over the Superintendent's garden shed was a big circular sign that had been used during one of the spring gymnastics festivals:

WIR WOLLEN KEINE CHRISTEN SEIN,
DEN CHRIST WAR NUR EIN JUDENSCHWEIN

When she squinted into the sun, it looked like a great, golden recording of Johann Strauss's waltz *Tales from the Vienna Woods*. The disc seemed to turn silently around its blinding center, the molten center of the sun. Hell. She closed her eyes quickly, afraid she'd go blind otherwise. But even with her eyes closed, the light seemed stronger than when she'd focused on the sun's center.

She turned her attention to Elzie Mayerfeld's dress—tight, shiny silk with large red roses and green leaves. The teacher was swinging her hips and admiring the reflection of her tall, dark, supple body in the window.

"Let's go on, *lieblings*," said Elzie Mayerfeld. Elzie Mayerfeld—known as the Dog Lady—paused in her explanation of how the frontiers of the Reich would expand over the next thousand years.

"In the struggle between wealth and poverty, which will come in the next ten centuries, the conquered and impoverished nations will have themselves to blame and not the Germans," she said. "Think of yourselves. Think positively of your own personal contributions to the welfare of Germany, rather than about who's getting rich from the suffering of others."

Through the open windows came the clatter of hobnailed boots striking the pavement—countless feet stomping in unison, marching away into the distance until only the echo of shrill fifes lingered behind. They were singing about earth and blood and the distant Fatherland, about what it meant to be a soldier in time of great crisis. The hoarse voices from the uniformed throats merged with the strict beat of the marching boots: *Hei-di, hei-do, hei-da!*

Elzie Mayerfeld's nostrils quivered. Her blond hair was pulled back in a chignon, held in place with a big tortoiseshell comb. She had smooth, pale skin; with her hair up, her bare neck was long and white. From the distance, the fifers' whistles still pierced the air and drumbeats merged with the thud of boots. The sound softened, becoming a pleasant cadence. This was the fifth day of such relentless heat. The pavement radiated the sun's warmth in waves, making the city like a furnace. The facade on the Superintendent's house was peeling, and the sills looked raw, their eagles and angels naked. Elzie Mayerfeld thought of General Rommel and the German armies in Africa.

The hard thudding of the hobnailed boots, the scent of the magnolias, and the tender sea of heat on which sound and order floated all seemed filled with the meaning of the song. The fifes, the drums, and the words—as long as they could be understood—recalled the distant Fatherland.

As the soldiers moved away, the hot air of Prague's German Quarter flowed in. Only a rhythmic echo lingered in the boundless space over the roofs of Otto Bismarck Street. Looking at the slate roofs, Elzie Mayerfeld saw an image of blood and of strong male legs—of men who pushed onward and onward, night and day, through heat and wind, to all four corners of the earth. It was an image of weathered faces with eyes squinting into the sun, faces set against a background of demolished cities and burning villages.

The sun beat down on the windowpanes. Through the silk of Elzie Mayerfeld's dress one could see the outline of her underwear. She was tall, even without high heels, and taller still when she wore them. She smiled without being aware of it. Her eyes were shining.

"There will be nothing to stop our access to grain and oil in the future. Poland and Russia will no longer block us in the east as they have for the past thousand years." The Dog Lady smiled as if she were saying that all the wealth of the world—from east and west—would begin to flow through the Reich, just as rivers flowed in their beds.

She closed her eyes. She saw herself at the military parade, the music playing. She wished to breathe into the girls' souls pictures of the fighting soldiers, consecrated to death as nuns are consecrated to God.

She felt responsible for the girls, who evoked in her desires that were forbidden.

In Elzie Mayerfeld's smile was Germany itself: the Fatherland, surrounded by the islands and the rough rocks of a German sea. In the end it always came down to privilege, and the question of who had the strength and stamina to seize it, to take it roughly the way a man takes hold of a woman, even at the price of German blood. A German cannot live in the same way as a Jew, a Pole, or a Russian.

Finally, there lingered in the scorched air only the fading refrain of a song that Elzie Mayerfeld and the girls in her classroom remembered, about how, in the far-distant lands, a German soldier would know when his time had come.

Elzie Mayerfeld turned to face her students and said, "*Lieblings*, I have a surprise for you."

"She's going to give us a test," whispered a girl sitting next to the girl with the scar.

Jenny Thelen looked down at the floor. The wooden tiles were angled like swastikas. The Dog Lady had explained to them the very first day that the bent cross was not only the symbol of the great German Reich, but also of the sun. In the old Aryan nations it had also signified the union of man and woman.

Every time the Dog Lady called them *lieblings* it was like the sting of a wasp.

"I bet she wants to leave early," Jenny Thelen's neighbor whispered.

"Third row by the window!" The Dog Lady immediately noticed. "Don't disturb the class! Kindly take out your notebooks." She lowered her voice, getting down to the business at hand. "Write the answers to three questions." She thumbed through the morning edition of *Der Neue Tag* looking for the marked articles. "I'm going to leave you by yourselves for a while. I have to leave a little early."

"I told you so," said Julie.

"How did you know?" the girl with the scar asked in a very low voice.

"He's waiting for her downstairs."

The girl with the scar felt the blood rush to her cheeks. "Who?"

"You sound like you envy her."

"The third row's asking for punishment," said the teacher. "I'm not here to discipline you; my mission's more important. I'm telling you for the last time to keep quiet."

The same fragments of images floated in Jenny's mind, images that went back to Tuesday, to her thoughts before the teacher's lecture had been interrupted by the marching songs of the soldiers. So someone was waiting for the Dog Lady. It wasn't hard to guess who. Jenny had been thinking about the sun, about hell and the restful shade, but now she thought about victory. Defeat she pictured as a net made of fire. To her, there was no more difference between them than there was between a butterfly and a moth. She was no longer aware of the classroom, but her lips whispered automatically, "I beg your pardon, I forgot myself" — the apology that the tall teacher demanded.

Jenny Thelen was no longer aware of the battered desk or the big map of the Reich, nor of the silk dress or the magnolias on the house across the street. She shut her ears to the teacher's irritated voice. All that was left were the tiny motes of dust and the sun, the soft play of streaming rays of sunlight. The sunbeams were long, thin, golden shadows. She felt herself glide down them, her eyelids half-closed, as if she were drifting off to sleep. Everything surrounding her was real, and yet she was aware of none of it. Nothing remained but the light and the thing she was learning to forget here in the Prague Institute for Girls of Pure Race from Non-German Territories: that in the year 1942 she had had a father and a mother. But she had not yet learned to forget what it was they had been executed for.

Something was streaming through her subconscious, like mud drifting on the bottom of a river, something connected with the damp day of March 15, with its snow and the motorcycles ridden by foreign soldiers who wore green cloth tunics under their raincoats, reminding her of uniformed frogs.

Father was wearing the nickel-rimmed glasses he'd just brought home from the health insurance company (as an employee at the waterworks, he was entitled to a yearly eye checkup and new glasses). He didn't want to see what was going on outside the window, so he took the glasses off. He said it was a wonder that the occupation soldiers weren't singing. And at just that moment they'd started to sing—songs about distant German lands, about earth and blood, with fifes and drums: *Hei-di, hei-do, la la.* Tanks tore up the road. After that, Father had taken her on his knee more often and told her about the times when he'd fought on the River Piava in northern Italy, where he'd learned to play *O Maria* and other songs from Trieste on the mandolin.

Drops of perspiration appeared on Jenny's forehead and above her
upper lip. She was hot and tired. She hadn't slept well the night before.
She hadn't slept well since Tuesday. In the morning the Dog Lady had
talked about what united children and parents and what divided them.
The rays of sunlight bore down on her.

"I know who's waiting for her," whispered Julie. "It's him. I'll bet
you anything. They made a date for Saturday."

"It's awfully hot," whispered the girl with the scar, as if admitting
that it was a possibility. She no longer felt that she could see her mother
and father in the rays of the sun.

She dropped her hands into her lap. The sun shone on the beads of
sweat running down her forehead. Suddenly she had an urge to get up,
without permission, and go to the window to see who was waiting for
the teacher.

She felt a flush of shame and, at the same time, an insatiable thirst.
For a moment her body felt like a big empty pitcher.

The open windows let in the smell of flowers. The fragrance aroused
her and brought back all the excitement she'd felt last Tuesday. Again
she remembered the Noncommissioned Officer's visit to Elzie Mayerfeld, and the touch, perhaps accidental, of his broad palm brushing over
her small breasts. She must have blushed immediately, her cheeks
turning fiery red. She'd felt the blood rushing to her head. Then she
heard the NCO promising to wait for her after class on Saturday. He
probably had no idea what punishment such a breach of the rules could
bring. She'd smelled the slightly acrid yet sweetish aroma of tobacco on
his breath.

"What do you say, lambkin?" he said.

She'd been glad when he'd left. Her heart had pounded as if she'd
been running. But when he'd gone she wished for something else. The
next day, Wednesday, the Dog Lady had made them line up in their gym
suits. He'd been watching them from the Dog Lady's room.

"You two over there," said the teacher. She folded up *Der Neue Tag*.
There was a long article in it about the Czechs that claimed they were
more concerned with their standard of living than with their national
goals. There was also a detailed article about dogs. Elzie Mayerfeld was
well aware of what was going on in the classroom. She looked sharply
toward the third row.

That was the moment their eyes met, those of the teacher and those
of the girl with the scar. The girl's eyes held the teacher's gaze until they

could no longer bear it, then moved to the windows and finally to the floor. The teacher again examined her face: the deep-set eyes, the narrow forehead with the long reddish scar that looked like a quickly sewn seam, her Slavic cheekbones, the pointed chin. An almost childish triangle of a face, it reminded her of a lamb's.

The scar turned pale for a moment. The teacher guessed that the tension inside this girl was not so innocent. The teacher's nostrils flared like those of a lioness. The girl knew that she could do nothing without permission, not even stand up and go to the window.

Everything came back to Jenny now—all Father had said and done when the Germans were occupying Prague. She felt numb, as if she were about to faint. Silently the words about the frontiers of the Reich echoed. *Alt Reich* and *Neues Reich*. In her fading smile, the girl felt the mature woman's disdain. She was avoiding Elzie Mayerfeld's gaze, but even so, she felt naked, as she did when they were measured and weighed, or when they were given blood tests.

"Keep your minds on your work," the tall woman admonished. "I demand silence, Jenny Thelen. It's not easy, but it's not so much to ask. Absolute silence. Voluntarily."

Finally she said, "Write as I dictate."

It took the girl with a scar a while to come back to reality. The sun was dazzling. A ray of light sparkled on the teacher's bracelet. She began to dictate.

"Question one: What's the *Curatorium* doing for us?

"Question two: Why must Germany—in the interest of Europe— defeat Bolshevik Russia, Jewish England, and plutocratic America?"

Elzie Mayerfeld folded *Der Neue Tag* on her desk. She smoothed her dress over her hips with soft, cushioned palms.

"Question three," she said. "Why is censorship progressive, when compared to the arbitrariness introduced in Europe like a Trojan horse by the Jews? What's the meaning of 'undesirable,' 'blasphemous,' and 'lewd'? How does the National Socialist German Workers' Party, the NSDAP, view the relationship between freedom and experience?"

The girls wrote the questions slowly, as she dictated them. Jenny saw the teacher's reflection now in the glass of the open windows. Everything about her looked full and dark; she seemed to exude an aura of animal magnetism.

"Now you may begin," said Elzie Mayerfeld.

Then she added that she expected silence and order in her absence. That's what obedience meant.

Elzie Mayerfeld's hips swayed. Her cushioned palms moved up and down the rustling silk, as if shaping her body into curves.

She said aloud, "I'll make it up to you. You won't miss anything. This evening I'll teach you how to waltz. Our soldiers are fond of waltzes."

She moved a few steps away from the desk. She wore another gold bracelet on her left ankle.

"There are three ways you can do the waltz," said Elzie Mayerfeld. "I have a new Lale Anderson record. She has such a wonderfully velvet voice. She's better than Marlene Dietrich used to be. Much better. She's also braver, of course. Lale Anderson's still our best frontline singer. I'll pick up your notebooks in the evening."

The girl with the scar found all this uninteresting and irrelevant. She was filled with a thirst that didn't burn, but that sapped the strength from her arms, legs, and brain.

Elzie Mayerfeld dilated the deeply sculpted nares of her long, thin nose, drew them in again, and walked slowly out of the room.

2

The noon heat permeated the classroom. Whispering filled the aisles. Julie said, "Lale Anderson's a slut. And so is Elzie Mayerfeld." The accusation hung in the air for a moment. Then a small girl with a tiny face said that at the German front there were probably a lot of such women, women who combined sex and song. The Little One started writing.

"We've got velvet voices, too, only we're not sluts like her," added Julie.

The girl with the scar listened to the whispered voices of the other girls. They called each other by old and new nicknames, names of animals or flowers, like the horses at the racetrack. The Dog Lady had taken them to the horse races once with Colonel Count von Solingen. Last fall they had made up nicknames solely from fruits.

She didn't even have to raise her head to know who was speaking. The father of the Fast One had been hanged for belonging to the Communist Party, although his brother had managed to go from the Communist Party straight into the NSDAP. The Dog Lady told the Fast One that before the hangman had tightened the noose, her father had betrayed all of his comrades. The Round-eyed Girl had come to the Institute because of an unsettled family situation. Her grandfather had shot himself in a brothel when her grandmother had come for him; then her father shot himself, too, so that he wouldn't have to go into the army. She had big brown eyes; the teacher promised her that for Christmas she could have them changed to blue, after the German laboratories in the east finished their latest experiments.

The Round-eyed Girl stood beneath the picture of the Fuehrer and Reich's Chancellor and grinned, showing her wide-spaced white teeth: "Who do you think is waiting for her, girls?" Then she imitated the teacher's voice: "You can go on writing, girls, while I, the Dog Lady, Elzie von Mayerfeld, walk my dogs in a gentleman's company. What's the mission of women in the Third Reich, Jenny Thelen? Bed, board, and breviary, Miss Thelen."

There were a few giggles.

"You must read *Der Neue Tag* more diligently, Jenny Thelen. Have you written your essay yet on why the British are called Jews by the Aryans?"

"Aren't you writing?" Julie asked the girl with the scar.

"I've written it once already."

"What's the matter with you?"

"Nothing. It's hot."

"Don't you feel well?"

The girl with the scar again recalled the strange excitement she didn't understand, the touch of the palm and her recurring dream of becoming a woman.

The Round-eyed Girl said, "Jenny Thelen's a dummy. A distinguished dummy."

The girl with the scar went to the window. The pavement reflected the light and sent up waves of heat.

"Is he young? Or is he old?" asked the Round-eyed Girl. "Don't tell me it's a civilian in a bowler hat. Isn't it that good-looking sailor she brought on Wednesday?"

"Do they have their arms around each other or are they just walking side by side?" asked Julie.

The girl with the scar closed her eyes. Elzie Mayerfeld was walking with the NCO. An invisible breeze passed through the street. It pressed the silk against the tall woman's thighs and tousled her hair. They were walking two slender, long-legged greyhounds. She had them on long leashes with studded collars. The dogs were white. They had slim haunches, brown spots, and long fishlike muzzles. The coats of the animals shone in the hot sunlight.

Jenny Thelen held onto the window frame, ready to duck out of sight if the teacher should turn around. But she did not turn. The girl with the scar tried to assume an indifferent air, but she felt faint. She heard words and phrases and laughter behind her. One of the girls said, "She has the tails cut off all her dogs."

The girl with the scar walked back to her desk. She felt shivers in her thighs and breasts. Her place at the window was taken immediately by the Round-eyed Girl.

"They look nice together," she said, evaluating what she saw.

"Quite," said the Little One in a resigned tone.

"You don't mean to say you'd like to prance around in silks?" asked the Round-eyed Girl.

"Why not?" snapped the Little One.

Julie turned to the girl with the scar. "We can go to the river this afternoon. She'll want to stay with him after lunch. Who knows where she's taking him?"

Jenny Thelen opened her notebook in silence.

"Will you go with us?" asked Julie.

The Round-eyed Girl was returning to her desk. "Hey, guess what? The Dog Lady's got Jenny Thelen's tongue."

"To the river?" the girl with the scar repeated absently. "Well, why not?" And then she laughed, just as absently.

"It's time for the bell," said the Little One.

"What time is it?" asked the girl with the scar.

She felt her body and her head swelling. Her own voice seemed strange. Again she was aware of being wet, literally everywhere, with perspiration. The Little One commented that women who wore ankle bracelets were fast. Someone else said she'd wear rings in her nose like the Africans did, if she felt like it.

The girl with the scar felt something within her wilting like a flower in the heat. The heat opened up her pores and filled them with perspiration. A deep languor stopped motion, time, life. Someone asked why the teacher had never been married.

Everything in the classroom around her seemed to have turned white. All she could see was Elzie Mayerfeld walking beside the NCO. They were both the same height. She tried to imagine what they were talking about. She imagined the rustling of fine silk, palms that caressed like a warm breeze, relaxing and stimulating at the same time.

Once again, she felt the touch of his hand, a sensation that mingled with the scent of the magnolias on the Superintendent's house across the street.

The Round-eyed Girl was scratching her name into the desk top: Catherine Faye. Then she sat there biting her nails. At last she said, "The Dog Lady was in the castle with some general. They had a reception in the Spanish Hall. She danced with Daluege."

"But Daluege's—you know," said the Little One.

"What do you mean—he's 'you know'?"

"I mean Daluege would be more likely to dance with another man."

"The Dog Lady couldn't care less," the Round-eyed Girl declared.

"It's the same with him as with Baldur von Schirach," somebody said.

"Baldur von Schirach? Well, he has a son. Either—or."

"Some are both, either and or. One of them must have hooked him. He's very good-looking."

The Round-eyed Girl recalled how, during the latest celebration, the air force officers lined up one after the other and sang *Hei-di, hei-do, la la.* They formed a long snake, always a man holding a woman around her hips and the woman with her arm around the man's shoulders. They marched from room to room. Among the officers was the father of the biggest furniture manufacturer in Munich.

The small girl confided: "As long as I can remember, my Father pretended he loved my mother. But that didn't stop him from throwing her best French dinners at her, dishes and all, or from throwing it all into the waste basket. When the slightest thing angered him, he'd lose his temper and shout: 'Where are the meat and potatoes?' When he was very drunk, which happened about three times a week in our house, he'd slap her or throw her down or push her against the wall and yell at her: 'Witch!' "

The girl with the scar caught only the sound of the voices, a name, an echo, and nothing more. It was all blurred by the heat, transformed into the sound of a palm sliding down silk. The smell of tobacco on the sailor's breath. His words. The way he'd called her a little lamb. The Dog Lady herself had said that one woman was seldom enough for a man.

She suddenly noticed that the page in front of her was wet. This frightened her. She quickly took out her scrap of beige handkerchief and wiped the page off.

"What's the matter with you today?"

But the girl with the scar had finally begun to write. She assumed most of the girls would want to go to the river. They'd be escorted there and back. That was the rule in this place intended for the orphans of those who'd been enemies of the Reich—whenever any orphans were allowed to remain. Meant for rehabilitation, these children had been carefully selected according to Nordic racial criteria. They were girls with Aryan forebears, girls whose destinies depended on academic accomplishment and on the testimonials of all the Institute officials.

Elzie Mayerfeld was their homeroom teacher. Prior to holding this post, the Dog Lady, in the company of three trained army dogs, had served in Sobibor near Lublin in the female guard. Now, for the girls' own good, she wanted them to forget their parents.

The first one to tell them was SS Obersturmfuehrer Hagen-Tischler, the General Inspector of Education. Their parents would have wished it, he said, had they been able to accept the inevitable. They'd have realized that their daughters were fortunate, all things considered, to have a chance of being sent to one of the old families of the Reich.

But for punishment they could be sent to the camps at the front, to the "house of pleasure"—as camp followers, or *Feldhure*—in the words of one of them who'd already been sent to the east.

The girl with the scar imagined her teacher again. She saw her wearing a lace dress, being married to Hagen-Tischler in Prague, and right after the wedding, flying to Majorca. As she wrote her answers to the questions, she kept repeating to herself that the teacher was kind, experienced, and a sincere admirer of Lale Anderson. Her two English greyhounds had brown and gray patches on their haunches. They had belonged to a Jewish family that had been moved out of Prague's German Quarter in 1940.

Once, at a spring party with German air force officers, the Dog Lady had had a little too much to drink and had begun singing military songs and smashing the crystal goblets in which they'd served the champagne. Another time, it was said, she'd received roses from Mr. Sollman, who used to leave her messages; she had occasionally left them in the lounge, perhaps trying to see who was curious enough to pick them up. Indeed, that might have been precisely what she'd wanted—as if the relationship would lose some of its importance if it were not public knowledge.

According to Tanya Grab, who'd been sent to the eastern front, the Dog lady had written some of the letters and messages to herself.

The teacher listened to everything; even when she pretended to be nonchalant, she was alert and on her guard—like the best of the Germans, like the members of the NSDAP, the SS or the SA—and as she listened she dilated the nostrils of her thin, Nordic nose. Sniffing, she took in everything that was in the air. The Fuehrer had said that nature was cruel, and so she was proud that she could be equally cruel. But she wanted to appear kind. It was in her nature to make the worst out of the best and vice versa. Her penetrating gaze saw right through the girls. The word "inform" meant the same to her as the word "honor." To believe in conscience was to give free rein to a Jewish ruse. Only the defeated found it necessary to kill in self-defense. The victor was the first to kill. In a higher sense, though, one could say that the whole German Reich was fighting a war of self-defense: defending itself against the pollution of its blood. The German Reich would last for a thousand years. Elzie Mayerfeld knew and understood why.

The windows were wide open. Heat poured into the classroom as if the boundary between the inside and the outside of a furnace had been obliterated. The Little One asked the Round-eyed Girl why Tanya Grab hadn't written since she'd gone east. It was doubtful that she'd been sent to a German officer's family. For a night, maybe, someone said. To "colonize" some officer's bedroom was more likely. The bell rang, slicing across the consciousness of the girl with the scar, ripping the silence.

The sound of the bell told her what was coming and what had passed; it was like a bullet that just barely missed its target. In it there were tender layers of light and dark, of silence and noise, of words and steps—of something that couldn't be perceived from the outside.

Finally the bell stopped ringing. Everything in Jenny Thelen seemed to fester, like a wound that had never healed: What she'd had to say to Elzie Mayerfeld—"Sorry, I forgot myself," or the days when the Dog Lady called Jenny to her or when she left to spend the evening and a part of the night with an officer from the SS division Wiking from the Army Group South. Or, when his fat wife was visiting in Berlin, with the Superintendent from the magnolia-covered house across the street.

It all reminded her of a man holding a knife who lets someone bend his arm until he's forced to stab himself.

"Jenny," said Julie.

"Don't worry about me."

"You're all wet."

Someone was talking about icebergs. One of the girls remembered the winter campaign and the gloves they'd donated to the *Winterhilfe*.

"You should dry off," said Julie. "Look at what you did to your notebook."

The girl with the scar slowly straightened out the crumpled page.

"You can copy off me if you want to," said Julie.

"I'll write it myself. She'd find out."

"I bet she won't even read them."

"She always reads them."

"Almost never. Just spot checks."

"I don't want to argue."

The expression on the face of the girl with the scar revealed both objection and agreement, and something unfinished, like when you get dressed to go out and then stay home. It had nothing to do with what she was writing. The heat of the sun didn't let up. Everything seemed to be coming to a standstill. For a moment she imagined that she was drinking water, and it gurgled in her stomach.

"She's got it in for us," said Julie.

"I couldn't care less."

"How much do you have left to do?"

Jenny Thelen's pen moved again, dipped into the inkwell, and then touched the paper in the notebook. Every line, every word, called up something that was darker than the dark blue ink, something that brought on another wave of shame.

"What are you thinking about?"

"About Lale Anderson," she lied.

"That's the end of the recess," said the Little One.

The second bell rang, piercing the girl with the scar like needles—needles threaded with heat and sunlight, with words and their most secret meanings, with silence.

She felt herself filling up with silence, like a balloon expanding with dense, hot air, and then rising, regardless of where it had been anchored, regardless of where it would have to land.

3

The images flashed through Jenny Thelen's mind again, as they had so many times before, images of the day that had begun like every day before it.

Images of the day that had brought her here. She'd had no idea then of what was to come: the punishments, the programs, the people with whom her new life was to begin. She didn't yet know that the Dog Lady—although she never beat them herself—derived considerable satisfaction from watching them in the bathroom, and seeing the traces of whippings on their naked buttocks.

She squinted into the sun and then closed her eyes tightly, as if the fiery disc had branded itself onto her brain.

She saw her father going to the door. Somebody was ringing the bell and someone else was pounding on the door at the same time. They'd guessed who it was. Father went quickly to open the door, and the visitor immediately struck him across the face. Father was stunned. He turned around, his eyes filled with fear and shame, as though he were embarrassed to be beaten in front of them. His face was bloody. Mother fell when they came for her, as though she thought this might be a way to defend herself.

Two men held photographs before their eyes and asked if they recognized the girl in the picture. "No," said Father. "No," said Mother.

After that day she never saw her parents again. The Dog Lady had once told her that she wasn't alone. In Germany and in the occupied countries there were many like her, many who didn't have parents, just as there were many women without husbands, husbands without wives, parents without children, and sisters without brothers.

She couldn't go to her parents' funeral because there wasn't one.

The morning of that day had begun as usual. Mother woke her up and called her to breakfast. Father was already at the table, which was spread with a clean tablecloth; he sat drinking his ersatz coffee and eating bread with strawberry jam. For the first time in her life, she had put on her mother's silk stockings. She could use Mother's things. And then the bell was ringing like crazy, and Mother was digging her fingernails into the crevices of the parquet floor.

Elzie Mayerfeld had come for her and brought her here. The first things she told her were to be tough, to learn how to forget what had been, and to start looking forward to what was coming. To learn how to adapt. A week later school began.

Her first class was with the Inspector, SS Obersturmfuehrer Hagen-Tischler, who admonished them not to underestimate an idea simply because they'd never heard of it at home. If they'd been brought up with religion, he suggested that they look there for guidance, for "proof" that it might even be a kindness for parents to die before their children.

He lectured on geography. He covered volcanoes, earthquakes, and other natural disasters. He talked about volcanic activity that began in unfathomable depths and couldn't be observed or measured beforehand, about disasters that didn't kill or destroy, and about others that wiped out all living things.

She remembered his saying that about 1500 B.C. there had been a great eruption on an island in the Aegean Sea. An enormous mountain had been thrust into the air—a mountain whose bulk measured some eighty billion cubic meters of earth and stone. Now only the tip of the rock remained above the surface of the water; it formed the center of a small island. In a matter of minutes all civilization on that island had ended.

He also described how earthquakes were caused by subterranean movements far from the place of the eruption and could be even worse than the volcanoes we know about. She remembered every word. Every word about the water changing in the wells, the terror of frightened animals, omens of the earth opening up as if waking from sleep.

At night, under the cover of darkness, she would see her mother and father in a rhythm with her breathing. Just like Elzie Mayerfeld, Hagen-Tischler said that children knew from the beginning that they would outlive their parents. He smiled, as if to say that he had made an effort to understand them and he expected the girls in turn to try to understand him.

Since then she was only able to see her mother disheveled and in pain, the way she'd seen her that last time, lying on the floor.

"You'd better make it short," said Julie.

"I'm making it short," said Jenny Thelen.

"Then why are you writing so much? Aren't fifteen lines enough?"

"I'm doing what she wants."

The stream of images was taking her away from her notebook and inkwell, away from the girls in the class, yet it seemed to be at one with the heat and the sunlight, reflected in the glare of light from the white walls, from the windows, and from the framed glass of the pictures—among them that of the Reich's Chancellor. Everything was white and sharp and penetrating: the white of the Dog Lady's skin. Her dogs. Glowing beads of perspiration. She was sliding away from the words she wrote. She inhaled the hot air.

She returned once more in her thoughts to Kralovska Street, to their old apartment in the house by the viaduct. The picture of the unknown girl was the only clue the German authorities had to track down the assassin who'd blown up the Reich's Protector, Reinhard Tristan Eugen Heydrich, at the end of May 1942.

The newspapers said that people would be praying for his recovery. For two weeks the police searched for the girl in the photograph. In the window of one of the shoe stores on Primatorska Street they displayed her briefcase, her coat, and a girl's bicycle. It turned out later that they were really looking for seven men from England who had parachuted in. But in the meantime, General of Police Heydrich died. Rewards running into the millions were offered.

She remembered the backs of the men in leather coats. When she tried to follow the people who were taking her parents away, they had slammed the door on her; the blow had split open her forehead. Later, only the reddish scar remained.

She remembered the nights in the cell at the headquarters of the Gestapo on Bredovska Street, nights when she was almost glad that her mother and father were dead.

"Were you going to say something?" asked Julie.

"No."

Mother and Father had been executed that June at the Gestapo firing range in Kobylisy.

"Are you talking to yourself?"

"What if I am? I don't owe anybody anything."

"I hope that's not what you're writing."

Before Elzie Mayerfeld had come, Jenny Thelen had been alone in

the apartment. Outside an armed police patrol guarded the door. Any
signal, the slightest knock, would have helped her believe that she
hadn't been abandoned; but it would not come, because the city was
gripped with fear. The Dog Lady told them in her second class how in
the east they killed sick dogs in special chambers with gas that
penetrated everything, every nook and cranny, so that there would be no
accidental survivors.

There had been the anticipated sound of approaching footsteps. Then
there was the first man, the one who had beaten Father and then Mother.
And the second, who had said approvingly: *Richtigbrutal*, really tough.
Later, she'd strained her eyes watching the doorknob in the Gestapo
office at Number 20 Bredovska Street. When the Dog Lady had finally
come for her, Jenny Thelen had bitten her hand.

On the stairs they hadn't met anyone from the house. Not even the
concierge, the lady who was always there, eager to pass on news from
London or Moscow radio. Two men had dragged Jenny Thelen into a
black Mercedes and thrown her onto the leather seat. They squeezed her
between them, while a policeman held her arms. Finally she'd stopped
scratching and biting.

She didn't wake up until much later, in the Julius Petschek Palace.
She felt eyes watching her through a secret spyhole. But it turned
out that Jenny Thelen had nothing in common with the girl in the
photograph.

That's how she had come to be here in the special Prague Institute for
Girls of Pure Race from Non-German Territories. It was probably
because of the Dog Lady. Elzie Mayerfeld had talked with the men in
the leather coats. When they were coming here by car, the Dog Lady told
her that she had a choice: She could stand with ninety million Germans
firmly in control of Europe, or she could stand alone against them. The
black Mercedes brought her here, to this worn desk, where every
morning, as a prayer, they said: Today Germany is ours; tomorrow the
whole world.

The army barracks were nearby. The marching soldiers would pass by
often on their way to routine drills or to ceremonial reviews. They
would be accompanied by Turkish bands, wearing plumes and carrying xylophones and lyres and shrill flutes. Sometimes they would only
be going to the drill field, led by the sergeant, but they always took
the band.

"Everything that's past is dead. Only the present and the future count," said the Dog Lady.

At first it was drilled into her incessantly: Her mother and father were no longer alive because they'd approved of the assassination. At the same time, it was also impressed upon her that she was under German protection now, and that the German authorities paid all of her expenses.

Her last sentence was short. It was in answer to the question of why individual freedom was the privilege of only a chosen few and a chimera for the many, and why suppression was not destruction, but rather its antithesis: The Reich is the whole world.

There was something about her name: Thelen. She probably had German ancestors. The Germans had been colonizing this country for a thousand years. The best people—aristocrats, knights, men with foresight—had been attracted to the German empire, much as the Poles had been drawn to Rome.

The girl with the scar walked slowly out of the classroom. When Julie asked her why she didn't want to go to the dining room, she said she wasn't hungry because of the heat.

"Give them my name and take my fruit," she said.

"Get my swimsuit ready, will you?" said Julie.

The girl with the scar lay down on the neatly made-up bed in her room. She closed her eyes. The heat was really getting to her. She could feel it again, just as on Tuesday—the touch of the man's hand. There was something she didn't understand, something she'd heard about often enough but was encountering now for the first time. Every word and every touch had layers of meaning. The air seemed to consist of hot crystals and pearls and it seemed to be inundated by the sound of Father's Italian mandolin. *O, Maria.* Father had known perhaps eight Italian love songs. She smoothed her body with her palms, imitating the teacher standing at the window. But then she heard the rattle of tanks on the cobbled pavement of Kralovska Street under the viaduct, and she saw the German camp and the soldiers who ladled soup out of the big army kitchen kettles and gave bread to children. She was thinking about the game all people played. According to the Dog Lady's rules, girls had to play it smart if they wanted to make it in the world at all. Once again she heard the NCO calling her little lamb. He'd asked if she'd go out with him. She heard herself tell him that she didn't know. He smiled and said people always knew whether they wanted to or not.

4

The afternoon sun permeated every breath of air. It was the hottest day of the summer.

Jenny Thelen joined the girls who were going swimming. That didn't surprise anyone. It wasn't the first time she'd changed her mind.

They crossed the bridge that had the columns with the golden birds with their wings spread wide. The birds were made of cast iron that had been spray-painted; they seemed to hold the bridge up over the water. The Little One was talking about the retired general who had been the Dog Lady's admirer. The Round-eyed Girl said that the general had helped the Dog Lady get the furniture she needed, allowing her to buy cheaply from the supplies of household goods taken from the "liquidated" anti-German elements (though in some quarters, their elimination was still thought to be only a possibility).

Julie called back to the girl with the scar that it wouldn't hurt if she tried to hurry up a bit. There was no sense in wasting such a fine chance to go swimming.

She realized that other people, to whom the swimming pools were closed on Saturdays, people who were walking through the streets, were alive only because they'd sensed when it was better to keep silent than to talk, and when it was better to speak than to remain silent, even if it meant going against one's conscience. The girl with the scar thought it possible that she might run into the Dog Lady and the NCO. She fell even farther behind, but at the entrance to the swimming pool the girls were waiting for her. When the group was complete, the lifeguards let them enter.

Usually all you could hear at the pool was German. There were almost four hundred thousand Germans in Prague. Some were only passing through, some served here, and some had already brought their families to occupy apartments vacated by Jews and the houses and apartments of the incarcerated and of those who had been executed. That summer there were more soldiers than ever in Prague. They lived here as if at a resort, since the exchange value of the German mark was very favorable compared with the Czech crown of the Protectorate.

"They sing well," said the Little One.

"You call that singing? Sounds more like croaking—like frogs in a pond," said Julie.

In the last few weeks there had been a lot of invalids at the pool: mildly or seriously wounded men from the army hospital, others without arms or legs, men who were blind or disfigured with scars from burns or frostbite, men without ears, noses or fingers.

They left their bandages, corsets, and artificial limbs in the dressing rooms. Though disfigured, they still looked hardy, and they would join the groups of healthy men who sang to the accompaniment of a harmonica or an accordion or maybe just someone whistling on a comb. The girl with the scar wondered if this was the reason why, for the second season now, Elzie Mayerfeld avoided the swimming pool.

The Little One said, "After the war they'll be stringing beads, weaving wreaths, and making baskets. Would you marry someone just because he was a hero?"

Near the kiosk the soldiers were celebrating someone's birthday and shouting.

They each took a long drink of beer and then began again: *Ernst ist das Leben, Ernst soll er heissen.*

The girl with the scar changed in the dressing room and then went to look for a shady spot. She tried to ignore the badly wounded soldiers and not to think about the NCO or where he might be. A few soldiers swam into the middle of the river. The logs that enclosed the authorized swimming area were walnut-colored, stained with oil and creosote; they drifted in the water, even though they were anchored with chains.

Above the swimming pool on the hill shaped like a jumping dolphin was a park. Still higher, from the flagpole of the castle, waved the banner of fulfillment—the swastika. The bronze statues of saints that had previously graced the bridge near the swimming pool had been taken to the Reich to be melted down into cannons. And no one had lifted a finger against it, thought the girl with the scar. Neither the believers nor the patriots. Why couldn't she have a bit of that detachment?

If things had turned out just a little differently, she might not have become the orphaned daughter of criminals. Not very long ago she had had parents. A thousand years ago. During some nearly forgotten age. In the same way, no one in the future would be able to imagine what it was like here and now. Had people really lived like fish in the distant past, as SS Obersturmfuehrer Hagen-Tischler had told them?

The logs undulated with the river. The heat seemed to call up silent echoes. She felt something building inside her, even though she couldn't name it. She felt the cool movement of the river.

Her head ached, and her fingers and eyelids felt swollen. The heat drained her of all her will. She watched the logs. The submerged portions were covered with green moss and slime.

She closed her eyes and thought about rocks and gorges, about ravines and caves, about deserts and seas and desiccated wastelands and people who'd died out long ago, as SS Obersturmfuehrer Hagen-Tischler had also explained. She thought about those now living who would die and nobody would know anything about them. She thought about all of these things to avoid thinking about the NCO and Elzie Mayerfeld. She looked at the iron birds, with their cheap coat of gilt, which seemed to soar over the bridge as if lifting and suspending it above the water. The iron wings of the birds were rusty underneath. Swallows had built their nests in the steel scaffolding.

She rose slowly, then quickly slid into the water and held onto a log. In the water she could dream about what had barely started on Tuesday, about what the continuation might be. The water caressed her, touching her and splashing rhythmically against the log. She remembered what Elzie Mayerfeld considered the most important physical attributes: a straight nose, blonde hair and blue eyes, a narrow waist. And an unencumbered mind. No trace of what, before the Germans came, used to be called "conscience." She closed her eyes. She slid down, submerging her head, still holding onto the log. The wood was cool, slick, firm. She felt her whole body open up to the streaming current, to the water flowing against her.

She felt the solid darkness. She began to touch herself with her free hand, and everything became darker still. When she could no longer hold her breath, she lifted her head above the water. The sun seemed to brand her once more.

She stayed in the water for a while longer, holding onto the log with one hand or the other. Then she got out and lay on the bank, a little higher up, where there weren't any planks. She used a large piece of flat slate as a pillow. A big tree covered her with its shade. She watched the changing colors of the water, the glint of sunlight, and the streaming air.

She closed her eyes without anyone noticing. She was half-asleep and half-awake, listening.

When she opened her eyes again, she saw Julie and Catherine Faye sitting next to her.

"We're still so skinny," said Julie.

"Only in swimsuits, don't you think?" asked the Round-eyed Girl.

"Just imagine what you'd look like in silks from the Dog Lady's wardrobe."

"Only if I didn't know where she got them."

"Would you like to lie here without anything on?"

"Why?"

"I did once. It's a nice feeling. Then I saw some soldiers on the bridge up there, and I started feeling ashamed."

"Only because they didn't know you?"

"Men are afraid of me," said Julie.

"Why should they be?"

"I can tell from the way they look at me. Men are animals."

"Women are animals, too, sometimes."

The girl with the scar thought about the NCO as they spoke. She felt a nervous tremor inside, as if she'd been suddenly struck with a virus. The heat, the quiet, and the water melted into the flickering of shade and sunlight that she could feel even with her eyes closed. She lay motionless. She had a feeling that the sun and the people, the voice and the river, were there and yet were nonexistent at the same time.

"The Dog Lady's already complete," said Julie. There was experience in her voice, and it made her seem older than the rest of the girls.

Once Obersturmfuehrer Hagen-Tischler had shown the Dog Lady a picture of a hundred or so Jewish women, already undressed and waiting to be shot down in front of a ditch dug thirty meters long and eight meters deep. There were eight of those pits in a row. The Dog Lady said it was disgusting.

"What do you mean by that?"

"She's a woman. But sometimes I have a feeling she's a man in a woman's shell."

"Do you feel sleepy, too, in this heat?"

Jenny Thelen was listening to their voices and to the splashing of the water. The river trembled between two strips of land. You could hear the sound of the current, the little waves lapping the sand and stones on the bank. She still had the feeling that it was all here and yet wasn't here at all, both at the same time.

"Wouldn't it be lovely if one of them drowned?" Julie asked suddenly.

The girl with the scar didn't open her eyes. She felt warmth in her cheeks and between her thighs. The air was as sweet as milk. You could hear laughter in the distance. Birds were chirping. The tree rustled with a dry sound. The sky burned.

Then Julie said, almost in a whisper, "I could never be true to any man."

"Why?"

"Tanya Grab used to tell us what the soldiers did in the east. They took out their pistols and forced girls to kneel in front of them."

"I'd bite. Even if it were the last thing I ever did."

"If you had a choice, which would you like to be, a girl or a boy?"

"I wouldn't hesitate for a minute." The answer was implied in her tone.

"I read that deep in the ocean, where life is very rare, there lives a strange fish that, when two males meet, the smaller male changes into a female." The girl with the scar lay still and the sinking afternoon sun lay heavily on her eyelids. She felt that all of this was taking place in a dream. She knew Tanya Grab had said that, out there, for every girl of pure race there were sixteen men from the SS divisions. The State took care of the children. She felt how warm her skin had become. It seemed that not only was the river moving, but also the earth, as if it were retreating with the current into some far distance. The stone on which she rested her head was hot.

Jenny Thelen felt dizzy and didn't want to open her eyes. She thought of fish cast ashore by the waves and then stranded and of how they died, leaving bloody marks in the sand and stones on the shore; and she thought of all the volcanoes that might be about to erupt.

"Why did they send Tanya Grab to the eastern front as a camp follower?"

"She didn't want to wash with the soap they used to give us before you came. Yellowish bars, like laundry soap. It came from factories near Kracków or Lublin and then from Danzig. Tanya Grab would sniff at it, as if it really were made from human bones."

The girls fell silent.

When the girl with the scar opened her eyes, she found herself staring with the others at a soldier who was sitting apart from the rest and rubbing the peeling skin from his shins. His legs seemed to itch and he was throwing the flakes of skin into the river. A banana peel, yellow on the outside and white inside, came floating down from the direction of the army hospital.

"Look at him scratching—isn't it disgusting?" said Julie, not sounding very happy. "It makes me sick. Why doesn't someone stop him?"

"What if it's catching?" asked the Round-eyed Girl.

"It's probably scabies. I had it once. They give you a sulphur ointment," said Julie. "They shaved my head, like they did once when they found a louse in my hair."

Then they watched the Little One trying to coax some ice cream out of an officer at the kiosk, just for fun. The officer looked her over like she was a heifer at the market; he sized up her legs, inspected her eyes, arms, shoulders. The expression on the Little One's face indicated that he might be asking too much for one ice cream. The officer was licking his cone, and his tongue hung out in surprise. He told the Little One she was some character.

"I guess I don't have the training," said the Round-eyed Girl.

The girl with the scar felt something in her soul shift, like the sun dropping in its afternoon arc. Like that rare fish deep in the ocean, changing because of a bigger male into something other than what he was. The city moved invisibly and time was somehow filled. The roofs were like burnished gold. There was a tinge of copper on the trees and on the houses in the distance. The blue streak of the horizon became more pronounced. The city lay quiet, crouched like a sleeping animal. Poplar trees grew on both banks of the Moldau. Here and there was a birch, slender and white. When the streetcar rode over the bridge, the whole rusty structure shook with a sound like rapid drumbeats. Birds were singing on the hillside.

When they were on their way home, the girl with the scar still felt as if she were lying in her swimsuit with her head on the hot stone, and as if at the same time she were floating in the water, touching the wet logs with her fingertips.

5

"It's your business if you want to starve yourself," said Julie when the girl with the scar refused to go pick up her cold Saturday supper. "I mean, what's the point of fasting all day?"

"I think it's going to turn cool," said Jenny Thelen.

"You look as if you were losing your willpower or something."

"It's just the heat," the girl with the scar sighed. "I don't like hot weather."

"I prefer the heat to the cold. It doesn't last forever, only till evening at the most."

"Why did the dinosaurs die out when they were so strong?"

"If even Obersturmfuehrer Hagen-Tischler doesn't know, how should I?" asked Julie.

The Obersturmfuehrer had explained to them once that sixty million years ago the earth had witnessed an inexplicable catastrophe, probably caused by the explosion of a star somewhere in the vicinity of our solar system, and all the big creatures perished, while rats, lizards, and small creatures, which could hide in the rocks or in the rivers or seas, survived. "It's just that there were illogical and inexplicable phenomena in nature, that's all," he had said. But it was another proof of nature's cruelty, and that was why the Reich's Chancellor was right in saying that people must be cruel, too. But another time he had told them that perhaps the dinosaurs disappeared because of a change in the weather, because it got colder, the trees stopped growing and they had nothing to eat.

She remembered what he'd told them on the Fuehrer's birthday, the twentieth of April. They were all assembled in the gym, and the army band came and played excerpts from Wagner. "You must be as proud as female eagles and as strong as lionesses. You are going to live in a world of German Aryans, and you will live like Aryans. Or you will not live at all." He never spoke of the Germans who were killed; it was as if they weren't even Germans. Once he told them that a man felt real pride only when he killed. Germany was a hammer that smashed weakness.

The girl with the scar watched the birds in the sky. They were less sharply defined now against the dark stripe of horizon.

Later, alone in the dormitory, she watched the electric clock on the wall. It said half past six. A rose-colored veil seemed to be stretched across the sky. It was just a tint, rather than the first real sign of the sunset. The sky looked like the sea. She suddenly felt a light chill, a touch of distant shivers brought on by the daylong heat. She was watching the sky change—like a mother dressing her child, removing its daytime outfit and putting on pajamas.

Looking at the sky, she thought of the sea she'd never seen, of ships she'd never known, and of islands she could only imagine, enormous rocks emerging from the bottom of the sea, their peaks surfacing above the water.

She put on her red dress, leaving the jacket on the hanger for the time being and not trying on the matching belt just yet. She thought about the heat and how it seemed to swell within her, and then subside. She felt the heat ebbing, leaving behind its many echoes and layers that had collected and were now falling apart. She could hear birds chirping in the garden. During the day they'd been quiet. Now from the window the garden looked like a green abyss.

She got up after a while and stood behind the curtains. She couldn't remember exactly what it was the NCO had said to her on Tuesday; in fact, each day that passed she remembered less. She no longer thought of how the sailor had betrayed her with the Dog Lady or why Elzie Mayerfeld had taken away her NCO.

But she couldn't escape the feeling.

Green ivy climbed the walls of the Superintendent's house across the street; the magnolias were clustered below them, with their faint but discernible fragrance.

She inhaled the cool air she'd been longing for all day, but she felt no relief, only the languor brought on by the day's heat.

The swaying of the trees indicated the direction and force of the wind. Birds flew out of their hiding places in the ivy.

The Superintendent was in the garden. He was appraising tomorrow's weather and inspecting the condition of the building's facade. Every summer he did the smaller repairs himself. He took only the faintest notice of his wife hanging out some clothes in the yard. She wore a spotted black dress. She was absorbed in herself and her laundry. He tried to avoid her glance, and anyone could guess that he wished she'd be off to her sister's in Berlin so that he could freely contemplate the Dog Lady and her older wards. The Superintendent was much fatter than his wife. When he wore his Bavarian shorts with suspenders, he looked positively ridiculous. They said his wife liked to see him that way, fat and ridiculous.

In front of his wife the Superintendent found it easy to hide his interest in the Dog Lady and his penchant for her students. He liked to ask them how they felt and he taught them things that—in their inexperience—they considered indispensable and unique. He laughed when his wife teased him about courting Elzie Mayerfeld.

The magnolias were white as swan's down in the center and their edges looked as if they were tipped with blood. They seemed a little darker now, like the evening itself: the green tenderness of leaves in an aquamarine sky that was like the envelope of a letter by an unfamiliar hand to an unknown addressee. The magnolias looked like swans, mortally wounded and bleeding from their necks. The sun had wilted them. They would soon be dead.

The paleness of the sky in the east was moving westward where it met a shadow, a darker reddish band. It looked like a woman dressed for the evening. The girl with the scar was afraid she'd stand here a long time and no one would come.

She held onto the drapes and imagined herself in a soft, bright silk dress, swinging her hips and lifting her breasts, looking confidently at the man who'd asked to take her for a stroll.

Her head was reeling. Every moment was gentle, like the breeze rustling in the magnolias, like the touch of silk on skin. The sky floated over the earth in clouds of fine mist. High in the evening sky she could see the birds flying. There were lots of them. She envied the birds. But it wasn't freedom she was thinking of.

She wished the sun wouldn't set so quickly. It was as if she were trying to gain time, to extend a deadline that wasn't hers alone. In a moment she saw the first star. The whole summer she'd watched that star in its duel with the sun. It was always the first and then the brightest, as if it came out of its shell just as the day departed, and then waited for the sun to go before it began shining. The star was still pale because the waning sun was still bright. It was Venus.

It occurred to her that, like memories, stars and planets resembled those lost islands that SS Obersturmfuehrer Hagen-Tischler talked about, whole lands that had submerged with the people who had lived there.

She had memories of her mother and father and of their life on Kralovska Street before the General of the Police had been killed. And also memories of Tuesday, when, making way for the NCO in the corridor to the geography room, she hadn't been fast enough to avoid his touch.

She smoothed her dress, automatically imitating her tall teacher.

Hidden by the heavy white curtains, she looked down again at the sidewalk. The sun felt different to her now—not the way it had in the morning. Now, it warmed and protected her and offered something she'd never had before. And she thought again of the NCO, as though she'd known him a long time and he'd just left her. That might be changed, just by willing it, to the possibility that he would come again.

From the living room she could hear the sound of steps and piano music. The Dog Lady was laughing. She was telling someone that prejudice brought suffering.

This was the second Saturday that Elzie Mayerfeld had worked at teaching them the waltz. The slow Viennese music engulfed everything. Lale Anderson was singing; it was a record of *Tales from the Vienna Woods*. She could hear it clearly, even with the living room doors closed. It evoked an image of polished shoes and women's slippers on the icy gleam of parquet floors, dancers in dashing uniforms and rustling evening dresses.

6

The music drowned out Elzie Mayerfeld's voice. She was saying something about the privilege of being able to dance while the world was seething in a fire from which a tempered Germany would rise. She talked of the happy hours when the most faithful find their best opportunities. The power of her voice sometimes robbed the girl with the scar of her will. She was happy to be away from her presence now. She could barely hear what the teacher was saying: to be patient, that they weren't old enought yet not to have to wait, but they weren't as innocent as when they'd come. The blood of German men . . . the self-denial of German women . . . One, two, three. One, two, three. The satisfaction of knowing that with what they were learning they could all graduate from the Institute into a good German family, either in the old Reich or in the annexed territories, as late daughters of some officer, camp leader, party functionary or statesman—someone who either couldn't have children of his own or who'd lost them at the front or during the air raids by the

British and Americans. Or they could get positions in the casinos in the newly conquered German territories that were still occupied only by soldiers.

Ten minutes later the girl with the scar looked down at the sidewalk and unconsciously grabbed at the curtain. The NCO was standing on the sidewalk. She felt again precisely what she'd felt on Tuesday. Blood rushed to her head. The scar turned pale and then ruddy again. She shivered, as if all the warmth of the hot day had left her.

"Miss Thelen," a voice called from the doorway. It was the night doorman. "Is that you?"

"What is it?" she asked.

"Lambkin," said the doorman in a friendly way. "Do you like the full moon?" He glanced around the room and put his finger to his lips, signaling that they must be quiet. The girl with the scar looked toward the window and the doorman nodded.

"There's nothing like being wanted," he said. "Good evening and all the best to you. You're to go on down. The sergeant sends his regards. Everything's taken care of. We don't have to worry about a thing."

He was bound by his word of honor, he said. It wasn't hard for Jenny Thelen to guess what he meant.

"Not a word to anyone, Miss. An order's an order, you know, and a sergeant in the navy is a promising rank, if you know what I mean." And he showed her a pack of Viktoria cigarettes, as if to remind her of the riches a sergeant could provide and of all that lay farther up the ladder.

"A minute more or less doesn't matter," he added, "but you ought to be back before midnight."

She left, flushed in the face and shivering uncontrollably. The doorman closed the gate behind her. Everything she'd tried to push down, expectations both old and new, now rose to the surface. She walked behind the building toward the NCO. She was frightened by all her mixed feelings—eagerness and satisfaction and fear, prejudice and joy—alternating waves of hot and cold. She felt a wild pain in her abdomen and tried not to think about the Dog Lady and her conquests, but to surrender instead to the pleasant breeze that pressed her dress against her thighs and ruffled her hair.

7.

The NCO greeted her by kissing her hand. Blushing, she gripped her poplin jacket in the other hand.

"What was your afternoon like, Miss?" he asked.

Again, his breath was sweet and tinged with the acrid smell of tobacco, but he seemed more handsome than on Tuesday.

She didn't know what she was supposed to say or what she wanted to say, or indeed what she actually did say in response. She didn't even know later, after she had come to her senses.

The sun was going down fast. They crossed to the other side of the river where the air was supple and mild, the breeze pleasantly cool, and the moon rose white like the tip of a column rising out of the dark blue depths of the sea. Birds were singing in the trees and evening was painting the city blue. The sun threw its last rays on the rose stripe of the western horizon. She was thinking of the ease with which Elzie Mayerfeld played the part of a woman.

"Did the afternoon drag for you, too?" asked the NCO.

"I didn't know if you'd come. Military men don't always keep their word." She smiled in embarrassment. Incongruously, she thought of Elzie Mayerfeld's explanation of how dogs growled at fleas.

"I'm not like the others. Or did you have someone read cards for you?"

She wondered what it was that the Dog Lady and the NCO had in common.

In a little while the sun came to rest on the green crowns of the trees and the highest spires; it had already left the river and the bridges, as if it were letting dusk fall from a high ridge to touch the lowlands and the depressions of the city. Suddenly the flame turned red and then paled like a reflection, and the city turned quiet and beautiful. Finally even the trees and spires were dark, and windows that had caught the rosy glow now lost their tinge of pink, blanching in the light of the moon.

"It's nice here," said the NCO.

"Yes."

"The sunsets here are different from the ones at sea. On the sea, night is born differently." He said he'd been in Prague a week now and

not once in the whole time had he looked at a newspaper. Then he said,
"The sky reminds me of a day in the North Sea. A day in the North Sea
is like night in Prague. Today was really a hot one. But I hear you went
swimming."

She knew immediately on what wind he'd heard that. And for no
reason at all she suddenly recalled a train ride she had taken with her
father and mother; she'd watched the passing scene through a frosted
window. She could see the villages flying past, the military encamp-
ments, columns of soldiers, the dirty snow.

Stars were emerging in the sky like shiny buttons on a dark coat.

"It was nice on Wednesday to watch you doing your gymnastics,"
said the NCO. "Girls look nice in gym suits." Then, as if to impress
her with his knowledge and experience, he added, "Do you know what
Socrates said? That whether a man marries or remains single, he can be
sure of one thing: that he will be sorry."

He smiled at her, but she couldn't find the courage to smile back.

"What do you want to talk about? Do you want to hear about the
ships I've been on?"

She asked him to tell her about himself, about what he did. She could
hear the constriction in her voice and the pounding of her heart,
knowing she was revealing her nervousness and wishing that something
she couldn't even name would relax and allow her to open up.

Then, when she realized she didn't have to talk because the NCO
would do most of the talking, it occurred to her that maybe man didn't
exist just to be fooled at every turn, and she smiled for no reason. The
NCO returned her smile. The full moon was reflected in her eyes.

"Don't worry. You can leave everything to me. You can't get lost
with me. I know every nook and alley. I know them like my own shoes,
little one." Then he told her about the ships he'd served on. He named
the unsinkable cruisers, *Tirpitz* and *Bismarck*. He'd painted them when
they were docked. He'd also been on two fast ships, a mine sweeper and
an antisubmarine vessel. Now he was glad to be back in Prague, where
he'd spent a few jolly nights. He was struck by the realization that here
he talked about what happened there, and there he'd talked about what
happened here. He smiled at the pleasant irony of it.

"Were you born in Prague?"

"Yes," she said.

"It's a beautiful city."

"Yes."

The NCO started telling her about all the ports and seas he had been through before coming here. He said there was no better place than Prague to take a furlough. Then he added that this was the last night of his leave.

"Where have you served?" she asked.

"All over Europe."

"I've never been anywhere outside of Prague."

"I know practically the whole continent by heart." He straightened up and unconsciously thrust out his chest.

She recalled her teacher, the silk dress with the green leaves. She could see the big roses stretched across the Dog Lady's bosom. She wanted to hold back only what was pure, only what she'd felt that morning. She was concentrating on this so hard that she couldn't quite understand what the soldier was telling her. Most recently he'd served in Kiel and before that he'd been in Prague officially, at the request of someone in the upper echelon, and had served with the unit that took part in the Heydrich action.

"That's interesting. I mean, it must have been interesting for you," she said, afraid that she didn't sound as casual as she wanted to.

The NCO felt her awkwardness and took her hand. "On my honor, *cara mia*. That's how it happened. Between breakfast, lunch and supper a man's life can begin, or change, or even end. We all had the same instructions. Kripo, Schupo, Gestapo. All three departments. It really didn't go very fast, but as I look back on it, it was a success. We were put onto the right track by one of them. Their own man." The NCO smiled, waiting for her to smile back.

"What does *cara mia* mean?"

" 'My dear.' Nothing bad. It's Italian. It's like when you sing."

"*Cara mia?*"

"Right. We took care of them that evening at the firing range at the edge of the city, *cara mia*. I believe it's where streetcars Number 3 and Number 14 go—the quarter called Kobylisy. Well, we didn't find anything in their apartment. They kept their mouths shut, the fools. When we pressed them about whether they approved of the assassination of the General—questions we were asking the whole populace a thousand times a day, ad nauseam—they just blinked their great calves' eyes. You know, honestly, the Slavs really look like cattle half the time."

He told her what it was they were most afraid of; he doubted they'd gotten over it. He said that putting the pressure on one man in one house in one street was enough to make all the others toe the line. It helped him understand why Germany would win the war.

She didn't ask for details and the NCO didn't volunteer any. He only remarked that brave men and cowards ended up the same way, even the ones who tried to hold onto words, as if words—just because you believe in them—could halt or change the direction of the bullets. Then he said he loved the fountains of Prague, even though he wouldn't drink from them because the birds made their nests in them.

When Jenny Thelen asked what the words were that they shouted, the NCO was pleased by her interest and by the urgency and the trace of fear in her voice, as though she were afraid to hear the full answer.

" 'Long live the republic' or 'Long live freedom,' as if they were trying to convince themselves. Some of them demanded a last request or to write a message home. One idiot was shot still swearing that a better Germany than ours would come to replace us. As if that would make dying any easier."

"Is it true what they say, that killing is beautiful?" she asked. Her words were barely audible.

"Usually their knees begin shaking before it comes; saliva runs from the corners of their mouths. They don't look like leaders of the anti-German Resistance. They don't look as elegant as their survivors would like to believe."

Then he added, "The greater their hope, the more frightened they are. Only those who stop hoping that something will happen—that they will be pardoned, or that some miracle will take place, the firing squad will have stopped-up gun barrels or the gunpowder will be damp—only those can stop ridiculously hanging on to life."

He went on. "Only those who no longer care, and have neither fear nor hope because they've lost everything and know it, only those are dangerous. We send them off directly to hell."

In a while he laughed: *"Wie der Vogel, so das Ei."* A mean bird lays rotten eggs.

The NCO interpreted Jenny Thelen's silence as a sign of approval. He said casually, "Even obvious cowards who'd be willing to live like mice for ten, twenty, or even fifty years, finally rush to get it over with when they're faced with our iron will."

"We aren't allowed to cry," she murmured.

The girl with the scar removed her hand from his and they walked side by side, slowly, like the other couples they met—mostly soldiers and their dates. She was glad the streets were almost empty. The NCO was quiet for a while, then took her hand again.

"Am I going too fast?" he asked.

"No."

She felt a gentleness in him that hadn't been there when he'd described the Heydrich action. He tried not to hold her hand too roughly, and it occurred to her that he had a big hand, a sailor's hand. It was smooth and dry.

"Whoever loses is always wrong," the NCO said, and smiled.

"I almost believe that," said Jenny Thelen. "You must never lose."

"How do you do that—never lose?" She smiled.

"A lot of our people make the mistake of feeling sorry for the enemy, even if sometimes they're children. There were a few irresponsible individuals who weren't only sorry for the murderers of our own soldiers, but even for young Jewish and gypsy snakes."

It crossed her mind that in his smile, as in the elegant smile of the Dog Lady, there was great pride, a pride that was great enough to destroy the last vestiges of conscience. She'd shown them a bracelet she'd been given by her sister, who was a pilot in the Luftwaffe and who was later shot down over London. It was a gold bracelet and on the inside was the inscription, "Next time both." What did she mean, "The animal is too big"?

They passed a group of sailors of lower rank who saluted the NCO. He returned the salute carelessly, not even looking at them; she felt he was looking at her. She imagined him as a member of one of the three units involved in the Heydrich action.

No one in Germany was particularly fastidious when it came to the children of the enemy, thought the girl with the scar; she left her hand in the NCO's although she didn't return his squeeze but let him lead her.

The NCO went back to his story. "Whether they were silent or shouting, they couldn't get the better of us. And silence is consent. Silence means complicity and vice versa, it. . . ." He coughed, as if gaining time to finish the sentence, but he must have forgotten what he was saying, because he started over: "There's something about it in very ancient law. Well, we're certainly as smart as they were. The ancient Romans even used this trick about silence. But I wish you could have seen them. The woman on the floor, whining like a whipped bitch. The old man leaning on the kitchen sink. And not a word from either of them. In the end people like that always have weak nerves. You stomp your foot or raise your fist and their resistance is gone. The guy had lost his glasses and he stood there blinking like an owl. Maybe he was trying to give his wife courage. So silly, just wasting time; we had plenty of bullets. The whole day I couldn't get rid of the smell of meatloaf. It's really funny sometimes, Miss. Their whole apartment, the whole building, smelled of meatloaf. A sweet and sour smell of meat, pickles and dipped bread. And then—can you believe it?—we had meatloaf for supper that night. We had a Czech cook. And then we had it for lunch the next day. Well, let me tell you, you can get too much of a good thing all at once sometimes. For a year you don't even see a meatloaf and then it's on the menu three times in a row. Your nose is full of it and you wonder where all this meatloaf came from all of a sudden.''

The NCO laughed. ''I like to come back here,'' he said. ''Prague has never disappointed me. A man needs to enjoy himself sometimes. When you're a sailor you don't know what's in store for you next.''

He was looking at the pavement, at the way the pale blue and white stones made a mosaic pattern: diamonds with circles or squares in the middle. The sidewalks of Prague were like stone lace.

''As one of my friends from the *Tirpitz* used to say, 'You climb Mount Everest only once.' '' Then he smiled. ''Every one of our men should have a chance to kill at least one of them. To purify his blood, so to speak, to earn for himself a place among the purest. It's like taking a bath.''

His voice was harsh, but it was softening, mellowing in the girl's presence.

''Would you like me to walk slower?'' he asked. He was thinking about her soft and at the same time pure Aryan face, and her forehead and neck—about her nice manners and about her shyness.

Then, thinking that she'd probably like to know more of the details, for him to elaborate—the way he had about the meatloaf—he added: ''There was a lot that happened, and if you have time I'm sure I can remember most of the details. We used to give very detailed reports— they're lying around somewhere—but I can't remember everything now. Sometimes it makes my head reel,'' he said with a little smile, lifting both arms over his head in a boyish gesture. She was happy he'd let go of her hand.

''There were an awful lot of people like that, *Fraulein*. We had to put the squeeze on quite a few. But people are like bedbugs. If you allow them to, they'll suck your blood. Particularly if they disgust you or make you afraid; then they'll suck you dry. You've got to have the courage to crush them."

Then he said, "I don't want to be too serious. That can spoil the pleasure of a walk. I hope I'm not boring you."

"Not at all," she answered.

And then he said that sometimes it took a long time before it was all over, and other times only a fraction of a second. "But I never envy them, *Fraulein,* whether it takes half an hour or just long enough to count to three, like it does when they use electricity to puncture the skulls of cattle in the slaughterhouse."

He knew how to command, he said, because he knew how to obey. He told her that their evening stroll through the city was just as stimulating for him as sailing the high seas, just as exciting as fighting and feeling death in your bones. Then he thought he might have overdone it; his voice mellowed and he asked her if she knew anything about the stars. When she answered no, he told her about the constellations over the North Sea.

The city was swimming in a cool, fresh breeze. The NCO inhaled deeply and exhaled slowly. He said the air tasted like honeyed wine. Some cities, he said, looked like resorts, as though their buildings were old gems. He was happy that the heat of the day had let up.

Everything he said seemed very familiar to the girl with the scar, as if she'd heard it all before.

"Every place in this city has memories for me, *cara mia.* Aren't you cold?"

"No," she said.

"Do you like saying no?" the NCO smiled.

"No."

"We can play a game: For every three no's, you have to give me one yes. All right?"

"I don't think so."

The NCO smiled again, as if he'd just trapped her, and then he returned to what had seemed to attract her attention from the beginning. "It took three months to paint the keel of the cruiser *Tirpitz.* Layers and layers of protective paint. Both of them—the *Tirpitz* and the *Bismarck*—are as heavy as any ship in the world. They're huge and unsinkable, like enormous floating ice floes."

The evening dusk was slowly thickening. Scattered clouds appeared in the sky and the moon penetrated them sharply, as if it were looking at them through a torn curtain.

"I'm leaving tonight," said the NCO.

"For where?"

"Kiel."

"Going to sea?"

"I'm a sailor," the NCO smiled.

"The sea must be beautiful," she said, like an awestruck child.

"Wonderful," he agreed. He knew it was beautiful, even for people who'd never actually seen it. You could hear all of this in the way he said, "Wonderful." Her silence seemed to indicate admiration and questions she was afraid to ask. Perhaps it was the helplessness of asking and waiting for a reply that frightened her, but her fear of eliciting suspicion never went further than her breathing, her voice, and perhaps a certain intensity in her silence. At the same time she was afraid of measuring everything by her own experience, since that had distorted all of her life, before and after. Her silence also held surprise and a different kind of helplessness and inexperience, as well as the satisfaction of knowing that she, after all, was the one here with the NCO and not Elzie Mayerfeld, even if she had to be second. And it was pleasant to talk about the sea. She was thinking about that strange fish deep at the bottom of the ocean, and how when two males meet in the dark, the weaker and smaller one changes into a female. But she let him talk on about the loveliness of the sea. He tried hard to stick to the topic and to emphasize how beautiful the sea was.

"You can never imagine what it's like until you've seen it with your own eyes," he said.

He was using his voice to stroke her—wooing her with the images and colors of the night sea, of the sea tossed by a storm, of the sea beneath a starlit sky—and then he took her arm in his. She didn't resist. His elbow was touching her breast and he'd become quiet.

She imagined the sea as the NCO described it; she felt a pressure in her temples and visions seemed to come out of the dusk. The whole day had so heightened ·her expectations that they had gone beyond the possibility of fulfillment.

Her thoughts drifted back to the blue of the sky that had dissolved now into darkness, back to the alabaster pearls of heat that had vanished in the cool evening breeze after having first been strung on threads of dust, lost now in the darkness over the city. The stars were beginning to disappear into the gathering clouds. She wanted to replace Elzie Mayerfeld just this once.

"I'd like to show you the sea close up," said the NCO.

"I don't know how to swim," she admitted.

"Would you like me to teach you?"

"That'd be nice," she said.

"Do you like fish?"

"Not particularly."

"Because they're cold-blooded, don't have a soul, and can't talk?" the NCO smiled.

He pressed against her, and the girl with the scar felt his tight, muscular body and his warmth. She could feel strength emanating from him. It was the first time in her life she had felt anything like this. She was aware of his will, and of her own as well.

Suddenly it occurred to her that any answer might give her away, even if she said yes three times in a row without a single no. She also knew she could tell him exactly why it couldn't be.

And so they walked for a while in silence; it was as though she were uncovering in her mind everything the NCO couldn't have thought of, or wouldn't have thought of in the same way she did. She felt she could never do any of the things she wanted to. In the Institute they were constantly told about the generosity and magnanimity of the Reich: the Reich that had taken them to its bosom like a true mother.

"You're trembling, little one," said the NCO. "Are you cold?"

"Not very," she said. "Just a little."

"You mustn't tremble like that," he added.

"There's a cool breeze this evening. It was so hot today."

"Come closer to me."

When she didn't respond, he added that she didn't have to be afraid. She thought she could hear real concern in his voice. He had his right arm around her shoulders and he held her close. Again she felt his strength and his warmth.

"Why are you so quiet?" the NCO asked.

"Where are those big, unsinkable ships now?"

"The *Bismarck* and the *Tirpitz?* Oh, they both went down."

"War is really cruel. And not just because everyone says so."

"War has to be cruel," the NCO asserted.

"Tell me more about the sea."

"What would you like to hear, lambkin?"

"How brave you were. How you and your friend rang the bell and pounded on the door of those people and how frightened they were and how everything smelled of meatloaf."

"I don't think we rang a bell or knocked on the door; we just pushed our way in," the NCO said with a smile. "Did I tell you about my friend? He's a sergeant now, too."

"Tell me why you've never forgotten it."

"Little one, you're so romantic."

His palm closed around her shoulder and she felt his whole hand, heavy and friendly at the same time. He looked at her and in the moonlight her eyes seemed larger. Moonlight streamed through a single gap in the clouds, as if it had been poured through a blue well.

The NCO was saying that there was a barrier between a man and a woman that a man could have difficulty surmounting. He said that when a man chose a girl, he wanted to be sure that she would be a credit to him when he took her out; he didn't want to be ashamed in front of his buddies, and he didn't want to worry about her when he was away for a long time because no sailor could avoid that.

The NCO told her that the icebergs in the North Sea looked like the white rocks along the banks of the Rhine, or like mountains with tunnels in them, or like castles, and that the water around them was always quiet and turquoise-blue and as clear as a German's soul. He smiled and told her that in war, as in nature, life and death were like brother and sister. She was more conscious of his breath than of his words.

The NCO felt a trembling frailty in her. "Lambkin," he said suddenly. And then, in the same soft voice, "You really are like a little German lamb." He told her she had a pretty face and small, feminine shoulders. And he said that he liked the way she held herself as straight as a candle, and that if she'd been born a man she'd have made a fine-looking soldier. And then he mentioned how clean she was.

She understood what was coming long before his voice broke and he told her that she looked like a lamb and that he'd never met a prettier girl. She understood it all before the first words passed his lips. Her whole life had been made up of lies; they were lies even when they were true, because everything began and ended with lies.

She started trembling as the sailor pressed her to him, repeating that she was like a little lamb. She let him lead her, obedient and docile, as though she were afraid to speak.

"You mustn't tremble like that," the NCO repeated. "Why are you trembling so?" And then he asked her point-blank, softly and rather gently, "Were you ever with a man?" There was a trace of hoarseness in his voice.

"No," she answered.

The lights of the city were drowning in a blackout. They were startled by the sound of a passing car, its lights covered with black cloth, and then they heard a streetcar that they couldn't see.

"It was so hot all day and now I feel almost cold," she said.

What did he want from her? What did he expect for a few sweet words and a *"cara mia"*? And what was she prepared to give him? She'd known for a long time that for every wrong there were a thousand and one explanations. Her father at the kitchen sink, collapsed in shame, her mother on the floor, and the whiz of a dog leash in the air.

Sometimes you wanted to forget so you wouldn't feel like a walking cemetery. But you couldn't, and the memories stayed inside of you for as long as you moved and felt and thought. You'd hear the sound of a mandolin somewhere, or you'd see a strange face with nickel-rimmed glasses and you noticed the likeness and it frightened you; or you'd recognize something in the chance sighting of a tree, a stone, or a star. Or you'd hear it in someone else's voice. You couldn't get rid of it as long as you lived.

According to Julie, people eventually stopped caring about where the soap they used came from when they couldn't get any other. She trembled at her own thoughts. She tried again to imagine the enormous ships, the freighters and cruisers. Were they like the steamboats with paddle wheels that used to run up and down the Moldau? Once her family took a ride on one of those boats—she, her father and mother, and their neighbor and his three daughters.

"A craftsman's girl would have it pretty good after the war," the NCO added to something she must have missed. "A trade is a handful of gold, as they say, *Fraulein*. If I had the opportunity, I could be a driver; I know quite a bit about car engines. And I could do quite well as a painter. Lately I've been thinking that the war will be over sometime and I ought to start looking around."

She didn't know how to respond, and the NCO added, "Of course, this isn't exactly the best time for serious commitments or marriage."

Then, as though reprimanding himself, he said, "I should try to warm you up somehow. What would you say to some tea with rum or a pastry?"

"Please," she said. "I don't want to trouble you."

"Oh, my little lady," he assured her kindly. "There's a nice place right here. Shall we go in?"

It was a self-service cafe near the viaduct. Close by were the slaughterhouse and the electric company and beyond the viaduct was the park. A freight train loaded with tanks and cannons rattled over the viaduct as the NCO led her inside.

The cafe was full of people and noise. The NCO wanted to order grog for both of them, but they didn't have rum, so he ordered a beer for himself and a Japanese tea for her. He made a point of asking specifically for green Japanese tea; he said it was as sweet as honey and good for the vocal cords.

He asked somebody at the next table for a light and began to talk quite loudly.

People were beginning to stare at them. She raised her cup and swallowed, almost choking in her haste.

She was happy when they were outside on the sidewalk again. He was saying that whatever is German is beautiful, and how difficult it is to describe it; you can only feel it. And how easy it is to recognize what is non-German. He laughed.

"Can I go back inside for a minute?" she asked. The NCO was putting his money away in his pocket and he looked up in surprise. "I need to go in by myself. Just for a minute."

He gave her a friendly smile and saw her lower her eyes and blush.

"I'll be right back," she said again.

He saw how shy she was. He smiled again. "We've got lots of time, my silly. A few minutes won't make any difference." She hesitated, and it occurred to him that maybe she was afraid he wouldn't be there when she came back.

Once she was back inside the cafe, she began to feel flashes of hot and cold; her teeth were chattering and she tried to tighten her lips. She thought of what Elzie Mayerfeld had said about living in the present, about remembering and forgetting, and about how now was always different from a while ago, as the future would be different from the present. She remembered what the NCO had said about the loser always being wrong, at least in the eyes of the victor. And she thought about his strong, warm body and his big hands and how willing he'd been to pay for her just a moment ago.

Although she couldn't stop shaking, she felt a calm deep within herself. She thought of the NCO's powerful body, recalled the touch of his hands and the sound of his voice, which was rough when he talked about the ships and about what he'd done during the war, and soft when he called her a little German lamb, and different still when he talked about what he might do after the war.

She tried to force herself not to tremble. She felt feverish after this long day. She tried to concentrate by remembering one of her mother's dresses, but she couldn't quite recall it.

Again she felt a cramp in her stomach. She was recalling the way he'd touched her on Tuesday, the feel of his heavy hand when he'd guided her in here a little while ago—all in an attempt to shake off the chill. She felt as if she were two people.

She inhaled the odors of the cafe, of the people and the food. She saw her reflection in the mirror, and the slightness of her bust surprised her. She addressed herself in her mind, scolding. The trembling in her stomach and thighs must stop.

Slowly she walked between the tables and chairs. She crossed the space between the last rows of tables and, without anyone's noticing, opened the door to the kitchen.

The dishwasher couldn't see her; she was facing the sink with her back to Jenny. Behind the cook there was a long board with several knives on it. Both women had their backs turned and were completely caught up in their noisy work.

The girl with the scar took a knife from the board and hid it under the jacket she was carrying over her arm. Her newly acquired skill at sleight of hand didn't even surprise her. It took only a second. Then she passed through a hall to the restrooms. The cook and the woman in the red rubber apron didn't notice anything.

Behind her she could hear the sound of running water and the sharp clink of porcelain. She entered the toilet stall and locked it. First she slipped the knife into her camisole, but then she changed her mind and tied it with her belt to the outside of her left thigh. She lowered her skirt as far as possible and tried moving to see if the knife would show. She remembered the NCO's saying that Prague was a capital city without fortifications. In the buttoned pocket of her jacket her ten marks lay untouched.

As she moved down the sidewalk next to the sailor, she was aware of the knife touching her body: it felt quite large, and that gave her a feeling of satisfaction. She had only to take slightly smaller steps. But she could still hold herself upright and she just had to check once to see whether the knife was held in place tightly enough.

"Here's the park," the NCO said. He'd been smoking and his breath smelled of tobacco. "I'm afraid it may rain. But the trees will protect us."

"It's awfully dark," she said.

"Are you afraid of shadows?"

He had the pleasant suspicion that she'd been preparing herself for him, the suspicion that deceives men as often as not. A man's desire, he thought, was different, simpler, than the desire or consent of a woman. And so he said, "We don't have to hurry."

He laughed without explanation. What he was saying was not really what he wanted to say, but he comforted her again. "You can trust me completely, *cara mia.*"

He led her farther into the park; his arm encircled her waist. She was afraid he'd feel the handle of the knife.

The NCO thought that in any situation a man could overwhelm a woman with images of the sea and islands, life and death, with a promise. Once more he laughed for no reason. Several times he called her "little lamb" and "lambkin" and "little one," and again he said it would be too bad if the rain spoiled things for them after such a long, hot day.

The park gate was made of wrought iron and had knockers with iron rings that were rusted from disuse. Inside the park, the air was saturated with the smell of the invisible river.

The NCO led her silently and carefully so she wouldn't stumble. She felt his hands as he touched her: her shoulders, her arms, her hips.

"It's really a beautiful evening," he said.

"Yes," she answered.

"Don't you agree that in the end everyone gets what he deserves?"

When she didn't answer, he added, "The soldier gets his moment of peace, the hungry man gets something to eat, and the lonely man gets a pretty girl."

"I don't know."

"In this darkness I can't see you unless you're very close." His voice broke again, somewhere between a full voice and a whisper, and he said, "Little lamb. My little lamb."

Then he held her close. "I'd like to ask you something. May I?"

"Why not?"

"I'd like this to be our evening."

"What do you mean?"

"Have you ever been kissed . . . by a man?" And then he interrupted himself. "Say yes, will you?"

"To what?"

"Just say yes."

"But to what?"

"Just say yes and then I'll tell you."

"No," she said slowly.

"That's enough," the NCO said softly. He said love was like a little death but he wouldn't know how to begin to explain it.

"You agree then?"

"To what?"

"May I kiss you?"

But before he could, she pulled back and asked, "Are you close to our teacher?"

The NCO hesitated. "Elzie Mayerfeld?"

She nodded.

"Oh, you lambkin. Elzie Mayerfeld is a distant relative, a fifth cousin or something. Our cow drank from their trough, as they say. She thinks I left hours ago. Why do you ask? Oh, yes. You'd better not tell her anything. Girls sometimes like to boast."

She said he didn't have to worry about her telling anyone. The NCO smiled at that; he was trying to find a properly secluded place for them. He held her so tightly that it frightened her; he misinterpreted her fear.

She could feel his hot breath and his strong hand. Then he was leaning over her, whispering, "Would you like me to be close to you?" His whisper was more penetrating and insistent than before.

"I don't know," she whispered back.

He led her away from the walk, over the grass and into some shrubbery. The ground was damp and crumbly, wet with the evening dew. She seemed to him compliant and soft, excited by the nearness and the increasing intimacy of a man who could no longer be refused. He knew that was why she was trembling. Her lips were pressed tightly together, which he interpreted as the anxiety of inexperience.

Her heart was pounding. And she could hear another pounding mixed with the sound of her heart.

She watched the NCO while he kissed her, and she saw images of other men in uniforms and leather coats, as if the many had become one, and each individual contained the first and the thousandth.

"It will be beautiful," the NCO whispered. "You'll see. It will be just like I promised." He caressed her with his palms and his fingertips, touching her cheeks and around her lips and then brushing his fingers over her forehead and stroking her scar.

She let him do it. She felt blood rushing to her cheeks. She was thinking of blood, terrified of what she could see in her imagination.

"Did they hurt you?" he asked. Then he added hoarsely: "I won't let anyone hurt you. No one will ever hurt you again."

With both hands he caressed her cheeks, and her shoulders, and finally her breasts. She knew what was coming and she was afraid he might find the knife.

"We're alone here," the NCO whispered. "I don't want anything bad. Only something we can have together, now, right now. Something we can remember. Nothing that would hurt you. You're lovely. You're so lovely . . . We should seize life while we're still young . . . a few stolen moments once or twice a year . . . don't think about anything . . . ugly . . . come closer . . . let me . . . lambkin." His voice was getting more and more hoarse.

The girl with the scar pulled back a bit. He thought she was merely confused by his whispered words, his caressing palms, his breath.

"No one's here," he whispered again. "The local people aren't allowed here in the evening. No one will disturb us here."

"Yes," she whispered. "Yes. But turn around for a second. Just for a second."

"Why? What's wrong?" he asked in surprise.

"I have to fix something."

The NCO heard her untie her belt; then he thought he heard the unmistakable rustle of a lifted skirt and the scratch of a fingernail against naked skin. He coughed in his effort to suppress an impulse to turn abruptly, take her in both arms and pull her down onto the grass. The blood was rising to his head. He imagined that her skirt was already off. He gave her time to take off her blouse and unfasten her underwear. It began to rain softly.

"OK?" he asked.

"Not yet," she whispered.

She had taken out the knife. Compared with the NCO she was small and weak; she'd have to give it a good swing, as far back as she could and then forward. She felt such excitement that she couldn't think of anything beyond the stabbing. She felt the pain in her abdomen, but she didn't allow herself to think about it. There was only a fraction of a second when she was paralyzed by a strange anxiety about the success of what she was about to do, like someone who had never killed before, but had lived, breathed, and grown up in the midst of killing. The anxiety left her as soon as she moved the arm with the knife, and so did any tremor that might have weakened her. She felt the point and then the wide blade enter his body silently, with almost unbelievable ease. She had struck him lower than she'd intended, and because the NCO had started to turn around, she'd struck him in the area of the kidneys. Then the movement of his body caused the knife to twist in the wound—as she held onto the handle—with a convulsive force that in only a moment began to ebb.

The NCO groaned hoarsely, as if he were trying to exhale without having drawn in a breath. The insistence of the sound was familiar to her. No final cry came from his breast. He was falling slowly, as if he were only lying down. As he fell, his body parted the thick bushes in front of him. The bushes opened with a plaintive, broken, rustling sound, and then closed over him again.

The NCO's hand grasped the knife, but he no longer had the strength to pull it out. He choked a little longer. The rain was soft and warm. The park was full of birds; they were roosting everywhere, on the ground, in the trees, in the bushes.

The girl with the scar straightened herself and walked out of the shrubbery onto the park road. She met no one on the way to the gate. The local people were forbidden to use the park, and anyway, no one would have wanted to come here in the rain. It seemed to her that she was strangely calm, as if she were divided in two. One was quietly walking, obediently trying to forget voices and faces, as she was daily advised by Elzie Mayerfeld. Inside was the other: She had lived with her a long time before getting to know her. Now at last she could recall her mother's wedding dress exactly. Her mother used to take it out at least once a year; she would shake out the wrinkles and air it before putting it away again.

Her father was walking with her, too, his nickel-rimmed glasses on the bridge of his nose. He looked like a professor, even thought he'd worked for years at the waterworks. He played the mandolin and sang *O Maria*. He told her that the tall trees bent with the wind and that the low trees could withstand storms precisely because they weren't so tall. And what a pity, he said, that the magnolia blossoms died so soon. She was telling him not to be afraid.

8

Drenched to the bone, the pale girl with the scar walked through the front hallway of the Prague Institute for Girls of Pure Race from Non-German Territories. Her belted poplin skirt and jacket hadn't protected her much from the rain.

"Home already?" asked the doorman. He was reading *Ost Front*, his face a mask of cordiality. "Lambs always seem to suffer from a lack of four walls and a roof over their heads," he said. "But if you can't do it under the open sky, you shouldn't do it at all."

"He left," said the girl with the scar. "For Kiel." She gave the doorman her ten marks. He quickly stuffed them into his pocket so they wouldn't get wet.

"Too bad," said the doorman, as if asking whether it didn't hurt. He smiled like a man who could draw his own conclusions. He was showing off his second pack of Viktoria cigarettes. "That's the way to do it, Miss. You have to elbow your way up in this world. We can't be like the English who missed the boat. That shouldn't happen to us in this dump." And then he added, "We must all answer for every opportunity we get, don't you think?" He was closing the gate behind her. "On my word of honor," he said slyly. "One good turn deserves another. Not a word. Not to a soul, ever." He raised his thick black eyebrows.

Upstairs in her room the girl with the scar untied her belt. There wasn't a trace of blood anywhere. All she could feel was the pulsing of her scar. She remembered the goldish bronze urn they'd shown her in Bredovska Street. The warm calmness within her did not leave. They were still dancing in the living room.

She put her jacket on the chair, then took off her red dress. She took out her comb and began to comb her hair. In her small bosom, which was quietly heaving up and down, there was no trace of what she'd feared. Nor did she cry. Next door, the record player was playing Johann Strauss's *Tales from the Vienna Woods*. The voice of Lale Anderson was velvety soft, and the melody was like an open embrace or a couple's joined hands.

In the darkness she thought of the soaked, softened earth, of the voices of birds waking at sunrise, and of worms, of earth and light. She imagined the magnolias opposite the window, blossoms whose centers were as wet and white as the throats of swans and whose edges seemed dipped in blood. Inside herself she was talking with her father and mother; the dead were the only ones she could talk to. Only the dead could be told the truth.

She combed her hair slowly with the easy, languid movements of a woman. She saw a white darkness in which she could imagine blood, perhaps spilled by a she-wolf biting through the neck of its mortal enemy.

She wanted to grasp the change in herself. But she couldn't. She felt her life was part of the rain, like a river or the sea. She knew she had done what she had to do to fulfill the secret purpose that existed in everyone's life.

She opened her eyes. Images of streaming water turned back into the furnishings of her room: the wardrobe, the desk, the bed on which she was sitting. The comb she combed her hair with. The waltz music filled the house, the garden and the night.

She took out some dry underwear and a clean dress and threw all that she'd taken off into the waste basket.

The belt lay on the floor.

Indecent Dreams

1

THE old woman's complexion was like the bark of a tree. She walked up to the cinema box office and handed two tin pots of food through the window. The cashier slid the long book of tickets for the next day's program to one side. "Thanks," she said.

"You're welcome," said the old woman. "You know how glad I am to be able to do this for you, honey. It's potato soup and in the other pot there's lentils and smoked meat."

The building was old and occupied a whole city block, like a palace. Italian masons had been brought here at the beginning of the century to build it. One of the owners had converted the former concert hall on the ground floor into a cinema. The middle floor, which had served as the owner's residence until he sold the building and moved to America just before the war, was now a courtroom. The basement, for reasons no one understood, was a dormitory where railway men from the three main Prague railway stations slept. A cloakroom with showers, a dining room, and bedrooms were located in a former massage parlor that had been forced to close when the owner failed to pay the rent.

Most of the verdicts handed down by the German judges in Prague in the spring of 1945, the last year of the war, were simplified to either life in prison or the ax. But the cinema below continued to show German operettas as it had before (except for five days when a state of mourning for a German defeat on the Volga was declared throughout Germany and even the occupied territories), and the theater was usually full, even during morning and early afternoon matinee performances, not to mention the evenings, when it was practically impossible to get tickets just before the film began.

The cashier was young and pretty, with fine features, perhaps a little melancholy even though nothing had happened to her during the war. Her fair, magnificently combed hair fell to her shoulders and her blue eyes never lost their ingenuousness, not even when she took a large banknote from a customer and carefully returned the proper change, concentrating fully on her job even though she was sometimes genuinely exhausted. The prettiest thing about her was her long neck: sometimes it looked like that of a purebred race horse.

"How are you, my darling little girl?" asked the mother.

"I've got some kind of rash on my neck," replied the cashier.

"Does it hurt?"

"No, it just itches."

It was the only animal-like thing about her, even though the animal it called to mind was beautiful. Perhaps not even that was just, because at the same time her neck was like that of a white swan. Something about her suggested loneliness, though her mother, with skin as wrinkled as an old tree, was never far away; and even now when she had a job, her mother never left her alone for very long. She would walk her to work every day from the working-class suburb where the most imposing structure was a huge round silver natural gas storage tank supported on tall sturdy steel lags. Together they would walk from the tangled labyrinth of small, ramshackle houses, some made of wood, others with stone or half-stone walls. There were no paved streets and they had to wear galoshes to avoid getting covered with mud before they reached the center of the city. To the old woman, her daughter meant everything that was valuable in life. She begrudged her daughter nothing, not even her fine clothes, in which the young woman looked above her station. Everything about the daughter suggested she was a person who knew how to look after herself well.

"I'm almost glad you never married," said the old woman through the window. For a moment her face relaxed. "I'm happy you're going to come out of this pure, not like those tramps who hang around with any rank at all—colonels, lieutenants, even privates," the mother added.

But her mind was full of thoughts she didn't confide to her daughter: There are a lot of young men hanging about with those vests made of rabbitskin turned inside out. Where have they come from? What are they looking for in the center of Prague? They all look like bums. You can't believe anyone. Perhaps the mother was genuinely glad that her daughter was still single, but it wasn't so certain the daughter shared her feelings, even though she didn't look unhappy.

The cashier sensed what her mother was thinking. The mother didn't trust people—people on the street or in the elevators of tall buildings where she occasionally went on errands for her daughter. Sometimes she was afraid even in the corridor of her own building before turning the key to unlock the door of her own flat.

"Will you wait till I finish eating?" asked the cashier.

"Some places they've already started taking German signs off the buildings," replied the mother. "Some of the trams have removed their route signs. And I'll bet it's not just so the Germans won't know where they're going." And her eyes said: There's something in the air. Something's about to happen, I can feel it in my bones, my little girl. We have to be careful.

"What's playing?" the old woman asked.

And she wondered why a person always felt threatened by something, like spring comes before summer and like summer comes before autumn takes its place, and like the wind and the rain come, or like the sun and the snow. A strange yet familiar anxiety came over the old woman, a feeling she'd never get used to, not even if she were to live a thousand years, and sometimes she felt as though she had been in the world a thousand years already, though she was scarcely sixty. Fear, thought the old woman. She sometimes trembled for no reason at all. As though fear had accumulated within her, not only fear for her own life, but for the lives of her mother and father, the parents of whole clans stretching far into the unknown, where only the rich or the famous are concerned for their destiny. What was she to them?

She looked at her daughter—at her swanlike neck, at her frank, somewhat timid eyes in which there was a light, dreamy haze, and she longed to penetrate her daughter's thoughts where unknown films were shown, different pictures. The old woman was afraid of the men who were interested in her daughter without her knowing about it. It wasn't just the Nazis who reserved the right to steal, kill, and lie. The poor thing has pimples just like a woman who needs a man; but she didn't trust her with anyone, not for anything. You have to be as clever as a fox, my little girl, strong as a tiger, and changeable as a chameleon. Not give yourself over.

What kind of storm would come bursting forth from the clouds hanging over the city, as though night were falling everywhere? She couldn't see properly. I don't like it when it gets dark. I don't like it when the day ends, when something is coming to an end. And no one knows anything, thought the mother. This is that unknown day, when no one knows anything, when everything can be first or last, last or first.

"Still the film about the two sisters," replied the cashier. "It's intermission just now. Do you want me to buy you some ice cream?"

"No, no, it's just made from water and artificial sugar anyway. Don't bother, darling."

Her mother's "no" was like an explosive tossed into the air to destroy something else. At least once a day, she said the more you trust people, the sooner they'll cheat you. The less you trust them, the better.

"You don't have any dish powder," she said finally. "Give me the dishes, I'll take them back."

What's the matter with me? she asked herself, because she could see the same question in her daughter's eyes. What am I really afraid of? What do I care about others? Why do I tremble when nothing is happening to me? That's how it's been for six whole years, she thought. Perhaps I'm just blaming it all on the Germans. I was afraid even before. But no. It's like the eclipse of the sun the newspapers are predicting for next week.

"I've never liked this building very much. Everything is too big. I've never been very fond of your cinema, either. The Morgenstern where I used to take you when you were a child was nicer. And I don't even like most of the programs."

"I'm glad I have a decent job," said the daughter.

"A decent job? Yes, at least you've got that," admitted the mother.

"It's warm in here."

"And it's not dangerous, that's the main thing, little girl."

"Remember that lanky guy, the one who moved out of our neighborhood and used to come here for sausages? He was just here looking for his brother. You didn't happen to see him on your way over, did you?"

"The one with the big teeth? Isn't he still selling papers?"

"Yes, he says he's worried about his brother. He says his brother saw God."

And the mother thought: To buy sausages? I'll bet I know who he was coming here to see.

The cashier laughed. Everyone has different visions. She had her own secret dreams, but instead of dreaming them at night, she dreamed them during the day while counting tickets or money or while sitting alone and eating, as she was doing now. Her own indecent dreams. But she couldn't tell her mother about them. She'd faint from the shame, because they were forbidden dreams. They weren't about Germans, nor about freedom. They were about men, and she was always in them, but they went beyond the bounds of what her mother would allow. They were terrible to imagine, and they made her dizzy with fright. She'd perspire all over. And that wasn't all.

Echoes of passions, of sin and sinning, went through her head, echoes of naturalness and shame. Visions of gallant love, romantic affairs or explosions of jealousy followed by shyness, shame and secret dissatisfaction; disillusion and even hate and injured pride at some moments. It was a haze of stories she had seen at the movie theater; but it was more than that. At the bottom of a stream no one knew about, there was something she wanted so much. She thought about a woman's courage. Why it means so many different things. Sometimes she dreamed that she was a river with many tributaries, flowing and flowing but never emptying into the sea—just circumnavigating the world and then emptying back into herself again.

"No, I didn't see anyone and I don't want to. Is the owner of the cinema here?"

"I have no idea. I haven't seen him," replied the cashier.

"Better that he's not here. I don't like it when he's around," said the mother.

And she thought: Each day I'm more and more frightened for you. Each hour. Why? Has it really been like this all my miserable life? Is there nothing beautiful in life? Is there only eternal, endless fear? Why does everything seem alien? I can see right into the owner's stomach. All I have to do is think of him and the feeling comes back. The richest people think the whole world is there to serve them. They're all the same, she said to herself.

"He's very polite to me," said the girl.

"Can you trust his politeness?"

"Why not?"

"Don't forget he once pestered you in a very nasty way," said the mother, and again she thought: He has eyes like a toad. I've never seen uglier eyes. He looked at your breasts so shamelessly, as though he were admiring you, but he envied you your beautiful breasts. Men envy a lot about women. I know men like that, I know what they want. White flesh, innocence, tenderness. The things I've had to do for them when they paid for it. The more money people have, the surer they are of themselves. They think they can do everything. You need a strong stomach. They think a girl will swallow anything, literally anything.

"Don't worry," said the cashier. "Come on inside. Why are you always afraid? What good does it do you?" She smiled. She had white, regular teeth. Her mother had taken great care to see she never needed a filling. "You end up being afraid to breathe."

He could charm you, thought the mother. She watched her daughter as she ate. And where would you get the money for decent cures? she thought.

"For years now we haven't been able to lead a normal life," she said out loud. "That's what it is." And she added to herself: People take great delight in murdering each other. They always have. People are animals, that's why they kill each other. There are only a few exceptions, people who respect themselves, like you, my little girl. Like me. The Bible says we were all created in the image of God, but only from the waist up. Open your beautiful blue eyes, my sweetheart, so you'll see all the shadows that follow you around. Hitler and Mussolini and Kaltenbrunner and Mr. Karl Hermann Frank. I could go on forever. The world has gone mad and we must try to go through it untouched, my sweet child. That's why we live inside ourselves, my darling, and everything that goes on outside doesn't require us for its doing. The world may be beautiful and yet it is terribly bad. No one loves anyone for long. That's why so many commit suicide, my darling.

"What are you thinking about?" asked the girl.

"Don't ask."

When have I ever not been afraid of something, can you tell me that? Only when I gave you my breasts and my milk. Then I felt the world was at peace. My breasts were firm and pliant. I was filled with love. But as soon as I finished feeding you, I was afraid again. And again it's in the air. The murdering will begin, child. It's here. Some things are beautiful only when you're young. Even though people try to persuade themselves that wisdom comes with age, it doesn't. The heart grows cold, that's all. I know what it means to have a broken heart. And I know what will break it: a long life. Waiting. Fear. Hopes. Lies. The truth, my darling. The naked truth.

The mother sat on a box containing old posters. She looked at her daughter as though she were expecting her to lay an egg.

"Why don't you rest here a while and then go home and lie down," said the cashier.

"Why should I rest? From what?"

"You look like you have a fever."

"Why aren't you eating, my child? I made it hot for you. You're letting it get too cold."

"Do you think this is the day we've been waiting for?" asked the cashier suddenly.

She didn't finish her food. Her mother always gave her more than enough, as though she didn't believe she'd be able to eat again the next day. She put the lid back on the pot and fixed it in place with a strong elastic band. She wiped the spoon off with a dish towel that hung on a peg. The towel covered a poster displaying the face of the German actor Heinz Rühman. The second pot had contained the potato soup, but the cashier had finished that.

"People are like animals," said the mother.

"People never get tired of enjoying themselves," said the cashier.

"Are you always sold out?"

"Pretty much."

"Something's about to happen," said the mother. "But you mustn't get mixed up in anything. You've never done anything to anyone and I don't want anyone to do anything to you."

"You said the same thing last year."

"It's in the air. Last year, this year, right now."

"Maybe."

"Someone said the staff of the British Embassy has moved up just outside of Prague." The mother watched her daughter, studying her mouth when she talked, her eyes when she looked at her. What do you know about debauchery? she thought. Luckily for you, you've never had to go through what I did.

"And the Germans pretend they don't see anything," added the mother. "As though Prague were an island of tranquility. An open city, as they say. A hospital city where they send the wounded to recuperate." The mother began to whisper. "As though they'd all forgotten, as though no one remembered anything, just because the Germans are getting beaten and their leader isn't recruiting fourteen-year-old boys anymore because he's dead and those who took over from him are urging them on and giving them rifles. And they still go to the movies and think that operettas will get them out of their fix."

The Germans are like rich people, thought the mother. They think they can do anything they want, not just kill, lie, and loot. When people think they can get away with it, they'll do things they ordinarily wouldn't dare.

"They'll be sorry once it starts," said the mother quietly. She had to wipe saliva from her lips. When her daughter was small, the mother thought, you could still believe that everyone was born the same, even though people are never the same, but they weren't worse just because they were different. The Germans beat that notion out of people's heads and now people are going to start beating it out of the Germans' heads. "That unknown day. That long-awaited day." Even those who are different will end up killing each other.

The mother shuddered and stroked her daughter's elbow. The girl had long arms and fingers, and supple skin. The mother thought: You might have played the piano beautifully, my child. That day. A mockery of anyone who has made himself at home here for six years with a pistol, a riding crop or a cane, carrying on with the local whores and beating up anyone he felt like.

On the street in front of the building that housed the cinema, an elderly German soldier with a raw, chafed neck appeared. He looked into the box office.

"He's in fine shape," whispered the mother.

"They'll be singing a different tune soon," said the daughter.

"Where do you suppose he came from?"

The man's neck looked as though they'd tried to hang him and the rope had broken. He shuffled over to the sausage stand and ordered a frankfurter. Then a second soldier appeared.

The second soldier ordered two tickets and paid in marks. Now it was obvious that a colleague was waiting for him a few steps from the box office. Both of them looked at the girl with appreciation.

"It's a fine building," said the first.

"Sure, but the cinema isn't the best thing about it," replied the other, and he laughed through a set of rotten teeth. "The teller's desk, the little nest." It was rather a nice laugh.

"I think I'd better wait for you," said the mother.

"No one will try anything," said the daughter. "They're just looking. They've probably had no company for a long time."

"On my way here, people were scraping the letters off German signs. They were standing on chairs, stepladders, and tables so they could reach the ones that were up high. There was a crowd on Charles Square."

And then she said, "One man there—it was near the Black Tower—was shouting that every soldier killed this Friday night by our people will make up for one of ours killed by them. I thought I recognized him. It was one of those two, you know who I mean? Both of them are tall and lanky."

"Were the police there?"

"No."

"Why didn't you tell me right away?"

"I wanted you to eat first. I put a spoonful of bacon fat in there for you. It's good for your complexion, child. I saw some young fellows in rabbitskin vests beating up a Hitler Youth kid. And there was a man shouting that they were doing it for Sonitschka Vagnerova. He looked a bit like the brother of that long-legs."

"I wouldn't be surprised if it was," said the cashier. She was upset that her mother hadn't mentioned it right away.

"Are things quiet here?"

"My boss told me crowds were gathering. He told me I could sleep in the cloakroom if I wanted."

Her mother never told her anything, not even how much money she had in her savings account.

"I hope you turned him down."

That's just what he wants, thought the old woman. A nice piece of young flesh in the cloakroom. He'd certainly filled his pockets during the war, and all because people wanted to forget (however briefly) and were willing to pay for amusement.

"I hope his ardor cools," the mother added. And she thought: Perhaps this is the day. How many times have I imagined it to myself? The owner certainly would love to have a nibble, that's for sure.

And she said to her daughter: "It's an odd thing in itself when the police are polite."

"Can you wait here for me?" the cashier asked. "Those were the last tickets. We're sold out now, both the balcony and the orchestra. The soldiers don't care if the film's half over. I'm going to hand the money over to the boss."

"All right, my sweetheart, but can you lock me in here? And don't be long."

The girl closed the window and the door. The mother stayed behind and thought: I don't want to remain alone. I know what it means to be alone. I know what loneliness is, my little chicken. It's like a cramp. It's like a splitting headache. It's that unknown day. That unknown day, the one you think will make up for everything, if only there's some meaning in it. What will that day hold? What will it have to hold? She knew herself what it would hold, apart from the mothers who lost their children and the children who lost their mothers and fathers, brothers who lost sisters, and sisters, their brothers. How many fathers had betrayed their own grandmothers because they feared the authorities might prove she had a drop of Jewish blood in her? How many people had been disposed of simply to accommodate the Germans? And then there was the personal aspect. The most personal thing of all, something that you'd never betray to anyone.

The old woman in her black widow's dress sat on a crate of posters in the box office and waited for her trembling to stop.

2

The cashier stood beside the tall fellow's brother. She looked at the German automatic pistol jammed deep into his belt, so that only the handle stuck out. The rest was hidden by his buttoned jacket. She went to turn the money over to the owner and when she came back, she looked down the passageway into the street at the sausage seller and the sweetshop opposite.

"How is your dog doing?" she asked.

"Law? I left him at home."

"Why didn't you take him along?"

"He's sick. I don't want them to shoot him."

The lanky fellow's brother smiled, showing his few teeth. He'd named his three-year-old Irish setter just after the assassination of the German secret police general, Heydrich, at the end of May 1942. A German truck, driven by a drunk driver, ran over the puppy's bitch-mother at high noon, just as it had run over a well-known Jewish poet near the National Theater earlier.

The lanky fellow's brother smiled at the cashier a little longer and smoothed out his creased and shaggy rabbitskin vest.

"How do you feel? Everything OK?" the cashier asked.

"It's OK," he answered.

"How could we have let it happen?"

"How? We were blind. Because we couldn't conceive of the horrors people just whispered about."

He thought of the dog and wondered why the animal was so faithful. He never felt quite worthy of the dog's love. It was lavish in its devotion. He believed the dog would actually die for him. Law wasn't timid. He met strangers head-on, level-eyed, never giving ground. With Law, the lanky fellow's brother's every movement was quietly observed, even when the dog was sleeping. If the young man moved, the dog's eyes would open and follow him. He could never get too far away because Law wouldn't let much distance come between them. He'd heave himself up, stretch and flop down beside him again, protective and content.

"You look pretty nice."

"Thank you. As you can see, my luck stopped there."

The cashier looked at the tall fellow's brother and thought the dog was an extension of his self-satisfaction. She liked this in the dog, but wondered why so few people had such a quality. Sometimes he was ashamed in front of his dog because he was shy and timid and held back when confronted, until he was really provoked. But then it was usually too late and he'd vent his anger alone, unlike Law, whose anger showed right at first. It was funny, she thought to herself: He could control his dog's destiny but not his own.

"What if it's too soon?" she asked the lanky fellow's brother.

"One of them dropped it," he said. "They gave him a real roughing up. I was the first to get to it."

"My mother saw you."

"I never noticed her there," he said, watching the cashier with his murky eyes.

"Your brother was here looking for you."

"I was in Bredovska Street, near that Jewish palace where the German secret police are, the Gestapo headquarters. They're ready for us. They moved tenants out of the best apartments and turned them into machine gun nests. They're armed to the teeth."

"He was with the owner here. He was looking for plans of the building. He wanted to know the layout of the basement."

"I sent him here. Maybe I missed him. I thought he would wait."

"He was a little nervous. He said you'd had a vision of God."

"That wasn't all I had a vision of, but it was the most powerful."

"What do you mean?"

"It's like a fire, spreading from person to person. I mean it, miss. It's like a disease, but it brings people together instead of tearing them apart. You don't happen to know where they buried him, do you? I never saw any mention of a funeral in the papers. Just that he died in his underground bunker. A million tons of concrete must have fallen on him. Tons of rock, granite."

"No idea."

"Did they get those plans?"

"Yes. The owner gave them to him. Your brother went away then. He was anxious to find you. He said if I saw you, you'd know where he went."

"I had a dream. We were in your theater. You sold me a box seat. She took her star off. We held hands. She was as beautiful as Venus, and as gentle as a sleeping volcano. She told me to come to the house with the marble facade after the movie was over, the house where they lived until Hitler came. She said she'd go first and get ready. Before she'd always been so standoffish. But when I wanted to touch her—I mean in the box with the red velvet—she pushed my hand away and told me not to do it and said, 'Such a muddle.' That's exactly what she said: 'Such a muddle.' Do you think I'm in my right mind?"

"I think you can probably make some sense out of it yourself," laughed the cashier.

The tall fellow's brother was wearing a vest made of uncured rabbitskin. He was talking, as he had the time before, of Sonitschka Vagnerova. They were standing at the end of the passage. Some young people wearing the same kind of vests were smashing the window of the sweetshop across the street. They took a sign that said, "No Admittance to Jews," turned it over, and one of them wrote on the back: "Long Live the Free Republic. Death to German Swine!"

"That's exactly it," said the lanky fellow's brother. "That's exactly the kind of thing they wrote about people like Sonitschka Vagnerova, except now it's the other way around." The sweetshop is going to be a wreck in a few minutes, he thought.

"I feel as if it had nothing to do with me," said the cashier, "but it's not because I don't want it to."

"I like watching it. It's as though you'd been angry with yourself for a long time and now suddenly you see you don't have to be anymore. I hope I never have the strength again to be as angry as they were."

"You should go looking for your brother so you don't miss him," said the cashier.

"Can I use the bathroom to fix myself up a bit?"

"Do you know where it is?" asked the cashier. She could hear people speaking in the railwaymen's dormitory. The courtroom overhead was probably empty.

"They're giving it to them for her, too," said the lanky fellow's brother.

"For whom?"

"For Sonitschka Vagnerova."

The cashier tried to guess what he meant. I mustn't feel jealous, she reminded herself.

"And for every one they humiliate, ridicule or beat from now on," he added. "For every one they rob of what he's worked for all his life, or deny what he has the right to. When they hold someone's mother against him, or someone else's father. And when they lie to someone, steal, and murder just because he wears glasses or is weak and sickly. They can take that sweetshop apart, if they like."

"Was she that nice looking girl who spoke like a ditch digger?"

"I couldn't get her out of my mind when they were taken away. They left that house with the marble facade. They had a used car lot."

"She was a very practical person, I remember that."

"For two and a half years, ever since November 13, 1942, I've kept watching that house just in case they come back. In that booth you sold us the tickets from, I pressed up against her. More than anything else, I long for her warm white belly."

By now the sweetshop had been ransacked and they were starting to wreck it. One of the young men began to smash the chairs against each other. They were shouting. The cashier looked at the inscription they'd written on the back of the sign. My mother is right, she thought. We're all animals.

"Do you think a girl who lives in a tiled house is suitable for a boy from the slums?"

"When I look back, it seems to me now, too, like calling a dog 'miss,' but anyway."

"I hope you manage to meet up with your brother," said the cashier, almost testily.

"I can even tell you where it's supposed to be: across the river, by the tracks."

She went back to her mother. The lanky fellow's brother left, and his last words were that he'd never seen chairs broken so beautifully before. He thought about the things he'd seen in his vision, just as real to him as those kids in the fur vests ripping apart the sweetshop, and he brought his brother a pistol to show him that while one of them was getting the plans of the cellar, the other had been assembling an arsenal. He knew what his brother had told the ticket seller.

He thought about two things. The first was that from the moment the Nazi defeat was certain, the Germans had chosen to feed their own illusions.

Hitler had given orders for the German Army to be divided into a northern part under Admiral Doenitz and a southern part under Marshal Kesselring. Both were told to expect a conflict between the American and Russian armies over who would control Germany. They needed a space that could be defended until the Allies started fighting among themselves. They created what they called the Alpine National Fortress and the Bohemian Zone. There was no demarcation line in Bohemia and that could well be one of the sources of conflict.

The other thing he thought about was how he'd pressed close to Sonitschka Vagnerova in the cinema and how she'd said, "Such a muddle."

He dreamed that he'd bought underwear for Sonitschka Vagnerova, just the kind he'd heard lovers bought for their favorites. But in his dream he had only a vague notion of what kind of underwear it would be.

Thinking of such things made him feel hot, as though he were slaving away in an underground shaft somewhere in Venezuela where it was seventy degrees Celsius. That's where everyone who has a Sonitschka Vagnerova on his conscience should be. And also those who let it happen, who pretended not to know what was going on. And then he had a vision of God. In return for the six years they were here, they should be made to work like devils for a million years in those Venezuelan mineshafts, with nothing on but their underwear.

3

"It's late," the cashier said to her mother. "The last performance is almost over."

"We'll have to sleep here in the dormitory," said the cashier later. "Downstairs there's someone from the railway we know. I don't want to risk walking home in the dark."

"I'm glad to hear you say it, my dear. But do you think they'll let us stay?"

"I can't say for sure, but I think they will," replied the cashier.

"What's making all that noise? It sounds like a generator somewhere underground."

At night it seemed to her that her mother was looking for the toilet, but she didn't know if it had been a dream or if her mother had really gone. She was already quite certain that the "unknown day" her mother was always talking about had already begun. In her mind—before she went to sleep—she saw the sweetshop. What was left of it looked like a woodshed. And there was the sign: "Death to German Swine." Outside she could hear intermittent bursts of gunfire and crowds of people moving through the streets. Why haven't I married yet? she wondered as she was falling asleep. Then she had three of her dreams, the kind she'd never tell anyone about: her indecent dreams, her indecent visions. She'd never have thought herself capable of such dreams. The blood rushed to her head whenever she thought of them.

In the first dream, the tall fellow's brother pressed close to her. It was before he'd exchanged her for Sonitschka Vagnerova, who was no longer alive. And he said to her, "I know what you want, what I want myself, what everyone wants. Sometimes there's so much else going on that love gets lost."

And then the tall fellow's brother said, "I feel we're together even though we aren't together and perhaps, since the Germans have killed so many of your people in the camps, we may not be. Your name alone is enough to warm, when I think about it or say it aloud. Sonitschka Vagnerova. Can you hear me, Sonitschka Vagnerova?" Suddenly, that scarcely familiar girl—known only by sight—had a voice, but she no longer had a face. What was her face like? She was pretty, that much is certain. Nicely dressed—that too.

And then Sonitschka Vagnerova answered the lanky fellow's brother and told him they ought not to have smashed up the sweetshop; and that she'd never, not even in the camps, have said that all Germans were swine, as though justice would have been served simply by turning over that sign banning Jews and scrawling a few different obscenities on the other side.

She felt as if she'd been touched by an invisible curse because of something her mother had done before she was born.

Her second dream was of a woman, ugly and fat. One night three men came to her door. The first said: "I have enough money to pay you to do everything." The woman replied that he would first have to do something for her. The man thought he hadn't offered her enough and stuck a roll of bills between her breasts. The woman laughed and pulled her blouse over her head, licked her lips and asked for more money. Then she told him what she wanted. The man refused. She said she couldn't force him, but if he were to leave he'd never know what he had missed. Then he left.

The second man asked how it had been. "Wonderful," the first replied. And the same thing happened to the next young man, whom she also rejected into the night. The third entered, an elderly man who was happy to have her tell stories. Only the cashier knew all the details, the words that were uttered, and the things that went on, the wrinkled face of the old man who'd come to her to get what he could not get. It was always the old men who wanted her to tell them how to live and how to die. Who can blame them for not wanting to die when they'd seen life before the war? How can they know when they're willing to pay nothing, neither with money nor with part of themselves? How do they expect to find out water is wet if they don't touch it? But she was laughing only with her mouth, not with her eyes, which looked like those of a piglet, clean from a fresh rain. "Everyone thinks the world was made for him; he doesn't remember that the world has been demanding the same favors all along."

Her eyes were grave, as if ten thousand years of wisdom and wrath and shame looked out from them. "What do they know about passion, which can destroy a person, silently and secretly?"

And then there was her third dream, about a red hole. The street was narrow, carved out long ago. Couples strolled the sidewalks, reading signs of invitation and stopping occasionally. Nothing to buy, they were told, but lots to see: girls, men, acts you'll never forget.

She woke and couldn't help thinking of her mother when she was young, and of what it was like to be up there, and what it was like the next morning when the raw, unswerving daylight flashed through the window and illuminated the recesses of the face.

Dreams were the cashier's freedom, as endless as a desert, a sea, a

night sky full of stars. Just as she was a living dream for her mother—
a dream of things that might be achieved or ways that fate might be
shaped—so were her dreams her own secret passions. They sparked and
fed on one another as if they were coal or wood, or a fire in the
wilderness, igniting bush after bush, tree after tree.

At the end of this, an image swept over the girl, as when the shooting
had begun outside. Tongues of blue and red licked her eyes, and then
she felt red explosions inside her. Suddenly the red became yellow. She
felt as if something were lifting her up and pushing her toward the
ceiling, as though it were her own hands, though she could no longer
feel them. She screamed silently. When at last all the colors had
vanished, black remained. But it was a soft black, like velvet, like a
caress. And when she woke up, she felt older than when she'd gone
to sleep.

She felt alone, even with her dreams. Her mother wasn't there. She
was afraid of the way her mother would look at her body. It didn't make
her feel good. And she thought about the massage salon that they'd
closed down. Who knows whether it was only because the manager
didn't pay his rent during the war? What went on there? Could she
imagine it?

In one of her fantasies she found herself in a room on the top floor
of the building with a view of the city at night. The room contained a
bed and a cot. The man, whom she'd met at the box office when he'd
bought tickets, lay on his back and she was sitting on a bench and a girl
knelt behind her brushing her hair. Nothing happened. There was a
quiet little song on the radio sung by girls' voices, about Sunday
morning. In the mirror on the ceiling she saw the reflection of flickering
candles and three people who didn't know each other and yet were
intimate friends.

She knew there had been a room like that in the former massage
parlor; once the cinema owner showed it to her. Could he possibly have
envied her because she was young, as her mother claimed? And once
she'd actually heard a song like the one in which girls sang of Sunday
morning, and it had made her feel like crying.

Outside, she could hear gunfire. It sounded like pistols or rifles.
Somewhere she heard a machine gun. Something seemed to go on down
below in the cinema, too. Perhaps the cleaning ladies had come early.
The railway men came and went. The trains arrived and departed

according to schedule, as though nothing unusual were happening. But the superintendent had closed the dormitory. There was also some excitement in the passageway.

She thought about the lanky fellow's brother and about Sonitschka Vagnerova. She connected it with what she sometimes thought about, how men and women are different between the legs. It seemed strange to her. Her mother was afraid, but she had her reasons. Everyone is afraid. The world is going through its final hour and I'm thinking about this.

Then, too, what disgusted her gave her pleasure at the same time. More than anything else, she wanted to touch—but only painlessly and without danger—an alien, incomprehensible world as intimately as she was touched by her own bedclothes. She felt the doors of paradise had opened for her, and she found that those same doors were also the doors of hell. From each tree you shall eat, save one tree, as she had learned in religion classes. She'd surrender to sleep with her new knowledge in the hopes that indecent dreams would come to her, regardless of whose life they belonged to. And then there was what the tall fellow had revealed to his brother: He'd wanted to lose his sex, the source of all his suffering.

The tall fellow used to go to Little Karlova Street to look at a mural painting of a monk who resolved a similar problem by cutting off the offending organ between his legs and throwing it to the dogs.

She could imagine her own picture on the walls of the buildings she used to walk past, though she had nothing to throw to the dogs but her fears, her terrors, her shame. The cashier dealt with her unanswered questions the way nearsighted people deal with their bad eyes. When she fell asleep—a deep sleep without the dreams, an empty sleep that gave her nothing and yet shamed her heart—it was to the accompaniment of music: either a waltz from the first act of *La Traviata,* so sad and beautiful that she felt like crying, or the aria from *Rigoletto.*

Where is Mother? What time is it? Maybe she's gone to the bathroom. She's left her shoes here. She can't have gone into the street in her stockings.

I'd like to love. I'd like to have my first love, even if it were the first and last love. Love—any love—at first sight or a quiet one, or maybe a stormy love so that men would make an effort for me. He'd understand my most secret signals and want to seduce me, court me, protect me, fight for me. I want to belong to someone, to stand at someone's side and have him at my side. To love a man more than my own life.

4

Walking along the corridor, the cashier's mother reached the emergency exit from the cinema, where she'd seen a light. Through the door, she could see two employees standing on the podium, on the audience side of the curtain. On the other side of the curtain, where the movie screen hung, stood a group of people, some in uniforms and some in civilian dress. An elderly man was talking to them. In the audience sat rows of German soldiers, deserters, with their hands tied behind their backs. The old woman gazed at the scene uncomprehendingly. Both orderlies were close enough for her to hear what they were saying, although they couldn't see her. She decided to stay and watch. Two other soldiers were guarding the prisoners. Except for the fact that one group was tied and the other held machine guns, there was no difference between them.

"You can rest the bench here for a while," said the first employee in a strong Sudeten accent. He was filthy from head to foot.

Only the safety lights were on. A draft came from an invisible window somewhere in a ventilation shaft. The first employee added: "Oh, God, what are they going to come up with now? Here, hold this for me."

He had a deep, hoarse voice. He paid no attention to the deserters whatsoever, nor to those guarding them, as though they didn't interest him in the least.

"*Dreckscheisse,*" said the second man. "We're all *Tiermenschen.* Just take a look around you. We'd better hurry up and get out of here. The sooner we get this over with, the better."

"You don't say."

"No point in shooting your mouth off too much. They're fools. You can't mess around with them. They're using a wedge to drive out a wedge and nothing can stop them. We're all *Menschentiere,* like I say. And it won't be any different as long as things are in their hands. You know what's going on at home? Bakeries in Berlin are looted. Dispersed

soldiers are organizing into Wehrwolf suicide units all over the Reich's
territory. Americans captured the German gold reserves in the salt
mines in Thuringia.''

"Reminds me of how we used to dig those ditches for silage back at
the beginning," said the first. "Did you read *Schwartze Korps?* There's
no sense in holding out militarily, but the idea must go on living under
any hell.''

He let the bench stand where it was, knowing that as long as he didn't
lift his end, his colleague couldn't carry it alone.

"Except that they weren't meant for silage ditches. First they were
fortifications, then they were graves. And we've got a million fresh men
in this sector. Where will it end? But that doesn't mean I'm not going
to be careful. What do you think they'll do with those fellows by the
cloakroom?''

"How should I know?" said the first, but they both knew the answer.
What they didn't know was how.

"If they can get three officers of the *Wehrmacht* or SS together, they
have the right to condemn them for anything they want, and there's only
one thing they want. They have the old man. He was sleeping upstairs.
He's the judge.'' He began to whistle *Der Elefant von Indien.*

"Why don't they do it upstairs?''

"They know no one's going to come wandering into the theater in the
middle of the night." Quietly he whistled *Kann das loch nicht findien*
this time.

The mother looked at the bound German soldiers at the side of the
auditorium, by the cloakroom; then she looked at the oak bench. There
were so many deserters. She felt a buzzing in her ears; it was the
underground generator again.

"Grab your end," said the second employee.

"Right.''

"Take it easy, the staircase is narrow and I don't want to cripple
myself after getting this far. I'm still planning to get home.''

"Right, I'll treat her like a Chinese empress," said the first. "Or was
it Japanese?''

It was a heavy oak bench that could accommodate twelve people
at once.

The mother looked at the old man on the stage. He was gripping a
golden tassel that was part of the dusty blue curtain. She felt as though
midnight were sitting in her soul. As though the eclipse of the sun

they'd written about in the papers were here already. She watched the employees handling the heavy oak bench with ease, like a toy. They were like draft horses. The one had stopped whistling.

The old man in a green hunter's outfit, the judge—probably with a private flat upstairs—watched the orderlies carry the bench onto the stage. They had already set up a table and two chairs with armrests. The old man was wearing plus fours and white woolen socks. He didn't look like a judge, though that was his profession; obviously he'd been just about to leave. Perhaps he really was going hunting.

Menschentiere, repeated the mother. That's a German word. *Menschentiere. Tiermensch. Tiermenschen.* What did they want to do with the soldiers? Why were their hands tied behind their backs? She shuddered. She could imagine only too well. They will kill them, because deserters aren't interested in *Lebensraum* anymore; they just want to go home. They don't want to shoot at people who never did anything to them, or even at those whose fault it all was. The two men she'd heard talking were Nazis at heart, and not just because of their uniforms and their insignia. The mother was overwhelmed by a sense of terror.

The old man looked delicate, and though erect, he gave the impression of barely being able to keep his balance. The expression of the first employee seemed to say: God, why are they dragging us into this? No one in his right mind would want anything to do with it at this point. The old bugger probably can't even wipe himself and flush the toilet without somebody holding his hand. And he's supposed to be watching over us?

"Lower it a bit, and I'll lift it up here," said the second employee.

The old man was looking for something in an open briefcase. It was a large, thick briefcase, the kind that the railway men used to carry their clothes and food. He pulled out a file with plans in it. The plans showed cellars and corridors, store rooms on the third floor where they kept the furniture and windows opening onto the street corners. The employees knew exactly where to put the bench. Now the open black briefcase stood beside the old man in the hunting outfit. The second employee, too, could scarcely bring himself to look at the old man, thinking: Can't he see that the water is rising, and those high-lace boots of his can't save him? He looks like he's ready for a trip to the mountains. Doesn't he know that the gravedigger is getting a grave ready for him not far from here, that the bell has already tolled?

The second employee, rather stout and not as grubby as the first, smiled respectfully at the old man.

The old man shifted the plans to his left hand, as though he were getting ready to point something out with his right. But it had nothing to do with them. He beckoned with his finger to a court secretary, who appeared to have just stepped out of bed. She was tired and unkempt, with a puffy face. It was already well past midnight.

"Yes, sir," said the first employee in his hoarse voice.

"I'm going to change," said the old man.

The mother had to strain her ears to hear. The old man looked at his large watch, which was on a gold chain that hung from buttonholes in his vest. He wound it up and then stuck it back in his pocket with trembling hands.

"Can you arrange it, please, miss?" he said to the secretary. "These two strong young men will be happy to help you with anything." The general should have been here already, he thought. But he didn't want to betray his nervousness. He went to a chair in the corner for his black robe. As soon as he touched the material, his listlessness seemed to disappear.

The stout employee sat down on the edge of the stage and let his legs swing back and forth over the floor with its footworn red runners. He pretended not to see the rows of seats full of soldiers. Whenever they brought in furniture for the stage, they came in from the left to avoid the cloakroom.

"Maybe he won't make such a big thing of it," said the first employee quietly.

"Life is not what you want but what you must do," answered the second. "Not what you expect, but what you've been ordered to do."

"Yeah, but now?'

"Didn't you hear shooting outside?"

"It's something else I hear."

The old man was explaining something to the secretary, who was listening with a sour expression on her face. He was telling her, in his soft voice, about the toughness that is the foundation of everything. We can do anything, miss, he reminded her, as though he thought she might have doubted it. "We are in the right, and we have our own will. We must demand toughness, miss, toughness and again toughness."

"Forget it," said the first employee a while later as he walked past the old woman, whose presence they either didn't suspect or didn't care about. "We should have gone over the hill long ago."

"Haven't you heard Germans don't die in bed?" said the second with a grin.

"It might well happen tonight, if not tomorrow."

"Be careful someone doesn't take you at your word."

"I could do with a cold potato right now."

"Let's clear out before they think up something else for us to do," said the second.

"Do you know what I saw in the cloakroom?" asked the first.

"Whatever it is, I'm not interested."

"Two of those doctors' handbags."

"So what?"

"So what do they need a doctor for?"

"How should I know?"

"I don't like it," said the first.

The mother watched as they walked toward the stairs where they'd brought the furniture down. They spoke in German so she could understand only vaguely. They pretended not to notice the soldiers. The soldiers were quiet. They couldn't have done much with their hands tied anyway, thought the mother. Oh, God, God, it's in the air, and what's in the air is killing. I don't have to be told that. We shouldn't have stayed here, and I'm afraid for my little girl, so I don't want to stay here and I don't want to go away, either. Why am I always so afraid? And if it's not death I'm afraid of, then it's life. Her skin settled in wrinkles she didn't have the day before. She looked at the stage from her hiding place. In his green hunter's outfit, the old man reminded her of "Little Red Riding Hood." I have midnight on my mind and in my soul, and I feel hot, as though this were somewhere in the Sahara. So my day has finally begun. She thought of when the Germans had first come and the newspapers had said that the time was past when anyone could attack defenseless German citizens and expect to get away with it. She'd also read somewhere that they were cultivating mushrooms for the Germans in the cellars of the Maginot Line. Those famous photographs in their magazines like *Der Stuermer* and *Der Angrijj* or *Der Adler.* The Germans had written that only those who'd suffered a just defeat could now have the audacity to demand peace. But they'd written that a long time ago. There must really be a generator whining away somewhere under the ground here.

The secretary was listening impatiently to what the old man was saying. Her nose was prominent and looked almost Jewish. She was bony but puffy. She probably found it hard to gain weight on a diet of lentils and black coffee, thought the mother. She's not as pretty as my little girl, whom I've looked after all through the war.

The old man snapped his fingers and wagged his trembling chin at the secretary. She glanced briefly at the soldiers with their hands tied behind their backs. They wore German uniforms and insignia representing various military branches. Most of them looked pretty slovenly. What the old man said hadn't sounded as grand as he'd intended. But the mother hadn't been able to hear what he said, except when he raised his voice.

"Who will keep the records, you?" the old man asked the secretary finally. "Where are those two musclemen who are supposed to bring you a typewriter? Have they gone? They probably think we need more chairs."

He turned to some people who were standing behind the curtain. She guessed from their voices that one was a woman, the other an officer.

The old man spoke to them: "What the Fuehrer had said . . . Anyone who would propose or even approve measures detrimental to our power of resistance is a traitor. He is to be shot or hanged without delay. I have here also my *Der Panzerbar* from the previous Monday. God is with us and our defense of the Reich. *Noch etwas, meine Herren. Jetz mussen wir uns aushelfen und vorlaufig die Tage des Ruhmes vergessen. Solange jedes unser Haus, jede unsere Wohnung und jedes Fenster eine Festung sist, so werden wir hier stark sein.*" The mother didn't get it, except for a few words.

The woman wore cotton stockings. She didn't betray what she was feeling by the slightest movement of her face. She might have been thirty. She told the old man she was a lawyer. She added something else and then said, "Mr. Chairman, I am here voluntarily." At the main station, she said, she'd seen the bodies of German families that had been shot and fortunately, she added, the bodies of dead bandits as well. About two hundred people on both sides had been killed. *"Ich wollte sie darum bitten, das ist das Gebot diesser Stunde."*

Several people in civilian clothes arrived with a man in the uniform of a colonel of the SS. That must have been the owner of the medical base because the judge addressed him as "Herr Doktor." He shook hands with the civilians and greeted the other officer in military fashion. Both the civilians had hats with hunter's ribbons on them; the officers had briefcases. The doctor requested that his two bags be brought from the cloakroom. The civilians put on buttons bearing the insignia of the National Socialist German Workers Party. It hadn't been a good idea to wear them in the street.

The secretary summoned both employees and asked them to bring the typewriter along with the doctor's bags from the cloakroom. Then she sent them for one more table. The judge looked contentedly at those present. His white collar was just a bit too tight for him. He had a shriveled neck, like an old rooster.

"Close the door," said one of the men in civilian clothes to one of the employees, pointing to where the mother was standing.

It turned out that among the civilians was a general out of uniform, which must have seemed strange to both officers present. The judge bowed and said, "Herr General," as though he were dubbing him with the title. There was nervousness mixed with respect in his voice.

"We have placed units of the defense police on watch at strategic places, Mr. Chairman."

"*Jedem das seine,*" said the old man. To each his own. "I have learned that the station and the approaches to the city have cost us the blood of several dozens of our soldiers."

He took a tin box of digestive tablets from his side pocket and offered them to the group on the stage, then closed the box again and stuck them into his pocket.

"We are safe here," said one of the civilians.

"They are not unimportant provinces," said the general later.

The eyes of the old judge betrayed an effort to convince the others that his loyalty, enthusiasm, will, and energy hadn't faltered. The cause he'd devoted his life to would continue.

"These are mere rebellions that have not yet been suppressed. The Empire is safe," said the old man.

His voice trembled. His whole body trembled. The palms of his hands emerged from stiff white cuffs with mother-of-pearl buttons. The skin of his hands was red, with brown and bluish blemishes. Blue veins stood out on his skin in high relief, looking in places like ancient purple strips. "Our laws are still in force here."

The cashier's mother became more and more convinced that somewhere deep beneath the floor a generator was operating. Her head ached. She could hear it even when the door was closed, although the noise was weaker then.

"Most of them are citizens of the Reich, not Hungarians, Romanians, or Ukrainians," said the first officer. He didn't look at the soldiers with their hands tied as he spoke.

"I'm only concerned about our families," said the old man. "Our apartments, however, are under military protection. I'm glad to hear our police are in the streets holding down strategic positions. That's just as it should be. So far, no evacuation order has been issued. Naturally we'll all remain at our posts—until the very last minute, gentlemen and ladies. In any case . . ." It was obvious that he had no doubts about his ability to convince the accused of their own guilt.

"Certainly," said the first man, who wore a green hat.

One of the soldiers with his hands tied was overcome with a fit of coughing. Several of them looked at him. He was almost choking. Something had become lodged in his throat and he couldn't get it out.

"We are the powerful," said the old man. And the rest in German, happily. "*So, Ich bin wirklich sehr glücklich, das Ich mit Euch bis zu Ende arbeiten und auch nuetzlich sein Kann. Alle sind wir hier.* I will take you all under oath, ladies and gentlemen. We shall proceed as the moment dictates. Gentlemen, arrange yourselves according to rank." The chain of his pocket watch swung back and forth on his stomach. "The purpose of the court is to issue verdicts. Of course."

Finally the soldier's coughing fit stopped.

From somewhere near the cloakroom, they led in more soldiers. A draft pushed the door open and the old woman could see some more of what was going on. The soldiers had obviously been beaten. She saw the two who had purchased the last tickets to that evening's show.

"You'll carry those who fall asleep to one side," said the doctor to both employees. He told them precisely where. When he was saying something that concerned the soldiers, he spoke succinctly, but more quietly.

"Should we wait here?" asked the first employee hoarsely.

The second employee looked as though he felt like vomiting. He turned pale, then red.

The colonel looked around and said to the second officer, "When it's over we can simply burn the place down. Have some gasoline brought in.'' He coughed without looking at the soldiers.

The judge looked as though the words had some kind of magic power. He could just imagine it. Nothing burned quite so well as gasoline. Gasoline burns even when it's damp. It burns in the rain and in the snow. The orderlies brought the gasoline up from the basement.

The doctor opened both his bags. They were full of hypodermic needles and bottles with all kinds of serum. The second bag was lined with vials of phenol. He counted the number of soldiers, including the new arrivals. He had serum enough for ten times as many. *"Menschentiere,"* the mother thought. They spoke in a fast German and she didn't catch everything and some things she didn't understand at all.

"Are you ready, miss? Is there paper in your machine?'' asked the judge.

The man wearing an NSDAP pin turned to the judge. "Would you administer an oath to the employees?''

The old man in the hunter's jacket took a flag with a swastika and the sign of the sun on a reddish brown and white background from the second civilian and spread it on the table like a tablecloth. They had the first soldier brought up. It was the one who'd bought two tickets from her daughter, for himself and his friend. So they're starting with them, thought the old lady. What is that noise coming from the deepest underground? Generators? It sounded stronger and stronger.

It lasted a minute. Had he deserted in an hour of danger? Had he lost his unit, his platoon, his regiment, his division? Had he lost the whole German army? The old man pronounced him guilty. The doctor gave him an injection. He nodded to the employees. The secretary, the officers, and the civilians maintained intent, calm, matter-of-fact expressions. The general out of uniform seemed indifferent. The cashier's mother was holding her palms over her ears in order not to hear what sounded like generators in the center of the earth beneath her.

5

The cashier thought about her mother, about her indecent dreams, and about the shooting outside. She wondered where the lanky fellow's brother was and what they were doing with their stolen pistol. She could only hear occasional random sounds coming from the cinema. The cleaning ladies were probably finishing up. They always worked quickly, sweeping up the papers and cigarette butts and, sometimes, from the box seats, condoms. Sonitschka Vagnerova, the daughter of a used car dealer. She shuddered.

So Mother's day is finally here, she thought. But I'd like to know where those two brothers are. Maybe they're sleeping. Maybe they decided to go to bed and wait for morning. And morning can't be far away. The cashier could hear bird songs coming from the nearby river. The whole mess is collapsing and the world is still on its axis, the river is flowing and the birds are singing. Somewhere a dog barked. I wonder where the brothers are.

At that moment, they were on the other side of the river, and the lanky fellow's brother asked, "Do you see that stable?"

"Yeah," replied the lanky fellow. "But I also see they've got a soldier watching it."

"He looks tired. He's asleep on his feet," said the brother. He had his hand on the butt of the pistol. It was drizzling slightly and he didn't want the weapon to get wet, as though he believed the dampness would penetrate to the powder in the cartridges. Only eight rounds were in the weapon. The man who lost the pistol had already fired four of the twelve, and hadn't had time to reload the magazine.

"It's a wonder I'm not asleep on my feet, too," said the lanky fellow's brother. "I haven't slept for several nights. I've been talking with Sonitschka Vagnerova day and night. And when she started to tell me all that had happened to her, God appeared."

"Tell me about it later," the lanky fellow cut him off. "Let's not drag women into it. Let's not even drag God into it. Just concentrate on what we have to do right here and now. I don't even want to hear about how you don't need sleep. You can tell me all about it later."

"I'll tell you something about horses."

"Not now."

"And about dogs."

"Neither about horses nor about dogs, now."

They advanced along the railway track. At every bridge and crossing there was a soldier. The lanky fellow's brother thought: My God, they all look like scarecrows. These fools are guarding everything, even themselves, because they're scared shitless. Before, when they still had faith in themselves, five or six thousand Gestapo were enough to make nine million people tremble, the whole nation. As soon as they stopped believing, they started guarding everything, as though they thought people would steal their bridges and their railways in their own country. The fools. Do they keep an eye on each other when they take a leak? He remembered how they'd taken up railway tracks and shipped them to Germany.

"What are you looking for in the stable?" asked the lanky fellow.

"You don't know how much I like horses? And why?"

"Stop clowning around."

His brother looked up at the cloudy sky. All I have to do is think of you, Sonitschka Vagnerova, and I feel such a tenderness in my soul, like when I tense my muscles to lift a rock, the muscles in my arms, in my legs, in my chest or my shoulders. I have no words for it. Words make everything common. I'm charged with it, like these eight cartridges in my German revolver. As long as I think of you, I don't need sleep. God is with me. Isn't that right, God? As long as you were alive, everything was light inside me. Now that light has gone out. I search for the old fire but the only fire I have now is in my eight cartridges. That ticket girl looks a little like you, Sonitschka Vagnerova. I mean, she looks different, but who cares if she's light-haired and you had dark hair? When the Germans sang of blue-eyed maidens, did you seem different, special, set apart, because you have—had—walnut-colored eyes? Ever since yesterday evening when I met that girl in the passage, when I think of you, I also think of her. You'll forgive me, I know, because love is forgiving. Only hatred never forgives. Bitterness never forgives. Humiliation never forgives, as long as love doesn't take its place.

"The girl in the box office thought I was off my rocker when I told her I'd seen God."

"Maybe she wasn't far from the truth."

"Do you think I'm nuts for talking about it so openly like this?"

"I'd bet my life on it," whispered the lanky fellow. "Why don't you want to give me the pistol?"

"I've got a steadier hand than you do, I'm not as tall, and my knees don't have a habit of giving out on me. You'll get a rifle. Just give me time."

"I'll bet you're off your rocker," the lanky fellow insisted. His rabbitskin vest was as wet as his brother's. "What are you going to do?"

"You still don't know?"

"We don't need horses, that's for sure."

His brother looked at him with his cloudy eyes. I may not have had any sleep, he thought, but something else is giving me a headache. I'm soaking wet. He ground his teeth. He had strong teeth. If teeth were enough to chew your enemy to bits, he'd have no trouble.

The lanky fellow was holding a stick with a large hook attached at the end of it that looked like the arm of an anchor. His brother handed him the pistol, said he was going out there with his bare hands, and asked him to cover him. The soldier would see that he was unarmed and would be off his guard. Then the lanky fellow would step out of the dark with the pistol, and that would be that.

"This will be the first thing I've done for Sonitschka Vagnerova. So far I've only talked about it. Now comes the time for action."

"I'm surprised you're still interested," whispered the lanky fellow.

"We both know what we're doing," replied his brother. "It's raining. Not like in those mines in Venezuela. And if God is with me, I've got nothing to worry about."

He was interrupted by a train coming down the tracks. In the dark, it was a long time before they could tell what kind of train it was. It was moving slowly, a freight train with several wagons marked with red crosses. This was probably the main line, since the rails hadn't been torn up and sent to Germany.

"A hospital train," sighed the lanky fellow's brother. "Where's it going, Germany?"

"What?" asked the lanky fellow, leaning close to his brother. He could feel his hot, fetid breath.

"You can never tell whether a German train is coming back from a victory or a defeat. This one's probably coming from one of their Alpine National Fortresses, bringing the wounded and the dead. It's not an armored train, like they threatened on the radio last night."

"I can't hear you," said the lanky fellow.

"I'm off, while the train's making a racket."

"Go ahead, I'll cover you."

The tall fellow gripped the pistol in his fist and in the other hand held the pole with the hook attached to it. Both men stood up. They were wet to the skin. The lanky fellow shuddered.

"Hang on there," said his brother.

"Nothing to worry about."

"In a little while you won't be cold and neither will I."

"On your way."

The tall fellow's brother walked past the sleepy guard, who was hunched over in a standing position in a primitive guard hut with a wooden roof. The rain was falling heavily now, and it splashed into the hut through knotholes in the roof. The brother waited until the rain came down harder. Then he walked through the mud and puddles into the stable. The guard didn't notice him. He was huddled against the wall of his hut, where the rain couldn't reach him, and streams of water poured through the holes in the roof, making a noise that covered the sounds of the lanky fellow's brother going by him.

The stable smelled of last year's damp hay, of rotting leather, harnesses, barley or oats, and acidic horse urine. Chill breathed out of a stone trough, and lying on an oak bench, out of the reach of the horses, were horse blankets full of holes. Every once in a while the horses jerked when the fleas or damp flies irritated them. Dampness permeated everything. In the troughs lay the remains of a haystack; a pitchfork, leaning against the wall, stuck out of the hay. Besides the horses, urine and hay, there was a mousy smell there, cobwebs woven many years ago, and the sweetish smell of cats. Everything was wet and cool.

The tall fellow's brother stroked the horses only lightly with his large, coarse palm in order to make sure that these were horses and not just an illusion. He went from one horse to another, but he didn't touch the last one, the black stallion. He left the stallion out as if, by not touching him, perhaps he could make the stud not exist. He wanted to separate himself from the stallion, in this way at least. Even in the dark, the stallion's blackness stood out, though everything was enveloped in the shade and twilight.

The stable was empty except for the horses. Some began to whinny, but the guard didn't notice anything until later when the tall fellow's brother appeared in the stable door leading two white horses by their halters.

There's a feeling you get when entering a barn in the early morning, the tall fellow's brother thought, like walking in on some secret gathering. War or no war. Uprising or no uprising. Somewhere in the space between the shafts of light he could hear the movement of the animals. Suddenly, there was a commotion, and the many tiny birds that made their home in the barn during the rainy nights rose up in

agitation and fluttered past him to the nearest exit. But the lanky
fellow's brother's thrill came from the greeting he received. Stillness
came to life and from each box appeared expectant, eager faces. These
horses know me, he thought, they know my walk and my voice, in spite
of the fact that I'm here for the first and last time. They've been waiting
since dawn, since night, since the beginning of the war. I ask you, he
said silently to the two white horses and aside to no one in particular,
who else waits so eagerly for my arrival? Each horse greeted him; some
neighed out loud, some regarded him silently and intently, but in all of
their eyes, except for the ebony stallion's, he saw an openness and trust.
He used a heavy chain lead which he twisted through the halter and
brought under the chin, over the nose. This is one of the most sensitive parts of the horse's face. He could control each step of these
thousand-kilogram animals with a jerk of his hand. An older horse
boxed next to a lovely mare had probably spent hours watching her.

From the more affectionate horses there was a special greeting, a
quiet nuzzle as he passed by, a touch that was intimate, honest, and
kind. Not looking for the morning's ration of grain, they reached for a
familiar word and stroke meant for only them.

Their bodies excited him and he loved to run his hands over their
smooth powerful sides. It always amazed him that such a large animal
could have such tender skin, responsive to the touch like a woman. He
dreamed of horses often and they always reminded him of women:
strong women, moral and independent; soft women, conquerable with
patience and gentle hands. But he liked to think that every spirited
horse, like every woman that ever lived, could eventually be won over;
though they could face brutality and roughness with fierce animal
vengeance. Shaggy and coarse, they turned their large watchful eyes on
him, an intruder in the early dawn.

He loved huge draft horses, he thought, but then he loved all horses.
Their eyes gave them away. He'd approach each one and look for the
gentleness in the soft folds of their eyelids. Beyond that, a light in
the dark depths of the eye itself would reveal intelligence and trust.
But the black stallion had the unreadable eyes of a hard woman whose
suspicion and distrust radiate from inside. The body would be warm
and supple to the touch, but the eyes remained dead. He saw the eyes
of death.

The lanky fellow was watching the guard and saw his astonishment
at what his brother was doing with the horses. He saw him raise his

rifle, its bayonet fixed, ready for firing. Everything was covered, watered down by the rain. My brother is nuts, thought the lanky fellow. He has cloudy eyes and he's been nuts ever since they locked up that Jewish girl from the used car lot. Sonitschka Vagnerova. But he'd never even spoken to her. He'd only seen her from a distance. He doesn't even know her. And she definitely doesn't know him; she never had the chance to. My God—they were from different sides of an abyss, deeper than all the abysses of the world put together. And by now she is probably dead. Dead as a Jewess.

So he really has gone off his rocker. But he did manage to get the pistol, and that's what counts now. Whoever has a pistol has a chance to do something. He has only two things in his head—that Jewish girl and revenge. His obsessive notion of justice. They keep changing places in his mind, like those submarines with chambers that fill with water to submerge and then fill with air to surface, over and over and over. He's nuts.

The tall fellow saw his brother spit in the mud in front of the German soldier. Both of them looked like wet hens; only the horses looked beautiful in the rain. Even in the dark they looked magnificent. Horses are the most beautiful animals in the world. They're neither too large nor too small. They are beautiful, like everything that's just the right size. And at night they look as though they were made of darkness itself.

The brother walked to the corner of the yard and tied both white horses to a tree. A leaky wooden barrel stood by the tree, and the lanky fellow thought about the ways in which a man is like that barrel, of how for six years the German occupation had got on his nerves and why Friday was the last day—today was Saturday—and why it's like a barrel that can hold no more rain. The guard might have thought the lanky fellow's brother worked for the stable. The brother disappeared into the stable once more, but he left the doors open and immediately afterward led two bays out and tied them up to the tree by the overflowing barrel. Altogether he brought out eight horses in this way. The lanky fellow counted them. Back in the stable, he caught a glimpse of a black stallion which his brother hadn't untied. They were racing horses. They probably belonged to some German officers.

The soldier was watching the brother from his guard hut and had probably decided it was time to ask him why he didn't leave the horses in the stable. But the lanky fellow's brother knelt down in the straw at the edge of the stable and unrolled a waterproof piece of canvas that he'd tucked inside his vest. He thought of the underground mines in Venezuela, where it's so hot that people sweat blood and urine, until at last they sweat out their hearts and their souls, for Sonitschka Vagnerova.

"Sonitschka Vagnerova," said the lanky fellow's brother—and the soldier didn't know who he was talking to—"you were as beautiful as those curtains when I looked down from the hill onto your balcony and into the back room where you slept. And you were sweet as candy. Because of you I feel enough strength in each arm to lift a hundred kilos without my legs giving out. Only yesterday I could scarcely have lifted twenty without both hands."

The lips of the lanky fellow's brother moved without his saying anything. He spoke only for himself, like a ventriloquist. I love you, Sonitschka Vagnerova. Your love for me and my love for you is like a gorgeous fire that warms and shines on everything, but doesn't burn. Love is a fire, in which everything that makes a man and our lives dirty burns to ashes without dirt, choking smoke coming out of it. You cannot therefore ever die and disappear from the world as if you never existed.

"How would you like to lay off that," said the lanky fellow quietly to his brother, when he saw what he was up to, but there wasn't anything he could do to stop him. The soldier finally went to see what he was doing and to whom he was talking.

The bundle of straw caught fire and the brother stood up. The first wisp of smoke curled up into the air and out of the stable, where it mingled with the rain and sank to the ground.

The ebony stallion in the back of the stable roared like an animal does when it senses a fire or a flood or an earthquake. It was a terrible sound and the other horses by the tree outside took it up. The stallion began to kick out around him, jerking to pull himself loose. The lanky fellow's brother was struck by the power of the animal. Where's the heavy chain? You could tell how the horse had been handled because of welts and the swollen uneven profile showing on the face of the stallion. Where was the chain lead?

The hard eyes wouldn't soften and the dilated nostrils didn't relax. The boy both admired and feared the horse, and therefore hated him.

The soldier ran quickly into the stable and started to untie the stallion. He began shouting at the lanky fellow's brother, who stood up and, in the midst of the fire that was rapidly spreading through the stable, spit in the soldier's face. The soldier raised his rifle with the fixed bayonet, ready to lunge at the brother, but was paralyzed by the sight of this madman. The brother slapped the soldier's face hard on both sides. And as the soldier jerked forward, the lanky fellow stabbed him in the side with the hook. Like the tine of an anchor, the hook lodged in the soldier's body and couldn't be pulled out. With every movement he made, the hook did more and more damage to his body.

"Pick up his gun," said the lanky fellow. "I don't want to shoot unless I have to. We might bring someone running."

Both of them were lit by the fire. They were surrounded by the whinnying of the horses and the anguished cries of the black stallion, which had finally managed to pull itself free and rushed like a maddened creature out into the rain and night, where it ran around and around the yard until it finally tired and stopped, exhausted and perspiring, beside the other horses, which were glowing in the light of the fire.

They saw they were alone. Thanks to the rain, the fire didn't spread beyond the stable. When it died down, they could smell only smoke in the rain.

"We're alone here," said the lanky fellow's brother. "I'd be happier if she could have seen it."

"Who, that girl in the box office?"

"Sonitschka Vagnerova."

"How would you like to lay off that for a while."

"I'll let the horses go. Maybe our people can round them up. If I knew how to ride, I'd ride till the earth shook clear through to Venezuela. They could hear the thunder of their hooves down in those hot mines under the earth. Those eight light-colored horses are all right. The black one is a devil. I was afraid to touch him but I finally managed to tie him up tight. But you can't tie the devil down. You heard it yourself. He roared like the devil."

He thought of the soldier lying in his own blood, which was running out into the mud and the water. "He tried out his bayonet attack on me, just like their defense police. They teach them to do it that way. Nothing like this will come back anymore."

"Come on, we'll talk about it some other time."

"Do you want the pistol or the rifle? You can keep the hook," said the lanky fellow's brother, and then took his pistol back. They hadn't even fired it.

The rain had slowed to a drizzle once more. It was almost morning.
On the way the lanky fellow's brother said, "Do you know how cold it
must have been in Poland when it froze, and how hot when the sun
shone? Just like those mines in Venezuela."

"Keep your discoveries to yourself," said the lanky fellow. "You'd
end up reminding me of Goebbels and the murder of those Polish
officers in Katyn. Forget it for a while. We've got too much else to
worry about. This is a fantastic German gun. Is this what they called
scheisse? We can go back to the dormitory. We'll get sorted out there,
and see what to do next. The girl's there."

"Right," said his brother, and he thought: I hope she isn't jealous of
Sonitschka Vagnerova, even though they're both beautiful. But that girl
must still be a virgin because her mother won't let anyone lay a hand on
her. She keeps her safely wrapped up in cotton wool. As though she felt
her virginity weren't between her legs, but in her head, in those eyes
that always look so frightened.

"You know what Sonitschka Vagnerova told me? That there are no
happy endings in life, just happy stations. Life is an ugly joke. You
must accept it, though, and bear it with dignity. It's the dignity that's
the hard part. But happiness isn't always in stations, either. It's
sprinkled throughout, and we live by looking from one sprinkle to the
next. If it comes, it goes away fast, causing more panic than before."

"Yeah."

"They started with their own weak people."

"Yeah."

"Am I not a lucky stiff?"

"Till the death," said the lanky fellow's brother as they went on
their way.

6

Soldier Number 9 stood before the doctor, the officer and the civilians
in hunters' fedoras with ribbons and feathers in them, and the old man's
black judicial robes lay tossed across the chair beside him. He looked at
his flat pocket watch on the gold chain. It was almost five in the
morning. This was the second soldier, the companion of the one who'd

bought tickets for the last show the night before. After the first had been sentenced, they'd started at the other end. The judge wiped his lips. They wouldn't be finished as quickly as he'd reckoned, he thought, because they'd brought in more soldiers. But these were probably the last, because in the meantime the telephone wires had been cut. They had lost contact. The soldiers were lined up like sheep. Not only were they imprisoned here, but they had imprisoned themselves from inside.

The cashier's mother stood frozen to the spot. She'd forgotten about time. She narrowly avoided being seen by the employees as they brought cannisters of gasoline from the garage. She was listening to the underground generators.

"Who are you?" asked the judge in a tired voice. "Where have you left your weapon?"

The employees dragged aside a soldier who'd been put to sleep with an injection. They did it the same way they'd dragged the furniture into the cinema earlier in the evening.

The old man pulled out the box of lozenges and offered one to the general: "Would you care for a mint?" he asked politely. "They don't even know how morally crippled they are."

Then he turned to the soldier and went on, "Do you have your identification with you? And do up your buttons and straighten up your clothes. A uniform is a symbol. Don't you know how to behave properly before a military court?" With some difficulty, he unfastened his pocket watch from his vest and lay it on the table in front of him. "Do you still have papers, or have you sold them or thrown them away?" He tried to raise his voice and shout, but it sounded like the shrieking of a child.

His chin sank to his chest. Now it seemed he had no chin at all. He began to wind his watch; then something happened. Maybe he'd broken a spring. A good thing I'm sitting down, he thought. He had a very small head, like a child's. "Didn't they warn you what would happen if you lost or sold your weapon?" So his old pocket watch had finally given out. How long had he had it? Fifty-two years.

The rest of the people in the court, through their expressions and whispering, showed their displeasure at the old man in the hunter's jacket and plus fours for having lost a sense of time and proportion, and even for having lost his inventiveness, because he was still waiting for the soldier's reply. Finally the soldier said, "They robbed me and beat me. Then I ran into a buddy and we went to the movies."

"Do you know what you can expect?" asked the judge.

"I couldn't help it. They beat me. I was outnumbered. They stole my weapon."

"No need to deliberate over this one, gentlemen," said the judge. The folds of skin on his throat trembled.

The secretary watched the judge's mouth, as though she were taking dictation. Her face was even more swollen than it had been at the beginning. Her sheeplike back was bending.

Power has only a beginning and an end, thought the general. It has no middle. Power cannot bear moderation. The doctor thought only about how many vials of serum he had left in his bag. The judge thought about his pocket watch. Those two employees should be given something strong to drink so they won't wear themselves out. Both civilians looked at each other and, after a silent agreement, removed their NSDAP pins.

"We'll give you a shot for energy," said the second officer to the soldier, who looked about suspiciously, as if he wanted to attack someone despite his hands being tied. They untied him and he didn't move.

"Sign this for me here," said the doctor.

It took him a while. They let him take his time.

It was, as the mother saw, only a matter of technique. They put him in a chair, told him to roll up his left sleeve and hold out his arm, and cover his eyes with his right hand. He'd be given a pick-me-up shot. Fruit sugar. And then an antityphoid shot. They'd inject that straight into his heart. What can it be? the mother asked herself. What do they shoot into their hearts that makes them die so suddenly? They look as though they were asleep. It reminded her of the way they kill old, sick, or wounded dogs that are beyond help.

The secretary had lit some candles when the telephone wires had been cut. Now, when the electric lights suddenly went out, it became evident how much foresight she'd had. Suddenly the noise from the underground faded. So it must have been a generator, thought the cashier's mother.

The guards struck matches, but they needn't have worried, for the prisoners had nowhere to go, though the noise of men suddenly shifting in their seats came from the audience.

"You will all be transferred to the Reich," said the judge. "Take them away."

The prisoners could hear nothing and they were surprised by the silence, the absence of shooting.

They sentenced all those on the stage who now were lying side by side, a row of corpses behind the curtain. The old woman could see only a portion of what was going on.

The judge half-closed his eyes, but it was the old woman who seemed to see only the candle flames and the deserters lying beside each other. The judge stared at the dead men and his chin began to tremble again. The old woman thought of dead dogs and wondered why the Germans had created words like *Menschentiere* and *Tiermenschen*.

"Pull yourself together," said the general to the soldier.

The expressions on the faces of the civilians showed they were lost in their own private thoughts. But something was happening. The old man's eyes appeared to bug out. He caught himself by the throat and chest, and then appeared to stiffen. His will was broken. It was as though he no longer wanted anything. All of his energy had evaporated. The box of lozenges fell from his hand and, for a moment, his watch could be heard rolling away into the silence. The old man had apparently had a heart attack. The trial was over. The doctor closed his bags. Those who had taken part in the trial went to the cloakroom and ordered the guards to leave with them. They also told the employees to leave everything as it was and go. The general and the second civilian stepped aside to allow the doctor, who was carrying a medical bag in each hand, to leave first. Suddenly the cinema was empty. The old lady looked at the candles, the old man and the dead soldiers. She was wearing a wrinkled black mourning dress and she stared into the dark.

She was thinking how quickly the world had changed in a few hours, and about the plague. About what she'd heard of the plague from her mother and father, at school and from the talk of people. She also thought about the rats and mice who spread the plague. The judge, his people on the stage, the deserters, and their guards in the audience made her think of the plague, even though they didn't have swollen glands or high fever.

That's what rats are after: if they themselves must die, then no one should live.

Suddenly, the soldier with the chafed neck stepped from behind the heavy black velvet curtain and grabbed the old man, the judge, who blinked as though he were waking up, then opened his eyes wide. He felt the soldier gripping him. Then something in his body crunched. Again, his head fell forward. He blinked like a terrified bird.

"My God," said the old lady.

The old woman's words fell into the silence of the cinema. The soldier with creases and raw red patches on his neck sat down on the bench. He looked at the flag draped over the long table and at the bench, now empty, and at the judge. He thought for a moment about what to do with him. The old woman was finally able to pull herself away from her spot at the emergency exit. She went back toward the dormitory to see if her daughter was still sleeping. She could hear the spluttering of the candles as they burned down and were extinguished in pools of wax.

7

At five o'clock in the morning, just when it was beginning to turn light, about five minutes before her mother returned, the cashier left the building. She intended to look for the lanky fellow and his brother. She wanted to go by herself, not because she was afraid for her mother, but because she wanted to do something on her own to show that her mother need no longer worry about who would look after her when she no longer could. But the cashier talked with her mother in her mind and told her, Yes, you were right, it's like an infectious disease. We all have it, as though something were being handed out for nothing and even people who don't need it want it, because normally you have to pay for it with your own skin, with your neck, but now it's free. A little piece of something everyone is fighting over. The Germans really did make *Tiermenschen* out of people.

She also felt she was rushing into something she only half understood and, at the same time, she feared. But, like a flash of light, it wasn't to be missed.

It was a pleasant spasm, not unlike when you touch yourself and long to be touched by someone else—an unknown someone—a man you may not even be fond of, since until that moment you hadn't known him.

She might have gone to see the owner of the cinema, but she knew he had locked himself in as soon as she'd turned in the money from last night's three shows and not even a pair of Belgian draft horses could drag him out now. The only men she knew, apart from those in her fantasies, were the lanky fellow and his brother. Why should anything happen to me? Even though it wouldn't necessarily be unpleasant, she thought. All night long she'd tried to determine what the sounds coming from the different quarters of the building were—from the cinema, the dormitory, the garage. She was cold; she needed something to keep her shoulders warm in the morning. An afghan, or at least a blanket. It's better to be outside than to have to put up with dreams about old men who couldn't understand her, who thought she was an easy woman like all women, and simpleminded, who thought that every woman or girl would do everything. But that, too, was far away, like the roses strange men, at this very moment, may be offering to strange women, as they contemplate an invitation to go on an outing, to a hotel, to a spa, or to Paris, which even during the war was like a vast amusement park, or so they said on the radio.

The cashier no longer thought about how she'd open herself up to everything a woman could if she were approached by someone she could only have dreamed about all those years with her prudish mother. Those blue pools or bluish spots that swim at the bottom of her eyes when she thinks about it, and her hands, not the hands of a man, do with her what comes of itself. And then the red explosions that burst to the surface and suddenly transform red to yellow and invisible hands grasp her and lift her to the ceiling, which she will touch with her hand and cease to feel. Inner cries join in and finally black, velvet black, like a soft and tender caress, like when you're touched by the soft tips of invisible fingers.

She was fortunate enough to have blue eyes and fair hair and she knew what a passport that was, allowing her to breathe, walk, exist. Survive.

She walked past the demolished sweetshop where not even a tea-spoon or a light bulb remained because everything had either been looted or broken.

This was something she both deplored and approved. It disgusted her, yet she agreed with it. It made her feel a horror and an enthusiasm she didn't understand. The *Lebensborn* organization was given a palace on the other side of the Vltava to which they brought girls from France, Germany, Norway, and many Czech girls about whom very little was known. After Heydrich's assassination there were orphans wherever you looked.

So the tall fellow's brother is taking Sonitschka Vagnerova with him into the revolution, she thought. But no one is taking me; I must bring to everything the swirling confusion I feel within me.

She was passing by the House of Romania bar. Last winter she had gone there with her mother. The Gypsy had sung a song called *Fire*.

> Even in the darkness of my village
> A part is missing from my body
> Oh, it's withering away, and hurting
> My body's on fire
> Oh, I still want to love
> Even if I burn to ashes

She would never forget the song.

The cashier was dreaming about love she never learned of, love the gypsies sang about, love so strong that people would kill for it without feeling guilt. Only the image of such passionate love, for which one is able to die, betray, and desert everyone and everything, all people and all things, hypnotized her. It was as if she were in a trance. She had a feeling she was losing her balance. An expression of single-mindedness, of looking inward, came into her eyes. God, I hope I don't faint here, she said to herself. She didn't. She only appeared to be enchanted, as if she were walking through a world other than that of the Prague pavement, with her pale face, blue, unseeing eyes, and her angel-blond hair.

The entirety of her mother's advice, even the color of her mother's voice, whirled around in the mind of the cashier, who would prefer an unhappy love to no love at all. Why did her mother think so badly of men?

Oh, my little girl, she could hear her mother in her mind. The fabricated nonsense that men devise against women, and dumb women against themselves, doesn't last, even in the most magnificent of affairs. It's nothing but a trap—some money or a mountain of impossible wishes and unfulfilled promises. It's like walking barefooted across a frozen river, on thin ice, my little girl. Nobody shares anything when he doesn't have to. Don't let them make you believe anything about the human heart where it concerns men, or money, or the future. It's only your sweet body and their pleasure seeking, little girl. After they get what nature condemned them to, they feign not having the time, as if it would be a greater sin to lose another second with you. Business, war, the job of a streetcar driver or a conductor are like a thicket for them in which they want to hide. They'd rather go to war than stay with you for another minute. I don't want to blaspheme. What they call passion, you'll forget all about it long before you grow old. It has no echo, like bad perfume, or cheap garters. It is yesterday's sunset, last year's snow. Oh, if I weren't ashamed to tell you what I have been, what I have gone through, what I had to do for money in order to be helpful to you a little. We are spared nothing, my little girl. You have to be practical, and understand that love will not wrest you out of your loneliness. A family? The foreman on the construction project next to the Adria Palace told me: It's good to have a family and a house like a castle. But then build a back door and sneak out. Oh, child, even what looks at first glance like the happiest family is a nest of treason. Men will sleep with just about anything, even animals.

The cashier felt shame wrapped in fear, like a piece of headcheese enveloped in greasy paper. And worry, which in turn was cloaked in the courtesy, restraint, and decency required of young women. She couldn't get over her fear of being despised.

There was a woman who came to the cinema once a week and bought a ticket from the cashier. She was pretty and always well dressed, but the cashier knew she wasn't employed, so she could guess how she made her living. Later she found out the woman lived in a nice three-bedroom apartment in Carpenter Street, on the third floor, with an advisor to the Minister of Justice, an older man whose mother wouldn't allow him to marry this woman. She was always very friendly to the cashier. She came once a week to the cinema, always by herself, and she and the cashier spoke a little each time she came, so they became acquaintances. The woman fascinated her.

Sometimes the cashier would tell officers the box wasn't available (her mother would have fainted on the spot, had she known) or she would say to herself that if she were forced to choose between giving the box seat to Sonitschka Vagnerova or her new acquaintance, she would not have hesitated for a second.

She tried to imagine—even now, as she was walking—what it would be like to be that woman.

The cashier was glad it wasn't her life, yet she envied her. It was like a magnet that attracted and repelled her at the same time, a force that tugged at her body and mind, her veins and her bones.

But the outcome of all the cashier's thoughts was that the dead Sonitschka Vagnerova, without any personal guilt in the matter, had taken from her the man she was thinking about and whom she wanted to see, even with his murky eyes. It was a fortunate thing he'd told her where he and his brother would be, so she could find him.

For a while she thought about the small salamanders and frogs she'd collected as a little girl in the puddles left by autumn or spring rains. The tiny tree frogs had eyes like bits of glass. They were no bigger than a child's thumbnail. Their eyes were angular.

She thought about Sonitschka Vagnerova, who even in death was fortunate enough to have someone in Prague think about her, for whom she is like the sun. She at least was worthy of being transported, but what am I worthy of? But then—oh, no, thought the cashier. I can't envy the poor thing in her death. Or can I?

She thought about her mother. I always felt disgusted when you silenced me all the time, Mother. My little darling, my honey. The cashier shuddered. A cold wind was blowing up from the river. She sensed what she was afraid of and why she was comparing herself with the dead Sonitschka Vagnerova. And then she heard the sound of her mother's voice, and the voice said: I haven't sung for a long time, dear. And she sang a few chords from *Danube Waves* and then burst out crying. Why are you crying, Mother? Other people are happy. That's why, my precious girl. Because other people are happy. I want to be like others. I want to join in. In my mind I hear a song about being together, about how we keep together. There must be a door to enter, Mother, isn't it so?

How can you be happy when you're afraid of everything? How can you be happy when the nearest person is so far away? When people hurt each other, even when they don't want to, even when they're not aware of doing it? It's so easy to hurt someone else. Do you think I don't know that, my sweetheart? I feel guilty and I don't know why, said the cashier. And she laughed at herself and saw all those colors once more, including black, which was like velvet and meant caressing.

Everyone is hidden as if in a box which is impossible to open. One cannot live this way. I don't want to live like this. And, with every move of her white arms, with her every stride, with a clenching of her hand into a fist, she went straight ahead, as if she were opening the doors to somewhere, to another place, where she would live her own life.

She thought about why people did what they did: the things the movie theater owner did in order to grow rich, and the lanky fellow's brother, in order to be remembered should he be hit by a bullet, sought danger in order to reassure himself and the others that he was no worse than the Germans. Her mother wanted her to meet a man who would make up for what Mother never got.

A moment later, in the window of a five-story apartment building in Parizska Street, she saw someone, probably a German woman, waving a white flag. The woman was about thirty years old and she wore a green German army sweater. At first the cashier didn't know whether she was surrendering or signaling someone. She remembered the sweetshop. Those signs. "Death to German Swine." "No admittance to Jews." And then it occurred to her: I probably shouldn't cross. And she didn't, because just then shooting started. Suddenly she could neither advance nor retreat. This is a silly thing to be doing, she thought, but I knew I'd end up like this. Absently, she stroked her lovely fair hair, washed in the chamomile her mother gathered each summer. Like an echo in her mind came the thought that she hadn't succeeded at much of anything in her life, and this wasn't just because the Germans had been in the land for the last six years. And she thought: I'm still pretty, but perhaps not as pretty as I used to be; and I'm a virgin. And she thought of what that meant.

She stopped on the corner. No farther, instinct told her. Not another step.

Something made the cashier's ears buzz. The German woman was no longer in the window. From the lower end of Parizska Street, from the direction of the Vltava River, an armored vehicle on tank treads crawled toward the center of the city like a caterpillar. It was a Hackel, firing toward the town hall from its cannon. A girl who looked like a peasant grabbed the cashier around the shoulders and drew her sharply in towards her.

8

"Don't give them your body to shoot at," said the country girl. "We're not here for a fashion show, miss." And then she said, "Since you're here, hang onto this thing for me, would you?"

She pressed a bazooka into her hand. It was heavy, and the cashier had trouble holding it. "It weighs enough," she said.

With some people she tried to make her conversation sound like dialogue she might have heard in a film. But this time it was her own voice, and she felt as if she were hearing it for the first time in her life.

"It does that," replied the country girl. "It penetrates even the thickest armor plate and explodes only inside the tank."

She adjusted something on her skirt and then took the weapon back. She grabbed the bazooka's wooden handle as though she'd been in the army for years. The cashier's hands felt empty. Something had happened at last, she felt, even though it wasn't much. It was a beginning. Something that was flowing towards her like the Vltava River. It was different from how she felt when the owner of the cinema had said she should experience something before it was all over, but what he meant for her to experience was himself. No hard feelings, miss, whatever you'd like. Who knows what's coming, miss. He had a dog. It reminded her of the time her mother had taken her to visit a family that had three dogs. They stank terribly. The family pretended that the smell was all part of having dogs.

"Don't be afraid," said the country girl, or perhaps she was a city girl who merely looked as though she were from the country. She sounded as if she really believed there was nothing to be afraid of, and not just as if she were trying to convince herself.

"Of what?"

A burning wall of the clock tower on the town hall came crashing down in front of the former grave of the Unknown Soldier, which the Germans had removed. The armored vehicle continued to fire at regular intervals.

The country girl put the bazooka down on the sidewalk and tried to pull up a manhole cover. The cashier thought for a moment and then went to help her. In doing so, the girls put themselves directly in the vehicle's path, but it continued to fire at the town hall. Maybe they were trying to destroy their archives, the lists of traitors. The cashier grabbed her side of the manhole cover with lovely white hands and prayed to God to give her strength to help the other girl lift it, because it wouldn't budge. The stench from the sewer reminded her of the cinema owner's dog, of those three dogs of the family her mother had taken her to visit, and of the lanky fellow's brother's two dogs, one dead and one still alive. Finally they managed to loosen the cover, but they still couldn't move it to one side so they could climb down inside the sewer. There were no men around, or rather there were, but they were on the other side of the street and they couldn't cross as long as the armored vehicle kept firing.

The apartment building where the woman had stood in the window with the white flag had apparently been evacuated. It wasn't until a machine gun started shooting that the girls realized a firing post had been set up there.

Suddenly everything seemed laughable to the cashier, though not enough to make her want to laugh out loud. She could smell the stench of the sewer and the smell of the river in the distance, the fragrance of the fields and the hillsides with their trees and parks. But mainly the stench. By the Law Faculty Building, where a German garrison was headquartered, a platoon of riflemen in full field gear, helmeted and armed to the teeth, was moving into action.

They finally managed to free the manhole cover. The country girl was red with the effort. The veins in their necks stood out. The tank, still firing, was coming closer and closer. The gunner was still aiming at the tower and walls of the town hall, but he had only to dip the cannon and swing it to one side to pulverize them as though they'd never been born. If the vehicle continued on its way, it would drive through the town hall as through butter, and the flames wouldn't harm it.

When they finally slid the cover off the hole, the stench of the sewer seemed like the sweet smell of a park, and the iron, rough and dirty with more than rust, seemed smooth. They scarcely noticed the rough edges that scraped their skin until they bled. The bazooka made of wood and iron lay inert beside the manhole. The riflemen were advancing behind the tank towards the town hall from the Law Faculty Building, where others were now fighting.

The country girl climbed down the ladder into the manhole. She did so nimbly, though there was scarcely room to move. The cashier didn't hesitate. The girl in the country dress, with the body and face of a peasant, was already covered by the stone shaft, and the cashier moved as quickly as she could to get inside as well. She understood what was going on, even though most of her understanding was only approximate, but what did that matter? Something told her this was how it should be. She no longer thought of Sonitschka Vagnerova, or of how the dead can steal men away from the living; she didn't even think much about her mother. She was utterly absorbed in what she was doing with her new acquaintance, whose name she didn't even know.

Until this moment, she thought, nothing has worked out for me, but now we'll see. She realized she was no longer conversing in her mind with her mother, only with herself.

"Hand me that thing," said the country girl. "Carefully."

When the cashier grasped the main part of the bazooka and handed it down so that her new friend could fire it, the country girl repeated her warning.

"Come down a bit lower, it'll be easier for you," said the country girl. "You can hang onto me. I won't fall now. Come here beside me. I'll try to fire it."

"My God," said the cashier, as though she doubted the country girl could actually work the contraption. She had to shout to make herself heard. The country girl didn't seem to notice her, but only in the way we don't notice people to whom everything unites us.

Gases were seeping from the sewer, reminding her again of when her mother had taken her to see those people with the smelly dogs. Below them flowed a river of sludge, with bubbles popping on the slimy surface. At night, when no one was looking after them, the dogs probably made messes all through the flat, thought the cashier.

"Come on," urged the country girl. "They're too close already."

The tank was coming nearer. The country girl had a pimply complexion and green eyes with circles under them that cut deep into her face. She held the butt of the weapon. She began to hiccup.

It occurred to the cashier that the peasant girl was holding the weapon like a kitchen utensil. Like what? Ah, she thought. And then there was a roar that filled the street where the men were standing.

The girl above her crouched down and fired. The whole thing, including the explosion, lasted about two seconds. The cashier expected everything to explode—windows, cobblestones, the wide avenue that suddenly looked like a field of blood. Then, in the third second, came the reverberation, spreading through the underground corridor of the sewer. A wave of pressure poured over them. The cashier thought she had opened her eyes, but they were closed the whole time and she saw nothing at all.

She thought she saw the country girl and her own mother and the lanky fellow before her. They were all lying together, but the lanky fellow's brother lay with Sonitschka Vagnerova. They exchanged a few words. Someone was covered with blood, a face was tightened in pain. Everything was dark and then brightened before the cashier's eyes. She didn't see the woman in the sweater in the fifth-floor window firing a military pistol, round after round, towards the sewer from where the country girl had successfully fired her first bazooka and blown up the tank. The woman kept firing, even though the tank was already in flames with its crew still inside it. The cashier felt as though she were hanging dead from the ladder, and she saw all the colors. No more than ten or twelve meters away, the tank was in flames and the metal was turning red hot. It was like when she'd come here, alone but to be less alone, and she thought of the colors that sprang from her memories, from recollections of something beautiful, of being happy, even though it had never happened. Only the colors remained. Only then did she remember her mother. Regret filled her. And that was all she remembered.

9

The cashier's mother sat on a chair until eight o'clock and waited. It had begun on Saturday, and then it was Sunday, and then Sunday evening and then Monday, but now she didn't know what day it was. It's not over yet, she thought. No one has to tell me, I can hear it from the street and I know what's going on from what happened in the night. She'd worn the same black widow's dress for several days, and she hadn't changed her underthings. She hadn't changed anything. She could wash and change her clothes when it was all over, when the other day came. Who knows what's become of my darling little girl, my precious little girl. I hope nothing bad has happened.

Shortly after nine the lanky fellow and his brother appeared in front of the box office, which was closed. Both wore red arm bands with the letters RG on them, for Revolutionary Guard. The lanky fellow had a fever and a rifle with a bayonet, and his brother had a pistol stuck in his belt. The pistol was visible whenever he opened his rabbitskin vest, by now beginning to fall apart, as the cashier's mother had predicted. They tapped on the glass and were surprised when an old woman with skin like the bark of a tree opened the door a crack. When she saw who it was, she let them come in and locked the door behind them.

Again she could hear the whine of a generator somewhere deep underground. It never stopped. It was deep under the cinema. It's probably just because my head aches and my ears are ringing, darling, she thought.

She felt as though she were carrying the whole huge building, as big as a palace, on her shoulders. She'd lost her sense of time and her thoughts had become confused. The things that must have gone on here, she thought. Only I know everything that happened here that night, she thought. But what happened last night? And who knows what will happen during the day? She looked at both unshaven men in their vests of unmatched and hastily sewn together rabbitskins. They'll probably fall apart on their backs, she said to herself.

What is it that tells a person something terrible is about to happen? the old lady asked herself. What is it? Why are we spared nothing? What accumulates all that corrosiveness that eats away at you, telling you something awful is going to happen but you don't know what and wouldn't know, not even if you were to tear yourself apart? Just as she'd felt the weight of the building, with its floors, corridors and staircases, with the cinema and what she'd seen in it, so she felt the weight of the light, the weight of the day, the shadow or echo of what she'd experienced that night. That night? Which night? And her daughter gone without even leaving a message. Where have you gone, my sweet precious one? What pulled you away, my dearest child? She felt as if everything that made people beasts of prey were clinging to her. It was their invention, the Nazi Germans, the word *Menschentiere* or *Tiermenschen*. But it's so close you can reach out and touch it. You don't even have to be a German. They only came close to the ideal, the way they tried to make Saturdays and Sundays into ordinary weekdays. In her mind she saw the employees, the judge, the deserters, the doctor, the general and the colonel, and the people from the NSDAP in the cinema.

She asked the tall fellow and his brother to go out and look for her little girl, her sweet child, her darling, the only thing she had in the world.

"Go, for the love of God," she said, "and find her before something happens to her."

And she thought, oh, my child, I knew you from head to toe, and I'd even find you a cripple for a husband, if only he'd say, "I love you, I'll do everything for you that one person can do for another." She knew that despite her good looks and beautiful hair, her daughter would be capable of finding a legless or armless cripple on a little cart, if only he'd love her and respect her and never desire anyone but her, and she could know he'd never defile her the way the Nazis had defiled the grave of the Unknown Soldier. Where do you get it from, honey? the old woman asked herself.

Aloud she said, "I've never liked this cinema."

"It's a palace," the lanky fellow said.

"I wouldn't live here for all the tea in China," said the cashier's mother.

She looked at the tall fellow and thought: What kind of person are you, living from hand to mouth, forever relying on someone else's favors? Existing without regard for human dignity, without respect for justice, behaving like children who'd renounce their freedom for a glass of lemonade? You'll forget everything, and you'll forgive everything, you pigs.

"You could live in this place for ten years and never set foot outside, that's how big it is," added the lanky fellow's brother. They all knew he meant the owner, who'd bought enough supplies for two weeks and locked himself in his elegant flat, where he'd remain until it was all over.

Both brothers looked at the mother; they appeared to be worried about her. Where should they look for the girl? Do they know something already? the old woman asked herself. Are they trying to keep something from me or do they genuinely not know? And will they really go and look for her?

"There's been shooting again this morning in Parizska Street," said the lanky fellow. "A German armored car was destroyed there, but they say two women were shot."

The lanky fellow's brother looked at the demolished sweetshop across the street. Someone had pulled the metal shutter down over the store front.

"One of their soldiers, a fellow with a raw neck that looks as though they'd tried to hang him, locked an old man up in the projection booth downstairs. The old man's a judge. He sentenced twelve German deserters to death," said the mother.

"Downstairs in the cinema?" asked the lanky fellow, surprised.

"But the main one isn't here," said the brother.

"I heard he was shot in front of the Kolovratsky Palace," said the lanky fellow. "I also heard they sent away the soldiers serving under that phony Russian general. Apparently they were wearing half-German uniforms. I couldn't figure for the life of me how they managed that. But if they'd stayed, it might have ended sooner."

"A lot of people kill these days for revenge and even more for money," said the old woman. "There are some days I don't like. Saturday, Monday, and sometimes Tuesday and Wednesday, although Wednesday is usually all right."

"It was a beautiful Saturday, and Sunday and Monday were even better," said the lanky fellow's brother.

The cashier's mother looked sharply at the lanky fellow's brother and thought: They think we're all fallen maidservants that the masters can play with whenever they're in the mood, while the ladies mercifully close their eyes to it all because there are some things that every woman, secretly, is fed up with. Up to her neck. Makes her stomach turn. Many people enter by the side door and go straight to the kitchen. They don't always come through the salon into the dining room. Up the back stairs, so as not to cause a scandal. God, where can you make up for it? Where could I possibly begin to make up for it?

The tall fellow looked at the sausage stand, now closed and covered with a sheet of canvas, and thought of the man who owned it: For the whole war you tasted good, hot meat, not like my brother here, who sold newspapers and was worn away by tuberculosis.

A fire will come and destroy all of it, thought the lanky fellow's brother. It will sweep away what used to be to make room for what is yet to come. Sonitschka Vagnerova. She should have lived to see it, she should at least have lived to see it. But perhaps she could imagine it for a brief moment before she began to suffocate and tear at herself with her fingernails. At first it may have seemed that she had a chance, but as it turned out, those who had less chance than you, Sonitschka Vagnerova, survived. They say that some Jewish survivors have already reached Prague. They hustled them into some hospitals or hotels. They must have been running like that famous guy at Marathon. Only no one was starving him along the way, or gassing him or hanging him, or taking shots at him at every step. And for them it was a hundred times farther. Nor did these people carry any victorious message.

"What's going on out there?" asked the old woman.

"Their general asked for air support," replied the lanky fellow. "Near the radio building, one of their women with only a brassiere on was firing a machine gun all night from a balcony on the top floor. They made a nest there. When they picked her off with a grenade from the roof, her son came out of the flat and took over, but he got it, too. He was scarcely thirteen. At the general hospital kids like that were shooting at pedestrians from the emergency room."

"Only birds have nests," said the mother. "I was always afraid of that. But I believed we'd live to see the unknown day together. And what comes afterwards, too."

"You should go and lie down, lady. You can hardly keep your eyes open," said the lanky fellow.

Human eyes are too weak for all that evil, thought his brother. He looked at his stolen boots from the Afrika Korps, and when he saw the old lady looking at them, too, he explained: "They belonged to a rat we stripped everything off of. It sounds like there's a river roaring through the basement here, lady."

"The underground newspapers wrote that Reinhard Eugen Tristan Heydrich was a passionate airman before they blew him up with a grenade. He wouldn't let a Czech doctor treat him, and by the time they found a German doctor, it was too late. Hitler got angry because the two of them were hand in glove and he eventually wanted Heydrich to take his place if anything happened to him. But he was lucky," added the lanky fellow. "Nothing much ever happened to him, except that he couldn't write without his right hand shaking and trembling. They say Benito Mussolini was a passionate airman, too. And the members of his family were passionate airmen; his daughter Edita, wife of the Count Cian, and his sons, Captain Vittorio and Bruno, who were combat pilots in the Ethiopian campaign and the Spanish war, which is where they won their wings and their ranks. Maybe what we're hearing right now are passionate airmen at work. The last of their passionate airmen."

He thought: It has given strength to many who were weak. It has given back a bit of good conscience to those who were tarnished. But people like the owner of the cinema and the sausage seller will try to go on living like parasites in the future. Many of them will slip through. But we'll know who they are, he thought.

"Leave me a box of matches," said the mother suddenly to the lanky fellow.

"Sure," said the tall fellow, handing them to her. "But you'll have to get your own candles."

"What else have you seen?" asked the old woman. It still seemed to her that generators were whining somewhere underground. But it must be in my head, too, she concluded.

"I only saw the evacuation. On the left bank of the Vltava the Revolutionary Guard gave them passes. The condition was that they had to surrender their heavy arms at the Prague city limits. They are allowed to take small arms with them on their way to give themselves up to the Americans. They believe the Americans will forgive them, that everything will quickly be forgotten, just like after the First World War. For those who went, they opened the barricades a single tank width. But they had to leave their tanks behind, empty. Yesterday, they tied our people to the gun barrels of those tanks and said they'd blast them to bits if we didn't stop pouring gasoline on them. But the line was so long I was amazed we were able to hold out against them at all. They have reserves in the barracks and they're covering their retreat. They have armored cars, cannons and tanks, trucks full of machine gun brigades, hundreds of trucks and cars. And civilians are bringing up the rear on foot, as if they were following the Pied Piper. There isn't enough room for them all in the trucks. They were running alongside, tying baby carriages to the trucks and then they ran behind to keep up, all covered with sweat like in those underground mines in Venezuela, my brother says. I'm almost beginning to believe it. They're terrified, shrunken, sick with fear, dragging their personal junk behind them. And there are sick people and children among them. Women with bundles on their backs. They don't want to lose sight of the one column of soldiers they have, otherwise there would be no one to protect them. It looks like the last armed units they have, lady."

"What day is it, anyway?" asked the cashier's mother.

"This is the fifth day you've been here, mother," said the lanky fellow. "Tuesday."

"The fifth day, Tuesday, and my little girl still isn't with me," said the mother. "If only I could turn it around."

"Love has no frontiers," said the lanky fellow's brother.

"Love?" asked the old woman spitefully. "Only the instinct to survive has no frontiers."

She was looking at both brothers and thought: How many times have you helped an old woman board a tram, my dear brothers? As far as I remember, you haven't helped me even once. How many times have you walked unconcerned past cripples, beggars, deserted mothers with babies? Isn't it like this with you always? Won't the one who won't burn his fingers have a greater chance to survive than the one who sticks his nose into other people's business?

"People watched like in a theater," added the lanky fellow. "Crowds of people. Like when there's an accident or a fire. They poured out into the streets from nowhere, God knows where. Since Saturday the streets were empty, and suddenly—it was an amazing show. And it's not over yet."

"I remember people staring out the windows across from the Holesovice-Bubny train station at the Jewish transports when they were collecting for departure," he went on. "Like a show in a theater. And now they're watching the Germans. As long as they have something to watch. You're telling me this is all a theater for people? Folks were staring at Jewish families while they still were allowed to ride the back platform on the streetcars. And when they crowded together at the Radio Market Hall of the Grand Fair Palace. It was a wonder people didn't applaud like in the theater. They were saying to themselves: It serves them right. To see those fat cats carrying sacks, dragging along two-wheel carts. A circus. They'd been living too good for too long. They envied them even the noses between their eyes; otherwise the Germans couldn't have gotten away with it that easily, after all. Before the Gestapo sealed their apartments, the servants would stretch their arms out and run their feet off, carrying away as much Jewish property as possible."

"People always like to watch when it's turning around," said the lanky fellow. And he thought: Perhaps you were watching, too, old woman. "Tomorrow is also a day, lady. You know what that priest used to say: 'God will take care of the impossible things. We'll take care of the possible things ourselves.' "

"I hope so."

"Don't panic, lady. Don't give in to it. It's better to feel sorry for all the other people than for yourself. The wild dog has to be kept on a short leash. Sometimes more happens in a day than in a year. My grandpa used to say that if you can last till you're nineteen and don't drown till you're twenty, you won't get lost anymore.''

The old woman looked out of bloodshot eyes full of the sleep she had denied herself for so many days. Maybe it was five days already, she thought, five days, my dearest sweetheart. Well, we weren't alive yet, my darling. Only now will we start living. It's all still waiting for you. Your life is ahead of you. I'm on my last legs. I love you, little girl, even though you're rebellious. I was at your age. I don't want you to be gentle like a lamb. You can believe me. I accept you as you are. It has begun for you, and these are not good times.

''I could tell guilt from innocence Saturday, Sunday, or any day of the week,'' said the tall fellow's brother. ''When the final reckoning comes, I won't let anyone leave out Sonitschka Vagnerova, no matter what day it is. That's if anyone were to ask me how the whole world could stay sitting at the table and have Sunday dinner and Sunday supper and allow what we allowed to happen.''

''She never let me wait for her this long, like a blind woman,'' said the mother. ''So this is the wonderful day.''

''Only those who actually did something wrong are evil,'' said the lanky fellow's brother. And he was thinking that before they asphyxiated Sonitschka Vagnerova with Zyklon-B, they suffocated her with silence. They wanted their *Lebensraum,* and they suffocated her to make more room. They used words like *Ausrotten, Vernichtung durch Arbeit.*

''You should take a rest,'' said the lanky fellow to the mother.

''We're all prematurely worn out,'' said his brother. He looked at the posters with the stars of pre-war films.

''You said there was shooting in Parizska Street. What happened there? Did they kill anyone?''

''Yes, two women. But that doesn't mean anything,'' added the lanky fellow quickly. ''It's just a rumor. We didn't actually see it happen.''

''What would I do if they killed her? Where are you, my sweet little girl?'' asked the old woman. The thought startled her. I mustn't bring down bad luck, my darling, she thought.

She wished her daughter would come to her, and she had other thoughts as well.

''The sausage man closed up shop,'' said the tall fellow. ''All he said was that on Friday they bought his sausages and Saturday morning they got a shot of phenol in the heart. On Sunday they don't bury the dead.

The newspapers said the stags have already shed their antlers. What were they trying to say?''

"The same as what Sonitschka Vagnerova was trying to say, that's all," said the brother.

"They're probably cut off from the world, in their own little nests," said the lanky fellow.

"What nests do you mean? Those aren't nests," the mother corrected him. "They don't even live like animals. They don't understand anything. They're worse than a storm. They've gone wild. I was always afraid of what would happen when that day arrived. We always did everything together. Why did she leave by herself?"

"Don't worry about it," said the lanky fellow.

"What would Sonitschka Vagnerova have said?" asked his brother.

The mother's look could have penetrated a stone. A bitter dampness filled her eyes. "She always clung so close to me," she said again.

"It'll all turn out for the best," said the lanky fellow.

"I'm afraid," repeated the mother. "I'm afraid of everything now, even my own shadow. Of sickness, of being alone. That I won't last. Oh, my God, what would I do alone?"

"You see, when they were wiping out people like Sonitschka Vagnerova, they weren't able to wipe out their names," said the brother. "When I had that fever on Thursday and God appeared to me, I realized why only this will give people back their tarnished honor and allow the humiliated to walk straight again. But only those who sacrifice themselves and don't try to drive out evil with evil, hatred with hatred, will be spared, or will spare others. And we won't let it get out of hand. Every one of them who murdered will work in the deepest mine shafts of Venezuela, with no respite. And those who were murdered will live on and their names will be with us."

The mother absentmindedly rearranged her dress, covering her ankles with the edge of her skirt. It's easy for you to talk, she thought. You have teeth that could tear a rabbit to pieces. And eyes that see only what they want to see.

It's 9:30, she thought, and it's still cool, even though it's May and the elders are blooming and the lilacs are fragrant. There's a dampness coming off the river. I can feel it when the wind blows through the passageway.

The old woman had hard eyes like the lanky fellow's brother's dog in

winter. They were indifferent and cold. They had shadows, reading as
deep as a dark well and yet as shallow as a dry field.

"It's cold. The furnaces aren't working," said the lanky fellow.

"We have to go," said the brother. "A few people have to sacrifice
themselves and get dirt on their hands so the others won't have to corrupt
themselves with all that evil."

"Your eyes are red; you should rest," said the tall fellow.

10

The cashier's mother waited until evening. Then it was eleven
o'clock and her daughter hadn't reappeared all that time she was
dressed like a widow, wearing black from boots to collar. She stopped
the ceaseless inner conversations in which she tried to persuade her
daughter not to get mixed up in any mob activity. They've killed
her, she repeated. Wolves are always just wolves. Wolves will never
change. Why didn't you listen to me, my angel, little girl, when I told
you about the shadows that follow you everywhere? My sweet rain-frog,
my precious jewel.

She talked to no one, looked at no one. She tried to walk erect and
resolute, the way she had when she was young, coming home through
the streets in the early morning as it was getting light and when, despite
everything, she felt young and healthy. Young and healthy, my girl, she
repeated.

The soldier with the raw neck that suggested a last-minute reprieve
from the gallows was holding onto the cord of the dark blue velvet
curtain and looking through the little window into the projection booth
where he'd locked up the old Nazi judge like a rat. He didn't know what
to do next.

She walked by him without a word. Maybe she saw him as he
crouched there in the light of a single candle. For the past few days
the judge had eaten only bread crusts and dry cookies the soldier
with the raw neck had tossed to him.

She looked through the window beside the circular opening through
which the lens of the huge projector stared like the eye of a dead fish.
The bodies of some of the murdered soldiers were lying on the floor.

The old man had hairy arms and the skin on the back of his hands was covered with dark blotches. His shirt sleeves, visible under his hunting jacket, were no longer clean. His jaw was sunken and his eyes were streaming with tears. He must have been thirsty because his mouth was partially open and he occasionally thrust his tongue between his lips. A set of dentures had fallen out of his mouth and lay on the floor. His teeth and gums had turned yellow. Around the fly of his trousers there were yellow stains. He was terrified of what the deserter with the raw neck might do, but he hadn't been beaten.

"You rat," said the mother. "You plague." So this is my unknown day—the day of the animal, not the day of victory. What can I do to make up for it, since you didn't come back to me? Nothing, nothing, or little, if I can find the strength, and I'll do the only thing I can, something I should have done long ago, when you were still with me.

She was talking to herself while she took the lid off the cannister of gasoline. She poured the gasoline through the small window onto the old man. He was terrified and retreated into a corner, stepping on his false teeth and crushing them. Then she poured the rest through the window and watched it spread across the floor. Even in the gloom the gasoline made small rainbow eyes. It ran into a large pool on the floor and it smelled very strong. She took a match, struck it and tossed it through the window. Something was telling the old woman not to do it. But it was only a vibration, a heartbeat, the wink of a swollen eyelid, the look of fatigued eyes. It became an echo before an idea—a breath, a word which would reverse what she was committing, many yeses and only one no which she didn't hear anymore. She was looking at the old man's face and, in it, suddenly discovered the reason she didn't like herself anymore.

Saliva was running down from the corners of her mouth. Am I punishing myself for what doesn't cleanse one, doesn't redeem one, doesn't help anyone? The good ones will die, the bad ones remain, she was repeating to herself. How can I live? How will I live? She sensed a dark connection between her memory and that which carried her name, her countenance, looked through her eyes, spoke her language. I have lived long. Why?

She was pale, with deep circles under her eyes, like people whose hearts are sick and who have lost respect for the world and for themselves; who have lost the awareness of their own worth. With an absent expression and her mouth slightly ajar, the old woman closed her eyes. Right without God, she was whispering. Justice without God. Or is it the other way around, God without Justice? You will tell, my little one. You'll see.

Her whispers were unintelligible. First the pool of gasoline caught fire and was covered by a blue flame that was reddish in the middle. Then the flames spread. The old man in the hunter's jacket and plus fours began to shriek. He sounded like a child crying.

The mother sank to her knees so she couldn't see what was going on in the projection booth. The fire cast rays of light on her only when the flames were high enough, ruddy reflections that became brighter as the darkness in the empty cinema deepened. She knelt as though she were praying, but she wasn't praying. The old man in the booth cried out hoarsely. She had colored reflections in her eyes, red explosions that shot outwards. Suddenly they became yellow and finally black, like the smoke that now enveloped her.

In her mind the old lady spoke to herself, but at the same time, she addressed her lost daughter: It had to come, to him, to all of them. Her mouth stiffened. She could no longer speak, not even to herself. Her lips became encrusted, as though the fire had already scorched them. Then she began to cough and choke and she closed her eyes, which were streaming with tears.

She felt nothing when the soldier with the raw neck dragged her away and she heard familiar voices, because the fire from the burning door had already reached her.

❖

About the Author

Arnošt Lustig was born in Czechoslovakia in 1926. After internment in Theresienstadt, Buchenwald, and Auschwitz, he escaped from a train of prisoners bound for Dachau. He returned to Prague to fight in the Czech resistance in 1945. When the USSR invaded Czechoslovakia in 1968, he was vacationing in Italy; thus began his life in exile. Lustig lives in the United States, where he teaches writing, literature, and the history of film at American University. He is the author of the collections *Indecent Dreams* and *Street of Lost Brothers* and the novel *Dita Saxova,* all published by Northwestern University Press.

❖

Jewish Lives

THOMAS TOIVI BLATT
From the Ashes of Sobibor: A Story of Survival

HERTHA FEINER
Before Deportation: Letters from a Mother to Her Daughters
January 1939–December 1942

IDA FINK
A Scrap of Time and Other Stories

LALA FISHMAN AND STEVEN WEINGARTNER
Lala's Story: A Memoir of the Holocaust

LISA FITTKO
Escape through the Pyrenees
Solidarity and Treason: Resistance and Exile, 1933–1940

PETER FURST
Don Quixote in Exile

SALOMEA GENIN
Shayndl and Salomea: From Lemburg to Berlin

RICHARD GLAZAR
Trap with a Green Fence: Survival in Treblinka

ROBERT B. GOLDMANN
Wayward Threads

HENRYK GRYNBERG
Children of Zion
The Jewish War *and* the Victory